Meg Hutchinson left school at [illegible] and [illegible] to education until she was thirty-three, when she entered Teacher Training College and studied for her degree in the evenings. She lived for sixty years in Wednesbury, where her parents and grandparents spent all their lives, but now has a quiet little cottage in Shropshire where she can indulge her passion for storytelling. It is a passion that has reaped dividends, with her novels regularly appearing in bestseller lists.

Praise for Meg Hutchinson:

'Hutchinson knows how to spin a good yarn.' *Birmingham Evening Mail*

'The mistress of simmering sagas.' *Peterborough Evening Telegraph*

'Meg Hutchinson's storytelling skills are attracting a bigger and bigger audience.' *Newcastle Evening Chronicle*

Also by Meg Hutchinson

Abel's Daughter
For the Sake of Her Child
A Handful of Silver
No Place of Angels
A Promise Given
Bitter Seed
A Love Forbidden
Pit Bank Wench
Child of Sin
No Place for a Woman
The Judas Touch
Peppercorn Woman
Unholy Love
The Deverell Woman
Sixpenny Girl
Heritage of Shame
Pauper's Child
Ties of Love

Non-fiction

A Penny Dip: My Black Country Girlhood

Writing as Margaret Astbury

The Hitch-Hiker
The Seal
Devil's Own Daughter

MEG HUTCHINSON

For the Love of a Sister

Abel's Daughter

HODDER

For the Love of a Sister first published in Great Britain in 2005 by
Hodder & Stoughton
A division of Hodder Headline
Abel's Daughter first published in Great Britain in 1996 by
Hodder & Stoughton
A division of Hodder Headline
This omnibus edition first published in 2006 by Hodder & Stoughton

A Hodder paperback

2

A CIP catalogue record for this title is available from the British Library

ISBN 978 0 340 93289 6

Printed and bound by
Mackays of Chatham Ltd, Chatham, Kent

Hodder Headline's policy is to use papers that are natural, renewable and recyclable products and made from wood grown in sustainable forests. The logging and manufacturing processes are expected to conform to the environmental regulations of the country of origin.

Hodder & Stoughton Ltd
A division of Hodder Headline
338 Euston Road
London NW1 3BH

For the Love of a Sister

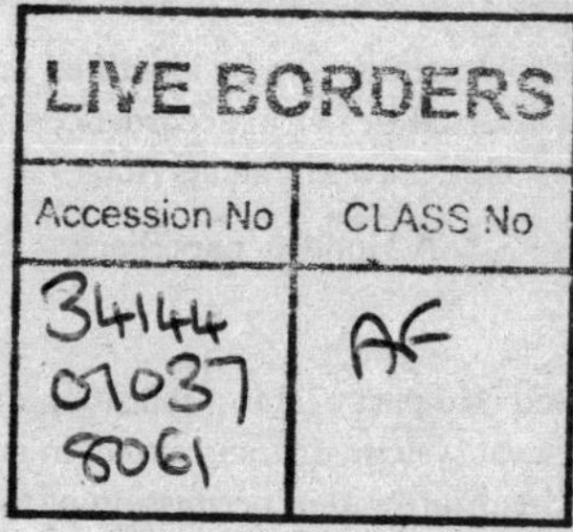

I

'I told you never to come to this house!' Myra Brent's eyes blazed with passion. 'I told you,' the words throbbed, 'never, never come here!'

'Myra, I . . .'

Quick and stinging, her reply a whiplash of words, Myra's mouth tightened.

'No excuses, I don't want to hear them. I told you to stay clear of this place, to stay away from me, I told you but you didn't listen. You never learn do you, Eden? But perhaps this will help you.'

The final word squeezing between clenched teeth, Myra Brent's hand struck hard.

Myra had never struck her before. Sitting now in the tiny house which had seen the growing of herself and her sister, Eden Brent seemed to feel again the sharp blow which had sent her reeling.

Why? She stared at the grate, dead and empty of fire for more than a week. Why had Myra's eyes blazed, why had her whole body shaken; why had she been so angry? It wasn't as if she had acted boldly; the very opposite was true. She had taken care to avoid the main approach to that house, coming to it by way of the surrounding fields and asking at the stables if one of the hands would let her sister know she was there.

Myra had run across that cobbled yard, the skirts of her dark blue dress flapping beneath the crisp starched cotton of her apron, her eyes throwing darts of fury. She had not even asked the reason of the visit.

Numbed as much by her sister's treatment of her as by the January frost, Eden made no move as the door to the scullery opened and a thin woman, shawl knotted tight beneath flat shapeless breasts, bustled into the darkened room.

'C'mon now, wench, it'll do no good yoh sitting there catchin' your own death o' cold. It be over and done, your grandmother be laid to 'er rest and though you mightn't think so this minute you 'ave to get on wi' life.'

'I tried to tell her . . .'

'Ar well, yoh done your best, can't nobody do more.'

Dora Benson drew the closed curtains a few inches apart following the custom of returning the household gradually to the full light of day after the burying of a family member.

'I would never have gone to that house . . . never gone against her word . . .'

'Like I says, wench, yoh tried, can't never be said as yoh didn't. But that sister o' your'n wanted no hearin' of what yoh went there to say, so that's it an' all about it. A man can lead a hoss to the brook but he can't push its head 'neath the water.'

'Gran would have liked her there.'

'I'll make no denial o' that,' Dora nodded, 'but it ain't always given that what a body would 'ave liked be what a body gets.'

'But why would Myra not listen?'

Fetching sticks and coal from the bucket beneath the shallow brownstone sink in the scullery, Dora set to laying a fire.

'The answer to that be knowed by none 'cept the wench 'erself and I 'ave no doubt you'll hear the tellin' o' it in time; 'til then you must carry on as your grandmother trusted you would. Now, go fill the kettle from the pump while I gets this fire to lightin'.'

'*I told you to stay away from me . . .*'

Taking the kettle into the yard shared with three other households, the words her sister had hurled at her echoed in Eden's mind.

'*. . . you never learn do you?*'

Eyes brimming, she swallowed hard. That had been one lesson she would never forget.

'Who was the young woman paying you a visit, Myra?'

Ava Russell's sharp eyes stabbed at the chambermaid she had summoned to her sitting-room.

'I . . . I've had no visitor, mum.'

Ava's smile was cold. 'But it was no servant of mine you spoke with yesterday out there beside the stables.'

How did she know? Which one of the staff had told of Eden's coming to Moorcroft House? Keeping her glance on the beautiful carpet, Myra hid the quick alarm triggering along her veins.

'It was not any staff of this house, was it?'

Could she go on denying the visit? Myra's brain sought for a way to do just that but her mistress's swift intervention gave her no time.

'I have the right to know the identity of any person calling at this house! You will furnish me with that knowledge or . . .'

The pause was deliberate, heavy in its meaning. Either Ava Russell got what she asked or a servant got the sack. Myra could not risk dismissal. She kept her glance on the carpet while her thoughts flew desperately in and out of her mind. Without her wage, Eden and their grandmother would be unable to manage, but to tell this woman of her sister . . .

'I'm waiting!'

Myra felt her insides twist. She could hear laughter in that voice, the taunt of malice. This woman knew her own power and revelled in it. With one word she could take away another's living, destroy a family dependent upon work as domestic servants. But there was something else, infinitely more cruel, of far more unmitigated evil, and that something must not touch Myra's family.

'I think p'raps you be referring to the gypsy woman, mum,' Myra answered with the only feasible thought she had, 'there was one called yesterday.'

Smoothing the skirts of her jade-coloured moiré taffeta gown, Ava Russell observed a few moments of silence, a silence she knew would tear at the nerves of the young woman standing before her, and enjoyed it to the full. The feeling of superiority, of dominance, the thrill of having another at her mercy never dissipated, never failed to set fire to her blood, and today she would feel that burning.

'A gypsy you say.' The gown smoothed of its non-existent crease, Ava's hand rested on her knee, the smile remaining on her lips, frigid and static as if held there by the grip of ice.

'Yes, mum, called at the house about three o' clock.'

Poor stupid fool! Ava's enjoyment heightened. Did the girl truly think she would be believed? Did she expect to fool Ava Russell with so lame an explanation? But what better could be expected of the lower classes? Really . . . Her inner smile as cold as that on her face, Ava chided herself . . . You should not have looked for a more intelligent lie – the girl just does not have the brain for it.

'A gypsy,' she repeated. 'And it was she who spoke with you before the stables?'

'Only for a minute or so, mum.' Relief at having her explanation accepted, Myra raised her glance to the woman regarding her with dark eyes. 'I told her she would have to leave, that the mistress didn't tolerate gypsies calling at the house.'

'I see.' Ava nodded, the light shooting blue darts from her elegantly coiffured raven-black hair. 'Then I must be mistaken, for the person I saw you with was dressed like no gypsy nor did she carry any basket of pegs or laces. In fact, she was dressed quite respectably as I recall, most neat and tidy in her maroon coat and bonnet. You are certain she was simply a gypsy, someone you had not met before that moment?'

She had seen! Myra's nerves jumped again. She had seen Eden, had watched them together in the yard. How else would she have known of the maroon-coloured coat and bonnet that were Eden's Sunday church clothes?

All of this reasoning showing clearly in her servant's blue eyes, Ava Russell's appetite for vindictiveness sharpened. But she must not satisfy that particular need too soon; she should exercise patience. Fruit savoured most was a fruit one had waited the tasting of. Tomorrow was another day and that would be followed by as many as Ava Russell chose. Lifting one well-manicured hand from her lap, she held it at chest level, each finger splayed in an affected gesture. Her tone conveying none of the satisfaction running inside, she addressed the servant.

'As you have said, Myra, I do not tolerate gypsies or vagrants. You did right in telling the woman to leave.'

She thought she had got away with it. Ava Russell's cold smile warmed to one of self-appreciation as she dismissed her maid. But that girl was merely on a leash, one which would be reeled in when the time was right!

The world was no different, the house was as she remembered it; her bedroom was the same small room with its chest of drawers, one plain wooden chair and her bed with a rag rug beside it; yet everything was different.

Unable to sleep, nerves quickening at every sound the night brought, Eden Brent stared at the darkness above her head. Somewhere up there should be a ceiling, to her left should be a door, yet all the knowledge of the past sixteen years of living in this house seemed to have evaporated, to have gone from her mind, leaving a blankness, an emptiness which held no marker, no indication of where she was or where she should go.

She had never thought she would feel like this, to feel so isolated from all she had known; now for the first time in her seventeen years she was afraid.

There had been no sign of her grandmother being ill. Vision lost in the black of moonless shadow the pictures in her mind showed vividly clear. The day had gone as so many before it, the cast iron range blackleaded to a silver sheen, the living-room polished and dusted, the quarry tiles of the scullery floor scrubbed, and the yard swilled down with buckets of water to which had been added the usual copious amount of 'Auntie Sally', the strong-smelling, dark, oily liquid bought weekly from the carter and used, Grandmother said, to keep down vermin.

As a child Eden had delighted in watching Grandmother add a little of the liquid to the water with which the floors of the living-room and bedrooms got their weekly scrubbing, laughing her pleasure when allowed to stir the bucket's contents with a wooden stick, asking, 'What makes it go all creamy?' and getting no answer other than a brusque 'Stop blethering, child, the water be gettin' cold.'

It had always been that way, Gran being abrupt and pretending to be too busy to answer. It had taken a long time to realise, a long time to acknowledge, that the woman who had been their mother, father and grandmother was not an oracle, that she did not hold the answers to all things. It had come as a shock.

Surrounded by darkness, silence heavy in her ears, Eden remembered. The teacher had asked 'What are shooting stars?' The children had looked questioningly at each other, none daring to say aloud the thought in their minds. 'They be shootin' stars, just like yoh says.' The teacher had waited a few moments and, when no reply was forthcoming, had tutted her impatience and told them she would ask the same question the next day. Eden had released the breath caught anxiously in case she was ordered to stand up and give her own answer. Myra would know, her sister knew a lot of things because of being older; and if Myra didn't know, then Gran would because she was even older. But Myra had no explanation and Gran had grumbled of 'kids bletherin' on when they could see a body were busy.' So she had gone to school the next day with no more knowledge of shooting stars but with an understanding that to her child's mind was far more profound. Her grandmother had offered no solution, given no definition; she had not taken Eden on to her lap after supper and given a reason as to the why and wherefore of a thing which puzzled a young mind. Could it be that, contrary to her long-held belief, her grandmother was not all-knowing?

Somehow it had seemed like a betrayal. How could she think thus of her grandmother? It was a sin and she, Eden Brent, was the vilest of people.

But once she had not been so. The pictures in her mind changed, flashing from a thin, scraggy eight year old to a taller girl, her shape more defined, buds of breasts soft mounds beneath her cotton frock. Blue-green eyes clear and sparkling with interest in life, fair hair gleaming like a spring sun, thirteen-year-old Eden Brent was a pretty child.

The headmistress of twenty years had retired, her place taken by a middle-aged, gaunt, sharp-featured, razor-tongued woman whose every word conveyed her feeling that her new post was beneath her, that the running of a school whose pupils were the offspring of colliers, nailers and foundrymen was entirely unsuited to someone of her class. Miss Jones! Eden's eyes closed trying to erase the memory, but it remained, stubbornly imprinted on her inner vision.

Three years Eden's senior, Myra had already left the all-girls' church school and secured a post as house maid at Moorcroft House, home of one of the town's prosperous industrialists. Eden hoped the same might be given herself.

She had missed her sister terribly.

Eyes wide open now, Eden stared into darkness which had no power to hide the visions of her mind.

Myra's monthly afternoon visits home were something Gran and she awaited with pleasure, her own a tingling excitement that tickled all over. Gran had allowed her to stay off school, calling next morning to state the reason for her grand-daughter's absence in her flat 'don't you go arguin' o' me' tone. But on each occasion the headmistress had later summoned a frightened young girl to her private room plying her with questions. What had Myra talked of . . . ? Had she spoken of her mistress . . . ? What did the other servants gossip about? And all the time those keen ferret eyes had watched her face.

Why had she been interested in what Myra talked of? It hadn't been as though her sister were still a pupil. She had kept her answers brief, resenting what, to her young mind, seemed interference in something not the headmistress's business. She had said none of this to Gran, and the interrogations had gone on until one day she had been asked if she would like a position as a domestic servant.

This had been Eden's dream. Not that she wanted to leave Gran . . . but to have a smart uniform, to be able to bring money home as Myra did, that was all she wanted. Miss Jones had said that were she prepared to work hard, a post could most probably be procured for her. A week later she had been summoned again.

Eden shivered at the memory. Dressed in a thin cotton frock her grandmother washed at the end of every school day, drying it before the living-room fire and smoothing it with the heavy flat iron to ensure a neat clean appearance the next day, she had tapped at the door bearing the name 'Miss Jones' above the awesome title 'Headmistress'.

'You have a neat hand with the sewing needle, so I am informed.'

The girl had nodded, hands held behind her back, as school required, eyes nervously lowered to wooden floorboards that shone from nightly polishing by a caretaker and his wife, both of whom viewed the headmistress with the same trepidation as did the students.

'That is a quality which will serve well in a position of ladies' maid.'

Ladies' maid. A jolt of pleasure had raced in her blood. Did this mean a post had been found for her?

'But a girl of your years, and with absolutely no experience of the requirements of a finer way of life . . .'

Miss Jones had paused and the pleasure had dropped away from Eden like a stone.

'. . . however . . .'

Again that dreadful pause, animal-sharp eyes assessing the girl whose fingers twisted anxiously.

'. . . however,' the thinly marked lips compressed before her next words, 'if you are prepared to do as you are taught then it is possible to get you to that standard of requirement. Are you willing?'

She had been more than willing. She had danced all the way home in a dream of smart uniforms and deliciously frilled caps and aprons, bubbling her words until Gran had told her sharply to 'Stop your fidgetin', you be jumpin' like a flea on a dog's back.'

It had been agreed, Gran giving her blessing. But within a month the bubble had burst.

Turning her face into the pillow, Eden hid the trembling tears.

The bubble had burst, but the shards of it were still stuck in her heart.

2

'That be the lot, there be no more in the copper.'

Beads of perspiration glistened like diamonds in the light of several candles on the flushed face of the scullery maid. Her cheeks deepened to a further shade of red as she emptied a bucket of steaming water into the bath housed in an exotically appointed room adjacent to her mistress's dressing-room.

'It'll take time to boil another copper . . .'

'No need for that Letty.' Myra Brent glanced at the girl whose breath heaved noisily in her lungs. 'I will let you know when the bath is ready to be emptied.'

'Fill the bath, empty the bath, fill it, empty it! Be the same one day after t'other! Why for 'eaven's sake? Why do a woman need to wash all over every day? T'ain't natural . . .' Empty bucket in hand, Letty Holden grumbled her tiredness. '. . . t'ain't as though 'er does anything to soil even 'er 'ands; 'ain't never 'ad to do nothin' for 'erself, not in all 'er born days, 'er would even 'ave a body wipe 'er arse for 'er, supposin' any o' we was willin'.'

The door closed on the girl's ire. Myra Brent gazed into the whispering flames of a fire around which she had draped white fluffy towels.

'. . . 'er would even 'ave a body wipe 'er arse for 'er, supposin' any o' we was willin' . . .'

Letty Holden's words echoed in Myra's mind but immediately became swamped by her own, saying what they had so many times before: '*There are worse services than wiping another woman's backside.*'

Worse services! Myra's eyes screwed tight against the thought. Worse services! And she, Myra Brent, had to perform them.

'I think perhaps Desert Dreams – the perfume is so very sensuous.'

Myra's eyelids flew open. She had not heard the footfalls of the woman now standing behind her, a woman whom she knew watched her with spite-filled eyes. But spite was not all Ava Russell desired.

Hands shaking, Myra reached for a pink crystal flagon from the cabinet and emptied a little of the heavily scented contents into the bath.

'Yes, it was the right choice.' Ava Russell, the hem of her silk robe whispering against the floor, swayed across the room and halted before her maid. 'The perfume is so alluring, so heady . . . so full of promise.'

Returning the delicately wrought stopper to the flagon, Myra's nerves jerked. The pause between words had been fleeting, subtle, but the inference was heavy. Tonight was to be no different to so many others.

'The water is the correct temperature? You have tested it?'

The voice was soft, smooth as the silk its owner was

wearing, but each word rubbed like gravel against Myra's heightened nerves. Replacing the flagon among others equally pretty, struggling to control the quiver in her voice, Myra answered quietly. 'It is hand-warm, mum, just as you like it.'

Just as she liked it. Ava Russell's inward smile spread. But all of her life was just as she liked it . . . and it would never be otherwise. Allowing the robe to slip from her, she twisted and turned to admire her naked body reflected in mirrors draped about with vibrant silks. Yes, life would always be as Ava Russell wanted it.

Stepping into the bath, lowering luxuriously into the perfumed water, she watched the slim figure of her servant take the robe and drape it carefully across a blue velvet chaise-longue half-hidden by sweeping drapes echoing those partly concealing the mirrors. Then as the figure turned, she waved a hand languidly.

She glanced at the soap Myra had brought from the cabinet. 'Rose of Shalimar! A perfect accompaniment for Desert Dreams; they both have that captivating enchantment of the Eastern world. Together they breathe love and desire.'

Love . . . What did this woman know of love? Myra's glance rested on the palely tinted soap. Love meant caring for people around you, whether servant or kin, yet Ava Russell harboured such feelings for none other than herself. But desire . . . yes, her mistress knew that well enough: it ran as permanently in her as the blood in her veins, desire which had to be satisfied in whatever manner she chose . . . but the desires of Ava Russell were merely pacified, quieted for the moment, never totally satiated.

'There will be no need for this.' A fingertip flicked the pink face flannel Myra held with the soap. 'We will use our hands, it is so much more enjoyable.'

Laying the flannel aside, Myra felt the breath bubble in her chest. If only she could run from this house . . . But she couldn't . . . she could not bring more hardship to her grandmother and sister. Bending to dip the soap into the water, her teeth clenched as Ava's hand rose once more.

'No, my dear . . .'

The affected sweetness of the tone brought a sickness to Myra's throat.

'. . . not like this, they get in the way. We enjoy our bathtime much more without their hindrance, do you not agree?'

How could she not agree? How could she tell this woman of her true feelings, of the disgust, repugnance and loathing that filled her each time she was made to partake in Ava Russell's nauseating self-satisfying pastimes.

Sickness solidified into a choking lump in her throat, Myra looked down at the fingers touching the frilled apron covering her dark blue dress. Like the claws of a hunting hawk. And she was the prey. She shuddered.

She could not look into those taunting eyes, must not look into them! Putting the soap into a dish shaped like a wide-open lotus she forced her trembling fingers to release the ties of her apron, then the buttons of her dress, removing each of her undergarments until she too was naked.

Eyes resting avidly on mirrors which portrayed every angle of Myra's slim body, Ava Russell breathed approval. She had done well in getting rid of her previous ladies' maid. This one was younger and prettier, altogether more to her taste . . . and when it palled? Then she would find another. Money was the key that opened any treasure box . . . or the legs of any poverty-stricken girl!

Relaxing her head on the towel placed for that purpose against the rim of the bath, she let her eyelids close slowly. Ignoring Myra's half-choked sob, smiling as she slid a little further beneath the water, she purred, 'Now we are both ready, my dear, let us begin.'

There was no way out. Myra touched the bar of soap to the scented water. Hadn't she tried, hadn't she applied for another position, any position that would take her away from this house? But without a reference no mistress would employ her, and Ava Russell would furnish no such paper; even dismissal from her service had never been tainted by that particular brand of spite, as others who had once laboured under this roof had testified. This woman kept folk beneath her thumb even though she had no further use for them; that was how it would be with Myra Brent. Yes, she could walk out, turn her back on this demeaning life . . . and take what? Perhaps she could accept abject poverty, even the workhouse . . . but Eden and their grandmother?

She could never inflict such terror on them. She must accept the horror, continue in this house and in the abomination of its mistress.

Tears sliding over her cheeks, teeth clenched against the repugnance of the ritual she had to undergo, she soaped her hands then, mouth trembling, passed them over the other woman's breasts, squeezing gently, playing over the erect nipples as she had been instructed.

Eyelids lifting, Ava Russell's dark animal eyes glinted a pleasure which spoke of more than physical satisfaction; they glowed with the deeper gratification of knowing the humiliation her maid was suffering.

'You have such soothing hands, their touch is so seductive, you give pleasure . . . a pleasure we both share, one we can share now . . . like this.'

Her glance riveted to the reflections of the many mirrors, Ava stretched a hand to the trembling girl. Cupping each of the tight breasts for a moment she trailed a finger over the taut stomach to nestle in the soft silky hair of the vee at its base, her free hand pulling that of Myra to touch between her own parted thighs.

One candle lit the room given as her own, its pallid glow flickering over a narrow bed while, beyond its reach, shadows enveloped a chest of drawers and a washstand. Myra Brent's eyes, drowned in tears, saw nothing of these, she saw only a naked girl, an older woman's hand caressing her slender body.

She had tried, as she did each time, tried to wash

away the touch of Ava Russell's hands, scrubbing at her breasts and between her legs, scrubbing until the bite of carbolic soap stung the lacerated skin; but the touch refused to wash away, the horror of it remained, a vileness which caused her flesh to creep.

Had it been like this with the girl who had previously filled the post she held now? Had some other maid been subjected to the same terrible degradation? None of the household staff had ever spoken of her. The few times she had enquired of the girl, mouths had firmly closed and backs had turned. It seemed as if no such person had existed, yet there had to have been someone, a woman like Ava Russell would not deny herself a ladies' maid. Then why dismiss her? Was it that she refused to take part in her mistress's games? Had she resigned rather than be abused as she herself was?

If only she could do the same. Trembling from the effects of the treatment she had been made to endure, her flesh crawling with the memory, Myra snatched up the candle, carrying it to the washstand where she began the scrubbing all over again. Doused in icy water, skin raw and bleeding from the harsh brush, she sank to the floor oblivious of everything save the tearing of her heart. Curled into herself, her face hidden between frozen fingers, she sobbed brokenly, 'Lord, please! I can't go on . . . I can't . . . I can't . . .'

But the words, whispered so desperately, were swallowed by the silence. There was no one to help her, no way to escape the evil of Ava Russell; Myra was trapped at Moorcroft House, trapped by the love of a grandmother and a sister.

The girl had visibly trembled on being informed her assistance would not be required with tonight's bathing. Shivers of relief? Ava Russell watched through her table mirror as her maid lifted a heavy satin gown from the wall-length cupboard of the dressing-room. Yes, the quick look darting over the girl's face had told beyond doubt the trembling was that of relief. But it had needed no shaking limbs, no quick look of thankfulness crossing that drawn face, to tell her that.

It had been amusing at first; the shyness, the blushes, the obvious sense of unease at what she was instructed to perform. It was that way with each girl at the beginning but they had all learned, learned that Ava Russell must be satisfied in all things . . . but satisfaction was waning!

Stepping into the gown, standing still whilst deft fingers fastened the back of the close-fitting bodice, fingers which no longer sent the swift arrows of desire shooting along her veins, Ava's lips tightened. Myra Brent had proved amenable and docile, but mere compliance was not enough.

Seating herself at the dressing-table, Ava looked at the young woman adding a spray of feathers to the coiffure she had painstakingly arranged. She was clever with the duties of ladies' maid, she took good care of gowns, saw to it that every aspect of her mistress's wellbeing was taken care of . . . But maids to do only that could be found anywhere; the maids she relished needed to have fire, needed to have desires that matched her own.

'Which necklace will you be wearing, mum?'

The question brought Ava's glance to the jewellery box held out to her and suddenly she wanted to chase away that expression of relief she had seen flash over the tired face, to see it replaced by uncertainty and . . . and yes, by fear. Touching a hand to Myra's she pressed gently her reply a whisper of soft intimacy.

'I will leave that to you, my dear . . . whichever you choose will please me, just as you please me in other things, as I know you will be eager to do again when I return this evening.'

The box had almost dropped from the girl's hand and the look as their eyes had met had been one of revulsion, and despair.

Seated in a box at Wolverhampton Theatre Grand, Ava smiled to herself. Maybe she should wait a while, keep Myra Brent a little longer; to act hastily, to dismiss the girl now, could have its disadvantages.

Raising her fan to her mouth, Ava hid the smile reaching her lips. A change of entertainment, a small *divertissement*, it had its attractions; after all, instilling fear could be as amusing as tipping the skirt.

'I agree entirely . . .'

The whisper behind its own covering fan brought a swift colour to Ava's cheeks. Had she spoken aloud? Had her thoughts somehow found their way to becoming words?

'. . . I too find this whole thing boring.'

She had not spoken aloud. Ava's startled nerves subsided as the second whisper emanated from behind the fan.

'I had hoped my feeling did not show, but now I feel so terribly guilty.'

'I know that feeling only too well.' The fan fluttered with the woman's reply. 'But we must all be seen to do our duty . . . unpalatable as it sometimes proves. But for myself, well let us say this is not to my taste; no, not my idea of a pleasurable evening.'

What *was* her idea of a pleasurable evening? Closing her own fan, Ava directed her glance to the stage on which three over-dressed and over-large women were singing the maids' chorus from the Gilbert and Sullivan operetta *The Mikado* but her attention was concentrated on the figure beside her.

Lenor Medwin was plain. Her skin faintly sallow, red-brown hair owing more than a little to the henna bottle, she tried to hide these obvious shortcomings beneath gowns of outlandish styles and a deluge of expensive jewellery, the result of a husband's manufacture of iron. They had met several times at dinner parties given by Wednesbury's industrial élite, and also at occasions such as this – charity evenings – the proceeds of which were given in aid of comforts for soldiers serving abroad.

With the curtain lowering for the interval, the house lights glittered on jewellery adorning every woman in the audience. Real or paste? Ava mused, her gaze wandering over the crowd. Whichever, they were worn as much to impress as to dazzle . . . each gleaming piece a testimonial to a man's wealth. Had those gems been earned by a wife's love shared in the marital bed or were they a salve to the conscience of a man indulging himself outside?

Fidelity! Ava's mouth twitched, holding back a laugh. It could be betrayed in so many ways . . . and not every one of them by the husband; a wife too could play that game of chance. But her own – which carried more risks than simply playing mistress to some man – that behaviour was frowned upon. Yet when it came to the push infidelity was somehow overlooked by society, the man being smiled upon as an 'old dog' while, at worst, the woman lost a few friends. What Ava Russell played at would not, if discovered, be overlooked; society would not turn a blind eye. Being mistress to a man was accepted, being lover to another woman was not.

How many of the folk in this theatre could possibly guess? How many could have the faintest idea of her particular proclivities? How many, looking around at the beautifully gowned and coiffured women, could have any notion she preferred sexual pleasures not with her husband, or any other man, but with a female? Lesbian! Her breath slid through nostrils flaring with the thrill of all that the word entailed. Woman in love with woman. But Ava Russell was never in love with her companions in fornication, she was in love only with the sensual pleasures they afforded.

A whore! The fan rose to hide a breaking smile. Yes, she supposed she was. A whore, whom if found out, would be hounded from the country, shunned by the so-called respectable; therein was the danger . . . but danger was the cream on the cake, adding flavour to an already enjoyable sweetmeat.

A whore! Ava applauded quietly as the curtain rose for the second half of the operetta. She was all of that . . . and she would enjoy the fruits of being so again tonight.

3

There was no more to be done. Eden Brent wandered through the empty rooms of the only home she could remember. Gran had brought her and Myra here after their parents' death. 'Who knows what took 'em?' her grandmother had said years later. 'Be God's will an' we must bide by it.' But the platonic words had hidden a heart broken by the loss of an only living child. Now grandmother as well as parents had been taken and her sister had chased her away.

She had hoped Myra would come home, be there to say goodbye to the woman who had loved them both, but Myra had not come . . . Why? There had to be a reason! But then there was a reason, her sister had not known . . . she had not waited to be told but merely shouted at her to go away. Now she was doing as Myra wanted; she was leaving Hobbins Street. Monway Colliery was taking the house. They had allowed Grandmother to remain there for her lifetime, Grandfather having been killed in an accident underground, but now that her lifetime was ended the house could be used for a working family.

There had been no use in contesting the decision.

The house, as all of those in Hobbins Street and the others surrounding it, was the property of the colliery. They had given Eden a week in which to vacate and now, with all of the bits and pieces gone, every floor-board shining from the scrubbing they had received, it was ready to be handed over.

Bits and pieces! Eden's eyes brimmed. With no place to go she had been unable to hold on to the few items of furniture so cherished by her grandmother. They had been bought for a few shillings by John Kilvert, the pawnbroker, and the gloat on his face as he drove his cart away said he had got the better of the bargain. But things might have been worse – John Kilvert could have refused to buy the furniture and that would have meant leaving it to the bailiffs who would have paid nothing.

Bits and pieces! Tears which had brimmed now spilled on to Eden's cheeks as she came to stand in the living-room. Bare and silent, cold biting up from the quarry-tiled floor which had lost the rugs she and her grandmother had pegged from worn-out clothes whenever they could afford to replace them with a twopenny skirt or a threepenny jacket bought from the second-hand stall in the market-place, the room seemed to wait.

For what? Eden pressed her hand hard against trembling lips. To swallow more lives and leave no trace? Where was the warmth, the love that had surrounded two small orphaned children, and the laughter they had shared? Where the gentle kisses which had soothed away tears, the delight of summer evenings with a grandfather naming flowers and insects between puffs of a clay pipe? Where the pleasures of making little men from pastry given by Grandmother, her head shaking with disapproval when two little girls ate the raisins meant for eyes and buttons so more had to be given from the crockery jar kept in the cupboard beside the fireplace.

Throat choked, Eden cast a slow look about the barren room. Nothing! *That* was what remained of the lives lived in this house, *nothing* to say they had ever lived.

'You be goin' then wench?'

Brushing away her tears, Eden turned towards the figure who had joined her in the cheerless room. They had been close in friendship, this woman and Grandmother, helping each other through thick and thin, through the joys and through the sorrows; but how many joys had her grandmother's life held? How many had any family of the men labouring in mines and foundry for hardly enough wage to feed them? Joy was a scarce commodity in Wednesbury.

'Yes,' she nodded, 'I'm going, Aunt Dora.'

'Where to, wench? You 'ave no kin 'cepting that sister over across to Moorcroft an' you says you won't be a'goin' o' that house.'

Eden reached for a woollen shawl from the line of pegs her grandfather had fixed on the back of the living-room door, the one item of her grandmother's she had refused to let go, and wrapped it about her shoulders, tying the corners around her slender form.

'I said you can stop along o' me.' Dora Benson's work-worried eyes played over the young face. 'Our Jack an' the other three can sleep afore the fire, it'll do 'em no 'urt and give you time to sort y'self.'

Sort herself! Cold fingers stumbled with the tying of the shawl. No home, no work, a sister who had rejected her, how did she sort that? Fear that had steadily grown over the days since her grandmother's death, the fear of facing the reality of her situation, surged in Eden's throat. She was alone!

'No, thank you, Aunt Dora, it is kind of you to offer but I think it best to leave now.'

Dora held the slight figure close, her voice trembling with emotion. 'Well, if you be sure . . . but should you find things be too much then you comes back to Dora Benson, we'll find room for you, wench, be no second thinkin' to that.'

A house filled to bursting with a family of her own, yet Dora had offered to take her in, to give her the room occupied by her own sons! Shawl drawn tight against the bite of a sharp wind, frost crunching beneath button-sided boots, Eden walked away from Hobbins Street, from the only life she had ever known. She could have accepted Dora Benson's offer, stayed a while longer, but what would have been the use of that; it would have served only to delay the inevitable.

'You should ought to wait a while,' Dora Benson had advised on hearing Eden's decision to leave. 'When Myra comes, you know 'er alliz comes once a month, what do I tell 'er? Where do I say to look for you?'

She had said that she would write to Myra once she was settled. The lie still sat inside her like a stone. Truth was, she would not write to Myra, she would not contact her in any way. Myra had chosen her life . . . a life she did not want saddled by a younger sister.

Reaching Union Street, the smell of hot food brought her to a standstill. Pangs of hunger pulling at her stomach, she touched the pocket of her skirt feeling the few coins nestled inside it. Most of what she had received from the sale of her grandmother's household furnishings and from the pawning of linen and personal clothing, including her own Sunday church suit, had gone to pay the undertaker for the coffin and the use of a horse-drawn hearse; 'a waste' some folk in Hobbins Street had called the use of that hearse and the coffin could ''ave been brought to the buryin' on a 'andcart same as it be by other folk'! Eden's fingers touched her pocket again. What had been muttered by neighbours, other than Dora Benson, was no doubt sensible – pennies saved were pennies that brought food to another day's table; but her grandmother had deserved better than being wheeled through the streets on a handcart.

The expense of a 'proper' funeral, a wreath bought from O'Connel's shop, the glass-panelled hearse drawn by two black horses, black feathers on their heads, and the payment for the services of the priest, had swallowed all but these last three shillings. It was all that stood between herself and the workhouse, three shillings to ward off an existence she had often heard people speak of as 'hell on earth'.

A picture of a low, forbidding building sprang to her mind, its heavy oak door crossed with iron hinges, tiny windows seeming to refuse the light of day. How many times had Grandmother hurried herself and Myra past that place in Meeting Street? How many times had she crossed herself and called on the mercy of God to keep them from being taken into it?

Three shillings! Eden's hand closed protectively around the coins. She must not waste a single farthing. But not to eat! How many days could she go without food?

Wrestling with her thoughts, Eden's mouth watered as she looked at the display of meat and sausages set in trays of steaming gravy in the window of the cookshop. She had to find work. That might involve many days of walking, days which, without nourishment, would sap her strength, and nobody would be fool enough to employ a girl half-dead from hunger.

Pork and two slices of bread – threepence.

Beef and two slices – threepence.

Sausage, egg and two slices – fourpence.

Eden read the words written with whitening, their letters beginning to trail pale tears down the steamy glass.

Piggy in a bed. That was what Grandmother had called a sausage sandwich. But for Eden Brent there could be no piggy in a bed today; fourpence for one meal was far beyond resources which had to last heaven knew how long. But for a penny . . . the shop sold a slice of bread dipped in gravy for a penny. It was common sense.

Slice of bread in hand, fighting the guilt of spending her money, Eden walked on to the Market Place, wiping her fingers on her handkerchief as she came to the stalls grouped closely together. Carters and wagoners shouted at people to move out of the path of their lumbering vehicles; harried women, babes in arms and toddlers hanging on to skirts, returned the same in like measure. It was a scene she had witnessed so many times when shopping alongside Grandmother, enjoying the bustle of it all, the jaunty comments of stallholders, Grandmother's swift repartee. But that had been when there was buying to be done. Would any stallholder be as friendly knowing there was no money to be spent?

It had not taken long to find the answer to that question. Hands tucked beneath the shawl seeking warmth her body did not have, Eden turned away. No one wanted an assistant. 'A body 'neath the feet, that be the last thing I be needin', be more nuisance than they be a blessin'!' That had been the reply given by most when she had asked for employment; others had proved not quite so polite.

What had happened to her world? The question that had grown so familiar over the days, flashed again in her mind. A few hours was all it had taken for that world to be stolen from her, to be shattered completely. First had been Grandmother, dying so unexpectedly, then Myra turning her away, and finally the loss of her home.

Tears glistening on her lashes, Eden lifted her glance

to the two church spires, one black, the other green, the landmarks of Wednesbury.

Like her grandmother and her sister they were part of a life, past and over; she would never see either of them again.

Next week she could go home. Myra Brent gathered the towels which Ava Russell's guest had used. She had thought the humiliation of being pawed by her mistress was the most degrading thing she would ever encounter . . . but that was not so. Last night's 'amusement' had been shared.

Putting the used towels aside for laundering she replaced them with fresh ones, her hands shaking; her mind tingled with the memory of those sickening hours.

Myra had been told to wear her best apron, the one with broderie anglaise inserts on the frilled bib and shoulder straps, to make certain her matching cap was spotless and her sleeve cuffs well starched while her dark dress was to be exchanged for the rarely used lighter blue bombazine.

Closing the door of the bathroom tidied to perfection, she stood with her back slumped against it, eyelids pressed tight, towels clutched tight. If she could shut out those pictures . . . just for a moment . . . but they stayed with her as they had stayed the whole night through, tormenting, plaguing, suffocating her beneath the nightmare of shame. And still they were with her . . . They would be with her to her grave!

Being told to wear her best uniform had meant only

one thing. Her mistress was to entertain a visitor she wished to impress. The visitor had been a woman, someone Ava Russell had met at the theatre.

A guest room had been especially prepared with fresh flowers, its linen scented with rose-water, a fire completing the air of welcome. She would help the guest freshen her toilette, Ava Russell had told her; she would take care to see to it that any request was dealt with immediately.

Any request! A sob rising in her chest, Myra's eyes opened. Forcing her legs to move, she walked through the dressing-room and bedroom, averting her glance from the bed her mistress had shared.

There had been no pretence, no effort made to hide the intention.

It had been an intimate supper, no other guest, the dining-room lit only by candles, and every dish chosen and prepared, as with the guest room, to impress.

'*I don't go askin' who 'er be, an' neither should you. Do as you be paid to do an' don't go askin' o' questions be the motto I lives by, an' I reckons it be safest!*'

The cook had been abrupt when asked if she knew the identity of the mistress's visitor. Her reply was short, her lips had clamped shut and that was how they had remained, at least until Myra had finished her own supper and returned to her duties.

Having deposited the towels in the laundry room, Myra stood staring out over the gardens at the rear of the house. Like Moorcroft itself, the grounds were immaculate but, unlike the house, they hid no evil; the men who worked in them were required to do no more than that, their duties were to please only by keeping the grounds . . . but hers, her 'duties' involved more, much, much more . . . and now those duties were to be extended.

A keen breeze caught at Myra's dress but the coldness of it was not the cause of her shudder. Long and hard, it rose from her very depths.

She had been helping the guest to retire for the night; as ladies' maid that was expected, but not what followed, no ladies' maid nor any servant should be called upon to . . . Myra shivered again but the pictures in her mind were relentless.

The woman was already dressed in her white satin nightgown, red hair loose and brushed ready to be braided for the night when Ava Russell had entered the bedroom.

Would her guest care to bathe before retiring? She herself always found a warm bath so relaxing, so conducive to a restful night's sleep.

There had been no demur on the part of the visitor and the expression in the mistress's flint-sharp glance had warned Myra: there would be no demur on the part of the maid!

'*Myra's hands are so gentle and relaxing,*' Ava Russell had cooed watching her guest lower herself into the jasmin-scented water. '*I must ask you to excuse my choice of word but really "seductive" is the only one that does justice to Myra's expertise; really my dear, you should let her wash you . . . I always do.*'

And so it had been, but only after Ava, giggling coyly, had suggested her friend be bathed in the manner she herself preferred . . . by a maid stripped bare of every stitch of clothing.

And the woman had enjoyed her bath, flattening her shoulders and lifting her breasts to the stroke of Myra's fingers, her breath quickening with every sliding movement over belly and legs, her eyes closing, a cry ripping from her as a final gasp left her quivering. But that was not the end; it was not all the hospitality her guest must be given, not while other entertainment was on hand. And so the process was repeated. A large bowl of freshly scented water at her feet, Ava had shed her own nightgown to stand naked on a large towel. Then, the other woman's eyes burning with the same desire as moments before had burned in her own body, she had cupped Myra's breast, licking a tongue over the nipple while her free hand had nestled between her legs. And her mistress had laughed as she invited her eager guest to do the same.

It had been a nightmare worse than any other. Tears clouded Myra's eyes but not the pictures they saw.

The touching of her body had gone on, first one mouth and then the other, hand following hand until her clenched lips had parted in a scream, a cry stopped by Ava Russell's sharp blow.

'*Appetite, Myra, is filled with craving . . . and we both know how strong is the passion such feelings arouse, do we not, my dear?*'

She had smiled when speaking, her dark eyes vibrant

with a meaning not lost on the woman whose rapid breathing and hot eyes revealed the ravening of her own appetite.

'*But we must not pamper our domestics. They must know what is and is not permitted, they must learn to be satisfied with what they are given.*'

The tone had hardened on the word 'permitted'. It had been a way of telling her maid that any dissent, any refusal to take part in these 'amusements', would result in dismissal . . . dismissal with no hope of further employment. But even seeing the tears squeeze beneath Myra's tightly closed eyes, Ava Russell had not hesitated to add to the embarrassment and shame she knew flowed in the girl she had caught in her web of immorality. Cupping one small breast, she had touched it with her lips before murmuring, '*Tomorrow . . . I promise tomorrow all of your longings, all of your cravings, the desires you so long to be quenched, will be utterly satisfied.*'

A vicious squeeze of the breast she had kissed bringing a gasp of pain, Ava had turned away, a lecherous, almost carnal, glow to her dark eyes, a smile still curving her mouth.

'*But now, my dear,*' the murmur had been soft, an invitation, couched in velvet promise as she had reached to take the hand of the woman already trembling with the strength of her own arousal, '*I think it is time for bed.*'

The bed prepared for Ava Russell's guest had not been slept in, the scented sheets smooth, the pillows showing no indentation. But her mistress's bed had displayed the ravages of frenzied activity.

An activity to be enjoyed again?

Hands covering her face, Myra gave way to the despair that grew with each new day.

Yes, the events of that night would be repeated and she, Myra Brent, would be forced to take part in them.

4

Ava had never asked if her ladies' maid visited her own home during the precious few hours of freedom which came only once in every month.

Dressed in the plain brown coat and bonnet allowed for 'visiting', side-buttoned boots polished to a high gleam, Myra almost ran from the precincts of the house she had grown to hate.

No, Ava Russell never enquired as to where she would spend her afternoon, but as to *how* it was spent she gave explicit instruction. She was to speak to no one of her duties at Moorcroft. She would tell no person anything of the mistress of that house, and always she finished with the same words: 'There arc those in the town who would relish nothing more than to gossip about Ava Russell; be sure, be very sure, you do not provide them with the opportunity.'

Household staff *did* talk of their employers. Hadn't she often heard those from other houses chatter about a master or mistress when visiting Cook? Did Cook ever speak of her own mistress's likes and dislikes, of what happened during her bathing?

The shame that thought aroused brought a burning

to Myra's cheeks. She had long since stopped hoping others at Moorcroft did not guess what transpired, her own unhappiness must have been an indication, even supposing the previous maid had not divulged the awful truth before having left. Then they – cook, scullery maid and gardener – must all have asked why she, too, had not resigned, they must think . . .

The awfulness of the thought brought her to a standstill . . . they must think she liked what went on, that she, like Ava Russell, enjoyed those disgusting episodes!

'But it's not true, dear Lord, you know it's not true!'

Her cry rang across the frost-bound heath, bouncing off the outcrops of limestone that jutted from the ground, echoing and re-echoing on the cold, sunless afternoon.

'It's not true!' The cry dropping to a whisper, Myra's hands came together lifting to her lips. 'Help me,' she prayed to the silence. 'Show me the way, show me how I can leave that house without bringing suffering to Gran and to Eden . . . Help me, Lord . . .'

Words trailing away, hands falling to her sides, Myra felt the futility of her prayer weigh like a rock in her stomach. She had no right to ask that of God, no right to ask deliverance; what she did was wrong in the sight of heaven, it barred her for ever from the mercy of the Lord.

No forgiveness! No deliverance!

Four words. They chimed like a church bell in Myra's mind. Four words that said she was beyond redemption. Four words which spelled damnation!

*

'Grandmother is dead?'

Myra's brows drew together, her blue eyes widening in disbelief.

'Ar, wench, been dead this last week an' more.'

'But . . . but how, why? Gran was never ill.'

Thin to a point of disappearing, Dora Benson touched a hand to her face and brushed away a stray strand of hair turned prematurely grey by her hard life. Continuing to hammer and cut nails from a narrow strip of iron, she answered the girl.

'It don't be for folk to go questionin' the ways o' the Lord. 'E chose the time o' tekin' your grandmother, God rest 'er, an' though passin' of 'er brings grief to your 'eart, you should thank 'Im, 'E d'ain't see fit to 'ave 'er lie on a bed o' pain for months afore 'er goin'.'

Her grandmother had suffered no pain. That was a blessing she should give thanks for, but the pain in Myra' s own heart drove away all thought save one: she had not been there, not been with the woman who had raised her, not been able to speak of the love she had for her; not been there to comfort Eden.

Shock of learning of her grandmother's death had driven all else from Myra's mind, it had kept her from realising her sister had not yet appeared. Now, glancing towards the kitchen, a few yards from the brewhouse which need had turned into a nail-making workshop, and asked if her sister was there.

Dora Benson's arm rose and fell, hammer striking

iron in a regular rhythm, an accompaniment to the words sounding between.

'No, wench, Eden don't be to the 'ouse, 'er don't be along o' we.'

'Not with you!' Disbelief which moments since had gleamed in Myra's eyes darkened to confusion. 'But she has to be . . . Grandmother's house is . . . is filled with strangers . . .'

Laying aside her hammer with a brief glance at her sons saying the work was to continue, Dora wiped her stained hands on the dark apron swamping her wasted body.

'C'mon, wench,' she said gently, 'come to the kitchen, a cup o' tea be what we both needs.'

'Aunt Dora, I don't understand, why was I not sent for, why was I not told . . . and where is Eden?'

Spooning tea into a teapot – its cream enamel pock-marked from years of wear – Dora scalded the leaves with water from the kettle hung constantly over the low fire before replying.

'You *was* sent for, though sent might not be the word in a true manner o' speakin', for it were all over afore anybody could be sent for . . . As for your sister, I can't be tellin' where 'er be. Listen,' Dora shook her head as Myra made to speak again, 'as you yourself said out there in the brewhouse, your grandmother never showed sign of no illness, was nobody guessed as there were aught amiss wi' 'er; not me, not your sister, not nobody in all of Hobbins Street. Kept things to 'erself did Rachel, least said soonest mended were 'er way, an' that way 'er held to the end. 'Eart, that were what the doctor said when 'e were called, a complaint of the 'eart, weren't nothin' as could 'ave been done about it so you needn't go frettin' yourself as to what you should or shouldn't 'ave done. You was workin' along of Moorcroft House, it were the money you earned kept a roof over your family's 'ead and 'elped put food in their stomach, so don't you go a finding of a rod to whip your own back. You've always been a credit, Rachel knowed that, 'er took a great pride in you and what you do over to Moorcroft.'

A great pride! Suddenly the tears welling inside were too strong for Myra to hold back, and they erupted in great heaving sobs. Grandmother had been proud . . . but she had not known the truth, had not known what her granddaughter was called upon to do for the money she brought home. Where would her pride have been had she found out? How much love then for the child of her own son . . . how much disgust?

'Cry it out, wench,' Dora's eyes, moist with sympathy, played over the sobbing girl. 'Tears be a way o' easin' away sorrows; though some teks more than others, they all gets less painful as times goes on: I telled the same to your sister when 'er cried over your not wantin' to be listenin' to what 'er come to tell.'

That day Eden had come to Moorcroft House, the day she had shouted . . . had slapped . . . Oh God! Breath caught in her throat, Myra recognised the reason for her sister going against the request she never come there. Eden had come to tell her of

Grandmother's dying, to bring her back to Hobbins Street so she might kiss that dear face one last time, to walk behind the coffin to the churchyard where together they would see it laid to rest in the same plot of ground that held their grandfather. But she had refused to listen, she had simply driven Eden away.

'I never thought . . . I never dreamed . . .'

'O' course you never,' Dora answered the murmur, ''ow could you 'ave, like I telled Eden, you would 'ave come 'ad you knowed.'

'I would have if only I had given Eden the chance to speak, but I didn't!' Myra's head lifted sharply. 'I gave her no time to explain, I wanted her gone, wanted it so much I slapped her.'

That had been the most unbelievable part of what Dora had been told. She sipped the hot tea she had poured into a mug as chipped as the teapot, Myra's drink having been served in the one china cup used only for visitors. Myra had not taken time to hear what her sister had run all the way to tell, she had not wanted the bother. Dora sipped again, thoughts replacing each other rapidly in her mind. But if Myra Brent hadn't wanted the bother, why were she here now? And if, as Eden had sobbed, Myra had turned away, wanted no more of her family, why the tears? And they were real enough, there was no play-acting at back of them.

'I was so angry . . .'

Myra Brent spoke now only to herself; her words were not for ears other than her own, knowledge of that bringing her to her feet, Dora rose from the table to stand before the small cast iron fireplace, but the cramped space that was both kitchen and living-room was not enough to close off the half-sobbed murmurings.

'. . . I could only think of the danger to her, of what would follow her being seen . . . I couldn't risk that happening . . . of her being drawn into the same dreadful . . . I couldn't chance Eden being seen by . . .'

Replenishing the water in the kettle, Dora pretended she had not heard, but the ends of her nerves suddenly tingled. What was the danger the wench murmured on? Why was her afraid of her sister being seen along of that house? What was it had Rachel Brent's granddaughter trembling like a leaf in the breeze?

But all of this were the wench's business; to hear her when none of the telling was intended seemed to Dora to be sly and underhand. Uncomfortable with the feeling she rattled the lid of the kettle noisily into place, reminding Myra she was not alone.

'There,' she turned to face the girl at her table, 'that'll be nicely on the boil come supper. You be welcome to eat wi' us, my Jack will walk you back to Moorcroft.'

Fingers curling into her palms, Myra felt ripples of revulsion run along her spine. Return to Moorcroft . . . The very thought made her want to run and run and never stop. She prayed each night, even coming here to Hobbins Street this afternoon she had asked the Lord to show her a way of leaving that house for ever, she had begged . . . The thought broke and with its halting a great weight seemed suddenly to lift away from her shoulders: she had asked and she had been answered. Heaven had seen fit to take her grandmother but it had given a gift in return; the gift of freedom! The responsibility of keeping a roof over the heads of her family was gone, she could take Eden, they could leave Wednesbury, find a place where they could live together. She was no longer under any obligation, she need no longer suffer the obscenity, the debauchery, of Ava Russell's 'little entertainments'. From this moment she was free, no more would she place herself in the service of anyone . . . and neither would her sister. There was other work they could do, they were both good at sewing, Eden as well as herself had shown an aptitude for needlework.

A smile shining where tears had glinted, Myra glanced at the woman she had been taught to address as Aunt even though they shared no blood.

'I won't be troubling Jack to walk me to Moorcroft, Aunt Dora. You see, I am not going back there.'

'Not going back!' Faded eyes opening wide, Dora Benson stared at Myra. 'But you 'ave to, it be your livin'.'

Her smile travelling to her mouth, Myra shook her head. 'Not any more; if I can wait here for Eden to come back I intend we go find work elsewhere.'

'You can wait 'ere, that you knows without the askin', but Eden don't be comin' back. Her left after your grandmother's 'ouse were emptied of its bits o' furniture.'

Newly discovered delight and the elation of release

from the abuse of Ava Russell drained rapidly from Myra.

'I said as 'er weren't to this 'ouse.' Dora watched the colour drain from the face that for a minute had smiled. 'I did tell you, wench, I said as 'er don't be along o' we.'

Eden was not here? She was not living with Aunt Dora? But it was *obvious* she was here, of course she would be with the woman who had helped mother them both. Perhaps she had misunderstood . . . Yes, that was it, Aunt Dora could not mean Eden had left for good.

For one brief second, hope bloomed in Myra's heart but was as swiftly killed by the cold breath of reality. Dora Benson was too poor to waste anything, even words. What she said was what she meant. She had said that Eden had left after Grandmother's house was emptied of its contents . . . that had been days ago! So where was she? Who was she with?

A picture of herself standing naked beside the bath, Ava Russell's hands stroking her body, brought Myra to her feet, words trembling in her throat.

'Did . . . did Eden say where she was going . . . who . . . who she would be with?'

The answer had been no. Myra ran from street to street and shop to shop asking of her whereabouts. Eden had taken that slap as a complete rebuttal, she had seen it as repudiation. To her it had seemed that she, Myra, no longer wanted any connection with sister or grandmother, that her failure to attend the funeral had implied they were no longer family.

Effect of the thought sapping her strength, fingers pressed hard against a rising sickness, sobs the reflection of the pain slicing through her, Myra folded into herself, her cry a whisper in the growing darkness.

'What have I done? Oh dear God, what have I done!'

5

The night's lodging would have cost ninepence.

Eden clutched the pocket which held the remainder of her three shillings as she left the White Lion Inn. She had not thought to have to pay so much: ninepence would have kept Grandmother and herself for two or three days, yet the landlord of the inn had shrugged when she had questioned the cost. 'You takes it or you leaves it,' had been the terse reply and she had left it. Darkness had already set in. She felt it would be unsafe to traipse the streets enquiring for a cheaper lodging yet she could not afford a hotel or inn.

She must find some place less expensive for, as well as a bed, she must buy food. Admitted the landlord had offered a decent supper but, at ninepence a night, she could not stay there. Perhaps if she had asked for some employment . . . A place providing rooms and meals must surely have linen in need of repair, but the sideways glances of the man who had spoken to her had set her nerves quivering so she had thanked him and left; even so she had not breathed easily until she was once more out on the street.

Her shawl was scant protection against the biting

cold. She glanced the length of the road lined on both sides with shops selling a variety of wares, and once more her stomach churned with hunger.

She had lingered too long at the house, wandering from room to empty room, wanting to be gone yet somehow unable to leave, unable to break the ties of the heart. Even when she had closed the door for the last time, she had stayed awhile with Aunt Dora, afraid to part from the one person she felt had any love for her. If only Myra had come, if only she had listened, then she would have come and not returned to Moorcroft. They would have found a place to live together, sisters sharing as they had always shared before Myra had become a ladies' maid. How grand they had both thought that . . . a ladies' maid! Yes, it was grand for a girl from Hobbins Street, so grand it had turned her away from her family.

'You best move yourself if it be you don't 'ave a likin' for bein' knocked down. Wagoners hauling iron to the canal don't 'ave too much care of folk standing in their way.'

'What?' Eden blinked, feeling a tweak at her skirt.

'I was sayin', you best step outta the 'oss road if it be you still wants to be livin' termorrer.'

A hoarse curse and the crack of a whip recalling the last of her wandering senses, Eden felt herself pulled sharply backward.

The hand releasing her skirts balled into a fist

shaking at the rumbling wagon, a louder curse echoing after it.

'Told ya!'

A face sprinkled with freckles and topped by sand-coloured hair, grinned at Eden.

'. . . told ya them wagoners gives no mind to folk daft enough to go standin' in their way.'

'I see that.' Eden felt an immediate surge of liking for the boy grinning at her, brown eyes gleaming like polished mahogany. 'Thank you for pulling me from the path of that one.'

'Weren't nothin'.' The grin spread. 'Seth Butler be a mean bugger, don't give a sod who he runs down, but there be ways of dealing with him, like tekin' the peg from a cart wheel so it works its way off the shaft and the whole lot tips sideways, spillin' its load.'

That was a dangerous thing to do. Teeth clenched against the cold held back Eden's response. This boy had saved her from what might have been a serious injury; could he also cause one by doing what he spoke of?

'Joby Timmins done that . . .'

Eden's shiver hid the quick breath of relief. She did not know the boy smiling at her but she was glad he had not interfered with the wagoner's cart.

'. . . Joby pulled the peg from the wheel of Butler's wagon after his little wench were knocked down by it; nobody said as much but everybody knowed it were Joby done it, said as how it should 'ave broke Butler's neck same as that little un's leg were broke . . .'

A steam whistle shrieking in the distance made the boy turn in its direction.

'Wait,' Eden touched his sleeve, several inches shorter than the arm it covered, 'please, could you tell me where I can rent a room?'

'Tek it you don't mean one along of the White Lion or its likes?'

A shake of her head affirming his guess, the boy's mouth twisted thoughtfully.

'There be old mother Marsh . . . her has a room empty since her son were killed fightin' in the Crimea, but whether or not her'll tek you in I can't be sayin'.'

He had given her directions, his words tumbling over each other as the steam whistle screeched again.

Huddled into herself, nose and mouth covered by the shawl protecting her face from flurries of snow beginning to fall, half of Eden's mind tried to remember the way the boy had told her to follow, the other half praying the woman would rent her the room.

She had refused!

Beneath the covering shawl Eden's mouth had trembled.

'I can be tekin' no lodger!' The woman had snapped when asked. 'That there room be my lad's, he'll be a' wantin' of it when he comes from the war . . . that'll be soon now, he be on his way, he'll be 'ome soon.' She had closed the door then, words filtering faintly as she shuffled away.

Trying hard not to give way to tears that would

freeze on her lashes, Eden stumbled through the thickening snowstorm. The cottage had proved to be a fair distance from the town but she must go back or spend the night beneath a hedge, to do that would mean her likely freezing to death. Stumbling over a jutting stone the coins in her pocket jingled against each other. Two shillings and eleven pence . . . At ninepence for a bed and supper and food during the day it would cover less than three nights . . . and if no employment was given her in that time?

'*God in His mercy keep we from that place.*'

Her grandmother's heartfelt words seemed to cry on the wind. The workhouse. Snowflakes thick on her eyelashes, Eden struggled on. Two nights . . . and then she would have to apply to the workhouse!

Blinded by whirling snow, head bent against a driving wind, her limbs so numbed they no longer seemed part of her, Eden gasped for breath which brought no relief. If only she could rest, just for a little while, then she could go on. Rest . . . just for a minute . . . just for a minute . . .

'*You be tired, my little wench.*'

It was a voice she knew, a voice she loved.

'*Come set along of me, it be warm here against the fire.*'

The fire was so bright . . . the flames rising from its scarlet heart danced like tiny birds, exotic in their plumage of carmine tipped with blue and gold. So warm, so beautiful . . .

'*Rest you now.*'

At her side. the familiar voice was low and gentle.

'*You be safe here . . . you be safe along of me.*'

It was so warm, she could feel the heat of the fire on her face, feel the softness of a pegged rug beneath her feet.

'*Rest you now.*'

Soft and tender, benign with the love she had always known, the words brushed her ear.

'Gran?'

Seized in a flurry of wind-driven snow, the whisper was whirled away, but the answer, itself no more than a murmur, sounded clear in Eden's tired mind.

'*. . . Ar, my little wench . . . it be Gran . . . I be here along of you . . . rest, my little love, rest you beside me . . .*'

Sighing with contentment, Eden lay down, her eyes closing, her mouth curved in a smile beneath the huge, soft flakes laying a covering of white over her body.

'Where did Myra say she was going?'

'Her didn't, mum, her just said as her would be back same time as usual.'

But she had not returned at her usual time, she had not returned at all! Hiding her annoyance, Ava Russell glanced at the pretty ormolu clock set on the mantel above the glowing fire.

'I am becoming concerned,' she said, allowing a faint crease to settle between her brows. 'I wonder if we should send the stable hands to look for her, after all she might have tripped . . . she may be lying injured somewhere.'

This woman wouldn't worry if the wench were hurt,

not even were her dyin'; the only worry Ava Russell ever had were for her own comfort!

The cook hid her thoughts beneath a shake of her head. 'I reckons that be a waste of time, mum. It be snowing heavens hard out there.'

'That is my worry!' Ava cut in sharply. 'Myra could be lost in that storm.'

'If you'll forgive the saying, mum, that don't be my thinking. Seems to me to be more like her seen the extent of the storm and, guessing it could well be on for the whole night, decided to stay put where her be and come back here once it be mornin'.'

'I hope you are right . . . we must pray that you are right, that Myra is safe.'

Pray! Hands clasped across the front of a spotless, heavily starched apron, Polly Jupp concealed the disdain that remark brought. Ava Russell prayed for nobody other than Ava Russell, and any true concern her might be feeling would be for herself.

'Myra be a sensible wench,' she said, grey eyes displaying no sign of her inner feelings. 'Her won't have set off in no storm. No, mum, I thinks you should put your mind to restin' on that account.'

It was that very safety that was the cause of the disquiet niggling inside Ava. She glanced again at the clock. The girl had always returned on time, never more than a few minutes after six, and now it was nearing nine. Almost three hours, time enough to have reached the house regardless of the storm . . . But if she had decided not to return . . .

A flush of alarm tingling her nerves, Ava almost started to her feet but recovered herself. It would not do to allow even a hint of the trepidation beginning to form in her mind to display itself. Servants gossiped, and gossip spread, and if that happened some people were apt to ask why . . . Why was Ava Russell so concerned over a maid, when any of a dozen could be hired next day?

'Of course,' she nodded. 'Myra is far too sensible to set off in weather as bad as this. However, if she should have done so, if by some mischance she should not return in the morning, then we must know where to look for her. Are you quite certain she did not say where she was going?'

There was a bee in Ava's bloomers and it were about to sting her arse. The thought brought a degree of satisfaction to Polly. Holding it warm to herself, she replied, 'If her did, mum, then it were not to me. Should I ask the rest of the staff did her say it to one of them?'

'No!' The answer was quick, too quick! Seeing the glint in her servant's eyes, Ava realised her mistake covering it with a small shake of her head. 'No, there is no need, I am probably fretting over nothing.'

That were a lie an' all! Polly kept her own look inscrutable. Ava Russell were frettin' all right, but why, when her had never given a tinker's cuss about anybody who worked in this house? Hands still grasped across her middle, she glanced towards the clock and said briskly, 'You will be wanting your bath tub filled, mum; the water be hot, I'll have the girl bring it up?'

Once again Ava shook her head, a brief dismissive movement as she rose from her chair. 'I shall not be requiring the bath this evening nor will I take supper in the dining-room. You may have a tray sent to my room.'

'Very good, mum.' Bobbing the merest assent, Polly Jupp left the room. Why was Ava Russell not wanting of that hot water? The answer were 'cos that wench were not here. Rapid as raindrops in a thunderstorm, thoughts raced through her mind. Bathing every night . . . tcha! Her had never done that while the master were living, a sponge down each morning and a bath once a week had been her routine, but since her husband had died (of a broken neck following a fall from his horse) things in this house had taken a very different turn.

Reaching the half-moon-shaped hall, Polly's glance travelled around it. *This* was all as it had been before the master's death: the gleaming mahogany of coat cupboards; the wall tables each supporting marble statuettes of lovely women half-covered in floating draperies, the names of their creators too foreign for her tongue; paintings by artists the master had named as Stubbs, Landseer and Turner. Oh yes, all that was still here – the first glimpse of the interior of Moorcroft that was seen by visitors, meant to impress . . . and to deceive!

Not all of this house was as it had been left by Ava Russell's husband. It had not taken long . . . In the five years of widowhood she had disposed of much of the contents, leaving empty those rooms once used by guests staying for party weekends or longer summertime visits; more than half of this once beautifully furnished home was now no more than a sham, a pretence . . . just as its owner was a sham.

Following along the short corridor which took her to the kitchen, Polly Jupp's mouth tightened. The mistress of Moorcroft led a life of deception. To the people beyond this house she might well appear the soul of propriety living the widow's role of a quiet, slightly withdrawn woman, reluctant to partake in society without the support of a husband. But nothing could be further from the truth.

Pouring herself a cup of tea, Polly sat at the table.

The love between a man and a woman, the love heaven had ordained, had found no place in this house; wherever Samuel Russell had found satisfaction it had not been in the bedroom of his wife. And only months after he had been buried, those carryin's on in that bathroom had started.

Staring into the fire burning in the well-polished range, Polly sipped her tea, only the pressure of her fingers around the large cup belying the acrimony of her thoughts.

Oh, the mistress believed none below stairs knowed of what went on, but Polly Jupp knowed. It were Polly Jupp had held a young wench sobbing of the terrible things Ava Russell had had her do, things never meant to be done woman to woman; a young wench who'd run away only to be found days later floating face-down in the canal. No, Myra Brent were not the first to be caught in the talons of that woman, not the first young wench to be sullied . . . and neither would her be the last.

'Brushing the muff' were what them carryin's on were called among Wednesbury folk and they gave short change to any woman thought to have a fancy for it; that much were known to her upstairs and that, like as not, were responsible for the death of that maid.

Death by misadventure! Polly's fingers tightened further pressure turning them white against her cup. That had been the verdict of the coroner but it weren't the verdict of Polly Jupp. To her way of thinking there had been no misadventure; the drowning of that young wench had been deliberate and the one behind the doing of it sat in this house. And unless Myra Brent returned tomorrow, then the canal would take another young life in its dark waters, for Ava Russell would suffer no risk of scandal.

Blue-tipped flames danced upward, drawn into the black void of the chimney. Gone as that young maid had gone. Lowering her cup, Polly heaved a long sigh. To tell what were held in her mind would do naught but bring a prison cell for herself. There were no proof Ava Russell's hand were at the back of that drowning. Likely her had paid well enough for a secret to be kept; but naught stayed hidden from the eyes of heaven, and one day it would take its reckoning.

6

Where could Eden have gone? From the window of the room she had rented Myra stared into darkness. Relentless, the storm raged, whirling great white flakes painting all that lay beneath. Was her sister out in this? Surely not. Eden would have found shelter somewhere. But Myra had not discovered where that somewhere was. She shivered against the chill which, despite the fire, pervaded the tiny room but she remained at the window, hoping even now that she might see the slight figure of her sister. She had enquired at every place she had passed but no one owned to having seen Eden. Then, as evening began to darken into night, she had been forced to find a place to stay.

She had seen the scrap of card. The proprietor of a small general shop had lit a lantern hanging over the goods displayed in the window and as its light caught the glass pane she had seen the advertisement. Scrawled in flimsy writing, it had proclaimed a house for rent.

'Ar, I knows the place . . .'

Blue-striped apron reaching from chest to feet, the

man behind a counter strewn with all manner of wares fingered a generous moustache.

'It be the first turning to the left, last 'ouse in the row, but there be nobody along of there, folk who lived there be gone to their daughter along of Dudley.'

'But the card . . .' She had looked with despair at the shopkeeper his face sallow in the sickly glow of that one lantern.

'Means what it says.' He had twiddled the moustache, enjoying the moment. 'Be for rent.'

He had said no more, but his eyes had run the length of her, taking in the drab coat and bonnet and, no doubt, the look of anxiety she knew etched her face and gleamed in the depths of her eyes. Had he thought her without the means to pay for a lodging? Or had he thought her a woman of the night, a prostitute looking for a dry place in which to ply her trade?

Despite the chill of the room, Myra's face flamed again in the sudden rush of heat which had suffused her in that shop. Indignation, offence and disgust obvious in her terse 'thank you', she had left.

Snow hurling itself at her in a wild frenzy, she had glanced towards the well-lit façade of the Talbot Hotel facing on to the market place. Maybe she could use a little of the money she had intended giving Grandmother, take a room in that hotel for just one night? But even as the thought took shape it was followed by another, one which warned against that or any other of the hotels Wednesbury boasted, for any one of them might have a guest who knew Ava Russell.

But would that guest recognise her ladies' maid? Common sense had argued against such a possibility but another, which her grandmother would have called a sixth sense, was stronger. Heeding the fears it kindled, she had trudged her way to the High Bullen. Only the length of Trouse Lane lay between this point and the heath. To be caught there, and in a snowstorm, was a hazard she must not put herself in. This time common sense had prevailed and she had entered the Grapes Inn.

'There be a room,' the landlord had said, running a quick look over the figure brushing snow from her eyelashes. 'But it be for one person only, so should you be thinkin' of entertainin' . . .'

'I require a room for myself only.' She had mustered every shred of dignity, her reply cuttingly sharp, but still the flood of heat had coloured her cheeks.

'So long as that be understood,' he had answered.

'Pay no mind to Jesse.' The landlord's wife had smiled apologetically, showing Myra upstairs. 'He tells the same to any wanting lodgin'; as he says, Jesse Newman runs a clean house, don't hold with no 'anky panky.'

The woman had put a match to the fire already laid in the tiny grate then, advising as to supper, had turned back to her duties in the kitchen.

Myra drew the curtains, shutting out sight of the snow-covered street; the mound that was Church Hill, robed now in pristine white; the dark shape of the spire of Saint Bartholomew's rising into a sky beginning to accept the silver touch of the moon. Myra crossed to the bed. Slipping between sheets smelling of soap, she closed her eyes, whispering the prayers her grandmother had taught in the firelight. But tonight another was added . . . a prayer that asked tomorrow she would find her sister.

'Be 'er goin' to be all right . . . ? 'Er don't be goin' to die, do 'er?'

'No, 'er don't be goin' to die, not if I can 'elp it, though it'll be no thanks to you. Of all the daft things to do sending 'er along of the Marsh cottage! You knows nicely the woman be a bit strange since the losin' of that lad of her'n.'

'I said as 'er mightn't tek a lodger.'

'You shouldn't ought to 'ave said anythin''. I've told you times afore about talking with strangers!'

'But . . .'

'This don't be the moment for buttin''!' Body as cold as her humour, Sara Melia snapped at the lad standing at her side. 'Help me get this poor soul along of the 'ouse.'

Risking his mother's ire no further the lad did as she bid, half-supporting the figure they had found lying almost hidden by snow. He had known of old mother Marsh's strangeness; all the lads at school had known and often gone to stand and shout at her gate, scampering like flies when she came from the cottage wielding a broom.

'That be a besom,' Cyril Hawkins had once said on

hearing what they had been up to. 'That be the true sign of a witch. Her flies on that at night to catch them who've annoyed her, an' her'll come for you when it be next full moon.'

'That one be soft as a brush and not near as useful!' his mother had said on finding why, at the very next full moon, he had been too afraid to go to bed alone. 'Frightenin' little 'uns be the only thing the noggin-'eaded lout be good for. I'll take a stick to his backside when I catches up to him, and I'll take it to your'n an' all for being daft enough to pay mind to 'im!'

But he *had* paid mind. For months the fear had remained with him, holding him rigid in his bed each time the moon reached its full. The thought of some avenging witch coming at him out of the darkness had never left him.

The weight of the burden slumped against him pressing his feet deep into the cloying snow, Davy Melia glanced at the great silent orb spreading the black sky with a silver radiance. It was with him now!

'Here, close against the fire.' Sara caught the expression on her son's face as the door of their home clicked shut behind them. At thirteen, he was street-grown, wise in the ways a boy without a father had needed to learn, but in others life had yet to oust the child in him.

'Take the bricks from the oven and put them to warming my bed, we'll put the wench in there. I can sleep afore the fire tonight.'

Gently easing the ends of a damp shawl from fingers

cold as those of a corpse, Sara did not catch the next look to pass across the boy's face, a look of fear at war with determination, but she heard the strength of the outcome in the reply.

'The bricks will be going into my bed. I'll be the one sleepin' afore the fire.'

The child was losing ground to the man. Sara felt the warm touch of pride. His father would have found no fault in their son.

'Be 'er going to be all right?'

Having helped his mother to carry the half-conscious figure to the bedroom, Davy voiced his question again.

A sharp retort rising to her lips, Sara checked it. She had tongue-lashed him for his thoughtlessness but, without his help, the girl would have been laying out in the open all night . . . maybe dying from cold, for the clothes she wore were no match for a winter's night. It had taken courage to tell of his encounter with a young woman, of sending her on what he had known to be a fool's errand, a brave step to confess in the face of a mother's anger . . . one more step of the man! A proud smile on her face she replied quietly.

'God 'as lent his hand to your'n, seems it be His will the wench will live. Now it be mine, you gets y'self from this room while I puts 'er to bed. You'll find broth simmering on the hob; bring me up a dish of it in five minutes.'

'I don't want to . . . I don't want to. . .'

Damp skirts gathered in her hands, Sara turned at

the muffled whisper. Beneath closed lids the eyes of the girl she and her son had brought in from the night moved restlessly.

'I don't want to . . . it don't be right . . . you shouldn't be asking that . . .'

Stepping closer to the bed, Sara watched shades of emotion flick across the pale face, the agitated turns of the head. Whatever was at the back of this girl's being away from her home were behind her still.

'. . . that isn't what I have to do . . .'

Caught by the intensity of the murmur, the sheer denial echoing in the words, Sara listened closely.

'. . . it can't be, Myra would have told me . . . my sister would never do what you ask . . .'

Seeming to watch moving pictures the closed eyes continued to move but Sara made no move to wake the girl who moaned softly.

'. . . Myra wouldn't do that and neither will I . . . you can't make me . . . I won't, I won't!'

What was it this girl had refused to do, what had given rise to such revulsion?

Disquieting questions, Sara thought, taking the bowl of broth her son had brought and handing him the wet clothing to be strung on the line tied above the fire-place. Disquieting enough in themselves but more disturbing yet was the one which followed; who was the cause of it?

'She has not come back?'

Lenor Medwin broke off as tea was brought by a

maid who bobbed a curtsy as she was waved impatiently away.

'No!' Ava Russell's reply was as tight as her mouth.

'But you said . . .'

'I know what I said . . . that she would return to Moorcroft.'

Hands shaking, Lenor poured tea into dainty china cups spilling as much again into the saucers. 'But she has to come back,' she whimpered, 'she must be made to return.'

Refusing the proffered cup, Ava Russell looked disdainfully at the woman seated opposite. Lenor Medwin liked the games but not the consequences, and there would be some painful ones should a whisper of what she indulged in reach the ears of her husband.

Keeping none of that disdain from her tone she answered. 'I am confident the girl can be persuaded to return!'

Lenor's plain face suffered under the worry of that reply. 'Persuaded!' she mewed. 'You mean she may not wish . . . she might no longer want her position!'

There was no 'want' about it, no maybe. Myra Brent had long desired to resign her post as ladies' maid. Only threats of what would happen to her sister and grandmother had kept her returning to Moorcroft. So why was it different this time? Ava tossed her head impatiently, keeping the question to herself.

'An unfortunate choice of word,' she said sharply. 'Of course the girl has no wish to leave her post.'

'Then why hasn't she come back?'

The intervention, quick and sharp, caught Ava off guard. She must speak and act with caution; Lenor Medwin's anxiety bordered on lack of control. Should it break it would mean more than her own fall from society . . . so it must not be allowed to break!

'I would have thought that to be obvious, my dear.' Adopting a softer tone, Ava's hard mouth relaxed to the hint of a smile. 'The girl's guardian is not a young woman, she has taken with some illness, the influenza so I am told. That is the reason Myra is not yet back at Moorcroft.'

'But could not someone else nurse the girl's guardian?'

Obviously unmollified, Lenor's anxious stare posed the unstated. What if the girl should inadvertently mention anything of those activities . . . those very private activities . . . shared with her mistress and the friend of her mistress?

Friend! Ava's own glance showed nothing of the acrimony that description aroused. Lenor Medwin was a tool, a means whereby amusement might be found, a plaything to be used then tossed aside without further thought . . . but a friend? Ava Russell wanted no friend!

'That is being taken care of.' She smiled more openly. 'I have arranged for that. I would have done so earlier but Myra asked to be given leave to stay home a few days longer.'

'Is that wise? I mean given what she knows . . . what she could reveal about us.'

About *you* . . . given what she knows about *you*, is what you really mean! Ava's glance rested momentarily on the hands twisting together in the other woman's lap. Lenor Medwin was concerned for Lenor Medwin and that concern was too near the surface. Drawing on her gloves Ava retained her composure.

'Myra is a sensible girl.' She rose from her chair. 'She knows that speaking of our little romps could bring dire results for herself. Think of it, my dear: a maid dismissed her position on being caught stealing, a girl attempting to revenge herself upon her mistress by making some preposterous allegation she had been subjected to indecent behaviour – what magistrate would believe that? Especially were an item of jewellery to be discovered beneath the mattress of her bed. You can put all fears from your mind, Myra Brent will not be disclosing any secrets.'

No, the girl would not be disclosing any secrets! Sitting in her carriage, Ava thought over what had passed between herself and Lenor Medwin. The talk of a guardian being ill of the influenza, of Myra being afforded a few days at home in order to nurse her had been lies; but not everything she had said had been lies. What she had said about there being no disclosure of secrets had been the truth, that she would make certain of . . . but not by accusing the girl of stealing jewellery.

Staring at the landscape yet seeing none of it, Ava's mind worked busily.

A girl in the magistrates' court, whether believed or not, the taint of it would settle. Ava Russell, though pronounced innocent of such wicked accusations, would nevertheless be whispered about behind women's fans, speculated about by men talking over cigars and brandy.

But that must not be allowed to happen. Lips compressing hard together, Ava's cold eyes gleamed.

It would *not* happen.

But, in order to ensure the girl's silence, the girl must first be found. That was no problem for she was not lost. She had told none of the staff at Moorcroft of her destination but where else would she go other than to see her family?

Was her ladies' maid so naïve? Did she really think the location of that home was secret? She had guarded it well enough, not speaking of it to anyone, but that did not mean Ava Russell did not know.

Poor Myra! In the privacy of her carriage Ava laughed softly. Had she forgotten the letter of recommendation she had brought with her on applying to Moorcroft for a position as domestic, a letter which spoke clearly of her background?

Hobbins Street. The name stood clearly in Ava's brain. She had read it only yesterday. Written in the neat hand of a teacher at Myra's school it was stated as the address of Rachel Brent, grandmother.

But had that grandmother changed her place of living? Had she, in the three years of Myra's being at Moorcroft, moved to some place else? Ava's hands tightened on her bag as a flicker of doubt edged her mind. If that was so, then where *had* Myra gone?

Dark ribbons of smoke-blackened houses stretched either side of the narrow streets through which the carriage passed, yet they remained invisible to Ava. Her eyes saw only one image: a young and pretty girl, a frilled apron tied over a dress the colour of her deep blue eyes, a starched lace-trimmed cap perched atop hair which shone like morning sun. She saw only Myra Brent.

Was she at Hobbins Street?

The time had come to find out.

7

'I didn't do it, Gran . . . I didn't do . . .'

A long sob bringing life to the words rushing through her sleeping mind, Eden woke.

'Gran,' she whispered, 'Gran . . .'

Teeth clamped hard on the tears trembling in her throat, Eden tried desperately to stem the truth, to keep reality from her mind, to hold the illusion, to believe the dream which said her grandmother was asleep in the next room, said Myra had not disowned them, said her life was as it had always been.

But the dream, the beautiful dream which gave her happiness, was a lie, a trap which closed about her each night, a safe, secure place hiding her from all that was truth. Yet every morning the pain of its falseness became an ever-sharpening knife twisting in her breast. Her life was not as it had always been. The love, the security, the joy of it was gone, shattered and broken beyond hope of repair.

'Gran . . .' Despite the pressure of tightly held lips the words fell into the silence of the dawn-filled room. 'Why . . . why did you leave me? Why does Myra no longer love me?'

Beyond the window, light spread across the sky as silent as the tears trickling down her cheeks, light which brought with it a new fear. Whose bed was this she lay in . . . who had placed her in it . . . and with what intent?

Her heart beating rapidly, a hand brushing away her tears, Eden threw back the covers with her grandmother's words speaking in her mind. *'This be no time for maudling, wallowing in pity for y'self; if somethin' be not suitable to you then you sets about puttin' it right.'*

And this was not suitable. She must dress and leave this place as quickly as she could.

'I sees you be awake, that's good.'

Her head twisted so rapidly on her neck she heard her bones creak a protest. Eden met the smile of a spare-framed woman, auburn hair faded and streaked with grey, her face touched by lines attesting to a life not filled with ease; but the eyes, the deep brown eyes held understanding, a look which stated she knew loneliness, heartache and fear, that they were companions which had travelled the years alongside her.

'I brought you up a sup of tea.' Sara Melia smiled. 'But you should get y'self back into bed for the day don't yet be aired.'

The day don't yet be aired. The same words her grandmother had used when two small girls had bounced on her bed eager to open a birthday present or to discover what delights lay in a grandfather's sock draped from the mantelshelf. Eden gulped the emotion of memory.

Though she had stepped no nearer the girl to whom

she had given shelter, Sara saw the nuance of unhappiness flit across the sad little face. The wench had gone through the mill, life had dealt a blow her was not yet recovered from; yet seemingly she had suffered no thraipins, no bruises spoke of physical violence; and the clothes her wore, though they were naught as 'adn't seen the insides of a pawn shop, were clean, the patches on petticoats neatly stitched and the gusset of the bloomers carried no trace of a monthly cycle. Was that the result of a good scrub and boil or of a babe in the belly? Could that be the reason of this wench being out on the 'eath? Had her been turned out . . . left to cope with the fruits of her sin?

Sin! Placing the cup on a table barely big enough to hold it, Sara felt resentment thicken in her throat. Who gave folk the right to say what were right and what were wrong? Who were it deemed a woman carrying a bastard child were the only one treading the path of evil while oft times the man responsible suffered no such judgement?

The girl wore no ring, no golden band on her finger. If it were her were carrying, there were no sign of its legitimacy, no attestation of a father proud of a child to come. More seemingly it was the leavin's of a fly-by-night, a man who had taken his pleasure then run, leaving behind a wench who would know a lifetime of condemnation and a child forced to wear the same badge, the stigma of being born a bastard, a child whose every step through life would be taken beneath the shadow of shame.

Was this wench no better than her should be? Sara looked at the girl she had dressed in one of her own cotton nightgowns, itself bought from the pawn shop. Denial born of instinct rose to answer Sara's thought. There was nothing of the whore in that face, drawn and frightened, yes, but given the trials of last night, lying out on the heath with no mortal soul for company and no shred of comfort, what young wench wouldn't look so? But there were no hardness of the mouth, no calculation in them eyes and, what of them cries made in her sleep? Did them be the cries of a prostitute? No! Sara reached her decision. Whatever had pushed this girl from her home, it couldn't be business of the night.

'I put a spoon o' honey in that there tea. You should drink it, whether or not you takes it sweet for honey gives a boost to the body.'

Again her grandmother's philosophy. Eden glanced longingly at the cup, steam spiralling from its contents.

'You be wonderin' where you be and how it be you come 'ere.' Sara saw the flash of anxiety cross Eden's face and nodded. 'Well, that don't be surprisin', but standin' in a chilled room wearin' naught save a nightgown don't be the best way to hear the tellin', and seems you have no likin' to put y'self back in that bed I best go fetch up your clothes and then we'll talk over a bite o' breakfast.'

She had left the house, said goodbye to Aunt Dora. Shivering, Eden dressed quickly, the clothes the woman had left with her still warm from the fire. She had walked away from Hobbins Street to go where?

Fastening the buttons of her skirt, she tried to halt the flow of memories, but one on the other they flowed in her brain like ripples on a stream.

Myra's slap . . . her failure to attend their grandmother's funeral . . . the house being taken back by Monway Colliery! But even had it not been repossessed she could not have stayed; the memories and the unhappiness of them would have weighed too heavily. Yet she had dawdled along the streets, looking in each and every shop window, using any excuse to step inside . . . for what?

Smoothing sheets and pillow case she tidied the bed, then folded the nightgown neatly. Standing with it in her arms, she stared at another, fresher picture in her mind; the picture of two little girls dressed alike in dresses of sky blue trimmed along the bodice with small pink bows, matching ribbons tied about long plaits of fair hair, heads bent over the serious business of making daisy crowns.

She had wasted time walking the streets of the town she was ready to leave for ever, dawdled with one hope in mind: to meet her sister. But there had been no Myra, no sight of the sister she loved.

Nightgown clutched to her, Eden blinked away the tears she felt resting on her lashes. Myra did not want her any more, that she would have to accept. The life they had lived and shared together was over, snatched from her in a single day, but nothing could rob her of what was in her heart, of the love she had, the love she would always have, for her sister.

*

'You'll do no such thing!' Sara Melia shook her head vigorously. 'Whoever 'eard the like, a day's work 'cos of bein' given a night's lodgin' . . . where be the charity in that!'

'The charity will lie in your allowing me to repay what I was given.'

Her outburst halted by the quiet dignity of the girl facing her, Sara Melia felt that same instinctive certainty she had felt the previous night; this wench were no trollop, her had been reared gentle and with the teachin's of good manners.

Faltering on how to answer, not wishing to tread on the girl's feelings, yet considering her own – feelings which said never to look for payment when doing a body a good deed – Sara took the neatly folded nightgown.

'That be all well and good,' she protested, 'but the giving of shelter shouldn't need no repayin'.'

'Kindness does,' Eden answered simply. 'I was taught always to repay . . .'

'And I was taught never to seek a shillin' after givin' a farthin'! I hears what you be sayin' but this be Sara Melia's 'ome and while her be mistress of it there'll be no askin' of payment for a kindness! Now get you to eatin' that porridge afore it be stone-cold.'

The woman had refused to give her some form of work which would pay for the night spent beneath her roof. Now she was offering breakfast! Eden glanced at the dish set on a table covered with a spotless cloth.

Porridge sweetened with honey and smothered in warm milk – it had ever been a favourite of hers and Myra's on cold winter mornings.

Defying any control the tears that memory brought rolled down Eden's cheeks. Returning from putting the nightgown with the rest of the weekly wash, Sara heard the deep sobs and stepped back into the scullery. Give the wench a minute or two, let her cry out her hurt for kept inside it never healed.

'Be it too forward of me to ask where you be goin'?' Minutes later, sitting together at the table, Eden's tears subsided, Sara posed the question that had been on her tongue the past hour.

'It isn't too forward at all, it . . . it's just I don't know.'

'You don't know!' Sara frowned. 'Then if you don't be knowing where it be you're goin' how will you know when it is you be there?'

She sounded so like Grandmother. Eden smiled inside. A great deal of logic but said in a roundabout fashion.

'Look, wench,' the reply she waited for not having come, Sara leaned across the table, touching her lined hand to one which showed no sign of nail-making nor chain-forging. 'If you be in trouble . . . if you be with child . . .'

'No!' Eden's blue-green eyes gleamed a truth Sara knew impossible to fake. 'I am not . . . I mean I never would . . .'

'Then that be one cause we can dismiss. But there be somethin' giving you heartache and if Sara Melia be good at nothin' else her be good at listenin' and holdin' locked away any confidence be her so asked.'

'It . . . it might all seem so silly, so childish.'

'Ar, it might.' Withdrawing her hand, Sara stood up. 'But what 'pears trivial to one be a matter of purpose to another. All I will say be this, a burden shared be only half as heavy as one carried alone.'

'It happened so suddenly . . . there was no warning.' Eden had not intended to speak but the first words breaching the barrier the rest followed, tumbling without pause until she had told it all.

Sara had not sat watching the girl tell her story; it would come easier were things carried on as normal. Pouring the tea she had freshly brewed in consequence of that line of thought, Sara placed a cup near to Eden.

'It be hard losin' loved ones,' she said, resuming her chair as the whispered explanation tailed away. 'But that be part of living. We can face it or turn from it but we don't 'ave the altering of it; death be the one fair thing given in this life, it be shared equal . . . whether pauper or king all gets the same. You says your grandmother loved you, that her cared for you from your being a babby. Now answer me this. Last night when you was caught in the storm, what made you lie down, what persuaded you to walk no further?'

'Nothing persuaded me, I . . . I suppose I was just too tired to walk any more.'

'But supposin' that were not the way of it?' Sara pressed quietly. 'Supposin' it were summat else halted your feet?'

You be tired, my little wench.

Startling in their clarity, the words returned.

Come set along of me, it be warm here against the fire.

Her face paling, Eden remembered.

'A voice,' she said, 'a voice, I heard it so distinctly, it . . . it said to rest, it said . . .'

She was suddenly back in the past. Her head bent against driving snow, her limbs numbed by the cold, she was alone in a world of darkness, but in that terrifying world a voice of comfort called.

I be here along of you . . . rest, my little love . . .

'Go on, wench,' Sara urged when it seemed Eden would say no more. 'Speak the rest . . . tell what it be your mind heard.'

'It . . . it . . .' Half in the past, half in the present, Eden stumbled. 'It said to rest, to sit beside the fire . . . that I would be safe.'

Sipping from her own cup Sara watched the nuances of emotion cross the pallid face. The wench were struggling with more than just words.

'What was said to you?'

'I was alone! There was no one with me to say anything!'

Halted by the confusion so obvious in the cry, Sara chose her answer carefully.

'The words you felt in your heart, those your mind spoke, they was gentle? They said no harm?'

'No.' Eden's frown quickened. 'They . . . they were only kind.'

'And the voice, though naught but the thinking of

your brain,' Sara was quick to reassure, ''ave you the remembering of it . . . of how it sounded?'

'Comforting . . . it sounded comforting.'

Returning the cup to the table, Sara stared at it for several moments. 'It told you to rest,' she said, looking up, 'it said you would be safe . . . but the voice which spoke them words, it be known to you.'

Startled, Eden met the woman's steady gaze. How could she know that which she had not admitted, even in her own heart?

'You knows, wench, tell y'self it be an untruth if the telling gives you ease, but Sara Melia sees it in your face, it be in your eyes; the voice that spoke from the darkness brought you no fear 'cos you had the recognisin' of it.'

. . . Ar, my little wench . . . it be Gran . . . I be here along of you . . .

Knuckles pressed against her mouth, Eden fought the rush of emotion, the rising need for what could not be, the need of her grandmother's loving arms.

'You 'ave to bring it out.' Sara spoke gently. 'Put words to what be inside.'

'It was imagination . . . only that, it could have been nothing more.'

'Imaginings be powerful things, they can soothe or they can worry, best way be to bring them into the open, 'appen they won't seem so frightenin'.'

Fingers gripping the cup she had been given, Eden stared at its contents trying to find the courage to answer.

'I thought . . .' She paused. The woman would think her mad, think her deranged.

'P'raps it be better should I tell it.' Sara's lined face smiled compassion. 'You thinks the voice speaking to you out of that storm were the voice of your grandmother.'

. . . Ar, my little wench . . . it be Gran. . .

Eden caught her breath. She *had* heard those words, she *had*!

'I sees by your look I be right.' Sara nodded. 'An' it be my guess I be right in saying you was told the very same.'

'How could it have been?' Eyes bright with tears clung to Eden's. 'My grandmother is dead.'

'But her spirit don't be.' Gentle as it was, the woman's quick response lost none of its emphasis. 'Her be with the Lord an' it be His mercy give leave for her spirit to walk beside you, to comfort and keep you from danger, the danger that waited not many yards from where you laid yourself down.'

'Danger?' Eden's frown returned.

'Ar, wench, you was in danger from more than the cold. A few more steps an' you would 'ave been among the gin pits, holes left from the diggin' of coal, shafts left open and without cover. Anybody not knowin' the whereabouts of such treads a dangerous path. Folk 'ave been lost in them more times than a few. That were what the spirit of your grandmother kept you from.'

The fingers gripping the cup were white with pressure, the lips trembling, the breath jerking from a throat held tight as Sara went on.

'Your grandmother cared for you, reared you tender as any mother could 'ave done, so think, wench, think on what you be about, what her would 'ave wanted you to do. Would her truly 'ave said to turn your back, to run from the first hurdle life has thrown at you, or would her 'ave told you to face up to them? Told you that only by facing trouble can it be overcome?'

Yes, Grandmother would have told her that. Tension breaking under a shudder that rippled the length of her, Eden's fingers released her cup.

But would she have told how to face the heartbreak of a sister's rejection?

Myra Brent was not at Hobbins Street! Her tightly corseted body ramrod-straight, Ava Russell sat in her elegantly furnished drawing-room, her features displaying none of the tension building inside her as she listened to her cook.

'Birks was sent, mum, as you instructed. Said as the woman at the next house told him the grandmother had passed away more'n a week since and that the house had been taken back by Monway Colliery, that another family entirely was living there.'

'And Myra?'

The cook's head shaking briefly gave the answer Ava dreaded, but she listened, her face displaying none of that inner worry bordering so closely upon anger.

'Myra d'aint never go to Hobbins Street, least that were what be told by Birks. He says the woman who were neighbour to the Brents from long afore them two granddaughters were brought to live at that house told him clear; Eden had gone to give the tidings of the grandmother's passing to her sister Myra who was in service along of Moorcroft, that when her returned her were in tears. Seems Myra had slapped her, saying her were never to come to that house again . . .'

The girl in the yard, the one Myra had professed to be a gypsy! Ava's fingers tightened in her lap. She had been no wayfarer and her neat clothing had shown her to be no vagabond.

'. . . well, Myra never showed to the funeral.' The cook's sharp eyes had caught the minute movement of Ava's tightening fingers but her mind, equally sharp had years before taught she remain blind and deaf to anything not specifically shown or instructed by the mistress of Moorcroft. '. . . and as for the younger wench, her were gone from Hobbins Street in less than a week . . .'

'To go where?' Incisive as a blade, Ava's snapped question cut across her cook's report.

'Nobody knowed, mum. Birks asked special like, says he put that self-same question, the answer being her were bent on leaving Wednesbury altogether, p'raps them two wenches met up and decided to go find a place together.'

Ava kept her expression even, though beneath the tight corset her stomach lurched. Of course they had gone off together, two sisters to plot and scheme, two sisters to threaten Ava Russell!

'Perhaps,' she answered levelly. 'In that event I cannot be of assistance though I would have preferred to help should it have been needed.'

It be y'self you would 'ave preferred to help! Dismissed from the drawing-room, Polly Jupp smiled knowingly. Ava Russell had got the wind up, her were nervous of what might come of Myra Brent's just up and leaving, not only this house but the town. The wench had slung her hook, not that Ava were piddlin' her bloomers over that; no, Ava were all of a cummujin due to something else entirely . . . and Polly Jupp knowed what that summat were!

Passing along the narrow corridor which led to the kitchen, Polly nodded to herself. Yes, her knowed what were bothering that woman upstairs; it was fear of who else might come to know of them capers in that bathroom. Who else, now Myra Brent were free of this house, might learn the secrets of Ava Russell!

8

'I don't be asking of it and I won't be taking of it.' Sara Melia pushed the silver coin back across the table.

'But, please,' Eden's distressed look lifted to a face whose work-worn lines were deepened by a frown, 'I have to repay the kindness you have shown me, you would not let me share in your work so . . .'

'So nothing!' Sara pushed the coin further, her tone adamant. 'I'll not take a shilling, I'll not take a farthing. After all, it were my lad with his thoughtless ways sent you off to old mother Marsh's place . . . eh, the daftness of him! Sometimes I wonder will he ever leave the way of childhood behind? But one thing I don't be wondering on is that his ears be stinging still with the boxing they got last night after I got you put to bed, though I must tell in his favour that, were it not for his guiding, you would surely have laid out there all night, or else staggered into one of them gin pits. Either way you wouldn't have lasted long.'

'I would like to thank him.' Eden glanced to a window through which the sky looked grey and leaden.

'He don't be here,' Sara followed the glance, 'he is always up at first light and off to help with the loading of carters' wagons or to stand the line in hopes of a day's labour. Usually comes home with coppers enough to see food on the table, but then that don't be until well after dark for he says carters pulling into the Turk's Head or Golden Cross taverns be willing to pay sixpence to have him take the horse and cart to the stabling yard, leaving them free to get to their night's comforts the sooner. And sometimes he is given the same by gentlemen arriving at the George Hotel or even the White Horse, but either way I don't see him back to this house until after nine at night.'

So late! Passing about her shoulders the shawl which had been her grandmother's, Eden caught the corners together in a knot beneath her breasts. She could not wait so long.

'I'm sorry there don't be a room here to offer you for good but we could manage for a day or two.'

'You have already been more than kind,' Eden's smile reflected her gratitude, 'and I thank you as I would like to thank your son. Please will you do it for me?'

Sara Melia's nod was gentle. 'I'll do that, wench, and the lad will be right glad to hear you bear him no ill will for sending you where he did.'

Picking up the coin, Sara followed Eden outside and pressed it into her hand. 'Take your money, for your need be greater than mine. The Lord walk with you.'

The last echoing in her ears, the shawl pulled close against the sudden shock of cold, Eden followed the way she had been directed. She had tried to repay as she had been taught. Maybe one day the chance would be given again.

Bell Street. Myra walked slowly through the rooms of the house she had rented. She had left the Grapes Inn and, on the advice of the landlord's wife, had hurried to the Market Place. 'You'll likely get a ride with one of the carters, many of them sets off from there, but you need hurry for once their wagons be loaded they don't waste time.'

She had hurried, her boots crunching the snow lying crisp and hard as she ran the length of Upper High Street, her lungs aching from the bite of frost-laden air as she raced, panting, into the yard of the Turk's Head, a prayer repeating over and over in her mind that a wagon would still be there.

She could ride with him and welcome. The one remaining carter had looked at her, his glance questioning beneath heavy caterpillar eyebrows. For a moment she had thought he would ask why she did not take a tram or even a train and her throat had tightened. Had she answered she could not risk being seen by anyone who might recognise her, that her best chance of leaving Wednesbury unnoticed was by way of a carter's wagon, the man might have thought her to be evading the law and refuse to take her.

But he had not asked. He had simply said he was travelling only as far as the next town, Darlaston, and if it were her destination also then she was welcome.

It was not only a way of protecting her face from the sharp sting of a dying winter that she had held her hands across her nose and mouth but a way of hiding her features from anyone disposed to glance at the figure huddled beside the driver of the heavily laden cart. Moorcroft was often visited by tradesmen making deliveries, and staff enjoyed a few minutes gossiping with them, a casual mention of a young woman dressed in brown coat and bonnet asking a lift of a carter . . . Ava Russell had sharp ears and long arms; it would not prove so difficult for her to trace where her maid had gone and bring her back!

The thought had sent a shiver through her body and beside her the man had felt it. Taking the thick woollen muffler from his neck, he had passed it to her, making no comment as she wound it about her head.

He was going to Darlaston but there were calls to be made first in Moxley. It would take a longer time so if she was in a hurry . . .

She had shaken her head at the implied suggestion, murmuring there was no rush for her to reach that place. But what was that town like? It could have been the moon for all she knew of it, but to ask him would have revealed she had never visited it and thus had neither friend nor relation among its people. That in itself would arouse suspicion, so fears of what she might or might not find had remained locked inside.

The journey had been slow. The ancient horse the carter called Solomon trod carefully on the ice-covered setts. Face covered by the muffler, Myra had watched buildings and streets familiar from childhood as the cart rumbled to the junction fondly called after the large cream-coloured stone built hotel, the White Horse. Either possessing the wisdom of his namesake or the knowledge gained from years of following the same route, the horse needed no touch of the rein to guide it to the right where they joined the Holyhead Road.

She had fought the impulse to look at the police station standing solidly opposite the imposing Wesleyan chapel. Had Ava Russell discovered she was not at the house in Hobbins Street? Had she reported her missing? Were the constables even now on the watch for her?

Biting deep into frost-crushed snow, the wheels of the cart had rumbled like thunder as they passed the gleaming red brick of the ornately façaded Town Hall. Grandmother had taken her to watch the opening celebration, a man among the crowds hoisting her on to his shoulders while Grandmother held Eden in her arms. Had it really been only seventeen years since that bright day in 1872? And was it really only three of those years since she had gone to Moorcroft? Years which had proved an eternity! A river of questions poured into her mind, each bringing the visions of memory. Like sitting in a quiet, sun-filled classroom of the school stood in a street to the left, her mind in another place, another age, as the teacher read aloud the deeds of Ivanhoe, or the adventures of King Arthur's Knights of the Round Table? Then the sympathy she had felt for the pigs she had known to be taken to Hollingsworth slaughterhouse at the corner of that same street. Pawn shop, grocer, draper, confectioner, the cart passed them by, memories following like spectres calling her not to leave. But she had to leave, not only to safeguard herself from Ava Russell but to find Eden, to find her and take her far from Wednesbury; to go somewhere they could live together in safety.

But was this town far enough away? The carter had asked nothing as he set her down at the Bull Stake, and she had told him nothing, not her name nor her reason for coming there for what he did not know he could not repeat. Nor had she asked any passer-by for assistance; she could see and she could read, she must find for herself what was needed.

The resolve in mind she had trudged several streets, her boots wet from snow turned to slush. She had found what she looked for at James Belcher, Estate Agent, in Pinfold Street.

'*A small property*.' A heavily whiskered man had smiled across a vast desk. '*But adequate for what you describe and not too far from the town centre, I think you will find it suits you very well.*'

She had refused the offer of being escorted, asking instead that the address be written for her. The less noticeable her arrival at Bell Street, the easier she would feel. Opening the scullery door she looked out over the communal yard. She would share one of two privies with two other families. Not so different from Hobbins Street. She closed the door turning back towards the room which, as in her grandmother's house, must serve as kitchen, dining-room and living-room. But it was all she needed.

Shivering against a cold dampness that drove into her bones, it took all of her strength not to give in to the misery inside her. But that she must not do, she must stay strong if she were to find Eden, and she would find her . . . Please God, she would find her.

'It is all taken care of, there is absolutely nothing to worry over.'

'Thank goodness for that!' Lenor Medwin's plain face relaxed visibly. 'I have been so . . . I dreaded every moment might bring an accusation, that Arthur may in some way have found out about . . . about . . .'

Ava smiled. An inner prayer thanked the Fates for freeing her from the ties of marriage and the subordination a wife was expected to show a husband. Widowhood suited her very well; being answerable to no one suited her even more.

'You can put it completely from your mind.' Across the comfortably appointed bedroom, Ava's smile was reassuring. 'Arthur will not find out . . . There is no one beside ourselves and Myra who knows anything.'

'But the girl is not here . . . She hasn't come back.'

'No.' In the light of gas lamps turned low in their ornamental brackets Ava's dark hair shimmered like blue diamonds at every shake of her head. 'I thought it kinder to let her remain a while longer with her grandmother.'

Lenor fiddled with the ribbons of her silk nightgown, its bright emerald colour serving only to highlight her sallow complexion and the falseness of her hennaed hair. She felt far from reassured. The wench could spill her secrets, tell them to God knows who. Money! Her fingers pulled hard tearing away the slender tie of silk. The girl had nothing . . . she was simply a maid but Ava had said she was sensible, intelligent even . . . The tie dropped from suddenly shaking fingers . . . Intelligent enough to realise the possibilities? The money she could demand for not relating what she knew to Arthur!

'I don't think it wise, I . . . I think she should be brought back . . . I mean we can't be certain she won't speak of . . .'

Lenor Medwin's anxiety had not abated. Ava felt a flutter of irritation. Despite the assurance that everything was as she would wish, that the girl would do or say nothing which could cast a slur, Lenor Medwin was still nervous. The smile remaining soft on her thin mouth, Ava crossed to her companion but, as she touched her lips to the pallid cheek, her mind closed like a vice about just one thought. Ava Russell did not tolerate threat, whoever it came from! That would be dealt with just as Myra Brent would be dealt with, but not yet; after all, where was the sense in disposing of something which was of use? Lenor Medwin might not give the same pleasure, her body not shapely and firm as a young woman's, her hands not building fires which scorched along every vein yet still she was of use.

Lenor Medwin provided some, if only a little, of the solace needed to ease that particular desire . . . to give the thrills which came from brushing the muff.

Calmly and gently, as if she were soothing a difficult child, all trace of irritability subdued behind the deceptive smile, Ava guided the fretful Lenor towards the wide bed.

'If you feel Myra should be brought back to Moorcroft then that is how it will be, I shall give instructions first thing in the morning; in the meantime let us not waste the few hours given to us, we have to wait so long for that which delights us both.'

It *did* delight; Lenor had never known such enjoyment, such gratification with Arthur. A small breath escaping her throat, she felt a swift liquorice rush, a quickening of the stomach, a tightness of chest and throat that held her breathless, gasping for the pleasures to come. Ava was right, they must not waste these precious hours. A soft moan was muffled by Ava's mouth on hers, her eyes closed on her silk robe rustling to the floor, Ava's lips transferring to her breast while her naked body was pressed slowly backward on to the bed.

She should have stayed. Sara Melia had offered to have her stay a while. Resting against the curved wall of a bridge, Eden stared into the waters of a canal. Grey and still as lead, they reflected a sky threatening yet another storm. Eden shivered, her teeth clenched against the cutting wind. Why had she refused? She could have slept on the floor beside the fire, there would have been no need for the boy to give up his bed. The boy, Sara's son . . . She stared at the dark sluggish water. She had not seen him since he gave her directions to the Marsh cottage, she had had no chance to thank him for bringing her in from the heath or for the use of his bed, but Sara would do so, she had promised as much.

Why had she not made that an excuse for remaining at that house? Why had she not said she wished to stay to thank the boy herself? It would have been logical.

It would 'ave been an untruth.

Clear and sharp as the frost rimming the heath, the words of her grandmother rang in her mind.

Comfort of the body be no comfort if bought by a lie, and the mind can never rest easy under an untruth.

Those words had admonished two small girls caught in some mischief or other and it seemed they admonished now.

Grandmother had been so wise, so practical. Gathering her skirts close about her, Eden slid to the ground, the body of the bridge a shelter against flurries of snow driven before the strengthening breeze. She would have known what to do, known where to go.

Head pressed to her drawn-up knees, Eden felt warm tears trace her cheeks. How would Grandmother have reacted to being rejected? How would she have dealt with being disowned by one she loved?

Not by running away! The voice in her head answered sharply.

Problems don't go away simply 'cos you refuses to face them, nor does turning your back mend a broken heart.

'Gran!' Beneath the shawl, it was a soft cry, 'Oh Gran, what can I do!'

'Well, you could stand on your feet . . . Unless of course you are trying for a bout of pneumonia.'

'I tried, Gran, I tried . . .'

'Then I suggest you try a little harder or the next person to come along will find you frozen to that bridge.' Even as she heard the words in her head, Eden's arm was grasped firmly and she was hauled upright.

'Don't you have more sense than to go sitting on ground solid with frost!'

That was not Grandmother's voice, nor was it her touch. Dazed by the sudden jerking to her feet, her mind not yet sorting the real from the imagined, Eden stared at the man still holding on to her.

'Lucky I came along.' He shook her roughly. 'Another hour and it could have been too late. Has no one ever warned you of the danger of sleeping in the snow . . . or could it be you just ignore advice!'

'I . . . I was not asleep.'

'I don't suppose you were sitting on the ground huddled against a canal bridge either!' Brittle as ice crunching beneath his feet, the reply cracked out.

Stung by the harshness, Eden's senses returned with a jolt, making her retaliation equally sharp. 'And I don't suppose you enjoy playing Sir Galahad!'

The hand dropped from her arm and a smile

appeared in dark eyes. 'You know me already, and there was I hoping my play-acting would go unnoticed! But I suggest we both move on before we freeze.'

Drawing the shawl close, seeking every atom of warmth it allowed, Eden met the smile with hostile eyes. 'Thank you, but your suggestions are not needed, I can manage quite well for myself.'

His smile dying as quickly as it had sprung to life, his hand moved like quicksilver to grab her in a grip of iron.

'Manage what!' Harsher even than before, the words grated from lips suddenly drawn tight. 'To throw yourself into the canal? To sit down until the cold sucks the life from you? Or to run a little farther away? That is what you are doing isn't it, running away? Well, I can't see that being of much help with your problems. Turning your back and refusing to face what life dishes up solves nothing and neither will it mend a heart you think to be broken.'

What did he know about her heart? What did he know about her feelings? Anger flaring, Eden tried to shake the hand from her arm but the grip remained firm.

'I see I have struck a nerve,' he said brusquely. 'At least that is a start.'

A flicker of apprehension, despite her efforts to hide it, gleamed beneath the anger in Eden' s eyes. 'A start of what!'

Had he heard that tremor of quandary in her voice? Did the sudden trepidation she was feeling show in her eyes? She was alone with a stranger, with a man whose grip on her arm told of strength her own would be no match for. Nerves dancing, Eden tried not to show the fear beginning in her stomach.

'A start of returning you to your senses.' The terse declaration was accompanied by a tug on her arm which snatched her free of the bridge. Her squeal of protest faded in her throat as she was dragged away.

9

He had not asked her name, he had not asked where she was from or where she hoped to go; in fact he had asked nothing.

Irascibility alive inside her, Eden watched the tall figure stride away.

He had not asked what brought her to that bridge, he had simply assumed . . . assumed she was running away!

But in that his thinking had been correct; she *was* running away.

The admission cooling her irate feelings she stared after his fast disappearing shape. There had been no asking would she accept his help, allow him to accompany her to a place more appropriate to her wellbeing than a canal bridge. Instead he had merely grabbed her arm and, despite her protests, had virtually dragged her along beside him. He had said nothing as they walked and, within a few yards, her own words had ceased, only small puffs of breath glistening white on the frosty air conveying her struggle to keep up with his long easy stride.

He must have known! Eden pulled tight the shawl

which had worked itself loose. He could not fail to have noticed her difficulty in matching his gait, must have felt her stumble over snow-hidden stones, yet he had not reduced his pace in the slightest.

Nor had he apologised for his handling of her. He had halted as they came in sight of a range of buildings rising stark against the wide, snow-covered emptiness. '*The Coppice*,' he had said. '*You will find somebody there who will give you directions to where you want to be . . . that is supposing you know yourself* . . .' With that he had left.

Drawing the shawl over her mouth and nose, she watched the figure now indistinct in the distance. He was gone and, strangely, so were her feelings of vexation; stranger still was the perplexity their fading left behind. Was it resentment tingling in the wake of anger . . . indignation at being treated as she had been? Or was it disappointment at his leaving?

But that was nonsense. She was cold and hungry and those were her only feelings!

Somebody there will give you directions . . .

The deep musical voice seemed to mock. Turning to the buildings, Eden hesitated. How did she ask the way when she didn't know where it was she wished to go? But she had to find a place somewhere and, as that stranger had said, to make that place a stone bridge would be to freeze to death in her sleep.

Renting a partly furnished house was an extravagance. Myra placed the coins she had counted several times into various small piles. There was so little left of the yearly salary she had been paid a month ago; salary she had intended for her grandmother. Looking at what remained of it, she wondered how two people had managed to live on such a sum. But they had and so must she.

Taking a house rather than a single room had accounted for a large slice of her twelve pounds. '*Thirty shillings a month*,' the bewhiskered estate agent had already dipped his pen into the glass inkwell given pride of place on a well-polished desk, '*but the property can only be let on a three-monthly basis. I trust that is acceptable to you, Miss Brent.*'

It hadn't been . . . Myra stared at the coins. Four pounds ten shillings to put a roof above her head. But she had needed privacy, somewhere she could come and go without question, without a landlady prying into her affairs. So she had signed the agreement and paid the three months' rent. Would that prove enough time in which to find her sister? But she could not allow that to become a question, it *had* to prove enough. Funds would not stretch to another three months even supposing she took employment. But there could be no supposition about that either; if she were to survive she must find work . . . but never again as a ladies' maid.

'I hopes you don't mind . . .'

Myra scooped the coins into her palm as a voice called from the scullery doorway.

'I've set a bucket of coal against you wanting a fire . . . there be a few sticks and some paper along of it.'

Going quickly to the scullery, Myra smiled at the woman standing in the yard.

'You can give it back when you gets your own,' the woman's glance ran over Myra, taking in the neat though drab-coloured coat, 'the jagger will be round in about an hour. He sells coal bought from pit bank wenches but don't pay near what it be worth, considerin' it can take close on a day to pick enough from them waste heaps to fill a sack. And mind . . .' halfway back to her own door, the woman turned, '. . . neither do you go payin' what old robber'll ask. It be well known that every sack he buys he splits to make two so you give no more than sixpence. Any arguin' and you give me a shout, he won't have no argy bargy with Ada Slater.'

The fire lit and the kettle hung from a bracket above it, Myra dried her hands. She had washed in water that had been covered by a thin film of ice. Privacy was one thing, an act of kindness another. She could not keep herself totally in isolation from her neighbours, for that in itself would arouse curiosity, but they would not be told all of her reasons for coming to live in Bell Street.

Pulling her chair close to the hearth, Myra went once more over her finances. She had bought sheets and blankets from a pawnbroker. She had almost walked past its sign of three brass balls, covered with snow, but then a bent figure carrying a cloth-wrapped parcel had alerted her to the business of the small, dingy shop.

'*Come from a clean house.*' The pawnbroker had opened a large parcel allowing her a glimpse of the bedlinen it comprised. '*An unredeemed pledge.*'

They had cost two pounds. Towels, tea cloths, two cotton tablecloths and cooking utensils had accounted for a further ten shillings, while the same amount had been asked for personal linen. Counting the rent she had paid, the cost of her night's lodging at the Grapes Inn, together with the food items she had bought and the coal she would be buying later today, her twelve pounds had already fallen to less than four.

In her rush to get away from Moorcroft she had given no thought to the expense it would involve. Food and clothing had been provided there and she had needed to spend none of her yearly twelve pounds. It had always seemed such a large amount when handed to her by Ava Russell; only now with three-quarters of it spent in a day did she realise the paucity of that sum.

She should have given thought! She should have had more sense! Remonstrance of the sort her grandmother would have given sounded loud in Myra's conscience. Would the estate agent perhaps release her from her contract? Would he return the money she had paid? And if his answer were no?

Caught in the dilemma brought on by her own thoughtlessness Myra dropped her head into her hands as another more worrying thought followed. What if Eden were not in Darlaston? What if she had left Wednesbury for a different location altogether?

'You'll find no charity here!'

He had stepped from the first of what had turned out to be three small houses, each a twin of the other. Eden stared, taken aback by his animosity. Old as Grandmother had been, hair more white than brown, his spare figure leaning heavily on a strong cane, a man glared back at her, eyes glinting like old copper.

'I said you will find no charity here!'

Loud on the crisp air, the repeated words cracked like pistol shots, clearing Eden's mind. Holding her stare, her tone as cold as the morning, she answered steadily. 'Thank you, but I was not aware I had asked for charity.'

'Just as well,' the reply whipped back, 'for there is naught of that in this place. Beggars find no welcome at The Coppice.'

So cold she could not prevent the shiver which made the whole of her body tremble, Eden made no effort to calm the storm suddenly stirring inside. Poor as they had always been, not once in her life had Grandmother stooped, or allowed her grandchildren to stoop, to begging; every crust they had eaten had been worked for, every farthing earned by the labour of their hands! Indignation flashed in her eyes, emphasis weighing icily on every word she spoke, slowly and clearly leaving no room for misunderstanding.

'You, sir, should recognise a beggar when you see one for it appears obvious you have driven many away, but I am no beggar, I ask for no charity.'

'Then you'll not be disappointed!' There was no hesitation in the answer. 'This be no almshouse and I be no philanthropist.'

For the briefest of moments Eden hesitated but that

moment was sufficient for the swords that flashed in her eyes to be sheathed and the ice which had weighted her voice to melt.

'No,' she said quietly, 'there is no charity here, and you, sir, are the poorer for it.'

Had it been a hiss of anger, the breath he had drawn so sharply, or had it been surprise? Shawl held protectively close, Eden walked on, the snow covered ground sucking at her feet as though reluctant to have her pass. First one man and then another! First the young and then the old! Both had spoken rudely, the younger assuming her on the verge of suicide, while the elder branded her a beggar. Neither had the solicitude or the compassion her grandmother had always shown towards those she thought in need; quite the opposite. They had each displayed a hardness of heart she found difficult to comprehend. 'A kind word lightens no pocket' was the maxim lived by in Hobbins Street, but here a different approach was made to strangers.

But then her own responses had hardly been of the kind that would have brought approval from her grandmother or from Myra; they would have thought her as ill-mannered as those men. And so she had been!

A tingle of reproof coursed along Eden's veins. Bad manners on the part of one person did not condone their use in reply. She had acted no better than those men.

Eden clutched the corners of her shawl. She was no longer in Hobbins Street! She no longer had the comfort of her grandmother or the love of her sister.

She was alone in the world and unwise to its ways, but she would learn . . . yes, she would learn.

Ava had lied to Lenor Medwin. What she had said about Myra Brent nursing her grandmother, that she would have the girl brought back to Moorcroft the very next morning, neither were the truth. But since when had telling the truth ever bothered Ava?

Sitting in the room her husband had used as a study and which she now used on those occasions when she wished to impress her authority upon those with whom she may have to do business, Ava Russell's fingernails tapped on the mahogany desk.

Never! The answer was never! Lying had been an ally in her life, a tool she always found useful and one she would not fail to employ whenever the doing suited her; and she was a master of the art!

Not that it had taken much proficiency to overcome Lenor Medwin's doubts. Ava's tight mouth thinned with contempt. One touch of her lips on Lenor's over-large breast, one flick of her tongue across the nipple, one stroke of those bare thighs, and all protest had faded. The woman's first shy acquiescence, the flush of colour to the cheeks as the clothes were gently eased from her body, the quick intake of breath that had become sighs of sensual pleasure, the soft hedonistic moans which had gradually turned to screams as hand or mouth had found the secret place between her legs, had at first provided . . . Ava's fingers stilled. What had Lenor Medwin's rapture provided for Ava Russell?

Delight? Only in the subduing. Satisfaction? Only in the domination. It was the power, the power she now held over the other woman, that was her own enjoyment.

Poor Lenor! The thin smile held no amusement and no pity. Lenor had run so willingly into the trap which caught and held, one which blinded the senses and prevented her from seeing the path she was following and the end to which it must lead. But Lenor Medwin was too lost to the pleasures of brushing the muff . . . and Ava Russell would not discourage the indulging of it. Let the woman have her pleasure . . . it would, after all, be paid for.

But on one thing Lenor made sense; Myra Brent must be brought back to Moorcroft.

'You asked Birks be sent along, mum.'

Bringing her hands to her lap Ava nodded, her glance travelling quickly over the man standing before the desk.

'You went to Hobbins Street some days ago. Tell me what occurred.'

The hard-faced bitch knew what had occurred! Polly Jupp would have given her word for word what had passed between him and the woman he had talked with . . . So why ask again?

'I told Polly . . .'

'Now you can tell me!'

The razor-sharp words snapped across the desk. Polly Jupp had said the mistress were edgy and that were no exaggeration, and lessen' he were mistook it had than somewhat more to do with that maid of her'n than just the wench's welfare.

'I went as you said,' he answered, his eyes alert to any reaction to his words. 'The house I were given to call at were lived in by others, they knowed nothing of a Myra Brent.'

'So you returned to Moorcroft.'

Her were trying to trick him, catch him out in a lie! The stablehand's fingers tightened on the cap they held. Her were checking what her had already been told, but for what reason?

Careful not to allow that curiosity to colour his answer, he shook his head. 'Not right away, mum, I thought p'raps the folk in the next house might be able to say where I could find Myra.'

'And did they?'

Catching the glint of anger in Ava's steel-hard eyes the stablehand smiled inwardly. He would act the dunderhead, let her think him a fool, make her ask for every item of information.

'No, mum.' He twisted the cap again, his glance falling as though he were afraid, but what he felt was not fear, not even curiosity, but a sense he could not yet define.

Exasperation pressing hard in her chest, Ava fought the impulse to sack him on the spot; but that could come later, when this dolt was of no more use. Control of her temper as tight as the corset laced about her body, her breathing deceptively even, she asked. 'Did they say anything at all?'

Holding to the charade, Alfred Birks glanced quickly at the mistress he pretended fear of, then just as quickly let the glance fall back to the cap clenched in his hands. 'Yes . . . yes, they said somethin' . . . well, the woman did, for it were a woman I talked with.'

The idiot had paused again! Hidden by the desk Ava's fingers twined painfully in her lap. Lord how long could she stand his stupidity!

'Her said as how Myra d'ain't never come to Hobbins Street.' Judging Ava to be near the end of tolerance and that by pushing her beyond that point would somehow be to his own detriment, he went on. 'Her said the younger wench, a sister by the name of Eden, had come to Moorcroft to tell Myra of their grandmother having died, but Myra sent her off with a slap to the face.'

'That was all the woman told you? There was nothing else?'

'No, mum, nothin' else . . . 'cept for . . .'

'Except for?' Ava's teeth gritted.

Feet shuffling, a slight choking of the throat adding to his air of nervousness, Alfred Birks hid his smile.

''Cept for sayin' Myra never was at the funeral and that the younger wench left from Hobbins Street less than a week after.'

'Did you by any chance enquire as to where the other girl had gone?'

This was no case of a mistress concerned for a maid. This probing were too deep for that . . . there was something more behind Ava Russell's questioning.

Pushing the thought to the back of his mind yet not entirely dismissing it, he answered, maintaining the illusion of a dull-witted brain, the smile he lifted to her deliberately inane. 'Oh, I done that, I asked special, I said where was her gone to? But the woman hadn't no knowing of that . . . said her d'ain't have that knowing at all.'

The story matched, though the delivery of its repeating had taxed her patience.

Alone once more, Ava's fingers untwined but her mouth held its tension.

So, Myra Brent had made no mention of any intended destination. That could point to only one conclusion. She hoped by leaving no track, by leaving no word of where she was headed, she could become lost to Ava Russell. But in that Myra was wrong . . . Myra was very wrong.

10

The man at the bridge had said there would be people here, someone from whom she might ask direction. But there was nobody.

Cold biting into every bone, Eden stared at the house the stranger had called The Coppice. Rising three storeys, the small glass panes of arch-shaped windows glittering in a struggling sun, it stood face on to a wide stretch of ground that reached to the group of buildings where that elderly man had spoken so rudely.

So much space, so different from Hobbins Street. Covered now by a sheet of snow it was beautiful, but in summer, with its bordering trees clothed in leaves, it must be a green paradise.

But why no people? The building showed no sign of disrepair, the windows, though shuttered, were intact. Could it be she had not been heard? Returning to the rear of the house she knocked again at the door she presumed was that of the kitchen, but as with that first time it brought no response.

Misery adding to the cold, Eden glanced across the spacious yard to where a line of low, wide-doored buildings edged yet wider grounds. Carriage houses and stables. Grandfather had told Eden and Myra stories of himself as a lad working as stableboy in a house big enough for a lord of the land to live in while its grounds would cover half of the town of Wednesbury. It had been like listening to wonderful tales of magic and fairy castles and she had never thought to ask why would he have left so beautiful a place to go and live in a tiny house in a town constantly overcast by the smoke of iron foundries and the dust of collieries. But then that house had never seemed tiny and the inside had held no trace of dust. For two young children it spoke only of love, of being cherished and cared for, and that aura had never changed.

But, memories drifting into her mind, Eden felt the hot sting of tears. The sense of being loved, of being part of a family, had suffered a dreadful blow with her grandmother's passing; then with Myra's slap it had died, leaving in its place a stifling emptiness. What had given rise to that slap? What could have been the cause of Myra's anger, of her rejection? Was it . . .

But she would not think of that, not now, not ever! Myra had chosen her own life, a life without the ties of love, and she must do the same.

'Been nobody lived there this twenty years. Place be empty all but one week each two month, that be when the house is cleaned and aired.'

Why couldn't he have said she would find no person in that house? Was there some sort of satisfaction in seeing her trudge all that way only to trudge back?

Repressing the comment rising bitterly to her tongue, Eden glanced back the way she had come. Standing at the head of what, during that long walk, had seemed an interminable distance, yet now she guessed was the drive up to the front of the building, the house stared back at her. It looked lost and lonely; abandoned by all it had known. A dart of sunlight played for an instant across a window and, to Eden, it seemed like a glittering tear and, despite herself, she felt a swift tug of sympathy. The house, beautiful and obviously cared for, was a place of unhappiness.

'The cleaning was finished a week gone, won't be folk there again until Lent be passed.' Several weeks! She could not wait that long. Conscious that the drawing closer of her shawl did not completely disguise the shiver she had not wanted seen, Eden turned her glance to the man who had stared at her as she drew level with his garden gate. Lips too stiff from cold to smile, her 'Good day' no more than a murmur, she made to continue but a movement of his cane had her pause. Maybe he relented his not speaking of that house being uninhabited, maybe . . . but her 'maybe' died as he spoke sharply.

'Be a fair walk to Tipton, should that be where you are headed, and some half mile the other way should it be Wednesbury you want; either will seem a lot further given the drag of snow 'neath the feet.'

What would her grandmother's attitude have been

towards someone so obviously cold and distressed? A hot drink, a bowl of soup and, as welcome too, a kind word! A hot drink . . . a bowl of soup! Eden's insides quivered at thought of the comfort they would bring. But to ask for charity *and* to have it grudgingly given, would stick like a stone in her throat.

'Thank you.' She forced out words which did not want to come. 'I am grateful for the directions you point out. Please give my regards to your wife.'

She had looked openly at him while speaking, seen the nuance of anguish flash across copper-coloured eyes, the tight pain-filled clench of the mouth, a look complete in its despair but which was gone as quickly as it had come.

'I have no wife.'

He spoke calmly but the essence of pain seemed to linger beneath the words. He too was lonely, as lost and lonely as that beautiful house, as she was herself. She had not seen that loneliness when they had talked earlier; her only awareness had been of a brusqueness she had read as rudeness.

'I live alone,' he was speaking again, 'I look to none and I depend on none.' Did he think her about to ask for a lodging here at this cottage? Did he perhaps expect her to beg for his charity? Eden shuddered, frozen to the marrow, more hungry than she had ever been. A long walk either way was exhausting to think about; but to ask anything from this man, so averse to giving even a word of warning that she would find no one at that house . . . the thought choked her.

'Like I said,' copper eyes as bright and sharp as a hedge-sparrow's held fast to Eden's, 'I give nothing. This cottage be no charitable institution.'

Sympathy which had welled only seconds before drained swift as water over a sluice. She had been right in her assessment of this man, there was not a charitable bone in his body.

Huddled into herself, muscles tensed and cramped against the cold, Eden winced with the ache of drawing her body to its full height.

'I observed that from speaking with you earlier.' She thrust one hand into the pocket of her skirt. 'I thank you for your advice regarding the distance to the nearest towns. That, I think, should pay for it.'

Withdrawing her hand, Eden placed two coins on the gatepost and, without another word, walked quickly away.

She had tried to make her questioning appear to hold no cause except for a mild curiosity as to the reason her maid had made no return to this house, but her efforts had failed.

Alfred Birks broke the thin film of ice on the surface of a trough adjacent to the stable of Moorcroft House, and filled a bucket from its contents.

If Ava Russell had thought to pull the wool over his eyes, then she had best think again. Alfred Birks were not the fool she might take him for. There was more to that business than that woman was willing to speak of;

business, if luck played on his side, he intended to make his own.

Carrying the bucket to the one stall still housing a horse he placed it in one corner. In the days of Samuel Russell every one of these eight stalls had held horses and the coach-house two carriages and a governess cart, but these, as with the rest of the stables staff, had long been got rid of and, according to the snippets Polly Jupp allowed to drip from her tongue, *he* might be in line for the next dismissal. But he would not go with nothing, and instinct said this affair of Myra Brent could go a long way in providing him with the financial rewards he deserved.

Forking hay into the feedbox he left the stall, slipping the bolt across the half-door before crossing the yard to the kitchen of the house.

'Asked had I been to Hobbins Street then had I talked with the folk in the next house, but her already knowed all of that for you told her, didn't you, Missis Jupp?'

Boots left outside the kitchen door, hands and arms scrubbed to the elbow, a piece of ragged cloth covering the seat of the hard wooden chair he sat on, Alfred Birks held the large mug of tea which accompanied his meal.

'I told her all, just as you said it to me.' Answering as she came from the larder Polly set a large fruit cake on the table. 'I said as how you had done all her had instructed.'

Alfred watched the knife slice cleanly through the cake. Did Polly Jupp know the reason of Ava Russell's wanting to see him? Had this woman told the mistress all he had said or had a bit been left out here and there? Saying nothing of the thoughts riding inside, he took the plate with its generous portion of cake.

'I don't know why it be her had to have the seeing of you herself for I'd already told all you said.' Seated now with her own piece of cake, Polly answered the unspoken question. 'But then her don't have to have no reason for anything her does, not since the master died; can do as her likes and answer to nobody.'

Swallowing a mouthful of tea, Alfred kept to the dull-witted way he adopted while at this house; a man they thought had only half his marbles was spoke more freely in front of than one with the whole of a brain.

'Must be wonderful to be servant to nobody,' he said, mouth full of cake. 'I wish I had money such as the mistress has got, and a house like as this to go along of it.'

'So do I, lad, but had I a house such as Moorcroft it wouldn't see the carryin's on this one . . .'

This one sees! Swallowing hard, the deliberately noisy appreciation of hot sweet tea covering the cook's slip, Alfred finished the sentence for himself. The carryings on . . . What exactly were they, and did they have anything to do with Myra Brent's leaving her post without notice? The more he thought of it the more likely it seemed. But he would ask no more questions of Polly Jupp though he would bet a year's wage her could give answers to them all, were her so minded. But a stablehand prying into matters not of his concern would raise its own enquiry and that were the last thing he wanted. He'd keep his mouth closed and his head down . . . until he'd discovered what it were had Ava Russell as nervous as a cat with its arse a'fire!

'This be the wrong direction to be walkin' in if it be Wednesbury you wants.'

The wrong way! Eden's breath caught in her throat and she knew that to release it would release the tears surging behind it.

Turning your back on a problem don't be the solving of it.

The words of her grandmother had flung themselves at her as she had walked away from that old man and with them had come others, those spoken by a much younger yet equally acerbic man accusing her of running away; an accusation which had caused her to reconsider. She should not give in, leave the town of her birth because of being alone. Other women left to fend for themselves managed to live, to find a way of earning their bread. She was no different. But the pathways worn across the heath had been hidden by a covering of snow and she had missed the way.

'This here be Gospel Oak. We be quite a step away from Wednesbury and seems you've walked every one of 'em.'

'Yes.' Eden nodded as the smith laid aside his hammer.

'Well, you don't be in no state to walk 'em back, least not afore them bones o' yours be thawed out. Set you there alongside the forge while I pours you out a sup of tea.'

Too cold to refuse and too grateful to worry about charity, Eden took the chipped enamel mug, holding it between both hands as she sipped.

'I trusts you ain't come by way of the 'eath, that be a risk when the weather be fine, but the way it be to-day . . .' He paused, using the cloth tied about his neck to wipe the perspiration from his brow.

'I came by way of the towpath.' Tears warmed away by the hot sweet tea, Eden answered, 'that is I followed it after leaving a house called The Coppice.'

'Ah, then you turned left when it was to the right you should 'ave gone, but The Coppice . . . Were a time I got work aplenty from there but that be many years gone, The Coppice . . .' he mused, '. . . but ain't been a soul there for twenty year or more . . . I be surprised to hear it being lived in again.'

Relishing the warmth of the mug and the heat of the forge, Eden glanced at the well-muscled man replacing the strip of cloth about his neck.

'It isn't lived in,' she said, 'but I was not given that information, rather the opposite. I was told there would be someone there would give me directions.'

'Don't tek no guessing who that be – gettin' on in years, leans on a stick, spoke to you from a cottage at the end of a wide avenue leading to the big house?' Looking at her over a large enamelled jug as chipped as the mug he refilled, the blacksmith's eyes reflected the glow of the fire in the bed of the forge. 'Be that the one failed to tell you?'

Needing no answer, he filled a mug for himself, then set the jug on one side of the forge, placing a saucer over it to keep out the dust.

'I've heard folk talk of him afore this,' he said, using the anvil as a seat. 'Waspish be the kindest account given of that one, though I teks that on hearsay for I ain't never had the meeting of him for myself, nor can I say I have the missing o' that!'

Waspish – was that what the elderly man had been? But had she behaved any better?

'You'll have found no meal along of the towpath . . .'

Her thought interrupted, Eden glanced at the face streaked where the cloth had rubbed a line in the black dust of iron and soot.

'No.' She shook her head. 'I passed a small house some halfway between here and the path which led to The Coppice but it also was empty.'

'I knows the place and as you says that be empty, much to the dislike o' many a bargee hoping to buy his meal or pick up provision for his journey. Been sadly missed has old mother Shipton, 'specially so by the cut folk, her dying be a loss to many.'

'But why have her family left the house empty?'

'That be no riddle.' The smith laughed, his huge hand reaching for Eden's empty mug. 'It be 'cos of her 'aving no kin to live in it. Childless her were and no relative o' no sort with which to spend her days, not that her would have left the cottage her husband built and her were brought to on the day they were wed. That being the way it is, the place has remained empty since her being took from it.'

Loath to leave the warmth of the smithy yet reluctant to keep the man any longer from his work, Eden got to her feet one hand reaching into her pocket.

'You have been very kind,' she smiled, 'and the tea was most welcome.'

'Eh, wench!' His own smile fading, the man shook his head slowly. 'I don't have the knowing of ways o' Wednesbury folk, but them along o' Gospel Oak asks no reward of a kindness 'cept that the Lord alone can give.' Folding her fingers over the coins held on her palm, his smile returned. 'I sees you've been reared so as not to expect to be given free from other folk and that be fitting, but your sharing a minute with me be a kindness o' its own and I gives you the thanking of it.'

He had not taken offence at her offering to pay for the tea she drank, and his manner had been pleasant and friendly. The other side of the coin! Drawing her shawl about her, Eden glanced towards the village the blacksmith said lay a short distance away. Today had taught her the meaning of yet one more phrase used by her grandmother.

11

Ought she to have knocked on every door? Should she have asked at every single house?

Fatigue dragging at her, Myra sank on to a chair drawn against an unlit fire. Had she been misled in thinking that to be unnecessary, had it been a mistake? But the streets she had walked all day, the houses she had called at, had been so very like those of Wednesbury; cramped and small, many of them back to back, sharing a communal yard which housed privies and water pump, while others boasted a pig sty with its pig snuffling and grunting as it gorged some household scraps.

It had felt like she was coming to another world as she had sat on that carter's wagon, a place she would find strange and hostile. But the strangeness lay in its familiarity, its similarity with all she had known before entering into service at Moorcroft. The people of this town, those to whom she had spoken so far, were no different to those she had known during her years of growing. Their clothing was patched and the all-purpose living-rooms she was cordially invited to step into as sparsely furnished as Grandmother's had been and, like that house, they had shown no trace of the smoke which, like Wednesbury's, belched from the throats of factories or the dust of collieries which left the vomit of black soot across every building. All of it had been as she would have found in Hobbins Street and its surroundings, one household knowing all that went on in others the length of the street, one woman telling what every other would tell. It had seemed pointless to ask at every door. Yet it might have been the wiser thing to do. Maybe someone among those warren-like streets might have seen Eden, someone who had spoken with her and dismissed it as of no importance.

Rising to her feet, each movement agony in her aching limbs, she reached for the matches, the small box the only ornament on the mantelpiece above the cast iron firegrate.

She had been at fault presuming every woman would say what the previous one had said. She should have asked them all!

Tiredness quickening a sob in her chest, Myra sank to her knees, the matches dropping from fingers lifting to the tears she had not the strength to hold back.

She should have asked them all!

Despair folding her body into a tight ball, regret giving life to the cries choking from her lips, unhappiness rocking her back and forth, Myra heard only that sentence shout again and again in her head.

She should have asked them all!

*

She had walked to the cottage set back from the towpath. Mother Shipton's cottage, the blacksmith had named it.

Eden gazed at the smooth waters of the canal, a grey velvet ribbon stretching away on both sides.

She had stood staring at the small house. Shutters closed across the low windows, chimney devoid of smoke that gave it life it seemed . . . not dead . . . no, not dead . . . sleeping, waiting for someone to awaken it.

But she had not that right; the cottage was not her property. So why had she come? The words of that stranger at the bridge, the words her grandmother would also have said, '*You are running away*', had rung in her mind as she had walked away from that other small house set at the entrance to the long pathway which led to The Coppice, they had echoed sharp and accusing branding her mind. Yet still her steps had turned towards this cottage.

Drawing closer along the towpath she had felt it almost knew she was coming. Though the windows were shuttered it seemed as if eyes watched her every step. So strong had that feeling been she had wanted desperately to walk on, to leave the house far behind, yet, as she drew level with the tiny garden in which beneath the covering of snow might sleep the flowers of spring and summer, her feet refused to carry her farther.

It had been so strange. Eden's glance remained on the still waters of the canal. She had wanted to go on but a stronger force than her own had held her. Then had come the whisper. Faint at first, hiding in a corner of her mind, soft as a baby's breath, a murmur on a summer breeze. But as she stood, the murmur had grown, become a sigh, become a word . . . Welcome!

The cottage was unlived in, it had no owner. But it was *not* hers. The latter thought had held her beside the wooden gate, but stronger still came the repeated word . . . Welcome.

It was almost as if the house called to her, as if an essence of something cried out to her to enter.

Something . . . or someone?

Overhead the blanketing clouds parted, allowing a pale yellow promise of sun to dapple the grey water.

Had she unwittingly leaned against the gate or had it really been as it had felt? That gentle hands had closed warm and loving over her own cold ones, hands which drew her to a door which yet again seemed to need no help from herself before opening.

She should not have entered. It was trespassing, it could even be construed as burglary – a crime which could have her sentenced to prison should anyone claiming ownership discover her there. But, as the door had swung inward on its hinges, that one word beating in her brain had intensified until the very walls around her had seemed to echo with the same . . . Welcome!

She had opened the shutters and daylight had streamed in at the windows, filling the room, touching furniture, lamps, fireplace, as if with a blessing. For long moments she had stood listening to the intimate whispers seeming to emanate from every article, from each corner; rustles and sighs answering the gentle touch of light, whispers of a shared love.

How long had the blacksmith said the house had stood vacant? Recall had been vague, lost somehow in the shadows, as though its telling had been insignificant. Standing in the living-room, bathed in the welcome that felt tangible and real, she had whispered back and, to her heightened senses, it seemed the cottage took its first breath of a new life.

The house was vacant but it was not empty. The thought had brought no fear. The body was gone of the woman the blacksmith had named Mother Shipton, but her spirit remained. Bricks and mortar could not whisper, they could not account for the feeling, so real inside her, a feeling which said she was wanted here. So what else could it be but the quintessence of that woman's love, so strong as to remain part of the very walls themselves?

What had Sara Melia's answer been to her saying it could not have been her grandmother's voice seeming to speak from the heart of that storm . . . that her grandmother was dead . . .

'. . . *but her spirit don't be . . .*'

Clear as when they were first spoken, the words returned. '. . . *her be with the Lord an' it be His mercy give leave for her spirit to walk beside you, to comfort . . .*'

Could the same thing be happening again? Was the spirit of the woman who had lived so long in this small house, who had known happiness and tears here, somehow passing care of it to her? Was she somehow saying, Live here as I once did, love the cottage as I loved it?

Fantasy . . . a dream borne of the desire for warmth and shelter?

Eden turned to face the cottage.

Maybe it was all of that . . . but, as she had walked through the tiny rooms which, apart from a light film of dust, appeared as they must always have been, even to sticks and coal laid ready for a fire, the feeling that it waited for her became even more positive. So she had asked. Sinking to her knees beside the fireplace her words a whisper in the silence, she had spoken what was in her heart.

'If what I feel . . . what I sense . . . is wrong, that I am not wanted here then I ask God in His benevolence allow the presence in this house, the spirit I feel to be that of Mother Shipton, to impart that knowledge to me; to tell me so I might apologise and leave.'

She had not known what else to say but in that moment a stream of sunlight had smiled into the room and, from its golden heart had whispered the word . . . Welcome.

'Same way as them others, mum, you asks me they all be done by one man; stands to reason . . . I mean if one be exactly like the other . . . Lord what be the world coming to when a wench don't be safe!'

'We all ask ourselves that.' Ava Russell took the newspaper the cook had brought to her sitting-room.

'I asks meself somethin' beside! I asks when do them

there constables be goin' to catch whoever it is be doin' them wenches in, be a disgrace that's what it be, folk don't feel safe walking the streets.'

'I'm sure the man will be apprehended soon. In the meantime . . .'

'In the meantime, how many more poor souls goin' to be murdered?'

Aware her outburst had been uncalled for, Polly Jupp followed it with a quick apology then,with a bob of a curtsy, left the room with the same speed.

'*Ripper Strikes Again!*'

Bold black letters spread across the front page.

'Third woman found murdered.' Ava's eyes followed the rest of the report. 'A young woman thought to be of the age of twenty years has been found dead in an alley connecting Great Western Street to Potter's Lane. Police have as yet issued no formal identification but a member of the public present at the scene of the discovery said the woman was a prostitute who plied her trade in the vicinity of the railway station and the Great Western Hotel. It was also related the body appeared to have been mutilated in a similar fashion to two other women whose bodies were found last year, each slashed with a knife. When asked for a statement, Inspector Silas Perry refused to comment, saying only he must await the coroner's report.'

Same way as them others . . .

Polly Jupp's remark returning to her mind, Ava laid the newspaper aside.

No trace of the killer of those women had been

uncovered. Someone maybe coming into the town by train and leaving quickly by the same way. That had been the only conclusion the constabulary had drawn. But which train . . . from where . . . and did the killer return to the starting point? These questions had been posed by the newspapers and none had received a satisfactory explanation.

If only that dead woman were Myra Brent! If it were the corpse of her maid lying in the morgue, then a source of worry would be lifted from her shoulders, for the dead can make no accusation of the living.

But that was like wishing for the moon, a dream which could never know reality. She could not afford to dream.

Her mouth a grim line, Ava rose to her feet.

She must have the satisfaction of reality. Myra Brent must die!

Yes, Myra Brent must die, that was the only way her secret would be entirely safe.

In her bedroom Ava paced like a caged tigress, her mind seething. Every minute the girl remained alive was one more minute Ava Russell stood in danger of being exposed. What a field day a story like that would provide the newspapers with.

'*Wife of Samuel Russell, late proprietor of Russell Coach Axle and Spring Manufacturing, denounced*!'

Headlines bold and dark as those read minutes ago seemed to blaze before Ava's eyes.

'*Maid tells of abuse by mistress. Ava Russell and her lover Mrs Lenor Medwin . . .*'

'No!' Ava spat the word through teeth clenched hard. Should that ever happen there would be no life for Ava Russell in Wednesbury, no life worth the living anywhere in the country. A rake, a libertine or even a lecher, a man could be accused of any of these and the country turned a blind eye; but for one woman to make love with another, to 'brush the muff', that carried a social death sentence.

But those headlines would never grace any newspaper. The time of dreaming was over. Myra Brent had to be eliminated . . . but first she had to be found!

12

It had seemed the answer to her troubles. The cottage having no occupant, everything being left as it was before its owner died, it was the granting of a prayer. But though the house provided warmth and shelter it could not feed her. True, the garden, visible now the layer of frost and snow had melted, would no doubt have herbs and vegetables planted in the autumn already poking their heads above ground; it would be weeks yet before most were suitable for eating, but early spring cabbage and tall sticks of sprouts could be picked now.

But ought she to pick any of them? The woman the blacksmith had said was elderly, had she been able to plant them herself? The answer would most probably be no. But somebody had, and that somebody would come to reap them when time was right. Would that same somebody order her to leave? That was more than a possibility and it was one she must be ready to face.

Then where would she go? Eden blinked against the strand of hair the breeze blew across her eyes.

'You will see more clearly if you allow me to take those from you.'

Deep in her thoughts, Eden had heard no step. Startled now by words which seemed to come from nowhere she turned quickly.

'You need to see when walking in these parts, whether it is the towpath you are on now or the heath. Neither of them is to be treated indifferently.'

The man from the bridge! Eden blinked again, her arms tightening about the bundle he tried to take from her.

'I am not about to rob you!'

Even against the glare of the sunlight reflecting from the waters of the canal, Eden saw the strong jaw stiffen, and for a moment it seemed he would turn away, but then he spoke, mockingly quiet.

'Anything I might have wanted from you I could have taken at that bridge, but then, as now, my only interest is in saving you from a possible accident. My advice . . .'

'Your advice is not asked for! But tell me what pleasure do you get by creeping up on people?'

Inches from her face, his sable-dark eyes gleamed. 'None!' he returned coldly. 'Nor do I get any from speaking with a woman who doesn't recognise a kindness when it is offered her. But wanted or not I will give my advice. This towpath, or that of any other canal, is not for daydreamers. The heath is pock-marked with disused mining shafts and the paths between them are mostly overgrown. Take your mind from your feet if only for an instant and your next step could very easily be your last. Do I make myself clear? And one more piece of unwanted advice: get yourself a small cart in which to carry your shopping, that way you will have your hands free to brush the hair from your eyes.'

. . . *a woman who does not recognise a kindness* . . .

The shawl in which she had carried the goods she had purchased lowered thankfully on to the table, which almost filled the cottage's small living-room, Eden breathed a sigh of relief at being able to rest her aching arms, but it was a sigh mixed with a fair amount of irritation. That man had mocked her. What other connotation could she place on his tone, on his attitude? She was a daydreamer, a woman without sense enough to look out for herself, wasn't that what he had meant? Well, kindness or otherwise, she could do very well without advice from him!

But a polite thank you, that should not have been too much for her to give. A twinge of guilt plucked at Eden's mind as she stared disconsolately at the items she had bought from the village of Gospel Oak.

She was no better than the old man who lived in the grounds of that graceful house, and certainly she had not the warmth of spirit or the kind manner the blacksmith had displayed towards her that day she had rested beside his forge.

'. . . *your sharing a minute with me be a kindness o' its own and I gives you thankin' of it.*'

It had been said genuinely, and the smile accompanying it was just as honest. The twinge of guilt sharpened, colouring her cheeks with self-reproach. What had been offered to her on the towpath had been more than simply a word of advice, infinitely more; it had been an act of kindness . . . one she had snubbed.

Grandmother would have been ashamed of her. Putting the last of her meagre provisions into the food cupboard, Eden swallowed hard.

She was ashamed of herself.

'You are sure you are up to it?' Trim in pale blue cotton, piped at collar and cuffs with white, brown hair drawn back from a small harassed face, Miss Sophie Brooke, dressmaker at Bull Piece, looked keenly at the young woman asking for employment. 'I accept only the best stitching, my customers expect it and I pay for nothing less. The piece you show me, is it your own work?'

Weary from days of walking and of nights going hungry because money spent on food meant less for lodgings once the rental on the house in Bell Street expired, Myra Brent tried not to let her tiredness show as she nodded.

'And might I ask where you learned to sew like this?'

How many more questions before the woman decided to give her work or tell her to leave? Myra met the suspicious stare. 'I was taught needlecraft at school in Wednesbury, but more so by my grandmother. If you wish confirmation of that petticoat you hold having been stitched by myself then I would ask you to give me a piece to sew. Tomorrow I will return it and you can judge the work. If it does not answer to your satisfaction then I will pay the cost of the cloth.'

'You obviously have high regard for your handiwork.'

'I have high regard for my grandmother's teaching, she would accept no second best.'

'Mmm.' Sophie Brooke glanced again at the petticoat. Spotless, well-ironed, each stitch small and perfect. If this was truly the work of this woman then she had indeed been well taught, and her manner and way of speech confirmed that that teaching carried over into more than needlecraft.

Handing back the petticoat, she took a half-worked blouse from a table and carefully wrapped it in tissue paper.

'This is delicate work,' she said, 'the material is the finest voile and the client it is for is particular in her requirements. Can you have it finished by tomorrow?'

Hurrying through the streets still busy with black-garbed women, small children holding to their skirts, Myra clutched the parcel. How could she finish that blouse and still search for Eden?

Reaching the house, smelling the musty dampness which one small fire in the evening could not cure, the hopelessness of Myra's life closed like a tomb about her. Why did she go on, why try to find Eden? Her sister would not want her, she had broken that relationship, ended the love that had been between them from birth, ended it with a sharp slap to Eden's face. Letting the parcel drop to the table, she stared at the dark hole of the empty firegrate.

Why go on! A sob, deep and wracking, rose in her

chest. She crossed the tiny space to the shabby dresser. What if she *did* find Eden, what if she knew of those bathtimes at Moorcroft? Eden would not only reject her, she would despise her.

No sensation of wood beneath her fingers, mindless of everything but the desolation of that thought, she drew open a drawer.

Perhaps Eden had been told . . .

The blade of the large kitchen knife glittered like silver raindrops as tears blurred.

Perhaps Eden had been found by Ava Russell . . .

Myra's hand closed over the handle of the knife.

Perhaps her sister was already caught in that woman's vile web!

The knife slid easily from the drawer.

It was her fault . . . if she had gone with Eden when she had come to the house . . .

Held between her fingers the knife blade gleamed as it rose.

Eden had spent the last of her money. Rolling pastry on a board she had fetched from the scullery and scrubbed with boiling water, she calculated her resources.

The penny she had spent at the cookshop and the tuppence she had left on that gatepost had reduced her three shillings to two shillings and ninepence, and that had slowly dwindled as with each day she had been obliged to buy food. Now all that was left was the shilling she had put aside to pay to any relative of

Mother Shipton should they come; payment of rent could offset an accusation of using the cottage without permission. But how many more days would a shilling pay for?

You *will* find work, you *will* be able to add to the shilling in that pretty vase on the mantel. That had been the promise she made to herself every morning when she woke and the prayer she said every night before sleep. But the hope went unfulfilled. Each day she bought a few sausages or a cut of meat from a family who had slaughtered a sheep or a pig, a bag of flour and a halfpenny worth of yeast from the mill, and sometimes a few potatoes or a turnip from the farmer's wife who also sold her milk. Every day she spent more of her precious coins; now, but for that one shilling it was gone. And if that should not prove sufficient to appease the righteous anger of any owner of this house? Covering the dish of meat and potato with the pastry, Eden pressed the edges with her thumb . . . Then she would be sent to prison.

But maybe it would never happen, maybe chance would be given to add to the shilling . . . she could dream. But carrying the pie to the oven, Eden knew in her heart that dreams, so like many other things in life, were only for childhood.

And her childhood had been so sweetly filled with dreams. How could she ever have foreseen they would be broken, replaced by the heartache of her grandmother's death, by the misery of her sister's alienation? But they had, and all she had left were memories.

Adding chopped leeks to the suet and seasoned flour already in a heavy pottery bowl, Eden's mind repeated words her grandmother had spoken.

Dreams be all well and good, but they best be left on the pillow for, though they feeds the mind, they don't never feed the body. You can't live the dream.

The answer would have sufficed a few weeks ago but now it was replaced by a thought to which even her grandmother's down-to-earth reasoning might have provided no answer. What was life when dreams failed?

Adding water to the bowl she mixed the ingredients together then rolled the resulting dough into small balls between floured hands.

What was life when dreams failed? Had she not had a taste of that already? Spooning leek dumplings into a broth of barley and mutton bones which had simmered in the oven for the best part of the day, Eden held the sting of her own answer in her throat. She had been given a taste . . . What was yet in store?

It repeated again and again as she cleared the table, as she washed the implements used in her cooking, and asked yet again as she rinsed her hands and face then tidied her hair.

What could her future hold but more of the unhappiness she was experiencing now? Grandmother had been right; you could never live the dream.

Nor could she go on living in the comfort of this house. Knotting the corners of a cloth she had wrapped about a basin of broth, Eden cast a glance about the small room. This cottage had embraced her, the breath of it had whispered of friendliness but, though the reception it seemed to offer had nourished her spirit, it could not nourish her body. And now the last pennies she had allowed herself were already spent and, once the food it had bought was gone, what then?

It would not go so quickly if you did not give half of it away!

Remonstrance jabbed incisively as she picked up the basin holding it beneath her shawl.

That was a logic she could not argue with. Basin held against her midriff, Eden set off along the towpath. Her food would last twice as long if she kept it to herself, the worry of what to do when finally it ran out deferred for many days.

But the teachings of childhood were stronger than logic. A kindness done to a stranger . . . an act of charity when given from the heart counts more with heaven than all the wealth of kings – again her grandmother's words, words which smiled in her heart.

Reaching the track that led away from the towpath and across the heath, Eden kept strictly to its path, aware of the pitfalls the man from the bridge had warned of. Who *was* he? Where was it he went when he strode away from her . . . and why did he figure so often in her thoughts? Did her subconscious use him as a means of keeping other thoughts away? Did her brain substitute the misery of losing a sister with the anger of being accosted by a man?

That was a logic she had no wish to dwell on; she

would forget that man, forget his rudeness, forget she had ever met him!

Resolve quickening her step, holding at bay thoughts struggling for recognition, she drew level with the huddle of houses at the entrance to the drive of the graceful house she knew as The Coppice. Bathed now in the pearl-pink gleams of a sun that had banished the last traces of winter and now warmed the days of spring, it stood as if waiting, beautiful windows glittering as if with anguished tears. Its heart is broken. Try as she would, Eden could not push the thought away, she could only listen as it came again; its heart is broken . . . just like your own!

It was the same powerful feeling she had experienced on entering Mother Shipton's cottage, the feeling that it waited for the return of love. But *she* could not enter that house as she had the cottage, *she* could never be given care of it, but she shared its sadness.

Away in a copse of tall trees, sentinels to the silent building, a wood dove cooed and was answered by its mate, the gentleness of their call serving to add to the aura of melancholy. What had happened there? What could have caused so beautiful a house to be left abandoned? She would not know the answer, the same as she would not know why a sister had been abandoned!

'I tell you as I have afore, I've naught to pay with!'

Snatched from her reverie by the abrupt call, Eden walked the last few steps to the gate. Leaning heavily on his stick the man, who might well be caretaker of the larger property though he had not said he was, regarded her with a sharp almost accusing stare. She had met with that same unfriendly stare, the same flat antagonistic greeting each evening she came. At first he had banged his stick on the gate saying he wanted no charity. A smile hovered on her lips as Eden remembered her reply and how it had taken him aback. He had expected her to turn tail and run but instead she had met that fierce copper glare saying evenly, 'And I tell you as I have afore, I require no payment.' With that she had placed the meal of sausages bedded in mashed potato firmly on the square-topped gatepost and, wishing him goodnight, had left without a further word.

There were so many queries to this place. She scooped up the dish she had left yesterday, washed clean as before, and walked swiftly back the way she had come. Not only did that elegant house emanate a sense of despair, of infinite loneliness, but so did this man. What had made him so bitter as to see the world through a mist of hatred? But no, not hatred! Eden checked the thought . . . it was pain; he saw the world darkly, saw it through the shadows of pain. What had hurt so much? What was behind the caustic manner, the harsh uncivil words? She would not ask, but they would not deter her from coming to his gate, from bringing him a share of her food as she had from the first she had cooked, as she would continue to do for as long as she remained in the cottage.

13

Ava Russell's concern were for somethin' other than a maid, they could be got anywhere in this town. Why then were Myra Brent so special, what were different to any other wench?

Alfred Birks' squinty eyes stared moodily into his half-filled tankard, the questions he had asked himself time and again since being called to that sitting-room revolving in his brain.

It weren't the safety of the wench had Ava Russell fretting, no, that cold-'earted bitch fretted over naught save the wellbeing of 'erself. The worryin' were for herself which meant the Brent girl must be holdin' somethin' over Russell's head.

That hadn't took a lot of figurin'. Alfred took a swallow of beer. He had worked that out at the start. What he couldn't work out were what it could be kept that wench away from Moorcroft. If her did have a cudgel to beat a mistress over the 'ead with wouldn't her be there at that house doin' it instead o' disappearin'?

That were another mystery . . . Why the moonlight flit? A shout of men's laughter drew his glance to the other side of the smoke-filled taproom of the beer house. He had asked around, asked if anyone might have come across her when looking for a doxy to spend sixpence on, but if Myra Brent had taken on business of the night then it seemed her had found her custom elsewhere than Wednesbury.

Emptying the tankard with one gulp, Alfred strode out into the street. There were money to be made from this, he could feel that in his bones, and it would be a sight more money than he would ever earn skivvying in a stable! But to eat the fruit you had to first find the tree.

Making his way along the Shambles he glanced at the near empty stalls besieged now by children begging for left-over meat.

He had done that, fought for scraps thrown like bones to dogs; ragged-arsed kids who, having grabbed a bit of scrag end or mebbe a couple of sausages, ran home faster than the Prince of Wales' best racehorse. But he would fight for no more leftovers and, once he found what it were had the mistress of Moorcroft piddlin' her fancy silk drawers, then Alfred Birks would live high on the hog.

'You give me an hour to slake my thirst then I'll be ready an' willin' to pay you sixpence.'

'Sixpence! You'll be lucky!'

'Ar, I will that . . . a lot luckier than you if your price be higher . . . I pays no trull more'n sixpence.'

'You'll get no woman open her legs for a tanner, nor play with your tool for that much neither.'

'Then I be sixpence better off.'

'Keep your tanner . . . and that you got in your trousers, stick it up your arse for a jug 'andle.'

The slanging match over, one which caught no heed other than his, Alfred watched the woman flounce away and her potential customer turn into the building stood on the corner. He had seen that man before, seen him in the Market Place with a wagon.

A sharp flick of the hand accompanying a snarled invective driving away a second woman bent on adding to her nightly earnings, Alfred entered the same building. He had talked with carters, shared ale with them in several of the town's hostelries but not here in the Green Dragon. If luck were with him then tonight he might find what he was looking for . . . and it wasn't any daughter of the night!

He had been no more friendly than on the other evenings she had walked to his cottage . . . but he had not forbidden her to come again. The dish which had held the previous evening's meal . . . had he washed it after eating the grey peas and bacon bits she had cooked or had he thrown them away? If the latter were true then why not tell her not to bring any more or was it a pleasure to him to have her walk to that cottage simply to throw away the meal she brought? Did bitterness spread so far?

The pottery dish clutched beneath her shawl, Eden followed the towpath, a narrow band of grey beside waters that glowed green-gold in the last of the setting sun.

But she did not share her meal with him for the reward of praise, she had no desire of payment, only a word of thank. '*The giving of charity be no gift when payment be looked for.*'

Grandmother's words to two young girls giving their precious halfpennies, saved for a visit to the fair, to a beggar at their gate spoke again in Eden's mind. Like the old man living at the entrance to The Coppice he had expressed no thanks yet grandmother had suffered no word to be said against him, adding only to her own.

'*A kindness gladly done brings a smile to the face of heaven, but if given only in exchange then the angels weep.*'

It had been a salve to their feelings, a calming of ruffled feathers, though not all the wisdom behind the words had been understood. But I understand them now, Gran, she smiled inside. Give willingly with no mind to what that giving brings you, or else do not givc at all. Yes, she understood . . . and she would go on sharing with that sad, embittered old man until her last crumb was gone.

Which could not be many more days. She had used her money frugally, buying a handful of potatoes, the cheapest of meat, to which she had added sprouts and cabbage taken from the garden behind the cottage. Mother Shipton's vegetables or someone else's? Either way, her taking them was stealing. She was a thief! Shadow touching her as the sun slid away from the horizon, Eden shivered. Thieves paid a dreadful price. But it was done, those vegetables could not be replaced, but her taking them would always be a guilt in her heart.

'I told you to watch where you place your feet when walking these parts. The canal makes a cold lover and its arms rarely let go.'

Totally oblivious of being followed, Eden gasped, her fingers releasing the dish.

'A towpath is no place for dreaming just as a bridge is no place for sleeping.'

A flash of fear leaping to her eyes, Eden turned to stare into a pair which held no smile. Sable-dark, they glinted, catching the grey of a darkening sky.

'You!' She tried to make her tone one of anger but knew it echoed the relief flooding into her.

'As you say . . . me!' There was no softening of the voice which was as cold and angry as the eyes and seemed to cut into her.

Fear already dissipated, relief becoming the anger she had striven to achieve, Eden snapped. 'Have you no thought . . . creeping up behind . . .'

'Hardly creeping.' He glanced at his own sturdy boots then reclaimed her eyes. 'As for thought, it is obvious I have more than a young woman who walks the towpath alone ignoring any advice telling her that to do so could be courting danger.'

'Your advice,' Eden snapped again, 'is not welcome, neither is it necessary. I have walked this path for some time and not once have I been accosted . . . until now. It seems you feel you have some God-given right to interfere in my business but that is a delusion you should rid yourself of. I do not need your assistance . . . in *any* way.'

Bending easily, a movement as supple and feline as his walk, he gathered the pieces of broken pottery.

Standing erect once more, head and shoulders above her, his eyes glittered like black ice and when he spoke it was quiet thunder. 'Then I apologise . . . for this.'

Thrusting the remnants of the dish into her hands, he strode away, the shadows of the heath wrapping him until he might never have been real.

But he *was* real. The shards of what had moments before been a perfectly useful dish still held in her hands Eden resumed her way. He was so real, he plagued her mind; even when asleep, he was there in her dreams. But she did not want him there, and as for her being in any sort of danger . . . who but himself had ever voiced more than a 'good day' as she walked to and from Gospel Oak or followed the track to The Coppice? No one approached her, no one barred her path . . .

The thought freezing in her brain, Eden came to a halt. There, coming from the door of the cottage, a man . . . a man who watched her, who waited . . . and it was not the man whose advice she had chosen not to follow.

This time he had struck gold, gold that would soon be in his pocket. How much . . . how much should he ask, fifty . . . a hundred? A hundred pounds! Alfred Birks hugged the thought as he left the Green Dragon. What did it matter how much he asked? If Ava Russell wanted to find Myra Brent as badly as he felt she did then he would get his money; that or she could whistle for the information he had gleaned from that carter . . . and it would be a hell of a long tune.

It had taken two pint tankards of ale plus a shilling to wash the carter's memory clear, two pints Ava Russell would pay dearly for.

'A *wench*!' the man had answered, the look that came with it clearly expressing the calculation going on in his mind, one that said how much of a charge could his information bring . . . how much silver to his pocket?

'*My sister, her run away from home and our mother be taken ill of the worry of it. If you 'ave met with her I asks in God's name you tell me.*'

The lie had run easily from Birks' tongue, the forced tear he had scrubbed from his eye having the effect he had hoped for; yet it had taken that second tankard and a shilling to part the man from what he knew.

'*Was a wench such as you describes, picked her up a few weeks since.*' He had clutched the handle of the pewter tankard, guarding against the possibility of its being snatched away once his talking were done. Alfred Birks frowned. That was precisely what *he* would have done but the carter had proved too smart. '*It were down at the Turk's Head, I were finishing takin' on a load when her asks could her ride alongside.*'

'*What name did her give?*'

His answer had been ignored while the carter sank his nose into the tankard, then wiped a line of froth from his lips with the back of his free hand.

'*D'ain't give no name . . .*'

Walking quickly along Church Street, Alfred's frown returned, seeming to bring with it the taste of sourness of breath the carter's loud belch had blown into his face.

'*. . . her d'ain't say and I d'ain't ask.*'

Was he going to have to lure the man outside, draw him into the narrow confines of the Shambles and kick the rest out of him? Irritation combining with the rancid taste of the man's breath curdled to a ball in his throat Alfred had gripped his own tankard with both hands, wishing it was the throat of the carter.

'*Seemed her were upset by summat,*' the man had resumed after another swallow of ale. '*But if as you claims her were runnin' from home then that don't be startlin'.*'

No, it wasn't! What had been startling was managing to hold back the urge to choke the man! Having reached the point where the road became the beginnings of the rise that was Church Hill, Alfred slipped through a low wooden gate set in the high walls surrounding Moorcroft House.

'*Said 'ardly a word the 'ole of the journey.*' Slurred by the rapid downing of ale, the carter's words had come thickly. '*I told her where it would be I was goin' and that it would take time for I was goin' by way of Moxley.*'

Going where? He had wanted to hurl the question, to follow it with a fist, then shake the rest of it loose of that froth-lined mouth. Patience was no virtue of Alfred Birks and it had stretched about as far as it would go.

'Darlaston don't be the other side of the world,' the carter had continued in the nick of time. *'But it be far enough for my old hoss, and far enough for that wench so it seemed for that were the place I left 'er.'*

Darlaston! Crossing the spacious ground which skirted the once immaculate gardens of the brick house, Alfred stood a moment staring at its silhouette dark against the moonlight. He had kept his patience with that carter and it had paid off. Tomorrow he would be paid again . . . but not with words. Tomorrow he would be the man with information to sell, and it would be more than two tankards of ale and a shilling would see the buying of it.

Satisfied with his night's work, Alfred Birks crossed to a minute building set a little way from the stables, and slipped inside. Once an extra feed store, now the one tiny room was his home.

One room! He stared around him. One room in which to eat, sleep, to live his life! But not for much longer. Alfred Birks was going places, he was going to have a better life, a very much better life . . . and Ava Russell would pay the cost.

What would it take to get some sense into that girl's head?

Andrew Denby angrily pulled the shirt from his back.

Was it obstinacy that made her disregard his warnings or was it sheer stupidity? Stripping away the rest of his clothes, he climbed into the tub. Relaxed by the warm water, he closed his eyes and mulled over the confrontation that had taken place on the towpath. Lord, he could have picked the girl up and thrown her into the damned canal! Maybe he ought to have done, perhaps that would have cured her obstinacy, for it was that and not stupidity that lay behind her reactions.

She had answered him tit for tat, countered his words with her own, the edge of them as sharp as his own. Some might construe that as stupidity: a young woman alone, daring to invoke a man's anger . . . or something infinitely more hazardous to herself. But she had dared and, were he to admit it, he admired her for doing so.

Warm water soothing tiredness from his bones, he let his thoughts run. Settled herself in the old Shipton place, that much he had heard gossiped between bargees pulling into the basin and the men who unloaded and re-loaded their narrowboats with cargo. That in itself was a source for concern; he would place his life against any of the men he knew bothering that young woman . . . but he did not know every man who passed this way. Try telling her that, try explaining the risk she might be taking? Andrew Denby smiled. It would be like spitting in the wind. So he must do what his own father would have counselled: 'Act on advice, don't just talk about it.'

Stepping from the tub he rubbed his body with a large towel. Taking the decision and augmenting it had presented no difficulty . . . but should she find out! But then he must make quite certain she did not.

Dressed in a dark suit, a pearl-coloured silk cravat at

his throat, he reached for matching gloves. Glancing at his reflection in the mahogany-framed cheval mirror his mouth firmed. His appearance was orderly enough . . . pity his damned mind was not!

What was it with that girl? Worn boots, patched skirt, a shawl over her head . . . the towns were filled with such women. Lord, he had seen hundreds . . . yet he had not seen one like her. There was something about her, something that shabby clothes could not hide, something he could not define, yet it was under his skin, in his mind. Whoever that girl was she had made an impression on him he was finding difficulty forgetting.

And what of those visits to that cottage in the grounds of The Coppice? Why did she go there each evening? Perhaps more of a question was why did *he*? Impatient with the answer, which like other thoughts of that girl plagued him.

Dismissing his coachman he took the reins of the light chaise. Guiding the horse between the tall, stone-built gateposts of Woden Place his mind immediately slipped to that other house, those other gateposts.

The first time he had seen that girl go there and watched her speak for a few moments with the old man, he had smiled to himself. The lady's intentions would bring her no reward there! That man's sharp tongue could make bitter aloe seem sweet; she would pay no second visit. Yet she had, and to his chagrin so had he.

Allowing the horse to find its own pace along Ethelfleda Terrace and on into Church Street, he gave his mind the same freedom. He had watched her come to the gate of the cottage, seen the walking-stick lift ominously; but she had not flinched, nor drawn back from the threat: quite the opposite, she had stepped forward, placed a cloth-wrapped bundle on the flat-topped post then left . . . she had simply turned and walked away.

That first evening had been a coincidence. He had spotted the slight, shawl-wrapped figure while returning from Lower Wood Colliery. Had it been curiosity that caused him to follow her? Refusing to admit to a stronger drive, Andrew pushed the thought aside. What he had seen had left him wondering. It was obvious the man had nothing to give apart from harsh words; she would learn that and not go there again.

Yet she *had* gone again . . . and so had he. But it was the errands of business had him pass that spot each evening.

Bringing the carriage to a halt outside the George Hotel, he nodded to the polite greeting of an ostler running to take the vehicle and walked into the chandelier-lit lobby.

He had been returning each evening from business which had him pass The Coppice. This was what he told himself. The only problem with that was he knew it to be a lie.

14

The doctor had diagnosed Lenor with an illness of the heart.

Returned from visiting her friend, Ava Russell paced her own private sitting-room.

'There must be no stress, no worries of any kind.'

Stress! Worries! Ava's fingers clutched each other in the anger she could not show whilst at the Medwins' house. What did Lenor Medwin know of either? Wasn't Arthur Medwin well placed, was not his business one of the most lucrative in the town? Yet something was pulling at the over-dressed Lenor. The saffron gown had been the usual expensive creation, its abundance of frills and bows serving only to highlight a figure of equal excess, and the jewellery, the rings on every finger, the pearls surrounding the fat throat all had confirmed that any worry Lenor Medwin may possibly experience could not come from a financial source. So why had Lenor stressed the doctor's words?

Ava's fingers pressed tighter, driving her fingernails into her palms but the pain went unnoticed beneath her agitation. She had asked the question and had known the reply before it was spoken. Lenor Medwin was afraid of her husband finding out . . . afraid he would get to know of her extra bedroom predilection.

But how could he? Neither of them was foolish enough to let slip any clue and only they knew of those delights shared at Moorcroft and in Lenor's own bedroom.

'*No, Ava, we are not the only ones who know.*'

The alarm which had come with that answer had struck like a physical blow blocking the breath to Ava's lungs, cutting off the flow of blood along her veins until her brain swam.

But it was not swimming now.

Lowering herself into a chair, whalebone corset holding her ramrod straight, Ava stared at the window overlooking the rear gardens of Moorcroft. But she saw only a sallow-complexioned face, eyes alight with alarm, full lips trembling. Lenor Medwin's face!

The woman had gabbled, dismay raising her voice until Ava's own, sharp and dominant, had quieted the flow.

What caused her to believe them discovered? What proof was there?

She had expected more of the fear-driven rambling which had stampeded from the terrified Lenor, but the plump figure had withdrawn a single sheet of paper from the bodice of her gown.

'*This.*'

It had been one simple word but the trembling of the hand passing it spoke vividly of the anxiety coursing through that plump body.

Ava's thin lips clamped hard, short breaths of temper snatching into her nostrils.

The note written in script had carried two sentences.

'*Two hundred pounds or your husband knows of your brushing the muff. Leave the money in the third pew of the parish church nine o'clock Saturday evening.*'

She didn't have any money, Lenor had wailed. Arthur said she had no need of it, seeing everything was paid by himself.

Jewellery . . . sell some of your jewellery. Ava's face darkened remembering the reply that suggestion had brought. Arthur Medwin had long since sold any jewellery of worth using the proceeds to bolster a failing business. Every piece adorning his buxom wife was fake as no doubt were many of the paintings and statuary in the house.

Asking Arthur was out of the question. Lenor had collapsed at the suggestion. Yet the money must be paid or . . . but there could be no 'or'; the scandal would destroy them both . . . not that the fate of Lenor Medwin worried her in the slightest.

But her own fate, her own standing in society . . . that was a different matter.

Behind thinned lips, Ava's teeth ground her fury. Paying some filthy blackmailer was galling no matter whose the coin, but when it was Ava Russell's then it became unthinkable. Yet she had been forced to think. If her own reputation was to remain stainless, then the money had to be paid and, without help from Lenor, it was Ava Russell must do the paying.

There was only one way of raising so much. Her glance passed to a document lying on a small elegant Sheraton table.

'You be certain her don't know it be yourself has shopped her, it don't be you that's given the game away?'

The voice had not been loud but the words had carried on the somnolence of the spring afternoon.

Returning to her carriage Ava had halted, the arch that gave on to the steps of the Medwin house shielding her from view of the speaker.

'Course I be sure.' The reply had been softer, feminine. 'I told you didn't I . . . I were passing the bedroom when I heard it, the mistress agasping and agroaning somethin' awful. Well, knowing as the doctor had said her heart were not strong as it might be I was set to go in, but then I heard the other one, I heard Ava Russell warning her not to make so much noise . . . but noise about what? Not bein' able to think what it might be had the mistress going on like her was, I peeped through the keyhole . . . that were when I seen what I seen.'

'And that be goin' to make our fortune. I asked for two 'undred pounds.'

'Two 'undred!'

Ava heard the gasp . . . She also heard the answer.

'Two 'undred, an' that be only the start.'

They had jumped apart as they caught sight of her coming down those steps, Lenor's personal maid and her avaricious accomplice, the girl darting away on the errand she had been sent to carry out, her glance at her man friend asking had they been overheard. But Ava had climbed into the carriage without looking at either of them. So far as they could be aware, Ava Russell had heard nothing.

Nor could they know what she had left behind!

Her mind had worked quickly in that bedroom. Lenor's dread of having Arthur discover her affair was fast becoming panic and that could not be allowed to develop into confession.

She had spoken softly to the overwrought Lenor, as a mother might speak to a frightened child. But Lenor Medwin was no child, and no mother would do what she did next.

She had led her friend to the velvet day-bed telling her she must rest. Rest! Ava's clenched teeth released their pressure and her tight mouth eased. Lenor must not become overwrought, her heart must not be subjected to any kind of pressure, Ava would see the money was paid. They would not meet again except in the presence of others.

In the privacy of her sitting-room Ava smiled. That had been her moment of triumph, the moment her quickly conceived plan had begun to bear fruit.

'*This would be the last time we can touch each other so tenderly, the last time our lips can meet in a kiss,*' she had whispered, brushing one hand over the befrilled bosom. '*We can never share our love again.*' It had been the perfect *coup de grâce*, the blow under which Lenor had crumpled. She enjoyed brushing the muff, the thrills she never got from Arthur's love-making, and the thought of it being snatched away for ever had had her weeping.

The memory of what happened next made Ava's smile broaden, displaying the contempt inside her.

Lenor had lifted her face to look into eyes she thought sensitive with the emotions she herself was feeling. Stupid fool of a woman; the only emotion coursing through Ava Russell's veins had been that of cold hard anger. But it was an anger she had kept hidden. Allowing a sham of a sob to escape, she had pressed her mouth over Lenor's. A moment later she had whispered, '*Once more . . . one last time let us hold each other.*' The hand resting on the plump bosom had tightened as their mouths touched again, the shudder rippling through Lenor one of longing for the rest of that delight.

And she had not disappointed her friend. Still holding the other woman' s mouth, she had released the fastenings of dress and bodice laying bare the full breasts. Then as her mouth transferred its caress to Lenor's hard nipples, Ava's hands had lifted skirts and pulled silk drawers free of a body pushing itself to meet the fulfilment of passion.

It had been passion kept long from satisfaction. Ava's entwined fingers laced more tightly. The movement had been one of satisfaction.

Lenor had cried her need, whimpered her desire for that all-encompassing, heart-stopping thrill, but the wonderful agony of suspense was made to play on.

Fingers tracing past the knees and up over quivering thighs, the caressing of that moist vee at the base of the plump stomach had brought cries of pleasure each held by kisses. All the time Lenor's body had squirmed and lifted, seeking that ultimate fulfilment, that uncontrollable flare which swamped the mind, ripped away the last vestige of control before at last allowing final gratification. And, as intended, it had proved Lenor Medwin's final gratification. Her desire had been slaked . . . and her life extinguished.

It would all appear as the doctor had feared. Lenor's heart had stopped . . . but the reason why would not be discovered.

Going over her subsequent actions, Ava checked each detail as carefully as she had before leaving Lenor's bedroom. Her clothing had been replaced, the gown decorously covering her feet, her bodice securely fastened. Ava's own handkerchief, sprinkled with eau-de-cologne, had patted the tiny beads of moisture from the dead face. Her friend having expressed a tiredness she, Ava Russell, had left. That would be her reply should any question be asked.

It had worked perfectly. Lenor had suffered a heart attack and died in her sleep . . . and no one had questioned the cause.

Rising to her feet, crossing to the tall sunlit window, Ava stared out over the expanse of grounds of the house deeded to her by her dead husband's will. One source who could expose her own sexual proclivities had been removed, but another still remained. She had brought the letter home with her, had torn it into a thousand pieces then burned them. But that was no safeguard. That pair knew the name of the other woman involved, they knew Lenor's lover and they would not forego the benefits that knowing could bring them. The maid and her greedy friend would not let such an opportunity slip easily from their grasp. The next demand for money would be sent to Ava Russell and it was certain it would not be long in the coming. Ava's mouth resumed its tightness.

When it did she would be ready!

He had stood beside the door of the cottage. Pausing in the peeling of the last potatoes purchased from Gospel Oak village, Eden glanced at the window beyond which the canal lay as smooth as green velvet.

She had not noticed the stocky figure until he was almost at the gate then her mind had rocked beneath a barrage of questions. Who was he . . . why was he here . . . had someone sent him to evict her . . . was it his house? All and more had raced in her brain until one more question had drowned the rest, had stilled the mêlée in her mind but left her body trembling: Was the purpose of his visit darker than any of those reasons? Was his quarry not the house, but herself?

The thought and the horror beneath it had her rooted to the spot. Transfixed by her own fear she could only stare. Then he had moved, come to stand on the towpath only yards from her . . . yet still her legs had been like stone.

'I seen the smoke risin' from the chimney . . .'

At last he had spoken but her own tongue was cleaved to the roof of her mouth.

'. . . the place . . . it bein' empty since Mother Shipton's passin' . . .'

He had paused then, snatching the worn cap from his tousled head, holding it folded between hands stained with the labour of years.

'. . . if it were kin to you the old woman were then I asks pardon for callin' her as I did, but everybody on the cut knowed her as Mother Shipton.'

He had received no answer but, as he made to move towards her, the pieces of broken dish had dropped from her hands. Recognising the fear pulsing through her, he had halted saying quickly.

'I means you no 'urt. Like I says, I seen the smoke from the chimney and wanted to be sure there were no mischief afoot, ain't a bargee plying the cut would turn a blind eye to that. They all 'ave reason to thank that woman for one thing or another and never once were one turned from her door. Boatmen be grateful of a kindness and don't ever go forgettin' of it. None would see this house ill treated; t'were to mek sure it hadn't been taken by vagabonds that I took the liberty I 'ave. I knows now that don't be so in which case I will be takin' leave of you.'

'Wait!'

There had been something about the man made her call to him. A quietness of speech? The candid look in the eyes which did not leave her own? Even now, more than a day later she could not decide; she only knew that in that one moment she had felt all fear evaporate and in its place a warm trust.

'Wait!' she had cried as he turned back to her. 'I am not kin to the woman who lived here.'

'Don't make no odds.' He had returned a strangely penetrating glance. 'You be welcomed by that house and by them as travels the canal. You'll come to no harm while you bides here.'

He had gone then, but today others had called, among them wives of the narrowboatmen and all had endorsed the sentiments of that first man. They were happy she was in the Shipton place and, unless she had objection, the practice of mooring one or two narrowboats alongside for the night would begin again.

She had no objection. She had caught the friendly smiles of those hard-working people. She had not been seriously afraid alone in this cottage but, with the comfort of folk so near at hand, she could know the pleasures of leaving open the shutters of her bedroom, to watch the moon, as she had loved doing from childhood, paint shadows on the wall.

But moon shadows were not the only ones that had danced, others less fleeting now played in her mind. Her food could not last much longer unless . . . but she would not do that . . . she would not spend the shilling she had set aside to pay a claimant to this cottage.

So what would she do once that tiny larder was totally without food? There was only one thing she could do . . . leave or starve.

Resuming her task, the potatoes washed, sliced and layered over scraps of beef scraped from bones given her from the abattoir close by the village and which she had slowly cooked with onion and barley, she covered the dish with its lid and carried it to the side oven of the fireplace. It would continue to cook slowly while she was making her regular journey to that other small house set beside the driveway of The Coppice. Maybe this evening, the old man who had not offered his name, had never passed a truly civil word with her, might greet her with a smile.

There had been no smile!

Last evening's dish, wrapped in the cloth she had carried it in, tucked beneath her shawl, Eden walked the mostly overgrown track which led to the towpath.

There had been no civil word nor had any name been spoken. He had stood as on each previous evening, leaning heavily on a cane, mouth firm and eyes piercingly sharp.

She in turn had smiled, placed the dish which held a portion of boney pie on the gatepost then, wishing him 'goodnight' had left.

It took only a matter of moments yet in that time, as every other time she had visited, she sensed the old man's loneliness. But she could not push a friendship he obviously did not want. He may not eat the food she brought but that would not prevent her bringing it but, at the same time, she would respect his wish; she would not infringe further upon his privacy, but do only as she had before: place the dish at his gate and leave.

The crack of a dead twig breaking her thoughts, Eden's quietness of mind changed swiftly. The man from the bridge, the one who had accosted her a second time on the towpath . . . He was once again behind her . . . following her!

Vexation lighting her eyes she wheeled about. A man was indeed standing behind her . . . but it was not the man from the bridge.

15

The sewing she had been given to do had been accepted, the dressmaker nodding approval of the fine stitching before giving her a delicate lawn petticoat to be sewn for the day after next. But the money she had been paid for her labour was paltry. Tears of weariness pressing against drooping eyelids, Myra rested the cloth on her lap.

Was it lack of sleep that made her vision blur? Or was it the poor light of the lamp by which she sewed that was affecting her sight?

She could not spend more money on lamp oil. She needed every penny if she were to pay the rental on this house. But she would not be able to pay it! She had gone without food, without fire to cook by or to warm herself, all in order to save the amount necessary, but to no avail. Starving herself of food, saving every copper she earned . . . still she had not the money it would require to stay on in this house.

The folk in Bell Street were amiable whenever she met them, but they, like herself, were struggling to make a living so her limited socialising only when in a shop or in the street was not viewed unfriendly.

Shivering from cold she glanced at the cheap tin clock set above the empty grate. Almost two o'clock. In four hours she would be out and about the streets, scanning the faces of women scurrying to take the hand-made nails and home-forged bolts to a nail-master or those returning with a fresh load of iron rod. The women of Darlaston, like their counterparts in Wednesbury, had hard lives; and what of *her* life? True, it wasn't spent bending over a hot forge or hammering endlessly on an anvil, yet what did it hold but hunger and emptiness? Was what she was living now punishment for the way she had lived at Moorcroft? Was heaven punishing her for the wicked things she had done with Ava Russell and Lenor Medwin?

Tears which had pressed all day for release spilled down pale, drawn cheeks. Blinking against their persistent flow she laid the needlework aside and carried the lamp upstairs.

The bedroom felt colder than the living-room. With hands almost numb Myra struggled free of her clothes, and slipped a cotton nightgown over her head. She gasped at the cold touch of it against her body. She would say her prayers in bed . . . Grandmother had never allowed that! Trembling, she paused.

'*Honour the Lord by kneeling when you prays, an' thank Him you 'ave strength of body to do it.*'

Her grandmother's words seemed to whisper from the night shadows. Myra's heart twisted. What would her grandmother have said had she known of her granddaughter's duties in that fine house? Of the demands of its haughty mistress?

Sinking to her knees beside the bed, fingers pressed hard against a trembling mouth, holding thoughts in silence her own words formed.

I did it for you, Gran . . . for you and for Eden.

It was not the man from the bridge. A sudden fear paralysing her limbs, Eden clutched the empty dish more tightly beneath the shawl. She had not seen anyone on this track before, yet surely men coming and going from the collieries or the iron foundries must use it? Eden's brain searched for a reason why the man was watching her but returned only a question: if that were so, why did he not continue on his way? Why just stand there?

'Now, there be a sight does a man's 'eart good.'

Followed by a leer that had Eden's heart lurch sickeningly he took a step forward. The tip of a tongue licking along his lips, his speech thickening he spoke again, the leer now an evident threat.

'But it don't only be the 'eart a man likes gladdened, it be other parts, an' you be just what parts of me be a needin' of.'

Speed denying the stockiness of his build, he covered the remaining space separating them, the force of him bearing her heavily to the ground.

Breath knocked from her, the blow of the hard ground to her head knocking her nearly unconscious, she could offer no opposition to the man intent on ripping away her clothing.

'That be the way I likes it: no backchat; and tits be what I likes to play with while I takes me a ride.'

Blouse torn open, chemise pulled away, the man laughed, the sound low and feral like the growl of an animal.

'There'll be no ride for you!'

Astride Eden, the man turned, a cry of anger issuing from his throat as he was snatched away.

'. . . and no walking either!' A closed fist smashed heavily into the surprised face. '. . . there'll be nothing for you but broken bones!'

The speed which had brought down his victim, the strength which had borne her to the ground, proved of little use against the hand which held him. A cry coming from a mouth spurting blood, the stocky figure tried desperately to squirm free but the grip in which he was caught held like steel.

'Thought to have yourself a good time, did you!'

Every word accompanied by a blow, Eden's attacker jerked like a puppet on a string. 'Well, I hope you are enjoying what you are getting now!'

A final blow sending him stumbling, the man was off across the heath.

'You think to have got away with what you were about,' Eden's rescuer murmured as he watched the fleeing figure, 'but that notion is as doomed to failure as your attempt to rape an innocent girl. The morning will see you in a police cell.'

Thank God he had called at that cottage, thank God even more that he had been in time.

Drawing the shawl from beneath the still-dazed Eden, Andrew Denby covered her with it then, as a moan indicated her senses were returning, he turned his back and walked off to stand a few yards away.

Anger against the man who had been set on raping Eden swung rapidly into another channel and, as he heard the sounds of her rising to her feet, it spilled over.

'When in God's name are you going to take notice of what you are told!'

The voice vibrated with wrath but to Eden it held the reassurance of safety. The man from the bridge . . . it was the man from the bridge. Hands trembling, hindering the fastening of the few buttons left to her blouse, she drew the shawl tight about her shoulders, tying the corners in a knot beneath her breasts. It was not this man had sought to harm her and something seemed to tell her he never would . . . not in the way that other one had tried . . . but the anger in his eyes! Blinking through tears, Eden saw his blaze as dark and fierce as burning coals. He would not rape her, but the fury of him . . . what form would that take?

'You damn little fool!'

She did not have to wait long for the answer to her question for, with that expletive, he closed the gap between them and shook her hard.

'When the hell are you going to learn!'

Released from his grip, confused by the effect of sudden heart-stopping fear, followed rapidly by the swift, breath-snatching surge of relief at hearing his voice, of an inner confidence that her ordeal was over, suddenly gave way to resentment. Her own eyes blazing through the filmy veil of tears, Eden threw words at him.

'Whatever I need to learn I do not need you to teach it!'

Vexation rasping on his tongue, Andrew Denby hurled back. 'Somebody has to, if you haven't the sense to listen to others!'

'To yourself you mean!'

The snapped intervention was no longer hardened by anger. Andrew held back the irritation ready to colour his own reply. The words had broken on a sob and the hands clutching the shawl were shaking. Reaction to what had happened, to the fear she had undergone, was turning to shock; she needed to be got back to the Shipton place. There would be time for argument in the days ahead. But of one thing there would be no argument; she would visit that old man only if she was accompanied there and back, and in that the feisty miss would have no say!

He had said no more, the man from the bridge.

The hot drink given her by the wife of a narrow-boatman he had called to assist her, the knowledge the woman had promised she and one of her sons would stay the night in the cottage living-room, should have soothed the tension which had built out of that awful happening on the track leading from The Coppice. But, lying in the bed that sympathetic woman had helped her into, Eden's eyes were wide and her mind restless.

He had not spoken a word from her hurling the accusation she would not listen to him, not even to say his name or ask her own; but his anger had seemed to throb, to emanate from him in ice-cold waves. But why had he felt so strongly? Was it masculine pride, had his authority been flouted? But he had no authority over her . . . she did not have to abide by anything he said.

'You can't make me do it!' Eyes wide moments before began to droop, a restless mind wandering towards the edge of sleep.

'I won't do it . . . you can't make me!'

Soft, trembling with emotion, the murmurs hovered on the edge of silence.

'Gran doesn't make me . . .'

Claimed by sleep, the dream which had plagued so often in the years from her leaving school returned in vivid detail.

'*You are learning very well.*' Hands folded across a pencil-straight body, sharp features seemingly drawn tighter by snatched-back hair, eyes small and ferret-bright looked at a girl not yet clear of childhood. '*But becoming a ladies' personal maid involves more than the learning how to set a breakfast tray or the correct mode of speech. To better serve a mistress we must be certain our own personal hygiene is of the very best. In order to ascertain that yours is you must remove your clothes.*'

'*They are clean, Gran had me change every stitch before I came.*'

'*Your clothing always appears clean.*'

'*Then why must I remove them?*'

The drawn face seemed to close, the voice became clipped.

'*That is one more thing you have yet to learn, a ladies' maid never queries her mistress! Now, stop being foolish, child, and remove your clothing.*'

Held in the chains of sleep, Eden watched the fair-haired girl hesitate then, as the headmistress tutted her irritation, slowly began to unfasten her dress.

Hands caught together across a corseted stomach clenched more tightly together, animal eyes glinting while the woman's tongue touched across tight lips as the dress and petticoat were laid carefully aside.

'*And the rest!*'

Eyes though closed seemed to see the young face lift to the older woman, perplexity drawing a line between finely marked brows.

'*Come along, child!*' the imperious voice commanded. '*Do as you are told. I cannot put my name to a reference without ensuring you carry no sign of illness.*'

'*I'm not ill, you can see.*' The young girl held out both arms.

'*Not all disease shows only on the face and arms. There are those which affect the private parts of the body. A mistress will expect a reference stating you are in* total *health and the only way I can attest to that is to examine you myself. Really, Eden, there is no need for shyness, we are both of the same gender.*' A forced smile hovering about taut lips, but eyes still holding their animalistic gleam, the woman's voice became breathy and rasping. '*Come, my dear, I only wish to help you attain a post as ladies' maid . . . to do so I have to see all your body. Now, remove your bodice and drawers like a sensible child.*'

'*No!*' The word cried loud in her dream whispered on Eden's lips as long, pencil-like fingers reached for her. The refusal hurled again, Eden jerked into wakefulness.

Rigid from tension that nightmare always left behind, her bones aching from the effects of the attack in which she had been knocked to the ground, Eden lay absolutely still, only her mind racing from question to answer.

Could what her teacher had said be true? No. If it were, Myra would have told her of it! Did a prospective mistress demand such an intimate examination of a girl? Of course not; Myra was a ladies' personal maid, and she would never have agreed to such treatment! It had to have been lies, all lies . . . but told for what reason?

Moonbeams gliding through unshuttered windows danced to silent music but Eden saw and heard only what was in her mind.

She had grabbed her dress and petticoat, struggling into them as she ran from the house. The voice of the headmistress had called to her but she had not stopped running, not until she was back at home, safe in her grandmother's arms.

Lies! Eden's eyelids lowered, the silent reprimand sending a tingle of guilt along her spine. The woman she had run from was not the only person not speaking truthfully that night . . . she too had lied.

'*I don't want to be a ladies' maid,*' she had answered her grandmother's concern, her demand to know the reason for tear-streaked cheeks. '*I thought I did but it was no more than a frilled apron and a lace cap I really thought about. The other things are so silly. Why is it important for the handles of cups to each face the same way, why towards the teapot and not away from it . . . and why be it so positive a hairbrush be laid before a comb on the dressing-table? Petticoats and drawers to . . . to be folded one way and not another?*'

Her voice had faltered on the words 'petticoats' and 'drawers'; that had been when Grandmother had held her at arms' length, the sudden stricture of her mouth speaking its own suspicion.

'*Tell me the all.*' She had spoken in that particular tone which warned she would stand no nonsense. '*I wants the full reason of your changing your mind!*'

But how could she say she had defied the headmistress? What if what had been asked was a normal requisite of obtaining a position of ladies' maid? Wouldn't Gran be angry with her . . . make her carry on with a training which now distressed and disgusted her? There had been only one way, lies! And she had told them.

She did not want a life of pandering to one woman, of being at her beck and call all hours of the day and night, of regarding petty little things such as forgetting to scent her mistress's pillow before helping her to bed as an absolute unforgettable essential; she wanted to do the things she had been taught to do, to cook and sew . . . but most of all she wanted to be here at home with her grandmother.

The last had been indisputably true . . . but the rest! Whether believed or not, she had been put to bed. But next morning Grandmother had accompanied her to school.

'*Don't come no truck wi' me!*' Grandmother had said, facing the headmistress' autocratic stare. '*I hears what my granddaughter telled as to her reasons for wanting no more of becoming a ladies' maid same as I have my own reasons of doubtin' the truth of it; so there'll be no more of her visiting of your house!*'

A look of alarm had flashed across those ferret eyes but the answer given was cold and haughty.

'*Then that is unfortunate for Eden, for without training she will not attain anything like the position of ladies' maid, in fact . . .*' cold and venomous the eyes had flicked to Eden '. . . *she will never amount to anything other than she is now, she will never do any good!*'

Had the headmistress thought that reply to cow Grandmother . . . to have her behave in the submissive manner she was accustomed to receiving from those she thought of a lesser station than herself?

Watching the pictures in her mind, Eden saw the very opposite happen. Her grandmother's back, always as straight as a beanpole, had stiffened, her stare becoming colder than winter ice. '*Doin' any good, or amountin' to nothin' be yet to be seen, but this much be already certain,*' Grandmother' s voice had risen then, carrying clearly through glass partitions to classrooms where teachers tried in vain to pretend it could not be heard. '*Rachel Brent don't be so gullible as to believe all a frightened young wench be tellin', neither does many another woman in this town; they 'ave their own surmising and like my own it tells them all don't be as it should in this school. Since your comin', young wenches 'ave avoided meetin' their mothers' eyes and many be cryin' in their sleep. You 'ave had your say as to my granddaughter's future, now you harken to my prediction of your own. Should that which be niggling the back of my own mind – and doubtless that of many another – ever come to be spoke by a child brought to tears at treatment meted by your hands, then you'll find yourself lyin' at the bottom of a pit shaft with a rope tied fast about your neck!*'

She had never entered that school again. The pictures fading from her mind, Eden's eyelids lifted. Grandmother had not questioned the truth of what she had been told . . . but had doubt been there all the time? Had she thought her granddaughter to do something of which she was ashamed?

'But I didn't, Gran!' In the quiet solitude of her bedroom, the words whispered out as they had so very many times before. 'I didn't do it, Gran . . . I didn't do it!'

16

Lenor Medwin was buried. The service had been lavish, the floral tributes opulent, the mourners expressing their sympathy to the widower. But was that sympathy misplaced?

Ava laid aside the newspaper in which the whole episode was reported. She had watched Arthur Medwin closely from behind her fine chiffon mourning veil. True, there had been no smile, no indication of anything but sadness at the loss of his wife . . . yet, regardless of the outer display, she had sensed a relief, a liberation. Lenor had said she had enjoyed little satisfaction from her husband, that he did not give the delectation or the gratification she enjoyed from brushing the muff . . . Could it be Arthur Medwin also had a penchant for playing the other end of the field? Were his own preferences those of homosexuality . . . did Arthur Medwin's choice of a lover take the form of a man?

'Excuse me, mum, young Alfred be asking could he 'ave a word with you.'

She had known this would come. Alfred Birks and that personal maid of Lenor's had lost the chance of getting money from that quarter, but they still had another. They knew the identity of Lenor's female lover, knew she would not chance their speaking out; they realised the fruits of blackmail were theirs for the taking and they meant to reap the harvest sooner rather than later.

Her expression showing none of this, Ava nodded.

Reaching again for the newspaper, she made a pretence of reading it when, moments later, Alfred Birks was shown into the room with a warning 'not to go tekin' too much of the mistress's time'.

'There be no need.' The answer followed the closing of the sitting-room door behind the departing cook. 'What I 'ave to say will tek no more than a couple of minutes.'

'Then you had best say it,' Ava replied coolly.

'Ar, I will.' Alfred Birks smirked. 'An' it be this. I knows the things you an' Lenor Medwin got up to in this house and hers, I knows all about the filthy games you played an', lessen you wants the whole town to hear of them you'll pay me to 'old my tongue.'

Folding the newspaper with slow deliberate movements before laying it again beside her on the silk covered couch, Ava looked up. 'I see, and what is your "holding your tongue" going to cost?'

The savour of victory already sweet in his throat, Alfred spoke quickly. 'Five 'undred . . . five 'undred pounds an' that be it, you won't never hear from me no more.'

'Five hundred!' The gasp also was pretence. She

had known he would come and she had known what he would demand and she had also guessed the price would cover the loss of money he had hoped to come from Lenor.

'Be little enough for a lifetime of silence.'

Silence! Ava's thoughts were acid. A silence which would last only as long as the money did and then he would be back for more. Aloud she said, 'I do not keep such sums in the house, I shall need time to get it.'

'Third pew of the parish church, nine o'clock Saturday evening or else I tells what I knows!'

That, too, she had expected, a repetition of what had been written in the note she herself had destroyed, except that the ransom of silence had increased.

At her nod he turned, then paused as she spoke again, her voice cold and ice-bound as her eyes.

'Mister Birks . . . as from this moment you are no longer in my employ. You will be gone from Moorcroft in one hour.'

Gone . . . yes, he would be gone, but not far. Ava stared at the door which had closed behind the departing Birks. He would not forego what he must clearly see as a life which held no more need of labour . . . He would return . . . and so would his demand for money.

'You be sure you be up to bein' left?'

The woman who had slept the night in the cottage looked keenly at Eden, at the shadows below the eyes which said the girl had slept badly. Living alone was not good for a wench of such tender years but, judging by the look on the face of the man who had brought her here last evening, there was no need of her being alone.

'I am quite sure, thank you, and thank you for staying here.'

'I'd stay longer were the choice my own, but if the cargo don't reach where it should when it should then my man loses the boat . . . and that means no 'ome; gaffers don't give no mind to whys nor wherefores, their only thought be the money in their pocket and a late delivery can 'ave that lessen. That be more'n reason to take a man's living from him.'

'Of course you must go on. As for my being left here, that will be only long enough to put everything as I found it.'

'You don't be stoppin'?'

'No.' Eden met the surprised glance. She could tell the woman the reason she must leave, that every penny except for the shilling set aside in payment for using this house, was gone. She must move on or starve.

'That be a pity. Word was the Shipton place was same as it 'ad been, an' there be more'n a few boat families glad to 'ave the hearin'.'

'They thought its owner was returned?'

Glancing to where a man whistled from the narrow-boat the woman called her answer as she walked towards it.

'Weren't that. They knowed it were not Mother Shipton, but they 'oped it were a body would carry on the same and this cottage be again a place where a meal could be bought. A boat with no woman aboard counts that a blessing, while others be glad of the chance to buy supplies. But then you knows your own way best . . . though I still thinks your leavin' be a pity!'

Lifting a hand in answer to a wave from two children, Eden watched the horse-drawn boat glide slowly away. Turning, she let her gaze drift over the small house. Spring flowers studded the tiny patch of garden gleaming like jewels in the morning sun while windows, freed of their shutters, seemed to smile at their reflection shining on water that lay like a ribbon of satin. This house had welcomed her, she had felt the warmth of it seep into her . . . it would break her heart to leave.

'*A place where a meal could be bought . . .*'

The words echoed like the house itself shouted them.

'*Counts that a blessing.*'

Was this her own blessing? Was she being given a second chance? Perhaps . . . but could she accept it?

Indoors once more, Eden asked herself the question again. Could she remain here on the chance of the boat people buying her cooking?

'Me father says to ask will you put a meal for two in this along wi' a loaf of bread? 'E says do this be enough to pay forrit?'

Standing in the open doorway of the cottage,

sunshine a nimbus at his back, a lad clutched a cap in one hand while the other held a coin which glinted on his coal-blackened palm.

A smile welling deep inside, Eden took the metal billy can and filled it with broth.

Her question had been answered.

'You are the young man whose mother brought me in from the snowstorm.' He was also the same one who had sent her on what he had known would be a wild goose chase!

Leaning nonchalantly against the gate of Shipton cottage, a sandy-haired lad smiled. 'The same, but afore you rips me off for what I done that day let me say I'm sorry, it won't never 'appen again.'

Maybe not, but only if she did not give him the chance. Eden remained wary.

Recognising the distrust made plain in the giving of no reply, the lad's smile broke afresh. 'That be the honest truth. I 'ave more sense than go against word given to Mister Denby.'

'Mister Denby? Who is he and what does he have to do with your being here?'

'You knows 'im, he be the same as walked you from The Coppice an evenin' back. Said he wanted somebody he could trust . . . an' that somebody be me.'

He straightened as he said it, a tug at his jacket an indication of pride. He was taller than she remembered, stronger looking, the glint of pride adding tangibly to his stature.

The stranger on the bridge, a man she had met several times since, but who had not given his name . . . why would he send a lad here?

'I don't understand.' Eden's brow creased. 'Why should this . . . this Mister Denby send you here?'

'To walk you to and from that house along of The Coppice. Says to be here at this time every evenin' and not to leave your side 'til you be back safe in your 'ome.'

How dare he! How dare that man presume! Vexation rising hotly, the crease on Eden's brow deepened. Words rattling like hailstones, she returned, 'I have no need of an escort! You will kindly go back to your Mister Denby and tell him so!'

'I'll do that, miss, tell him what you says, but not 'til I've done what were told me to do.'

'But I don't want you to walk with me!'

'So I understands, but then I don't relish goin' against anythin' Andrew Denby tells to do, nor would anybody else if they knows what be good for 'em.'

Was that a warning for herself? Irritation a flare in her eyes, Eden made to answer but the lad's words came before she could.

'I'll be no trouble to you. I won't even speak unless you asks it, that be a promise, only don't refuse . . . for Mister Denby . . . well, he be payin' good. It be more'n I can earn in a whole day along of Wednesbury. Them there carters pays no more'n a copper or two, no matter the load to be shifted.'

Wednesbury! In an instant Eden was in the market

place, a small child holding her grandmother's skirts while she haggled the price of an already worn-through coat, small feet tapping the setts as she followed to The Shambles where the bargaining was repeated, Grandmother complaining a breast of lamb or a knuckle end of pork be far too costly, standing resolutely until it was reduced to suit her purse. Memory a living ache, a pain that tore her heart, Eden's irritation died.

Wednesbury held no easy living for folk of her walk in life, nor would it for this lad and his mother; they would earn their bread like the people she had lived among from childhood, the families herded together in so many tiny houses, so many narrow streets, each man and woman, so many sons and daughters, all labouring dawn to dusk in order to live.

'I be sorry for misleadin' you the way I did, truly I be. Please miss, say you'll let me walk along of you, the money will be of great help to me mother.'

Drawn from the tide of memory threatening to swamp her, Eden caught the look in those brown eyes. No longer the brightness of mischief, the twinkle of roguishness; what they held now was a plea, the hope behind it burning like a flame . . . a hope she could not deny. She had once thought opportunity might come by which she could repay the kindness of Sara Melia; this, it seemed, could be that opportunity.

'Five 'undred pounds!' Alfred Birks caught his accomplice in his arms. 'Five 'undred and not even the makings of a protest. That were something I 'adn't expected. To agree to pay what were asked an' no bones made!'

'Ava Russell said her would pay?' The late Lenor Medwin's maid freed herself from the hug.

'Couldn't say otherwise.' Shifty eyes gleamed. 'Her knowed I holds the upper hand, that should I speak of her carryin's on, then her would be finished, not only in Wednesbury but everywhere's else; brushin' the muff don't go down well with any sort 'cept them as plays it! 'ere! Does you dip your fingers?'

Laughing at her outraged gasp, Alfred caught the girl to him, his hands clasping her buttocks.

'But you don't needs to, you gets plenty of the other. Alfred Birks be generous with what nature give 'im.'

'Just so long as he be generous with me and no other girl.'

'You don't share with anybody.' Alfred kissed the panting lips. 'What be in my trousers be for you . . . in fact I be goin' to give you a little bit of it right now.'

'No!' The girl giggled as he caught her hand. 'I can't, I'm supposed to be sortin' the mistress's things.'

'You'll like sortin' this better.' Pressing the hand he held in his close up against his crotch, he laughed again, a thick throaty sound that stayed in the mouth.

The girl beneath him in the stable loft, her breasts bare and her legs spread wide, Alfred felt his hard flesh jerk. His generous endowment was all hers . . . until inclination proved otherwise!

She was a fool! Lust satisfied, Alfred watched the

girl skip across the large cobbled yard then disappear into the kitchen of the imposing house. She was a fool to believe herself the only wench to savour the delights of Alfred Birks, and she was an even bigger fool to believe he would share any part of that five hundred pounds with her. True, he had enjoyed what she had given so often, enjoyed the feel of her body beneath his; but five hundred pounds would buy him many more . . . and not one to hold a threat over his head.

Slipping from the stable, checking there was no one around to see him leave, he ran for the cover of a nearby copse. Resting a moment among the trees he breathed hard. He had thought long on that problem. It was the one flaw, the one crack which could have the whole plan collapse. He had tried telling himself it would not happen, that she would be too afraid to disclose the part she had played in blackmailing Ava Russell, but something at the back of his mind had warned him otherwise, something he had heard but could not quite remember . . . something about 'a woman scorned'.

Leaving the shelter of the trees, his breathing level and even, he crossed the wide expanse of ground lying to the rear of the Medwin house. Going by way of the front approach was too risky, there were still visitors coming to give their condolences to the distraught widower, visitors who might just wonder what an all too obvious servant was doing walking along the main drive.

Distraught widower! He snorted softly as he came

on to Hall End following the road to where it joined Ethelfleda Terrace. If that maid were to be believed, and there were no reason of her not being, then Arthur Medwin were no more distraught than Alfred Birks would be when his present titillating partner was removed. And she would have to be.

Away to his left the clock of the parish church of Saint Bartholomew rang nine times. Glancing at the spire, no blacker against the night sky than it was in the light of day, Alfred smiled. It would be there in the place he had specified. Ava Russell would not chance the world learning of her dirty game; it would be there, all five hundred, and soon it would be in his pocket.

'Give an old soldier tuppence for a bite o' bread . . .'

From a narrow alley a cracked voice called from darkness the moon did not penetrate. That way lay Trouse Lane and a few yards from where he stood now those few stone steps locally called the Church Steps.

A beggar! Alfred made to go on his way, then paused. In less than two minutes he would be a rich man, he would be well able to toss tuppence to an old man . . . In fact he would be well able to afford a lot more.

'Wait you there, old 'un.' He grinned in the direction of a bent figure hobbling from the gloom, a stick tap-tapping on the ground. 'Wait you against the Church Steps. I'll be passing that way in a minute or so an' I promises you'll 'ave more than enough to buy yourself a bite. You will 'ave enough for a whole bloody meal with money left over to buy the same for a couple of weeks.'

The beggar's grin expanded by the murmured, 'God bless you sir, God bless you,' Alfred glanced once more along the rise of the hill to the spire rising against the sky.

17

The shilling the boatman had paid for the broth she had ladled into that billy can (together with a loaf of bread and several slices of beef cheek she had pressed the day before) had bought enough ingredients to make more broth, and some faggots that she could team with the quart of blue peas.

Blue peas! Eden mused over the term. She had often asked why they were called blue when in fact they were a greyish green, and always Grandmother had clucked sharply, ''cos that be what folks calls 'em, an' that be all about it!'

Myra and she had shared knowing looks when answered in that testy 'don't bother me now, child' fashion; yet they had not dared to voice the suspicion each guessed niggled in the mind of the other, the incredibly wicked supposition that Gran was not the holder of all knowledge. It had been one of childhood's fantasies that Grandmother was the very font of wisdom, one she and Myra had not held quite so true once they had left those childhood years behind; yet even so they both held that recognition to themselves.

'Following your usual occupation, I see.'

Startled by the quietly spoken interruption, Eden clutched the provisions she had parcelled into her shawl.

'Daydreaming. You really ought not to indulge whilst walking alongside a canal.'

'So you have said . . . several times!' The first element of surprise faded, Eden snapped tartly.

'So why is it you continue to do it?'

The groceries seeming suddenly to weigh more heavily in her arms, Eden felt herself flush beneath a startlingly clear gaze. How did this man always manage to come upon her when her mind was a thousand miles away? Holding tight to it now, refusing to let it wander an inch, she answered in that same acid tone.

'Because it pleases me to do so, almost as much as it would please me not to have you continue to give what I have previously pointed out to be most unwanted advice. In short I wish you to . . . to . . .'

'Keep my nose out of your business! Is that the phrase you were looking for?'

'Exactly!' Eden hitched the parcel-filled shawl higher in her arms.

Inches above her head, sable eyes echoed the smile curving a sensuous mouth. 'I don't think I can do that . . . at least, not before I am absolutely sure you have learned those lessons needed to be learned by all folk living on or beside the canals.'

'Or those walking the path to The Coppice!' Eden hitched the shawl again. 'Tell me . . . what is it has you thinking I am not capable of seeing to my own safety?'

As if wiped by an unseen hand the smile vanished leaving eyes and mouth chiselled granite. 'Haven't you had proof of that already? Is it going to take yet another attack . . . yet another man's lust to convince you? We are not living in Paradise! The quicker you get that into your head the better!'

The flush which, until that moment, had tinged her cheeks pink, now flamed scarlet. She shrivelled inside with each memory of that attack, memory which always left the questions: Did her rescuer think she was a willing partner in the scene he had come across? Did he think her guilty of such obscene behaviour?

'Give me that before you drop it!'

Hands brusque as the voice took the bundle from her, holding it easily in one arm whilst the other propelled her forward.

Inside the cottage Eden had made her home, the bundle of provisions lowered to the table, his eyes locked once more with hers.

'I advise . . . no, I *suggest* you remain more aware when out walking . . . leave your dreaming until you are in your bed.'

Colour gone now from her face, Eden held the tenebrous stare. Growing up in Hobbins Street, among the rough and tumble of neighbours' children who, from the earliest age, were taught to stand on their own feet had taught her the same. Now the defiance she had so often shown to those boys who thought to play the bully stirred in her as she replied quietly.

'Thank you, Mister Denby . . . it is Mister Denby, is it not? Thank you for your suggestion; now, *I* suggest . . . no, I *require* you no longer send the Melia boy to walk with me to The Coppice.'

Would he argue with her, raise a threatening hand as those childhood adversaries had done? Eden dismissed the thought with speed. They were not children to squabble and fight, but the slight tightening of the mouth said plainly that the man watching her was not one to negotiate terms.

'Forgive me, Miss Brent . . .'

Eden's senses quickened. How did he know her name?

'. . . Davy Melia furnished me with your name, as no doubt he gave mine to you . . .' he paused, a hint of amusement rising behind his dark stare, '. . . the lad is quite communicative; however, to your requirement . . . I regret I cannot agree to it.'

'Then I will pay him myself.'

The intimated smile died instantly, leaving a stone-hard glare matching the hardness of his voice. 'Davy Melia, as is his mother, is in my employ. Whilst that situation remains, he will do as I instruct. However, should you prefer the services of both be terminated then that is something I can agree upon.'

It was a threat, much more refined than those made by childhood protagonists but, nevertheless, a threat. There was no question he was well aware her circumstances were not such she could reimburse the Melias' loss of income. Andrew Denby was not so different after all; he was determined on his way every bit as much as the Hobbins Street boys had been.

'Well!'

It was a strident, unequivocal demand. To refuse would bring hardship to a woman who had helped her; that was something she could not do. Using every reserve of dignity, though the spark of rebellion still flared, Eden nodded acceptance.

'Eh, mum, it be a terrible shock an' no denyin'.'

Ava Russell reached for the newspaper held out by a weeping cook. 'I couldn't help seeing,' the woman raised a corner of a spotless apron to dab red eyes, 'I couldn't help but see, what with it bein' right on the front page. Oh, it be terrible! Who could 'ave done such a wicked thing, who? I mean he were a good lad. Why it be our Alfred, Alfred Birks?' Behind the apron, buxom breasts heaved again.

'So what has he been up to should cause so much grief?'

The apron lowered with a swish. 'T'ain't so much what he's been up to as what somebody else been up to.'

'Then what is it someone else has been up to?'

'Murder!' The word hiccuped behind a fresh torrent of tears. 'Murder be what's been up to. Found with his chest stabbed and throat cut across, poor little bugger; wouldn't harm a fly, wouldn't Alfred Birks, nor never do nobody a bad turn.'

Not unless it resulted in doing himself a good one!

Ava left the newspaper folded on her knee, the glance she now gave her cook that of disbelief. 'That is absurd! You have made some mistake . . . no one would want to murder Alfred Birks!'

'Want to or no, that be what somebody been gone and done . . . ain't no mistake, as you'll see yourself when you reads the paper. It be young Alfred Birks, an' him with his throat an' chest cut through. Be like them murders along o' London, p'raps it be the same killer come to our streets.'

'Now, that is enough of such talk,' Ava said as the apron flapped up again. 'For all we know the newspaper could be quite wrong in its report . . . it certainly would not be the first time.'

'But, mum . . .'

'No!' Ava's customary snap served to halt her cook's sniffled reply.

'If it should be as you fear, then no doubt we will be informed by the constabulary; until then, I expect you to attend to your duties as normal.'

Alfred Birks dead! But had the victim, a man killed by foul means, been positively identified as Birks? Polly Jupp seemed convinced; but then her cook was hardly someone to seek fact over gossip. Taking up the newspaper, Ava glanced at the heavier black heading of a column halfway down the front page.

'*Body Found Slashed*!'

Polly Jupp was right so far, how much more of the woman's snivelled story would prove the same? If it *all* did, if it *was* Birks who had been found dead, then two obstacles to her continued social standing had been removed; first Lenor Medwin and now Alfred Birks . . . both a threat . . . both gone. Drawing a deep breath, she took up the newspaper.

'. . . *the body found beside a small flight of steps midway between Trouse Lane and Church Street was identified as being that of a Mister Alfred Birks . . .*'

Ava's pent-up breath escaped slowly. Birks was dead. She was free of him and of his blackmail. Fate had favoured Ava Russell. Now, if only it would reveal to her where Myra Brent was to be found.

Myra Brent! She thrust the newspaper aside. That fool Birks! She had sent him to the grandmother's house; she had phrased her own conversation with him in such a vein that he would think her concerned for the wellbeing of the girl; surely he would have enquired of his acquaintances! But if he had, he had said nothing of it to her and, if he had brought word to Polly Jupp, then the woman would have said so.

Two people who could betray her no longer lived. Ava's fingers curled into her palms. But another most probably was alive, and that probability spelled danger. She was not completely rid of the threat of exposure. What benefit was there in two sources of jeopardy being removed while one even greater hazard remained!

Rising to her feet and walking to the window, Ava glanced to where a corner of the stable block showed above the screening tiles.

Birks! Her brain spat the name acidly. The dung the

man shovelled from the stables had been of more use! He had failed to find Myra Brent but the hunt would not end with his death. It would go on. Her missing maid would be found and, when she was, then the threat to her mistress's secret would indeed be over!

She had agreed. It had been achieved only under pressure . . . his pressure.

Andrew Denby's long strides carried him swiftly past workmen hammering and sawing, men who worked for him every one of whom had a word of greeting.

'There be a request for carriage of a shipment from the Moxley Iron Works up to the India docks along of London.' A heavily starched winged collar seeming to support a whiskered face, the clerk of Denby Boat Builders handed a sheet of paper to his employer.

'Will you be requiring me to write that we can't oblige?' The clerk fingered the pencil permanently lodged behind his right ear.

'Turning custom away does not make good business.' Andrew glanced at the clerk. 'Are you absolutely sure we can't handle the Moxley freight?'

Removing the pencil and running the tip over a list of names written neatly in a black-bound ledger, the whiskered man took a moment to answer. 'There be no boat standin' in the basin, and them as makes the London run don't be due back afore Wednesday next.'

'Isn't *Midland Queen* due in today?'

It was a question that had not needed to be answered.

Andrew Denby knew the times of arrival and departure of every one of the boats he owned as well as the weight and content of cargo, but dutifully the man again touched pencil to ledger.

'Ar,' he nodded, still with his eyes on the page, 'the *Midland Queen*, her be due t'other side o'midday.'

'She will be here an hour before that. I passed her as I came along the towpath. Her skipper is a good boatman and not unfamiliar with the London run, he did it many times for my father. Ask would he take the Moxley iron . . .' he smiled as the clerk looked up, 'be sure to tell him it is a request.'

'He'll know that for 'imself, all the bargemen as works for you knows they don't never be ordered.'

'Then assure him also my request does not come without a token of gratitude . . . the pay for that run will be doubled.'

Yes, the cut folk in Andrew Denby's employ knew their master for his fairness in his dealings with them. They also knew he had taken more often to walking to the boatyard or the basin, and that had them asking why? The question in his own mind, the clerk returned to the outer office unaware the same question played in the mind of his employer.

He had used the threat of withdrawing employment from young Davy Melia and from his mother, used it as a means of extracting an agreement from a young woman he scarcely knew and with whom the few dozen words exchanged had been less than friendly. His head resting against the high-backed leather chair,

Andrew Denby ran a hand through thick dark hair. Why had he engaged in such tactics, why use other people in order to get one young woman to agree to his proposals? It was a practice entirely foreign to him . . . but then so was wrestling to keep thoughts of her from creeping into his mind during waking hours as well as before falling asleep at night.

She had been caught in that last vicious swipe of winter, had lain down during that snowstorm then found and given shelter by the Melias. Apart from her name that was all he knew with any certainty. He had guessed she was running from something . . . maybe someone, but that was only a guess.

Fingers resting on his head, he stared at the picture forming across his vision: the picture of a shawl-wrapped figure huddled against the wall of bridge spanning the waters of the canal. She had seemed so fragile beneath that shawl, so vulnerable, half-frozen and blue with cold, yet she had found enough inner fire to argue with him . . . and resolve to make her own way. Staying alone in that canalside cottage proved the courage of that; not many young women he knew would be prepared to live that way.

But she was like no other woman of his acquaintance. There was no air of affectation about her, no coy smiles or exaggerated helplessness, no feminine wiles; so what attracted him so that he often walked between his business at Willingsworth and that at Gospel Oak . . . and why come by way of the towpath or past the grounds of The Coppice? Lowering his hand, he breathed out slowly. Why ask questions he already knew the answer to!

'*Ar, Mister Denby, I knows Shipton Cottage.*'

Davy Melia was young, but life had equipped him with a sharp brain and a nose which could smell a sixpence were it buried in a midden. He had carried out the task assigned him and reported.

'*. . . it be the same wench took up livin' in old mother Shipton's place, the one Mother and me found lyin' out on the 'eath. Near enough froze her were. Her name be Eden Brent, but that be all Mother told.*'

Pictures fading, Andrew Denby reached for the pen set on a brass inkstand but still his brain would not free him.

'*That be all Mother told . . .*'

The phrase had played many times since his first hearing it and it repeated now. Could it be that the lad's mother knew more? Did she perhaps know where the girl in the snow had come from, what she was running from? He could ask, he could even order Sara Melia to divulge any other item of information she might have gleaned regarding Eden Brent, even threaten . . . but no more of threats! Mind snapping shut at the thought, he dipped pen nib into the ink.

Whatever he may learn of that girl it would not be at the expense of anyone's peace of mind.

18

The fry – liver, heart and kidney – she had purchased from the abattoir that morning was almost cooked. Bringing it from the oven, setting the hot dish on a cloth protecting the table she scrubbed twice every day, Eden strained the diced meat. Setting the gravy aside she mixed freshly boiled onion with a slice of bread broken into small pieces. What more had her grandmother added when cooking faggots? Touching her hot cheek with the back of her hand, she glanced beyond the unshuttered window to where a narrow-boat was mooring. Shipton Cottage was becoming a regular stopover for ever more barge people and the food they bought there received high praise, especially the dish she was preparing now.

'*That always be supposin' it ever does get done!*'

The admonition given two little girls 'helping' with grandmother's preparing of a meal sounding in her mind, Eden returned her attention to the table.

She added a sprinkling of sage and a couple of bay leaves taken from the tiny rear garden to the bread and onion and seasoned the whole with salt and pepper. Then, adding the meat, minced the whole together before fashioning it into palm-sized balls. Now came the part Grandmother forbade tiny hands from touching. She and Myra had stood, noses almost touching the table, fascinated as the kell, the delicate lace-like lining of a pig's stomach bought with the fry, was wrapped around the balls of meat. Smiling to herself, Eden carried out the procedure allowed her in later years then, faggots set in neat rows in the large roasting pan, placed them in the oven.

Straightening, Eden glanced about the room. In reality it wasn't so very different to the house in Hobbins Street, a living-room that must also serve as kitchen, a scullery leading to an outhouse and privy while upstairs held two bedrooms. But outside could be a world far removed from that she had known, that world of narrow streets their houses cheek by jowl with foundries . . . those endless foundries and workshops that belched their black streams of smoke over Wednesbury. Surrounded by open heath, the canal a silent highway, Shipton Cottage was a haven of quiet peace.

If only Myra were with her. Unbidden, the thought slipped into Eden's mind and, for a moment, she allowed it to play freely. They would have shared the work of cooking, enjoyed the pleasant moments of conversation with passing boat people . . . But she must not dwell on what might have been, those were dreams she should not harbour. Myra had left the life they had once shared, she had chosen a home very different to the one given by their grandmother, chosen a new life with new friends. It was what she so obviously wanted; freedom from the drudgery of Hobbins Street, from that tiny house . . . But, freedom from her sister? Yes, that slap had said as much.

A tap at the door recalling her attention, she opened it to a smiling Davy Melia.

'Eh, that smell be a banquet on its own, it be waftin' all along the towpath, fair makes the mouth water. Be faggots or my name don't be Davy Melia.'

A smile touching her own mouth Eden nodded. 'You have the nose of a gourmet.'

A hand brushing vigorously over his face, the lad looked crestfallen. 'I . . . I washed afore I come, me mother says to always wash afore comin'.'

Now *she* was embarrassed; he thought the words she had used meant he had a dirty face. Apology bright in her eyes as it was quick to her tongue, she explained the term she had used.

'I ain't never 'eard no such word, but if it means as you says it do, that I be an excellent judge of food, then I reckons I be a . . . a . . . a what you said.'

'Then I think we should put you to the test.' Reaching a plate from the dresser, Eden spooned a faggot from a batch taken earlier from the oven. Covering it with rich gravy she handed it to the watching Davy.

'I thought never to taste cooking the equal to me mother's,' he said, a forkful of the savoury meat already in his mouth, 'but yours be; no wonder the cut folk be talkin' of it the way they do.'

'Well you had best stop talking until your mouth is empty. Your mother will be asking where it is you learned such a habit.'

A grin his answer, the lad gave all his concentration to his plate.

She had grown very fond of Davy Melia. His company, and his flow of gossip picked up in the town, were like sunshine after rain; they refreshed and warmed her mind. Washing the utensils of her cooking, she nodded as he brought his empty plate then asked could he dry for her. This was how she thought Myra. . .

Refusing to let the thought linger, she removed her apron as they both returned to the living-room.

'I takes it you be goin' along of The Coppice.' He watched her wrap a dish in a clean white cloth. 'Why is it you goes there every evenin'? T'ain't as though that old man be pleased of seein' you . . . leastways he don't show it. Be he some relation?'

'No.' Eden shook her head. 'He is no relation.'

'Then why . . . I means, why bother? He be a grumpy old bug . . .'

'That is one more thing you are going to have to watch! Let your mother hear that kind of language and she will . . .'

'Tan me hide!'

'Until your backside bears a very good imitation of leather.'

Her reply bringing a grin as wide as his face, he took the dish she had wrapped. Leading the way from the house, he waited while she placed a broom diagonally across the doorway indicating temporary absence, then fell into step beside her.

Easy in her company, he walked a while in silence but his mind continued to question. If the old man were no relative then why these visits? Why take him food that were never paid for, not even with a smile or a thank you? Words bubbled from brain to tongue and slipped from his lips.

'Payment is not important.' Eden answered the impromptu question. 'A smile or a word would be nice, I admit, but it is not necessary. I will go to that gate so long as I live in Shipton Cottage, and I will continue to offer food. He may not eat it, but that also is of no consequence.'

'The man might be old . . . and mean-tempered he certainly is . . . but I reckons him not fool enough to be throwin' away what you brings.'

'Perhaps.'

Flicking a pebble with the side of his boot, Davy watched it curve out over the water then drop, spreading widening circles on its smooth surface. 'Ain't no p'raps about it, but what do you mean when you says his lack of thanks be not necessary, and not eatin' what you brings of no consequence?'

Were the questions put by the man paying this lad to walk at her side would she answer so readily? Knowing she would not, Eden nevertheless replied. 'I do what I do because I feel the man is lonely . . . that it is a broken heart responsible for what some see as churlish behaviour. He is full of sadness. The beautiful house he may watch over has an air of that same unhappiness, of despair. I think he may have suffered a loss great as my . . .'

Was she about to say a loss great as her own? Glancing sideways, Davy saw the quiver of Eden's mouth, her fingers draw the shawl closer as if shutting out some unwanted intrusion. Each evening of walking with her he had wanted to ask what had brought her to live by herself. What was it caused the look he sometimes caught on her face? A look which said she had lost her world.

The words formed in his brain but, as on every other evening, that was where they remained. 'Ask naught that be no concern of your'n,' was his mother's counsel. 'Ask no question and you'll be told no lie.'

Glancing again at a face he thought prettier than that of any wench he saw in Wednesbury, Davy Melia's lips closed.

He would ask no question . . . but that was not from thinking Eden Brent would lie; it was because . . . because of what?

Colour rising in his cheeks, he turned his gaze to the placid waters of the canal.

The problem of Alfred Birks was removed, there would be no more ransom of silence . . . not unless that maid of Lenor's . . . but she would not dare!

Secure in the thought, Ava Russell allowed herself a smile then dismissed it as a tap to the sitting-room door heralded her cook. It had been several days since the finding of Birks' dead body and still she snivelled. Not on account of sorrow! Ava's lips firmed. The woman was not the heartbroken friend she pretended; she was simply enjoying the drama.

'Be a police hinspector asking of seeing you, mum.' It was followed by the loud sniff Ava had expected. 'Will I tell you be home?'

The police! Ava's brows drew together. Why would a policeman call at this hour?

'I will try to be brief as I can, ma'am, but questions must be asked . . . you understand.'

Polite, but by no means servile! This man would not be dismissed as would any servant. Ava glanced at the accompanying uniformed constable standing just within the door, a pencil poised over a notebook.

Ava indicated a chair and, when the inspector was seated, asked, 'Questions . . . to what purpose?'

'The death of a Mister Alfred Birks. I trust you have heard of it.'

'Of little else from my cook these few days. She has been quite upset by it all.'

'Understandable, ma'am, understandable.'

'Quite.' Ava nodded. 'But your coming to this house is not, so why are you here?'

'Corroboration, ma'am, corroboration. We has to be certain facts, as we have them, be correct. Your cook tells me the deceased worked here as groom and coachman for a number of years.'

'Six,' Ava answered. 'He was hired by my late

husband. His service and manner were always commendable.'

'Tell me if you will, ma'am, the evening of his death . . . had you given permission for him to be free of duty?'

Behind the inspector, the constable touched the tip of the pencil to his tongue. Why all these questions . . . did these people think she had murdered Birks! Keeping the fire of irritation doused beneath a frigid tone, Ava replied evenly.

'As a widow I rarely have need of my carriage in the evenings, Inspector; an annual charity event, midnight mass on Christmas Eve, but very rarely more so, unless directed otherwise, my groom had permission to spend his evenings as he would.'

'My thanks, ma'am.' The inspector rose. 'That be all I needs to ask. I hope it hasn' t been too painful. You won't be troubled again.'

She would not be troubled again! The policemen departed, Ava smiled, the pleasure inside her warm and voluptuous. That inspector could not know how true his words were; she would not be troubled again, her dirty little blackmailer was gone.

'It be the same one, I be certain of it, the newspaper said he were groom along of Moorcroft an' that be the name of the 'ouse he said were his place of service.'

'I don't care to know his place of service, same as I don't want you to speak of what you 'eard being talked of. You keep your mouth closed, Davy Melia, the dead be dead an' they be best left to lie in peace.'

'But . . .'

'But nothing!' Sara Melia's lined face showed a new source of worry as she rounded sharply on her son. 'You don't be a babby no more, you knows well the consequence of owning to knowin' or even hearing of a man killed in the street. It would have them constables afetching you to the station for to answer questions and only the Lord hisself knowing how long that would take or the results of it. Some things have a funny way of turning out. What be thought of as helping has a way of bouncing so it hits you on the head. You owns to knowing anything and it could be *you* gets the blame . . . you be the one landed in court on a charge of murder.'

'That couldn't never 'appen, the police . . .'

'The police needs to be seen to 'ave done what they gets paid to do!' Sara cut short her son's response. 'They needs to reassure folk they be safe and there be no more danger lurking the streets, that the killer be caught . . . and if they can't do it one way then chance be they'll do it another. That be one chance I won't have you take . . . you hear me, Davy, I won't have you take no chance!'

He had promised. Heaving the last of six dozen crates of soap and candles on to a wagon, Davy stood to catch his breath. His mother was mistaken in her claims but, even so, he had promised to say nothing of what he had heard that evening of a man asking questions regarding a woman. The Green Dragon was not a place his mother would approve of but the landlord allowed him to stand inside the taproom while nights were cold, and it had been chilly that night.

'*My sister, her run away from home . . .*'

The words had caught his ear and he had looked to where a younger man sat talking with another he had recognised as a carter who sometimes gave him work. Hoping that might have been the case that night, he had edged closer. The carter had given a ride to a woman, but she had given no name.

The younger man had seemed riled by the answer . . . a young man whose description seemed to match that given in the newspaper. But wenches often run away and it were natural a brother should be seeking her . . . so why was it the more he thought about what he had seen and heard the less natural the younger man's behaviour had appeared?

'Be you finished, young 'un?'

The shout bringing his mind to the present, Davy jumped from the cart, surprise having him almost miss his footing as he landed. The owner of the wagon and the carter in the Green Dragon were one and the same.

'Bit of a to-do along of Church Street the other night, so I hears.' The man wiped the remains of his breakfast from his whiskers with a brightly spotted cloth. 'Fella done in wi'a knife . . . what be the world comin' to?'

His mother had voiced the same. Davy watched the wagon's owner bring several coins from a pocket, fingering through them and selecting two.

'There ya go, young 'un,' he flipped the coins,

'reckon that bloke were done in for his money for talk hereabout. Reckons there were none in his pockets when he were found . . . but then what some don't know for sure they invents. As for meself I be certain he had a bob or two more'n he paid for ale.'

'You knowed him then!'

'Not personal.' The man heaved himself to the driving seat, gathering the reins in weathered hands. 'But I seen his picture in the paper, it were a face I'd seen afore . . . that I would stake a sovereign on! Asked me right there,' he tipped his head towards the tall cream-coloured building, one wall emblazoned with the name, Green Dragon, 'asked 'ad I given a ride to a young wench some time back, seemed 'er were runnin' from 'ome. I told him I 'ad . . . but it cost him two tankards of ale and a shillin' beside.'

A young wench . . . runnin' from 'ome.

The coins he had caught dug into Davy's palms as his hands closed tight. Eden Brent had been running from something, could she have been fleeing from home? Was the man found with his chest and throat slit Eden Brent's brother!

19

There was no place left to enquire. Myra eased off her boots, grimacing with pain. The soles were almost non-existent, worn away by the hours of tramping the streets asking if anyone had seen Eden. She could well have been asking had they seen the Queen, for their answer would have been the same.

She had hoped this town might hold her sister, that if she searched hard enough she would find her. But all of the searching, all of the praying, had been to no avail. Eden was not in Darlaston, she couldn't be; otherwise someone somewhere would have known of it, told where she could be located. But there had been nothing, not one single word of hope.

Boots laid aside, she glanced at the grate set with coal and sticks, at the kettle hung on a bracket. She could light the fire, make herself a hot drink . . . but the time spent on doing was time she could not spare. Forcing herself to her feet, wincing at the sting shooting through them, she went into the scullery. It was already dark, the sun having gone down well before her return to Bell Street, but she ignored the candle. Rinsing her hands in cold water she returned to the living-room, the dampness of its walls thick in her nostrils.

Lighting the lamp, she placed a clean cloth across her knees to ensure the pale lemon silk for a blouse did not become marked, she threaded a needle. The lease she had taken on this house was up. She had tried to save enough money to renew it but had failed. Tomorrow she would return the key to the estate agent and take her finished needlework to the dressmaker. The money earned would feed her for a few days, a few days more of searching.

But in which town? She held the delicate cloth closer to the lamp, blinking as her tired vision blurred needle and stitches. Where could Eden have gone? The answer was anywhere . . . Her sister could have gone to any town. She would have had money with which to purchase a tram ticket, the selling of Grandmother's belongings would have given her that.

A train ticket! The cloth she was working fell from her cold fingers. Trains travelled the length and breadth of the country and Eden could have taken any one of them!

It had been only weeks . . . just weeks since another woman's hands had fondled these breasts, since soft lips had closed over nipples teased to hard points, weeks since gentle fingers had played between wide-spread legs . . . yet it seemed years.

Standing naked before the long mirror of her dressing-room, Ava Russell stroked slowly along her hips and across her stomach, breathing deeply as she cupped each breast.

She had denied herself the pleasure of a lover for what reason . . . respect for Lenor? Hardly that! The thought that Myra Brent would return? But she had known deep down that would not happen.

Releasing her breasts, trailing her hands slowly, voluptuously, over her waist and stomach, breath catching in her throat as her fingers touched the silken bush of pubic hair, Ava smiled at her reflection. The days of denial were ended!

Reaching for clothing laid ready, she dressed languidly, holding drawers several moments below the vee of her legs before drawing them slowly over it. That was the way they would be removed, a woman's lips following their long slow withdrawal.

She could buy a woman of the street; half a crown would have any one of them do what was asked. But women of that calling might be as liberal with their tongues as with the selling of their bodies. She could go to a place where men indulged their sexual excesses whilst believing their wives to know nothing of their fornications; a brothel would doubtless cater for all tastes while being less forthcoming with gossip – the continuance of their business depended upon discretion.

Fastening the buttons of a dove-grey suit, Ava toyed with the idea of visiting such a house of pleasure. She could go to Wolverhampton, Birmingham, any town where she would not be recognised . . . but what would she return with? Prostitutes were not exactly sisters of the church, their faith was not as pure nor their habits as clean, and she was not in the market for a dose of the clap!

Securing a band of black velvet about her left arm, she took up a bonnet circled about with ostrich feathers, then discarded it. Bright colours and feathers would draw attention. Selecting instead a hat of the same grey as her suit, its low crown allowing a fine black silk chenille veil to fall to her chest, she picked up black gloves and bag and took a final look at the result in the mirror.

It would look well her being present at the funeral of Alfred Birks; a caring employer paying respects to a trusted servant. Ava glanced again in the mirror, the veil was an excellent touch . . . it would hide her smiles; and when that delight was over she would go shopping. But the goods she purchased would have no disease, they would not be procured at any street corner or bawdy-house, nor from the school which had furnished her with Myra Brent. Why pay that head-mistress when she could obtain the same merchandise for nothing? The workhouses were full of young girls, any one of whom would gladly exchange that life for one as ladies' maid.

Ashes to ashes . . .

Beside the open grave, a priest, in white lace-trimmed cassock over dark robe, raised a hand in final blessing. Standing a few yards away, Ava silently intoned the irreverent accompaniment heard muttered once in childhood.

. . . The Lord won't fetch you
So the Devil must.

'It was good of you to come, ma'am, I know Alfred would have appreciated it.'

Already walking away from the graveside, Ava paused as Lenor's maid caught up with her.

'Who'd have thought,' the girl sniffed, 'who'd have thought such a thing could happen?'

Who indeed? Ava watched the lace-trimmed handkerchief lift to dab tear-stained cheeks. No doubt it had belonged to Lenor as had the coat the girl was wearing. But the killing of that man was a blessing for Ava Russell!

'We . . . we was going to wed. Alfred had asked would I wed with him.'

'And what will you do now?' Ava kept her tone sympathetic.

'That be it, ma'am,' the girl sniffed again, 'with the mistress having passed away I no longer be required as ladies' maid so I thought to wed right off, but now with Alfred gone then that be gone with him.'

'Was there no other position for you at the Medwin house?'

'None were vacant, ma'am, 'sides which, the rest of the staff will be finished soon for the master be selling up . . . going to live abroad if what I hears be true. . .'

Arthur Medwin selling up . . . going to live abroad! Ava's interest kindled. Now why was that, do you think? And would the handsome young buck so often seen in his company be going with him?

'. . . the house is almost ready for closing . . . The master couldn't live there with his grief . . . but we will all be living in grief supposing we can't find other employment.'

'You should encounter no difficulty. Your mistress spoke well of you.' Ava watched the priest, the only other attendant at the funeral, walk quickly towards the church.

'That were kind of her, God rest her soul.' The girl crossed herself piously. 'But with her passing quick like her did I be left without statement, and no mistress be like to employ a maid who don't have such; they asks proof of standards.'

The priest had disappeared into the confines of the large soot-covered church. Ava glanced about the enclosed graveyard. Except for herself and the girl it was deserted.

'I see your difficulty,' she answered, her glance returning to the face being dabbed yet again with the lacy handkerchief. 'Without reference a post will be unobtainable. However, I am myself without a personal maid and knowing your late mistress's regard of you I am inclined to offer that position to you, to become permanent only, if after a period of six months, you prove to be satisfactory.'

Cutting off the profuse thanks with a wave of the hand and instructions to come to Moorcroft House the next evening at eight, Ava walked away.

Watching the figure pass beneath the lych-gate the tear-stained face broke into a smile. So, that haughty bitch had seen her difficulty; well, she would soon be seeing her own. She thought the claim made by Alfred Birks had died with him. Walking slowly towards the ancient gate through which so many mourners had passed, the girl's lips moved in a whisper: 'That is where you are wrong, Missis Ava Russell, that is where you are so wrong.'

'I still can't fathom why you bothers wi' the old bug . . .' Davy Melia caught back the word but not the grin, 't'ain't as he appreciates it.'

'We have been over that before and I gave my reasons then.'

'But not to speak a word don't seem natural.'

'*We* speak.' Eden smiled at the strapping lad walking easily beside her. 'We both speak to him, Davy.'

'Good evenin'! Two words! Don't see how you can call that talkin'.'

'It's enough. He knows we go there in friendship and nothing more.'

'Wouldn't get nothin' more of that miserable sod!' Davy Melia's sunny face hardened. 'Mother offered to clean forrim once and he waved his stick at her like her were a burglar. Drove her off with words so harsh her were in tears. I wanted to go break his bloody neck, and I would 'ave had Mother begged me not to. So I made her promise in return, promise that when the cleanin' along of that big house were done her wouldn't call at that cottage nor speak to the man should her see him.'

Surprise overriding a reprimand for his swearing, Eden asked. 'Your mother cleans at The Coppice?'

The dish the old man had placed ready for collection tucked in one arm, Davy reached with the other to pluck a leaf from an overhanging branch.

'Goes in there every few weeks. No real cleanin' . . . I mean scrubbing or the like, ain't nobody to leave footmarks or muck things up . . . Her just has to air the rooms and dust what don't be covered wi' sheets. I went along wi' her once, but not no more . . . It be a miserable place, just like him who thinks he be its guardian!'

'The house is not miserable, it is sad; sad and lonely as the old man, sad as we all become when we are no longer loved—' She broke off abruptly. She had not meant to speak that way, to intimate her own lack of love.

Folding the leaf nimbly between the fingers of his free hand, Davy bit a tiny piece from the central crease then, holding the leaf to his lips, proceeded to blow into it. She hadn't needed to say her were lonely, livin' as her did spoke for itself . . . but her had said 'we' . . . 'we are no longer loved'. That included herself. The rasping whistle of air passing through the tiny hole in the leaf grating on the balmy softness of the evening, Davy let his thoughts run.

Had somebody stopped loving her, was that what she had meant? Was that somebody a man, a boyfriend? A brother! The whistling died suddenly, the broken leaf falling from his fingers. Eden Brent had run from something, that much he was certain of, and the young man he had overheard talking with the carter in the Green Dragon had been asking of a runaway sister. But the newspaper had named the man Birks . . . while Eden . . . but wouldn't using her real name lead to her being found, didn't it make sense to give another?

Walking now in silence, he went over each thought again, his mind searching for points he may have missed yet, as before, it returned to the same final question. Was that murdered man brother to Eden Brent? If so, her had made no mourn of what had happened to him! The thought gripped, holding his brain for several seconds before releasing it to another equally disturbing. Did love between kin die so easily? Did lack of mourning mean Eden no longer held feeling for a brother? He couldn't, he *wouldn't* believe that of her. Davy's defences rose, protecting the girl he had come to like so much. So why had he seen no trace of tears? Unless, of course, Eden did not know of that death? That were the more believable. He had seen no newspaper when calling to walk with her to The Coppice and there were no other way news could travel out to Shipton Cottage . . . but that were wrong! Davy's brain hurled the next thought like a stone . . . that were reckoning without the cut folk!

'You are very quiet, Davy.' Eden broke the silence, glancing at him as she spoke. 'Did I offend you when I spoke of the house being lonely and not miserable? If I did, I'm sorry.'

Sandy hair caught the scarlet rays of a setting sun and gleamed like fire as he shook his head. 'You give no offence.'

'Then you think me silly saying a house can be lonely.'

'I don't think no such thing.'

The answer did not come with his usual laugh. Eden felt the abruptness of it and the fact he did not follow with his usual banter added to a sense of something troubling him. Though what it could be eluded her. About to ask a reason she was prevented by his own question.

Coming to a halt, his face lit by those same scarlet rays, he asked, 'Eden, can I ask somethin'? But afore you answers I 'ave to tell you, there'll be no 'ard feeling on my part should you tell me to stop pokin' me nose . . . That be what Mother would say were her standin' along of us now . . . and like to catch me round the ear to go with it.'

'Well, I will not catch you around the ear,' Eden smiled, 'I don't want another dish dropped – I have broken enough already – so ask what it is you wish to know.'

'I were wonderin' . . .' The words reluctant on his tongue, it seemed he would say no more, then in a torrent they rushed out. 'I 'eard two men talkin', one middle age, the other younger, it were the youngest, he were askin' of a wench run from home, said he were seekin' after her . . . that he were brother to her an' . . . an' I knows you 'ad run from somethin', be it that man? Be he your brother?'

Was that the reason for such unaccustomed silence, the unusual reticence? Eden caught the laugh before it reached her lips but the smile of it remained evident in her reply. 'Davy, I have no brother.'

'Then it don't matter none.'

The words had come with more than a light breath of relief and the grin spreading its width across his pleasant face echoed what she heard. Davy had thought some man to be her brother . . . but why the swift return of spirits on finding he was not? Falling into step beside him as he walked on, Eden waited for some explanation of what it was he had dismissed as of no consequence then, when he reached again for a leaf, folding it as before, she put the question quietly.

'Don't matter none,' he repeated, blowing into the folded leaf. 'Seein' Alfred Birks don't be brother to you, then there be no reason of your mournin' 'im bein' dead.'

Eden jerked to a standstill, her eyes wide as she stared uncomprehending at the lad snipping at the centre of a leaf. 'Alfred? No . . .'

A frown of confusion drawing lines across his brow, Davy watched the inconceivable become the impossible, the nuances of those emotions shadowing that pale face.

'No!' Eden's words were a whisper. 'It can't be true, there has to be some mistake . . . a terrible mistake. Alfred can't be dead!'

Reaching Shipton Cottage Davy settled the shaking Eden into the chair he drew closer to the fire.

The man were not her brother.

Swinging the bracket with its kettle over the glowing coals he set to making a pot of tea.

'*I have no brother . . .*'

They had been her very words; yet, being told of that man's death had her trembling. A task he had performed many times before, brewing tea needed no concentration, so Davy's thoughts were free to play on.

Not her brother . . .

But a sweetheart? Nothing had been said in that regard. So was that what Alfred Birks had been to her? Was he the man responsible for her having left her home? Had he been at the root of those words, 'sad as we all become when we are no longer loved'?

Taking the cup from him, Eden met the boy's troubled eyes and it seemed she read the questions behind them.

'Alfred Birks was not well known to me.' She rested the cup on her knee. 'He came a few times to my grandmother's house in Hobbins Street. He came to walk Myra back to Moorcroft House those evenings it was too dark for her to return there alone.'

'Myra?' Davy stirred sugar into a second cup, sitting with it on the opposite side of the fireplace.

'My sister.' Eden swallowed the lump rising in her throat. Even now it was painful to speak of Myra. 'She was ladies' maid at Moorcroft and Alfred was the groom. It . . . it was knowing him as Myra's friend . . . It came as a shock hearing he had died . . . But how did you hear of it?'

One upset was enough. Davy's mind reacted swiftly. He would not tell her the manner of the man's dying. A slight shrug and a brief shake of the head adding to the innocence he trusted was in his look, he answered. 'Read it in a newspaper . . . it said only he had *passed away*, d'ain't give no cause.'

The newspaper had given no cause, was that not unusual?

Troubled by thoughts which had persisted since Davy's leaving, Eden climbed the narrow stairs to her bedroom.

Alfred Birks had been a groom, no one of importance to other than family, so why had a report of his death been printed in a newspaper?

Full and brilliantly golden the moon bathed the small room in light. Turning out the lamp she had carried with her, she crossed to the window. Below, the canal glittered, a sparkling band winding across a shadowed somnolent heath, a barge moored almost at her door dark and comforting.

It was all so beautiful, so different from anything she had known in Hobbins Street, the scenes she and Myra had seen when peeping from the window of the room they shared. And what of Myra now? The views from the windows of Moorcroft would be gentler than the roofs of houses, the forest of tall, smoke-blackened chimneys of iron foundries and the winding wheels of collieries seen from Grandmother's house. Even so, they could be no more peacefully serene than the view from this tiny cottage.

Reluctantly leaving the window, Eden prepared for bed. Her prayers said, she added a further one for the soul of Alfred Birks. God would not mind her asking he be given eternal rest even though a relative stranger asked.

Lying in bed, she watched the ballet of shadows dance to soundless music, her mind restless as the moon glided shapes.

What had caused the death of Alfred Birks? Why did no mention of that appear in the newspaper report?

Beyond the window an owl hooted, joining song to the rhythm of the night, but Eden did not hear.

Had there been an accident? Had he died of an illness? Fingers tightening on the sheet, Eden's mind asked a more terrible question still. Was that illness one Grandmother had a fear of? Could it be that the cholera or maybe the smallpox that had ravaged the town many years ago had returned? A chill, sudden and frightening, ran along every vein.

What of Myra . . . could she be infected? Was her sister fighting death!

20

Eight o'clock in the evening was not a time she would have expected to be told to present herself for an interview, but then the only master at Moorcroft House was its mistress and she could suit herself in all things.

The late Lenor Medwin's personal maid lifted a deep blue coat from a cupboard in her own room. Arthur Medwin had been dismissive of his wife's clothing. Her maid could keep anything she might wish to have; as for the rest they could go to charity.

Charity! She smiled. For Dilly Madely, charity began at home, *her* home, and that was were it would stay. Those of the dresses, suits and coats she had no liking for would be sold, and the money they fetched would lie beneath her mattress.

Glancing again at the coat she had altered to fit her, Dilly replaced it in the cupboard. It might not be wise to go asking for the post of ladies' maid looking as well-dressed as the lady herself . . . and certainly it wouldn't be wise so long as it were that stuck-up Ava Russell was being asked.

Dressing quickly in the featureless fawn that was the walking-out suit she regularly wore, the same plain brown bonnet and cotton gloves teamed with it, the girl glanced at her reflection in the cheap mirror hung on her bedroom wall. Perhaps for the moment it was better to look drab as always; that way would draw no comment from the other staff she would pass leaving the house. Picking up her bag, she passed the cord of it over her wrist. She had told no one of Ava Russell's offer, that way no one would have the delight of sniggering if she wasn't given the post; but soon, post or no post, nobody would snigger. Dilly Madely would wear every one of that cupboard's fine clothes and more besides; the money keeping Ava Russell's secret would pay . . . it would pay for a very long time.

Could that woman possibly know of her walking out with Alfred Birks, that it was Lenor's own maid had told him of the doings in that bedroom? So what if her did! Dilly tossed aside the slight fear that edged along her nerves. There were nothing her could do! A jaunt in her step, she walked quickly through the kitchen returning comments with saucy answers and, once outside, allowed a smile to spread greedily across her mouth. No, there were nothing Ava Russell could do . . . except to pay.

Hidden beneath the drab fawn skirt of Dilly's costume, the pretty green leather shoes taken from Lenor's wardrobe tapped the footpath. Whoever had killed Alfred had taken the money from his pocket. Of course, no mention had been made of *that* in the newspaper, no report of robbery. But then nobody would suspect a man of Birks' class to have such an amount, and Ava Russell would not admit to paying him a farthing more than his yearly wage.

It must have puzzled that woman as much as it had puzzled herself. Dilly's thoughts were brisk as her steps. Had he talked to someone of going to collect the money from the church, bragged to them of how smart he was? But he was not that much of a fool. He would have known the dangers of that, known words said were words repeated if the listener were not given coin enough to hold the tongue still . . . and Alfred Birks were not a man given to sharing. But now he would not have to . . . and neither would she!

Coming to Ethelfleda Terrace, she paused. Maybe she should walk by way of Trouse Lane. There would be folk about, the road would still be busy with men leaving their place of work or going to the ale houses; and women . . . there would be those also, children clinging to their skirts while they haggled for the cheapest cut of meat or the last few chops before the butchers closed their stalls in the Shambles; then there would be the others, those women of the night waiting for any man who would pay sixpence to take their pleasure, and maybe not just men! Dilly smirked remembering her late mistress . . . maybe women were also willing to buy their pleasure.

Trouse Lane! She could go by way of Wellcroft Street and join it there. But that was a long way around whereas the Terrace . . . indecision chafing, she stood a moment. It was half the distance!

Overhead, the moon sailed from a sea of cloud, its brilliance bringing back the day, while atop the hill the clock of Saint Bartholomew's church rang out.

A quarter of an hour, that was time enough to go by way of the longer route . . . but Lenor's shoes pinched, the woman had been stout but her feet had been small. Trying to ease her toes, Dilly grimaced. The less walking she did the better . . . but going by way of Ethelfleda Terrace meant passing the alley where Alfred had been . . .

Toes pinched together throbbed painfully. Bloody shoes! She glanced at her feet and then again at the sky. The moon was brilliant, it had the whole length of the road lit up . . . She could be at the other end in a few minutes . . . besides nobody would hang around the place where they had killed a man . . .

A sharp sting lancing both feet, Dilly's mind was made up. Footsteps echoing in the silence, she began to walk.

'Spare an old man tuppence for a bite o' supper.'

A cry of fright rising to her lips, Dilly whirled to meet the voice, then gasped her relief at the sight of a figure bent low over a walking stick, feet shuffling in steps more painful than her own.

'Lord, but you give me a scare!' It was a half-laugh, one of solace on realising the speaker was old . . . so old a stick was needed for support. For a moment she had known real fear . . . but an old man could do her no harm.

'Tuppence would buy a supper . . . I ain't 'ad a

decent meal for I don't know 'ow long . . . nobody cares about the old.'

Alleviation of that sudden fear, consolation of its being unfounded, of hearing the weak, cracked old voice, wakened a streak of pity in Dilly. Tuppence wouldn't empty her purse . . . and with the bounty soon to be hers she could afford to buy an old beggar a supper.

Turning to where the bent figure dragged itself towards her, she took the bag from her wrist, opened it and took out the small purse. There were two pennies among the coins it held; he could have them.

'You be welcome . . .'

The words stilled on her tongue, the real fear of moments ago becoming a terror she could taste in her mouth, an abject horror which had her rooted to the spot and filled her wide-stretched eyes with an unspeakable truth. A scream passing no further than her throat, she stared at other eyes . . . eyes glittering like a serpent's from the shrouded face, watched the bent figure move, watching as, soundless in the silence, shining silver in the moonlight, a blade rose . . . and plunged!

'A young woman should have called here last evening.' Ava Russell looked up from the household accounts book as her cook entered the study.

'D'ain't nobody come 'ere last night, mum, least not afore I went to me bed an' that were not a minute afore I should ought to 'ave done.'

'She should have called at eight o' clock.'

The older woman's head shook briefly. ''Ad her 'ave called, mum, I would 'ave knowed for I sat in the kitchen same as I always does . . . sat 'til goin' to my bed.'

'The young woman who should have called.' Ava closed the book decisively. 'She is probably known to you, Dilly Madely by name, she was the late Mrs Medwin's personal maid.'

'Young Dilly . . . yes I know 'er, mum, bright young wench wi' a sensible 'ead on her shoulders.'

Sitting at the heavy desk which had been her husband's, Ava's mouth tightened visibly, her face displaying a displeasure not lost on her cook. 'I had arranged with her to call in respect of obtaining a position here.'

And I bets I know what position that be? The thought kept suitably inside, the woman's head shook again. 'I can't go thinkin' why it is her d'ain't show up, not after you was kind enough to think of her regarding employment; it don't be like Dilly Madely to turn her back, there must be a reason at back of it, mum, that be all I can say.'

'But that is not all I can say!' Each word cracking like breaking ice, Ava slipped the closed book into a drawer. 'Should the girl call, you are to tell her the offer of possible employment is withdrawn, that her services will not, after all, be required. Failing to keep an appointment, especially one that is no less than an act of charity than dropping coins into a beggar's hand, shows an acute lack of manners. Maybe it bodes well she did not keep that appointment for rudeness is something I can tolerate in no one, and much less so in a paid servant.'

'Charity!' Returning to the kitchen the cook mumbled to herself. 'Ava Russell don't know the meanin' o' that word . . . and, as for manners, they should apply no matter your station in life; but does the high an' mighty Ava Russell practise as her preaches? That one sees rudeness in others while thinkin' herself pure as a lily!'

Reaching the kitchen she slammed the door behind her. Young Dilly Madely had done the wise thing in not coming to Moorcroft, and her would be wiser yet to get as far from it as possible.

Alone in the study, Ava withdrew the accounts book from the drawer. Opening it she ran a glance over figures already cemented in her brain. Even with only a cook left as permanent staff the drain on finances showed little relief. Could she dispose of the help brought in once a week? But laundry was something that had to be done. The gardens then? The fellow who came a couple of days a week, his wage could prove a saving; but what would that tell the outside world?

Why were the proceeds from the axle works falling every month? Didn' t she run them as her husband had run them . . . didn't she call to account every penny laid out in the buying in of raw materials as well as the paying of wages . . . and had she not reduced those wages not once, but twice?

Would Samuel Russell have done that? No, he would have been too weak, he would have worried for men having too little to support their families; and when the colliery had finally given the last of its coal would he have done as she had? Would he have left those miners to their fate? No, he would have paid them until he himself became a pauper. But not so Ava Russell; she would become no pauper nor would her house show sign of lack of money, the grounds would continue to be cared for . . . As for the inside, only those rooms used to receive visitors need show affluence.

But there was no real affluence left at Moorcroft! She glanced again at the truth displayed in columns of figures. What wealth Moorcroft had once contained was long gone, and profit from the iron works was almost non-existent. How much longer could she maintain this house?

Returning the book to the drawer her eye fell on a folded parchment. How long could she expect to live in a house no longer hers? That paper lying in the drawer was one she had signed; a paper giving ownership to the bank of Moorcroft and all it held if the mortgage was not repaid in the time specified.

Five hundred pounds! One finger touching the folded sheet, Ava breathed deeply. She had raised that money in the only way possible . . . money she had needed to pay a blackmailer. But Alfred Birks was dead and with him his hopes of a comfortable life lived at her expense . . . And his lady love, the maid of Lenor Medwin? She would not dare attempt the same.

The threat had been removed from her life. The book returned to the drawer and the key turned in the lock, Ava rose to her feet.

The threat of Birks was no more, but that of Myra Brent . . . that as yet was not!

She had spoken to the people of Bell Street, those who had shown her friendship in the few minutes they could snatch from lives centred on making a living. She had said goodbye to them, now the key to that drab damp house was returned to the estate agent. Tiny pieces of stone broken and partly crushed by the constant movement of wagon wheels bit painfully through the worn-out soles of Myra's boots. All that remained was to take the blouse to the dressmaker and she could leave Darlaston.

Three shillings. The cloth-wrapped parcel held against her chest, she crossed the busy Bull Stake, oblivious of the threatening hiss of a steam-driven trolleybus and the shout of an angry carter, the wheels of whose vehicle barely missed the thin, hurrying figure. The dressmaker had promised three shillings for the stitching of that delicate blouse. She had sat the entire night fighting the blindness of eyes longing for sleep, hunching over the candle in order to see, each minute stitch an agony of worry that it might be placed wrongly or else be a fraction too large and, as a result, her work being pronounced unsatisfactory therefore bringing no payment.

Too weary almost to walk, she caught her foot

against the kerb, stumbling against a woman who pushed her away, muttering loudly of the evils of drink and the hell Myra could look to when death came for her. But what hell could be worse than the one she endured now, what death worse than the life she was living?

Her murmured apology ignored, Myra rested a moment beside the window of a small shop. Should her fear be realised, should that three shillings not be paid . . . Myra's free hand touched the two pennies pushed deep into a pocket. How long would that save her from the workhouse!

The thought trembling on her lips, she forced herself to walk on.

'I am with a client.'

The dressmaker's pert mouth firmed as she saw who it was had entered her establishment, her nose wrinkling at the sight of the tired clothes and pale, almost deathlike, quality of the face that looked back at her. She had a client, a very important client who might well take her custom elsewhere should she catch sight of the woman standing there, holding a parcel. It would be realised no person so obviously poor would be purchasing an *à la mode* garment . . . and a woman as wealthy as the client now in the private fitting-room would not frequent the same premises. That would be loss of a valuable source of business. This uppermost in her shrewd calculating brain, Sophie glanced towards the door at her back at the same time reaching for that which gave on to the street.

'As I said, I have a client,' she said, her tone hushed, 'you can wait outside.'

'But I have brought . . .'

'I said you can wait outside!' Sharp as the snap of a vixen's jaws the dressmaker's lips clamped together, a quick push sending Myra stumbling out through the door.

It would have taken no more than minutes to have looked at her work. Myra felt a wave of tiredness sweep the length of her. A few minutes to inspect the stitching then to pay the shillings; but they were minutes the like of herself could not be given when a client was present, and those shillings . . . What did the paying of those matter when attending a customer who might well be spending many sovereigns.

'The blouse I ordered . . .'

Imperiously loud, the words reached to where Myra waited.

'. . . it is ready, I trust.'

The dressmaker's reply was indistinct but the halting prevarication of it was quite clear.

'I said I would want it when next I called.' The voice reaching Myra brimmed with arrogance. 'If it is not finished then the order is withdrawn.'

'It is finished, ma'am . . .'

Obsequious in its apology the quieter voice floated to the pavement as the shop door was thrown open and the parcel snatched from Myra's hand.

'. . . I asked it be kept back until you had finished dressing.'

The door had closed again. Myra shifted her position but her aching body gained no solace from the movement. Please, she whispered in her mind, please let the blouse be acceptable, let me be given the price promised.

'. . . if you wish it, ma'am.'

The end of a sentence reaching her as the door opened yet again, Myra looked into the harassed face of the dressmaker signalling she enter the shop.

'The client is trying the garment.' It was a murmur, her glance going quickly to the closed-off fitting room. 'She asked to see the woman who had brought it . . . though for the life of me I can't think why. She may not speak to you but should she do so then you curtsy and address her as ma'am.'

Her clothes were not those of the wealthy and her appearance not at all that might be desired but they in no way affected the manners she had been taught from childhood to observe. Too weary to put the same into words, Myra simply nodded.

'Wait here,' the dressmaker hissed as her client called. 'And remember, you curtsy and call her ma'am.'

Why would that customer want to see the person who had stitched her blouse? What did it matter who had had the sewing of it? Myra stared at shelves filled with rolls of pretty fabrics, cases holding ribbons of silk and velvet. If it suited, then the woman would take it and if it did not meet with her approval she would refuse it; either way it could not be affected by who had made it.

'Of course, ma'am, it will be delivered this evening.'

Emerging from the fitting-room, the dressmaker laid the blouse on a highly polished counter, her fingers fluttering like anxious moths as they reached for several sheets of deep violet-coloured tissue.

'One moment.'

It was no request. Haughty, imperious as before, the voice brought a halt to the fluttering fingers.

'I shall not be purchasing this garment . . .'

A small gasp broke from the dressmaker but its distress made no impact on the client who had stepped into the body of the tiny shop, a client who looked with cold eyes.

'. . . I find the work most unsatisfactory. I suggest you follow my example, Miss Brooke. I suggest you refuse to pay whoever is responsible for such shoddy work.'

'Shoddy.' Myra looked up, her exclamation falling away as she looked into the face of Ava Russell.

21

'*The work is of a poor standard . . . were I you I would not accept* it . . . '

Ava Russell's eyes had stared into hers, the message they conveyed easy to read: you will pay one way or the other!

Walking away from the town Myra felt a bitterness such as never before.

'*Do you not wish to hear of your sister? The girl whose face you slapped the day she came to Moorcroft?*'

Ava had followed her from the shop calling quietly but the words had sounded loud as church bells beating in Myra's brain as they beat now. She had swung around to meet the cold sadistic stare of the woman who had been her mistress.

'*What do you know of my sister?*' She had thought the question loud but it had whispered from a throat dry with fear.

'*A more fitting question would be what do I* not *know of her . . . She is young, pretty as you once were, and she shows every potential of becoming a most satisfactory ladies' maid . . .* '

'*No!*'

'*Oh, but yes.*' The reply had come with the smile of evil. Tears clouding her eyes, Myra stumbled on.

'*You chose to leave my service.*' Satisfaction had throbbed in every syllable, dark eyes gloating. '*I, therefore, was put to employing a new personal maid. I was happy to give the position to your sister, and I must add that so far she has proved a very amiable choice. She is settling to her duties, and I expect that quite soon now she will carry out those more delicate ones, the services you yourself performed so "pleasurably".*'

'*There was never pleasure for me . . .*'

Ava Russell's hard laugh had cut away the rest. Coming a step closer she had hissed. '*You! But who is speaking of pleasure for you? What you did or did not feel was of no consequence, just as it will be of no consequence what your sister will or will not feel.*'

'*No . . . please, you can't . . .*'

'*Can't! Remember who is mistress of Moorcroft! No stricture governs what I wish to do within its walls, or with whom I share my pleasures.*'

'*Not Eden! She is . . .*'

'*If you were about to say your sister is not yet fully out of girlhood then your experience should have taught you, Myra. The young learn more quickly . . . and Eden is a most adept pupil. She will suit my requirements . . . every aspect of my requirements . . . But of course should you wish to return to Moorcroft, to resume your duties there, then I might have to reconsider your sister's employment.*'

The implication had been plain, the threat of it stark. She could go back to the hell she had left or Eden would be subjected to that same horror. There had been no pity in that hard face, no softening of those sharp tight features, only a glitter in the eyes that watched her, a glitter of triumph.

Women passing glanced curiously at the thin hunched figure, sobbing as it walked, but paid little attention to a spectacle they had witnessed so many times before; life was hard for the folk of Darlaston. If a pit disaster or a foundry accident didn't claim a loved one, then poverty or disease waited with impatient hands.

But none of those things was responsible for the tears Myra shed now; it was fear for a sister . . . fear of the evil that hovered over Eden, an evil that would suck her into a hell of depravity, a hell which would only be banished if she, Myra, returned to it.

And she *would*, return to it. Beneath the moisture clouding her eyes, Myra seemed to see the face of a girl several years her junior. Fair hair framed a small heart-shaped face, eyes fresh and green as a spring meadow, a skin so clear it might have been translucent, no mark of the smallpox which had killed her parents. Eden was touched with a beauty which even in childhood had set her a little apart; but it was not looks alone that created the difference between Eden Brent and her sister. Eden was a dreamer . . . she lived inside herself.

That was the reason of her own returning to Moorcroft. Myra blinked, her vision clear. Eden would have no defence against the wiles of Ava Russell. She was still that innocent of childhood, a young girl who knew nothing of a world beyond Hobbins Street. And she must never know!

A cough bubbling in her chest, Myra rested against a wall. Grandmother had always said they must care for each other. That was what she had been doing when she slapped Eden. Only the shock of the blow could prevent her visiting that house again . . . and now she must show that care again. She must return to Moorcroft; only that way could she keep her sister safe.

Pushing away from the wall, Myra's fingers brushed the pocket of her skirt, feeling the coins nestling inside it.

A ragged breath brought the cough rising in her throat. It had troubled her more and more in the weeks of living in that damp house, sapping her strength. Tuppence! The coins were hard beneath her fingers. The dressmaker had taken her cue from Ava Russell, she had needed no further urging to withhold payment for the work of that blouse, work they had both known was of perfectly acceptable quality.

But what did that matter now? Myra coughed again. She could walk back to Wednesbury. The tuppence in her pocket . . . She glanced to where she had rested against a wall, the wall of a shop, its bullseye windows almost concealing the wares displayed there . . . tuppence would be enough . . . Please Lord, let it be enough!

'I tells you, mum, it fair has me feared to step into the streets! A body don't feel safe no more, don't know should it be you will be the next one to be done in.'

'Done in?' Irritation at being disturbed laced Ava Russell's reply. Returning a folded sheet of parchment to a drawer of the desk, she looked at the woman worriedly twisting a corner of her starched apron.

'That be what I said, mum, done in . . . another poor soul found dead . . . I tells you, I be feared to sleep nights.'

Fingers resting against the closed drawer, Ava looked at her cook. 'Are you saying someone has been found dead?'

'That be eggsactly what I be sayin' . . .' The cook's bosom heaved. 'Found just as poor Alfred were found.'

Pressing her apron to her wet eyes delayed the woman's telling for several seconds, the interval filled with a moan and the shaking of shoulders. Then, the apron lowered, she began again. 'Killed.' Polly Jupp sniffed. 'Killed as were poor Alfred Birks, an' for what reason? The wench could 'ave had naught worth the stealin' of, same as that lad 'ad naught the worth of killin' for.'

Another murder! Upright in her chair, Ava regarded her cook with fresh interest.

'The town be full of it, they be talkin' of nothin' else.'

That was something she could well believe. Ava's fingers dropped to her lap. Gossip flew on rapid wings and none flapped harder than those which flew over Wednesbury.

'You should know better than to listen to rumours.' She spoke sharply. 'It will probably turn out to be no more than that, a silly tale told to scare people all over again.'

'Oh Lord, I does hope so.' The sniff sounded loud as before. 'I hopes it don't be as folk were sayin', that some poor wench be lying with her throat slashed.'

That was the second time of using the word 'wench' . . . the supposed victim of a murderer was a woman! Ava kept her silence.

'Be a terrible thing for folk to lie about.' Taking her mistress's silence as an invitation to continue with her news the cook went on. 'But it be even more terrible, supposin' what they be saying be the truth.'

'So, just what are they saying?'

Lifting the apron again, holding it beneath trembling lips, Ava's cook drew a long breath. 'They be saying . . .' the cloth pressed against her mouth, the woman paused, '. . . they be saying a wench were found this mornin', found by a man on his way to his work. They reckons he thought it were a drunk lying by the roadside but when he looked . . . Oh God, mum, if it be as folk says it must have shocked him summat awful.'

Ava's fingers folded together, a brace for the irritation rising in her. Why didn't the woman come right out with it, say what she had heard in the market place?

'Can you think, mum . . .' half-hidden by the apron the woman's mouth contorted, 'can you imagine what it must have been for to find what he did? Be a wonder if the poor soul ever knows a peaceful night's sleep again! I only knows if what has been said turns out to be truth then I won't never rest easy, not no more I won't.'

'You say this . . . this woman was discovered this morning?' Ava watched her cook nod assent. 'Then there has been no official report. So, until there is, until confirmation of what is no more than gossip is given then I suggest you forget what you have heard. There are people who enjoy nothing so much as putting fear into others and this story you have heard will no doubt prove to be just that, a scaremongering that has absolutely no foundation.'

'Please God you be right, mum . . . May the Almighty grant it be no more than that.'

She had not visited Moorcroft.

Lifting the cast iron pot from the bracket on which it had hung almost all day, Eden carried it to the table setting it on a cloth spread to prevent marking.

She had wanted to so badly, fears of Myra being taken with some illness plaguing her every moment.

Removing the beef cheek from stock she would later use for the making of gravy, Eden stripped the layer of skin from the interior of the mouth setting the meat aside to cool.

But if Myra had not been ill . . . she would have been so angry at having the demand for her sister stay away ignored. The thought had stayed, but the desire to see Myra, to know whether or not she was well, had remained.

Reaching for the parsley and chives she had washed

and set to dry beside an open window, she chopped them, the fragrance releasing a mouth-watering aroma to blend with the meat.

She had known she could not call at that house, yet the worry of what it could be holding had not left her for a moment. It had plagued her so much she had at last asked Davy Melia to enquire in the town. Had anyone fallen ill, had either of the diseases her grandmother had so feared returned again to Wednesbury?

Tender from its slow stewing, the meat chopped easily into tiny pieces. Adding them to the fresh herbs, seasoning with salt and pepper, Eden spooned the mixture into a variety of small pots, pressing it with the back of a spoon before covering the surface with melted butter.

There had been no report of any such illness. Eden felt that same relief she had felt on hearing Davy say so. But relief, sweet and welcome as it had been, did not remove the ache always in her heart, the questions which had never entirely left her mind. What was it had made Myra turn from her and from their grandmother? What was so unacceptable it had even kept her from seeing that same beloved grandmother to her grave?

Ought she have gone back to Moorcroft, ought she to have defied Myra, demanded to tell her of their grandmother's death?

'But I didn't, Gran,' she murmured, covering the pots with greased paper, 'I didn't do it.'

A key opening a locked door the whisper brought

memories flooding in. A girl running from the house of a headmistress who had demanded she remove every stitch of clothing, of that same haughty face, that autocratic denouncing that the girl 'would never do any good, she would never amount to anything'.

Turning her attention to the making of a kidney pudding which could be left atop the fire to steam for an hour, she added two cups of breadcrumbs to parsley, a grating of nutmeg followed, with a small amount of suet together with the sheep's kidneys she had prepared earlier. But the preparing of food did nothing to chase the spectres in her mind.

The prophecy had proved correct.

Binding the whole of the ingredients of the bowl with an egg whisked into a cupful of milk, Eden's thoughts travelled their own path.

The words spoken so savagely by that headmistress had been an ordination of truth. Her life had followed what had been predicted.

Placing the mixture into a fresh basin Eden covered it with a cloth. Tying the four corners into a knot she set it in a pan of water then hung the whole above the fire.

She would never forget the words across the chasm of years.

'*She will never do any good . . . she will never amount to anything.*'

And so it would be. She had done nothing except work alongside her grandmother, naught other than scrub and clean, learn the preparing of food. It was true she had not amounted to anything, not even the position of the lowliest scullery maid. A lump hard in her throat, she stared at the dull red coals of the fire. She had not given her grandmother the pride Myra had afforded, she had not attained the grand post of ladies' maid, one which had written pleasure across that loved face; and now she never would. Her grandmother would never have that same gratification from her youngest grandchild.

'Eh up, wench, that smell promises a meal the angels would 'ave the leavin' of heaven for.'

Turning quickly, Eden brushed a hand across eyes moist with the threat of tears, then touched her brow with the hem of the large apron which must once have belonged to Mother Shipton.

'Ar, wench, it be warm . . .' The bargee smiled at the gesture he presumed caused by the heat of the small room, '. . . but the heat of the devil's own furnace wouldn't keep me from the eatin' of a dish of what it be you 'ave cookin' atop that fire.'

'That will not be ready for eating for an hour or more.' Eden returned the smile. 'But there is boney pie ready for lifting from the oven, should you wish a hot meal, or fresh baked bread and newly pressed beef cheek should a sandwich be all you prefer.'

'I'll take the pie.' Handing her an enamelled plate the man counted out several coins while Eden cut a generous portion of pie setting it alongside a helping of potatoes and cabbage.

'Add to that a pot of that pressed chawl I 'ave the

smellin' of and a loaf of bread. That will mek a supper fit for any king, ar, or that little lady a' sittin' on England's throne; give 'er a taste of that and I reckons her'll be wantin' no more of what them there palace cook a'serves her up. But then the cut folk be 'oping that there queen don't go gettin' no tasting of what you provides, for that would mean our 'aving the losin' of you.'

Taking his plate, a pot of pressed meat and a small loaf balanced precariously in his hands, he grinned widely. 'There be them wouldn't tek no crown in exchange for what you cooks, t'were a blessin' for the cut folk the day you come to this cottage.'

A blessing! From the window Eden watched the man jump lightly aboard a laden narrowboat. She would not begrudge anyone that . . . but why could heaven not have bestowed its grace upon her? Why had she not been able to bring a pride to her grandmother's heart? Now she never would; the most she would ever be, the most she could hope for, was to be what she was now: a nobody, an interloper who had taken another woman's home.

22

'Mother be along of The Coppice. If you don't mind, I can fetch her 'ome from there.'

Davy Melia looked at the young woman walking beside him. She had hardly put two words together since they had left Shipton Cottage.

'Won't tek no more'n a minute to run up the drive an' if old misery guts thinks to stop me then he's got another think comin'.'

The remark had brought no defence of the old man. Davy frowned, the freckles on his forehead falling together. Eden always stuck up for that old 'un, had a word to say as to the reason of his forever 'aving the bear on his back, so why not this time? Could it be her were also gettin' fed up of his never 'aving a good word? That don't be likely. Davy answered his own question. Were that the case, then her would hardly like to be bringin' him a supper. Then what were it had her behavin' different?

'Mother was sayin' just this mornin' . . .' Davy tried again, '. . . her were sayin' same as meself, why bother with him as lives beside the big house when he don't never 'ave a decent word to say to you. T'ain't as though it would tek a penny from his pocket, or d'ain't he ever learn civility costs naught?'

'I . . . I'm sorry Davy, what did you say?'

Even her voice didn't sound the same. Wanting to ask, yet somehow not wanting to know, he let the moment pass, saying instead, 'I were remarkin' on him you brings a meal to every evenin' and on his never speakin' a kind word for the trouble of it.'

'It's no trouble.'

'Nor ain't it no trouble to speak a thank you!' Where Eden's reply had been lifeless, Davy's was full of fire. 'Good manners don't cost not a brass farthing yet the way he refuses to use 'em they might as well cost a thousand pounds a word. He be a mardy old bug . . . Well, that's what he be!'

The essence of a smile rose to Eden's lips. 'The man is not bad-tempered, Davy, but he has been unhappy for such a long time it seems to have driven away every other feeling he might have had.'

'We don't know he be unhappy, and even if he is, then himself like be the cause of it. Probably drove folk from him with them sour ways of his'n.'

No, they could not be certain of what lay behind the man's churlishness, yet something inside Eden told it was an all-encompassing sadness, a sadness arising from something he blamed only himself for. Was it the sourness Davy had spoken of? Her glance travelling along the track, she saw the now familiar figure standing beside the gate, a bent figure that leaned heavily on a cane. Was it simply an irascible temper had made this man cut himself off from society, or was it something deeper, something which cast a long black shadow?

'The house be open, I suppose you will be wanting to take a look inside.'

Eden looked at the man regarding her above the gatepost. The face was drawn, the cheeks hollow, and dark circles ringed the eyes, but they were eyes that probed, sharp and keen as a knife.

'No . . .' She shook her head. 'I would not intrude.'

'Intrude!' He snapped at her. 'How can you intrude when there be none there to intrude upon! If it is the cleaning woman you are averse to disturbing, then there is no need. She will welcome another person with whom to speak.'

'And be civil in the doin' of it unlike some as be needin' no mention.' Davy's clouded features spoke all of the resentment inside him. 'Some folk don't 'ave the knowin' of a kindness when it be hitting 'em in the face! Come you on, Eden, come along wi' me to fetch me mother.'

The dish of kidney pudding and potato set on the gatepost, Davy turned to Eden but she shook her head in refusal.

'The lad be protective of his mother, that is good, it is what a son should always be.'

There had been a softness in the usually hard voice, a gap in the wall of bitterness with which he had surrounded himself, but in an instant it was closed. The cane rising, he growled, 'Fetch your mother, lad, and then be off before you come to regret giving freedom to that tongue of yours . . . And you . . .' the cane swung in Eden's direction, the tip hovering a yard from her chest, '. . . you go along of him. Do what you have a desire to do, go walk through the rooms of that house.'

Aware of the cane that could so easily strike, Eden glanced coolly at the lad beside her, his fists doubled, his features mutinous.

'Go on, Davy,' she said calmly, 'go bring your mother. I will wait further along the track.'

'I said for you to have the seeing of the inside of that house.'

Watching Davy sprint along the wide tree-lined avenue, Eden answered quietly. 'And I said I would not intrude.'

'Pah!' The cane struck the stone of the gatepost, setting the lid of the dish rattling. 'I tell you there be none there save that lad's mother!'

Already a few steps along the track, Eden turned. The pale essence of a smile that had hovered on her mouth when answering Davy touched her lips again. Her glance resting on the drawn face, she swung her head briefly. 'We both know that is not so.'

'Not so? I tell you that house be empty. I be . . .'

Again the chink in that self-built barrier! Eden watched the mouth clam, cutting off the rest, the veil that dropped over those sharp eyes.

'But not of love.' She spoke softly. 'I have not been inside, yet I feel that love. It reaches out, it calls for its voice to be heard. There may be no living being within its rooms yet they are filled with a presence, a sorrow which it cannot banish. There may be no physical evidence, no figure or body which can be seen, yet my whole heart told me, told me that one time I stood looking up at its windows and tells me again now: there is a love in that house, a yearning to find what once was but became lost. I think you feel that way also . . . I think you have suffered that same deprivation, that you also yearn for what is lost, but to find it you have to face your heart.'

He might have answered, he might have spoken of what her words triggered, of the cause of the emotion his face could not disguise or his copper-bright eyes keep hidden. But he had not, he had simply picked up the meal she had brought him and walked away.

Looking at the door he had closed firmly behind him, Eden felt a wave of pity. He could shut out the world, close himself away behind locked doors, but that would not heal the hurt or mend the heart her own told her was broken. It seemed that for that elderly man, love, as with herself, was set too deep; maybe, as Myra had done, someone had withdrawn, taken that love from him, snatched it away for some reason he might not understand. But, though he had been devastated by such cruelty, love still lived in his heart as in hers; as it lived yet within that silent house.

Three days. Ava Russell gloated quietly as she walked into her dressing-room. Three days and then . . . Her glance rested on the bath tub . . . and then her pleasure would begin again. That was how many days until Myra Brent returned to Moorcroft. There were things she had to do; that was what she had said; to disappear from the place she lived in without speaking of leaving to those who were neighbour and friend would arouse suspicion.

And what of her leaving this house whilst telling nobody of her intention? What did she think that to have aroused! But nobody in Ava Russell's employ would dare to speak of any business of her house. The thought calmed the spurt of anger ready to rise. Yes, that toad Birks had tried his hand, had threatened her with extortion, but the fruits of that blackmail, the harvest reaped, had not been the one expected. Yet Birks had been correct in one assertion, false though she had felt it to be. She would not hear from him again . . . and neither would anyone else!

A thorn which had threatened to prick . . . a thorn which had been cut away. Satisfaction spread its trail over a thin mouth. The man's death had erased the spectre come to rest on her shoulders, lifted the threat he had placed there. And as for his little flight of fancy, that maid of Lenor's, she would pose no problem, the assurance of any accusation she might make resulting in twenty years of penal servitude in a house of correction for herself . . . The smile of satisfaction deepened . . . there would be no accusation.

No, it would not come to that! Removing the gown

she had unbuttoned she stepped in front of the long mirror. Once again fortune had smiled on Ava Russell leading her to find Myra Brent. The girl had not known the dressmaker her mistress visited, no one had. She had guarded that secret as she guarded that other; so far as was allowed to be known, the gowns Ava Russell wore were created in an exclusive London salon, the railway train she professed to taking her there being in fact a train taking her to Darlaston.

Myra! Chemise loosened, Ava spread her hands over her breasts. The girl had realised her little fight for freedom was ended. Oh, it had been a lie she had heard, there had been no truth in the telling her sister was in service at Moorcroft, but what did a lie matter.

Fingers squeezing the soft mounds Ava felt her pulses quicken. Service! Yes, that girl would be returned soon, returned to the task that brought her mistress so much pleasure. But that would not be all she would bring. True, that younger sister was not here, but time would rectify that for, where one was, the other would call, and when she did . . .

Trailing her hands voluptuously along her waist, pushing away silk drawers, the thin mouth opened in a gasp, every nerve becoming a pinprick of fire, a flaming that enveloped in a seething ferment of passion, a craving desire as her fingers played in the moist vee between her legs.

When that sister called, then Ava Russell would have two personal maids . . . two young women to serve her.

*

She had bought herself a woman. Ava scrubbed at her body with the soap and hot water it had taken another shilling to have brought to this tastefully furnished room.

Her own hands, her own fingers, they had set light to her senses but when that light had faded the fire was not extinguished. It had smouldered, simmered and flared until she could think of nothing but the ecstasy of another woman's body, another woman's hands. So, for a second time she had come to this house, a place she had heard whisper of one evening she had visited the theatre. The two women had not been aware of her secreted in that tiny cubicle, but she had been aware of *them*, listening with attentive ears as they talked of Church House. '*It is no distance from this very theatre*,' one woman had murmured to the other, '*I am told it is a few yards from Mount Pleasant in the direction of Willenhall Road*.'

It had been more than gossip, more than an item of titillating chatter; it had been a passing on of information, and it had passed to ears other than those for which it had been intended. But, having a maid to attend to her special needs, having a woman friend eager to participate in those bathtime games, Ava had not needed to visit the place those two had spoken of; but with Lenor Medwin dead and Myra Brent no longer at Moorcroft, desire had proved too much. She had taken a train to Bilston and a hackney to Church House and today had repeated the journey.

Church House! It was a name that deceived, one which hid from society those practices society would not accept.

'Are you sure you have to leave?' A young, full-breasted woman pressed her own naked body against that of Ava. 'There is so much yet we can do together . . . so much more pleasure to be had.'

Lips closing over her breast, the tip of a tongue teasing the nipple, Ava's senses lurched and for a brief wonderful moment she opened her legs to the fingers exploring the soft intimate cavern. But then she had thrust the girl away, a girl who laughed with quiet exultation.

'You'll be back . . . you like brushing the muff too much to stay away.'

Yes, she liked it, but, no, she would not be taking the journey to Bilston again. From now on the pleasures paid for so expensively at Church House would be hers for no more than it took to pay a ladies' maid . . . And for the sister of that maid? One wage would suffice for both!

'Eh, mum, did you hear while you been out?'

'Hear . . . hear what?" She did not want to listen to the woman's drivel. Ava brushed past the fluttering cook.

'About the killin', mum, that I spoke of only this mornin', have you heard of it?'

'Only what you yourself told, and I want to hear no more.'

'But, mum . . .'

'No!' Ava's eyes warned of her irritation. 'I will hear no more tales of the market place. Silly, irresponsible gossip is all it is. You should have more sense than listen and much more than to pay heed to it!'

In her own room, coat and gown removed, Ava stripped away underclothes, tossing them aside for laundering, then walked into the bathroom where she poured water from a tall rose-painted jug into a matching bowl. She had scrubbed herself with the soap supplied by that house but she would not feel truly clean until she washed again here in her own room.

She had thought not to have frequented Church House after that first time but temptation had proved too strong. Demands of the flesh! She touched a towel to the body still crying out to taste again what she had left behind. Needs of the body that men thought a woman never felt! But they *were* felt, the necessity for fulfilment was as strong in female as in male; but where men could satisfy that passion with wife, mistress or street whore, the same was denied a woman. She must never own to a husband's attention leaving her wanting, never speak of the desire left unsatisfied, and certainly not seek that sweet delectation with another woman.

The towel falling from her fingers, Ava cupped her breasts, throbbing with the memory of a moist tongue, while her gaze ran over a stomach aching still for the gratification of a touch other than her own. But all of that would come again soon. Tomorrow Myra Brent would be back in this house.

The thought did not alleviate the pincers of desire squeezing every nerve but only added to its heat. But the normal practice of the day had to be observed. Dressing quickly, she went downstairs seating herself only minutes before tea was brought to her.

Setting the tray on to a Georgian cabriole-legged tea-table, one of the few items of any real value still gracing Moorcroft, Polly Jupp sniffed. This perfume were not that as had drifted into this house with Ava Russell's returning, that had been washed away an' replaced by another . . . It needed no guessing to tell the kind of establishment the first had been acquired in, whore houses catered not only for men, there were those where brushin' the muff were also to be had for a price. That bathroom 'ad seen no frolickin' since the passing of Lenor Medwin, an' Ava Russell were no woman to deny 'erself them pleasures for long . . . No, it needed no guessin' as to where the mistress 'ad spent her afternoon.

'T'weren't no gossip.' Standing straight, her hands together across an ample middle, Polly faced the woman only a salary had caused to be treated with pretended respect. 'That which I tried to tell you of this mornin', t'were no tale bandied about the market place, seems it be no tittle-tattle after all.'

Not lifting her glance from the tea she was pouring, Ava toyed with the idea of dismissing the woman without answer then changed her mind, asking instead, 'What chit-chat would that be?'

Not the sort you been listenin' to, none of the drivel

I'd bet a pound to a penny been a' pourin' into your ears the whole of the afternoon! Repugnance held behind tight lips, Polly Jupp sniffed again.

'Ain't just chit-chat neither,' she answered firmly. 'That which you called market-place tales were no less than the truth.'

There was a difference in the woman's attitude. Ava stirred sugar and milk into her tea. There was none of the deference, none of the respect she was usually so careful to show. Lifting the porcelain cup, Ava sipped twice. What was it? What was this truth the woman so obviously wanted her to hear?

'So.' She lowered the cup. 'What is this terrible truth?'

'It be terrible all right . . .'

The cup replaced in its saucer, Ava noted the lack of the word 'mum', the ignoring of that essential protocol.

'. . . be what I told afore, there were a wench found in the town, a wench wi' her throat slashed an' her chest ripped open, an' that not a dozen yards from where the body of young Alfred Birks were found an' him ripped in that self-same way.'

'A second killing!' Ava set her tea aside, her attention now given fully to the woman standing before her.

'That be right, an' what with them as 'appened last year that meks four, four people murdered right here in this very town. I tells you, it be the work of that Ripper that were doin' all of them murders along of London, the constables d'ain't never catch him along of Whitechapel an' nor they won't, 'cos he don't be there no more, he be here in Wednesbury a satisfyin' of his evil lusts on folk the like of Alfred an' that young woman who were maid along of the Medwin house.'

'The Medwin household?' Ava frowned.

'That be what I heard.' Polly Jupp's head bobbed. 'The wench they found dead along of the Church Steps be the same as you said to be expectin' to call here at Moorcroft. It be young Dilly Madely.'

'Dilly . . . Dilly Madely is dead!'

'As a doornail. I spoke with a woman as lives next to her poor mother . . . God help her . . . was fetched by the constable to identify the body . . . to have to look upon a daughter cut to ribbons by a maniac. Dear God what be this world comin' to!'

'There can be no mistake?'

'None.' Polly's head swung decisively. 'Same as can be none as to the sort that killer be lookin' to find, though heaven alone be privy as to the why of that.'

'I don't understand. Surely a murderer would not specify a particular kind of victim?'

'Wouldn't he though . . . wouldn't he!' Hands which until now had remained still, twined with anxiety. 'Then why pick on two who it were obvious had no wealth behind them, who it could be seen were working-class? And them whor— them women of the streets slashed to death in London, they had nothing save what the sellin' of their bodies brought and that would be nobbut a shillin' or two. No, I says this killer, whoever he be, be looking to the serving class, the only difference atwixt what he done in London to what he be about here being he don't strike only at wenches, he will strike men an' all. But man and woman, they were both servants same as me, though that be ended here an' now. I'll be taking what be due to me an' leaving right now. Polly Jupp ain't going to hang around waiting for no knife to slit her throat. My bags be packed so I'll be asking for the money I've earned be paid now; and if you teks my advice you'll get yourself away from this town 'til such times as that murderer be safe behind bars.'

23

He had forced himself to stay away from Shipton Cottage. Setting young Davy Melia the task of walking the girl to and from The Coppice, hearing reports from him every day, there had been little need for him to see her himself and certainly no cause to visit that house beside the canal.

No need! Andrew Denby smiled grimly to himself. Why then was he here? This was not the route he took to the wood mill at Willingsworth or the coach and axle works along at Monway Field. Answering the polite greeting of men passing on narrowboats, he knew they also would be asking themselves the same question: why was the owner of Denby Boat Builders walking the towpath?

Reaching the cottage, he glanced at the heath running on all sides wild and empty of any other building. She should not live here alone. Even having arranged for a boat to moor here every evening and for that lad to walk with her to and from The Coppice he still worried for her . . . But why did he? That was yet one more question Andrew Denby was loath to answer.

'Mornin' Mister Denby, sir.'

From a little way ahead a man leading a large shire horse touched his cap, then grinned as the horse came to a halt.

'Old Pharaoh 'ere won't budge another step afore he gets his titbit from the little miss living along of that there cottage . . . I don't never have no argying with him no other place, stops and starts meek as a lamb, but when it be the Shipton house he be nearing, there he stands his ground as you might say . . . refuses to budge, does Pharaoh 'til he gets what it is he's set his mind to havin'.'

'Like his namesakes of old, they knew what they wanted and made sure they got it.'

'Don't know nothing of that,' the man smiled as Andrew rubbed the horse's nose, 'but if they were sensible as that hoss then I reckons they got what it were they set their mind on. Mind, it ain't just Pharaoh looks forward to reaching 'ere. The wench be a fair hand with a cooking pot and her charges be the same; if'n you ain't had a mornin' meal, Mister Denby . . . or even if you 'ave . . . you couldn't do better than purchase a bite from this 'ere cottage.'

'Something to eat would be very acceptable . . . but perhaps only narrowboat folk are welcome here.'

'Only people who lack good manners find no welcome at this door.'

One hand still on the animal's nose, Andrew Denby turned to see a young woman, her fair hair gold-spun in the clear sunlight, coming down the short garden path, her heart-shaped face wearing no smile. She was no more pleased to see him than on those other days, days when she had literally told him to mind his own business.

'Then I shall make sure mine give no offence. Maybe then I, like Pharaoh here, might be allowed a titbit.'

'He knows when we be comin' this way, knows a mile off, does Pharaoh, I swears he quickens his step no sooner we be turnin' off the main Navigation and following along the cut from Wiggins Pool.'

'Well, folk do talk of horse sense,' Andrew answered, stepping away as the horse swung its head expectantly, 'and it is quite obvious Pharaoh has an ample amount. A man can do no better than to follow his lead, always supposing I am allowed. May I, Miss Brent . . . may I purchase a meal from you?'

Acutely aware of the tall figure stooping to enter the cottage, feeling those sable-dark eyes on her, Eden filled the basin the other man carried then, wrapping a fresh loaf in the bandana he passed to her, accepted the coins he held out.

'Is that sensible?' The bargee having left, Andrew frowned, watching her count a number of coins into a box she lifted from a drawer, then put several in a pretty vase on the mantel.

'I beg your pardon!' Eden's own frown held more annoyance than question.

This was a good start! Andrew Denby held the mutinous stare. The girl looked more ready to throw him out than ask him to sit and eat. But she had proved on several occasions to act without thinking; this it seemed was one more of those times.

'I asked, Is that sensible, keeping a money box where it can so easily be found? And a jar is not exactly a safe.'

'It is safe enough, Mister Denby, or so it has been up to now!'

Tart as a sour apple. But this girl was not the picture she painted. She was sweeter, more tender beneath the façade of cold indifference; that he had learned from the praises Davy and so many others sang of her. Sweet maybe, gentle perhaps, but mindful of her own safety . . . definitely not!

'Up to *now.*' He emphasised the word. 'But people pass this spot every day and while I would not count the majority of folk dishonest there are exceptions.'

'Exceptions occur in many aspects of people's behaviour, Mister Denby. Some may take money which does not belong to them, while some take the liberty of making the business of others their own. Both are a grievance.'

As he had thought. Andrew Denby hid the smile threatening to curve his strong mouth. Tart, and certainly not easily cowed; nevertheless her idea of safeguarding the proceeds of her labours was as sensible as sitting against a stone wall on a freezingly cold day.

'Grievance or not,' he glanced to where the window was opened to the air, 'it has to be said, a box in a drawer and a pot on a mantel are hardly the most secure of hiding places.'

A kettle which had started to sing taking her attention, Eden swung it away from the fire. She should show this man the hospitality her grandmother had taught be observed no matter the caller: 'Rich as a Lord or poor as a beggar they deserve no less than a sup of tea.' Never before had she wished to ignore those words of her grandmother, but with this man . . .

Sensing her hesitation, he turned back to the door. She had never displayed any pleasure in his company, it would be unfair of him to impose it on her any further.

'Miss Brent.' He paused, swinging his head to look at her. 'Unacceptable as it is, I offer my advice yet again. Do not leave your money where it can be so easily found.'

'But that is the precise reason of my placing it where it is,' she replied quickly, 'at least that is the reason of the coins being placed in the jar. You see, Mister Denby, I do not know who it is owns this house, neither do I know the sum which might be required as rent. I have asked among the people of Gospel Oak but it seems they also do not know the present owner, they only know it belonged to an elderly woman they called Mother Shipton. But, being unaware of the owner of a house does not mean a person may live in it and pay no rent at all; it is for that reason I place a share of all that I myself am paid into that jar. If the owner of Shipton Cottage does not call before my leaving then the jar and its contents will remain where it can be found . . . and hopefully what it holds will prove sufficient.'

. . . *before my leaving* . . .

The words rang in Andrew Denby's mind as he strode across the heath towards Willingsworth wood mill. Of all the times he had thought of that girl he had not once thought of her leaving that cottage. But *why* leave . . . and to go where? If she had had somewhere to go, why was it he had found her huddled against a bridge? And, if there were some other place waiting for her, why stay all these weeks in that cottage?

But she had said, '*before my leaving*'. Why say it if she did not intend to go? And why had her words resulted in this feeling, this sudden sense of his world falling apart?

He had not asked for food. He had not once smiled or even wished her the time of day before leaving. Walking beside Davy, who whistled happily through a leaf, Eden let her thoughts dwell as they had all day on a tall figure whose sable eyes had held hers before he had stooped through the doorway and strode away. It had been abrupt, his leaving; he had looked for a brief moment as if he might say something but he had simply walked away.

It should not have bothered her; she should have welcomed his going but, instead, she had stared at the empty doorway, and somehow the day had lost its glow. That had been absurd, she had told herself, returning to the process of preparing another batch of the faggots so favoured by the bargemen with no wives to cook for them. But, work as she had, the day had retained a shadow, a gloom which even now lay over her like a cloud. Why had he come to Shipton Cottage? The question had plagued her all day but, as with so many others Andrew Denby aroused in her, she could find no satisfactory answer.

'He don't be there!'

The sharp note of surprise piercing her thoughts, Eden looked towards where Davy pointed.

'That old 'un,' he said again, 'he don't be there. Now that be a turn-up an' no coddin'.'

Like Davy had said, it was no lie. There was no figure at the gate, no man waiting for his meal.

'But he is always there.' Eden peered against the shadows daringly attacking the sky as the sun lost its hold on the evening, shadows strengthening and made bolder by trees and bushes lining each side of the narrow track.

'Well, this is one time he don't be.' Davy threw away the leaf.

Alarm replacing the torpor that had lain over her, Eden hurried forward. Maybe the old man was ill, maybe . . .

'The empty dish be there, washed as usual.' Davy had easily kept pace with the running Eden.

The dish she had given him the night before was indeed placed on the lintel of the gatepost, but the man himself . . . Eden cast a quick glance at the surrounds of the small house . . . where was he?

'Don't be usual, don't be usual at all.'

Davy voicing what was in her mind, she glanced at

the windows. No face looked back from any one of them, neither did the door open. Had their conversation of the previous evening annoyed him so much he had taken exception? Did he no longer want what flimsy relationship he had allowed to develop between them to continue? She ought not to have spoken as she had. Eden stared again at windows that showed no light of a lamp. Gran had often said her tongue ran away, leaving her brain to follow on behind. That was what she had done last evening, let her tongue run on without thinking.

'Might as well go back.' Davy, too, glanced over the silent house. 'He don't be goin' to come out, that be easy to see.'

For all her surmising of the reasons the man was not at his gate, Eden felt uneasy. Perhaps he was turning his back, saying without words that she was no longer to come here. There had never been any smile in those copper-hued eyes, no hint of any welcome on that drawn face, nothing to say he found pleasure in her brief visits, yet she felt a sharp dejection in his not appearing. Even his words of anger, or his cane rising to drive her away, would have been infinitely better than the feeling she had now, the feeling that once again something precious had been snatched from her.

Turning away, leaving her to pick up the empty dish while he carried the full one, Davy was already some way along the track when Eden's sharp cry brought him racing back, his brown eyes gleaming concern.

'Be somethin' wrong?'

'No . . . I mean yes. There is something not right about all this.'

'You mean the old 'un not showing here at the gate? But that be the way of 'im. I said he were a surly bug . . . Well, I said as he 'adn't a civil bone in his body and tonight I be proved right; can't even be bothered to come outside and say he don't be wanting no supper! I says to leave 'im to it, let 'im stew in his own juice for a while, mebbes he'll come out of it a mite tenderer than when he went in!'

'But how can we be sure his not being here at the gate is simply the result of ill humour? How can we be certain it is not something more than that?"

'More?' Davy frowned, then drew a short breath as the meaning behind Eden's reluctance to leave became clear.

'You means p'raps he be sick or . . . or worse?'

'We ought not to leave before finding out.'

In the last of the light Eden saw the look which crossed the lad's face. It was apprehension. But of what? Was Davy afraid of the man who lived in this house, or was he afraid of what he might find inside it?

'We can't do that wi'out going in, and that be one thing me mother don't have the tolerating of. If I goes into that place without the inviting her will have the hide off me.'

Lost among the swift-growing darkness, Eden's smile remained unseen. It was neither of the fears she had thought made Davy Melia reluctant to step into that cottage. It was a fear of his mother's anger and, knowing his mother as she had come to do, Eden owned it was not something anyone should take lightly.

'There is no need for you to go in,' she said pushing open the gate, 'I will do it.'

'And 'ave me mother wallop me for lettin' you! Seems I be in for a clout about the ears either way, so I might as well be the one to look inside.'

Where was the moon? Alone beside the gate, Eden probed the shadows with anxious eyes. It was so dark she could see nothing but the black outline of walls and roof. Please, the thought rippled on the silence of a mind only too aware of a cane wielded by an irate hand, please don't let Davy be harmed.

Dilly Madely would not be calling at Moorcroft, not for interview for the post of ladies' maid, and not to try her hand at the same stupid game her erstwhile lover had tried to play.

Ava Russell extracted two five pound notes from a box, locked it and deposited it in a bureau in her bedroom.

First Birks and now Dilly Madely. Fortune was certainly playing in her favour. Only Myra Brent remained and now that she had been found she would prove no threat. For, with the belief that that sister of hers was here in this house, she would return as arranged. Of course, as her mistress, Ava could have demanded the girl return with her, travel with her from Darlaston, but she preferred it this way.

Ava's feral smile touched the edges of her thin

mouth, making it even more hard and unattractive. Yes, she preferred it this way, somehow it added spice to the game. What was the childhood rhyme? She laughed quietly. 'Will you walk into my parlour said the spider to the fly'. Myra Brent would certainly do that, and so would Myra Brent's sister.

'I am sorry you feel you have to leave.' Returning to the sitting-room, all trace of the smile banished, Ava held out the banknotes. 'Ten pounds is the wage due. You did not complete a twelve-month.'

Miserly old cow! Polly Jupp's thought reflected her look. After fifteen years of dancing to this woman's tune her couldn't make a gift of the other two pounds! But nothing given meant nothing the needing of thanks, and Ava Russell would get none of those from her. Taking the money, she pushed it low into the bag hanging from her wrist.

'There be a hansom callin' for me in five minutes.' Polly looked at the woman whose house she had virtually run for so many years. 'Seeing you'll be by yourself after that time, I would advise you lock the doors. Like I says, nobody be safe in this town no more.'

'. . . *you'll be by yourself* . . .'

Her clothes removed, Ava looked again at her body reflected in her dressing-room mirror.

Yes, she was alone in this house, but not for many more hours; tomorrow Myra Brent would be back, the two of them together.

Hands sliding voluptuously over her stomach, Ava let the feline smile return.

The two of them together, two naked bodies, two sets of touching, caressing hands, a moist tongue to tease a nipple, a mouth to kiss, and most of all fingers playing in that warm vee bringing each to a gasping explosion of passion. Oh, yes. She gazed at the reflection watching from the mirror. Myra Brent would learn to play the whole of the game, she would learn all of the delights brushing the muff could bring . . .

Lips parted, eyes closing, fingertips stroking a soft slippery mound, Ava drew a breath of pure satisfaction.

Yes, Myra Brent would learn . . . and so would her sister.

24

Myra Brent was returning today. She would see to the managing of these two women who came daily to help with the general cleaning of those rooms still in use, and deal with the laundrywoman and the gardener and, of course, the tradesmen. Myra was a competent girl, well able to add the duties of housekeeper to those more entertaining tasks.

Standing in the kitchen, a part of the house into which she had rarely ventured, Ava looked with distaste at the reedy woman and equally unattractive girl. Mother and daughter, no doubt, and both nervous their employment was about to be terminated.

'There will be a new housekeeper arriving later today. In the meantime you will continue with your usual tasks.' Hearing the release of breath, knowing the reason for it, Ava smiled to herself, then continued. 'I shall inspect the kitchen and other rooms after you have left, rooms I expect to be thoroughly cleaned.'

'They . . . they will be, mum.' The older of the two twittered like a nervous bird. 'As . . . as to the midday meal, Missis Jupp give us both a dish of summat or other. Be . . . be we still to be given. . .'

'There is food in the larder, you may make a meal of that.'

Turning on her heel, taffeta skirt swishing, Ava swept imperiously away. She did not know what was or was not in that larder and she cared even less; food was not her main interest, right now there were other more important things on her mind like the letter received that morning.

The study door closed carefully, she crossed to the desk. Sitting in the chair that had once been her husband's, she allowed her gaze to pass around the room. She had not once entered here in the years of their marriage; it had been Samuel's inner sanctum, his place of privacy. From here he had dealt with all but the running of the household, that having been left to her. '*Business is not for a woman, she is not strong enough for the burden of that.*' Remembering, Ava's thin lips curled with contempt. Who, if not Samuel Russell's wife, had kept that business going since his departing the world? And the forging of iron had not been the only business he had relieved her from; that of the marriage bed had followed quickly. Samuel liked a woman beneath him while his wife had made quite clear she did not care to be that woman. The ensuing arrangement had suited them both: she would see to the comforts of his home whilst a mistress, or several mistresses, saw to the comforts of his body. But with Samuel's death she had become not only mistress of Moorcroft but of Moorcroft Ironworks, but they were failing.

Taking a key from her pocket she unlocked a drawer of the heavy desk and drew out a ledger. Opening it, she ran a glance over neatly recorded numbers. The requests for iron had begun to fall within two years of her becoming the foundry's owner. Because of her being a woman . . . because it was thought she had not wits enough to run an iron foundry? She had believed that, and why not? Didn't every man think the same of any woman? But it proved not only Moorcroft iron was failing . . . every manufacturer of that metal had seen their orders reduced. Arthur Medwin had sold up and so had many others, taking what they could salvage before every last penny followed the rest down the drain.

But she had not sold. Ava's glance followed the columns of numbers. She had held to the belief the setback was temporary, an overstock of iron which, when used, would see those orders flocking back. That had not happened. Metal was still wanted, huge amounts of it, but the metal required was not iron but steel; steel was the new god, only steel would do for bridges, for girders, for the making of axles, wheels and boilers, for more and more railway trains: steel! She slammed the ledger shut, she should have changed over to its making . . . now the money needed to pay for that change, to bring in new furnaces, rolling beds and all the other equipment necessary, was no longer in the bank.

In fact there was no money there at all, hence the letter. '*Repayments due on the mortgage taken on the property known as Moorcroft House have not been forthcoming . . . the bank strongly advises . . .'*

The bank strongly advises . . . Ava leaned her head against the back of the chair, her eyes closing.

Returning that five hundred pounds was one more thing she ought to have done . . . it was one more thing she had not! Now most of it was gone. Settlements of accounts to suppliers of iron ore, of coal needed for the smelting of that ore and the paying of wages, though that bill had become less as men had been dismissed from their jobs. The drain on those five hundred pounds had not ceased there . . . household suppliers had also threatened action should their dues not be settled.

Scandal! Ava's eyes opened. That was a slur she would not tolerate! Scandal of any kind would not be allowed to touch the name of Ava Russell. To avoid it she had put the foundry up for sale. How much would that realise? Would the proceeds settle the amount loaned by the bank?

And if it did not? Locking the ledger away, Ava walked slowly upstairs. But it would . . . it had to! Maybe had she not spent so much on gowns. Cheap as that dressmaker was in comparison to those salons she had patronised during Samuel's lifetime, they still were responsible for more than she should have spent, but appearance mattered and hers mattered a great deal. She would not be seen to appear reduced in circumstances, it would appear as it always had. The times she visited the theatre, charity events or even Sunday morning service in church, her clothing would be of the finest materials and the latest fashions.

And that other expenditure?

Taking the small box from the bureau she opened it. The expense of that visit to Bilston. It had been more than she could afford, she had not guessed a service bought in that establishment would cost what it had.

But it was a payment she would not need to pay again. The services of Church House would not be necessary any longer.

'Told to me while we was lying over at Monway Basin tekin' on a load of iron. The only time a body gets to speak with another is when you be picking up or setting down of a cargo, that or waiting to be passed through a lock, either way it be no more than a few minutes can be given . . . I'll tek a couple of pots of that pressed chawl, be right tasty does that, my man and lads reckon it be the best anywhere on the cut . . .'

Standing at the doorway of Shipton Cottage, a woman took coins from a pocket. She was dressed in faded blue cotton poke bonnet and equally faded cotton blouse, her dark skirt bearing marks of helping to load the boat that was of necessity home to her family, while the ankle-length apron covering it was of a whiteness that bore witness to the woman's efforts at keeping that family clean.

'. . . I tells you, wench, it must be fair worryin' to the mothers of young folk living in that town. Two dead within no time of one another. Has me glad me and mine lives on the cut.'

Another person dead! It could not be the result of some dreadful contagion . . . but any other cause of death would not have news of its happening passing mouth to mouth, so why this one?

Taking coins from the woman, handing her two pots of pressed meat, Eden felt the question press on her mind, only to be intensified by the woman's next words.

'The whole town be buzzing with it, first a man and now a young woman . . . both found with their throats cut across and their chests slashed. Lord, it fair meks the blood run cold a' thinking on it. Reckon it must be some lunatic broke from an asylum . . . stands to reason nobody in their right mind would go doing what be done to them poor young souls. Will be a blessing when he be caught, for folk can hardly rest easy knowing there be a killer on the loose.'

Stunned by what was said, Eden could only stand staring as the woman ran back to the narrowboat moving slowly along the canal.

A killer . . . two young people . . . a man and a woman . . . both found with throat . . .

The horror of it only now registering in her brain, Eden caught her breath. Davy had talked of a death, Alfred Birks' death, but Davy had not spoken of the cause, only that no awful disease had come to the town. But this woman had spoken of murder . . . and not of only one, but two.

'*. . . first a man and now a young woman . . .*'

Had Davy Melia known the man he spoke of had

been the victim of murder? Had he known, yet decided not to tell her, for fear of frightening her?

'*. . . a young woman . . .*'

The words seemed to scream at her, to pound in her brain as if they carried some warning.

'Myra!' It broke in a gasp, riding the crest of a fear, rising stark and terrifying, holding her breath, stifling her throat. Myra was in that town, Myra was a young woman!

No . . . no, please no! Fear now a riot gripping her mind, she snatched the shawl that had been her grandmother's and ran with it across the heath.

'There don't be nobody of that name 'ere.'

'But there has to be.' Holding one hand to the spot aching beneath her ribs, Eden half-sobbed. 'Myra Brent, she is ladies' maid to Missis Russell.''

Wiping her hands on a dark apron, a needle-thin woman looked, with lacklustre eyes, at the girl leaning for support against Moorcroft's kitchen door.

'Was a wench 'ere, looked a lot like y'self; I seen her sometime when her were sent on an errand for the mistress, her would pass by the scullery or the wash-house just so as to speak to folk, nice young thing her was . . .'

'Please,' Eden interrupted desperately. 'Please, when will she be back?'

Hands rough and red contrasted against the dark cloth of the apron the woman smoothed into place. 'I don't be knowing this as fact but it might be as her won't be comin' back at all.'

'. . . *first a man and now a young woman.*'

Words which had drummed with every footstep as she had run across the heath became a harsh, jarring screech, a cacophony from which three words stabbed again and again.

'. . . *a young woman . . . a young woman . . .*'

The screech laughing into a thunderous roar, Eden slid into blackness.

'Eh wench, but you caused a body a right turn, faintin' away like that!'

Anxious but gentle, a voice lifting her to the light, Eden opened her eyes. 'Gran . . . Gran, I . . .'

'Don't be your gran, wench.'

Senses not yet returned, Eden glanced about the large room. A huge dresser filled with dishes each of a match, pans shining like dull suns hung in a row against one wall, a gleaming black range ambled along another. This was not home! This was not . . . 'Gran!'

'No, wench, I don't be your gran . . . but there be no need of alarm, you just had a faintin' turn, no doubt be 'cos you was out of breath, seemed you had been runnin'.'

Everything rushing back at once, Eden rose shakily from the chair she had been helped to. 'You . . . you said Myra . . .'

'You shouldn't go moving just yet.' The worn-out face took on a worried look. 'The mistress don't be 'ome but should her be, then it's certain her would say for you to sit awhile and tek a cup of tea.'

It weren't certain at all, the cleaning woman admitted to herself, relieved when Eden refused. Ava Russell were not a woman noted for the giving of anything to them thought beneath her.

'*. . . a young woman . . .*'

Eden drew a deep breath. It had to be asked. Holding the air a moment in her lungs, a moment keeping at bay an answer she dreaded, she clutched the shawl the woman had thoughtfully draped about her shoulders.

'I . . . I heard in the town, a young woman had . . . had been . . .'

'Killed. That be true. A young wench, seems her were maid along of the Medwin place, name of Dilly Madely if what folk tell be right.'

It was not Myra! Her sister was not dead! It sang in her like a hymn, a glorious song of thankfulness. Her sister was not dead!

'But that were not the name you spoke, not the wench you first asked after.'

Eden shook her head confirming the woman's words. 'It was Myra Brent, she is my sister.'

'And you thought . . . well, seems it be a different wench . . . God give peace to her soul and torment to the one who killed her . . .' the woman crossed herself piously, '. . . as for the one you speaks of, her that were ladies' maid here at this 'ouse; well, like I told it could be as her won't be back at all.'

'But I don't understand, Myra has been here for several years . . . has she been dismissed . . . has she done something wrong?'

Untying the straps of her apron, the woman handed it to the younger, equally tired-looking replica of herself. 'Can't be answerin' as to what that wench might or might not have done 'cept to say the rest of them as worked in this place must have done similar, for the all of them be gone along of her, including her as was cook for fifteen years. Be nobody left save for me and my own wench. We comes a few hours a day as does the old man come to see to the 'orse and do a bit to the garden.'

Breaking off, the woman listened to the chimes of a clock reaching from the hall.

'Be time for we to finish.' She glanced at her younger counterpart appearing from the scullery a shawl already drawn over her head and held beneath non-existent breasts with one hand, while the other passed a second shawl to her mother. 'I 'pologises for hurryin' off but it don't do to be out after dark, not with that killer stalkin' . . . You teks my advice and get y'self 'ome, same as we be doin'.'

'But the mistress, I have to speak with her, ask her about my sister.'

Enveloped in the shawl despite the warmth of summer, the woman answered quickly, her desire to be gone plain in its brevity. 'Then you'll have to wait in the yard. Don't be for me to say wait you in the 'ouse.'

They had left without another word, scurrying like two frightened mice, disappearing quickly from sight among the trees and bushes that bordered the grounds of Moorcroft House.

From the tower of Saint Bartholomew's church, a single bell rang the hour. Eight o'clock. She had stood in the yard for two hours. The breeze rustling through the trees had her glance nervously into reaches of the garden swathed now in the ink-like darkness of a moonless night.

'*. . . don't do to be out after dark . . . a killer stalkin' . . .*'

The woman's words twanged against nerves already taut as a bowstring.

'*. . . get y'self 'ome . . .*'

Somewhere in the shadowed depths a sound deeper than the rustling of leaves reached to where she stood. Fingers twisting the corners of her shawl, Eden stared, her own anxiety as evident as that of those cleaning women.

Myra was not in this house, she was not expected to return . . . And her mistress, what was to say she, too, might not return, that she was not gone to stay a while at some other place? She had not been told so, but then neither had she been told otherwise.

The sound, one she could not identify, came again. Anxiety turning to fear, she stared into that threatening blackness, stared at a darker shape emerging from the bushes.

25

'She was not at the cottage?'

Andrew Denby put down the pen he was holding, his gaze on the lad twisting a cloth cap between his hands.

Davy Melia saw the frown nestle between dark brows and answered quickly. 'No, Mister Denby sir, there were no broom across the door to say Eden were out so I called and when there were no answer I went in; the door it were open and . . . and Eden has said for me not to stand at the gate when I calls to walk her to The Coppice . . . but her were not nowheres in the place.'

'Did you check the garden?'

Davy Melia's head bobbed rapidly. 'I done that but her weren't there neither.'

Had she been taken ill? Not allowing the concern that thought aroused to show in his voice, Andrew Denby's next question was falsely calm. 'Did you go upstairs? Did you look for Eden in her room?'

He were allowed use of her name! Davy was also cautious, allowing none of the surprise it engendered to colour his reply.

'I thought of that . . . thought her might 'ave been tekin' a bit of a rest.'

'But did you go upstairs?'

This man could be sharp with words . . . and even sharper with action. Hearing the astringency contained in the tone of that demand, the cap twisted again.

'I . . . I thought mebbe her were sleepin'. I hollered Mister Denby, I hollered real loud . . . me mother says that betimes I shouts fit to waken the dead . . .'

The apprehensiveness of an answer filled with unspoken apology telling of the boy's own discomfort, Andrew Denby curbed the disquiet once more rising inside him. 'Davy,' he said calmly, 'tell me, please, did you look for Eden in her bedroom?'

Deep colour staining his face, Davy nodded. 'I did 'oller, be God's truth I did, then gettin' no answer I got feared Eden might be teken poorly so . . . so I went . . .' he swallowed hard, his fingers torturing the cloth cap, '. . . I swears on the Bible, I swears I knocked on both them doors, I banged 'em 'til my knuckles was sore but weren't no answer so I peeped in . . . honest to God, Mister Denby, it were fear for Eden had me look in them rooms . . .'

'I believe you, Davy, and it was the right thing to do. But did you not wonder had she gone to the village?'

'I did wonder, so I went there, but folk along of Gospel Oak said as her had been there that morning but not after that, nor had the cut folk seen her for I asked every one as passed but they all said the same thing; they'd called at Shipton Cottage but Eden weren't there.'

What time had it been when she was last seen? To ask the lad that question might serve to make him even more jumpy.

'I went from Gospel Oak straight back to the cottage in case Eden were back from wherever it were she was at, but the place were still empty. That were when it come to me her might already be gone along to The Coppice and that her were talkin' to the old sod . . . the man who lives nearby. Eden tries speakin' with 'im though he be so surly I wouldn't spare 'im the time of day. But her weren't there neither, and the man were missing an' all. Same as the evening afore. That were when I went 'ome but Mother said I should ought to come tell you, seeing as how you pays me to walk along of Eden. Her said I were not to tek money when it were not earned.'

It sounded exactly like Sara Melia. Andrew nodded, but his thoughts sped like windblown leaves. Eden Brent had said the money placed in the pot on the mantel was put there against her leaving. Was that what she had done? Had she gone as quietly as she had come . . . was she still running away . . . or had the fear she was running from caught up with her, had it come to Shipton Cottage? But what use were questions no one could answer!

His voice calmer than his mind, he closed the book he had been writing in when the lad was shown into the room that was the office of the boatmaking yard. Thank Heaven he had worked later than intended . . . Had he left sooner . . . !

Pushing away the thought of what could have been, he looked again at the sturdy figure waiting before him. 'Davy, you and Eden, you get along well?'

What did that mean? Davy Melia's hands became suddenly still, his pleasant mouth tightening. Did Andrew Denby think him responsible for the wench not being where it were thought her should be?

'Eden and me was friends . . . I would walk along of her without pay from you and I would kill anybody as dared lay a finger on 'er!'

The shoulders had squared, the polite deference to station had gone, the lad had made way for the man.

'So would I, Davy . . . so would I.' More of himself in the words than he should have shown, Andrew went on quickly. 'The evenings you walked with her to that house below The Coppice, did she perhaps speak of where she had lived before coming to the Shipton place? Did she say anything which might provide the answer to where she is now?'

'Like I says, I'll kill any man bringin' harm to her.'

There had been moments of waiting for him to answer, moments when he had seen conflict in those brown eyes, now he saw promise, and more . . . he saw threat. Where Eden Brent was concerned, this young man would acknowledge no master. His reply no longer that of a lad, Andrew Denby met the threat.

'I understand the feeling you have for Eden,' he said, 'but believe me when I say mine are a thousand times stronger.'

'You . . . you and Eden!'

Dark head shaking briefly, Andrew Denby smiled. 'No, not Eden, only myself. I cannot claim the friendship you enjoy with her. I fear she feels nothing other than animosity towards me, and most certainly not what I feel for her.'

'You have feelings for Eden?'

Again the man! Andrew smiled to himself, then at the figure whose hands no longer mangled the cloth cap. 'Yes, Davy, I have feelings for Eden.'

Had he expected the threat in those honest eyes to deepen, to become a challenge? Did young feelings run as hot and burning as his own? Relaxing into a grin, Andrew felt relief. His confessed feelings had not placed a wedge between himself and a lad he admired.

'That be wonderful! Eden . . .'

'Eden does not know of my feelings and you must not speak to her of them!' Rising to his feet as he spoke, Andrew watched the wide grin become a frown of puzzlement. 'I would have your word, Davy."

No trace now of the boy who had been shown into the office, though not all confusion had gone from his brow, Davy nodded. 'You 'as it.'

Thanking him as he rounded the desk, Andrew asked again: Had Eden spoke of her life before coming to Shipton Cottage?

'Her never said much, and Mother . . . well, you knows Mother, Mister Denby.'

The respect was back. Striding across the cobbled yard, Davy keeping easy pace alongside him, Andrew Denby recognised a respect shown one man by another; like a chrysalis the shell of boyhood had broken and the man had emerged. Sara Melia sent a youth to Denby Boat Builders but she would receive back an adult!

Returning the respect, he answered, 'Yes, David, I know your mother, her tenet is: Ask no question.'

A flush of pleasure brought on by the use of his given name, the freckled face found yet another grin. 'Ar, them be her words and they were followed by me. I asked nothing and nothing were told me, not until . . .'

'Until?' A hand on the saddle of the horse brought to him by the watchman, Andrew turned a sharp look to the figure half-swallowed by shadow now encompassing the yard.

'It were when I spoke of a man being killed along of the town . . .'

Waiting until there was no more to tell, Andrew Denby swung into the saddle. 'She said her sister was maid at Moorcroft but her grandmother's house was in Hobbins Street?'

'That be what her told. I be going to both them places now . . .'

'No.' Andrew' s sharp tone made the horse prance. A soothing hand stroking the arched neck, his words came more softly. 'No, David. It is best you return home. With talk of murder your mother will no doubt be uneasy; she will be happier having you there to take care of her.'

It had not been meant condescendingly. This young man had a strong arm and the courage to use it. It would be a brave man or a fool who threatened Sara Melia.

Cloaked by night gloom, Davy pulled a wry mouth. Eden Brent were a friend, and young women needed tekin' care of same as his mother . . . but to leave one for the other . . . !

'I understand your difficulty. You want to be with your mother yet feel an obligation to search for Eden.' Andrew recognised the cause behind the failure to answer.

'That be it, but . . .'

'You can't be in two places at the same time, no man can. Do as I ask, return to your mother and I promise I will go look for Eden.'

He had meant what he had said. Andrew Denby drove the carriage he had hurriedly collected from his own home. Dark and squat, huddled like so many frightened sheep, the houses of Lea Brook Square seemed to seek the shelter of the pottery kiln rising tall above them while on the opposite side of the road the lone black shape of a chapel seemed to shrink into the darkness. But though concern for Sara Melia had been genuine, it had not been all of his reason for sending her son home.

Then what had? Was it that he also felt an obligation to search for the girl he wished he could call friend?

Guiding the carriage along a still busy Dudley Street, his inward smile was grim.

He was not searching for a girl he would have as a friend. He was searching for the girl he loved.

*

'I waited at Moorcroft. A cleaning woman there told me Myra had not been at that house for some time but that I could wait in the yard against the mistress's return: I wanted to ask if it was that Myra was no longer employed in service there then could she perhaps tell me where I might find her. I waited so long but then, then I thought maybe the mistress was gone away and might not be returning for some time . . . but I had to try to find where Myra was, I had to, so I came here, I came to ask you, Aunt Dora.'

There were more than thought of the mistress of Moorcroft not returning had this wench afeared. Was it the same thing had filled them other two young 'uns with fear? Had this one had a brush with that killer? Dora Benson watched the girl gulping in air. No, it were not Ava Russell had the face of this wench pale with fright.

'You did right to come. Don't do to be on the streets by yourself, not these nights it don't.'

'I heard about Alfred Birks . . .'

'A bad business . . . he were a decent lad, so your grandmother told, always polite an' respectful.'

'It was a dreadful shock to hear, I thought it might have been some illness . . .'

Turned to the kettle simmering over the fire, Dora Benson felt her blood chill. The wench didn't know!

'. . . then today I learned it was not . . .' Dora's breath eased, '. . . today a woman told me a young man had been murdered. That was dreadful enough, but when she said a young woman had suffered the same it fair stopped my heart. All I could think of was Myra, could it be Myra had been killed!'

'Weren't Myra.' Dora turned from the fire, leaving the kettle on its bracket. 'Weren't your sister that maniac done for.'

Relief which had sung on hearing that same news from the woman in the kitchen of Moorcroft became tinged with guilt. It was not Myra's life had been taken, but did that give right to her own feeling, her own joy!

But she could not help feeling the wonderful comfort those words had given; she could not prevent the consolation of knowing the sister she loved was safe and well. Surely heaven would not blame her for that?

'I was so happy when I heard that woman say the name . . .' Eden's quiet confession was almost lost beneath the clang of hammers coming from the tiny workshop where the others of Dora's family worked at the nailing long into the night. 'Is that so wrong, Aunt Dora? I don't mean to be unkind.'

'Nor you ain't, wench, nor you ain't.' Eyes filled with sympathy rested again on the kettle, sympathy which turned to dread with the next quiet words.

'The woman could not tell me had Myra been dismissed her position. She said only that she had not see her at Moorcroft for some time. I thought you would know, Aunt Dora, I thought Myra would have come to you, maybe . . . Maybe left some word for me or . . . or perhaps said where she could be found.'

There was a mountain of grief in Eden Brent . . .

Dora swung the kettle from the heat of the fire . . . but the wench had higher mountains yet to climb.

'Did she, did she come here?'

At Dora's back the question was soft in its pleading but each syllable pricked her heart. She had seen this wench brought to Hobbins Street when nobbut a babe in arms, watched her grow, shared the caring of her and yes . . . felt the loving of her, like she were a daughter born of her own body. How then . . . how to tell a wench you loved as your own . . . how to break her heart? But seemed that were a burden placed on Dora Benson by the Lord hisself . . . who but Him? Drawing a long breath she turned to face the girl sitting beside her at the table. Who but the Lord . . . may He grant her strength!

A lull in the medley of hammering brought a moment's blessing of silence but Dora's ears were filled with the beat of her pulses. She had known that one day this might happen but had prayed that day be far in the future, that Eden Brent would have a man beside her, a man to hold her when night forced open the gate of tears, to comfort sorrow the slow passage of years could ease, yet could not erase. But Eden Brent was here now, and so was the time of truth. It would be a savage truth, cruel and heartless, one against which no barrier could be forged, no wall built high enough to close out the horror, to shield against the nightmare . . . It would be a gospel of truth, a gospel of pain!

The hammers resumed their clanging but to Dora,

caught by love for the girl watching her and the despair the telling of that truth would bring, it seemed each blow was a laugh of the devil.

But the devil's work had been done out there along of the Church Steps! No, this was not his ordaining; this was the moment chosen of the Lord, the moment of His bidding, and she must keep faith with it. Though the bitterness of that would be aloe on her tongue, she must tell all, there could be naught held back, naught left to question that would grow and fester in the darkness of doubt. But not to say what was known only to her, to keep secret what would always lie like a sword in her own heart, would that protect Eden Brent for ever . . . or would the ransom of silence be paid in vain?

'Yes, her come here.' Despite the clamour of the workshop the reply was quiet, each word showing pain on Dora Benson's thin, lined face. 'T'were a while since. Come to ask did I know of your whereabouts, where it were you might 'ave gone on leaving of your grandmother's house; but I could give no answer savin' the telling of your intent to leave Wednesbury altogether.'

'But where?'

'No, wench!' Dora lifted a hand against the interruption, 'Bide you quiet 'til the telling be done. Myra were all but spent when her reached this house. The walk from Darlaston had her exhausted, least so I thought. But it were not a fault of tiredness; that I realised next day when her couldn't rise from the bed I had laid her in, but the result of a sickness. The parish doctor were called for; we 'adn't the money to pay another. All credit to him, he examined her thorough. Myra had a sickness of the lungs, he said when that examinin' were over. It were one had been hurried in its path by lack of food and warmth, the neglect had been such that there were no escapin' of its result . . . Myra was dying. Cold had eaten into her, becomin' the pneumonia. That, together with the infection of the lungs, meant there could be no more'n a two day afore the end would come. Doctor said he would arrange for her to be taken into the infirmary along of the poorhouse . . .'

Eden's agonised sob brought Dora to her side. Holding her, feeling the emotions trembling wave upon wave, Dora's own mouth trembled. She had known the heartbreak her story would bring, she also knew she must give all of its telling.

'. . . I . . . I told him . . .' her voice cracking, she went on, '. . . I told him Myra Brent would lie in no poorhouse, that her would stay in this house with folk as loved her. I sat with her the rest of that day and though I begged her stay quiet, so her strength would last, her would 'ave none of it. Every word were pain to her, the coughing takin' her breath so it were longer and longer afore her could go on, but the look in her eyes, it were a look that pleaded time in which to tell. The all of what I could do for her was to listen and that I did though it had me pray the powers of heaven strike vengeance on the mistress of Moorcroft.'

Arms tight about the sobbing girl, Dora told the rest of her story. Of Myra's reason for the slap she had given, of her not knowing of her grandmother's dying, the abuse she had suffered only so there would be enough money to help her family and the futile search for her sister, one which ended when she had met Ava Russell in a dressmaker's shop.

'That woman vowed you was at Moorcroft, that should Myra not return to service there, then you would be made to practise all the vileness, perform them acts of wickedness herself had been forced into. That were summat Myra couldn't live with, nor turn her back on. Her would return to that house of hell but first her would come to one who might understand, one who in time could explain should her sister ever enquire why it was that slap were given and why it was the position at Moorcroft had been snatched from her. It was done of love.' Dora touched a hand to the head pressed to her chest. 'It were done to protect you. You asked did her leave some word for you? The answer be yes; her used her last pennies to buy pencil an' paper to write a letter, but there were no address on the envelope I found among her things so I kept it, kept it against the chance of meetin' with you.'

The envelope a blur amid tears, Eden lifted her glance. 'Myra, where . . . where . . . ?'

Her own throat so thick she could scarce answer, Dora dabbed her own tears with a corner of her apron. 'Her be alongside o' your grandmother. The folk of Hobbins Street, they all given of their ha'pennies and pennies. Together we scraped the cost of a box, plain though it were; and the little 'uns, them still at school, lads an' wenches both, they gathered the flowers that grows wild in the fields, bunched an' dressed them with leaf an' with ribbon took from Sunday frocks until every inch of that box were lost beneath the blossom: then the priest along of the church, him an' old Tom Higgins who digs the graves, they asked no payment. It be no consoling of the hurt the knowing of that will give now; the hurt you feels inside will go on for many a year, but this might, with the Lord's mercy, bring a comfort. Your sister were given a Christian burial, maybe not of the sort afforded your grandmother, for money d'ain't stretch to a stone to mark her, but the love that went along of Myra Brent, the respect with which her were laid to her rest can have no surpassing.'

Love and respect. Eden's eyes closed against the pain. Myra had been shown love and respect . . . but neither had been paid by her sister.

26

Moorcroft had been in darkness. No butler had answered his hand on the door and no scullery maid had answered at the kitchen. Where else was Eden likely to have gone? His fingers taut on the reins with anxiety, Andrew Denby's glance raked the street each side of the carriage. The one leading into the town from Lea Brook had been busy, as expected, but here in the heart of Wednesbury the difference was glaring.

The butchers' stalls in the Shambles were empty, no women hoping for a cheap cut of meat and no straw-hatted butcher tempting customers with calls of an extra couple of sausages with every pound bought. The narrow street was deserted as was the market square, its stalls lines of black-boned skeletons etched against the gloom of shadows retreating from the lantern lights of hotel and tavern, leaving darkness to gather over the empty square.

The town was afraid. What he had been told by David Melia, what he had heard from others when going about his business, the brutal murders of two young people had the whole of Wednesbury in fear.

Two killings . . . and the second victim had been a

young woman! Andrew Denby's blood chilled. Eden Brent was a young woman . . . and she was here in this town!

The hiss of steam from a train beginning its journey from the market place had the horse buck nervously; the jolt of the carriage jerked at Andrew's attention. He must not give way to the alarm lurking on the perimeter of his mind; he must stay alert if he hoped to find Eden.

Moorcroft was the house where her sister was employed. Murmuring softly to the still fractious animal, Andrew forced his brain to think calmly. That girl had obtained the position of ladies' maid whilst her sister had remained at home with their grandmother. Home! A frown of concentration heavy on his brow he strove to remember. Lord, why had he not paid more attention to what the lad had said. He had been eager to be gone, avid to begin the search for the girl who more and more claimed his thoughts . . . But rashness, as often he had found during boyhood, resulted in cold comfort.

Think! Fingers tight about the leather reins, he willed his mind to the conversation he had held with the Melia lad.

'. . . *Eden had remained with their grandmother* . . .'

Carts rumbling past, their drivers shouting their disapproval of 'folk daft enough to 'ave a carriage stood in the middle o' the road a' blockin' of folks' path', made no impression on Andrew.

'. . . *remained with their grandmother* . . . *lived at* . . .'

Lord, where was it David said she had lived?

Owen Street? A mental shake of the head rejected

the name. Think, man, think! What name did the lad say? Breathing deeply, Andrew pushed back the dread, once more sending cold fingers probing along his veins. It was 'O' something or other. The lad had been so anxious his words had fallen over one another. Oldbury Street . . . Ogden Street . . . No, it had been neither of those!

''Ow long yoh o'bin a' goin' to keep that there carriage a' blockin' o' the street!'

That was it! Relief sweeping through him, Andrew called an apology to an irate carter complaining loudly at his path being obstructed. Like his contemporaries, this man failed to give the beginning and ending requisite letter to many of their words.

''Ow long yoh o'bin!'

Tautness released from his fingers, he flicked the reins putting the horse to a trot.

'O'bin.'

He breathed a smile. The name he had tried to remember . . . it was Hobbins . . . Eden's grandmother had lived in Hobbins Street.

Too many days had passed. Ava Russell's mind swirled, a pool of acid. The agreement had been for one day . . . one day and then Myra Brent would be returned to Moorcroft. But that day had passed into two, then three, then . . .

But counting, like the waiting, would not bring that girl back . . . She would have to be brought, and she would!

Reaching for the bell pull beside the ornate fireplace, Ava felt the bile of anger surge fiercer. It was no use ringing for a cook who was no longer here, and that cleaning woman . . . She did not want the like coming to this sitting-room; the smell of carbolic soap, the patched clothing and dreary face were too distasteful. She could go herself to the yard and tell the gardener to harness the pony cart. Yes, it was a task she could perform, had not her husband had the teaching . . . But since when did Ava Russell keep a dog and bark herself! Besides . . . eyes glinting like ice-covered rock despite the heat burning inside, it did not do to let all and sundry know her skills.

Would it be more propitious to wait until those two cleaning women had finished for the day, until they had left the house? But that would be evening, dusk would already be falling; by the time she reached Darlaston night would have the streets dark. She could hardly look for Myra Brent at night.

A hesitant tap supplementing her irascibility Ava glared at the door. What could the fool of a woman be wanting? Had the orders given her not been explicit . . . even an idiot could have understood!

Timorous as the step of a church mouse during mass, the tap brushed the door a second time, bringing a sullen snap from Ava.

'Beggin' pardon, mum . . .' The speaker did not enter and Ava did not invite. '. . . be a young woman askin' for to see you.'

'I will see no one.'

'Yes, mum, but her asked to tell you . . .'

Was the woman a complete imbecile! Ava's nostrils flared her impatience. How long could she go on without a housekeeper, without a personal maid? The cleaning woman hadn't the brain of a flea!

'. . . her asked to say her called last evenin'.'

Mouth open to order the woman back to her duties, Ava closed it slowly. A young woman . . . called last evening . . .

Irritation becoming the dull glow of satisfaction, tight mouth curving, Ava stared at the partly open door.

Myra Brent had returned! Ava drew a long breath, feeling it carry the savour of satisfaction deep inside. Myra Brent had returned! Once more the fates had favoured Ava Russell.

Going to stand at the window, staring out towards the trees and bushes bordering the grounds, she smiled, a vindictive, vengeful movement of the mouth. Myra Brent had returned . . . she would be sorry she had ever left!

'Why did my sister leave this house?'

Flung with the force of stones the words hit, spinning Ava about. This was not the woman she had followed from the dressmaker's shop! The hair, the bone structure of the face, the way of holding the head all were the same; only the eyes were different, Myra Brent had blue eyes where as this girl . . . her eyes were blue-green, a beautiful turquoise. But there was one more difference: Myra's eyes had lost their fire while the ones that stared at her now spat repugnance, spewed loathing as a volcano spewed lava. But if this was who she was certain it must be then that repellence would add pleasure to pleasure. She would enjoy breaking this girl as she had enjoyed breaking her sister . . . and in the process enjoy more . . . Yes, she would enjoy *much* more.

Hiding this behind an affected glance of bewilderment, she gave a slight shake of the head. 'Forgive me . . . your name?'

'I think you know that already!'

The girl had fire. Ava nodded to herself. But there were many ways of dousing fires . . . and she would use them all.

'. . . but I will tell you. My name is Eden Brent. Myra was my sister.'

Was? Ava's pulse tripped on the word. Had this girl made a slip of the tongue, used the wrong tense . . . said 'was' in place of 'is'?

'I will ask again,' Eden's voice throbbed, 'why did my sister leave this house?'

Was that cleaning woman still standing beyond that half-open door, her ears flapping to catch every word? Words that would find their way into half the houses in Wednesbury.

'A moment!' Ava lifted a hand. 'I think you would not want every person in this household hearing what it is you may wish to speak of.'

Skirts whispering over thick turkey carpet, she crossed the room, then standing in front of the door she closed, faced a girl whose every fibre spoke hatred.

The pulse that had tripped a moment before took on a drumbeat. What did this girl know? Had Myra gone to see her? Was that the reason of delay in her returning? Had the fool of a girl told of . . .

'I have no objection to anyone hearing what it is I have come here to discuss,' Eden was speaking again, 'in fact I intend it become public knowledge!'

She must go carefully . . . find out exactly what had Myra's sister so incensed.

'My dear,' she said quietly, 'surely you must know your sister is with your grandmother? She is not in this house simply because she is on annual leave.'

Bitterness of a strength she had never known before, lanced the reply from Eden's taut lips. 'Myra is with our grandmother but she is not on annual leave . . . Myra is dead!'

Dead! Like choral music the word swelled in Ava's mind. Myra Brent was dead! The last threat to the safety of Ava Russell, to the keeping of her secret, was removed! But she must not allow the jubilation of that to show. That same affectation of a moment before creasing her brow, she gasped. 'Myra dead! But . . . but how . . . when?'

Eden's stare blazed pure fire. 'You might do better to ask the cause, but then you know that . . . and so do I.'

There was more than resentment burning in this girl, more than fury had her trembling; there was passion, the passion of hate. Ava felt the cold of warning touch her spine. She must go carefully indeed.

'I know the cause?'

'Yes!' Eden hurled the word. 'Yes, you know, for it was you, you and your vile practices. That was the reason for Myra's leaving, she could stand no more of your abuse!'

So Myra Brent had told of those little pleasures! But it would have been told only to this girl . . . Myra would have been too ashamed to divulge it to anyone else.

The lies of a chit of a girl against a woman of property! She must be made to realise the harm that could bring upon herself. But not only upon herself. The drumbeat continued in Ava's veins. Mud could stick as easily to silk as to cotton, as easily to the wealthy as to the poor.

All pretence sliding from her like a cloak, Ava's eyes were black ice. 'Take care, Miss Brent. Justice wields a heavy hand and accusation not justified has it strike hard.'

'Then you should be prepared for the blow. My sister is dead!'

A laugh of pure venom cut Eden's words, Ava's own spitting like a cobra ready to strike. 'Your sister is dead . . . Am I supposed to show sorrow?'

The sheer indifference, the total lack of compassion, caught in Eden's chest, squeezing away any trace of excuse she might have found for this woman's behaviour.

'No.' There was no exoneration, no pardon. Cold and implacable, Eden's response came quietly. 'No, you should not show sorrow, that would be only one more deception. But you will show fear, and believe me that will be no falsehood.'

'Fear!' Ava's laugh slid deprecatingly. 'Fear of you!'

Her glance steady, though the intensity of it blazed, Eden gave a brief shake of her head. 'No, not of me but of what I will bring to light. Your fear should be of the proof I have, the letter my sister left showing you for the creature you are – a vile parasite feeding on the needs of others, a viper whose poison is injected into any who come in contact with you. You carry the cancer of evil, the abscess of corruption. It is a canker of the soul, lust which knows no cure, no satisfaction except that of abusing an innocent girl, of using her poverty to lure her into carrying out your unspeakable demands and, once trapped, there was no escape . . . none but death.'

As will be your own only escape! Ice-cold, the thought sat in Ava's mind though her face showed no sign of its residence. Instead she answered calmly.

'I advise you take care not to let your words be heard beyond this room. Meantime, perhaps you would take with you the things your sister left behind. Please wait here and I will bring them to you.'

Fate had smiled, but the god of fortune laughed. Upstairs in her room Ava flung open the door leading to her dressing-room.

First Birks had met his death, then Dilly Madely had felt the embrace and now Myra Brent. All were dead, all threat they had held eliminated. But now that of Eden Brent hovered. Did she truly have a letter written by her sister?

Reaching inside a tall mahogany wardrobe, Ava found what she was looking for.

The god of fortune was laughing now . . . but the one who laughed last tasted success!

Halfway back to the head of the staircase, she paused. That cleaning woman! How dare she speak with a visitor to this house, even one as insignificant as the Brent girl. Mouth hardening, feet silent on the thick carpet, Ava walked several steps then halted. The voice . . . it was no longer that of the cleaning woman . . . It was not a woman at all. Body tense, every nerve alert, she listened to the words carrying indistinctly.

'Davy . . . he said you would not . . .'

'I had to . . . I could not go on . . .'

'Then you should have asked . . .'

That last was louder, deeper. The voice of a man! But what man? Husband of the girl or . . . Ava's hands tightened on the petticoat and drawers taken from the wardrobe . . . a member of the constabulary? Had Eden Brent spoken with the police?

She had said she had a letter . . . If that were true . . . if she had shown it to the magistrate! But doing so, would bring disrepute upon her own sister, have her name despised and herself shunned by everyone she knew. The girl was no idiot; she would have reckoned with the results of speaking with the police.

A breath calming her turbulence, Ava laid aside the underwear, one free hand smoothing the bodice of her gown. Whoever was the man with Eden Brent, he was no representative of the law.

'What could Myra have left in this house?' Closer to the head of the stairs, Ava heard the words clearly.

'. . . she would not have wished to keep anything that reminded her of this house.'

Deep and pleasant-sounding, despite the edge of anger, the man's response was equally audible.

'Then there is no reason to remain. I will tell that serving woman to inform her mistress we do not wish to wait.'

We! Ava glanced towards the sitting-room. Not a brother, Myra had no brother, nor had there been mention of a marriage within her family . . . but then Myra Brent had made very little mention of her circumstances.

'There is no need for you to stay. I can return to Gospel Oak by myself. I will be at Shipton Cottage when Davy calls.'

'You will not return alone. However, I respect your need to speak privately with the mistress of this house. I shall wait for you in the carriage.'

Not a brother . . . and, if not a husband, then who?

Ava remained perfectly still as the door opened, her eyes following the tall figure striding across the hall.

Andrew Denby! Ava's teeth clenched. He had been to this house before. Samuel had often done business with him, saying afterward he was a young man it would not do to trifle with. But why would he come traipsing after the Brent girl . . . was it simply the dog following the bitch?

Waiting until he was gone from the hall, she returned to the sitting-room.

'I'm sorry.' She faced the slight figure which had not moved. 'I am unable to find the things left in Myra's room. It seems my housekeeper has stored them away. If you will say where you are living I will have them sent on to you.'

Tense as her slight body, Eden's reply twanged the quiet of the once-elegant house. 'There is nothing here that I would want. I have not called for what I might take but for what I could give.'

'Give!' Ava's laughed return was scathing. 'What could a poverty-stricken slut give me . . . apart from lice!'

She had not been able to fully comprehend what she had read in Myra's letter. Part of her had not understood . . . not quite accepted the awfulness written there. Now, looking at the sneering face of the woman who had been her sister's employer, Eden felt the truth rise solidly in her throat. Ava Russell was all Myra had claimed. Malignity and malice gleamed in those stone-hard eyes, rank bitterness twisted a line of naked savagery about the mouth painting the face with a look of cold, heartless cruelty.

The cruelty she had shown Myra? Watching the thin lips compress in a vicious line, the eyes become hooded with threat, Eden owned to what sounded in her mind. Ava Russell was a woman of evil!

Eden's fingers curled tightly into her grandmother's shawl at the horror of what she now acknowledged. In that moment it seemed that beloved voice spoke.

'*Don't go lettin' her see you be feared, stand your ground, me little wench . . . show her the love of a sister.*'

Her head lifted with courage drawn from those inner words, and Eden's reply was steady.

'I can give you more than lice. I can give you that which will bite harder and be much more difficult to rid yourself of. I tell you, the time will come when you will regret the degradation you brought upon Myra, you will regret the vile acts you forced her to perform.'

Loud and snatched, a breath hissed between Ava's clamped lips. 'Are you threatening me?'

Tightness still holding her body, Eden looked into glittering serpent-like eyes and, for a brief moment, it seemed the evil of the woman reached out for her. Then, like a hand taking hers, the strength of her grandmother flowed warm along her veins.

'Not my threat but that of heaven. What you have done is judged by that power and it will not go unpunished. Retribution will be taken and from this day my every prayer will be that the Lord make me His instrument of revenge.'

27

'I thought he were goin' to strike me, I seen his hands curl into fists and I thought he were about to give me a beltin'.'

Walking beside Eden, a cloth-wrapped dish in his hands, Davy Melia related that morning's meeting with Andrew Denby.

'I told 'im, I said as I couldn't be at your side every minute, I couldn't go sleepin' at Shipton Cottage like I was your brother . . . but that d'ain't have the curbing of his anger. I swears I ain't seen him go up like that afore. Oh 'e has a temper, that's been shown more'n once along of the boatyard, but this were summat different. Mister Denby were not just angry he . . . he seemed frightened like. Why do you reckon that be? Unless he were feared of that killer that still don't be catched . . . reckon that be it. Mister Denby were worried for that man, couldn't rightly be no more'n that.'

No, it was no more than that, Andrew Denby had no more reason to be anxious for her than any decent man was for a woman's safety at this time. All of Wednesbury was anxious for their safety. But why come to Moorcroft himself? Why not send Davy to bring her home to Shipton Cottage?

'I said as I would go find you but he hadn't the listenin' of that, he were off outta that boatyard like the devil held a firebrand to his tail. I hopes this don't mean I won't get to walk with you no more.'

Her mind on words other than those now being spoken, Eden made no answer but, in the silence that followed, she heard other words echo clearly in her mind.

'*What did you think to gain in coming to that house!*' Andrew Denby had been silent until they had left the town centre and were on the way to the cottage, but then the anger held inside him had breached. '*Have you no sense . . . crossing the heath alone . . . For God's sake, girl, if you have no thought of yourself, at least have some for others! Consider their feelings instead of just your own!*'

That had been the torch which had put flame to the feelings churning inside her. She had wanted to avenge her sister, to tell Ava Russell she had come to Moorcroft to do just that. But that had been a siren song, a lure calling its promise . . . but that promise had proved false. Ava Russell had simply laughed her contempt and she . . . Eden remembered her helplessness . . . She could no nothing. Then, with Andrew Denby's accusation, the dam holding those feelings of inadequacy burst, letting free the torrent that swept away all of her grandmother's teaching regarding politeness to other people.

'*Feelings!*' It had snapped from her, a verbal onslaught, sharp and bitter. '*Just whose feelings would that be? Missis Ava Russell's, the woman who drove a young woman to her death? Or perhaps you mean those of an elderly man, one who cannot bring himself to speak a pleasant word? Or are the feelings you refer to those of a younger man whom it seems cannot keep from interfering in the life of another person, one who not only does not wish his attention but positively resents it! Allow me to tell you, Mister Denby, I find no reason or excuse for behaviour towards affairs that have no business with you. Your attentions are uncalled for and are most definitely unwanted!*'

'Be you angry with me, Eden?'

'What?' Drawn sharply from her thoughts by a tug at her arm, Eden glanced at the freckled face, its usual sunny look displaced by one of apprehension.

'I asked . . . be you angry with me?'

A quick smile meant to reassure having no effect upon the dismay evident in his eyes, Eden asked gently, 'Why would I be angry with you, Davy?'

'For going to the boatyard . . . For tellin' Andrew Denby you wasn't home in the cottage an' that I couldn't be finding you nowheres I looked, and for . . .'

'For what?' Eden prompted as the confession tailed away. 'We are friends, Davy, and true friends need have no fear of speaking of what they did to help the other.'

'That be what I thought I were doin', honest Eden. I were thinkin' only to 'elp, otherwise I wouldn't never 'ave told 'im . . . we be friends, you an' me, but you won't want that no longer . . . Not once you find I d'ain't hold to a confidence.'

A confidence! What could he be referring to? Seeing the slight tremor of a mouth he was trying so hard to hold firm, Eden hid her question behind a smile.

'Davy, whenever we have talked together have I once asked you never to repeat what I have said?'

'No . . . not so I recalls.'

'And you don't recall because such was never spoken, so how can you have broken a secret you were not asked to keep?'

'That be right, you d'ain't ask such . . .' the smile chasing the tremor from the boy's mouth faded as quickly as it came, '. . . but me mother, her won't judge what I said not near so gentle as you . . . It'll be a cuff around the ear an' no mistake, her says as I talk afore I think, an' it be right, I does . . . but I were feared for you, Eden . . . so feared that when Mister Denby asked 'ad you made mention of your life afore comin' to Gospel Oak I . . . I told 'im everythin'.'

That was how he had known to come to Moorcroft! He had followed her there not to interfere in her affairs but to calm a young lad's fears, to assure Davy she had come to no harm crossing the heath.

'. . . *I find no reason or excuse. . .*' That was what she had said of his behaviour.

Eden felt the sudden warmth of shame.

What would Andrew Denby think of her!

★

She had had the audacity to come here to this house . . . to threaten!

Her cleaning women gone for the night, Ava Russell stormed through the silent rooms of Moorcroft House.

A letter, she had said, a letter written by her sister. That, supposing any such letter existed, was the only real threat. Eden Brent was penniless, as her sister had been, a pauper who could only dream . . . but was that all she was? True, *she* may have no money but the man who had followed her . . .

A niggle of alarm brought Ava to a halt.

Andrew Denby was no pauper, neither was he without respect and influence . . . influence that would go a long way in this town, influence which, if brought to bear, could well have the mistress of Moorcroft standing in a court of law!

Damn the girl! Caught with a vicious kick, a delicate *guéridon* toppled, snapping a slender fluted leg against the wall. Glancing at the broken stand, its circular glass top shattered as was the Leroy et Cie clock it held, Ava swore again. That was one more of Samuel's treasures she had intended to sell; that, more than anything left in these near empty rooms, would have realised a decent price . . . something she expected from the sale of the foundry but as yet there had been no offers!

Why was it taking so long? Because it was a woman who was selling! Did they think her so gullible that should they hold out long enough that she would part with the business for little or nothing? They would roast in hell before that happened!

Roast in hell! Was that not the verdict of the pious given to those who 'brushed the muff', given by the oh-so-puritanical-holier-than-the-saints-of-heaven women, many of whom no doubt practised the same even as they whispered against it behind their hands? And was it not the condemnation meted out by those charlatans, men who took their pleasures with others of the same gender! Roast in hell. Ava laughed contemptuously. Hell would be pretty overcrowded!

But not all of that region's torments were experienced only after death; there were some that were visited upon the living, some like that which burned in her now, the desire screaming to be satisfied.

Having reached her bedroom, Ava stared at the door which led into her bathroom. She had dismissed all intentions of visiting the workhouse, of taking another girl to train to her requirements. With Myra's return and her sister to join her, the two of them living at Moorcroft, two to satisfy the need which pulled and twisted, to slake the ravening which flicked and whipped between the legs until she must try to appease the longing for herself. But the sedative of her own fingers, the remission they brought from that ferment of longing was fleeting; it did not impart that heady, exotic, breathtaking emotion, that wonderful sweep through the whole of the body which brought cries to the throat, cries which begged for more.

But Myra Brent was dead!

Going into her dressing-room Ava flung open the door of a large wardrobe.

Myra was lost and the sister also. There would be no chance now of having *her* come to Moorcroft as ladies' maid, not with Andrew Denby in the background. That would be taking too great a risk; as Samuel had once remarked, '*He was a man who did not happily concede what he felt to be his*'.

And he must feel that of Eden Brent. He must have some claim or else why follow her here?

The dog and the bitch! Ava's stomach jolted with the eroticism the thought aroused. She must find her own bitch.

She ought not to have spoken the way she had. Grating the lump of suet she had obtained fresh that morning, Eden's thoughts were on the events of the previous day.

Rudeness had never been allowed whilst her grandmother lived and all of her own and Myra's lifetime the lesson had been taught: 'Good manners cost naught.' But it was a lesson she had forgotten.

Reaching for the stale bread left to soak in water until it was soft, she squeezed each piece until the residue of moisture was removed, then broke it further with a fork.

She had snapped angrily at Andrew Denby, thrown her accusations like missiles. She had felt him stiffen beside her as he drove the carriage, but he had made no reply to her volleys. He had remained silent the whole of the way to the cottage then driven away, still without speaking a word.

She added the grated suet to the bread, folding the whole with sugar, mixed spice and sultanas, then stirring in a beaten egg.

She had been too angry, too absorbed in her own frustration, to care about the things she had said but that indifference had lasted only a short while. Now she found herself remembering the tightness of that face, the straight line of the mouth, but, especially, it was the look in those dark eyes as he had helped her from the carriage. He had hesitated before releasing her hand and, for a brief moment, his penetrating stare seemed to reach her very soul and in that stare had been . . .

Spooning the mixture into a well-greased roasting pan, then sprinkling the surface with sugar, she placed it in the oven.

. . . in it had been . . .

Straightening, she stared into the fire.

What had she seen in those eyes? She asked herself now as she had asked long into the sleepless hours of the night.

It had not been anger nor irascibility, it had seemed to be none of the feelings consuming her as she met that stare, there had been no irritability or waspish contention but only . . .

Eyes closing, a long breath drawn against what the silence of dawn had finally forced her to accept, Eden twisted the cloth held in tightening fingers.

. . . those eyes had held the look of a man filled with distaste and, as in those long wakeful hours, the realisation added to the sorrow in her own.

She opened her eyes, breathed out and returned to the task of preparing food.

She regretted her outburst, felt humiliated by the remembering of her bitterness, but one thought overrode all of that, one thought which had her heart twist: Andrew Denby despised her.

She had tried to dismiss the hurt of that, a hurt which matched that of knowing she could do nothing to repay Ava Russell's cruelty to Myra.

Long accustomed to the task of cooking her hands worked quickly, leaving Eden's mind to the misery of her thoughts.

'. . . *her every touch, the feel of her body beneath my hand burned inside like acid* . . .'

The words written in Myra's letter had branded themselves on Eden's soul.

'. . . *believe me, my dearest sister, I stayed at Moorcroft only so you and our grandmother be kept well and safe. What I did whilst under that roof can never be forgiven of heaven, nor of you. But I do ask, dearest Eden, that you believe me when I say, I did it for you, and for Grandmother, I did it out of the love I have for you both.*'

'I do believe you, Myra.' Eden whispered against the tears thickening her throat. 'I believe you and I forgive you as I know God also will forgive.'

But how to forgive herself? How to live with the

knowledge she could not avenge the wrongs done to her sister?

'Help me, Gran,' she whispered again, 'help me punish that woman for what she did to Myra.'

Tying a cloth about the basin holding the kidney pudding she placed it in the pan of water bubbling gently over the fire.

Her grandmother could not help. Nobody could!

I'm sorry, Myra. Her heart cried out as she washed the utensils used in preparing her dishes, the pain of her failure biting deep while she tidied the small room.

She could only speak those words to a memory, apologise to the sister she carried in her heart . . . but there was an apology she could speak aloud, speak it to a living man, and it must be made now.

Quickly ensuring all would be well with her cooking until her return, she placed the broom diagonally across the cottage door, her steps rapid as she ran along the towpath.

'Be a woman out in the yard.'

Andrew Denby looked at the boatyard overseer who had come into his office. 'A woman?'

The man nodded. 'It don't be nobody I knows from the boats, I ain't never seen her here afore.'

Pen resting between his fingers Andrew allowed the ghost of a smile. His overseer knew every wife, daughter, sister and granddaughter who helped man the narrowboats yet this one had him puzzled.

'What does she want?'

'Be a bloody cheek her askin' . . . no, her tellin' of what it be her wants.'

'Which is?' Andrew's tongue remained firmly in cheek.

'Her said her be here to speak with yourself and that her wouldn't be takin' her leave until her had done just that.'

An ultimatum . . . and to his yard overseer! There were not many *men* with nerve enough for that. The hovering smiled reach Andrew Denby's eyes. How would his reputation sit with the others of the yard hearing the demand of a woman! Keeping the thought to himself he asked, 'A name . . . did the woman give her name?'

'Ar, Mister Denby, sir,' the overseer nodded again, 'her said her name be Eden Brent.'

Eden Brent! Andrew's fingers whitened with the force suddenly gripping the pen. What had brought her here? Had she been . . . the man who had attacked her that evening along of the path leading from The Coppice, had he returned . . . found her alone at Shipton Cottage . . . had he . . . ?

'Will I tell her you be too busy to go speakin' with her?'

'No.' Snapping off the thought that made the blood run cold in his veins, he coughed to disguise the tremble of the reply. 'Tell . . . tell Miss Brent I will see her. Have her come in.'

Miss Brent! Returning to the yard, the overseer pursed his lips. He had not used the title 'Miss' even though it had not gone unnoticed the girl wore no ring on her finger, yet Andrew Denby had used it. Now, how come he knew her were no man's wife? And why the tremor in his voice when he had answered? The wench come to the boatyard might be unknown to some but her were certainly knowed by Andrew Denby.

28

What had she expected to find at that boatyard? The last of the day's chores completed and the next day's planned and catered for, Eden climbed the stairs to her room.

Her mind had been filled with the memory of the look she had seen in Andrew Denby's eyes and the nearer she got to his place of business the more she wanted to turn and run. But she had not turned, she had gone on, though it had taken every last ounce of determination to actually step into that yard and ask to see the owner.

The man she had asked that of had stared. In amazement that a young woman should demand he do as she requested? Or was it simply surprise that demand was to speak not with him, and not even through him, but to address herself directly to a man so obviously above her own station?

But, reluctant as he had been, the man had carried her request to his employer and, on his return to where she waited, he had touched a finger to his dust-laden cap before conducting her to that small room he said was 'the gaffer's office'.

She had never been in an office before.

Removing her clothes, laying them neatly over a chair, she sponged herself all over with water poured from a large jug liberally painted with pink briar roses.

She had lived almost every day of her life in Wednesbury, a town of a thousand workshops, metal foundries and coal mines. Yet, apart from Aunt Dora's brewhouse which served as a nail-making shop, she had never set foot in any one of them. Yet she had gone to that boat-building yard.

Fair hair, lightened by summer sun to pale gold and now released from restraining pins, shone in the light of the lamp placed beside the bed.

Her nerves had been stretched so much she had almost felt them twang.

She drew the hairbrush in steady rhythmic strokes through long silken strands.

The yard had been noisy with the sounds of saws and hammers, filling the air with the medley of sounds she had heard a distance away. One by one the sounds had ceased and the eyes of several dozen workmen had fastened on the figure of the young woman come to stand on their ground. Then, the one so obviously in charge had walked towards her and, in that moment, she had been terrified.

Eden set down the hairbrush, both hands pressing down on it to still the trembling that came with the recall of those few moments.

She had watched the figure approach, but it had not been the workman she had seen. Eden swallowed, the restriction building even now in her throat. The yard around her had faded, its place taken by a room with cotton lace curtains closed across its windows, a dark heavy sofa and, in one corner, glass-fronted cages of stuffed birds that added to the overall gloom. But it was not the room with its tiny dead birds that had her trembling; it was a woman . . . a gaunt sharp-featured woman, cold eyes gleaming, voice harsh and breathy as she reached for a young girl, a girl she ordered sharply to '*Remove your bodice and drawers* . . .'

Deep breaths stilling the shake of her hands, chasing the ogres of childhood, Eden stared about her own small room, resting a glance on chair, washstand, bedside table, each object giving reassurance that this, and not those pictures in her mind, was real.

Had she been trembling when that workman had reached her, when he had asked what was her business there at the yard? Perhaps not visibly, but it had to have been that old fear, a fear she had thought buried so deep inside of her that it would not rise again, that had made her answer as she had.

Grandmother would not have approved. Going to kneel beside her bed, Eden's smile was faint but her heart beat strong with love as she whispered, 'I apologised to that workman, Gran, I said I was sorry to have been so rude.'

And she had also apologised to Andrew Denby.

Her prayers said, Eden turned out the lamp, then crossed to the window, drawing open the shutters to a gentler, almost silver, light.

He had risen from behind a wide desk as she had entered that office. Broad and tall, it was he, not the wooden cupboards set along the walls, seemed to dominate the room and again she had felt the urge to turn away, to run back to the familiar surroundings of Shipton Cottage.

She might even have done that except he was around the desk and helping her to a chair before her feet would move.

Was something wrong? Had she been hurt in any way? Had someone come to the cottage?

Eden stared down at the silvered ribbon of water winding into the mystery of the darkened heath, but the mystery that held her was not that of night-shrouded land but of the look she had seen in Andrew Denby's eyes as he touched her. It had not been the stare of distaste; she had been wrong. He did not despise her.

A small cloud skipped across the huge silver orb sending shadows skimming across the water.

Shadows, too, had skimmed across those dark eyes. Shadows that had disappeared quickly, but not before she had seen what they held. It was not the look she thought she had seen the day he fetched her from Moorcroft. Today she had caught a glimpse of something far removed from that. Concern? Disquiet? No, his look had held . . .

Forehead touching the cool glass of the window-pane, Eden felt the rush of warmth to her cheeks.

It had held what her grandmother's look had held

when comforting a grazed knee or a cut finger . . . Those eyes had gleamed not with reproach but with affection.

But that was as much of a fantasy as dragons under the bed had been to a child, and it must be banished as she had banished other imaginings!

Moving from the window, Eden climbed into bed.

The man had been concerned to know her reason for going to the boatyard and on hearing it had accepted her apology with polite words.

But they were not the words of his eyes.

Heat flooding again into her veins, Eden turned her face towards the glittering window.

No, they were not the words of his eyes!

'I tells you, wench, them there faggots and that pressed chawl be a meal folk on the cut be happy to pay for. Ar, and many the folk as don't work the cut would be just as glad of the chance of buyin' or I be a Dutchman . . . and I ain't that.'

Handing his coins to Eden, then taking up his plate of faggots, the boatman breathed the delicious aroma of the steaming meat.

'I don't be coddin' when I says what I just told,' he smiled back from the sun-filled doorway. 'There be many a folk be glad of the chance to buy theirselves a meal the like of this. You just tek a few to market and see if I don't be right.'

He was not pretending. Eden watched the lithe figure leap aboard a narrowboat. Her food would find ready sale. That was no more than the word of a hungry man! But there were other hungry mouths . . .

'Help me . . . show me the way.'

Whispers so often spoken in her prayers returned vividly. Was that prayer being answered? Was she being shown the way? But even should it be as that boatman had said, should her food sell, how could that help avenge the wrongs done a sister? How could it help show Ava Russell for the evil woman she was, help prevent the horror Myra had lived with being visited upon some other unwitting young girl?

'You said I might call when passing this way.'

Immersed in her thoughts, Eden had not heard the light tap on the door.

'I hope you meant it.'

Flustered by the appearance of the figure which had troubled her sleep, Eden stumbled a reply. 'Of . . . of course . . . Would you care for some tea?'

It was all that would come to her tongue and she took refuge in it, turning to lift the kettle and scald the tea leaves placed ready in the little brown teapot.

'That would be most welcome, especially were it accompanied by a piece of that bread pudding David Melia sings the praises of.'

Those smoke-dark eyes . . . had they held that look . . . could it have been . . . ? Stop that! Censuring herself sharply and silently. Eden clattered cup against saucer. Fetching milk from the coolness of the scullery, the self-reproof continued to ring in her head. She must not allow that thought ever . . . she must wipe it from her mind . . . she was not a child and she could not harbour silly childish thoughts! Andrew Denby had looked at her with concern, nothing more than that . . . nothing!

'David was not exaggerating.' The tip of a finger rescuing a sultana threatening to fall, Andrew Denby smiled, pushing it into his mouth. 'This is truly delicious. Might I buy some to take with me? There are those at the yard who would really enjoy a piece with their mug of afternoon tea.'

'*. . . there be many a folk be glad of the chance to buy . . .*'

'But that is presumptuous of me.' Andrew caught the essence of a frown.

'No,' Eden answered quickly. 'It . . . it is just so strange.'

'Strange?' He laughed. 'What is so strange about men enjoying a delightful snack?'

'Nothing.'

Taking the tea she had poured, Andrew's smile gave way to a frown.

'I thought we had agreed upon no more misunderstandings between us.'

'It was a narrowboatman.' Eden knew a logical reply was called for. 'He called a while ago to buy faggots . . . they are something of a favourite with the canal people . . . He said there could be a market for some of the dishes I make and . . . well, it seemed something of a coincidence when you also asked could you buy some.'

'Boat people are well known for their common sense. If they say a thing is good, then you can rely on the fact that it is and, in the case of your bread pudding, I agree with the man. You should take his advice.' Andrew's smile returned. 'Take some of what you make, offer it to a wider market. You never know what can be achieved unless you try.'

They could almost have been a match for her grandmother's words; she had always said, 'A body don't have the knowing of what they can do if they don't never try.'

Wrapping a dozen slices of the fruity pudding in a fresh white cloth, Eden placed it in a basket alongside two trays of faggots and several pots of pressed chawl.

She had thought a long time on the words of the narrowboatman and of Andrew Denby. She had also thought on her own grief at Myra's suffering and her overwhelming need to ensure it happened to no other girl. Was this that way?

She had asked herself that same question, her mind repeating it again and again in the quiet hours of the afternoon until at last she had admitted the answer. Only heaven can tell.

The market place was as she remembered it. Eden's throat tightened as she looked at stalls familiar from her earliest days. She knew many of the women by name and, as she passed, they called their pleasure at her return and Eden smiled her own. Even if not one ounce of what she set out now on an empty stall should sell, her journey would have been worthwhile.

But it had sold. Every last crumb, every last scraping

of potted chawl, and many of the customers had asked would she be here again tomorrow?

Empty dishes placed in her basket, the cloth folded neatly on top, she called her goodnights.

'You tek care now, wench,' an elderly woman called as she packed her goods on to a small handcart. 'You get yourself straight 'ome and don't go dawdlin' . . . You don't want to be found as another young wench were found last night . . . found with her throat slit and her poor body laid open from stomach to chest . . . Rumour has it an old man usin' a walkin' stick were seen near where her lay . . . But an old man needing a stick to help him walk wouldn't 'ave the strength to go attackin' no young woman, now would he?'

Another murder! Eden felt her stomach contract. The day was already turning to evening. The streets were filling with shadows . . . and somewhere among them a killer watched and waited.

She had promised Davy she would always wait at Shipton Cottage, that she would not make that evening walk along the towpath unless he were with her. The basket clutched tight to her middle, Eden walked as quickly as she could. It had not been evening when she set out, the sky had not been filling with shadows, but she should have taken account of the time it would take walking to and from Wednesbury market place.

'. . . *When are you going to think of other people's feelings and not just your own?*'

She could imagine Andrew Denby hurling those words at her, but what words would he hurl at Davy?

Would he accuse him, say he was not doing that which he was supposed to do? But it was not Davy's suggestion she had followed, not his recommendation she take some of her cooking to sell in the market . . . but then neither had Andrew Denby advised she do so that very afternoon!

It had felt good having him sit at her table, having him smile at her instead of frowning, of seeming to enjoy their new-found cordiality . . . but how much of that would be left tomorrow? How would that fragile friendship stand when again he found her to be the same thoughtless, self-centred person he had found huddled against a canal bridge?

An ache pulling beneath her ribs, Eden slowed her steps to a steadier walk but her thoughts raced on.

What did it matter how Andrew Denby thought of her? She did not rely upon him for her living whereas part of Davy's and his mother's income did; should that be taken from them . . . should she be the cause . . . !

Halting abruptly, Eden was elbowed aside by a hurrying woman, several small children holding to her skirts, her voice echoing a trace of fear as she mumbled 'Some folk don't have common sense enough to get themselves 'ome nights!'

She had not used common sense. She had given no thought to not being back at Shipton Cottage by the time Davy called . . . of the consequences. Would Andrew Denby take away the Melias' living?

The grind of a steam train halting alongside, the call of its conductor to several alighting passengers to 'be safe 'ome', settled any argument her mind might have given. She would not allow the Melias to suffer on her account. Glancing only once the way she must take, she turned off Lea Brook Road to run quickly along the track that would lead across the heath, past the sad and beautiful house that was The Coppice and on towards the towpath.

She had hoped to run all of the way. The ache she had thought to be easing pulled more savagely, allowing each breath to be only short and shallow. A moment . . . a hand pressed to the pain throbbing beneath her ribs . . . a moment to catch her breath . . .

But in that moment, breath locked in her throat.

There along the track a few yards ahead of her, stepping free from a bank of grey shadow . . . an old man leaning on a walking stick.

She could go back . . . she could turn around and go back to Lea Brook Road. Transfixed by the sudden freezing of her limbs, Eden's stare remained on the figure slowly closing the gap between them.

'*. . . An old man needing a walking stick . . .*'

Fear transforming the words to ice blocks in her chest, Eden fought for breath that would not come.

'*. . . old man . . . walking stick . . . old man . . .*'

Like a hammer on an anvil it clanged in her brain, screamed in her mind and beneath it all was the urge to run.

He was coming closer. She could see him clearly now. Lungs tight and burning for breath she could not take, mesmerised by fright, she watched the slow approach. Etched against the fading light, the colour of clothes was indistinguishable, the face drooped to the chest invisible, but the stick . . . the stick moved in determined rhythm . . . in rhythm . . . but the sound!

Like a pencilled sketch, the shadowed scene she looked at became a night-veiled garden, a garden of trees and bushes black silhouettes against a charcoal sky, and the sound reaching her became the sound she had heard the night she had waited in that garden, waited for Ava Russell to return to Moorcroft, sounds that had helped send her hurrying away. She could hear them again now; a step, then silence . . . a step, then silence . . . The step was an old man's foot crunching on the pathway . . . the silence the result of his stick falling on grass!

'. . . *an old man needing a walking stick* . . .'

Breath returning on a cry, Eden saw the head lift, watched the stick rise, but the blackness that swallowed her closed the face away.

29

'Eh, you 'ad me all of a sweat . . .'

Davy Melia looked at the girl he had half-carried to Shipton Cottage.

'. . . I seen you lyin' all of a heap and I thought for sure I would need be callin' Webbs.'

'No.' Eden managed a pale smile. 'No, Davy, I wasn't needing the attentions of the undertaker.'

'So I found when I reached you, but Lord, you give me a turn. How come you was there . . . an' after promisin' never to tek that grumpy old bug . . . that old man a meal lessen I walked you there.'

There was reproach in the tone but Eden recognised the underlying concern.

'I was not taking a meal to him.' Accepting the tea in which he had stirred a spoonful of honey, she told of the narrowboatman, Andrew Denby's visit, of her subsequent journey to the market at Wednesbury and of her wanting to be home when he, Davy, came to walk her to the old man's gate.

'That be all well an' good,' he answered as she finished speaking, 'but bein' here the time I come for you shouldn't 'ave had you tekin' the way across the heath. Did nobody tell you. . .'

What had he been about to say? Eden accepted a second cup of honeyed tea. Had nobody told her she should have sense enough to stay off the heath with the approach of evening? Or that a killer had once again struck in Wednesbury?

'Still, you be safe 'ome now, so that's it and all about it.'

'No, Davy, that is not all that need be said.' Eden lifted a glance to the young face she had seen bending over her on that darkened pathway. 'As usual, I acted without thinking. It was foolish, I know that now, and, believe me, I am sorry I caused you concern; as for Andrew . . . Mister Denby, I will explain. I will tell him of my not being in the house, I'm sure he will not take employment from you and your mother.'

If only himself were as sure. Davy hid the thought behind the sipping of hot tea. That look on the man's face when told Eden could not be found . . . the way he had ridden from the boatyard as if all the devils of hell were at his back . . . it proved that, where Eden Brent were concerned, Andrew Denby were capable of more than giving two people their tin.

'You needn't add worry of that to your fears,' he said, putting his cup aside. 'Mister Denby be sharp at times but he don't be a man to let spite rule his head; but summat ruled your'n to 'ave you faintin' as you did. Was it summat you seen?'

He had not seen the figure on that path? He had not

seen an old man raise a walking stick? But he was there . . . the man was there, Davy *must* have seen! But Davy had made no mention of seeing anyone, not spoken of a bent figure walking with a stick! Eden's brow creased in a frown. Davy had said nothing of seeing anything or anyone except herself. That meant the whole thing had been a figment of her own imagination, an illusion built out of fear; unreal, a figure formed of shadows . . . but shadows made no sound as they moved!

'No . . . no it was nothing I saw. I was running . . . I caught my foot against a stone and tripped.'

It was a lie. Had she told it for Davy's benefit or her own? Told it to allay his fears or hers?

'Reckon you don't feel you wants to walk along of that house tonight. That old man can go without a meal . . . he don't deserve it anyway.'

She did not want to walk that dark path, to watch the shadows loom and merge, their black arms reaching for her. But not to go might arouse Davy's suspicion that it had not been a trip over a stone that made her fall senseless to the ground.

'You have reckoned wrongly, Mister Davy Melia.' Forcing a smile, she took a freshly laundered cloth from a line strung above the fireplace. 'It is a little later than usual so I would rather you went home, I don't wish to have your mother worry.'

'It be me needs worry should I let you go along of that house by yourself; I wouldn't get to sit down for a week after the tanning my backside would get.'

Not to mention the tongue lashing he would get from

Andrew Denby! Keeping the thought to himself he took the dish of faggots from Eden. Laying it in the centre of the cloth he gathered the four corners together and tied them into a knot.

'I thinks it be a waste o' time goin' to that place.' He glanced to where Eden was ensuring the fire was safe to leave. 'That old man, he were not to the house when we called last night so what's to say he won't be there again tonight.'

. . . He were not to the house . . .

. . . A young wench with her throat slit . . .

Poker in hand, Eden stared into the heart of the glowing fire.

. . . an old man . . . a walking stick . . .

Pulses pounding, fingers gripping the poker, Eden felt fear prick like broken glass against her throat.

. . . an old man . . . a young wench . . . last night.

Words shouted in her mind.

A figure in the shadows.

Shadows made no sound!

'Will I do that, Eden? Will I go take this on my own?'

Dragged from her thoughts by Davy's words, she replaced the poker with trembling fingers, rattling it against the grate.

'. . . it might be best I should. Seems to me you don't be up to trekkin' along of that house tonight.'

Either Davy had not noticed her trembling or he was tactfully overlooking it. Swallowing the razor sharpness in her throat, a breath steadying her shaking nerves, she turned.

'A walk in the fresh air is just what I need; it will blow the cobwebs away.'

'You be sure you be up to it?'

His look could not be mistaken for dislike. Eden smiled into clear brown eyes. It was open and honest, it spoke words of the heart, words which said he felt true concern.

Her own look gentle with gratitude, Eden nodded.

'Quite sure, Davy.'

It was a denial of what churned inside. Walking beside him along the towpath, she took no comfort from the light of a high moon, no reassurance from the black hulks of moored narrowboats.

She had not wanted to take that meal. Turning off the towpath, Eden felt cold fear against her spine. Trees she had taken no notice of before seemed to lean their branches over her head, twining them together until she was enclosed in a whispering tunnel of darkness.

A figure in the shadows.

Stifling a sob of fright, she drew closer to the lad walking beside her.

'T'were a shock to me, an' no mistake. For a minute my brain wouldn't have the tellin' of who it were stood in that kitchen, an' then I realised. It were him from the cottage along at the entrance to the drive.'

'The elderly man?'

'I felt like that when I turned to see who stood behind me.' Sara Melia answered the surprise in Eden's question. 'I tell you, I couldn't 'ave been more taken aback were I sittin' in the Queen's chair being crowned with gold. I hadn't been cleaning no more than an hour when he come.' Breaking the explanation only long enough to observe the ritual of drinking tea, brought from home, she went on. 'D'ain't give no reason of asking and I called for none. All he said were would I come to Shipton Cottage and ask would you walk along back with me and this were given along of the request.' Digging into a pocket of her dark skirt, Sara held out an open palm displaying a half sovereign. 'Reckon he must want to meet with you summat serious to pay such a sum. But that don't go meaning you 'ave to go along there should you not feel you wants to . . .'

A figure in the shadows.

A frisson of alarm settled along Eden's spine.

'He be there still; I felt I shouldn't ought to have left him sit a' waiting in the kitchen, not with me being entrusted to see the contents of that house come to no harm, but then a man of his years can't be like to do damage.'

A figure raising a walking stick . . .

Alarm became trepidation, bringing a tremble Eden tried to hide.

A shadow whose footsteps carried sound!

Davy might not have seen. Anxious in his searching for her, he could easily have missed a figure in the shadows . . . But she had not missed it . . . she had not missed seeing a figure raising a walking stick . . . the figure of the man who lived below that large house.

'You don't needs to go.' Sara caught the shudder. 'I'll just tell him as you be busy along of your cookin' . . . A wench can't be expected to leave off doing what brings her living just 'cos he asks it. Whatever he might want the sayin' of can have no spoiling by the waiting for evening . . . No doubt yourself and my lad will be walking there with a dish of summat though were it me in your place I wouldn't give the surly old soul the time o' day much less a meal.'

Those few moments enough for her to banish the thoughts bringing a shiver to her spine, Eden pretended a frown. 'Now, why is it I do not believe that?'

Her cup emptied, Sara Melia carried it into the scullery, long years of tidying after husband and son having her wash and dry them despite Eden's protest.

'It were a welcome sup.' The older woman smiled. 'I don't go making myself tea while I be to that house. I don't feel it to be my place and as for using that there crockery . . . Lord, I be terrified even to look, let alone touch! I swears it be finer than a moth's wing. But standin' here gossipin' won't buy the babby a new hat, as my mother used to say, so I'll be off back to my cleaning and this . . .' she took the coin from her pocket, the gleam of it glowing against her palm, '. . . well, he can have this back. Reckon that man thought the giving of such a sum would have me coax you against your will. But the old bugger can give 'imself a headache with the thinking, for coaxing a wench to do aught her has no will for doing don't be Sara Melia's nature.'

'I know that well enough,' Eden answered, as they

returned to the living-room. 'I will come with you, it should only take a few minutes.'

'But your cookin'?'

Had Sara seen her fear? Was the woman offering her a way of refusing to go meet with that man? But a half sovereign was more money than Sara might see for weeks of cleaning . . . and saying she would return it was no lie. The Melias were poor as herself but they had that same pride, pride which said 'Take only what has been earned'; and Sara had earned it by doing as she had been bidden. But this woman's mind worked, much the same way as Grandmother's. She, too, would have thought by returning alone the man might suspect her of simply finding a spot to sit ten minutes then returning with a reason to say why the girl had not come . . . and Grandmother's self-respect, like that of Davy's mother, would have her refuse to accept any payment overshadowed with suspicion.

All of this fleeting through her mind, Eden covered a large shallow roasting pan with a clean white cloth. 'This will keep until I get back and the faggots have only just gone into the oven so they will take no harm.'

'Bread pudding.' Sara nodded towards the covered pan. 'Now, there be a favourite of my lad . . . Has a sweet tooth same as did his father . . . God rest him . . . They would both eat a pan to theirself hadn't I been there to whip it from their hands, but I don't be sayin' nothing you don't know already for I hears every night of some titbit or other he be given along of your kitchen. I tells him it don't be polite to take without giving but I swears a brick wall has sharper ears than that one when he don't want to hear.'

'The pleasure of Davy's company is all the giving necessary. Please don't forbid him accepting those titbits.'

'Fat lot of good the trying would do.' Sara waited until the broom was placed across the door. 'That rogue would just get himself along to Denby's boatyard to be given a piece of pudding from there.'

Sara knew of the tray of bread pudding which went every day to that boatyard. Eden's cheeks coloured. Did she also know it was Andrew Denby himself who fetched it, that each time of calling he seemed less inclined to leave . . . and could he ever guess she wanted his visit to go on, wanted him to stay? But, of course he could not, nor must he! They had become friends, she would not have that friendship embarrassed by showing what daily was growing inside her . . . her love for Andrew Denby.

'That is offensive!'

Ava Russell's gloved fingers tightened, clutching the bag resting on her knee.

'Am I supposed to find it amusing? Was the offer supposed to have me smile? I assure you I find it quite the reverse and you may tell the bidder so.'

'I will, of course, do as you say, but might I suggest you give some thought . . .'

'Give some thought!' Resounding from the walls of the quiet room, the explosive response had the solicitor's clerk look up from his own desk beyond the glass partition. 'Give some thought to that? The offer is preposterous!'

Stubby fingers touching in a pointed arch, a plump bland face rested a chin on their tips, but the eyes regarding Ava held no such aspect. Sharp, acute, with an intelligence not detected by a first glance at the neatly whiskered face, they watched the annoyance play over the angry face. Ava Russell was a woman heavily in debt, a mortgage loan of five hundred pounds, not a penny of which had as yet been paid . . . and there was as much chance of seeing pigs fly as seeing that happen!

Expression bland as before, the solicitor lowered his hands. 'Of course, that is how this must appear to you.' He touched the paper Ava had flung back across the desk. 'But I would remind you it is the only offer to have been made.'

'So far! The only one so far!'

'The only offer made so far.' An inclination of his balding head acknowledged the outburst. 'That, if I might say so, speaks for itself. The property you have placed on the market has attracted one enquiry, the one which has resulted in the offer made here.' He tapped the paper with a forefinger. 'That would indicate what I have suspected for some time.'

'And what might that be?'

'The market for iron has declined. The demand now is for steel. To adapt the foundry to the making of that commodity would require a large amount of outlay. Should you envisage the making of steel tubes, for example, you would need to install one of the new Bessemer furnaces, draw bench, screw press and dies, plus various other tools. I advise you weigh the cost involved against the competition of existing steel works, of which the town has several.'

There was no money for the alterations he outlined. Teeth clenched almost painfully together, Ava was silent. The loan made by the bank was all but spent and it was a certain fact they would loan her no more.

'Do you wish me to instruct this offer be unacceptable?'

Watching the stubby fingers take up the paper, Ava's brain flipped through the possibilities open to her. She could hold on to the foundry, wait for the market in iron to revive; she could try raising funds elsewhere, but those were dead-end ideas. Iron smelting might never revive and, as for raising funds elsewhere, she would need collateral . . . But the house was already mortgaged and there was nothing else on which she could raise money. But money was what she needed; funds enough to take her from Wednesbury . . . from England . . . a house in Italy, no scandal of unpaid debts would follow her there.

'Will I write the offer is rejected?' The paper held at an enquiring angle the solicitor's razor-keen glance watched the hard face of the woman who had squandered Samuel Russell's wealth and brought his business to ruin. She had consistently refused to listen to advice, now she was about to pay the price.

'No . . .'

The expected answer, long drawn out as if it had required much thought, found no sympathy with its listener. The wife of Samuel Russell deserved none.

'No,' Ava said again, 'you will draw up a contract of sale. I wish to be rid of that property.'

The buyer had wanted only the land. Outside in the street she stood a moment breathing against the bile of anger and the cold bitterness of disappointment and frustration. The sum agreed was paltry and that solicitor had known, as he had known she would not refuse to accept it. Only the land! She all but spat the words. How much truth was there in such a claim and how much would prove to be a lie? But, truth or lie, that offer had been the only one made and, galling as it was, she had known she must accept or have a dead foundry hang indefinitely about her neck.

Time . . . that was a luxury she could not afford, time would make public the straits in which she now found herself, could eventually show the level to which she had fallen . . . time could destroy her!

But not if she moved quickly, and money from sale of the foundry would ensure accomplishment of that. She would tell no one her plans, not even the few servants remaining at Moorcroft. And the remainder of debt outstanding? A smile cold inside, she proceeded to walk along Lower High Street towards the town centre. Debt outstanding . . . that too would be left behind!

30

She and Davy had come here last evening, brought a meal to the man's gate. Beneath Sara Melia's conversation Eden's thoughts ran wild. It had appeared that, yet again, he was not home. The thought had brought respite from the fear which had nagged at her, eased the urge to grab Davy and run; but the lapse had been short lived. With their coming to the gatepost, the exchange of one dish for the other not quite completed, had come the sound which brought back all the dread, all the terror which had swept away her senses a short time before . . . Crunch and silence, crunch and silence . . . the sound of a step on hard ground . . . the silence of a walking stick on grass!

Even now, in broad daylight, Eden felt the same shiver she had felt then, the dryness which had grabbed her throat as a figure stepped from the shadows surrounding the small house.

It was the figure she had seen on the path . . . the same figure which had raised a stick! Fear had leapt in every nerve, fear which had shown as she had met that old man's eyes, seen the look which had said he had known her thoughts, said yes, he was the figure she had met on that path, fear that had verged on panic as for almost the first time he had spoken. Quiet and soft the words had followed as she turned away. 'We will meet again . . . soon.'

Davy had made no comment and she had been thankful for that but, once he was gone and she was alone in Shipton Cottage, the words had preyed on her mind. Had his words been a threat, were they saying the attack foiled by Davy's arrival would be repeated? But why attack her, what had she done to deserve such?

But what had Alfred Birks done? What had the two young women who had suffered the same fate been guilty of?

'*. . . an old man needing a stick to walk with . . .*'

The stallholder telling of a third killing had said an elderly man using a walking stick had been seen in the area of the murder.

. . . an old man needing a stick.

It rang in Eden's brain as it had rung last night. The man living below The Coppice used a walking stick . . . and on the evening of that murder he had been absent from his home!

'He don't be there . . .'

Sara turned to where Eden's steps had automatically come to a halt.

'. . . least that don't be where I left him. He were up there.' She flicked her head in the direction of the house at the end of the wide tree-lined drive.

Pulled so quickly from thoughts tumbling frighteningly in her mind, Eden's brows drew together.

'I know, wench.' Sara Melia smiled, mistaking fear for confusion. 'Set me to wonderin' same as yourself. Come to that house bold as brass and nothin' to show permission forrit he did . . . Lord, I should 'ave had more sense than leave him sit there . . . and stands to reason that be where he is still or else he would be here a' waiting at his own gate . . . which my own two eyes tells me he ain't.'

Was he truly in that house . . . or was he here in this small cottage? Was he watching unseen from one of its windows, waiting until she returned to pass this cottage alone? And what then . . . would he attack her as he had attempted to do yesterday, was that to be the fulfilment of the threat behind his quiet 'We will meet again . . . soon?'

Would Eden Brent become the fourth victim of a killer?

He had apologised immediately for not staying beside her on that path. He had seen her approaching, had waved his stick to draw her attention; he must have startled her for she had missed her footing and pitched forward. She had been unconscious and, knowing he could not carry her, he had made for the canal basin. There would be men there to bring her home and the wife of a boatman to care for her, but by the time they returned she was gone. He had intended walking to Shipton Cottage to enquire as to her wellbeing and offering his apology there, then moments later she and Davy had come as usual.

So why had he not given his apology then? Her brain had asked but her tongue had remained silent while his explanation went on.

'An old man is not as agile as he would wish. By the time I came from the rear of the house to the gate you were already left. I needed to tell you all of this, that is the reason for my asking you to come to The Coppice.' But had that truly been his reason . . . or behind the apology was there another?

Questions had torn at her, their answers whispering in her mind, answers which now brought the mark of shame to her cheeks. Climbing into bed, Eden's eyelids closed hard on the memory.

Fear! She had given in to fear, allowed the nightmare of it to override all common sense. She had mentally accused an elderly man, one about whom she knew virtually nothing, had convinced herself he had been about to attack her . . . depicted him in her own thoughts as a vicious, mindless killer.

The shame of that still weighed heavily. What would Grandmother have made of her stupidity . . . and would she have termed what had happened in that beautiful house called The Coppice even more stupidity?

Eyelids lifting, Eden stared into darkness concentrated by lack of moon.

He had been where Sara Melia had said she had left him. The same man who had accepted gifts of food without a single word of gratitude but, as he had risen to his feet on her entering the huge kitchen, Eden had become aware all was not the same. Lines about the eyes and greying hair and drawn cheeks depicted the years but, though he still held the walking stick, his body was somehow straighter, the droop gone from his shoulders; but it was the smile had struck her most . . . it had been a smile of happiness. Where she had convinced herself waited threat had waited welcome.

Deep in the well of darkness that was her bedroom it seemed the smile shone out at her again.

He had thanked her for giving of her time, for pandering to an old man's request. His voice had held no gruffness, none of the surliness Davy had often complained of, but a gentle pleasant tone as he also thanked Sara for her errand, though it became firm when refusing to take back the proffered half sovereign.

'Do you recall?' He had turned to her but had not asked Sara to leave, '. . . once telling me that in order to find that which was lost I must need face my heart?'

She had used those words, words which in turn she had spoken to herself. To find the cause of the love she had lost, a sister's love, she must have the courage to face her own heart, the courage which had taken her to Moorcroft.

Not quite fully recovered from the fright of going to that house, she had answered with a nod and he continued.

'That is what I have done. Though it took many weeks I did at last come here to this house.'

'This house?'

'Yes, to this house.' He answered Sara's quiet gasp,

smiling at Eden's own look of perplexed expression. 'It was you who said it, you, my dear, who said you felt a love reaching out, a love which called for its voice to be heard. It was that love I yearned for yet that same love kept me away. The sorrow was too strong . . . the love had been too deep . . . and so I lived with my pain, nurtured my wounds, allowed them to fester until they were beyond healing. But though heaven be sometimes slow in executing its designs, its pity is boundless, and in that pity it sent you. You were the balm, the antidote to the canker of poison I had allowed to grow deep within myself, you who showed the way to recovery. For a long time I fought against heaven's compassion, I did not want that healing. But day and night the words a stranger had spoken refused to be banished from my mind, words which said I must face my heart.'

They had glanced at each other, she and Sara Melia, both looks asking the same question: 'Why tell it in this house and not his own?'

Had he interpreted that shared glance? The half-smile which had touched his mouth traced a reflection of itself on Eden's.

'I am not as used as I once was to the company of ladies,' he had gone on, 'I ask pardon of you both for my lack of manners. My name is Tobias Jevons and The Coppice is my house.'

'Your house!'

Sara's surprise had echoed in the large kitchen, Eden's had shown only in her eyes.

'Mine,' he had answered. 'But my explanation will

perhaps be too long . . . I have taken a deal of your time already, Miss . . . ?'

Half of her mind had wanted to believe what it was hearing but the other half was warning this was a false friendship, a lure to bring her from the safety of Shipton Cottage. Pulled both ways, she had murmured, 'Eden . . . Eden Brent.'

He had taken her hand, his copper-coloured eyes seeming to see more than her face as he smiled. Had she felt uncomfortable? Eden stared at the face she seemed to see in the shadows, a face which had looked so different to the hollow-cheeked, gaunt one she had become used to.

No. Silent now as when it first came, the answer repeated in her mind. No, she had not felt uncomfortable with that penetrating gaze; she had been . . . happy? Lying there in the darkness, she mused over the feeling . . . Yes, she had been happy he had overcome the anger which had seemed always to be with him, happy his sorrow would fade, the healing would begin.

'We have met many times, Miss Brent, but not until now have I allowed myself the joy of speaking pleasantly to you. I ask your forgiveness for my surly behaviour; and you Missis Melia.' He had smiled at Sara with that same bright glance. 'I also ask your pardon.'

'Me? You 'ave no cause to go asking no pardon of me,' said Sara.

'But I have, my. . .' he had swallowed as if on a half-sob, '. . . my dear wife would have been unhappy at my lack of courtesy in thanking you for the way you have kept this house . . . the house where we were both so happy.'

Colour rising to her cheeks, Sara had reached for the apron left folded on a corner of a long high dresser, saying the job she was paid to do would never get done if she stood talking all day.

'Missis Melia,' he had said as she caught up a duster, 'would this old house of mine have the makings of a cup of tea?'

'Ain't no such. But I brings myself a bottle of it for a drink should I feel the need. You be welcome to a sup of that supposing you'll 'ave the accepting of it.'

'I think we would each find it acceptable. I trust there is still china somewhere about.'

'. . . *Finer than a moth's wing* . . .'

Sara's hesitation had spoken of her reluctance to handle delicate tableware but the man who claimed ownership of the house swept open a cupboard and reached down three white china cups and saucers, self-embossed with a design of oak leaves and acorns.

'There,' he had smiled, 'now we will share your tea, Missis Melia.'

Sara's fingers had trembled slightly as she had wiped the china on a cloth taken from a drawer of that long dresser. Kitchenware it may have been to staff who had once taken meals in this spacious room, but to Sara it still seemed fragile.

She should have helped! In the silence of

approaching dawn, Eden reprimanded herself. It should have been she who had wiped those cups, poured tea and handed it to the others, she should have relieved Sara of the fear of dropping one of those pretty pieces; she was no more used to handling delicate china than was Davy's mother but if any of it had been damaged blame would have been hers and not Sara's.

But it had not been broken, and while they had shared the still warm tea, Tobias Jevons had continued to speak.

'It was thirty years ago I brought Miriam to this house as my bride. She was not yet twenty and was as beautiful as a summer morning. We thought ours a happiness even heaven could not improve upon but when we learned we were to have a child we knew we had been wrong, for the happiness we felt was increased a hundredfold.

'Increased a hundredfold.'

Tears had thickened the softly repeated words and the bright copper eyes had glistened with moisture, but hard as it must have been for him he had continued.

'They were the most wonderful months. We pondered over the names we might give our child, Miriam's laugh one of amusement whenever I would tease that perhaps Obadiah, Peregrine or Zachariah would be appropriate for a boy. . .'

He had paused, taking a moment to clear the emotion memory brought to this throat.

'. . . but always she would declare our son would be named for his father and grandfathers and should our child prove to be a daughter then she would be given the names of both grandmothers. Heaven did grant us a son . . .'

He had paused again, fingers tightening where they held the walking stick.

'. . . but the gift was taken back. In less than an hour my son was gone from me and heaven also took his mother. My dearest wife was dead and to all intent and purpose so was I . . . the life I was left with had no meaning. I left this house when she did; on her burying day. I could not bear to enter it again, to walk through rooms which once had held so much happiness and now were cold and empty; but the pain of leaving, the feeling of somehow breaking faith with Miriam . . . so I closed this house and took over the gatekeeper's cottage. My heart told me I could never find my Miriam, yet something deep within my soul held me to this place . . . and now I know why.'

Beyond the window of her bedroom the night sky was paling to grey but Eden saw only a kitchen with a man sitting at its table.

'As you said, my dear,' the voice spoke on in her mind, 'there are things we maybe cannot see nor touch, but on coming here that first evening I sensed a presence so tender and compassionate, a love reaching out to me, and it was then that I knew the reason I had never sold The Coppice. It is here my darling waited, here I would find the comfort of that love I thought lost for ever, here my broken heart might at last be eased.'

He had asked then would she walk with him through

those rooms he had once walked through with his wife. All the fright he had roused in her that previous evening now gone without trace, she had accepted.

The house was as beautiful as she had imagined that day she had stared at it. Room upon room filled with furniture such as she could never have dreamed of, carpet so deep it felt she walked in grass-filled meadows, while paintings glowed on silk-covered walls. Only one room did he not open to her, one she guessed had been the room he had shared with his wife.

'I returned to the house on several evenings,' he had said when they stood together in an exquisite sitting-room. 'With the light of a candle I sat in this room . . . too long I am afraid, for the meal left on my gatepost told of your visit . . . Again, Miss Brent, I must apologise.'

The times she and Davy had brought food . . . the times he had not been standing beside his gate . . . she had thought perhaps . . . but he had been in the house of his memories, of his love!

Beneath the covers, Eden felt her body glow from the swift rush of shame.

How could she have allowed such thoughts to enter her mind? How could she have entertained the notion of his being a murderer!

'Now I know where it is my remaining years must be spent.' He had smiled as she had brushed away the apology. 'To that end I shall re-open this house, engage the staff necessary to maintain it. But there is one I would have live here not as a servant.'

He had asked that she take a seat. Eden stared to where dawn shone pale and opalescent behind a muslin veil of transparent cloud. It was well she had accepted for what had followed had her shaken to the core.

'I watched you closely.' A smile had held the same confession of regret as had his words of a moment since. 'My rudeness the first time of our meeting was, I fear, spontaneous; it was the way I had come to dealing with anyone approaching The Coppice. But as time went on and still you came, bringing food, never asking anything, always polite despite the incivility and disrespect you were given in return, I began to see you for what you are and not what I had thought you to be. I came to admire a courage I myself did not have, to appreciate the way you tackled adversity. You did not give in to self-pity as I had, you did not turn your back on life as I had done but grasped it by the wrist and forced it to walk beside you at your own pace. You have a tenacity and strength I would ask you to share with me. The footsteps of servants, the sound of their voices as they go about the duties, will give life back to this house but you could give back its smile, the joy I stole from it, return it from the exile I forced it into. Miss Brent . . . Eden . . . I am asking will you share The Coppice with me?'

31

The amount paid in exchange for the iron foundry had been far less than she had expected. The tools, furnace, the crucibles, nothing it contained had been wanted by the purchaser. The building itself was small, too cramped for the process of steel manufacture . . . it would need to be knocked down.

Lies! The hairbrush Ava Russell had been holding flew across the bedroom.

The buyer would not pay for what he could not use, it was simply the land he wished to purchase.

Lies! Ava's mouth clamped against the rage churning inside her. She knew it was lies and so had that damned solicitor! Most likely the two had been in collusion, a nice little payment for that solicitor should he get her signature on a deed of sale which brought the other a foundry for two hundred pounds.

Two hundred pounds! Bristling with temper she swept a hand across the dressing-table. Silver-rimmed crystal pots of creams and elegant vials of expensive perfumes spilled across the floor. She snatched up the cheque she had been given no choice but to accept.

What sort of house would *this* provide? What style of living, whichever part of the Continent she chose to settle? Not the style she wanted!

Forcing the storm in her mind to quieten, she took mental stock of items remaining in the house which might be sold. There were precious few and what there was must be sold without the bank's knowledge. But nothing was impossible until proved so!

First, the Meissen Samuel had given her for her birthday. Determination adding to the tight line of her mouth, she took the delicate porcelain figurines she had preferred to keep in her own room and wrapped them in a silk shawl.

Downstairs, the hall cupboard, a carpet bag . . . swiftly her mind moved. The cleaning woman . . . if she saw? But what if she did? She would not possibly know what was carried inside it!

But the woman had not been in the hall nor had she come into the drawing-room to see the pair of Sèvres dishes added to the bag, dishes that the dealer had almost drooled over. His mouth had watered at the sight of the contents of the bag but his tongue had been hard and dry when stating the price he was willing to pay. He had smiled while counting out twelve five pound notes, a smirk of triumph!

Sitting on the train which would carry her home from Wolverhampton, Ava's fingers tightened angrily about the empty bag. Every way a woman turned she was taken advantage of by men, business or bed it was all the same.

'Bilston . . .' the call of the conductor sounded from the train's corridor, '. . . next stop Bilston.'

Business or bed.

The thought returned with the fading of the conductor's call. Ava glanced through the window at the passing forest of smoking chimney stacks. Bilston was the same as Wednesbury, a depressing little town choked in its own soot. But Bilston held one pleasure!

Wheels clanking noisily over the points of the metal rails seemed to chant *Church . . . House . . . Church . . . House* . . .

Returning her glance to the bag resting in her lap she wrestled with feelings already hot and demanding.

She had told herself after that first visit there could be no more, but resolution had melted in the heat of desire and she had capitulated, not once but over and over again. Church House was designed to give its patrons complete privacy and total gratification, no matter their tastes.

But paradise came at a cost. Its fees were exorbitant; they had proved an extravagance she knew ate away what was left of the mortgage she had raised, yet still she had paid, indulging her passions until the money had virtually run out. But desire had not drained as those sovereigns had. Nights spent tormented by the thought of what Church House had supplied; those young bodies soft and perfumed, those willing skilful hands, had at last driven her to find a woman of the streets.

Distaste rose in her throat.

The odour of cheap perfume, the smell of gin on the breath, the exaggerated assurance of the delights to come, had all curdled until disgust had almost had her turn away; but, strong as aversion had been, the burning inside herself had been stronger, the desire so avid it had to be satisfied and she had gone with the woman.

But passion spent in a doorway of a darkened street!

The grind of metal on metal, the loud hiss of steam as the train slowed to the station, made no impression on the thoughts circling in Ava's mind.

It had lasted only a few minutes, every sound from that gloom-enshrouded street stinging her brain. To be discovered there! To be found with a common prostitute! That would be humiliation enough, but to be exposed a lesbian . . . that degradation could hound a woman to her grave! Warning had sung its harsh melody but lust had sung louder.

The woman had fumbled beneath her skirts. Ava's breath caught with the memory.

She had pulled away the bloomers her low laugh blown on a breath of gin as the touch of her fingers in that warm moist crevice had brought a gasp from her client's throat.

Then it was finished. The prostitute's hand had clawed the half sovereign she had demanded for 'special service' but then had demanded ten more.

Ava's glance travelled again to the window, the scene beyond invisible through the grey-white haze of steam floating back from the engine.

'Ten more, dearie . . .'

The words seemed to laugh from the curtain of steam.

'. . . *after all, we wouldn't want the 'ole town to be a' knowin' of your little fancies now, would we?'*

The woman's hand had reached forward.

'. . . *ten be all it'll tek to 'ave your secret kept safe . . . ten sovereigns can seal a woman's mouth, that be little enough, you does agree.'*

She had agreed.

The lurch of the train coming to a halt jolted Ava sharply forward, then back against her seat.

The prostitute had received her payment.

'Bilston!'

The call reached through the steam-misted window.

'Bilston town!'

Fingers closing on the carpet bag, Ava rose to her feet.

'He told you!'

Hands covered in flour, Eden looked up from the pastry she was mixing in a large bowl.

'But I said not to, the blame was mine and I should be the one taken to task not Davy!'

His tall figure blocking the light of the open doorway, Andrew Denby frowned.

'Why would you think David taken to task?'

A smudge of flour remaining where a finger had brushed her cheek, Eden watched the frown draw dark brows together.

'He thought should you hear of . . . of . . .'

'Of his finding you on that path? Oh yes, he told me.'

'Did he say it was my fault? I was not at the cottage when he called.'

Frown becoming a smile, Andrew Denby's smoke-dark eyes gleamed.

'That is not the way of David Melia. If there is blame to be taken then he thinks he should take it and he is fast proving himself man enough to shoulder what comes. But, as you say, fault did not lie with him; it lies with me for advising you take your cooking to market. Had I not done so you would not have suffered that fall.'

'Had I stopped to think instead of rushing off to the market? Isn't that what you really want to say?' Eden's own smile curving her mouth, she returned to her pastry.

'Maybe I should at that!'

'But seeing as the primary cause lies with you?'

'Truce? Let the matter rest?'

Their laughter joined together, Andrew watched the slender figure, the quick deft movements of her hands, the slight sideward tilt of a head that sunlight from the window gilded silver-gold. Had it been more than a fall . . . had she been injured in any way . . . Lord, what would he have done!

The thought a knife blade in his stomach, he forced it away. Eden Brent had suffered no serious effect and he thanked God for it.

'Then my rashness is to be forgiven?'

'This time yes, but Eden . . .'

Catching his glance as she looked to what she thought to be a question, Eden's pulses tripped.

'Don't . . . please don't put me through that again.'

It was there again, her imagination playing tricks! Unable to control the surge of colour to her cheeks, she turned to the oven checking food which needed no check. Why did this keep happening? Why did her mind insist on showing what was really not there? It had been a joke, he had teased her and she had placed an entirely different light on it. Heavens, what a fool he would think her, could he only read her mind. But that at least she was spared. Her thoughts would be her own; she would never share them, not with him, not with anybody.

'I will not have Davy walk me to market.' She turned a determined face.

Raising both hands in a gesture of surrender, Andrew Denby gave a slow shake of the head.

'Then you had best tell David that for he has already made up his mind that is what he is going to do.'

'Without asking me!'

'Or me.' Hands lowering, the smile in his dark eyes gave way to a serious look. 'Believe me, I had nothing to do with this, it is entirely the lad's own idea. He said he walked into Wednesbury every day so why not the two of you do so together.'

Turning pastry on to a floured board, rolling it lightly to a rectangle, the decision she had reached earlier came back to her mind. She had not thought to mention it just yet but, first or last, it would need be said some time.

'There will be no call for Davy to disrupt his working day by waiting to walk to the town with me,' she said, lining a dish with pastry. 'I will not be going there after today.'

'Not going?' Andrew Denby's frown returned. 'Might I ask your reason?'

She did not have to tell him anything, but then she had acted upon his suggestion so it seemed only good manners to explain the reason behind her decision.

'It is really very simple. I cannot make sufficient amounts of food to serve both a market stall and the canal folk; it is those people, the boatmen and their families, their friendship means more than . . .'

More than what? There had been the threat of tears behind those words. Andrew sat in silence. It seemed something she had set her heart on had been snatched from her . . . but what was that something?

'Eden.' He spoke her name softly. 'The reason you give, it is the only one? There is nothing else that has frightened or upset you?'

Having brushed the lid of the pie with milk she set it in the oven before answering.

'If you are referring to my fall that was simply an accident.'

'No accident is simple!' On his feet and beside her before the words were out, he grasped her arms, his fingers biting into tender flesh. 'Can't you see? You are important to David, you are important to . . .'

Staring into her eyes for a brief moment he loosed her arms then strode from the house.

One more second and he would have been unable to prevent the rest of that sentence leaving his tongue; one more second to say what throbbed even now . . . '*You are important to me!*'

Striding towards the boatyard, Andrew Denby's thoughts ran chaotically.

He had wanted to say it, wanted to tell her what was in his heart, that he loved her. But what effect would that have had except to have her turn from him completely, to lose the relationship they had developed. Yet what sort of relationship was friendship when it was her love he yearned for?

'. . . *their friendship means more than* . . .'

Those words not spoken, would they have said the friendship of the canal folk meant more to her than that of Andrew Denby? Could he honestly have wondered at the answer being yes? Those first encounters . . . He had hardly presented himself as other than disapproving, his every word had been condemnation of or a reprimand for her behaviour. All in all it was surprising she even bothered speaking to him . . . and now that she did, now that she showed warmth however small he would not risk the losing of it. What he felt for Eden Brent must remain where it rested now, buried in the depths of his heart.

But that would not ease the ache of it. Like David Melia, he cared for the girl scraping a living at Shipton

Cottage and, like that lad, he worried that one day she might leave for good.

'. . . *against my leaving* . . .'

That was what she had said regarding coins kept on that mantelshelf. To pay in part at least the rent which may have been asked of the owner.

'. . . *against my leaving* . . .'

It rang like a warning bell in his brain. Would telling her no rent would be required have her forego any idea of leaving? Should he tell her who owned the cottage she lived in, that its owner wanted nothing in respect of payment?

But pride was almost a fault with that young woman. Crossing the cobbled yard to the boatyard office he allowed himself a smile. Hard as life had been for her, hard as it still was, he knew she would not have passed one night beneath the roof of Shipton Cottage without gaining permission had she known its owner and having him accept a rent. And now . . . should she be told his name now, would that same pride have her accept or deny . . . would it have her remain in that house or set her feet on some other path?

That was one more risk he would not take!

Sitting at his desk he stared at the papers left by his clerk but his mind was still on Eden Brent.

She had sprung to the defence of the Melia lad. The fault, if fault there had been, was not his!

How those lovely eyes had blazed! A turquoise fire, they had proclaimed her ready to fight for the youngster's good name. Defence of a friend . . . it was a quality not to be discredited. And when she had spoken of her accident on that path below The Coppice . . . it was the truth as told to David Melia, as she had told it again to himself, yet it was not all of the truth.

Rolling open the sheet of parchment he looked at it with unseeing eyes.

There were things Eden Brent chose not to share, either with himself or with David.

Through the glass partition, the clerk looked at his employer, his dark head tilted now against the leather of his high-backed chair. Deciding now may not be the most appropriate time to re-enter his office he returned his own attention to a blue-bound ledger.

She had given reason for not continuing to cook food for sale in the market, a sound and logical reason, but she had not revealed the disappointment he had sensed lay behind it. Andrew's eyelids closed, myriad questions dancing beneath them.

What could be so hurtful she could not speak of it, what so painful that thought of it brought the threat of tears? If only he could ask, but that would be to invade her privacy. She had chosen not to speak of whatever it was inside her and he must respect that decision . . . as he had respected that other decision, that other happening she had seen fit not to disclose.

Friendship! He stared at the ceiling. How much of what Eden Brent showed towards him was truly friendship and how much simply tolerance? Was her attitude towards him, her acceptance of his visiting Shipton Cottage, an indulgence designed for the benefit of

David Melia? Was she accepting one man merely to protect another? Was her friendship no more than a pretence . . . a pretence practised in order to safeguard the Melias' living?

No, he would not believe it!

Jerking upright in the chair, he snatched at the paper lying unread on his desk.

He was expecting too much of her, he was finding reasons simply in order to cover his own feelings, feelings that were absurd. So, she had not spoken of being asked to that house, of Sara Melia being sent to ask would she go to The Coppice. He had learned that from Sara's son . . . but even Sara's son did not know all!

32

He had asked her to live at The Coppice, to share that beautiful house with him.

Wooden shutters closed across living-room windows, Eden stoked the fire with sleck then doused the fine coal chippings with water so the burning embers would sleep through the night to wake with fresh life when she did.

Tobias Jevons . . . the elderly man she had held suspicion of being a murderer . . . She smiled to herself . . . How could she have entertained such a horrid idea! But *any* idea she might have had concerning him could not have been anywhere near as fantastic as the truth.

Familiarity born of months of living at Shipton Cottage, her hands reached down basins and bowls from the rickety dresser setting them alongside the dry ingredients she would need for next day's cooking.

Of all the notions she might have had, not one would have touched the reality of Tobias Jevons being owner of that house. Had anyone in Gospel Oak known that? Not Sara Melia, for she had gasped surprise loud as her own.

Checking the mutton which would simmer all night

in the side oven of the gleaming cast iron firegrate, she took a freshly laundered cloth from the length of finely twisted rope that ran above it.

And Andrew Denby, did he know? Her spine tickling with just the thought of the handsome man who offered her friendship, Eden flicked the snowy white cloth and draped it across the assembled articles on the well-scrubbed table.

She could have asked that question when he had called here earlier today. She could also have told him of her visit to The Coppice, of walking with Tobias Jevons through its gracious rooms, shared with him what that man had told her of his wife and newborn child; of the smile which had touched his mouth as he had spoken of feeling their presence, of a love waiting to be renewed. But she had said nothing of those things . . . nor had she told of that request that she go to live in that house.

What would Andrew Denby have made of that?

Baking tins and roasting pan set ready on the hob, she turned a glance about the room she had prettied with covers and curtains sewn from a length of honeysuckle-printed cloth found tucked away in a drawer. Cooking and needlework, skills bestowed more by the teaching of her grandmother than of school, they had stood her in good stead.

'*. . . she will never do any good . . .*'

Words, hurting now as they had when spoken, whispering shadows in her mind, she stood holding a cushion her gaze did not see.

'*. . . she will never amount to anything . . .*'

Sharp to the point of cruelty, pale eyes regarded a young girl, her petite figure seeming to draw back from the slash of a razor-keen tongue, her heart-shaped face lowered against a withering stare.

The headmistress who had ordered she strip away her clothes had intended the savagery of those words. In return for being disobeyed she had deliberately spat a malignance she had hoped would grow over the years, would become so deeply embedded that no amount of love would cure, that, like some hideous disease, would lie hidden deep within, eating away at a child's life.

'Once said never forgotten.' That had been Grandmother's gentle warning when either of her granddaughters had come close to speaking in temper . . . as it had seemed Myra had spoken that day she, Eden, had gone to Moorcroft to tell her of their grandmother's death.

But Myra had not spoken out of temper. Eden's hand gripped the soft cushion. The words had been hard only to drive a sister away in order to safeguard her from the evils of its mistress . . . an evil she, Eden Brent, must seek to redress.

She had been given that chance. Setting the cushion in its place on the wooden squab, a bench-like couch years of polishing now reflecting the pretty cloth like some dark mirror, she turned back to the table.

It was a heaven-sent chance! She would no longer need to count every penny, to scrimp and save on her own meagre living in order to put money from her cooking into the pot on the mantelshelf; she would have no landlord to pay . . . and with someone like Tobias Jevons on her side then the authorities would be bound to pay more attention to a complaint brought against Ava Russell.

But what complaint could she bring? A letter allegedly written by a dead girl . . . an accusation so terrible it would rock the whole town . . . Who would believe such of any woman, much less one of the social standing of Ava Russell! Would Tobias Jevons . . . would Andrew Denby? They would never be asked to believe . . . they would never be told of her sister's shame, of her persecution, nor would anyone; only Aunt Dora was privy to the degradation Myra had been forced to endure and she would not renege on that confidence.

Yet, if by the same chance she was offered now in being asked to make her home at The Coppice, its owner should believe the story of Myra's abuse it would be of no avail. She would not use his name in any attempt to avenge those wrongs, and most definitely not any financial assistance he might offer.

How then could she fulfil the promise of her heart? How could she ensure Ava Russell paid for her crimes?

The profit from her cooking would have grown at a faster rate by selling at the market and by following the further suggestion of Andrew Denby that his boats carry her food on to other towns to be sold in shops there; but no matter how quickly her savings amassed money alone was not enough. She could not buy justice. If she were to bring Ava Russell to book she would require evidence, but evidence of enforced lesbianism was something that woman would guard with her life.

Then how to keep the promise she had whispered at her sister's grave?

Taking the cup which had held her evening cocoa, she carried it to the scullery and washed it by the light of a candle in a jar.

How . . . unless she too asked for position of ladies' maid at Moorcroft House? Would she be strong enough to tolerate what Myra had lived through?

Hands which knew every inch of the tiny cottage reached for a cloth lying beyond the lemony perimeter of candlelight.

Would Ava Russell employ her?

The cup dried, that same inner knowledge of the space around her ensuring the cloth back in its place, she blew out the candle.

Given what she had read in Myra's letter, the truth she knew those words contained, then there was little doubt of the answer. A shiver ran needles along every vein. Why would there be? Becoming a partner in lasciviousness, no girl would own to willing acceptance, no girl would condemn herself to the years of imprisonment which would follow; of that the woman would be certain.

Stepping into the lighted warmth of the prettily curtained living-room, Eden's fingers tightened about the cup.

No, Ava Russell would not refuse . . . but then Ava Russell did not truly know Eden Brent!

Coming to the curve that led Lower High Street on to the rise which became Church Hill, Ava Russell slipped quickly through a low wooden gate set in high brick-built walls encompassing the grounds of Moorcroft House.

There had been no prostitute walking the street, no doxy stepping out to offer 'a good time for a sixpence'. It seemed any women selling those particular wares were parading them only in taverns, in well-lit premises where every potential customer could be seen and noted. The Wednesbury 'Ripper' had them all wary of taking a customer from the streets.

But she could not be seen entering an inn or tavern and, as for being observed speaking with a woman of the night! Crossing the darkened grounds made more gloomy by the absence of a moon, Ava hissed her irritation. The need which had driven her to look for ease among the local strumpets still burned and gnawed in her stomach. It was risky looking anywhere for her particular brand of pleasure, even more so when the search took her to the streets of her home town, but the visits to Church House had all but drained her purse. The money gained from the selling of figurines and dishes had gone into the coffers of that establishment and she had vowed to herself each visit would be the last.

But vows easily made had been the more easily

broken, and sovereigns had followed sovereigns down the same bottomless pit until once more little remained. Desire was a flame which refused the quenching. The heat of it grew, increasing with the days until it seemed it would burn her alive. That was how it had been for the past couple of weeks, a scorching red-hot flame feeding a craving so voracious as to have it burst into wild volcanic fire exploding along every nerve until it could no longer be controlled but became the stomach-twisting fervour which had tonight driven her first to the streets then on to the house of that schoolmistress.

The woman's sharp-featured face had exhibited no surprise. Ava's feet crunched the hard unkempt path which led to the rear of Moorcroft House. She had led the way to a vulgarly over-furnished front parlour where she had listened impassively. *A girl, one she was absolutely certain would utter no word of what she was made to do.* Ava had spoken quietly, the schoolmistress responding as she might the request for a joint of meat. She had such a girl, she was here in the house, Ava could take her pleasure. No money had exchanged hands, the unspoken fee being that of one woman's hold over another, the unspoken ransom of evil. Ava Russell would never be able to commit her accomplice to the hands of the judiciary without suffering the same fate herself.

The girl had been young, barely past her twelfth year. An orphan taken from the poorhouse, grateful to the woman who had rescued her from that life of poverty; but what of the life to which she must now resign herself, how long would she give herself to the slaking of another woman's lust before doing what Myra Brent had done? But no thought of that had interfered with the satisfying of Ava Russell's need.

Passing the line of bushes alongside the small outbuilding which had been home to her stablehand, Ava walked on, her thoughts unchecked.

Thin to the point of being all bone, the girl had shivered beneath the hands stroking her body. Her own fingers clumsy in performing lust-gasped instructions she had squeezed breasts larger than her own, trailed a tight-closed mouth over a stomach convulsing beneath its touch, then rubbed rather than caressed the warm, moist channel topping Ava's parted legs succeeding in bringing an explosive burst of passion which resulted in no real quenching of desire.

It had cost no money, but it had brought no relief. Maybe when she got to the Continent, maybe then she would once more train her own lover. Yes, she would train a girl of her choosing, teach her the art of making love, the skills necessary to satisfy another woman. The thought lancing a trail of heat from stomach to throat, a thrill of emotion that had breath a prisoner in her throat, Ava smiled her first smile of the evening.

'I've been a'waiting of you.'

Soft-spoken in the darkness, it made the breath burst free of the chains holding it in Ava's throat.

'I guessed you might come this way.'

'Who are you, what do you want!' Ava snapped,

anger at her private grounds being invaded overriding caution.

'Who I am will be seen once we be inside of the house.' The voice seemed to smile. 'As for what it be I wants then surely you don't need the tellin' of that, but in case I be wrong in presumin' then I will give the tellin''. What I be wanting is money . . . money to keep what I knows of you from being hawked all over this town.'

Blackmail! Ava's blood thickened to ice. Whoever was standing in the shadows carried the threat Alfred Birks had carried, was making the same demands he had made. But no one apart from him and his lady love had known of the liaison between herself and Lenor Medwin; and that dirty little stablehand and the pathetic maid were both dead. Yet here was someone else claiming that knowledge and its ill-gained reward . . . someone very much alive!

'Well, do we be goin' inside or do I take myself to that posh George Hotel along the street? I 'ave no doubts as to the attentions I'll get when I tells the doings of the mistress of Moorcroft House.'

'*The doings of the mistress of Moorcroft House.*'

Each word the loudness of a bell ringing in her brain, Ava tried to think. Had she been careless that first time of paying a woman of the street for her service? Had she been recognised while visiting the high-class brothel that was Church House? The first was a definite no . . . and the second? Any casual observer seeing her enter that house in Bilston could have no knowledge of its reason, and certainly one whose speech was as rough as that of this person would be no client there.

Encouraged by this, Ava returned sharply. 'You had best leave before I call for the constable.'

'Call him!' The reply no longer held the hint of a smile but an open sneer. 'I've no worries if you 'ave none.'

It was a challenge! Ava's thin mouth tightened. But one she could not take up. Should this intruder in her garden really have the knowledge claimed, then to risk it being voiced abroad was not to be dared.

Swallowing hard, hoping to clear all trace of supposition from her voice, she asked, 'What are these so-called doings you speak of and what on earth leads you to the belief I will give you money?'

'The 'doings' be that of brushin' the muff, and you'll give me what is asked 'cos you wants that secret kept tight as that little hole you likes fingered atwixt your legs.'

There could be no further doubt. Tight as bowstrings, Ava's nerves quivered. But how . . . how had she been found out? Birks? His lover? Myra? Impossible! The dead don't talk.

The dead don't talk! Breath hard in her lungs, teeth clenched so firm they hurt, the phrase sang in her brain. The dead didn't talk but a letter could. The letter Eden Brent claimed was written by her sister . . . Had it somehow been seen by the creature standing in the shadows, might it even now be in a pocket or a bag? Stolen! It had to have been . . . The other Brent girl would never have willingly allowed it to fall into the hands of anyone else.

'Well! You decide quick, I ain't about to stand 'ere all night.'

Sharp and demanding, each word vibrated along Ava's veins. How much would this one want? How regular would the demand be made? It would be no once-in-a-lifetime, of that she could be assured. Like Birks would have done, this blackmailer would come again and again . . . and when the last halfpenny was gone? Ava felt a laugh start low in her stomach . . . This one would no doubt do as she herself would do in their situation . . . Sell the letter to whoever was interested!

Thoughts darting like quicksilver, she searched for a way out then a rustling in the shadows warning of impatience, she said, 'I carry very little money with me. I will need to get more from the house, but first you will tell me how you came by your information.'

A loud sniff or a stifled laugh? Ava could not distinguish but the answer caused no doubt.

'I don't 'ave to tell you nothin' . . . but I ain't vindictive so I will. Not every woman at Church House earns her livin' by lyin' on her back for a man or by strokin' another woman's fanny. I be one who sees without bein' seen, one of them as cleans up the mess folk of your sort leaves behind. I seen you the times you come thinkin' a veil across your face to hide what your mouth watered for, then when you was done and left I heard the wenches laughin' and talkin'. Brushin' the muff was what they talked of. Now, I might be no more than a room maid, but that don't go to say as I 'ave no brain. I knows what a story like that could do to a woman should it get spilled . . . and I knowed the money could be earned by holdin' it the back of the teeth. That bein' so, I followed you, not once but three times, and on each you come here to this house. You be its owner, Missis Ava Russell. Oh yes, I found that out an' all . . . so if you wants to remain here playin' Lady Muck then you'll get me that which I be 'ere for. Ten sovereigns be the price. That don't be much to ask now do it? Ten sovereigns can seal a woman's mouth and you does want it sealed, don't you? Ten sovereigns and I'll be on my way, unless o' course you would like that muff of your'n brushed . . . Won't cost near so much as havin' it played with along of Church House.'

At Ava's back, soft enough not to be heard beyond the confines of the garden, a snigger seemed to scream contempt.

'What do you say? Shall we tek ourselves an hour in that bedroom of your'n, I could mebbes show you a few delights them there wenches along of Bilston ain't learned yet . . . I wouldn't be askin' of no extra payment. Call it showin' of satisfaction with our little arrangement. Ten sovereigns pleases me, a ticklin' of your fanny pleases you . . . we both be satisfied.'

Fingers clasped against the sibilant hiss of one more sniggering laugh, Ava's mind whirled.

'. . . *I knows what a story like that could do* . . .'

'*I knowed the money could be earned by holdin' it the back of the teeth* . . .'

'*Ten sovereigns can seal a woman's mouth . . .*'

But for how long? Paramount, that one thought rose above the others. Only so long as the sovereigns did, and then this creature would be back for more, threatening and sneering!

'Well!' The voice was louder, less patient. 'Do it be payment or do it be I teks my little titbit along of the George?'

'It will be payment.' Ava's whisper mingled with that of leaves dancing on the night air. Turning on the ball of one foot, a hand lifting to strike, she whispered again, 'Oh yes, you will get your payment!'

33

'The wife checked at the 'ouse afore we settled for the night; the wench were all right then, her said as her would be setting the things to readiness against the mornin' an' then would be gettin' herself to her bed.'

The operator of the narrowboat the *Gospel Maid* stood cap in hand in the office of Denby Boat Builders. He hadn't known why the owner had sent for him and now he waited nervously for the outcome of their meeting. Would it be the sack, would it mean his wife and family would be without home and the means of feeding themselves? Lord forbid the doing!

'The missis . . .' the boatman swallowed, an anxious, noisy movement of the throat which had his Adam's apple dancing, '. . . her had a look to that scullery an' also asked might her use the privy along of the back-yard just so as to check all were as it should be . . . Her wouldn't never go leavin' lessen her were convinced the wench were safe. If only Old Nick hadn't died, that dog were true to his name if any dog was; he could hear a butterfly fart from a mile off and 'ave its throat out afore it got to settlin' its arse on a poppy . . . beggin' of your pardon for the sayin'.'

Behind the heavy mahogany desk, Andrew Denby nodded. He had known this man from boyhood and knew the simple honesty of him. What he had said, coarse as it may have been put, would be the truth.

'Old Nick was one on his own,' he answered, allowing a brief smile.

'He were that, Mister Andrew. Like I says he could hear, smell and see sharp and clear as the devil hisself and he'd 'ave the gizzard outta any man a' tryin' to do what oughtn't to be; wouldn't 'ave nothing untoward 'ave gone on 'ad Old Nick been wi' the boat. Reckon it'll be a year or two afore I gets another dog the like o' that one.'

'There was no boat moored alongside of your own?'

The boatman shook his head. 'None but the *Maid* within sight, Mister Andrew, but if you be a' thinkin' that what were done were by the hand of one of we . . .'

The quick lift of a hand cut the sentence short and Andrew Denby's smile, though brief, was reassuring. 'No, Jed, I don't think any cutman would do what was done last night, and certainly not any who knew Miss Brent . . . But somebody attacked her, the question is why? For what reason?'

'You reckon it were done for money? That it were a thief lookin' for easy pickings?'

He had thought so himself when the Melia lad had come to tell him of finding Eden lying on her living-room floor, hands and feet trussed like market poultry her head and face streaked with dried blood. But though each room of that cottage appeared as if caught by a whirlwind, the money kept in a pot on the mantelshelf and that kept for the buying of ingredients for her cooking were still in place. So, if not cash, then what had any thief been looking for? There were no valuables in Shipton Cottage; that meant only one possible explanation. The girl herself! Whoever had entered that house had done so not to rob but with the express purpose of . . . his blood chilling, Andrew Denby's hands closed into hard balls . . . of harming Eden Brent . . . maybe of killing her!

'I brought the *Maid* from her moorings just as dawn light touched the sky. The trip along of London being a long one and the cargo I were hauling having to catch the India boat, I thought best to sail soonest I could see a stretch in front o' me. I never thought somebody to break into the Shipton place. All looked to be as it should afore we pulled away or we wouldn't never 'ave left.'

The man was blaming himself for what had happened. Recognising as much in the twisting of the cap and the anxious look of the eyes, Andrew Denby rose, circling the desk as he assured the other man no blame was attached to him but, with the boatman's leaving the office, he felt the cold fear hit his stomach the way it had when the Melia lad had come running in.

David had gone to Shipton Cottage in order to walk with Eden into Wednesbury as he had stubbornly declared he would. The shutters still closed across the downstairs windows had alarmed him and he had entered the house not bothering to knock. At first he could see almost nothing, the fire in the grate being all but dead. He had crossed to the window and opened the shutter and, as daylight poured in, he had seen the living-room scattered with the contents of every drawer and cupboard, then . . . the lad had gulped air before saying . . . '*Then I seen Eden, her were lying across the hearth, her d'ain't move when I called her name. I . . . I were feared her were dead.*'

So had he! Staring out across the busy boatyard, Andrew felt the chill of ice strike again at the pit of his stomach. His every nerve had jangled at the sound of David Melia's voice shouting to the clerk that he must see the gaffer 'now', but on seeing the stricken look on the lad's face it seemed his heart had stopped.

Leaving David to follow, he had galloped the distance to the cottage, his brain knowing only he might have lost the girl he had never told of his love, that Eden Brent might be dead and, through the pain of it all, had beaten one promise; the person responsible would suffer the same fate! That vow had been on his lips as he had strode into the tiny house and was silently renewed as he saw the girl lying asleep, one side of her pale face darkened with a purpling bruise.

'Shh!' Sara Melia's mouth had pursed the sound as he framed his question then she had slipped out of the room, leaving him alone with Eden.

He had wanted to lift that sleeping figure into his arms, hold it close against him, to whisper the love which had flowed like a fountain, the rush of it gathering in his veins hurtling into his throat until he felt he must choke on it. Then her eyes had opened and she had smiled at him.

Lord, what that smile had caused in him! Glance resting on the waters which ran beside the boatyard, he tried again to analyse the emotions which had raced with that smile but, if he lived a thousand years, he would still not name them all. Anger? Oh yes, there had been that, a whole burning river of anger . . . Desire for vengeance? That, too, in equal measure, but of all the sensations driving through him the overriding one had been love. It had risen from deep inside him, an all-embracing upsurge, a pulsing throb that was a drum in his brain, a pain in his heart that had him cry her name.

'Eden.' He whispered it now as he had then and, in his mind, saw again the swift look which had gleamed momentarily as those turquoise eyes had opened, a look which had been shut off but not so quickly that he had not caught it. But had it been what he thought . . . what he hoped? Albeit faint, could it have been a shadow, a semblance of the love he himself felt?

But then it was gone and she was thanking him for his concern but insisting there was no need and that he must not neglect his business on her account.

Not neglect his business. Andrew Denby laughed, a soft, hopeless laugh. He would bypass heaven itself if it meant a moment with her. Would he have told her as much, would he have spoken of that fierce longing chained inside him?

The moment had been snatched away with the

coming of Tobias Jevons. Turning from the window, Andrew returned to his desk, acid settling on his tongue; the acid he had tasted as Eden Brent's smiling words of welcome had met the other man. One man welcomed, the other politely told he must not neglect his business. The nib of a slender pen snapped against the surface of the desk. It had not been difficult to see which of the two Eden Brent preferred!

Which of the two she preferred . . . could it also be which of the two she loved? Unable to settle beneath the cloud of that question, Andrew Denby rode the path leading to The Coppice. It was not unknown for a young girl to take an older man, money was a powerful motive for such marriages. But what of love? Could Eden Brent love a man old enough to be her grandfather . . . be *in* love with him!

'That is a preposterous question.' Tobias Jevons laughed as it was put to him. 'You have no reason to think that. I am very fond of the girl, in fact I would say yes, I do love her, but not in the same way you do.'

An apologetic curve touching his mouth, Andrew met copper-coloured eyes. They were alive with a brightness they had not held in many years.

'No need to say what I can read for myself on your face,' Tobias waved a hand dismissively. 'You love the girl and I admire you for it,' he smiled widely, 'I'd call you a fool were you not to.'

'Won't do me any good.'

'It won't if you don't tell her! Though I don't take the girl to be blind, she can see for herself the feelings you have, they show clear on your face; but no maid takes it upon herself to speak the first words. That be up to you and I counsel you do it quick, my lad, or you be like to lose her to another.'

Sitting in a velvet-covered chair, the light from high-arched windows played across the tense line that was Andrew Denby's mouth. Was there someone in Eden's life, someone she loved?

Settled in his own matching chair, Tobias read the pain hovering on the face of a man he had watched grow from childhood, one who had known the true identity of an old man living in a cottage at the entrance to that long drive, and who had kept his secret.

'Andrew.' Hand resting on a malacca cane, he spoke gently. 'I was your father's friend as well as his partner in business and I claim that same privilege with you. I feel you to be the . . .' voice breaking, Tobias swallowed hard against the sting of his own pain, though the sheen of it gleamed a watery veil over his eyes, '. . . the son who was taken from me. That being so, I speak as I know your own father would speak. Go to her, tell her of your feelings . . .'

'But if there is someone else!'

'Then she will tell you.' Tobias answered the swift interruption. 'There will be hurt in it for you should she be given in love to another man, but that will be as the bite of a gnat compared to the anguish you could both suffer should you remain silent.'

'Both?' Andrew frowned.

Sunlight turning grey to silver, Tobias' head

nodded. 'Yes, Andrew, I say both, for it is my firm belief Eden loves you. We have talked several times since my returning to this house and whenever our conversation touched upon you a gentle flush would invade her cheeks and, though her eyes lowered, they could not hide what lay in their depths. She will not speak, though the holding back break her heart. That is a barrier that must be broken by you. Eden Brent has pride, pride to match your own, that much was shown by her refusal to accept my proposal she make The Coppice her home. It would have meant a life of ease for her but she declined, saying she had been taught to take only that which she had earned. It was gently said but the meaning of it rang clear; she would accept no man's charity.'

But would she accept his love? Andrew sat quietly, the thought reverberating in his mind.

'She told you of my asking her to share this house, to make her home here?'

Drawing his mind away from that one thought, Andrew shook his head. 'No, she did not.'

'Pride.' Tobias chuckled. 'I told you she had the same affliction you have. But Andrew . . . don't let pride get in the way of happiness. Regret sometimes comes so late that life has already passed by. Have the courage to take it in hand, to seek the thing you want most from it. Believe me, it is the only way. Sorrow is a bitter medicine and it brings no cure. I know for I drank it long and deep. Do not tread a path that leads nowhere except to heartbreak.'

'My father always said you were a wise bird, now I know what he meant.'

Pushing to his feet as his visitor rose to leave, Tobias Jevons leaned heavily on his cane. 'Eden Brent refused my offer to share my house as a daughter or even a housekeeper,' he said quietly. 'My hopes go with you she will not refuse to share yours as a wife.'

Share his home as a wife.

Andrew Denby's mind wrestled with the thought of what the asking might bring. It had been weeks before the friendship they had now developed. How could he expect it now to become love? Tobias Jevons was seeing things through different eyes. He did not know of the antagonism Eden had once held for the son of his old friend. Could he risk the return of those feelings, could he jeopardise that friendship on one slim hope? She had given him no cause to think him other than a casual acquaintance. Their meetings were pleasant, their conversation no longer spiked, but it was not the conversation of a man and his sweetheart.

Sweetheart! It was a word he might never hear from her lips.

'Evenin' Mister Denby, sir.'

Brought up by the call Andrew returned the greeting of the bargee mooring his narrowboat alongside Shipton Cottage.

'Be the young miss all right? Her ain't suffered no lastin' hurt I 'opes.'

'A cut to the head but thankfully no permanent injury.'

Jumping on to the towpath to where his own horse waited to be released from the tow line which pulled the boat, the man looked at Andrew. 'We thanks God for that, me and my missis both, but I'd be a' thankin' Him more should He grant me just two minutes with the swine as broke into that there cottage. I guarantees he wouldn't never stand on his legs again! And that don't just be a vow made by meself, Mister Andrew, but it be the word of every man jack o' we, every boatman as plies the canal be of the same mind . . . Find the bast . . . well, find the one attacked that wench and make him a bed at the bottom of the nearest lock. Don't suppose them there coppers have nabbed the varmint?'

'Not so far,' Andrew replied, swinging easily from his own mount.

'Bit too far for 'em to come likely, them chaps be too fond o' their comfort to trek across the 'eath looking for villains, but should I catch sight of the fellah I seen a' walkin' toward Wednesbury that night . . .'

'Which night?' The demand crackled on the quiet air, the force of it bringing the other man's attention from hobbling the horse.

'Why, the same night the young miss were broken in on. I left the wife and the lad to bring the boat to her mooring . . . They set for the night down around yon lock.' He pointed a callused hand in the direction from which he had come. 'I dropped off as we come through the town, I don't care for the missis to be walkin' across the 'eath after dark so I went for the supplies we was needing. To be truthful I had meself a taste o' the jug along of the Lea Brook tavern . . . keeps a good drop of ale does Thomas Challinor . . . but it were a clear 'ead I'd be needin' if it weren't a pit shaft I was to sleep in, so I took no more than two pints; that bein' the way of it I knows it were no trick of the mind when I seen that figure a' comin' towards me on the path, though from the look I could have been forgiven for thinkin' it a vision from hell. Old it looked, walked bent over a stick, and the jacket and trousers the colour of night.'

'The face,' Andrew urged as the telling ceased, 'did you recognise the face?'

'D'ain't see it.' The bargee swung his head slowly. 'Wore a flat cap low over the brow and the collar of the jacket were pulled up over the chin and though I wished the fellah goodnight he made no answer, just hobbled past like I wasn't there; but so sure I comes across him again he'll be glad to talk, he'll tell me did he see any other man a' walkin' of that path even if I 'as to choke it outta him!'

Walked bent over a stick!

The boatman, having tended the needs of his horse, had returned to the narrowboat, yet Andrew Denby stood, the blood in his veins chilled.

Those murders in Wednesbury . . . There had been talk of an old man being seen in the vicinity, a man needing the use of a stick to walk! Had that same man visited Shipton Cottage? Had the murderer widened his field in search of victims? Had he intended that next victim to be Eden Brent but had he been frightened away before he could finish the job?

Finish the job. The words were cannon fire in his brain. The bargee had seen no face . . . but Eden . . . He drew a long juddering breath . . . Eden must have seen, she could identify . . .

. . . *Finish the* job . . .

He would have to do exactly that to save himself . . . the man would be back!

34

A high moon painted the heath in shades of alabaster and pearl, the movement of wisps of baby cloud sprinkling the tussocky grass with spangles of silver while each outcrop of limestone was etched with light gleaming about it like a robe of pale silk. But none of the beauty of the night impressed itself upon the mind churning with questions.

Had the someone who had entered Shipton Cottage done so with the intention of murder? Why had Eden been bound hand and foot? What was it the intruder had ransacked the house in search of?

The first of those questions Andrew Denby could only guess at; perhaps something had startled the intruder causing him to leave the house with his task unfinished. The second of those questions he found simpler to answer. Unlike those poor unfortunates murdered in Wednesbury, Eden had been bound at wrist and ankle, but not been killed . . . That had to be because should whatever was searched for not be found then Eden would be needed alive, tortured maybe until she told what was necessary.

Tortured! Andrew's nerves jolted. Had that procedure already begun, was that the cause of Eden's bruises, the cut to her head? Had she known . . . been told of the fate she would suffer once the rogue had what he'd been looking for? Lord, it was a wonder she was still sane!

But the scaffold would see the one who had done that to Eden Brent, and it would see the one who no doubt had paid for it to be done. That was the answer he had for the third of his self-asked questions.

Shipton Cottage held nothing of value to anyone except a letter, a letter damning Ava Russell, and it could only be Ava Russell who had hired a man to burgle and possibly kill Eden. How the woman had found where she lived was unimportant now; all that mattered was going to Moorcroft House and facing her, of telling her should aught befall Eden then he himself would tell the authorities all that Dora Benson had confided to him.

Dora Benson had not wanted to tell him anything. Moonlight sketching shadows on the ground, stealing the pale shimmering robes from rocks dotted about the heath only to replace their silken glory moments later, went unheeded against the pictures filling Andrew's mind.

Thin, work-worn almost to a shadow, the woman had left the clamour of the small brick-built brewhouse which served for a nail-making workshop.

'*Yes, I knows Eden Brent but I don't know where her be living.*'

The woman had answered defensively, wanting to

shield Eden from anything which might result in trouble. It had taken some little while, Dora being convinced he meant no harm only when her husband came from the workshop and vouched for the honesty and fair dealing Andrew Denby practised with each man having the good fortune to work for him.

Dora had invited him into her home then, apologising for the frugality of it all, and after offering tea which he had accepted with thanks and listening to all he could tell of Eden, she had glanced at her husband and at his nod had told her own story.

Quietly, interrupted by the occasional pause as she searched for words in which to explain the more delicate situation Eden's sister had found herself in, it had all come out; all that Myra Brent herself had revealed and also of the letter she had written.

And it was that letter Shipton Cottage had been ransacked for. But it would do Ava Russell no good. If he could prove hers was the true hand behind the assault upon Eden, he would ensure the whole country learned of that woman's vile practices. Knowledge of what was being gossiped of while waiting to be sentenced would be Ava Russell's own torture.

. . . Ten sovereigns can seal a woman's mouth . . .

Ava Russell stared at the ceiling above her bed. That had been the payment demanded by that slut of a woman.

. . . I knows what a story like that could do . . .

Only there *would* be no story, for payment had been

given. But no sovereigns had changed hands. Ava's inner smile was pure hatred.

The woman's mouth had been wide beneath the leering grin, a brief shaft of clouded moonlight showing the gapped teeth. Ava's inward smile deepened. It had shown for one short moment before the mouth had opened to scream. But that scream had known no birth, nor would that mouth open again. She had waited there in the grounds of Moorcroft House, waited for money . . . but there was no profit in death. Nor had there been profit in her own journey.

Unmoving except for the glance playing over the ceiling, Ava recounted her doings of earlier that same evening. She had waited until after sunset before reaching deep into the wardrobe to extract a shoddy jacket, trousers and flat cap. Bought for a supposed fancy dress party, her cook had given no second thought to the procuring of them for her mistress, saying only they had come from a pawnshop so they needed hanging outside in the yard to air away the smell of damp. There had been no fancy dress, their use being that of making a woman look like a man . . . of making the mistress of Moorcroft appear as a working-class man worn out by his labours, and Samuel's cane had completed the illusion. Samuel had carried the cane every day since bringing it home from the Crimea, but it had never served him as it had served her.

Beyond the fringe of thought sounds echoed on the stillness but Ava remained with her memories.

Birks had thought to blackmail her. Poor stupid Birks!

'*Wait you there, old 'un.*'

The words he had spoken to a bent figure hobbling from the gloom, walking stick tapping the ground, came from the mouth of the man pictured so vividly by her brain.

'*I'll be passing that way in a minute or so . . .*'

And so he had. Alfred Birks had returned but not to pass, he had remained at the Church Steps, his chest and stomach slashed by the blade that 'old 'un' had drawn from the walking stick.

Her wit and Samuel's cane had saved her from the demands of a blackmailer as it had prevented Lenor's maid having the same idea.

It had happened as she had surmised. Ava's glance played on the white ceiling. Shoes that had most likely belonged to Lenor had tapped loudly, heralding the girl's approach. She had chosen the same route taken by Birks, coming by way of Ethelfleda Terrace, the way which brought her to that same alley where her lover had met his end.

'*Spare an old man tuppence for a bite o'supper.*'

The words she had called echoed now in Ava's head. Dilly Madely had gasped relief on seeing a bent old man grasping a walking stick in order to hold himself on his feet as he hobbled forward. But it had been no tuppence she had given, but her life! Samuel's cane had once more done its work and Ava Russell, disguised in the worn clothing of a working man, had simply walked away. But the clothes had not been disposed of, they had been stored in their hiding place, along with the cane. She had been sensible to keep them. Ava felt the smile spread in her chest. They had proved her salvation yet again.

She ought not to have sought the services of a woman of the streets, but the craving that was a flame in her stomach, desire lancing like blades, a hunger ravenous and consuming, a maelstrom of desire ripping away all common sense, had sent her in search of the only thing which would ease the longing . . . sent her in search of a woman. She had agreed, thinking to service an old man and be back at her trade in less time than it took to laugh over the doing; but there had been no return to the streets and the woman's payment had been the slashing of her chest and stomach. The Wednesbury Ripper was the term used to describe the perpetrator of those foul killings, but no one in Wednesbury had suspected the mistress of Moorcroft of being that killer.

Nor had the maid who cleaned the rooms of Church House! Above her head the shadows of evening began to inch across the ceiling. They would darken as those enveloping the garden of Moorcroft had darkened but these would hide no blackmailer.

The woman had played her game well. No morsel of regret, no trace of remorse or repentance for the murders she had committed, draped itself on Ava's conscience; only pictures fresh as if they had taken place but a minute since played clear in her mind.

'. . . *the doings be that of brushin' the muff* . . .'

Again a mouth seemed to move, to speak words only her mind could hear.

'. . . *you decide quick, I ain't about to stand 'ere all night.*'

Ava smiled at the echo in her brain.

The woman had not stood all night. She had stood only long enough for that blade to slice across her throat then she had collapsed, folding slowly, almost gently, from the knees as some player on the stage might curtsy to an audience. But there had been no audience and no applause, only a blade slashing and ripping at a body already beyond its feel.

She had laughed, a low exultant laugh of sheer triumph. Ava's eyes watched the encroaching gloom swallow the daylight. A feeling of exhilaration had swept like wildfire through her veins, had danced a wild dance of success, an exultation of victory. Once more she had defeated a challenge, destroyed the one who had made it and no other was witness. There was nothing and no one could call her to answer for what she had done. Ava Russell would never pay the price for murder.

She had laughed again but, as she had raised the blade to insert it into the body of the cane, the laugh had become a stranglehold, a choking blockage in her throat while her lungs had gripped convulsively on the handle of the swordstick. She had fallen there beside the door of her own house, fallen across the dead body, her own refusing to move. It had not moved since.

The smile which had spread so easily in her chest had died the same way.

The stroke had whipped across her brain taking with it the movement from arms and legs. But not the movement of her mind. Trapped where she lay, inert except for the flicker of eyelids, she had realised the truth and if she could have laughed one more time she would have done so then.

Nothing and no one could call her to answer for what she had done!

The thought had flashed.

Nothing and no one . . . except the will of heaven!

He had come immediately Davy had told him what had happened. Eden dressed slowly, pulling her clothes over aching limbs. Andrew Denby had called each day since . . . She pushed the thought away. Even now, a week from that awful night the memory of what had occurred brought fear to her throat.

Why had someone broken into this house? Eyes closing against the sting of moving her aching body, she sat on the side of the bed. She had come from the scullery, barely entered the living-room . . .

Pictures racing across inner vision, she drew a sharp breath.

. . . the light of the lamp had seemed strong after the pallid glow of a candle. Her spine had tingled, a strange feeling playing with her senses, the feeling of someone else being there in that empty room. She had made to draw back, instinct warning of something wrong and, in that same instant, from the corner of her eye, she had caught a movement, a dark shape lifting and in the seconds before it crashed down on her head she had glimpsed a pair of eyes.

Fingers twisting together, Eden tried to clear her mind, to erase the pictures from it; but, vivid in detail, hard and strong as reality, they clung on.

A coat collar turned up hid mouth and chin . . .

Relentlessly the memories returned, each demanding its moment in the theatre of her mind.

. . . a flat cap drawn low over the brow had held the rest of the face in shadow, but not the eyes . . .

Eden's whole body tensed.

Not those terrible glittering eyes! Her head had turned, drawn towards the shadow of movement at her side and, in that one fleeting second, her glance had locked with one spewing venom, a loathing so strong it had blazed like black fire, its message seeming to reach for her, wanting to pull her into itself, to destroy her in its own malevolence . . . and, more terrifying still, had been that awful conviction that the hatred came from someone she knew, someone she had met before!

But that was the result of shock. Gingerly, only too aware of the reaction of bruised flesh to any sudden move, she pushed herself to her feet. There was no one she knew who had eyes like those, no one in her life who had ever displayed the intensity of feeling, the hatred she had seen there.

Yet, tell herself what she did, tell herself a dozen times a day, that same feeling remained. Somewhere, sometime, she had seen those eyes before.

'You shouldn't be a' leaving of your bed . . . Mister Denby said you was to rest.'

Sara Melia turned to the figure coming slowly from the stairs, sympathy and anger mingling as she saw the bruising dark against pale skin. What no-good rogue could do such to a young wench? The cat were too good for the like of men like that, they should have the rope and so sure the culprit were caught then Andrew Denby would make certain that were what he'd get.

'Mister Denby is very kind but he is not my keeper.'

No, he ain't, but there is summat he would like to be. The thought kept safely inside, Sara tutted her disapproval as Eden settled thankfully to a chair.

'You have all been very kind,' Eden smiled, accepting freshly brewed tea, 'but now I am well enough to take care of myself.'

Sara's head shook slowly. 'That ain't what Mister Andrew will be sayin'. He cares about you, wench. You might not see but other folk does, Andrew Denby cares a great deal about you.'

Much as she wanted to follow Sara into the washhouse to help with the laundry, the ache in her limbs told Eden she would be more hindrance than enough.

'. . . *Andrew Denby cares a great deal about you.*'

Did he? Eden stared at the tea she had not tasted. She had dared to dream that that might be so, dared to hope . . . but hope, like dreams, had been fleeting.

'*Dreams does no harm, lessen you* mixes *them with the truth.*'

Another of Grandmother's sayings. Eden smiled ruefully. But was that not what she had done? She had allowed that which she longed for to become entangled with what was given, and that was wrong. She could not take friendship and weave it into love; Andrew Denby had offered her one, she could never expect to be offered the other.

Yet there had been moments. She took up the cup, gripping it tightly in an attempt to still the trembling that came with the thought. Moments she could not forget. Like the one when, the day following the assault upon her, she had wakened to find him standing beside her bed. There had been such a look of tenderness on his face, a depth in his dark eyes that she had felt her heart cry its own response. Then Tobias Jevons had been shown into her room and the look had vanished, replaced by one which could be read almost as anger.

How could real tenderness, even that of friendship, die so quickly unless it were simply imagined? Sipping the hot sweet liquid, Eden felt the same sadness which had risen at Andrew Denby's abrupt departure. He had seemed suddenly angry . . . but for what reason? And the evening he had called on his way to Wednesbury. She had glimpsed that same unreadable look deep in his eyes and for a heart-stopping moment she had thought he would take her in his arms . . . but then the moment was gone and so was Andrew Denby.

Replacing the cup on its saucer, she stared unseeingly at it.

He could not refuse what he did not know was his. He could not refuse her love.

Beyond the tiny living-room, the thump of the wooden maid beating linen in the heavy tub reverberated on the silence but Eden heard only the beat of her own turmoil.

And, if by some miracle, Andrew Denby were to love her? Nothing could come of it! Fingernails bit deep into the soft flesh of palms. She could never accept it, how could she? How could she ruin his life, for that was how it would be. A girl from Hobbins Street, a place so poor its inhabitants knew hunger from birth! That might be overcome. Andrew Denby did not give the impression of snobbery, of the possession of wealth being a dominant factor in his life. But lack of money was not the only thing made Eden Brent undesirable as a wife, not the only part of her background could give him cause to despise her . . . There was her sister!

But no . . . not Myra herself! Eden's mind revolted at the thought. Eden was not wicked . . . her sister was not dirty! It was what she had been forced to do, what Ava Russell had insisted upon, vile acts no girl should ever be made to partake in! But would Andrew Denby believe that? Would he believe Myra had done what she had in order to support her grandmother and sister? Or would he believe she had been a willing partner, one who enjoyed the games that were played . . . would he see Myra as no less a lesbian than her mistress?

But the test would not be put. Myra's past would

never be revealed. Andrew Denby would never learn her secret.

Myra's secret! A jolt ran the length of Eden's spine. The letter written by her sister . . . had whoever had ransacked this house found it . . . had it been stolen?

Pushing to her feet, she cried out as a shadow from the open doorway fell across her vision.

35

'I found her meself, out there in the garden, a' covered in blood and lyin' atop a corpse slashed almost to ribbons.'

Andrew Denby had listened to the woman who had cleaned at Moorcroft House.

'Whoever would 'ave thought it!' The woman had sobbed. 'Whoever would 'ave teken a murderer to be a woman.'

Who indeed!

Had Ava Russell been lying at the back of the house while he had knocked on the door at the front?

There had been no doubt in the minds of the constables the cleaning woman's screams had sent running to that house. The jacket and trousers Ava Russell was dressed in were splashed with blood, her hands were covered in it and the blade of the swordstick still clutched in her useless fingers was rust-brown where blood had dried on it. It was like a signed testimonial, an unspoken admittance to her being a murderess and one readily accepted by the magistrate.

'*All carry the same hallmark,*' The magistrate had declared. '*Each victim was despatched in the same manner, the throat being cut and the body ripped open by a blade. But with the accused being unable to answer to any questions the law can make no call for trial. The outcome, therefore, must be that until speech returns the woman, Ava Russell, will remain under medical supervision.'*

Medical supervision! Andrew Denby played a glance over the high walls and tall iron gates of the private sanatorium. That magistrate might just as well have acquitted the woman for, as things were, she could not be tried or sentenced; Ava Russell had got away with murder after all!

'Doctor is of the opinion that a major part of the paralysis is the result of shock.' The matron who had conducted Andrew to a small room holding only a narrow iron-framed bed, a chest of drawers and a bedside table with glass-topped lamp, touched a hand to the covers smoothing a non existent crease. 'Once that is gone he is convinced the use of the limbs, as the speech, will be restored. It should be remembered, however, that a stroke does often result in one side of the body being permanently affected. We should be aware of such a possibility. We should also be aware of visiting hours . . .' A sniff emphasising displeasure at having routine disrupted, the matron glared at Andrew. 'You may have one half hour . . . but future visits will be made at the regular time!'

With a swish of grey skirts beneath an apron whiter than God's own snow and starched stiff as cardboard, the woman had swept from the room, a whiff of carbolic circling after her.

Looking down at Ava Russell, Andrew felt the bile of distaste bite his throat. The woman could not speak with her tongue but her eyes said she knew the reason of his visit . . . They knew and they laughed.

'I know you can hear and I know you can understand.'

Almost black against the pristine pillow, the dark eyes gleamed.

'It was you, wasn't it?' he asked. 'You who went to Shipton Cottage, you who struck and bound Eden Brent?'

Ava's eyelids closed slowly, then opened.

'Is that your sign for agreement?'

The eyelids closed again, remaining so for a couple of seconds before lifting.

It was a yes. Ava Russell was answering.

'You were looking for something?'

Again the lowering of the eyelids.

'That something was a letter, a letter written by Myra Brent?'

Black against the pillow, the eyes regarded him. Would she answer again?

'I know there was such a letter. Dora Benson told me of it. Was that the reason of your going to that cottage?'

Slowly the lids dropped. She was hiding nothing but she would know that in the eyes of the law she had admitted nothing. What can't speak can't lie! The adage seemed to taunt in the stare once more fastening on his face.

'Did you find it? Do you have it?'

No movement of eyelids confirmed the answer, only that mocking laugh, that dark evil glittered in a coal-black gaze. Even now, malice was Ava Russell's master.

'If you will not answer that, then will you answer this.' He paused, feeling the acid of his throat spill on to his tongue. 'Did you intend to kill Eden Brent?'

There was no hesitation. With the last syllable not yet free of his lips the eyelids lowered, pressing hard against the eyeballs beneath. A swift intake of breath brought the next question. 'Were you disturbed? Is that the reason Eden Brent is still alive?'

The same sign telling him the assumption was correct, he glanced with exasperation at the door being opened. The half hour was not up yet!

'This is highly irregular!'

The voice of the matron cut shrilly across the room and, staring up from the pillow, Ava Russell's eyes laughed again.

She was aware all right! Andrew's teeth ground his frustration. Aware he could ask no more questions. But her being disturbed, and by whom, no longer mattered . . . It had meant the saving of Eden's life and that was all he cared about.

'Highly irregular!' Heels tapping on floors polished to a crystal shine, the woman swept into the room, her face flushed and angry beneath a wide starched cap. 'The time allowed for visiting patients is made very clear, and that time is not now!'

Dressed in a dark suit and tie, a tall thin-framed man

answered in the same acerbic tone which had addressed him. 'I am aware of that, as you should be aware, that being Missis Russell's solicitor, the law allows I speak with her whenever I deem it necessary; and the law, I might inform you, has precedence even over this establishment.'

A loud sniff her reply, the matron turned on her heel but could not resist one last curt rejoinder. 'Then I hope the law will take note a patient needs rest!'

'Please.' The solicitor touched a long finger to Andrew's sleeve as he, too, moved to leave. 'If you would not mind staying. What I have to disclose to my client I prefer to be said in the presence of a witness.'

Not waiting for an answer, the man drew a sheaf of papers from a leather Gladstone bag, his voice droning on.

'Missis Russell, the doctor assures me you are in possession of your hearing and that your ability to understand that which is said to you remains unimpaired.'

Andrew looked at the figure in the bed, at the eyes suddenly alert with apprehension. Ava Russell was no longer laughing!

'That being so,' the solicitor glanced briefly at his client, 'I have to inform you the bank has taken possession of Moorcroft House and the few items remaining within it. I am given by them to tell you the residue of the sum it sells for . . . if any residue there be . . . will be paid in due course. However, added to the amount of money found at Moorcroft House . . .' he flicked a page, running the tip of a finger over the next, until arriving halfway down, '. . . the sum of which amounted to . . . here is where I wish a witness present to testify my words should they be questioned at some future date . . . the sum of which amounted to eighteen pounds four shillings and threepence three farthings. I would add that of that sum ten pounds is due for legal services accruing over the past months and will be deducted, the rest will be given over to the sanatorium in order to cover the expense of the care you have received so far.'

Papers returned, the Gladstone bag snapped shut, the solicitor glanced once at Andrew before requesting an exchange of cards. Then, with a brief nod of the head, he was gone.

Ava Russell was destitute. Moorcroft House did not belong to her and what was left of her money was already spoken for. But private sanatoriums were expensive . . . and charity had no place in the running of them. Drawn again to glance at the face, white now almost as the pillow, Andrew could see she too was thinking that same thought.

The return of the matron, followed by two timid-looking nurses, seemed to fill the quiet room with a rush of sound, drawing Andrew's glance away from the bed.

'One moment!' He lifted a hand halting the order for him to leave immediately. 'Can you tell me, should this patient be unable to meet the cost incurred by remaining in this establishment then where will she be placed?'

A sarcastic laugh bedded in her throat, the matron sniffed. 'I can tell you that. She is to be given to the care of the parish. In other words she is to be sent to the place where all paupers are sent . . . she is to go into the poorhouse!'

The poorhouse! Andrew could almost feel pity as a glance caught the jerk of fingers scrabbling at the bedcover. No, Ava Russell was no longer laughing, the sneer and taunt had gone from those raven eyes. In their place gleamed panic, a dark silent scream of utter horror. She had felt the first tremor of her own returning ability to move, had heard the words of the matron and realised their full meaning.

Sentence had already been pronounced! Andrew walked from the sanatorium. Ava Russell had heard it proclaimed. She would hear, move and most likely speak, but only within the walls of the poorhouse; she was condemned to a fate more odious to her than death.

How many years would she live it? Climbing into his carriage, he turned the horse towards home.

Ava Russell was a true daughter of the devil and her evil had indeed reaped its own reward.

'Sara has her own home to care for as well as a living to earn. I will not take advantage of good nature.' Eden's determined look met the coppery smile of her visitor.

'Sara will be . . .'

'Paid . . . but not by me!' Sharper than was meant, it

was followed by a quick apologetic smile. 'Forgive me, but I will not take charity, though I thank you for your kindness.'

Determined as ever! Tobias Jevons smiled inwardly. It was an aspect of Eden Brent's character he had come to admire . . . even if sometimes he thought it to act not entirely in her best interests; but he could not blame her stubbornness; after all, did he not possess the same trait? Allowing the smile to show he said, 'You are a very independent young woman. A few weeks spent at The Coppice would see you fully recovered and it would afford myself great pleasure. Will you not give it some thought?'

From the towpath which ran before the small house the call of a boatman brought a horse to a standstill, then was followed by a second call asking permission to fill water pails from the well.

Sunlight gilding a slight frame, glistening on fair hair like golden fire, brought a tightening to Tobias Jevons' throat. The canvas in his bedroom . . . it might be a replica of what he was seeing now; but this was a living, breathing girl while his own dear wife . . .

'I have thought of it.' Eden turned from speaking with the boatman. 'I love The Coppice, it is regal and beautiful but at the same time gentle, filled with a love which seems to touch me whenever I enter. Your offer is tempting but I have to refuse.'

'But why?'

Eden's glance flicked to the window to where the narrowboat began to move. 'That is why. It is not only

Sara must make her living, I also must do the same. The people who work the canals buy the food I cook; without that I cannot feed myself or pay rent for this house.'

Bright as newly minted coins, Tobias Jevons' copper-coloured eyes narrowed, fingers gripping more tightly on the silver-topped malacca cane. 'Rent?' He frowned. 'You pay a rent for this cottage . . . to whom?'

'To nobody as yet, and I shouldn't really call what I put aside each day a rent for, not knowing the owner of the property, I could not agree a sum. I only hope that when someone does claim payment the money in that pot will prove sufficient.'

He had not been mistaken in his beliefs. Tobias watched the slip of a girl who had once left tuppence on his gatepost as payment for advice. She had the quick fire of pride, but she also had dignity. Andrew Denby was stupid not to ask her to wed with him, serve the young fool right if, as he had been warned, some other man scooped her from under his nose!

'I was afraid the person who . . .' Eden faltered, '. . . who came into the house that night might have taken the money in the pot but, thank heaven, it was not stolen.'

Thank heaven you were not severely injured. Tobias Jevons' own thanks were silently given while aloud he asked, 'Was *anything* stolen?'

'That is what is so difficult to understand.' Eden's brow wrinkled her glance showing puzzlement. 'Nothing was taken. I suppose I surprised him and that is the reason I was struck. Then, fearing I might run to the narrowboat moored at the bank, he bound my wrists and ankles.'

Then stayed long enough to turn the place upside down before making his getaway! As before, Tobias kept his reasoning to himself saying instead, 'Leads a man to ask, what would any thief expect to find in so tiny a house?'

'I don't know. I am only too glad he did not find the money in that pot . . . I really don't think I could have saved enough to replace that as well as the amount I already put aside. It would be a relief were the owner to come, to agree the amount he required in order for me to live here.'

Fingers relaxing, copper-hued eyes softening, Tobias answered. 'The owner has called here on several occasions and he tells you now: there is no rent required for Shipton Cottage.'

'You!' Eden stared. 'You own this house?'

'The land it is built on belonged to my father, the materials for its construction were provided by him, so yes the cottage belongs to me though it was built by Ezekial Shipton and lived in by himself and his wife from their marrying.'

'But you knew I was here! Why did you not ask for payment?'

'I needed none.' Tobias shrugged. 'Besides, the meal an old man was brought was asked no payment of.'

'I didn't want money!'

'Neither did I, my dear.' The lined face smiled. 'I

also thought I did not want friendship but, in that, I was wrong. Despite my sour ways you continued your visits until, in the end, I waited for them, wanting to see you, hoping you would come and you did, every evening without fail. That was your kindness. Allow my not speaking of rent to have been mine.'

The house in Hobbins Street was empty, the cramped brewhouse which had seen the making of the family's livelihood was empty, the fire in the forge dead and cold. Had that which had been feared for so long finally happened? Had the making of nails no longer brought money enough to feed them? That is what had to have happened; they had been near enough penniless when she had left Grandmother's house and now Aunt Dora and her family too were gone.

She ought to have called more often, maybe she could have helped. But she had told herself the pain of the past was still too great. Would Dora have acted that way . . . would the woman who had loved and comforted a motherless child have turned her back on that same girl, forgotten her as she had forgotten Aunt Dora?

But I did not forget! The thought was a cry of pure anguish but, as Eden walked quickly from the place of childhood, the feelings of guilt did not subside.

Where had the family gone? The sons were grown and capable of travelling to find work, but their mother . . . She had been so tired and worn, always sharing most of her own food between her boys until it seemed she was no more than one of the shadows which haunted the badly lighted house. Aunt Dora would need to find a home quickly, but where? Who would employ a woman so . . .

Striking so hard it rocked her on her heels, the answer slammed into Eden's mind. No one would give work to Dora Benson . . . and the only shelter she would find would be the poorhouse!

Clenched fingers pressed to her mouth holding the cries inside, Eden stared towards Meeting Street. Often with her hand clutching Grandmother's skirts a young child's feet had clattered to keep up as she was walked quickly past a building which even to so young a mind had appeared dark and forbidding. Was that where Aunt Dora was now . . . in that place so feared by the poor of Wednesbury? The institution spoken of as not breaking only the heart but destroying the very soul of those condemned to live within its walls.

But not Aunt Dora . . . she would not be left to such a life! Her grandmother's shawl propping a courage already threatening to fail, Eden crossed the Holyhead Road into Meeting Street.

36

'What the hell do you think you are doing, going off by yourself!'

Sobs which Eden had fought all the way home from that poorhouse flared into resentment as Andrew Denby's angry words met her. Stepping inside Shipton Cottage she retaliated, her whole frame throbbing with quick anger.

'And who do you think you are!' Green-blue eyes danced with fire. 'You have no right to speak to me that way.'

Already on his feet it took Andrew Denby only one stride to reach her. Hands fastening an iron grip on her elbows he glared down at her, his words coming hot and furious.

'I have every right, dammit . . . I'm in love with you!'

She had not heard right. The fire left Eden's eyes but she made no answer. She had thought he said . . . but that was her own foolish mind.

'I love you . . . you little fool!'

Dark eyes held the look she had seen before, the look she had told herself was yet one more trick of her mind.

'That gives me the right to worry over you, to want to protect you, to ask you to be my wife.'

She was not imagining, this was not a dream. Andrew Denby was real, he was here in this house . . . he was asking her to marry him!

'I have loved you from the very beginning,' his voice was softer now, husky with tenderness, 'from the moment I found you huddled against that bridge freezing to death.'

'You love me!'

A smile crossing his lips adding to the warm sable softness of his eyes, he drew her closer, his arms holding her against him. 'Is that so very difficult to believe?'

It was more than difficult, it was impossible. How could he feel love for her? She was from a different world, a world of poverty while he . . .

'I have wanted to tell you . . . to ask . . . but we seemed always to be at odds; then when I came here to find the place empty and you nowhere to be found, I realised just how much you truly meant to me, that without you my life is empty. I knew then I had to say what is in my heart: I love you and I want you to be my wife.'

They were words she had longed to hear, words she had dreamed of hearing. Held in that embrace Eden felt her heart crack. They were words she must refuse!

Pushing free she moved several paces away. Not daring to trust herself to look at him, knowing that what she must say would end any future relationship, that the friendship they had between them now would be broken for all time, but still she had to say it.

'I . . .' her voice trembled, '. . . I'm sorry but I . . . I cannot become your wife.'

Silence, breath-catchingly deep, seemed to Eden's agitated mind to go on for ever but at last Andrew Denby spoke, tension cracking his words.

'I beg your pardon, I have embarrassed you. It was presumptuous of me to think you could possibly entertain the idea of consenting to marry me, to believe . . . to hope you might return my love. I see now that cannot be.'

'That is not so!' Words she tried to hold inside swept past all resistance. 'It is not because I do not love you . . . I can't marry you because of . . .'

Not moving from the spot, only his glance moving across a face pale with emotion, Andrew demanded quietly.

'Because of what? Have you given your word to some other man?'

'No!' Eyes swimming with unshed tears lifted to his.

'Eden.' He moved close but did not touch her. 'Answer me honestly. Do you love me?'

How could she lie, how could she say words which would have him turn from her . . . how could she live without him? Yet how could she do otherwise when knowledge of what her life held would one day have him despise her!

'Andrew, I . . .'

'Don't!' He interrupted swiftly. 'I can read your answer for myself; you may wish to deny it but it is there in your eyes. You do love me Eden, refute it if you must but you cannot hide it.'

No, she could not hide it, but neither could she give way to it. His life must not be ruined as a result of hers.

'Say it.' His look gentle with love he reached for her, drawing her back into his arms. 'Say it, my darling, say you love me as I love you.'

Heaven could give her this one moment, a second of time to treasure. Breath held against the rapture of it, Eden let herself be held, allowed herself the bliss of lips closing on hers, the touch of his body strong and firm against her own. This was the paradise she had longed for, the desire of her soul; she could take it now, take the love he offered . . . But how long would love last . . . how long before paradise turned to ashes in her heart? To whisper the truth would be hard but, of all things, Andrew Denby deserved to hear that.

Taking one more moment, breathing the scent of him deep into her lungs, she whispered, 'I do love you, I love you with all my heart.'

Holding her even closer, Andrew laughed, a deep jubilant, thankful laugh. 'Then you will be my wife.'

Now for the pain! Knowing the moment must be broken, Eden pushed gently from his arms. 'No. . .' It trembled on the brink of tears but the storm did not break. 'No, Andrew, I cannot marry you and please . . . don't ask me why.'

'No, I won't ask you, instead I will tell you. You are refusing me because of Myra, because of what happened at Moorcroft House and the things Ava Russell forced her to do.'

In the quiet hush of the small cottage, his words calm

and unruffled, Andrew told of how on following her to Moorcroft, not finding her there he had gone to the house of Dora Benson and she had told him the whole of Myra' s story.

'It was that letter the intruder searched this house for,' he took her hand, holding it between both of his own, 'a letter which could harm only one person: the mistress of Moorcroft.'

'Aunt Dora told you.'

'Yes, but don't hold that against her. She could see I loved you, that I wanted only to protect you.'

'The man who came, the one who struck me . . .'

'Was no man,' Andrew cut in. 'That was Ava Russell. It was she in men's clothing and it was she who committed those murders in Wednesbury, killed in order to protect the secret of her vile practices. But all of that is over, the woman will never walk the streets again.' Quietly as before he told of Ava's incarceration.

'But that changes nothing.' Eden pulled her hands free. 'What Myra did cannot be erased.'

'But it can be forgiven and forgotten.'

'Can it?' Eden rose to her feet. 'I went to Aunt Dora's today to ask that same thing but the family were not in the house in Hobbins Street. They were gone, driven out by hunger and want. Don't you see, Andrew, I failed Aunt Dora as I failed Myra. I did nothing to help either of them; I brought my sister only unhappiness and that is ultimately what I would bring you should knowledge of this ever become known. That is why I will never become your wife.' Taking an envelope from her pocket

Eden held it towards him. 'Read it,' she said, 'read what it was my sister suffered . . . suffered for me!'

'You need hold no grief for Dora Benson or her family.' Andrew watched the stricken face. 'They did not leave Hobbins Street for the reasons you think but in order to work for Tobias Jevons. He wanted reliable hard-working staff and I recommended the Bensons. Dora and her husband will care for the house whilst the sons do the same for the stables and grounds. As for this,' he took the letter and held it for a moment, 'I have no wish to read it. I know that what Myra did was done out of love, for the love of a sister. You know that, too. Myra loved you and your grandmother enough to go through hell in order to keep you safe. Honour that love, Eden, honour it by burning this letter and living the life she would have you live.'

For the love of a sister! Her heart twisting, Eden took the letter and tossed it into the fire, watching the corners of the envelope crisp and curl, then burst into orange flame. Myra *had* gone through hell for her sake and she would tread those same paths to shield Andrew Denby from shame.

Turning to tell him so, she was forestalled by a call from the towpath.

'That will be the trainee manager of the new boatyard I've had built along of Wiggins Pool. He is taking the first boat built there to pick up a load of glassware from Stourbridge. Would you like to see it?'

At her nod Andrew caught her hand, holding her back just long enough to say, 'I love you Eden, no matter how you decide to live your life, remember always that I love you.'

She wanted his kiss, wanted his arms to hold her but, in taking her own happiness, she would eventually rob him of his. This thought all that held her together, she walked out to the towpath. There, an immaculately painted hull reflected its deep blue and lemon colours in the smooth sun-kissed waters.

'*. . . honour that love, Eden . . .*'

The words burned in her mind as she looked at the sleek narrowboat, Davy Melia pointing smilingly to its white-painted name.

'*. . . honour it . . . by living the life she would have you live.*'

That was what Myra would want, that was the love of a sister.

Catching the look she turned to him, Andrew frowned. 'You don't like her?'

'The boat is beautiful.'

'But?'

'The name,' she answered.

Andrew frowned again, 'The *Eden Brent*, I thought you might like that!'

Pure happiness lighting her eyes, Eden stepped close to the man she loved.

'Eden Brent was a nice choice,' she whispered lifting her mouth to his, 'but would you make it the *Eden Denby*.'

If you enjoyed
FOR THE LOVE OF A SISTER,
here's a foretaste of
Meg Hutchinson's new novel,
THE WANTON RED-HEAD.

PROLOGUE

She had to do it!

This was a chance that would never come again! Auburn hair streaming in a breeze that pressed a thin cotton dress against long colt-like legs, the slight figure ran across the open heath.

But if she could not make it happen!

If she were saddled with a child!

Thoughts clanged like the passing bell, the impact of them bringing the flying figure to an abrupt halt.

That would mean the end of everything. If this one opportunity were lost, this one straw Fate was holding out to her was allowed to pass her by, it would condemn her to a life of misery, a life such as her mother had lived in a poky terraced house back to back with faceless rows of the same.

To live a lifetime as she lived now, sharing a yard with eight other houses, the families of four of them using the same wash-house, the same water pump . . . the one privy . . .

Looking to where the winding wheel of Spindrift Colliery rose black against the vermilion of a cloudless sky, Thea Maybury's pretty young face twisted with repugnance.

That wheel rode the sky like the chariot of death and that was what it brought to many of the people living in its shadow; death to men choking their days away in the black bowels of that coalmine, children sleeping top to toe in beds shoved into rooms whose very air was laden with the dust of the coal they were forced to help drag from the earth, children who coughed with the sickness of the lungs that digging also brought. A life of torment and grime was what she would have, a life many women of Darlaston lived working until they dropped, then every night asking the Lord to keep them from falling with yet another child.

Breath catching in her throat, Thea's nerves tightened. Spindrift Colliery! It was aptly named. Every dream dreamed by men who passed within its black mouth, every dream of women who toiled pulling coal-laden bogeys from the pit head soon spun away; drifting mists of dead hopes.

That was what the child would bring to her.

Staring at the spirals of smoke rising from the chimneys of the houses built simply to serve that colliery, Thea Maybury anxiously twisted the cloth of her cheap skirt.

It would ruin everything, bring an end to her own dreams; they too would be lost like spindrift melting in the first rays of a summer sun, taking with them all she had longed for every day of living in that hovel of a house, what she had prayed for every night - and now that prayer had been answered, the chance she yearned for was offered and to let it pass . . . !

Disturbed by her presence a bird flew up from among the rough tussocks of grass, its song spreading over the quiet evening as it rose to meet the sky. Watching it glide effortlessly, graceful wings etched dark against the brilliance of a setting sun, Thea felt her heart lift. Fate which had offered the dream now offered the solution.

Thea watched the bird, its wings feathering the air holding it where it wanted to be. As she must hold to what she wanted.

To let it pass . . . She smiled beginning to walk on. No, she would not let it pass, she would not lose the dream . . . not even if it meant dropping the child down a mineshaft!

'You've got to help me, 'Lyssa, you are the only one I can turn to.'

Thea Maybury watched incomprehension become disbelief on the face of the young woman sat on the edge of a narrow iron-framed bed.

'You've got to, you do see that, don't you, it's the only way.'

Stomach nerves taut, Thea broke her pretence of a sob, threading the void of silence. 'Lyssa was not going to agree . . . she would not . . . but she had to be made to agree!

Beneath the cover of another sob Thea Maybury's mind worked like quicksilver. The offer which had been made to her had come like a gift from heaven; it was all she had ever wanted, a new life in a new country. She would no longer live in near-poverty, no longer skivvy carrying things to market, making do with the cheapest of clothes. She would have her own fine house and all that went with it . . . Thea Maybury would live like a lady.

'No one will ever know.' Allowing yet another false sob she crossed to a corner of the tiny room where she rested her hand on a chest of drawers before proceeding. 'Nobody will think twice, it won't matter for you, after all it's not like you have . . .'

Not like you have anyone interested in you. Alyssa Maybury finished the sentence in her mind. Alyssa the older sister, Alyssa the dowdy sister, Alyssa the girl a man never looked at once he had seen the pretty Thea.

'You must see,' Thea persisted, paying no mind to the hurt she saw before those other eyes were lowered, 'this is the only way, the best way.'

Best for all of them or best for Thea? Alyssa could not prevent the thought rising beneath the hurt. Her sister had always been self centred, the world must not simply revolve around Thea, it must revolve *for* Thea.

'This way I can help more with Mother than I can by taking stuff into town.'

Stuff! Alyssa's fingers clutched the bed's cold iron frame. That was all it was to her sister. Not for Thea the stitching which helped keep a roof over their heads, not for her the back-breaking hours of tending vegetables they sold to the kitchens of Darlaston's wealthy and certainly not for her to assist in the caring of a sick mother.

Across the narrow space dividing the bed from the chest of drawers Thea felt the weight of hesitation. Alyssa had not answered, she hadn't uttered a single word . . . and when she did would that word be 'no'? But it couldn't be . . . she would not let it be; there were ways and there were means and if one failed then the other must be tried.

'Don't say no, 'Lyssa, please . . .'

Breaking long enough to force a fresh sob, she pleaded. 'This is what I've hoped and prayed for, you can't let me lose it now, you can't!'

You can't! Refusing to be held back thoughts ran wild in Alyssa's mind. This was the way it had ever been between them, Thea doing exactly as she wished, the blame for any mischief it might cause being left to lie heavily on her sister's shoulders. Always the responsibility had been placed with her. 'You should have watched her' . . . 'You should have taken more care of her.' That had been the way of their mother; she could never bring herself to accept there was any fault in her youngest child. But then Thea had always come first in their mother's affections; the delicate, pretty red-gold-haired Thea must have the new dress, Thea lifted to a mother's knee each evening, Thea who must not be burdened with any but the very lightest of chores, Thea who could do no wrong.

But Thea had done wrong and now in typical fashion looked to her older sister to take the blame, to carry the guilt. This though was too much. Alyssa's fingers clutched even tighter against the cold iron. She could not do what her sister was asking. It was morally wrong, a sin against a child and a sin against God; she would not help, not this time.

'No.' Looking to where the slight figure waited, Alyssa shook her head briefly. 'No, Thea, I can't . . .'

The scarlet-gold of the dying sun filtering through the small square window caught the blue lightning flash of Thea's eyes, her answer spitting the flame of anger.

'Can't!' she snapped. 'Can't or won't! Oh, I see why you refuse . . . you haven't been offered the chance so why should I have it! That's the truth of it, isn't it? Oh yes, that's the truth all right, you are jealous, you have always been jealous of me, admit it, Alyssa, you have always been jealous!'

Had she always been envious of her sister? Alyssa felt the mental slump as she acknowledged the grain of truth the answer to that accusation must contain. Yes, childhood had been a time of envy and so many times a sadness. Not so much an envy of the lovely red-gold curls and pretty face, not even of the new dresses with their ribbons and bows their mother had sewed. That she had learned to deal with but the sadness of not being shown that same love, that special love which had always been Thea's. Yes, it was the love their mother had lavished on her younger daughter which the plain Alyssa had longed to experience; her mother's love she had wept for in the dark hours of night, prayed for the length of each day, but when evening came it was Thea lifted to their mother's lap, Thea held close to have her head stroked, hers the face receiving the last gentle kiss when put to bed: it was that, only that. . .

'Admit it!' Anger bruised the silence. 'Admit it, Alyssa, give the devil his freedom!'

Sharp as a blast of cold wind stripping trees of the last of their leaves the outburst blew away the shadows of guilt and for the first time Alyssa faced that which she had known for so long, known yet refused to know: for Thea it was Thea, it would always be Thea and nobody but Thea; in her sister's eyes only self was of any consequence.

'Give the devil his freedom.' Calm despite the emotions churning her mind, Alyssa looked at her sister, at the pretty face twisted now with temper and frustration. Always in childhood and even to this very evening she had drawn back from that look, allowed Thea her own way, but now all of that was gone. Thea must face her problems, own to her responsibility, accept the results of her actions. 'Give the devil his freedom,' she repeated quietly, 'that is what you have always done, that is what you did a year ago . . .'

'That's not true, I was forced . . .'

'No.' Alyssa shook her head again. 'Mother may have believed your story but I never have. You behaved then as you have behaved all of your life. You fulfilled your own desires, took what you wanted, gave freedom to the devil that sits inside you, the devil of selfishness;

but you forgot that demon gives his own rewards and he has given you yours. You knew what you were doing that day just as you know what you are about now, what you are always about, Thea, getting your own way, making things suit you . . . but not this time. Yours was the sin and yours must be the carrying of it.'

Across the room a slant of sunset touched red-gold hair lending a halo of flame.

That was how saints had been portrayed in those pictures which as children she and Thea had been shown at Sunday school, holy men and women their heads crowned with haloes of gold.

For the briefest of moments Alyssa was back in the small rectory room of St Lawrence Church gazing in wide-eyed awe at the paintings of people spoken of as the Blessed Apostles, of Saint Anne and her daughter the Virgin Mother of Christ, their calm serene faces captivating her young mind.

'I should have known that would be your answer . . .'

A toss of bright head threw a thousand gold-tipped slivers of light showering the gathering shadows like tinder sparks. The accusation snapped harshly in the gentle quiet. It broke Alyssa's reverie and once again it was her sister she watched. No face of gentle saint, no tender loving smile painted those delicate features. The look of anger and aggravation which, from their earliest years, heralded a fit of the sulks should Thea be opposed in anything. Then as quickly as the storm of temper had threatened so it cleared.

But Alyssa had seen this same swift cessation of

anger many times and always it had proved a prelude to another of her sister's wiles. This was not an end of demanding; it was not in Thea's nature to give up before gaining the last little bit of what she had set her mind to.

Across from Alyssa a fresh cascading of light danced like fireflies in the tiny room, a last gift of the disappearing sun touching a blessing to her sister's head. Watching her now, the delicate features no longer wearing the mutinous look of aggravation, the tightness of temper no longer pulling at the pretty mouth, Alyssa thought again of the painted saints. Yes, her sister was beautiful but there was a saying about beauty being skin deep . . .

Alyssa caught the thought before it could go any further but she could not prevent the sudden rush of feeling in her heart, a feeling of pity. Why? She tried to reason the emotion; surely her sister, the strong-minded, beautiful Thea, needed no one's pity?

'I should have known . . .' Fireflies fluttered with Thea's brief shake of her head. 'I should have known what you would say but despite your reason being pure jealousy, of your wishing to see my life ruined, of wanting me to lead the same life you will always lead, a soul-destroying poverty-ruled existence, I realise that . . . yes, it is best I clear this matter myself.'

Lowering her hand to a half-opened drawer of the chest Thea looked at the sister she had always been able to manipulate. The hair was the same, maybe a shade or two darker, the gold glinting among the rich heavy folds forever dragged back from the face which though not as pretty as her own, yet held a certain attractive quality; but it was the eyes, those dusky winter-violet eyes that had the real beauty, a beauty compelling enough to ensnare any man should her sister but try. But 'Lyssa did not try. 'Lyssa was not given to slipping away at every opportunity and she, Thea, had never encouraged her to. It served very well having her stay at home. Getting on with the business of earning their living meant no encumbrance on herself, instead it allowed that liberty which had ever been indulged to its fullest. In the softening shadows of approaching night the tightening of Thea's mouth remained imperceptible. Liberty! That was the one thing she craved over all else, release from the yoke of living hand to mouth, to escape the smoke and dirt of Darlaston . . . of the new fetters threatening to bind her! Her hand closing on the edge of the drawer, she breathed the sharp breath of resolution. She would never wear those chains . . . never!

Alyssa had watched . . . was watching. Deep inside Thea laughed. The sister she had always so easily twisted round her finger would do her bidding yet again.

'Thea!'

Edged with concern, the call merely had Thea's inner smile deepen, yes, 'Lyssa would do as demanded.

'Thea, what are you going to do?'

Lifting a blanket-wrapped bundle from the open

drawer, Thea faced her sister and now that inward smiled etched her lips. The battle was almost won!

Eyes brilliant as the minute lances of light sparkling in her hair, Thea shook her head in affected sadness. 'Do?' she echoed. 'Exactly as you said I should, face up to my responsibility.'

Concern becoming a needle-sharp prick of anxiety, Alyssa watched the smile, the cold glitter of eyes fastened on her own. This was a Thea she had not known before. A girl who had never accepted the results of her foolhardiness was now accepting consequence? No! A trip of nerves told Alyssa there was something else behind this sudden acquiescence, something infinitely alarming. Her sister had never tolerated denial and instinct warned she would not do so now.

'But you of all people, 'Lyssa, should know what I am *not* going to do!'

The very quietness with which it was said, the calm, even tone smooth as frozen ice added frissons of fear to Alyssa's tense nerves as she glanced at the bundle held in her sister's arms then at the face which gleamed an awful triumph.

'I am not going to allow this . . .' Thea gave a shake to the bundle, '. . . this mistake to ruin my life, so I shall get rid of it. You have no need to worry, no one will ever find it . . . but should you find yourself thinking in those hours when sleep refuses to come, then remember I told you . . . I told you nothing would take this chance from me. Remember also that you were as responsible as I, for you sat there knowing all the time I would throw this . . . this nuisance . . . down the first pit shaft I came to.'

Abel's Daughter

For my husband, whose patient encouragement and faith in this work remained when my own had failed. Thank you, sweetheart.

Chapter One

'Phoebe Pardoe, I find you guilty of wilful theft. I order you to be taken to a place of imprisonment where you will serve a term of fifteen years' hard labour.'

Phoebe pushed the soiled rags into the hot tub, wincing as the soda bit into the raw flesh of her hands.

'. . . *you be taken to a place of detention* . . .'

She scrubbed the rags against the ribbed wooden board, the menstrual blood of her fellow inmates turning the water red.

'. . . *fifteen years' hard labour* . . .'

The words circled endlessly in her brain as they had for the past eight months.

'. . . *guilty of wilful theft* . . .'

'Put yer back into it, Pardoe!'

Phoebe gasped as the slim wooden cane sliced across her shoulders.

'. . . them bleedin' jam rags won't wash themselves – or p'raps you ain't used to washin'? Yeah, I forgot you once 'ad a laundry woman to do yer washin' for you. Well, you ain't got one now, you bloody thief, so get stuck in or you'll be sorry.'

Phoebe's teeth tightened on her lip; she knew better than to answer back to Sally Moreton, superintendent of the laundry. Built like a man, her mouth was twisted up at the side due to some childhood illness, and her insides were twisted to match. Beating other women seemed the only source of pleasure she had, the cane she carried cutting into their flesh on the merest excuse, and often without any at all.

Squeezing the strips of cloth and dropping them into a cane basket, Phoebe pushed against her hair with a hand as bloody as the rags she had just scrubbed, then picking up the basket she carried it to one of the steaming boilers, dropping her load inside. Now she could take a recently removed batch to the yard and peg them on the lines stretched between the buildings. These were the only moments in her long days that she looked forward to. To see the sky, to feel the clean air on her face, to hear a bird sing . . .

'Leave them!' Sally Moreton's cane came down across Phoebe's raw hands, her cruel piggy eyes gleaming at the scream of pain it brought forth. 'Martha can peg them out. We don't want to risk yer delicate constitution by sending you out into the cold air, now do we?'

'But I always do the pegging out!' The thought of not going outside, even for the few minutes it took to peg the strips of torn sheeting to the lines, made Phoebe forget what so many blows of that cane had taught her. 'Martha does . . .'

The stinging cut of the cane across her mouth stilled the rest of the protest, sending Phoebe crashing backward against the cauldron of bubbling soapy water.

'Martha does what I tell 'er.' The cane rose again, swishing downward across Phoebe's legs, cutting through the worn grey calico. 'Same as all the rest of the thievin', murderin' scum in this place – same as you will, Miss High and Mighty Phoebe Pardoe! An' if you answer me back one more time you might find yerself missin' a tongue to answer back with. Now get that lot in.' Lashing out with her foot, she tipped over another basket of soiled cloths, stained crimson against the stone floor. 'An' get 'em clean. I don't want to see no mark on 'em when I come to inspect.'

'You better be ready to play tonight, you stuck up bitch!'

Liza Spittle dropped a fresh basket of laundry at Phoebe's feet as the superintendent moved away. 'Or Steel Arsed

Sal might find a bundle of these pushed up a chimney somewhere.'

'She wouldn't . . .'

'Believe me,' Liza cut in, the beetroot birthmark staining the left side of her face seeming to swell suddenly as though about to burst, 'that wouldn't stop 'er usin' that cane if we was to give her a good excuse. Loves to use the cane does Steel Arse. It's 'er only pleasure. Does for 'er what no bloke would – not wi' a face like that.'

'You're disgusting!'

'Am I?' Liza's large hand grabbed the basket Phoebe had lifted and, bundling several stained cloths together, she shoved them beneath the hessian sack tied about her middle. 'So tonight will mek two of us, won't it?'

The rest of the long day stretched out between jibes and advice as to how to please Liza, but there was no sympathy, that was something these women had had removed from them as cleanly as amputation severed a limb. Please God, Phoebe prayed when at nine p.m. the one gaslamp was turned off, leaving the dormitory in darkness, please God don't let her come near me. But instinct told her that God was not listening.

'So, you've decided to be nice to Liza, 'ave you?'

Liza Spittle sat on the side of Phoebe's narrow mattress, her approach from the far end of the line of ten tight-spaced beds lost among the snuffles and coughs of the women who filled them.

The dim light from outside had faded almost to extinction by the time it touched the beds but Phoebe did not need light to tell her who sat beside her; the rancid stale fish smell that always accompanied Liza, despite the compulsory baths with carbolic soap, told her her prayers had gone unheeded.

'I thought as 'ow you'd see sense . . .'

Liza bent forward, one broad hand pulling away the rough woollen blanket, the miasmic stench of her closing Phoebe's throat.

'Leave me alone,' she choked, swallowing the smell of the other woman. 'Please, leave me alone.'

Liza snatched the blanket further down, revealing white calico a pale shadow in the darkness. 'Is that what you said to the bobbies when they come fer you, or did you let 'em do this?' One hand undid the row of flat calico-covered buttons while the other pressed heavily on Phoebe's shoulder, the snores and moans from the other beds indicating that none of the other women cared what was happening. 'In fer thievin', ain't you?' The nightgown opened to the waist, the older woman pulled it wide. 'A necklace so I 'ear, a very valible necklace . . . Look good over these pretty tits I've no doubt. Did the bobbies tell you you've got pretty tits? Did they feel 'em like Liza's doin'?' A scaly-skinned hand closed over Phoebe's breast.

'Stop . . . please!' Tears poured down Phoebe's cheeks, salting her lips. 'Please stop.'

Liza bent forward, the stale fish smell of her gagging the girl beneath her. 'You'll be a-sayin' please again soon enough but you won't be a-sayin' stop. You'll be begging Liza to go on . . .'

'Somebody'll be beggin' but it won't be 'er.'

The voice was a hiss in the darkness as Liza was jerked from the bed and flung face down on the floor.

'I told you to leave the kid be, keep yer filthy paws off 'er!'

One hand pressed to her mouth to stop the vomit spilling out, the other holding the edges of her nightgown together, Phoebe recognised the tones of Tilly Wood; serving a life sentence, the gaunt-featured woman was the only soul in the whole prison who had shown her the faintest semblance of kindness in all of the eight months she had spent in this hell hole.

'Seems as 'ow you don't understand plain English . . .'

Suddenly there were no snores, no groans. The silence from the other beds announced that each woman was awake and listening though none moved.

'. . . well, Liza Spittle, I can mek it plainer fer you . . .'

Lifting herself on one elbow, Phoebe peered through the gloom. Tilly Wood had one knee between Liza's shoulder blades with both hands cupped beneath the woman's chin, forcing her head back.

'Play yer dirty bloody games wi' any other of the pissants you fancies but this one you leaves be, an' if you doesn't then you's goin' to be found behind one o' them bilers wi' a jam rag stuck in yer gob!

'Y'see, Liza, I ain't got nuthin' to lose – I'm already behind these bars fer life an' there ain't nuthin' Steel Arse or the likes of 'er can do to me they ain't already done in ten years. That's a long time, Liza, but you put one more finger on that wench, just one finger, and *you'll* be 'ere for eternity.

'Oh, you knows I pushed my swine of a man down the stairs, they told you that did the wardresses, but what they didn't tell you was I broke 'is neck fust. It didn't tek much . . .'

Pressing her knee further into Liza's back, she pulled the chin upward, bringing a strangled cry from the woman on the floor. 'Just a quick jerk and the spine was broke at the base of the neck. You don't 'ave to be no big bloke to do that, Liza, you just need to spend yer life fightin' off ten brothers an' a bloke you wus never married to in fust place.' The cupped hands jerked again. 'It would be easy, Liza, an' pleasurable, an' you would never know when it was comin', so if you wants to live long enough to get out of 'ere, you'll think on what I says . . . leave this 'un be!'

Rising, Tilly waited while Liza picked herself up and slunk back to bed, hearing the disappointed grunts coming from the shadows; there were many in the room who would have welcomed the snapping of Liza Spittle's neck.

''Er won't mess wi' you any more,' Tilly said, covering Phoebe with the blanket, then louder, ''cos Tilly Wood don't tell the Good Lord 'isself more'n twice.'

I order you be taken to a place of imprisonment where you will serve a term of fifteen years.

Lying in the darkness, Phoebe knew her life would not stretch that far.

How had this happened to her? Phoebe closed her eyes, letting the darkness press against her lids, and in that darkness saw again the summer ball and herself in a pink rose-trimmed gown dancing with Montrose. Montrose Wheeler, son of Gaskell Wheeler, owner of the Monway Iron Foundry, had asked for her hand in marriage and her father had agreed. The ceremony had been planned to take place at Christmas, Montrose vowing he could hardly bear to wait until then. He was so handsome and tall, his sandy hair and light blue eyes so different from the coarse overfed features of his father or his thin, sharp-faced mother. Who would have dreamed that an evening so warm with music and moonlight, so soft with the promise of love, would be the last time she would see her fiancé, for in the space of weeks her own father lay dead and with his death all her own hopes were extinguished.

'It's bad news I'm afraid, my dear.' Alfred Dingley, her father's doctor and friend, had come to Brunswick House to tell her himself of the accident in which her father's chaise fell to the bottom of a vertical pit. Old mine workings, the coroner had said. Wednesbury was riddled with them and dangerous shafts regularly opened without warning.

The funeral had been a week later, a family affair with just her father's brother Samuel and sister Annie, no one being left of her dead mother's family.

Against the darkness of her lids, Phoebe saw again the finely drawn face of Uncle Samuel, a carbon copy of her own father, and the sad blue eyes that seemed to know more than they revealed. Phoebe realised it was the only time she had ever seen her uncle outside the house he shared with his sister, and even on her rare visits to them she was never left alone with him: 'Because of his stone deafness, dear,' was what she was always told when she had asked the reason he never went out, an answer that even as a child she'd found unconvincing. Her Aunt Annie in her customary black, shrouded in the perennial air of bitterness Phoebe had recognised from an early age, sat straight-backed in the carriage that followed the hearse, black-plumed horses walking slowly to St Bartholomew's Church and her father's final resting place.

His death had been a blow but there had been worse in store for her, much worse. The reading of Abel Pardoe's will took place in the drawing room of his home, Brunswick House, the following afternoon. James Siveter, her father's lawyer, in a long old-fashioned tail coat that gave him the appearance of a crow, rose from his seat at her father's heavy oak desk, ushering Phoebe to a chair beside her aunt. His impassive face as he resumed his seat betrayed nothing of what was to come.

'"I, Abel Pardoe, being of sound mind . . ."'

Siveter's expressionless voice droned on through the bequests to servants, only changing when he came to her father's provision for Phoebe herself.

'"Next I come to my beloved daughter, Phoebe Mary Pardoe. By the time of my death you will have been Mrs Montrose Wheeler for many years and as such mistress of your own home and in need of nothing. Therefore I leave you what you have always had and enjoyed: my love.

'"Lastly, to my brother Samuel, and my sister Annie who has imprisoned him for the last forty years – to you, Annie Maria Pardoe, I bequeath the sum of one thousand pounds annually and the house you live in for your lifetime. To my brother Samuel Isaac Pardoe I bequeath this house and all its contents together with Hobs Hill Coalmine, Dangerfield Lane, the Crown coalmine, Moxley, and all lands, property, goods and monies pertaining to me. May God give you the courage to use them to buy the freedom I never had the courage to give you."'

The numbness she had felt since her father's death shielded Phoebe from the full impact of what the lawyer had said and she sat there while her aunt ushered him out. Mrs Banks, their cook-housekeeper, offered to help her upstairs.

Now, opening her eyes, Phoebe stared at the moon-filled squares of the windows, their regimented line like the yellow eyes of demons about to strike, while in the shadowed belly of the room figures from her nightmare continued to move.

'You understand, Phoebe, Uncle Samuel needs continual quiet. To have a young girl about the place, especially one with the comings and goings of a fiancé, would be much too upsetting for him,' her aunt had said not two weeks later. 'Therefore I am asking you to make other arrangements.'

'But Uncle Samuel is already in continual quietness, is he not, Aunt?' Phoebe remembered her own answer and the fulminating look that crossed the older woman's face as she added, 'Is he not chronically deaf?'

'And are you not chronically rude?' her aunt had retorted waspishly, then drawing black gloves over thin stick-like fingers, drove home her winning blow. 'I want you out of this house by one week from today, and be sure you take nothing that was paid for by your father.'

'But Father paid for everything,' Phoebe had protested. 'My clothes . . . everything.'

Her aunt moved to the door, waiting while the maid opened it. 'Then you will have less to carry. But your uncle would not want you to suffer any hardship. Therefore you may take two dresses and two changes of underwear, and to be certain you take no more, I will send my own housekeeper to pack them.'

'Surely I may take my jewellery?'

'All paid for by my brother, therefore part of his estate and now part of Samuel's.'

'Not all.' Phoebe followed the spare grey-haired woman, whom for all their family connection she hardly knew, out into the late-autumn sunshine. 'I have several pieces left me by my mother.'

Annie Pardoe did not hesitate in climbing into her pony trap. 'Paid for, no doubt, by my brother.' Picking up the reins, she clucked the horse forward. 'Unless you have a deed of gift you will be wise to leave any such pieces where they are.'

Phoebe concentrated hard on the tiny moon-filled spaces, willing the nightmare memories to go away, but on they went, passing before her eyes like some awful dance. She had been writing to Montrose when the Wheelers' carriage had arrived from Oakeswell Hall, and she had felt so relieved. Montrose had obviously been informed of what had happened and was arranging for her to be moved to his parents' home until after their marriage. Grabbing her bonnet and smiling at her maid, Lucy Baines, Phoebe rushed out of the house.

'Miss Pardoe . . .'

The formality of the greeting from Montrose's mother did not surprise Phoebe who had always found the woman cold if not positively unfriendly; neither did the absence of her husband who would be at his place of business at this hour of the day.

'Miss Pardoe,' Violet Wheeler sat stiff-backed facing Phoebe, 'have you written to my son informing him of your situation?'

'No.' Phoebe shook her head, wondering how such a sharp-featured, cold-natured woman could ever have been given the name of so lovely a flower.

'I thought perhaps you may not have, therefore I myself informed Montrose of your position. Under the circumstances I must inform you there can be no question of a marriage between you. As an officer in the Guards Montrose must be seen to make a good marriage – he cannot afford to tie himself to a wife unable to bring with her a good social standing.'

Phoebe remembered the physical sickness that had come over her at these words; how she had stuffed a gloved hand into her mouth.

'I know this must come as a disappointment to you,' Violet Wheeler went on with no more compassion than if she had been wishing her young visitor a pleasant walk about the gardens, 'but both Montrose's father and myself agree that it is for the best.'

Of course it was for the best – the best for Montrose.

'And your son, Mrs Wheeler,' Phoebe had managed, swallowing the sickness filling her throat, 'does he also think that breaking off our marriage is for the best?'

'Montrose will take the advice of his father,' Violet Wheeler's sharp features tightened, her nostrils flaring with controlled anger, 'whilst you would be wise to take mine and say no more than that you feel unable to go through with the marriage so soon after your father's death.'

Phoebe turned her head sideways, staring into the darkness of a room she shared with nine other women. In the space of three weeks she was orphaned, homeless and jilted. Violet Wheeler had said her son must have a wife who could bring with her a good social standing. What she really meant was Montrose must have a wife with a good financial standing.

Three days after Aunt Annie's visit her housekeeper Maudie Tranter arrived to supervise the packing of two dresses and two sets of underwear in a large carpet bag.

'Miss Annie says I am to see that all wardrobes and cupboards are locked in my presence and that I am to take the keys back with me.' The woman looked apologetically at Phoebe. 'She also said I was to take your jewellery box . . . I am sorry, Miss Pardoe, but that was what she said and I have to do it or lose my position.'

'Please don't worry, Mrs Tranter,' Phoebe had tried to reassure the woman, 'no one is blaming you, of course you must do as my aunt says.'

'I've made an inventory of everything in that box,' said Abel Pardoe's own housekeeper who had watched the packing. 'That sees us all safeguarded, Mrs Tranter. Your mistress can't go saying as how anything has gone astray. Tell her this sealing tape was set around the box in your presence and this here is the inventory I spoke of with a copy already sent to Lawyer Siveter's chambers in the High Street for her to check by.'

Fanny Banks's quick fingers passed brown sealing tape three times around the box before handing it to Annie's housekeeper. 'Now, as you've seen to all you came for, you best be off back to that crow you call your employer. As for me, I'll be leavin' when Miss Phoebe do.'

With Fanny Banks treading on her brown skirts, Maudie Tranter dropped Phoebe a quick bob and disappeared from the room, her footsteps almost at a run on the polished wood of the corridor and stairs.

Phoebe herself had left the next day, bidding goodbye to a tearful Mrs Banks who was joining her sister in Chester and a defiant Lucy who vowed to 'go into the workhouse rather than work for that sour-faced prune, Annie Pardoe'.

Try as she might Phoebe had never been able to remember more than walking down the long tree-lined drive away from the large house that had been her home since birth. She knew only that somehow or other she had walked the three miles across open grassland to Hobs Hill coalmine. There Joseph Leach had half carried her into the tiny brick building he called 'the office'. Injured in an explosion underground years before, her father had kept him on ostensibly as tally keeper, though the times her father had taken Phoebe with him on his regular visits to the pithead it seemed Joseph oversaw just about everything. Prising the carpet bag from her fingers, he sat her on the one chair, listening as tears and words poured from her.

'Joe . . . Joe . . .'

Even now, in the quiet of a prison cell punctured only by the breathing of its occupants, the shout seemed to throb against her ears.

'Joe . . . there's bin a cave in!'

'Christ Almighty!' Joseph Leach turned for the door as it burst open.

'Joe.' A figure black from head to foot with coal dust,

the white circles around his eyes the only patch of colour, announced, 'There's bin a fall – roof gone.'

'Where?' Joe asked tersely, all thoughts of Phoebe gone from his mind.

'North tunnel.'

'Bugger it!' he rasped. 'I knew that bastard would go, I said it would. Who's down there?'

'Manny Evans's gang.' The begrimed figure made no acknowledgement of Phoebe's presence.

'Eight men,' Joseph said instantly, with no reference to anything other than his own sharp brain. 'Right, you send young Billy for the doctor then meet me at the mouth.'

After that the girl was forgotten as Joseph organised the rescue.

Though no sound from the pit head told the women of the town what had occurred, the sight of the doctor's trap following the path across the heath told its own story and soon they stood just beyond the green-painted wooden gates with her father's name painted tall and white across them – Phoebe could see them clearly from the small office, women with chequered shawls about their heads, each face chalky with fear.

'How many, Joseph?' Alfred Dingley jumped from the trap, a black Gladstone bag in his hand.

'Eight, sir. Emanuel Evans, Evan Gittins, Charlie Norton and 'is lad Tommy, Sam Deeley, David Walker, Ben Corns and Meshac Speke.' Joseph reeled off the names as he swept papers and ledgers from the table that almost filled the office, clearing a space for the doctor to work on any injured men.

'Where?'

'North tunnel about thirty yards in. We can get to about ten yards of 'em at a guess. I've got a gang in now clearin' rest, but the shorin's be weak. We got to watch rest of roof don't come in atop of 'em.'

'You are sure there are no more than eight?'

Joseph had pointed to a line of nails hammered into the

brick wall of the office, each bearing a round metal plate the size of a penny. 'Tokens be all in an' Davy's be all gone for North tunnel an' there be nobody else in that part o' the mine. I'll 'ave the tokens checked again though, if you wants, for the other seams?'

'No need.' Alfred Dingley glanced at the wall where the Davy lamps were hung as each man checked in when coming from underground.

Phoebe ran out into the yard after the two men as a shout of 'They'm through' rang out, watching them make for the mouth of the mine. Her offer of help went unanswered.

Slowly, the iron cage was winched again and again to the surface, the cries of the women reaching across the yard as they recognised their men, but each in his turn waited for the raising of the cage until the last survivor, Charlie Norton, stepped out, his fifteen-year-old son carried in his arms.

In the darkness, Phoebe threw an arm across her face, desperate to obliterate the screams of the lad's mother. They had been lucky, Joseph had said later, but what use was that to Sally Norton?

'You did very well.' Dr Dingley had smiled at Phoebe as the last of the men's cuts were washed and bandaged. 'Now you'd better let me take you home, my girl.'

But Phoebe had refused, saying she preferred to walk, not wanting to admit the truth of having no home and Joseph said nothing of what she had told him.

'You'd better cum along o' me,' he said, watching the doctor drive horse and trap through the gates, 'my Sarah'll know what to do.'

And she had, leastways until Annie Pardoe landed on her doorstep.

It hadn't taken long. A fresh ripple of anger swept over Phoebe and she flung her arm from her face as if fending off an enemy. News had a way of travelling fast and it was news in the town that Sarah Leach had taken in Abel Pardoe's daughter. Days from the cave-in at Hobs Hill mine her aunt had driven down to the Leachs' cottage and marched in. The whole thing was over before it began: the house was part of Samuel's legacy, as were most others in this area, her aunt said, and either Phoebe went or they did – and with them Joseph's job at the mine.

'Yer father was good to me, I can't turn me back on 'is wench.'

Joseph's protest at her leaving echoed in Phoebe's mind. He and his family were reluctant to see her go but as Sarah admitted, jobs were hard come by, especially for 'a bloke wi' a bad leg'.

Phoebe stared upward. The light against the windows was changing as her life had changed, but where the sky was brightening her life grew ever darker. Turning on to her side she closed her eyes, squeezing the lids tight, fighting away a memory she could not escape . . . *fifteen years' hard labour.*

Chapter Two

Phoebe breathed deeply, savouring the warm July air, not wanting to return to the stifling steam-filled prison laundry. Last night had been only one more in a long line of sleepless nights but Liza Spittle's visit to her bed had left her terrified, too afraid to sleep even after Tilly Wood had half throttled the woman. Phoebe pegged the last cloth to the line, her hand shaking. Liza wasn't the sort to give in easily, sooner or later she would try again.

'Thinkin' of doin' a runner, Pardoe?'

Sally Moreton stood in the doorway of the laundry, the long cane swishing alongside her skirts.

Phoebe picked up the empty basket.

'Wait!'

The order cracked across the yard. Phoebe stood still, watching the other woman march the length of the washing line, her cane lifting each of the cloths in turn.

'Wot 'appened last night?'

'Last night?' Phoebe hedged, knowing Sally Moreton would already have been told everything.

'Don't play the innocent with me, you bloody thief! I want to 'ear wot 'appened.' The cane whistled past, close to Phoebe's ear.

'I didn't know anything had happened.' She waited for the blow she knew the lie would bring. 'We all sat as usual, mending linen after clearing the dining hall, then at eight-thirty we dispersed to the dormitories and prepared for bed. Then at nine the light was put out and everyone went to sleep – at least that is what happened in our dormitory.'

'"At least that is what happened in our dormitory,"' Sally

Moreton mimicked, bringing the cane down again. 'Listen to me, you little snot! If nothin' 'appened 'ow come Liza Spittle can 'ardly shift 'er 'ead on 'er neck this mornin'? An' 'ow come when 'er talks 'er sounds like a glede under a door? Got a touch of this new influenza as 'er or is it somethin' else grabbed 'er by the throat? Somethin' like another woman?'

The cane tapped warningly against the drab grey skirts of the laundry superintendent. Phoebe knew that it would take very little to bring it lashing across her face.

'Lost yer tongue, 'ave yer?' Sally Moreton grinned, showing large uneven teeth, bases blackening with decay. 'You nearly lost a lot more last night. 'Ad a visit from Liza so I 'ear. Enjoy it, did you?'

Phoebe gripped the empty basket, holding it close against her as Sally Moreton stepped nearer.

'Play wi' these, did 'er?' Sally's free hand closed over Phoebe's breast and squeezed. ''Er likes tits does Liza, especially young tits.' She smiled again, bringing her face close to Phoebe's. 'The sort that is still firm. But it ain't just tits satisfies Liza, 'er likes more, 'er likes a bit of what's down 'ere . . .' The hand holding the cane knocked the basket aside, allowing the other to press between Phoebe's legs. 'I know what Liza likes. We 'as the same tastes if you see what I mean!'

Dropping the basket, Phoebe pushed the woman, causing her to take several steps backward. 'You disgust me!' she spat.

'So I disgust you, do I?' Sally Moreton brought the cane to rest against the palm of her left hand, eyeing the girl whose mouth was still swollen from yesterday's blow. It was going to be more than her mouth would be swollen this time! 'Did Liza disgust you an' all . . . could it be we ain't good enough for Miss 'Igh and Mighty Pardoe? Or is it Tilly Wood 'as staked a claim?'

'Tilly Wood isn't like that!' Phoebe flared. 'She hasn't got your filthy ways . . .' She stopped as the cane found its mark, the force of it splitting her lower lip as it threw her backward.

'So Sally Moreton 'as filthy ways, 'as 'er?' The cane whistled through the air, slicing across Phoebe's shoulder. ''Er ain't to yer liking.' The cane struck again. ''Er disgusts you, do 'er?' The cane flashed downward, cutting across Phoebe's cheek, then lifted high into the air again.

'Stop that!' Agnes Marsh caught the superintendent's arm, halting the blows raining on to Phoebe. 'You bloody fool, Sally. Ain't you got more sense than to beat the kid senseless this time o' the day?'

'I don't let nobody mouth off at me!'

'Nor you should,' Agnes allowed, 'but daytime ain't the time to teach her a lesson, you should know that.'

'No, it ain't, Agnes.' Sally Moreton lowered the cane, her eyes on the girl still shielding her head with her arms. 'But it won't always be daytime, will it? Then this one will really find out what it means to mouth off at Sally Moreton.'

'That's it, Sally.' Agnes Marsh, deputy superintendent of the prison laundry, released the woman's arm. 'Do what you like in the dark – that way there's nobody can point the finger. As fer 'er,' she jerked her head towards Phoebe, 'Governess 'as sent fer 'er, wants 'er upstairs.'

'What for?' Sally looked quickly at the woman beside her.

'Didn't say, just sent Mary Pegleg to say as 'er wanted to see Prisoner Pardoe in 'er office, now.'

'You 'eard 'er.' Sally reached out with the cane, poking Phoebe in the ribs. 'Get yerself up there . . . an' mind, I'll 'ear of every word what's said so you better be careful what you tells our new lady Governess about yer little . . . accident.' She touched the cane to Phoebe's bleeding mouth then stood aside. 'Get yerself to the bathroom and wash afore you go upstairs.'

Her eyes clouded with pain Phoebe picked up the fallen basket, carrying it into the steam-filled laundry and depositing it beside her washtub. All eyes followed her as she walked from the laundry; all eyes registered the bloody mouth and weals like scarlet ribbons criss-crossing her cheek, among them the eyes of Tilly Wood.

'Wot did 'er say?'

The evening meal of bread and potatoes finished and the dining hall cleared, the women prisoners sat at the long wooden tables, each with a piece of mending.

'She said I wasn't to be assigned to the laundry from now on,' Phoebe answered in a whisper.

'A sined? Wot does that mean?'

'It means 'er don't 'ave to scrub no more bloody jam rags, that's what it means.' Mary Pegleg, her duties as general dogsbody for the prison Governess finished for the day, sat with the others, the wooden stump attached to her left knee thrust out beneath the table. Tilly Wood looked up from her place opposite Phoebe but said nothing.

''Ave you bin sprung, Pardoe?' a thin whippet-like woman asked.

'No,' Phoebe shook her head, 'I am not being released.'

''Er's goin' into the sewin' room.' Mary Pegleg supplied the information with an air of importance. 'I 'eard through the door. I 'as to sit outside Governess's room case I'm wanted, an' I 'eard 'er say as 'ow Pardoe was to work in the sewin' room from now on.'

'By all the Saints in Heaven, I wish it were me!'

'Governess ain't that daft,' the whippet-faced woman grinned. 'Tek you in there an' Christ knows 'ow many would get clobbered.'

'It's not bloody fair! A bloke lathers the 'ide off of a woman an' 'e gets away wi' it. A woman 'its a man an' 'er finishes up doin' twelve months in 'ell, washin' other folks' dirty linen.'

'That's true an' all, Bridie Trow,' came another whisper, 'but you hit the man with a wooden stool, nearly knocking his brains out!'

'Holy Mother o'God, an' that's a dirty lie.' Bridie looked up from the sheet she was mending. 'Oi could never 'ave knocked out the man's brain for 'e 'ad none in 'is 'ead to start with.'

'Hey up, Steel Arse is comin'.'

The sudden whisper stilled the women's giggles and all heads bent to the sewing.

''Alf-past eight . . . pack up.' The ever-present cane swished as the superintendent of the laundry surveyed two hundred silent women. 'Put the sewin' in its proper basket then prepare for bed. Each dormitory will be inspected before lights out at nine.' She stood watching the women file silently from the hall, her eyes following the thin figure of Phoebe Pardoe.

'So 'ow come the sewin' room . . . an' why you?'

Hands and face washed, a rough calico nightgown swamping her stringy body, Tilly Wood sat on the end of Phoebe's bed, the other occupants of the room covertly listening.

Phoebe glanced at her hands, encased in the white cotton gloves which Hannah Price, the prison Governess, had given her to protect them while they healed. 'It seems Mrs Price was invited to a friend's house at the weekend. While she was there they visited the Goose Fair at Wednesbury and Mrs Price purchased a petticoat from one of the stalls. She asked who had made it because she would like to buy more but was told that would not be possible for the girl who was responsible for the petticoat had been sent to prison in Birmingham. Being told the name "Phoebe Mary Pardoe", the governess guessed it might be me. When I told her my home was in Wednesbury she asked to see some of the sewing I had done here in Handsworth, then she said I was to be assigned to the sewing room but my duties would not begin until my hands were healed.'

'An' yer face?' Tilly asked, looking at the weals still red

against the swollen flesh. 'What 'ad the Governess to say about that?'

'She asked what had happened. I told her it was an accident, the drying racks had slipped and caught me on the face.'

'Best way,' Tilly nodded. 'This is a new government prison, it ain't like the old 'uns with everybody packed in a single stinkin' underground cell, an' Hannah Price is first woman to run a prison as I know of. It will be a 'ard job keepin' it if I know anythin' about men – one breath about 'er bein' unable to control we women an' 'er'll be out. Besides . . .' she threw a meaningful look at Liza Spittle '. . . we can sort out our own problems.'

'Find yer own bed, Tilly Wood.' Sally Moreton strode into the long room, her cane slapping the foot of each bed as she passed. Reaching Phoebe's, she paused. 'Seems you 'ave more than one visitin' yer bed at night, Pardoe.' She touched the cane to Phoebe's breast. 'Already gettin' more than tits to play with, are they? P'raps we better move you from more than the laundry.' She smiled, showing her blackened teeth. 'Mebbe that little room next to mine? Be nice an' private there you would, nobody to come pawin' you in the dark.'

In her bed, Tilly's strong fingers tightened on the rough blanket.

'Now the lot of you, listen!' The cane cracked against the iron frame of each bed like a series of pistol shots as Sally Moreton proceeded to the door. 'There'll be no lovers' meetin's tonight, no moonlight walks from bed to bed . . . you 'ear that, Liza Spittle? Each of you stays put where you am now. Ignore Sally's warnin' an' you'll wish yerselves dead!'

Turning off the one gaslamp, she left.

'Goodnight to you an all, Mrs Moreton,' Bridie Trow called softly after the departing wardress.

'An' arsehole to yer warnin',' another voice added, just loud enough to be heard.

'Ar, an' you can stick yer cane up that!' Mary Pegleg laughed in the darkness.

'Sure, Mary, an' that's not the place old Steel Arse will be pushin' 'er cane in 'er lonely room,' Bridie Trow said crudely. 'It's not that 'ole she'll be a pokin' stick into, may the Divil an' all 'is demons escort her into Hell!'

Tilly Wood pulled the blanket up to her chin, remembering the weals on Phoebe's face, the broken mouth swollen to four times its size. The Devil could have Sally Moreton but it would be Tilly Wood gave her to him.

Phoebe stared at the windows high above her bed. Why had her aunt turned her out of her own home? Why after that had she ordered Joseph Leach to turn her out of his? Why did her aunt hate her so much? Why had Montrose not come to see her or even sent a note? The questions kept sleep from her.

'. . . *I find you guilty of wilful theft* . . .'

The words seemed to echo through the quiet room.

'*I want you for my wife, Phoebe.*' The figure of Montrose Wheeler rose in her mind, so tall and handsome, so dashing and attentive. '*I want to take you to London . . . to Paris . . . I want to show you off to the world . . . I love you, Phoebe, and I want you to be my wife.*'

But he hadn't loved her enough to write, he hadn't wanted her badly enough to come for her when the home she thought hers forever had gone instead to her aunt and uncle.

And her aunt had made sure she went from it quickly, just as she had made sure she had also gone from Joseph's home.

But Joseph had not left her entirely without help. He had taken her to see Elias Webb, a stumpy irascible man who owned property on the edge of the town.

'I wants no truck wi' the Pardoes,' he had shouted, his face red and angry when Joseph told the reason for their visit. 'It was Abel Pardoe ruined my business when he sold Monway Field to an iron merchant – pulled my mill down, 'e did, a mill I'd ground flour in all me life, ar, an' me father afore that, an' then she . . . Annie Pardoe . . . I wasn't good enough fer 'er . . . wanted no mill owner fer a 'usband did that one . . . bloody stuck up bitch! No matter who got 'urt so long as it wasn't Annie Pardoe.'

'Then why let 'er 'urt another, Elias,' Joseph had asked, 'why when you can stop it?'

''Ow can my lettin' Abel Pardoe's wench 'ave my 'ouse 'urt that bitch of a sister of his'n?' Elias had demanded.

''Cos your 'ouses are about the only ones left in Wednesbury as don' belong to Pardoe or Foster or Platt, or else to folk who am beholden to 'em. Annie Pardoe not only turned 'er own brother's wench out of 'er father's 'ome, 'er turned 'er out o' mine. Said if 'er didn't go, I 'ad to – an' lose me job at the pit an' all. An' if Annie Pardoe 'as seen wench off two places, what meks you think 'er will let Abel's daughter rest in any if 'er can do anythin' about it?'

Elias had looked at her then, Phoebe remembered, his eyes bright and calculating in his red face.

'Why let the sins of the parents fall upon the children, Elias? Especially the sins of Annie Pardoe.' Joseph drove home the last nail.

'That 'un!' Elias had almost spat the words. 'Annie Pardoe is still the same heartless . . . done!' He struck the table palm down. 'You can 'ave the 'ouse but it will cost you two 'undred an' fifty guineas . . . tek it or tek yerself off.'

Joseph had tried to get Elias to lower his price but Phoebe had agreed. To own her own house, however small, a house her aunt could not turn her out of, would be worth two hundred and fifty of the three hundred guineas her maternal grandmother had left her.

Wiggins Mill stood some way out of the town, close to its own pool. Set in a hollow, it was sheltered from the winds blowing off the open heath, the Birmingham Navigation Canal at its rear. With a scullery, kitchen, large living room and smaller parlour, three fair-sized bedrooms, together with the usual outhouses and a stable, it had become hers the following day.

And a week later Annie Pardoe had arrived.

'And this is where you intend to live?' she had asked, looking down her nose at the furniture which the remainder of Phoebe's guineas had bought from John Kilvert's pawnbroker's shop in Union Street. 'And what do you intend to live on?'

Refusing the offer of tea, her aunt wiped a gloved finger across the chair Phoebe indicated then refused that too.

'. . . or is there someone prepared to keep you – for a price?'

Staring at the squares of moonlight high on the shadowed walls Phoebe felt again the heat that had risen to her face and the cold steady rise of anger in her stomach. She had despised Annie Pardoe then: before that moment she had held no real feelings for the woman who was her father's sister, but at that moment the seed of hate was sown.

'Aunt,' her voice had been steady though she was taut with fury, 'this house is my home and how I choose to make my living is my business and no one else's. My father's will did not name either you or Uncle Samuel my guardian, therefore you have no jurisdiction over me. That being so, you will not interfere in my affairs.'

Her aunt's face had twisted with what Phoebe had hoped was derision but knew to be hate.

'What do you expect people will say . . . a young woman living alone outside the town?'

'That I'm what you already think me,' Phoebe had answered, 'a whore.'

Sally Moreton strode through the prison laundry, thin cane swishing beside the skirts of her grey uniform, her hair scraped back to form a knot at her neck, adding to the severity of her features.

'Call them clean?' She stopped at a basket of cloths, their sides ragged where they had been torn into strips.

Martha Ames looked at the cloths she had scrubbed at for over an hour. 'They look clean to me, Mrs Moreton.'

'Well, they don't look clean to me. Look at 'em!' Sally Moreton's black-booted foot caught the wicker basket, tipping it over to one side. Poking the contents with the cane, she strewed them across the flagged floor. 'Look at this . . .' She ground a boot into a wet cloth. 'An' this . . .' Her boot came down on another, leaving a dirty mark on each. 'An' wot about these?' Hitching her skirts, she trampled the freshly scrubbed cloths, spreading a pool of water across the floor.

Martha Ames stared silently at the cloths that had had her knuckles bleeding. She knew better than to argue.

'They'm bloody filthy!' Sally Moreton shouted, her tall man-like frame towering over Martha. 'Filthy, like all o' you scum!' She glared at the other women, watching silently. Only Tilly Wood's eyes refused to fall before her glare. 'We'll 'ave 'em done again,' she shouted, kicking the cloths across the floor, 'we'll 'ave the 'ole bloody lot done again. You!' She pointed to Bridie Trow. 'Get them boilers emptied. An' you,' she bawled at the ferret-faced Nellie Bladen, 'get fresh water in them tubs. An' you lot . . .' she glared around the steam-filled laundry, '. . . you all do the same. You are going to start all over again.'

'But, Mrs Moreton . . .' The pale consumptive face of Nellie Bladen blanched further as the superintendent swung back to her. 'That'll tek the rest of the mornin'. It'll be afternoon afore we can start washin' agen.'

'Are you arguin' wi' me?' The cane lifted, coming down hard across Nellie's thin shoulders.

'Steel Arse ain't took kindly to Phoebe Pardoe bein' teken out of 'ere,' a voice whispered behind Tilly Wood, 'looks like we am all goin' to be made to pay.'

'When I tell you what to do, you do it . . .' The cane rose again, coming down across Nellie's bent back. 'You don't talk about it, you *do* it!'

Tilly's hand tightened about the thick wooden stick she used to lift clothes from the boiling water in the huge copper.

'You 'ear me, scum? You do it.'

Nellie was already on the floor when Sally Moreton fell across her, unconscious from the blow Tilly Wood struck to the back of her head.

'That bastard has dealt 'er last blow.' Tilly looked at the figure of the wardress almost covering the thin woman half-conscious beneath her. 'Quick, you lot, 'elp me get Nellie out from under this swine.'

Bridie Trow grabbed the shoulder of the woman who seconds before had seemed set to beat Nellie Bladen to death, and heaved her aside, rolling her on to her back.

'Christ Almighty!' Martha Ames breathed. 'What've you done, Tilly? We'll all be done for when Sally Moreton comes to.'

'Holy Mother an' all the Saints.' Bridie Trow crossed herself. 'We'll all be swingin' on the end of a rope, so we will, when 'er tells Justice about this.'

''Er won't be tellin' Magistrates nor nobody else,' Tilly said, grabbing a cloth from a basket standing ready to be taken to the washing lines in the yard. 'Steel Arse 'as caned the last woman 'er'll ever cane an' spoke the last words 'er'll ever say.'

The cloth stretched between her hands, Tilly sank to her knees at Sally Moreton's head. 'Sit on 'er,' she said, looking up at the women grouped around. 'Bridie, Martha, sit on 'er – an' one of you watch the door.'

Then as the two women sat on the unconscious wardress, Tilly placed the folded cloth over the woman's face and held it tightly until any sign of breathing had stopped.

'That's you got yer comeuppance,' Tilly breathed, getting to her feet.

'An' may the Divil 'ave the dealin' of it,' Bridie added, crossing herself again.

'We'll all be meetin' 'im when Governess sees that.' Martha

touched a foot to the dead woman. 'We'll all be as dead as this one.'

'No, we won't.' Tilly looked at the woman on the floor. 'Find Mary Pegleg an' tell 'er to report to the Governess there has been an accident in the laundry . . . an' tek your time.'

''Ow do we mek this look like an accident?' Martha asked. 'The woman's dead.'

'Sure an' 'as no one ever died of an accident before?' Bridie answered as the woman watching the door set off on her message. 'Try holdin' yer gob for a second, Martha Ames, an' listen to Tilly.'

'Leave 'er be.' Tilly held out a hand to the women who stepped forward, about to lift the whimpering Nellie. 'Let 'er lie. Now listen to me. Sally Moreton was tellin' Nellie to tek the cloths outside for peggin' out when 'er started to gasp. 'Er clutched 'er chest, staggerin' about knockin' that basket over, then 'er cried out, a funny stranglin' cry in 'er throat, an' then tumbled 'ead first over Nellie there, nearly knockin' 'er unconscious. You two,' she pointed to Bridie and Martha, 'an' meself rolled Sally over an' called out 'er name, but gettin' no answer thought we best send for the Governess.'

'What d'you reckon will 'appen then?'

Tilly looked at Liza Spittle who until that moment had remained a silent observer. 'Do you reckon as the Governess will believe you?'

'I do.' Tilly looked at the woman who revolted her. 'An' I reckon summat else, Liza, I reckon you'd better keep yer mouth shut, 'cos what Tilly Wood does once 'er can do again – only next time it will be *you* lyin' there.'

'Won't the Governess be after sendin' for the doctor though, Tilly?' Bridie's look was as anxious as her question.

'I'm bankin' on 'er doin' just that,' Tilly answered. 'That Poor Relief doctor as looks after this place is more interested in the bottle than in patients. 'E's drunk no matter when 'e's sent for, be it day or night. It's my guess 'e'll tek one look at Sally Moreton, listen to what we tells 'im 'appened, an' say 'er died of an 'eart attack.'

'Amen to that,' Martha murmured.

'Holy Mother o'God, smile on the man an' grant he be as drunk as a fiddler's bitch!' And Bridie Trow crossed herself again.

Chapter Three

'Are you all right?' Bridie Trow had watched Phoebe from the start of the evening meal. 'You've not touched your taties other than chase 'em round the plate like a bobby after a babby.'

'Yes . . . I'm all right.'

'Like my arse you're all right!' Martha Ames popped the last of her own potatoes into her mouth, speaking as she chewed. 'I seen you comin' from the sewin' room an' you was cryin'.'

'Cryin'!' Tilly Wood stopped eating. 'What about . . . 'as anybody 'ad a go at you?'

'No.' Phoebe didn't look up, unable to keep more tears from filling her eyes.

'Then what am you cryin' for, Phoebe?' Mary Pegleg eased her wooden leg to a more comfortable position under the long scrubbed table top.

''Er's cryin' for to go 'ome,' Liza Spittle laughed, the beetroot mark on her face seeming to darken. 'Well, you'll cry a long time, Pardoe – about fifteen year I'd say.'

'Shut yer gob, Liza Spittle!' Bridie's eyes flashed.

'"'As anybody said summat you didn't like, Phoebe? 'As anybody upset you, Phoebe?"' Liza Spittle minced, then laughed coarsely. 'You lot mek me sick the way you dance round 'er. 'Er ain't no different from the rest on we. 'Er was thievin' an' 'er was catched, now 'er's got to do time like we all 'ave so let 'er be . . . the more 'er cries the less 'er'll piddle.'

Tilly looked across the table, her thin face pinched with distaste. 'If you wants to chew yer next meal, Liza, then tek my advice and keep yer mouth closed.'

'Liza's right in a way, Tilly,' Mary Pegleg put in. 'Phoebe ain't no different. We all feel like 'avin' a cry at times, an' there be times when a good cry meks you feel better.'

'Give me half hour after lights out,' Liza smirked, 'then I'll mek 'er feel better. What Liza does is better for 'er than fartin' around wi' words. Ah bet you can remember 'ow it felt when that fiancy o' your'n touched you up, eh, Pardoe?'

Picking up her plate, Tilly tipped the remainder of her bread and potatoes on to Mary Pegleg's then swung the empty plate fast and hard, smashing it full into Liza Spittle's face.

'You was told to keep yer dirty mouth shut, Liza!' Tilly put the dented metal plate on the table as Sally Moreton's replacement began to move towards them. 'You should 'ave done just that, but then, they say there's no fool like an old fool.'

'What's going on here?'

Emily Pagett had been superintendent of the laundry for the month since Sally Moreton's death. She carried no cane but every prisoner in Handsworth gaol knew she was not to be played with.

'Phoebe . . . 'er's . . . 'er's a bit upset.' Nellie Bladen's consumptive face turned an even more sickly yellow.

'Why is that, Phoebe?'

Brushing at her cheeks with her fingers, Phoebe glanced up at the wardress. She had no occasion to see this woman other than at mealtimes, her place of labour being changed to the sewing room, but Tilly and the others had said she was not without sympathy.

'I . . . I was just remembering . . .'

''Er was saying that 'er father's bin dead twelve months today,' Tilly chipped in as Phoebe faltered. ''Er was very close to 'er father.'

'It happens to everybody, Pardoe.' Emily Pagett turned her

glance to Liza Spittle, trying to staunch the blood spurting crimson between her fingers. 'And what's happened to you, Spittle?'

'Sure an' 'tis the nose on 'er face, 'tis bleedin'.' Bridie Trow was angelic in her innocence. 'Sure an' it does that sometimes.'

'So her nose is bleeding. And what has happened to her tongue, why can't she use that? It's usually to be heard if she thinks none but inmates are around.'

'It'z juzt a doze bleed,' Liza snuffled through her fingers, 'it 'appenz zumtimes.'

'I see, just a nose bleed . . . not caused by anything specific like a snide remark or the promise of a midnight visit?' The wardress raised her voice so it carried over the clatter of forks. 'In the four weeks since my arrival in Handsworth I have come to know almost all of you women, and you have all come to know me and to know I will have no stepping out of line. Keep yourselves orderly, do your work well and there will be no trouble. That is *exactly* what I want and expect . . . no trouble.'

The clatter of forks resumed, no prisoner raising her head, each afraid that to catch the eye of the laundry superintendent might in some way constitute a challenge.

Her voice once more at a normal level Emily Pagett looked at Liza, blood smeared across her face, merging the beetroot mark into one red mask. 'Looks nasty, Spittle,' she said. 'Better get along to the washroom and get it cleaned up. You wouldn't want to get it knocked, now would you? That *would* be painful . . .' Then, her eyes still on the woman shuffling from the table, she added. 'And you, Tilly Wood, best try getting that plate back into shape. And next time, use your hand – there's less evidence that way.'

'How did you know?'

Phoebe slipped the rough calico nightgown over her head, fastening the flat cloth-covered buttons up to her throat.

'Took no guessin'.' Tilly fastened her hair in a plait, leaving it to lie across one shoulder. 'You've said one or two bits o' what 'appened afore you come 'ere, one o' em bein' as 'ow your father died sudden like.'

'God rest the puir man!' Bridie crossed herself.

'I never expected it.' Phoebe stared down at her hands, now lying in her lap. 'Father sometimes stayed away if his business took him to London or Southampton but he always told me first. I had no idea he had not come home that night until Mrs Banks announced his bed had not been slept in. Then when I heard about the accident . . .'

'Don't go over that.' Tilly fastened the buttons of her own nightgown. 'No use in rakin' spent coals.'

'Let 'er get it out if 'er wants to.' Martha Ames came to sit beside Phoebe on the low iron bed. 'Spit it out, wench, it'll feel better when you do.'

'It all happened so quickly,' Phoebe said quietly. 'Father dead, his will leaving me penniless, Montrose no longer wanting to marry me, and Aunt Annie turning me out of my own home . . .'

'By Patrick an' the Saints, ye puir girl! An' it's little wonder the Divil got his hooks into yous. So how did you manage, you never 'avin' to strike a blow yerself afore?' Bridie asked.

'I never would have managed without Joseph Leach and his family,' Phoebe answered. 'It was Joseph and his son Mathew who hired a horse and cart to transport the furniture from the shop to Wiggins Mill, and Sarah Leach and their daughter Miriam did most of the organising of the rooms. But it was providing food that gave me my worst moments. It was over an hour's walk from the house to the town and I would bring back only enough for one day. It was Sarah taught me to plan ahead, to buy in stones rather than in ounces, and it was she who got the carter to bring what I needed from the town and drop it at the crossroads on his way to and from Dudley. From the crossroads I had to carry it the half mile to the house. There were times I just wanted to give up . . .'

'I know that feelin'.' Nellie Bladen's sickly face looked death-like in the anaemic yellow light of the single gaslamp. 'But we keeps on goin' somehow.'

Phoebe smiled, recognising knowledge gained the hard way. 'Yes, Nellie, we keep going on. It didn't seem so bad once Miriam and Sarah finally taught me to cook . . . not so bad, that is, until I realised my very last pennies were gone.'

'Eeh, ma wench, 'ow did you manage?' Martha pressed a hand over Phoebe's, her eyes on the girl's face.

'I didn't know what to do,' Phoebe replied quietly, interrupted only by Liza Spittle's moans as the rough calico of her nightgown scraped her swollen nose. 'I only knew I wasn't going to take my trouble to Joseph and Sarah, they had done enough already and with my aunt only too ready to take their home . . . that was when Lucy Baines arrived. The carter had brought her to the crossroads then directed her to Wiggins Mill. I had not seen her since that last day at Brunswick House. She had found work at Sandwell Priory across the valley at West Bromwich. It was her first real day off, she said, and Sarah had told her how to find me.

'We talked a lot and laughed over some of the mistakes I had made while learning to fend for myself, then it came out about my last pennies being spent. She asked me about my jewellery, why didn't I sell it? I would get enough money to tide me over comfortably until I got work or was married.'

'But you said that fi-nancy o' your'n 'ad given you the push!' Mary Pegleg began, then stopped as Tilly's hand smacked against her backbone.

'Lucy seemed to think that was the least of my troubles.' Phoebe smiled again. 'I was better off without a "bloke with not enough oil in his lamp to light his way home", were her words, though what she meant exactly I don't know.'

'I do,' Tilly broke in for the first time since Phoebe had begun to speak. ''Er meant as 'ow your Montrose Wheeler 'adn't enough sense to hold on to a good thing when 'e'd got it, an' I fer one agrees wi' 'er. You be better off wi'out a bloke who only wants a woman for 'er money.'

'Tilly's right, Phoebe,' Mary Pegleg nodded. 'You be fortunate to 'ave found out what 'e was afore you married 'im. There be them among us as don't an' it's too late to do anythin' about it once you're wed. I know, that's 'ow I come to 'ave this.' She tapped her knuckles against the wooden stump below her left knee.

'So what did you do, Phoebe?' Martha asked, stealing Mary's moment of glory.

'I reminded Lucy of what my aunt had said. My mother's jewellery and mine must have been paid for by my father, and unless I had deeds of gift confirming they had been given to me, then they were part of the estate and as such belonged to Uncle Samuel.'

''Er sounds a proper old cow,' Nellie Bladen muttered. 'I wouldn't mind meetin' 'er one dark night. ''Er wouldn't bloody know 'er arse from 'er elbow when I'd finished wi' 'er.'

'An' the Lord give strength to ye,' Bridie Trow said fervently, 'an' the demons o' Hell be there to pick up the pieces.'

'And did you 'ave these deeds of gift?' It was Tilly who asked the question.

'No.' Phoebe shook her head. 'So when my aunt's housekeeper arrived to collect the keys to the house she was given both jewellery boxes, my mother's and my own.'

'So if your maid saw as 'ow the jewellery was took by your aunt's 'ousekeeper, 'ow come 'er asks you why you don't sell it?'

'I asked the same question,' Phoebe answered, 'then Lucy asked something else I found puzzling. What had I done with the dresses I had taken with me? I said I had not worn them since coming to Wiggins Mill, I had used only the underwear, the dresses were in a box in my bedroom. At that Lucy grabbed my hand and dragged me after her up the stairs. In the bedroom she flung open the box and threw the dresses across the bed. "Your bloody dried up fart of an auntie took your mother's jewellery but the old bag didn't get your'n," she said.' Phoebe halted. Less than a year ago she had never heard such words; now she could speak them without so much as a blush.

'But that 'ousekeeper of Annie's, 'er took both boxes, least tha's what you said.' Mary Pegleg sounded confused.

'So she did, Mary,' Phoebe answered, 'and I said the same to Lucy who laughed. She agreed Mrs Tranter had been given two boxes each containing pieces of jewellery – none of which, she said, was that given to me by my maternal grandmother. *That* she had removed from my box, replacing it with some of my mother's. She said Aunt Annie didn't know what jewellery my mother and I had so she would never know what or if any were missing.'

'Sure an' if that girl's brain is not the gift of the little people oi'll be after askin' what is?' Bridie Trow grinned. 'So tell me, what had she done wi' the trinkets an' all?'

'Sewn them in the hem of my dresses.' Phoebe looked at the women grouped around her. 'Mrs Banks and Lucy had taken my grandmother's jewellery out of my room as soon as Aunt Annie had left Brunswick House and together they had sewn it into the hem of two dresses, the two Lucy packed into a bag while Mrs Tranter watched.'

'Oi said it was the gift of the little people the girl had.' Bridie grinned again. 'Sure none but they have the guile to think of doin' the loike, sewin' baubles into a frock. Jesus, but Paddy O'Flaherty 'imself couldn't come up wi' better, an' him the smartest man in all Oirland.'

'So why 'adn't you sold the jewellery?' Tilly watched Phoebe's face, waiting for an answer.

'Because neither of them had told me what they had done. They both thought if I knew I would insist the jewellery go to my aunt, then Mrs Banks left for Chester, and with the worry of getting a new post and then not being allowed time off up until she came to see me that day, Lucy could do nothing but hope I'd found them.'

Seated on her own bed, Liza Spittle touched a finger to her broken mouth. 'If you found you 'ad jewellery to sell,' she said, trying hard to speak without moving lips swollen beyond recognition, "ow come you was 'ad up fer thievin'? 'Ow come you am in 'ere doin' fifteen years?'

'You sew very nicely, Pardoe.' The prison Governess examined the stitches Phoebe had put into a church Psalter. 'Father Heywood will be pleased with these, I'm sure. Tell me . . . who taught you to sew like this?'

Hannah Price's office was at the front of the plain purpose-built prison and from where she was standing Phoebe could see out across the heath, out where people were living ordinary lives, where they could walk with soft meadow earth beneath their feet, where they could stand with the sun and wind on their faces, out where her own life had once been worth living.

'Mrs Banks, Ma'am.'

'Mrs Banks was your tutor?'

'No, Ma'am.' Reluctantly Phoebe turned from her view of the outside world. 'She was my father's housekeeper. I did have a tutor,' she explained, seeing the Governess's enquiring look. 'Mr Caleb Priest was my tutor until I reached the age of thirteen then my father thought my education needed a woman's hand. He engaged Miss Stephenson who did not think I would need the skill of needlework, but I enjoyed it. When she left I used to sit with Mrs Banks and Lucy. That was when I learned to sew.'

'I see.' Hannah Price returned the Psalter. 'Tell me, Pardoe, do you prefer to work out your sentence in the sewing room, or would you rather be in the laundry or the kitchens?'

Phoebe's hand tightened on the beautifully embroidered Psalter. To have to return to the laundry, even without the presence of Sally Moreton . . . a cold sickness rose in her stomach; fifteen years' hard labour, the Magistrate had said, and the woman watching her across the room had the power to return her to a labour that paralysed the soul.

'I . . . I prefer the sewing room, Ma'am.' Phoebe swallowed the sickness of despair. 'I . . . I hope my work is satisfactory?'

'It is.' Hannah Price nodded, the slant of sun through the window catching the chestnut brown hair she had coiled into a knot on the back of her head. 'And so is your behaviour. Your superintendent tells me you have given no trouble while you have been here and I have received no report of any disturbance in your dormitory.' Crossing to the table that served as a desk, she sat down, her hands clasped on its surface. 'In view of that, Pardoe, and of the excellence of your work, I am placing you in charge of the work of the prisoners in the sewing room. I hope you realise the trust I am placing in you?'

'I do, Ma'am.' It took Phoebe long seconds to find her voice, the sickness of fear subsiding into relief. 'And I will do my best to honour it.'

She had not been returned to the steamy hell hole of the prison laundry and to the hated task of washing menstrual cloths, a task Sally Moreton had taken particular joy in making totally hers. Phoebe looked at the Psalter she was embroidering. Fifteen years . . . how many Psalters would she sew in that time?

'Eeh, Joseph, I can't believe it!' Sarah Leach looked across at her husband. 'I can't believe Abel Pardoe 'as bin dead over a year.'

'You can believe it all right.' Joseph peeled off his moleskin trousers, dropping them beside shirt and waistcoat on the floor of the tiny scullery of the one up, one down that housed them, their twenty-year-old son and fifteen-year-old daughter. There was little enough room to move in the place but there would have been less had the rest of his seven children lived beyond babyhood.

'I 'elped to gerrim out an' our Mathew 'elped to carry 'im 'ome.' He slipped into the tin bath Sarah had prepared for him, the warm water easing his crippled left leg, that being the only thing that had prevented him helping to carry Abel Pardoe's body.

''Ow did it 'appen?'

Reaching for the Sunlight soap Sarah kept on a cracked saucer, Joseph lathered his face, blowing like a seal breaking the surface. 'Crownin' in,' he spluttered, 'along of Bilston Road, I told you.'

'I know you did, but I still can't believe it.'

Picking up her husband's clothes, she carried them into the small yard they shared with five other families and threw them across the rope Joseph had fastened for her between two slim tree trunks he had trimmed and hammered into the earth. Proceeding to beat them with a cane carpet beater, she coughed, catching some of the billowing coal dust in her throat. There were those in Wednesbury did this once a week, same as their men took a weekly bath, but in her house it was a nightly affair. Sarah gave the finishing whacks then gathered the clothes, carrying them back to the scullery. Wealthy they were not, but clean they would be.

'Did anybody see it 'appen?' She took up the conversation from where she had left it.

'Don't think so, not many comings and goings up that end during the week.' Joseph scooped handfuls of water, throwing it over his hair, revealing brown beneath the black. 'Folks is all at work 'ceptin' fer Sunday, an' most o' that is spent in Chapel.'

'What did Miss Phoebe 'ave to say?' Sarah had heard it all before but felt the need to go over it again.

'Not a lot, too shocked I reckon, though 'er did say as 'ow 'er father didn't go 'ome at all that night.'

'Oh!' Sarah placed trousers, jacket and waistcoat across a wooden stool. Then, 'Joseph . . . do you reckon 'e wuz theer all night . . . in that 'ole?'

'I doubt it, Joby Hackwood would 'ave found 'im. Them dogs o' his'n could find anythin' – sharp as a razor be them dogs an' Joby 'isself not far off. No, if Abel Pardoe 'ad met wi' that 'ole that night, Joby would 'ave found 'im.' His bath finished Joseph dressed. ''Sides, 'e were facing wrong way.'

Carrying the tin bath out the back, Sarah emptied it into the communal drain that ran through the street of miners' houses then brought it back into the scullery against the arrival of her son.

'What do you mean, 'e were facin' the wrong way?' In the tiny living room she passed Joseph his clay pipe from the mantle then the precious tin with the last few strands of shag tobacco.

Joseph packed the tiny white bowl of the home-made pipe, pressing the tobacco firmly down with his thumb, testing the draw of it with loud sucking breaths before holding a taper to the fire. 'It were soft Johnnie as found 'em . . .'

'Wot! Minnie Pritchard's lad? I thought 'er kept 'im close, not let 'im roam about?'

'Lad 'as fits, Sarah,' Joseph held the lighted taper to the bowl, answering through short puffs, 'that . . . that don' . . . that don' mean as 'e's daft. Lad 'as a brain . . . it's folk around 'im as is daft . . . too daft to let lad be.' Knocking the taper against the bars of the grate blackleaded to a shine like silver, he extinguished the flame, dropping the taper back into a clay pot in the hearth. 'If that mother o' his'n let lad out to work . . .'

''Ow can 'er?' Sarah was quick to defend the woman. 'Lad 'as fits . . . 'e ain't responsible. 'E can't be trusted to act proper.'

'It's folk who believe that am the daft 'uns, Sarah.' Joseph leaned back into the chair set close to the fire, pulling heavily on the small pipe. 'Lad were responsible enough to come straight to pit an' tell me what 'e'd found. If that ain't actin' proper then I don' know wot is. Seems right responsible way of carryin' on to me, an' don' 'e always put isself down somewhere when 'e feels a turn comin' on?'

'I feel sorry for 'em both,' Sarah added coals to the fire, 'the lad an' 'is mother. What the good Lord was thinkin' on the day 'e was got . . .'

'Nobody knows the ways o' the Lord, Sarah, an' it's a wise 'ead that don' puzzle over 'em.'

'That be true enough.' Picking up her mending, Sarah carried it to the hard-backed settle beneath the small window. 'Any road up, it were lad found 'im, you say?'

Joseph tapped the white bowl against the palm of his hand, loosening the tobacco. 'Ar, leastways nobody else 'ad, not to my knowledge anyway.' He replaced the slender stem in his mouth, holding it between his teeth. 'Along about three o'clock he come runnin' into yard like a bat out of 'ell, babbling on about Bilston Road cavin' in and oss an' cart at bottom of 'ole.'

Sarah waited while Joseph tapped his pipe.

'I could see lad was upset,' a wisp of grey smoke curled from Joseph's lips, 'so I left office to Manny Whitehouse an' went wi' 'im.'

'What if gaffer 'ad come an' you not at the pit? You could 'ave lost yer job.'

'No fear o' that 'appening seein' it was 'im at bottom of that 'ole!'

You didn't know that at the time, tekin' off after soft Johnnie, Sarah thought, though was wise enough not to say it.

'Any road,' Joseph puffed, 'soon as I seen trap I knowed who it was 'ad gone in. I sent Johnnie 'ome an' went back to pit for men to raise Abel.'

'So, what about 'is facin' wrong way?' Sarah asked again as Joseph settled into silence.

'Well,' he removed the pipe from his mouth, his gaze on the glowing coals, 'if gaffer 'ad bin on his way from pit to the 'ouse, as Miss Phoebe thought, then oss would 'ave bin facin' t'other way, but it were facin' *toward* Bilston with its back end toward Brummagem.'

Sarah held the needle in mid-air, a puzzled frown drawing her brows together. 'What's wrong wi' that?'

'Think on it,' he answered. 'Abel Pardoe left 'ome that mornin' fer pit only 'e didn't come to pit that day. Miss Phoebe said 'e 'adn't come 'ome from pit in the afternoon nor 'ad 'e bin 'ome all night. Joby Hackwood is certain sure there was no 'ole in Bilston Road that night nor up to eleven o'clock next mornin' when he says 'e was runnin' 'is dogs along the edge o' cornfield . . .'

'Seein' 'ow many rabbits was runnin' likely,' Sarah said drily.

'Whatever 'e was doin', there was no 'ole in Bilston Road at that time or 'e would 'ave seen it, so Abel must 'ave run into it between eleven an' two. It would tek the hour between then an' three for young Johnnie Pritchard to sort out what to do then get isself over to the pit to get me.'

'I still don't see what you reckon is wrong?' Sarah stabbed the needle into her mending.

Joseph blew another stream of blue-grey smoke, the smell of shag tobacco mingling with the smell of coal. 'What's wrong is this. Oss 'ad its back end toward Brummagem,' he said, using the local term for Birmingham, 'that means Abel Pardoe was on 'is way back from there.'

'But 'ow can you be sure?' Sarah asked.

'I'm sure enough,' Joseph replied, his glance still deep in the heart of the fire. 'I 'appens to know Abel spent a deal of time there.'

'Doin' what . . . business?'

'Of a sort.' Joseph sucked on his pipe.

'What sort?' Sarah removed the thread from the needle, using the eye end to unpick an untidy stitch.

'Use yer 'ead, woman.' Joseph bit on the stem of the clay pipe. 'What sort of business does a man do at night? Not the sort 'e does in any office! It's my belief Abel Pardoe 'ad a kept woman – either that or he med regular visits to some knockin' shop.'

Sarah almost dropped the needle. 'Eeeh, Joseph! You mean Abel Pardoe . . .'

'That's just what I mean,' Joseph continued where Sarah's shocked voice left off. 'I mean Abel Pardoe had spent that night in Brummagem with a prostitute.'

'Thank the good Lord that never came out.' Sarah held the needle poised in mid-air. 'Phoebe Pardoe went through enough with that aunt of hers wi'out 'earin' such things about 'er father.'

'Seems nobody else figured it,' Joseph sucked once more on the slim white stem of his clay pipe, 'or, if they did then they'm keepin' quiet about it same as we 'ave.'

'That poor girl in prison these twelve months,' Sarah sighed, resuming her mending. 'I can't believe that neither, 'er would never steal anythin'.'

'Magistrate said 'er did.'

'Magistrate don't know everythin',' Sarah snapped, a catch in her voice. ''E don't know what a nice carin' wench young Phoebe was.'

'Magistrate don't need to know.' Joseph stared into the glowing heart of the grate. ''E knowed only what somebody wanted 'im to know an' in my opinion that somebody be Annie Pardoe. My guess is it be 'er as supplied that evidence, if what was said in that court could be called evidence, an' that were just enough to put Abel's daughter down the line for fifteen years.'

Chapter Four

''Er's sewin' what!' Martha Ames's face creased with a mixture of amusement and disbelief. 'Hey, Phoebe, you 'ear that? Mary Pegleg reckons you be sewin' salt cellars.'

'Psalters.' Phoebe joined the laughter of the women. Apart from a half-hour break for the midday meal she didn't see them until evening. 'I'm sewing Psalters . . .'

'That another of 'er new ideas?' Liza interrupted scathingly. 'Gets a good many of them does new Governess.'

'An' all of 'em to the good so far.' Martha looked at her fellow prisoner, the beetroot stain livid on her cheek. 'Though I reckon I could suggest one we'd all find to our liking.'

'Oh, ar, an' what's that, Martha Smart Arse?'

'That 'er 'as you put down.'

'What them Psalterers for then, Phoebe?' Nellie Bladen asked as the second flush of laughter died away.

'Jesus, Joseph and Mary!' Bridie exclaimed, making the regular sign on her chest. 'Sure an oi can't be after believin' what my own ears be tellin' me, Nellie Bladen.'

'So what am they tellin' you?' Nellie's ferret features tightened. 'One thing they ain't tellin' you for all the sign o' the cross you keep mekin' . . . they ain't tellin' you Bridie Trow is an angel nor ever likely to be!'

'That's where you be wrong altogether, so you be.' Bridie's native brogue thickened. 'If oi'm not after bein' an angel when oi'm dead it would be meanin' oi was to spend the rest of me after loif with the loikes of you – an' the good Lord will never be permittin' the loike of that.'

'And what is it the good Lord will not permit?'

The women's smiles faded as Agnes Marsh halted her patrol at their end of the long table.

Bridie, eyes still malignant, half turned on the bench seat. 'Nellie Bladen was after sayin' that oi'll be livin' wi' the loike of herself after oi be dead.'

'Well, you both have one consolation.' The wardress smiled spitefully. 'After you've finished in Handsworth you'll be used to each other . . . and to the place you'll both finish up in when you're dead. Now get this lot cleared and get ready for lights out or you might be wishing yourselves there now.'

'Sour-faced cow!' Nellie muttered, watching the wardress move down the room toward its one door. 'I know what 'er could do with.'

'An' p'raps you would like to tell 'er,' Liza Spittle dropped the apron she had been mending into the large basket set beside the table, 'to 'er face.'

'Why don't you when you am doin' it wi' 'er in the store room, you dirty bugger. Don't think we don't know what goes on in there.'

'It don't bother me what you think, none of you, I'll do what it teks to get by in this place.'

'An' that means mauling the tits off any woman who'll let you an' a few that's bin too frightened to refuse.' Martha Ames dropped her own mending into the basket then turned a disdainful glance on Liza. 'Yer nothing but a filthy swine, Liza Spittle, no wonder the Devil marked you one of his'n.'

'You still didn't tell me what a Psalterer was?' Nellie Bladen whispered to Phoebe as they left the dining hall.

'It is a book of Psalms.'

'A book! But you can't sew a book, Phoebe.'

'No, of course I can't.' She smiled, following Nellie out of the dining hall. 'What Mary should have said was that I am embroidering covers for Psalters.'

'Trust Mary Pegleg to get it wrong.' Nellie turned toward

the washroom. 'That woman couldn't get anythin' right, not if 'Ell fetched 'er.'

Soaping her hands and face with carbolic, Phoebe thought of the events of the morning. Hannah Price had sent for her, asking that she make two Psalter covers. She wanted them as a gift for the Vicar of St James's church in Wednesbury. Now Phoebe felt the same tug at her stomach she had felt when the Governess told her of her visit to a friend she had in the town. How long before *she* could visit friends? Phoebe buried her face in the rough cotton that served the prisoners as towels. She knew how long . . . fifteen years.

Phoebe stared at the familiar rectangles of moonlight, her brain refusing her the sanctuary of sleep. She had thought her troubles were ending when Lucy gave her the jewellery. If only she had known . . . her troubles were just beginning.

She had pawned a ruby ring first, choosing to take it to John Kilvert, the pawnbroker who had sold her the furniture, hoping to redeem it in a few weeks.

What a hope! Phoebe turned her face to the wall, finding no solace in the well of shadows.

The ring had been followed by a marcasite brooch and that by a cornelian bracelet. One by one the pieces had gone, John Kilvert giving her a fraction of their worth and that fraction swallowed by the purchase of food and the small amount of cotton she bought to make garments to sell, garments that brought her even less than her jewellery. Finally it was her grandmother's sapphire necklace. John Kilvert's eyes had glowed when she unwrapped it from her handkerchief and laid it on his counter. He had scrutinised it carefully then said, 'Two pounds ten, tek it or leave it.'

She had had to take it as the pawnbroker well knew. Two pounds ten shillings . . . careful as she had desperately tried to be, it had lasted less than six weeks.

Too proud to tell Sarah and Joseph of her circumstances, she had agreed to go with them to the Advent Fayre one

Saturday evening. 'The gentry will be there,' Sarah had said, 'mebbe they might buy some of your petticoats. Heaven knows they'm pretty enough.'

Only she had no material to sew petticoats and no money to buy more. But she would be expected to take something that could be sold to benefit the church. She hadn't thought about her two dresses until she went to bed. The next morning she had chosen the white one sprigged with tiny red flowers and carefully taken it to pieces, using the cloth to make two dresses for a child, trimming one with red ribbons and the other with pink.

Standing behind the stall allotted to her and Sarah Leach, Phoebe had seen Montrose's mother sweep into the market place and saw the doffed caps and bobbed curtsies of the townsfolk as the woman and her companions halted a few moments at each stall. Maybe they would pass her and Sarah by, maybe Violet Wheeler would not recognise her in the flickering light of candles set in jars, but even as she pressed into the shadows Phoebe knew it would not happen.

'Mama, look, how delightful.'

The two women and a girl Phoebe guessed to be around her own age paused at her stall, the cold November breeze fluttering the feathers of their bonnets.

'Look, Mama.' The girl touched a gloved hand to the dresses Phoebe had made. 'Don't you think they are pretty?'

'I do, my dear.' Lady Dartmouth smiled at her daughter then asked,'Who made these?'

'I did, Your Ladyship,' Phoebe answered, aware of the warning in Violet Wheeler's eyes.

'They are very pretty and well stitched.' Lady Dartmouth held one of the dresses closer to the lighted candles. 'Don't you agree, Mrs Wheeler?'

Montrose's mother made a pretence of examining the stitches. 'Yes,' she answered, already turning in the direction of the next stall, 'quite.'

'Mama,' the girl picked up the second dress, 'do you not think these would make the most admirable Christmas gifts for the children of the servants? You know how much you enjoy the giving of something useful.'

'They would indeed be admirable, my dear, always provided the children are not boys, eh, Mrs Wheeler?'

Forced to turn back Violet Wheeler managed an acid smile. 'As you say, Your Ladyship, useful only if they are not boys.'

'Tell me,' Lady Dartmouth returned her hand to the warmth of her fur muff, 'have you more of these?'

Phoebe shook her head. 'No, Your Ladyship.'

'Pity.' Lady Dartmouth made to move on but her daughter stayed.

'But you could make more.' The girl's cheeks glowed red in the cold of the November night. 'How many could you make before Christmas?'

'Two would be all I had cloth for.' Phoebe avoided the glare of Violet Wheeler. 'You see, Your Ladyship, I made those from a gown of my own and I have only one more.'

'You mean you made something as pretty as this out of an old gown?'

Not so old, Phoebe thought, that particular dress had been a gift from her father on her last birthday.

'Then there is no problem.' The girl turned to her mother. 'I have lots of dresses I do not wear any more. I may give them to be used may I not, Mama?'

'Of course, Sophie,' Lady Dartmouth nodded, 'that is a very good suggestion.' Then turning her glance on Phoebe added, 'My daughter and I will be returning to the Manor on Thursday of this week. You may call whenever my daughter wishes.'

'Oh, come the next afternoon.' The girl turned to Montrose's mother. 'I'm sure you too will find a few dresses for such a worthy cause, Mrs Wheeler. After all, the proceeds will go to the church, so when may she call upon you?'

Even in the darkness of the November evening Phoebe saw the colour drain from the woman's face. 'I . . . she . . . she may call Thursday afternoon of this week at three o'clock.'

'So,' Lady Dartmouth was clearly to be delayed no longer, 'bring the dresses to the Manor one day before Christmas Eve. I will send a list of how many and what sizes to the Vicar.' She turned to her daughter. 'And now, Sophie, I insist on returning to Oakeswell Hall, this night air is much too cold for either of us.'

'Looks like Violet Wheeler 'as designs, invitin' 'er Ladyship to Oakeswell.' Sarah Leach watched the departing trio.

'Designs,' Phoebe breathed, relieved when the carriage drove away, 'how do you mean?'

'Mean!' Sarah handed over a pot of her preserve, taking a threepenny piece and handing back a penny and a halfpenny to a woman with five children hanging on her skirts. 'A man wi' half an eye can see what I mean. Violet Wheeler 'as set 'er sights on that young un for 'er lad.'

'You can't mean . . .'

'I can an' I do,' Sarah said. 'That woman intends for 'er son to wed Lady Sophie, daughter of Sir William and Lady Amelia Dartmouth of Sandwell Priory.'

Phoebe remembered the feeling that coursed through her then; it wasn't pain, no, she couldn't call it pain, it was more like pity . . . pity for a young girl being prepared like a lamb for the slaughter.

She had gone to Oakeswell Hall at the appointed time to find a servant waiting for her at the gate, the dresses, two of them, draped across her arms. Phoebe Pardoe was not to be admitted even to the grounds of her former fiancé's home.

The visit to Sandwell Priory had been so different. Phoebe turned her eyes back to the greyish-yellow rectangles high up on the wall. She had looked down from the ridge of high ground on to the house nestling in the valley, its tall windows reflecting the pale watery November sunlight, windows that seemed to go on and on along the expanse of the huge building. Brunswick House was by no means small but it would fit a hundred times over into that house. She had stared until a flurry of snow blew across her face then set off down the path to the valley. A mile or so further on she had stepped aside, hearing the rumble of an approaching carriage.

'It is you, isn't it?' Lady Sophie leaned from the window, calling for the carriage to stop. 'You are the girl I spoke to at the Fayre, are you not? The girl who is to call today?'

'I am, Your Ladyship.' Phoebe bobbed a curtsy.

'Edward,' she went on to someone in the carriage, 'this is the girl I told you about, the one who makes such delightfully pretty dresses.'

The carriage door had opened then and a tall blond man of about twenty or so had jumped out.

'Forgive my sister,' he said, 'it is a failing of hers to keep people standing in the cold.' He smiled, a smile that lit deep blue eyes. 'Allow me to assist you into the carriage?'

'No.' Phoebe took a step backward. 'No, thank you, I . . . I'll walk.'

'Nonsense.' The man smiled again. 'I will not hear of such a thing, the day is far too cold. And besides,' he held out a hand, 'it is coming on to snow.'

'Of course you must ride with us.' Lady Sophie added her smile and voice to her brother's. 'There is plenty of room.'

Phoebe had made no more demur, accepting the man's hand as she climbed into the carriage.

'My sister told me of meeting you but she failed to tell me your name?'

Across the carriage the blue eyes had smiled deep into hers.

'My name is Phoebe . . . Phoebe Pardoe.'

'How do you do, Phoebe?' He said her name slowly as if wanting to hold it in his mouth, to keep it inside of him, a part of himself.

'My sister you have met already, allow me to present myself – Edward Dartmouth.'

He had introduced himself simply. Phoebe knew he was Edward Albert Richard Dartmouth whose family had owned the Priory for nearly five hundred years, but he had given himself no airs and graces.

At the Priory Sophie had heaped dresses into her arms, their colours mixing like some exotic rainbow, then laughed as Phoebe gradually disappeared beneath them.

She had not seen Lady Dartmouth, Sophie apologising for her absence, explaining that her mother's evening visit to the market had given her a chill. 'Poor Mama,' Sophie had laughed. 'She says the things she does for the church should guarantee her a healthy eternity, though she does wish it would do the same for her earthly existence.'

Four maids had eventually carried the dresses down the great staircase. Phoebe watched for a glimpse of Lucy as they passed but she was not among the servants who crossed the vast marble hall and down a wide fan of steps to the carriage Sophie insisted Phoebe should travel home in. Edward stood beside it.

'I could not forgive myself should I let you go home alone.' He had helped her into the carriage then, his eyes never leaving her face. Phoebe had not wanted him to accompany her, ashamed for him to see her dilapidated home and the tumbling outhouses, but once there he had kept her hand in his while the coachman carried the dresses indoors. 'You must allow me to call you Phoebe,' he had said softly. 'Please tell me I may?'

Phoebe closed her eyes but the face of Edward Dartmouth was printed on the lids. A handsome face, a face with more than admiration revealed in those deep blue eyes.

Lucy had been at Wiggins Mill one day when Edward paid a visit, one of many since Phoebe's going to Sandwell Priory.

'You wants to be careful, Miss.' Phoebe remembered Lucy's warning. 'Could be 'e's here after more than you should give 'im.'

'He's a friend, Lucy.'

'There's friends and friends.' Lucy's reply had been tempered with the same warning. 'The sons of gentry is no friend to the likes of us, Miss. Not unless they want a special sort of friendship. You take a tip from me an' tell 'im not to call 'ere no more.'

But Edward had not tried to take advantage of her. He had been so courteous and yet so full of life, insisting on her going out for walks along the canal bank, teaching her to skim stones across the water, piling logs on to the fire then sitting at her feet as she sewed. She had known he loved her, known even before he told her. In the darkness of the quiet dormitory, Phoebe remembered.

Samuel Pardoe put down his brush, turning from his latest landscape painting. 'It has been a year now since Abel died.' He spelled out the words on his fingers as he had been taught in childhood. 'It seems so very long, Annie.'

Annie Pardoe watched the brother she had lived with all of his fifty-two years. He had always been slight of build even as a child but of late had become markedly more frail, seeming to dwindle into himself, fading a little more each day.

'Twelve months is a long time,' she signed in return, 'but there it is. Abel is gone and we must learn to live with the fact.'

'But Phoebe is not gone,' Samuel's fingers moved quickly, 'yet we have not seen her since her father died. Why is that, Annie? Why does Phoebe not come to see us?'

'I told you, Samuel . . .' Annie walked to the window of the room that had been turned into a studio for her brother, avoiding the need to look into the face that was so like that of Abel, then after a moment turned to sign: 'Phoebe said she never wanted to see either of us again.'

'But I think perhaps if we went to see her . . .'

'No, Samuel!' Annie Pardoe signed rapidly then dropped one hand to her side as if the movement gave her pain. 'We will not go to see her. She made the decision to leave this house, hers was the choice and we must abide by it. If it be that she changes her mind then she will be welcome to return. Until that time we will have to wait and pray.'

Samuel applied another touch of paint to the canvas, his thin hand almost transparent, then signed again. 'I wonder why Abel left everything to us? It seems so very strange.'

'I see nothing strange in a man entrusting his business and property to someone old enough and wise enough to look after it.' Annie breathed deeply, holding her hand tight against the spot beneath her rib cage, then released it to sign, 'Phoebe was very young. Abel thought we would be the better guardian of what was his until she married.'

'The better guardian of what was his . . .' Samuel left off painting. 'Phoebe was his but he did not name either of us her guardian, did he, Annie?' His eyes reflected a sadness he could not voice.

'Our brother did not appoint anyone as guardian to his daughter,' Annie crossed to the door, 'simply because he thought to see her married long before he died. I have called to see our niece several times, Samuel, hoping to persuade her to come and live with us, but each time I have been met with hostility. It hurts us both to know that she has cut herself off from her family, those who have loved her from her birth, but we cannot force her to come home, my dear.'

'Annie,' Samuel signed as she opened the door, 'what happened to the idea of her marrying Gaskell Wheeler's son?'

She hesitated, the hand on her ribs pressing a little harder, then, 'I'm afraid she took the same headstrong, foolish action she took toward us,' she answered. 'She said she had been pressured into accepting Montrose Wheeler against her will, and now her father was no longer here to enforce the marriage, she would not do so. The Wheelers were understandably upset but agreed to say that following the unforeseen death of her father, Phoebe felt she could not marry so soon, therefore a postponement had taken place.'

'Is she alone?' Samuel's fingers fluttered like wounded butterflies.

Annie looked into the thin face and sad grey eyes of her brother and the pain beneath her hand worsened. It had not been his fault, he was not to blame for what fate had ordained for him or the life Abel Pardoe had ordained for her – he was not to blame yet she could not forgive him.

'No, she is not alone.' Her answer was sharpened by the pain. 'Abel's housekeeper went with her and so did her maid. They are all well cared for, I instructed Lawyer Siveter to pay an annual allowance. Phoebe might have turned her back on us, Samuel, but we will never turn ours upon her.'

Leaving the room before he could ask any more questions, Annie paused outside the door, her eyes closed, her hand pressed to the pain that refused to be ignored. Samuel had asked the same questions before and she had told the same lies.

Opening her eyes she walked to her bedroom, taking a small cardboard box from a drawer in the table that stood beside the heavy fourposter bed. Abel had slept in that bed, Abel and his pretty wife; so many nights, so much happiness. Taking the lid from the box, she put two of the white tablets it held into her mouth, swallowing them with water from the carafe on the table. Yes, Abel had shared this bed, this room with a wife while she . . . what had she had . . . what love had Annie Pardoe known, whose bed had she shared?

Putting the lid back on the box, she replaced it in the drawer, covering it with a layer of lace-edged handkerchiefs.

She had shared neither love nor bed with any man thanks to her brother. Abel could never be made to pay while he was living and death had carried him beyond her reach. No, Abel would not pay for a life he'd snatched away, a life he had destroyed so he could live his own. But Abel's daughter would . . .

Is she alone?

Samuel's question echoed in her mind, and in her mind she answered but this time with all the truth of vengeance. No, Phoebe was not alone. Some two hundred women shared her home, a home she would inhabit for the next fifteen years.

'Well, if it ain't the Governess's little pet.'

Liza Spittle's narrow eyes watched Phoebe coming along the corridor that led to the kitchens, a tray balanced in her hands. 'Ain't you goin' to stop an' 'ave a chat wi' Liza?'

'Move out the way, Liza,' Phoebe said as the other woman moved her large frame, blocking the narrow passage. 'You know prisoners must not hang around the corridors.'

'There's a lot of things not allowed in this bloody place,' Liza grinned, showing discoloured teeth, 'but the bastards 'ave to catch you at it first.'

'I have no wish to be caught,' Phoebe edged to one side in an attempt to pass, 'especially talking to you.'

'We don't 'ave to talk.' Liza stepped closer, the beetroot mark pulsing like some living thing on her cheek. 'You don't need to talk for what I want.'

'Liza, please move.' Phoebe was becoming alarmed. Why wasn't Liza in the laundry?

'Lucky me, bein' given the job of clearin' dinner plates,' she grinned as if answering Phoebe's unspoken question, 'otherwise we wouldn't 'ave this chance.'

'Chance?' Phoebe tried to control her trembling. She knew Liza Spittle had not given up in her twisted desire and for that reason took care never to be in her company without Bridie or Tilly.

Liza stepped forward again, wedging Phoebe against the wall. 'The chance for me to show you what you missed 'cos of that interferin' bitch Tilly Wood.' She leaned forward, pressing the tray into Phoebe's middle, her hand lifting the skirts of Phoebe's prison uniform, sliding high up over her thigh.

'Leave me alone!' Phoebe tried to use the tray in an effort to push the woman away from her, turning her face from the sour fumes of her breath. 'Please, for God's sake, don't!'

Liza laughed, a husky sound deep in her throat. 'They all says that first time.' Her voice was deep as a man's, her mouth touching the side of Phoebe's neck. 'But then it changes – it changes to, for God's sake, please do.'

'Stop!' Phoebe's cry cracked on a sob. 'Please, I . . . I'm not like that . . .'

'You will be.' Liza's tongue licked upward against Phoebe's ear, her hand moving toward the vee between her legs. 'You will be when Liza gets through.'

'No, please.' Phoebe's control had gone, the tears spilling down her cheeks. 'Please leave me alone. Please, for God's sake!'

'If you won't do it for God, then do it for me!'

Tilly Wood's voice rang out behind Liza as she was swung away, one arm twisted high up her back.

'I warned you,' Tilly snarled, her gaunt face twisted with contempt. 'I warned you afore, Tilly Wood tells not even the Lord 'imself twice . . .'

Grabbing the collar of Liza's grey calico frock, she spun her backward against the opposite wall.

'. . . but you don't tek a tellin', do you, Liza Spittle?'

Tilly struck out, the back of her hand slamming hard across Liza's face.

'. . . so yer goin' to 'ave to be shown that 'ands off means what it says.'

Across the narrow corridor Liza's small eyes glittered with a feral light as they flicked from Tilly to Phoebe then back to Tilly. 'I'm goin' to do fer you, Tilly Wood,' she breathed, wiping the blood from her mouth with the back of a hand. 'This time I'm goin' to kill you.'

She lunged forward, her large masculine frame threatening to obliterate Tilly who turned aside, thrusting a foot in her way. Liza stumbled but the force of her attack carried her forward, the sickening crunch of bone against brick covering Phoebe's sobs as she hit the wall beside her. Then Liza was falling, slipping sideways as she went down, her cracked skull sliding slowly over Phoebe's shoulder and breast, down along her skirt, trailing a long slow smear of red across grey.

'What did the Governess 'ave to say about it?' Martha Ames asked as the women prepared for the nine o'clock light out.

'I couldn't 'ear all that well,' Mary Pegleg answered. 'But 'er sent me to get Agnes Marsh an' that one looked none too 'appy when 'er went into the Governess's office, an' 'er looked a damn' sight less when 'er come out again.'

'But sure an' you must have heard somethin'?' Bridie said, slipping her nightgown over her head then folding the drab grey prison dress before placing it regulation fashion across the foot of her low iron bed.

Mary Pegleg unfastened the straps that held the wooden stump below her left knee, balancing it against the wall beside her bed. 'Well, I 'eard 'er tell Agnes as 'ow this was the first prison to 'ave a woman in charge an' that it would only tek summat like a brawl between the inmates to convince the Board that a woman wasn't fit for the job an' that 'er would be replaced wi' a man.'

'Sure an' that would be a black day for all,' Bridie said, buttoning her nightgown. 'Hannah Price has been fair in her dealin's with us women an' all. Could be we might have had a Governess the loike of Steel Arsed Sally Moreton, God rest her puir soul.'

'Did 'er say anythin' about Tilly?' Nellie Bladen looked across to Phoebe, sitting silent on her bed, her face pale and empty, then whispered, 'Is 'er still locked away on 'er own?'

Mary Pegleg rubbed a hand over the rounded nub of bone where her leg had been amputated. 'I 'eard summat about police, but I don't know if Governess said 'er was sendin' fer 'em or keepin' thing quiet from 'em.'

'Get the bobbies in 'ere an' it'll be more than Hannah Price will be teken out.' Martha Ames looked from one to the other of the women, their faces mirroring the tension that had held them all afternoon and evening. 'We'll all go, an' there's some of us in 'ere knows where to. 'Ell itself would be a better place.'

'Do you think Liza will die?' Nellie's normally yellow skin took on a deathly gleam under the sullen glow of the one gaslamp.

''Er looked near enough to it when we carried 'er to the infirmary,' Martha answered. 'Reckon 'er'll be lucky to last the night.'

'Holy Mother of God!' Bridie's hand lifted, making the sign of the cross several times in rapid succession.

'Did Agnes Marsh send fer the doctor, does anybody know?'

''Er couldn't.' Mary Pegleg eased her thin body into her bed, covering it with the one rough blanket before answering the question. ''Er 'ad to wait till Hannah Price got back from meeting with the Board an' that wasn't till after seven o'clock gone. 'Er said it was too late to get the doctor out then, that it would 'ave to wait till mornin'.'

'Too late my arse!' Martha spat. 'What 'er meant was the bloody doctor was too blind drunk by that time of the night even to stand up, let alone treat anybody.'

'Well, whatever 'er meant, 'er didn't send fer 'im,' Mary Pegleg stated flatly.

'Oi wonder what he will be makin' of it when he does come?' Bridie said.

'I don't know,' Martha shook her head, 'but this much I can say – drunk or sober there be no way 'e can call this a 'eart attack.'

'What will 'e call it . . . will it be murder?'

'Liza Spittle ain't dead,' Martha shot a glance at Phoebe but Nellie's words seemed to have passed over her head, 'so 'ow can 'e call what 'appened murder?'

Crossing to Phoebe's bed she pressed her back on the pillow, pulling the coarse blanket up to her chin before going back to her own place.

'But what if Liza do die?' Nellie persisted.

'If 'er does then any tears I shed won't be for 'er,' Martha said acridly. ''Er was nothin' but a filthy bitch sniffin' round women, 'er 'ad it comin' to 'er an' I fer one ain't sorry as 'er's copped it. The one I'm sorry fer is Tilly Wood.'

'What's goin' to 'appen to Tilly would you say, Martha?'

'Lord knows!' She looked at the other woman, death marked plain across her thin consumptive features. 'Depends on what the doctor and the Governess 'as ter say ter the Prison Board.'

Bridie crossed herself fervently. 'Then may the sweet Mother o'Jesus be puttin' the words into their mouths.'

Chapter Five

Phoebe lay awake in the hard narrow bed. She had not spoken since the affair in the corridor, she had not joined the discussions of the women, her mind empty, somehow detached, hearing nothing yet registering everything.

Tilly had offered no resistance when Agnes Marsh ordered two wardresses to take her away, only the eyes that had long forgotten laughter staying on Phoebe's face as they took her. What would they do to Tilly? She was already serving a life sentence for manslaughter . . . if Liza Spittle died Tilly would be accused of murder and it was certain she would hang. But she was no murderer; she had told Sally Moreton a lie about snapping her husband's neck to frighten her, it was the push down the stairs had broken it. No, Tilly Wood was not quite guilty of murder . . . yet.

Oh Lord! In the darkness, listening to the breathing of the sleeping women and the consumptive coughing of Nellie Biaden, Phoebe prayed, 'Oh Lord, don't let Liza die.'

High on the wall the windows showed a paler shade of darkness. Why was I sent to return that tray to the kitchen? Why was Liza Spittle clearing the dinner plates? Why was she in the corridor at that precise moment? Why was there no one else clearing the dining hall?

Questions vied for prominence in her brain. Lord, if only her father had not met with that terrible accident, if only her Aunt Annie had not acted as she had, if only she had never made those children's dresses, Lord if only . . . but how often had the Lord heard those words?

Above her the small rectangular windows lightened with infinite slowness, like lids lifting to reveal strange hypnotic eyes, and she turned her head away. But out of the shadows Lucy danced towards her, Lucy with eyes glowing and lips smiling.

'I'm getting wed.'

Phoebe heard the laughing happy voice rise from the depths of buried thoughts. 'Mathew an' me, we are goin' to be wed.'

Phoebe had joined in the girl's delight, returning the hug Lucy enfolded her in. They had talked a long time in the kitchen of the mill house, Lucy baking scones and mixing an amount of bread dough Phoebe thought must last a year at least, then she had asked about a wedding dress.

'I hadn't thought about it,' Lucy answered, setting the cloth-covered dough to rise besides the hearth. 'Well, not really thought about it, though I would like somethin' nice, somethin' new, I suppose, if the truth be told. But that's out of the question on what I get paid at the Priory.'

'And Mathew?' Phoebe had asked.

'Can't really ask him to sport me a dress from the money he makes, Miss Phoebe.' Lucy collected wooden mixing spoons, dropping them into the large brown earthenware bowl. 'Mathew had his wages docked same as the rest of 'em at the pit.'

'Docked?' Phoebe remembered the surprise she felt, but had it been surprise or disgust? 'Do you mean my aunt has reduced the wages of the men working at the mine?'

'Yes, Miss Phoebe, I do,' Lucy answered. 'Both of 'em, the Hobs Hill pit and the Crown mine at Moxley, and the folks who depend on it am feelin' the pinch real bad.'

'But why?' Phoebe asked. 'For what reason?'

'Annie Pardoe said as how price of coal had fallen an' men could take lower wages or take their hook.'

'She said that!'

'Well, not in them exact words.' Lucy carried the utensils

she had used in her baking to the long shallow sink in the scullery, returning for the kettle singing softly over the fire. 'But that was what 'er meant: the men could either accept a lower wage for a day's work or they could leave the pit altogether. And as you know, Miss Phoebe, that would leave them without a home as well as a job 'cos most houses in Wednesbury belong to Annie Pardoe, least at that end of the town they do.'

Phoebe might have asked what part her uncle had played in all of this but deep down she knew Samuel would know nothing of it.

'Mind you,' Lucy carried the kettle into the scullery, pouring hot water over a bowl and spoons then putting the kettle aside to be filled later at the pump in the yard, 'some of 'em couldn't be much worse off if they did leave. They 'ave little enough in their tins to feed a family *and* pay rent, and Annie Pardoe ain't one to let rent man call twice and get nothin', so some of the women an' kids am goin' more than hungry.'

'What of Joseph and Sarah?' Phoebe reached for a cloth to dry the dishes but it hung forgotten in her hands.

Lucy placed the freshly washed baking bowl on the wooden board Mathew had made to stand beside the sink. 'They are fairin' up to now though Joseph had his wage docked same as others, but they only manage 'cos Sarah can do most things herself.'

Sarah was a marvel, Phoebe thought, cook, housekeeper and gardener rolled into one, growing vegetables Joseph could no longer tend after the accident that had left him lame. But how long could she manage now money was short?

'So how will you and Mathew be fixed with him not earning as much?'

'It's going to be harder.' Lucy took the cloth from Phoebe and set about drying the bowls and spoons. 'There be no use in my denyin' that, but I'll have my position at the Priory and Mathew will 'ave his job at Hobs Hill. We can afford to rent a little house . . . just.'

'But you said yourself the wage at the pits had been reduced and what if you start a family? They won't keep you on at the Priory if you have children to care for. And if the situation at the pit gets any worse . . .'

'We've thought of that, Miss Phoebe, and we both know that if we wait for things to be perfect we will never be wed so we decided to go ahead. There will be hard times and worry for us whether we wed or not so we have little to lose except each other.'

Why had her aunt reduced the wages of the miners? Had the market price for coal really dropped or was there some other reason for her action? Phoebe picked up the bowls and spoons, carrying them back into the kitchen, replacing them on the rough wooden dresser set along one wall. Could it in some way have anything to do with her aunt's obvious dislike of Phoebe herself?

'So when will you and Mathew be married?' she asked as Lucy bustled into the kitchen, setting the freshly filled kettle over the glowing coals.

'Next month, the fifteenth,' Lucy's face radiated her joy, 'that's my birthday. Mathew said to have the wedding on that day then we would have two things to be happy for. Ooh, I am looking forward to it.'

Just as I was looking forward to my own wedding, Phoebe thought, watching the happiness light the other girl's eyes, only mine never took place.

'We want the ceremony to be at St Bart's.' Lucy lifted the bread dough on to the table, scoring it with a knife before placing it in the oven to bake. 'Just family and a few friends. We both hoped you would come, Miss? It won't be grand or anything.'

'I'm hardly grand myself, Lucy,' Phoebe smiled at the half apology, 'and I would like to come very much.'

'Would you?' Lucy placed the cooled scones on to a prettily flowered plate, embarrassment touching her cheeks with pink. 'I mean, could . . . ?'

'Would I . . . could I what?' Phoebe laughed.

'Well, Miss, me and Mathew thought . . . we hoped you might be my attendant.'

'Bridesmaid!' Phoebe grabbed the young girl, hugging her. 'Lucy, I would be absolutely delighted, and I think I have something upstairs you might be delighted with too.'

Holding on to Lucy's hand, Phoebe raced through the sitting room and up the stairs to a bedroom draped with the dresses Sophie had given her and which as yet she had not taken to pieces to make up into garments for children.

'What about one of these for a wedding dress?' she asked.

Lucy stood quite still, her eyes wide. 'You mean . . . you mean I could have one of these . . . to keep?'

'Of course to keep,' Phoebe laughed. 'Try them, I'm sure they will fit. You and Sophie are much the same size, and if need be we can soon make a few adjustments.'

'Which one?' Lucy stepped forward, touching first one and then another of the dresses. 'Which one can I try?'

'Try them all.' Phoebe snatched up a blue muslin gown trimmed with silk forget-me-nots, pressing it into Lucy's hands. 'And take whichever you wish.'

'Ooh, Miss Phoebe,' Lucy held the gown almost reverently, her eyes playing over the others, 'do you think I should?'

'No, I do not think you should!' Phoebe answered emphatically. 'I *know* you should. Now get out of that skirt and blouse and try every one of those dresses.'

Trying the blue gown, Lucy preened before a long cheval mirror that had come from Kilvert's pawn shop, then discarded it for one of pale creamy yellow, the skirt caught around the hem in half hoops of yellow tea roses.

'That looks lovely, Lucy,' Phoebe said, scooping up the girl's dark hair into a yellow silk ribbon, 'and we could make some silk rose-buds to dress your hair. The whole effect would be marvellous.'

'Oh, I do like it, Miss Phoebe,' Lucy breathed, touching a hand to the high waist, 'it's so pretty.'

'Then it's yours,' Phoebe smiled.

'But what if Miss Sophie should see me?' Lucy turned, her eyes filled with concern. 'Wouldn't 'er get mad seein' as how 'er give you these to make kids' frocks?'

Phoebe knelt, smoothing the creamy folds about Lucy's feet. 'I really don't expect the Dartmouths to turn up at Wednesbury Parish Church to witness the marriage of Mr Mathew Leach to Miss Lucy Baines, even though she'll be the prettiest bride in the country. And even if they should, I'm sure Miss Sophie would be delighted you chose to wear her gift on the most special day of your life.'

'Then if you be sure, Miss, I think I would like it to be this one. Only . . .'

'Only what?' Phoebe stood up.

'Only it do seem a shame not to try them others on, I'll not be gettin' another chance to wear such frocks!' Lucy grinned.

'And I will not be getting another chance to rescue the bread from burning.' Phoebe sniffed then dashed out of the bedroom. 'You carry on,' she called, hurrying downstairs to the kitchen, 'I'll be back in a minute.'

'Am the loaves all right, Miss?' Lucy asked when Phoebe returned a few minutes later.

'They look delicious. You are so good at cooking, Lucy.'

'Like you with sewing, Miss.' Lucy paraded a pale green sprigged dress. 'Those little frocks you've made for the kids look real pretty, I reckon Lady Dartmouth will be right pleased wi' them.'

'I hope I can get them all done in time for Christmas.' Phoebe helped to extricate Lucy from the swathes of pale green. 'There are more than I had expected.'

'Then you mustn't use your time making rose-buds or nothin' for my wedding frock,' Lucy mumbled from beneath layers of muslin.

'I shall make just as many rose-buds as it takes, Lucy Baines.' Phoebe took the dress, draping it across a chair.

'And anything else we think is necessary to make your day perfect.'

'P'raps I can 'elp, on my day off? I ain't much wi' a needle but I'm willing to try.'

'You already help enough, Lucy, I don't know how I would manage without your coming here. Sarah and Miriam tried hard to teach me to cook but I am still not very good, I'm afraid, so your help in that department is invaluable.'

'Mathew says my scones are as good as his mother's.' Lucy beamed.

'And Mathew is right.' Phoebe draped the green dress higher on the chair, leaving its folds free of the floor. 'Their only drawback being you want to go on eating them and that is not so good for a girl's shape.'

'Eeh, Miss, you need 'ave no worries in that direction.' Standing in white frilled bloomers and chemise, Lucy looked at her former employer. 'It might not be my place to say it but I reckon as you could be doin' wi' a bit more meat on your bones. You be gettin' to look right scrawny, beggin' your pardon.'

'Well, all that delicious bread of yours will soon remedy that.' Phoebe picked up the last of the dresses Sophie had given her and one which Lucy had so far refrained from touching. 'Now, Miss Lucy, I think you should try this on.'

Lucy looked at the gown, its folds streaming to the floor like a jade waterfall. 'Ooh, no, I couldn't, not that one . . . it's much too grand.'

'Nonsense.' Phoebe held it out. 'I agree it might not be as suitable to your colouring as the yellow but try it anyway. You will never know unless you try.'

'I . . . I don't think I should . . .' Lucy hesitated, a longing to feel the rich taffeta against her skin pulling her one way; a reluctance to dare try anything so grand and costly pulling her in the opposite direction.

'Oh, come on, Lucy.' Phoebe held out the dress, its fabric gleaming in the wintry sunlight, entering the tiny window sheltered by the eaves. 'Where is your sense of adventure?'

'Well, if you say so.' Lucy held up her arms for Phoebe to slip the gown over her head. 'Though I don't think it's goin' to suit me.'

'We will see.' Phoebe pulled the heavy fabric down over Lucy's shoulders then stopped as the girl cried out.

'It's somethin' in the frock,' she said, pushing the gown right down to the floor and stepping out of it. 'Somethin' cold and . . . and . . .'

'And what?' Phoebe put an arm around the frightened girl, leading her away from the dress folded in upon itself like a green island on the bare wooden floor.

'I don't know,' Lucy answered shakily, 'it . . . it felt cold and . . . and hard . . . across my chest.'

Phoebe stared at the mound of taffeta. She couldn't just leave it, she had to find out what it was lying coiled inside that dress.

'Stay here.' She pushed Lucy into the open doorway of the bedroom then, her own heart thumping, walked back to where the gown lay heaped.

'Eeh, don't touch it, Miss,' Lucy said, fear making her voice sound hollow, 'don't touch it!'

'Don't be silly, Lucy, it's probably nothing more than a dressmaker's pin that has been overlooked.' Sounding far more confident than she felt, Phoebe reached for the gown. Teeth gripped together she shook the material, then as nothing happened, lifted the dress, holding it at arm's length.

'Eeh, I could 'ave sworn there was somethin' in that frock,' Lucy said, courage returning sufficiently for her to step back inside the bedroom. 'I could swear I felt somethin'.'

'Well, let us look.' Phoebe laid the taffeta gown atop the pale green muslin draped over the room's one chair.

'I'll look.' Lucy came to stand beside her. 'I know whereabouts it was.'

Opening the bodice wide, she examined the inside of it. 'Oh my Good God!' she exclaimed, drawing back as though from the hand of death. 'Oh my Good God, will you look at that!'

'I want you to tell me exactly what happened.' The Governess of Handsworth Prison for Women looked at the thin figure of the girl standing in front of her desk. 'You were in the corridor at the time Liza Spittle was injured, were you not?'

'Yes, Ma'am,' Phoebe answered, her voice little more than a whisper.

'What were you doing there?'

Phoebe looked across the desk at the woman she knew held Tilly's life in her hands. 'I was returning a lunch tray to the kitchen, Liza blocked my way, she would not move when I asked her to let me pass . . . then . . . then she tried to force herself upon me.'

'She tried to do what?' The Governess's face blanched, her mouth pinched with disgust. 'Are you telling me Liza Spittle tried to behave like . . . like a man?'

'Yes, Ma'am,' Phoebe whispered, looking down at her feet. 'It happened once before and Tilly Wood helped me then.'

'As she did yesterday?' The Governess spoke as though she held a bad taste in her mouth. 'Tell me, Pardoe, where were the wardresses whilst all of this was going on?'

'Mrs Marsh accompanied me almost to the kitchens,' Phoebe lied, aware of Agnes Marsh standing just behind her, aware also that the woman had been asleep in her room instead of being on duty and knowing that to say so would bring vengeance not only upon herself but also on Tilly and the others. 'Then we heard the noise of a bucket being dropped on the stairs and she went to see what had happened.'

The Governess raised an enquiring glance to the wardress.

'It was one of the new intake, Ma'am,' Agnes Marsh took up the lie. 'She was scrubbing the top landing and knocked over the bucket, sending it down the stairs. I stayed to see to her mopping up before anybody could slip on the wet stairs, then I saw to her getting fresh water and soda to start again, and when I got to go to the kitchen Liza Spittle was lying unconscious in the corridor.'

'I see.' The Governess returned to Phoebe. 'You say Tilly Wood helped you? How come she was in that part of the building and not in the laundry?'

'I checked on that, Ma'am,' Agnes Marsh put in swiftly. 'She'd been sent to fetch the cooking cloths and towels from the kitchens ready for the afternoon wash.'

'Allow Pardoe to answer my next question,' Hannah Price answered coldly. 'Tell me, what assistance did Wood give?'

Phoebe swallowed hard, her eyes still on her shoes. Please God, help me to answer without making things worse for Tilly, she thought. Don't let me put her in greater danger than she is in now.

'She pulled Liza away, then when Liza tried to attack her, stepped aside. Liza crashed her head into the wall. It all happened so quickly, Ma'am, then Mrs Marsh came and had Liza taken to the infirmary and Tilly was locked away. That is all I know.'

Hannah Price glanced at the blank sheet of paper lying on her desk. Was that all the girl knew, or was it all she was prepared to say she knew?

'Have you seen Spittle this morning, Mrs Marsh?' she asked without looking up.

'Yes, Ma'am,' Agnes answered. 'There is no change from last night. She is still unconscious.'

'In that case there is no sense in sending for the doctor.' The Governess picked up a pen, dipping the nib into a glass ink-well and beginning to write on the paper before her. 'I will send an interim report informing the Prison Board that one of the inmates is unwell, and this evening I will ask the doctor to call. Spittle should have recovered sufficiently well by that time to relate to him what occurred.'

Spittle should have recovered by that time, Agnes Marsh thought, beginning to usher Phoebe from the Governess's office, or was Hannah Price giving the doctor time to drink away his senses? Either way it suited them both. The last thing the Governess or Agnes Marsh wanted was a murder inside the prison, and if Liza didn't make it then that would be another bonus.

'Excuse me, Ma'am.' Phoebe ignored Agnes Marsh pushing her towards the door. 'May I please ask a question?'

Hannah Price paused in the writing of her report and looked up at the young girl whose eyes no longer studied her own shoes but were on her, steady and unblinking. Was she truly a thief? Had she really robbed the home of Sir William Dartmouth? In all honesty Hannah could not bring herself to believe so; this girl was very different from all the other prisoners in Handsworth, so well mannered and polite, so obviously well bred it would be hard for anyone to believe her a criminal, but the law had pronounced her such and the law must always be upheld.

'Yes, Pardoe, what is it?' She signed to the wardress to wait.

'It is Tilly Wood, Ma'am,' Phoebe said, showing no trace of her true feelings. 'What is to happen to her?'

The Governess balanced the pen back and forth between thumb and forefinger as though testing its weight, her lips pursed tightly together. Phoebe waited, each tick of the tiny carriage clock sounding like the boom of a cannon in the still room.

'Ah, yes, Wood.' The balancing of the pen stopped as if some decision had finally been reached. 'I do not think it necessary to mention the involvement of any other prisoner at this stage, so for the time being Prisoner Wood will return to the laundry.'

'Thank you, Ma'am.'

Hannah Price looked up at the quiet answer and knew it was more than a simple thank you. Much, much more.

Chapter Six

Phoebe pushed the needle tiredly into the cloth, her eyes aching from a sleepless night, a night that had followed the pattern of so many since her confinement to Handsworth Prison, for though her body rested her brain refused to sleep. But last night it had not been for herself she had worried but for Tilly: locked up in solitary isolation, a place Phoebe herself had only heard of, a place the mention of which reduced the rest of the women to hushed tones.

But Tilly was free of that for the moment at least. Phoebe pulled the gold wire thread through the cloth, seating it with the tip of a finger. And what of Liza . . . would the Governess send for the doctor this evening, and if so . . . ?

'May I see?'

Phoebe looked up as a voice broke into her thoughts. She placed her needlework in the prison Governess's outstretched hand.

'This is very fine.' Hannah Price examined the Psalter cover. 'You sew very well, and such an elegant choice of colour, I know Phi— Father Heywood will be pleased when he receives them. You should be able to place yourself in some dressmaking or millinery establishment upon your release.'

Phoebe took the piece back as the Governess moved on along the line of sewing women. She should be able to secure a position. It was so easily said but who would employ a convicted thief?

'I find you guilty of wilful theft . . . you will serve a term of fifteen years . . .'

She pushed the needle through the cloth. Fifteen years for a crime of which she was innocent.

'Oh my Good God, will you look at that!' Lucy's shocked words rose to the surface of her mind and Phoebe saw again the bodice of the jade taffeta gown spread wide, revealing the necklace caught up inside it.

''Ow do you reckon that got there?'

Lucy's words replaced the quiet hum of the sewing women's conversations.

'I don't know,' Phoebe had replied, 'but we must return it to the Priory.'

'How come it hasn't been missed?' Lucy looked up from the floor of the bedroom. 'And it can't 'ave been or I would 'ave heard about it. Word gets round fast in that house.'

'It must have become caught when Sophie removed the dress,' Phoebe said, seeing how the mounting had become hooked into the dress lining. 'She probably wouldn't feel it through her petticoats, but surely when her maid came to put the gown away she would inspect it first for any mark or stain?'

'Not that one, Miss.' Lucy watched her free the necklace. 'I know 'er and lazy isn't the word I'd be using to describe 'er. She would 'ave had 'er marching orders long since but Miss Sophie is too soft. Everybody downstairs says they don't know how 'er gets away with half of the things she gets up to, but get away with it she does.'

'Maybe, Lucy, but to overlook something as valuable as this must be more than careless.'

Lucy looked at the necklace, emeralds dripping like huge green tears through Phoebe's fingers.

'Aye, Miss,' she said thoughtfully. 'Like you says, more than careless.'

They had taken the necklace to the kitchen where they both sat looking at it spread on the table, its stones gleaming in the pale sunlight, the gold of its setting turned red by the glow of the fire.

'Eeh, it's so beautiful,' Lucy sighed. 'A girl would feel like a queen with that round 'er neck.'

Phoebe glanced up, her mouth curved in a smile. 'Much as I want you to look and feel like a queen on your wedding day, Lucy, I couldn't offer to let you wear this.'

'Would make no difference if you could,' Lucy drew back as if the necklace were a living thing, 'I wouldn't dare to. Why, I'd be scared to death!'

'And rob Mathew of his pretty bride? Then it is as well this does not belong to me.'

'What *will* you do with it, Miss Phoebe?'

'Return it to Sophie as I said.'

'I 'ave to return to the Priory, do you want me to take it for you?'

'No, Lucy,' Phoebe answered as the girl reached for the cloak she had hung on a nail set into the kitchen door, 'I would not want to put such a responsibility upon you. The dresses were given to me and I must be the one to return the necklace. Not to do so personally would be most impolite.'

'If you say so, Miss Phoebe.' Lucy tied the ribbon of her bonnet beneath her chin. 'But you be careful you say nothin' to anybody as to why you be visiting the Priory. There's folk about these parts as can't be trusted.'

Lucy had left Wiggins Mill then, and for the first time since making it her home Phoebe had felt truly afraid of being alone. The next day she had wrapped the necklace in a piece of white linen, pushing it deep into the pocket of her skirt, then wrapping her cloak tight about her had set off across the heath toward the Sandwell Valley.

She had reached the rise above the Lyng Fields, so called for their covering of tiny purple wild flowers, when Edward had caught up with her.

'Couldn't you have sent someone with word?' he said, dismounting from the huge bay horse and listening to her reason for visiting the Priory. 'I would have sent the carriage for you.'

'I have no one to send.' For some reason Phoebe did not mention Lucy and her connection with his home. 'Besides I have no wish to impose, your family has already been very kind to me.'

'Yes, but out here all alone,' Edward took her hand, concern loud in his voice, 'there's nothing out here for miles around . . . anything might happen.'

'And nothing.' Phoebe smiled. 'Really, I am quite safe.'

'I suppose I know that,' he touched her hand to his lips, 'but I would prefer you didn't walk the heath alone, Phoebe. I only wish I could accompany you but I have an appointment with my father at two and it is almost that now.'

'I would not want to be the reason for your being late for Sir William.' Phoebe withdrew her hand. 'Please go, I will be all right.'

'Well, at least let me take the blamed trinket for you. It's near enough an hour's walk from here to the Priory and I can send a carriage to take you home.'

'No, Edward,' Phoebe returned firmly. 'No carriage. I want to walk back to Wiggins Mill. The fresh air will do me good.'

'If it doesn't kill you from cold first, and it will be dark before you get there.' He glanced at the grey snow clouds gathering over the valley.

'Then hadn't you better take this so I can be on my way home?' Phoebe drew the linen bundle from her pocket, unwrapping the necklace and handing it to Edward. 'Please would you give my apology to your sister and explain I did not know this was caught inside one of the gowns she gave me until yesterday evening?'

'My sister would lose her head were someone not there to fasten it to her neck.'

Edward tossed the necklace up into the air and Phoebe watched the tiny flashes of green flame dance circles in the light as it descended into his palm.

'I still wish you would let me send a carriage out to you.'

He dropped the necklace into his pocket before swinging easily into the saddle.

'I shall be perfectly safe, Edward.' Phoebe stepped back from the horse, a sudden breeze catching the animal's nostrils and causing it to prance restlessly.

Edward reined the bay, speaking softly and touching the animal's neck. 'Sophie will certainly wish to thank you herself.' He looked down at Phoebe, the breeze fanning her sherry-gold hair about her cheeks. 'May I bring her to Wiggins Mill tomorrow?'

The horse neighed loudly, its hooves stamping restlessly at being held in check, and Phoebe raised a hand to wave, relieved at not having to answer.

One week later she had been arrested.

'Governess wants to see Phoebe.'

Mary Pegleg limped into the sewing room, delivering her message to Agnes Marsh.

'What for?' The wardress's voice was sharper than usual and as she looked at Phoebe her eyes held a touch of concern and a heavier touch of warning. Whatever the Governess wanted, Agnes Marsh had better come out of it white as snow if she were to keep the promotion of Superintendent to the sewing room and not be sent back to that hell hole of a laundry.

''Er didn't say.' Mary Pegleg leaned against the door jamb easing her weight from the wooden stump attached to her left knee. ''Er just said to tell you 'er wanted to see Phoebe right away.'

'You better get yerself to the office then, Pardoe.' Phoebe put her sewing on the end of the long trestle table, feeling the eyes of the other prisoners on her as she went towards the door.

'Pardoe!' Agnes Marsh came close, her mouth merely a slit as she breathed, 'Mind what you tell 'er. Things could be made pretty bad for you . . . there are worse places inside this prison than the laundry.'

Mary Pegleg limping alongside her and Agnes Marsh marching behind, Phoebe walked along the gloomy corridors that led to the Governess's office. How many more years would she spend locked away? Her fingers curled tightly as the memory of flashes of green fire darted across her brain. She had not stolen Sophie's necklace, they had found it caught up inside a dress, she and Lucy, but neither she nor the maid had been believed.

Edward and his sister had not called the next day or any day. She had seen no one until the day the constable arrived. She had to go with him to the Magistrates' Court, he said, and no, he could not tell her why, the Magistrate would tell her that.

They had walked the several miles to Wednesbury where she had been taken to the Green Dragon Inn at the entrance to the Shambles. It was in an upstairs room there that the Magistrate had heard evidence against her.

It was alleged that she had visited Sandwell Priory and taken away several dresses, the gift of Miss Sophie Dartmouth; in the process she had stolen an emerald necklace, the property of the said Miss Sophie.

That had been the point at which John Kilvert had been asked if she was the woman who had pawned several pieces of jewellery at his shop.

'She is, Your Honour.' The pawnbroker's shifty eyes had fastened on her and his high-pitched reedy voice carried around the room. 'Some very valible jewellery, and where could the likes of 'er get such from lessen 'er stole it?'

'We will decide that, Kilvert.'

But the Magistrate's voice had held no rebuke and the pawnbroker had smirked at Phoebe as she stood up from her seat.

'Are you now prepared to tell us what you have done with the necklace?'

She had not been asked if she had taken Sophie's necklace, she had been told she had, told she had stolen from a girl who had helped her.

'The necklace you speak of,' Phoebe tried to stay calm, to keep the mounting fear out of her voice, 'I . . . we found it hooked inside a gown given to me by Miss Sophie.'

'We?' The Magistrate had looked at her over heavy spectacles. 'Do I take it someone else was with you?'

'Yes,' Phoebe answered, the trembling in her stomach increasing as she realised Lucy was not present and neither was Edward. Did he know she was being accused of stealing the necklace she had given to him? Of course he must know, the complaint must have come from the Priory, so where was he? Why wasn't he here to tell them it was a mistake . . . to tell them she had been returning Sophie's property when he had overtaken her, that he himself took the necklace from her?

'Well, was someone else involved in this theft?' The Magistrate leaned across the table that served as a desk.

'There was no theft.' Phoebe stared at the other three people in the room: the constable sent to bring her here, John Kilvert her accuser, and a woman dressed in black, her face hidden behind a heavy veil. 'Please, you must believe me, I am telling the truth. We found the necklace caught up in the bodice of the gown and . . .'

'*We* found?' The Magistrate leaned back in his high wing chair. 'You had better say who it is besides yourself makes up this we.'

'It was Lucy, my mai— my friend. She was visiting me and we decided to try on the dresses before taking them apart. We found the necklace inside a green gown. We guessed it belonged to Miss Sophie, seeing she had given me the gowns, and Lucy asked if she could return it that day when she went back to the Priory.'

'And did she?'

'No, Sir.' Phoebe swallowed hard, seeing the look of satisfaction cross the hard features of the man facing her. 'I thought that as the gowns had been given to me, mine was the responsibility of returning the necklace.'

'Which you obviously did not or we would not be here today.'

'I did not return it to the Priory.' Phoebe felt a cold desperation take hold of her: they did not want to believe her, this man had already decided she was guilty. 'The . . . the day after finding the necklace, I went to return it. I had crossed the Lyng Fields and was about to go on when Edward Dartmouth overtook me. I told him the reason for my journey and he offered to take the necklace for me as the weather was worsening and it would take me several hours to get home.'

For several minutes the room remained silent except for the anxious fidgeting of the pawnbroker. Across the table the Magistrate fingered long white whiskers then, leaning forward, he glared at Phoebe.

'You are saying that you returned a valuable emerald necklace to Edward Dartmouth, that he did not return it to his sister, and that therefore he is in fact the thief?'

'No! No, I . . . I'm not . . . Edward wouldn't . . .'

'No more.' The Magistrate's palm came down hard on the table. 'I have heard enough. You stole a necklace and now try to place the blame upon the son of a respected family, a family who have held their seat in West Bromwich for hundreds of years. You accuse a man who is not present to answer for himself against your lies. Well, I will answer for him. Edward Dartmouth would never commit such treachery against his own. You are a liar and a thief, and it is only out of regard for the young man's father, Sir William Dartmouth, that I will exercise leniency and not inform him of what you have said here, for to do so would result in your incurring a far heavier penalty than the one I am about to pass.'

He then reached out a hand to the wooden gavel lying in front of him.

'Phoebe Pardoe, I find you guilty of wilful theft. I order you be taken to a place of imprisonment . . .'

A rustle of black skirts told of the woman's leaving the

room as the gavel struck hard against the table. Behind her black veil Annie Pardoe almost smiled. Her meeting with Sophie Dartmouth's personal maid had paid off. That girl's attempt to extract money in return for her silence regarding a missing emerald necklace had failed, but the charge of theft Annie had forced her to lay against Phoebe had not. The Magistrate's final words followed her through the door.

'. . . you will serve a term of fifteen years' hard labour.'

'Wait there, Pardoe.'

Agnes Marsh held out a hand as they reached the Governess's office. Mary Pegleg limped to the stool set against one wall where she was allowed to sit between running messages.

'Why has she asked to see me, Mary, do you know?'

'No idea.' Mary Pegleg answered the question in a whisper. 'I ain't bin 'ere the whole time though I knows there be someone in there with 'er 'cos I 'eard 'em talkin' when I come up from the kitchen. Sounded deep, the other voice, like a man's.'

'Is it the doctor?' Phoebe asked worriedly. 'Has the Governess sent for the doctor, is Liza worse?'

'I don't know,' Mary hissed. 'Was some shemozzle goin' on downstairs, summat about a visitor, but I didn't 'ave chance to find out who it was. Though like I said, it sounded like a man an' 'er in there seemed in a right tizzy, 'er voice all excited, what I could hear.'

'Maybe it is Father Heywood.' Phoebe's reply was almost a prayer. 'Perhaps he has called regarding the covers for the Psalters.'

'Let's 'ope it is.' Mary Pegleg shifted position on the stool, one hand rubbing her amputated leg where it sat in the cup of the wooden stump. 'At least let's pray to God it ain't the doctor. We don't want to see 'im 'ere while 'is brains is still in 'is skull.'

The door to the Governess's room opened and Agnes Marsh stepped out, her mouth tight with resentment.

'You're wanted inside, Pardoe,' she said, barely allowing her lips to free the words. 'And you, Pegleg, get your arse off that stool and get down to the kitchen. Tell them Her Highness is wanting a tray of tea sent up to her office – *now*.'

Waiting for an answer to her tap on the Governess's door, Phoebe remembered the Magistrate's words: 'Out of regard for the young man's father I will exercise leniency and not inform him of what you have said here, for to do so would result in your incurring a far heavier penalty.'

Chapter Seven

Inside the Governess's office, its desk lit by a larger window than elsewhere in the prison and set about with comfortable leather high wing armchairs, Phoebe bobbed a curtsy to the woman standing behind the desk.

'Pardoe, this is Sir William Dartmouth.'

'*A far heavier penalty*'. The words screamed in Phoebe's brain, the room whirling around her in a mad dance of chairs, desk and people. '*A far heavier penalty* . . .'

'Are you all right, Miss Pardoe?'

Phoebe felt hands to either side of her as her legs began to crumple.

'Sit here,' the distant voice commanded. Then, 'Have you sal volatile, Mrs Price?'

'Smelling salts, Sir William.' Somewhere above the void that threatened to swallow her, Phoebe heard the Governess answer, 'I have smelling salts,' then coughed as a small bottle was held beneath her nostrils.

'No, do not get up!' Sir William Dartmouth touched a hand to her shoulder then walked to the fireplace that held a fire both winter and summer. 'I have something I wish to say to you.'

He hesitated, waiting for Hannah Price to acknowledge the tap on the door. A woman in the drab grey dress that marked her as an inmate entered carrying a tray, depositing it on a small oval table set against one of the wing back chairs. She glanced at Phoebe before leaving.

He had been told. Phoebe's fingers curled, pressing her

nails hard into her palms. He had been told she had accused Edward of not returning the necklace to his sister. But she had made no such accusation. Why hadn't Edward told them he had the necklace, and why after so many months had his father decided to seek his own revenge?

'You will take some tea, Miss Pardoe?' he said as Hannah Price poured the steaming liquid into a china cup. 'My presence here has seemingly upset you.'

A china cup! She had not drunk from a china cup in over twelve months. Phoebe made no move to accept the tea the Governess held out to her. A tin mug was all she had to drink from now and would be all she would have for fifteen years – and how many more? How many more years had this man demanded be added to her sentence?

'You were accused of stealing a necklace from my daughter . . .'

Phoebe raised her gaze, her soul in her eyes. 'I did not steal it,' she said softly, 'I was returning it to the Priory.'

'So I understand.'

Hannah Price returned the cup to the tray, leaving her own untouched as she studied the girl who had already served a year in Handsworth gaol.

'I gave it to Ed— to your son. He said he would give it to Miss Sophie together with my apology. They were both to call at Wiggins Mill the next day, but they never came.'

'Miss Pardoe . . .' Sir William hesitated, looking into the fire for several moments then faced her again, squaring his shoulders as if preparing for an unpleasant task he would have preferred to leave to someone else.

Frightened of what she knew was about to come Phoebe stared at Edward's father, standing tall against the fireplace, tan knee-length coat accentuating his powerful physique, hair that had once been black crested with a dusting of grey above the temples, and eyes that in the dim light of the room might have been grey or even black.

'Miss Pardoe,' he said again, as if searching for words, 'I

was told of what passed between yourself and the Magistrate the day after you were sentenced, but yesterday I was told more . . .'

Phoebe's throat closed and her head began to pound. Yesterday he had been told more and today he would have retribution.

'Yesterday,' he went on, 'I spoke to Lucy Baines, or I should say I spoke to Mrs Mathew Leach. She told me you would not allow her to return my daughter's necklace but said that you yourself would do so.' Breaking off, he turned towards the Governess. 'We will not go on with this any longer. Mrs Price, you have the Magistrate's signed document?'

'Yes, Sir William.' She touched the folded sheet of white paper lying on her desk as he moved to take up his hat and gloves lying on a small table just inside the door of the room.

'Then I will say good day.' He inclined his head the merest fraction as Hannah Price dropped a curtsy. 'Miss Pardoe.' The same slight movement of the head and he was gone.

He had spoken to Lucy. The pounding of her head mounting to a sickening crescendo, Phoebe gripped the arms of the chair. Why had he not mentioned Edward? Why had he not spoken to his son?

'Sir William took the trouble to bring this himself.' Hannah Price picked up the sheet of paper, holding it unopened in her hand.

Phoebe stared at it, the world slowly dropping away from her. He had taken the trouble to bring it himself, to see the girl who had attempted to accuse his son of theft, attempted to blacken the character of his family, to see the girl whose life he was taking away. How many more years were written on that paper? How many more years to serve in hell?

'It seems a mistake has been made . . .'

Hannah Price's face swam before Phoebe's eyes.

'. . . the necklace you were accused of stealing has been

found. This,' she tapped the paper against her fingers, 'is an authorisation from the Magistrate. You are free to go.'

'Sir William Dartmouth himself?' Sarah Leach looked in disbelief at her son and his wife seated in her tiny living room. 'Billy-me-Lord in your 'ouse? Eeh, it's not to be believed.'

'What did 'e say?' Joseph tapped his pipe against the bars of the fire.

''E said as how his family had returned from Europe the day before and 'e had asked his son if he knew anything of Sophie's missing emerald necklace,' Lucy answered. 'It seemed at first as though he knew nothing of it then he remembered taking it from Phoebe and dropping it in the pocket of his riding habit.'

'So?' Sarah urged as her daughter-in-law paused for breath.

'So 'e says 'e sent a footman or some such to search the coat an' 'e comes back wi' the necklace in 'is hands,' Mathew took up the story.

'Oh, thank God . . . thank God!' Sarah wiped her eyes on her apron. 'Now she'll be free – Abel's daughter will be free to come 'ome.'

'Oh, aye, I reckon as Phoebe will be free to come 'ome,' Mathew went on, 'but what sort of freedom will it be? Nobody will want to know a gaolbird, innocent or not. I reckon as Phoebe Pardoe ain't gonna be a whole lot better off outside o' that prison than she were inside of it, 'specially if that aunt of 'ers can do anythin' about it.'

'What does that mean?' Joseph scraped the bowl of his clay pipe with a slender bladed knife then blew down the stem.

Mathew looked over to where his father sat beside the shiny blackleaded grate. 'I mean that in my opinion Annie Pardoe is somewheres to be found in this business. She 'olds something against Phoebe, the facts tell that themselves – turnin' her out of her father's house, tekin everythin' that was hers 'cept what Lucy saved for her – an' it's my guess it was her in that Magistrates' Court in the Green Dragon.'

''Ow can you tell that?'

'I can't really, Mother.' Mathew turned his glance to Sarah, scalding tea in a large brown earthenware teapot. 'But I got talkin' to the bobby as fetched Phoebe to the Magistrate . . . 'e gets into the Gladstone most evenings when 'e ain't on duty . . . an' 'e said the woman come in a carriage – a carriage wi' A.P. on the door.'

'A.P.' Sarah held up the teapot, the first cup half filled. 'Abel Pardoe.'

'Yes, Abel Pardoe,' Mathew said. 'The carriage was Abel Pardoe's an' the woman as rode in it were Annie Pardoe. An' 'er went to the Green Dragon to hear 'er own niece sentenced to fifteen years an' never lifted a finger to stop it!'

'God 'elp us,' Sarah murmured.

'Ar, an' 'e will 'ave to an' all if anybody 'ears you goin' on like that.' Joseph glared at his son. 'Keep yer opinions to yerself, my lad. Annie Pardoe 'as done thee badly as it is but 'er's capable of doin' a damn' sight more so be ruled by one older and wiser an' keep yer tongue between yer teeth.'

'Did 'Is Lordship say what was to be done about Phoebe?' Sarah resumed filling the cups, handing a larger mug to Joseph.

'He said he would see to everything himself,' Lucy accepted the cup from her, 'but he didn't say what it would be.'

'Billy-me-Lord be a fair man,' Joseph said, using the name by which the locals addressed Sir William. 'If 'e 'as said 'e will see to things then see to 'em 'e will. Reckon we will just 'ave to bide our time til' Abel's daughter be 'ome.'

'There's no telling when that will be,' Lucy said, swallowing her tea, 'but when she does come I want to have a fire going and something hot ready for the table. So drink up your tea, Mathew Leach, it's a long walk to Wiggins Mill.'

'Aye, the wench will be wantin' a bit o' comfort,' Joseph nodded as Lucy dropped a kiss on his head. 'If you can let we know when 'er is back, Mother an' me will walk over to the mill.'

'I'll do that, Father.' Mathew grabbed his cap from one of the several nails hammered into the door that opened on to the street, respectfully holding it until he was out of the house. 'Bye, Mother.' He folded Sarah in his arms, feeling the thinness that had come in the last few months, and in his soul cursed Annie Pardoe afresh. Her money grubbing was robbing his mother of her life as surely as Phoebe had been robbed of hers. 'We will be back to see you on Sunday.'

Reaching the corner where the road curved away out of sight of the house, he turned to wave to his mother and in his heart he made a wish: May Annie Pardoe not live to see Sunday!

The heavy door banged behind Phoebe. She was free! There would be no more days locked inside Handsworth Prison for Women, no more backbreaking hours in that laundry or sewing until she could barely see the needle, no more wardresses barking orders at her. Closing her eyes she breathed deeply, feeling the fresh air bite at her throat. She was free, free to go home, but Tilly Wood would never go home.

Phoebe had not been allowed to say goodbye to any of the women who had shared her existence for more than a year; even Mary Pegleg had not been sitting on her stool outside the Governess's office when she had come out. Given the clothes she had arrived at the prison in, she had changed, Agnes Marsh in attendance, then had been taken to the door of the prison, passing no other prisoner on the way.

'Excuse me, Miss . . .'

Phoebe opened her eyes to see the man who had come to stand at her side, wearing a high black hat and knee-length boots teamed with deep blue coat.

'Sir William asks if you would be good enough to ride home in the carriage?'

'*Sir William took the trouble to bring this himself.*' The

words echoed in her mind. But he had not come to lengthen her eternity, he had come to bring her freedom.

'Miss!'

'What . . . what did you say?'

The coachman looked at the girl in the shabby brown dress and cloak, her bonnet tied over lifeless hair snatched back from a drawn pallid face. This was not the usual kind to ride in the Dartmouth coach, but then again it was certain sure she wouldn't get far on foot. 'Sir William, Miss,' he said again, 'asks if you would kindly take the carriage home?'

Phoebe glanced about her, seeing for the first time the outside of the high prison building. She had not seen where they had brought her in that black-painted cart with its iron-grilled window, nor even known apart from hearing 'the women's gaol in Birmingham'. Now she saw a bare stretch of heath broken only by a group of scraggy trees some distance to the left and a path leading to the right, and realised she had no idea in which direction home lay.

'Yes . . . yes, thank you.'

Holding both hands to her skirt, feeling every sharp stone through the worn soles of her boots, she half stumbled to where the carriage stood waiting. Then the door closed and she was on her way home. Home! Leaning her head against the cushioned upholstery, she allowed the pent up tears of months to flood her cheeks.

'Allow me!'

Phoebe felt the soft cloth pressed into her ungloved hands and opened her eyes to see Sir William Dartmouth.

Across the narrow space that separated them he saw the sudden fear return to her eyes and felt disgusted at a system that treated a young girl in such a way as almost to destroy her; but it was a system he himself had long upheld.

'Forgive me for not giving you an explanation,' he said quietly, 'but I felt the sooner you were out of that place, the better.' He glanced at her hands, nervously twisting the white lawn handkerchief, then went on, 'I was informed of the outcome of your appearance before Gideon Speke, and of the term of imprisonment to which he had sentenced you, and I felt no regret. My family's friendship seemed to have been abused and my daughter's property stolen. But yesterday I found that nothing had been stolen and that I had been wrong. Because of my action you have been made to suffer great hardship. I can only offer my most sincere apology. I will, of course, make reparation in any way you wish.'

Reparation! Phoebe stared out of the window but the passing streets and imposing buildings of Birmingham went unseen. How could any reparation make up for what she had been through . . . for what she knew was yet to come?

'Your home is at Wednesbury, I believe,' he resumed, covering her silence. 'If you will tell me where I will have Aston take us there.'

'Brunswick House,' she answered, only half registering what he had said.

'Brunswick House!' He leaned forward slightly, a small frown creasing his brow. 'You live at Brunswick House?'

'No . . . I . . . I'm sorry.' Phoebe forced her mind to attend her words. 'I do not live at Brunswick House. My home is Wiggins Mill on the outskirts of the town.'

'Then why say Brunswick House?'

For a moment Phoebe thought she heard the note of accusation so many voices had held over the past months and her head rose defensively. 'Possibly, Sir William,' she said clearly, 'because I once did live there.'

'Brunswick House?' The frown deepened, his eyes narrowing in concentration. 'That was Abel Pardoe's house . . . his sister got it if I remember rightly. And you . . . your name is Pardoe . . .'

'Yes, Sir William.' Phoebe looked straight into his dark eyes. 'Phoebe Pardoe. I am Abel's daughter.'

'So she is to be set free?' Annie Pardoe looked at the man

seated in her drawing room, one hand tugging nervously at long white side whiskers.

'There was nothing I could do,' he answered. 'Sir William Dartmouth himself came to withdraw the charge, said the necklace had been found and demanded the girl be set free at once.'

'And you signed the document of release?'

'I had to, Annie.' Gideon Speke had been unnerved at Sir William's appearance in his office; he was a powerful man and not only in West Bromwich, there was no telling what he would do if he found out.

'Yes, I suppose you did.' Annie stood up, black skirts rustling. 'But hear me, Gideon Speke. You took my hundred pounds to put her away and if anything comes of her being found innocent 'tis you will bear the brunt. I will swear before God I paid you one hundred pounds to try buying her freedom, and that you pocketed that money while hearing no evidence in her defence. One word, Gideon . . . just one word and you will never sit on the Magistrates' bench again!'

So Abel's girl was free! Annie Pardoe closed the door on the departing Magistrate. She had been denied little more than one year of her life while she, Annie, had had no life at all. Slowly she walked through the house and out into the garden. She would not let it rest here. She had taken her niece's home and all she possessed save the paltry sum her maternal grandmother had left her, but all that would not pay for what her own brother had taken from her. Revenge tasted sweet and Annie craved its sweetness. There was more yet to be had and she would drink it to the very last drop.

Turning, she walked back into the house and up the stairs to her room. Putting on her cloak and settling a black bonnet on her head, she went to the room Samuel used as a studio.

'I have to go out for a while,' she signed on her fingers. 'I do not expect to be very long. Is there anything I can get for you while I am in the town?'

Samuel shook his head, his mouth unsmiling as he regarded his sister. Annie had always worn a look of bitterness but of late that look had changed; to what he could not rightly say but it was a look he liked even less.

'Has Tranter brought your hot drink?'

Samuel rested his brush on the palette. 'No,' he signed back, his fingers moving rapidly, 'I told her not to.'

Annie did not question his answer, knowing that in the years Maudie Tranter had spent with them she too had learned the sign language that enabled Samuel to speak.

'Then we will have one together when I return.' Annie Pardoe looked at the brother she had cared for for so many years. His features were thinned and gaunt compared to a year ago but they were still a carbon copy of the man who had been a brother to them both, still with the same keen eyes, 'Take care not to get cold, dear.' Her gloved fingers fluttered like the black wings of a crow. 'You know how unwell you have been of late.'

Samuel picked up his brush, watching his sister leave the room. The house always felt easier when she was not in it.

Annie drove the small trap, guiding the mare along the Holyhead Road that linked Wednesbury to its neighbouring towns. Passing the Monway Steel Mill of which Samuel, thanks to their brother, was part-owner, she turned off across the heath towards Hobs Hill mine, stopping at the huddle of small houses some half-mile away.

'I will say what I came to say.' She had marched straight into Joseph Leach's cottage, ownership relieving her of the necessity of waiting to be asked. 'My niece has besmirched her father's name, she has been imprisoned for theft, therefore she will be unwelcome in any house of standing.'

'But my Mathew's wife says Miss Phoebe is to be set free.' Sarah Leach stared at the woman who seemed to fill her small room with darkness. ''Er says as 'ow they 'ave found out Miss Phoebe never done it, 'er never stole no necklace.'

'Nevertheless,' Annie drew in a long breath, the effort flaring her nostrils, 'the slur remains, my brother's good name has been stained, and I will not have it perpetuated by accepting the girl's presence in any property I and my brother Samuel own. And this house forms part of that property. I tell you, Sarah Leach, you have Phoebe inside this house for one minute and you are out, bag and baggage. What's more, I will see to it that the cripple you call a husband will get no job in Wednesbury.'

'There be only one thief in Abel's family,' Sarah muttered, watching the trap pull away, 'an' that be you, Annie Pardoe. You 'ave teken everythin' that should 'ave bin his daughter's an' may the Good Lord pay you for it!'

Chapter Eight

Sir William Dartmouth watched the face of the girl he had just seen released from prison. Its pallor and thinness did not completely hide its fine-boned quality, or the unhappiness shading her green eyes detract from their lovely almond shape. He had known Abel Pardoe for many years, they had done business together on a regular basis, he buying much of the coal Abel's mines produced together with steel from his Monway works, but they had not mixed socially. Now he was looking at the daughter he had not realised the other man had, a daughter whom he guessed bore a quiet beauty beneath the mark of Handsworth Prison.

She had not spoken since telling him she had once lived at Brunswick House and though she had stared out of the window for the rest of their journey he guessed it was not the passing scenery that held her attention.

'Is this Wiggins Mill?' he asked as the carriage rumbled over a stony path worn by the carter's wagon. 'Miss Pardoe?' He leaned across, touching a hand to hers, still twisting the handkerchief, then withdrew as Phoebe jerked backward, the shadow in her eyes deepening. 'I asked, is this your home?'

'Yes.' Phoebe looked across to where the old house began to rise out of the hollow that sheltered it, the stilled windmill standing sentinel on the adjoining high ground. 'Yes, this is Wiggins Mill.'

The coach drew to a halt and almost immediately the coachman was opening the door.

'Miss Pardoe,' Sir William waited until she stepped down, 'you are no doubt in need of rest but perhaps you will do me the courtesy of calling at the Priory as soon as you feel able? There is a lot I still have not said and we must discuss how you may be compensated.'

Phoebe looked at her home. She was free, she did not have to bite back her words any longer and never again would man or woman order her life.

'Sir William,' she turned back to him, a cool gleam of assurance clearing the shadows from her eyes, 'I will call at the Priory but only to return your handkerchief. As for compensation, there is no need of any. A mistake has been made and a mistake has been rectified, we need say no more on the subject. Will the day after tomorrow be convenient for me to return your handkerchief?'

'I will send the carriage for you at eleven.' Then, as Phoebe made to reject the offer, he smiled. 'And *you* need say no more on *that* subject.'

'Miss Phoebe . . . oh, Miss Phoebe, you're home!' Lucy raced around the corner of the house as the carriage drove away. 'Oh, it's so good to see you.'

'And you, Lucy,' she breathed as her friend's hug threatened to stifle her.

'Welcome home, Miss Phoebe.' Mathew Leach smiled at the two women, laughing and crying at the same time.

'Mathew!' Phoebe broke free to hug the man she had known from childhood. 'But . . . but shouldn't you be at the pit?'

'Come in, Miss Phoebe.' Lucy's voice lost some of its joy. 'There's a fire in the grate an' tea on the hob an' I'm dyin' to butter you one of my scones.

'You see, Miss Phoebe,' she said when at last Phoebe stopped wandering through the rooms of her home and settled in the warm kitchen, 'when I was sacked from the Priory and Mathew was given the sack from the pit we had nowhere to go like an' . . . well, I thought the mill could do wi' being kept an eye on an' you wouldn't mind us being in one of the outhouses. We never used the 'ouse, Miss, honest we didn't. I just come in every day to dust and keep the rooms aired.'

'You mean, you were both removed from your employment?' Phoebe left the scone untouched. 'But why? For what reason?'

'Mathew was sacked for questioning the reason for your aunt reducing the wages at the pit an' meself? Well miss, Sophie's maid said I must 'ave put the necklace in one of the dresses sent to Wiggins Mill, that I knowed you as a friend and would be able to retrieve it when I visited you and then sell it. So the housekeeper up and sacks me. Matters of the servants is left to 'er when 'er Ladyship is away, Sir William is never bothered with little things like sacking a maid.'

'They don't 'ave to give a reason,' Mathew said sourly. 'Pit owner or gentry, meks no difference – when either of 'em wants you out it's a case of pick up yer tin and go.'

'But how have you managed with no wage between you?'

'Well, like I said, Miss,' Lucy took up the thread, 'we had nowhere to go. We thought yer aunt might turn nasty if we lived with Mathew's parents an' we couldn't live here without being wed so we just got Father Heywood to say the words over us then we come here. Oh, Miss, I hopes you don't mind?'

'Of course I don't mind, but Lucy . . . your lovely wedding? Didn't you get it after all?'

'No, Miss.' Lucy smiled at her husband. 'But I got the man and that's all that matters.'

'We'll be gone in the mornin', Miss.' Mathew turned towards the door. 'I'll go see to our bits an' pieces an' when Lucy is finished over 'ere 'er'll pack the beddin'.'

'She will do no such thing!' Phoebe answered vehemently. 'And neither will you. You will stay here and glad I'll be of your company. I . . . I wouldn't want to stay here alone . . .'

'We understand, Miss, and we thank you,' Lucy cut in, seeing the shadow return to Phoebe's eyes. 'Mathew and me we'll mek it up to you, really we will.'

'There is nothing to make up.' Phoebe smiled. 'We are friends, and wage or no wage will survive somehow. In fact, you two seem to have found a way already, judging by the food on this table.'

'That's Mathew, Miss,' Lucy beamed. 'You remember he was quite handy with hammer and saw? Well, he gets a few odd jobs from folk in the town, mending a chair or mekin' a stool, little things like but they buy flour and vegetables. And I do a bit of sewing like you used to only I don't get no dresses from the nobs.'

'Neither will I again, Lucy.' Phoebe sipped the hot tea she had poured. 'Those doors are closed forever, I'm afraid.'

'But you didn't never tek anything!' Lucy's glance was bright with anger. 'Them at the Priory knows you never and so does Magistrate.'

'I don't think that will make any difference.' Phoebe shook her head as the other girl offered more tea. 'The very fact that I have been in prison will be sufficient for the nobs, as you called them, to reject my company.'

'Then bloody nobs ain't worth associatin' wi'.'

'Mathew!' Lucy glared at her husband. 'Language.'

'Beg your pardon, Miss Phoebe,' Mathew pulled open the door that led on to the yard, 'but that's the way I feel,' he said, going outside.

'Please don't tek no notice of Mathew.' Lucy gathered the used cups on to a wooden tray. 'But the losin' of his job 'as made 'im bitter. I keep tellin' 'im it's no use his feelin' that way but I might as well bang my 'ead against a brick wall for all the good it does. ''E just won't take a tellin', says all moneyed folk am the same: all out for themselves an' sod the likes of folk who grind for 'em. There be times I think he'll never be the same as he was.'

Never be the same. The thought lingered as Phoebe followed the other girl into the scullery. She understood Mathew's feelings. Things might never be the same for any of them. She was free, but what freedom would Wednesbury allow a girl who had been in prison?

Phoebe came up the rise from Lyng Fields, feeling the softness of the earth beneath her feet, and stood on the crest of the high ground cradling Sandwell Valley, looking down on the ancient Priory. Cool air fanned her brow and she lifted her face to it, revelling in its touch. She had deliberately not waited for the carriage as Sir William had told her to, ignoring his instruction. Never again, she told herself, closing her eyes to the delicious taste of freedom, never again would any man or woman order her life.

A breeze lifting out of the valley caught her skirts, lifting them like unseen fingers, and she pressed a hand to them, delighting in the touch of the brown bombazine after so many months of wearing drab grey calico. But the women who had been her companions of those months were still wearing grey uniforms. Her mind flashed to Tilly. She would be dressed in grey calico the rest of her life. If only they had given her time to say goodbye to the woman who had befriended her . . . but she had been rushed from Handsworth Prison as though she carried the plague and now she would never be able to tell Tilly how glad she was to have known her and to have been her friend.

Opening her eyes, she looked down at the house nestling on the floor of the valley, its mullioned windows seeming to stare back at her. Sir William Dartmouth had waited outside that prison, waited until she emerged through its heavy door; he had brought her home in his carriage, but for what reason? Reparation for what his son had caused to happen to her? Maybe, but any such feeling would be momentary, passed and forgotten in a week. As Mathew had said yesterday, all moneyed folk were out for themselves, they and they alone were all that mattered to them, and the more money they had the less those without it counted for. Well, she had none but she would count for something. Lifting her skirt, she set off down into the valley. Somehow, some way, Phoebe Pardoe would count for something.

At the foot of the high ground the valley widened into a flat swathe, the grass-covered earth rolling away to green eternity. It had been green around Brunswick House, Phoebe remembered, the lawns edged with beds bright with flowers, a shaded arbour leading to her favourite rose garden, but there had been nothing like these vast acres spreading endlessly, the ancient house at their heart.

Passing at last beneath a great stone arch, she began to walk along the sweeping approach, itself lined with magnificent beeches, their arched branches almost meeting overhead as if in imitation of the stone.

'Hey!'

The shout coming from the hushed silence of the morning took her unawares and she stopped, both hands clutched to her brown cloak.

'Where do you think you be goin'?'

A man in late middle age, his shoulders hunched, stepped from behind a tree.

'Don't you know this 'ere be private property?'

He stepped towards her and Phoebe saw his earth-stained hands move toward the heavy buckle belt fastened about his breeches.

'Of course I know.' Phoebe lifted her chin, putting every ounce of her failing confidence into her voice. There was no one around; in fact there might only be herself and this man in the world, so empty was the spread of ground. 'This is Sandwell Priory and I am here by appointment.'

'Appointment, eh!'

The man's hands still hovered about the fastener of his belt and Phoebe felt her heart jerk. What did he intend to do? Whatever it was there was no one to see.

'Yes, by appointment.' Phoebe stood her ground as he came closer. 'I am here to see Sir William . . .'

'*You*, 'ere to see Billy-me-Lord?' The man sniffed derisively, eyeing her plain brown dress. 'You'll be tellin' me 'as 'ow you be a personal friend of 'is next.'

'Hardly.' Phoebe stared into the man's eyes, pale rheumy eyes that seemed to swim in a mist of water. 'Though I do wish to return this.'

Thrusting a hand into the pocket of her cloak, she pulled out the freshly laundered handkerchief, its crested initial worked in pale blue, and held it towards him.

'Oh!' He stared at the handkerchief, his manner changing as if the owner himself had suddenly appeared. 'It's . . . it's just that 'er Ladyship don't like town folk using the main drive, an' with you not bein' in a carriage like I thought as you . . .'

'That I was one of the town folk?' Phoebe returned the handkerchief to her pocket. 'You thought correctly, I am.'

'In that case . . .' the hands stopped hovering, dropping instead to the man's sides '. . . you should 'ave come by the back way, up against Ice Pool. That way there would be less chance of them up at the 'ouse seein' you. You best go back. There be a path around to the left of the arch will lead you to the stables. You can get to the servants' quarters that way.'

'Thank you.' Phoebe's mouth did not relax.

'I ain't seen you afore,' the man went on as she turned away. 'You be the new maid?'

'No.' Phoebe halted then swung around to face the lovely stone mansion. 'I am not the new maid and neither do I enter a house via the servants' quarters.'

Feeling those watery eyes on her back she marched up the arrow-straight drive, her mouth set in a straight line. Her home might be a hovel in comparison to that of Sir William Dartmouth but she was mistress of it and servant to no man, and that was the way her life would remain.

She had almost reached the steps that led from left and right, forming an arc up to the main entrance of the Priory, when a footman in dark blue livery appeared as if from nowhere.

'You shouldn't have come this way.'

His voice was hushed, almost reverential; no servant in her father's house had been expected to speak this way.

'So I have been told,' Phoebe answered loudly.

Closing the space between them, the man glanced at the house before grabbing her elbow. 'Then why did yer? You must 'ave been told 'er Ladyship don't like servants usin' the main drive. C'mon, out of it, there'll be trouble if 'er sees you 'ere.'

The hand on her elbow tightened and for a fleeting second Phoebe was back inside that corridor with Liza Spittle's hand pushing her back against the wall, the old sickness rising in her throat.

'What is going on here?'

The words were not loud but they acted upon the footman like a starting pistol. His hand fell away from Phoebe's elbow and he stepped back as Sir William Dartmouth rounded the corner of the house.

'I asked what is going on here?'

The sickness that memory had provoked faded as he approached. Glancing at the footman, Phoebe saw the pale line of anxiety now lining that man's lips. So it was the same here in West Bromwich as it was in Wednesbury! Positions once lost would be hard to replace, especially if a man were to be dismissed with no references.

'I have a stone in my shoe,' Phoebe lied, 'your footman was about to assist me.'

'I see.'

I know you do, thought Phoebe, catching the look of gratitude in the servant's eye as he was dismissed. First you think me a thief, now you see me as a liar.

'I will send for one of the maids.'

'Please don't bother.' Phoebe bent, and removing a shoe, shook it, displacing the imaginary stone. Then she slipped her foot back into it. 'A woman learns to do these things for herself in Handsworth Gaol.'

'Take him back to the stable.' Sir William turned to the groom who had followed him from the back of the house. The man began to lead away the magnificent black horse and its master turned back to Phoebe.

'That will keep them in conversation for a few days.' He smiled.

Phoebe glanced at the departing groom, remembering how the slightest deviation from the usual could set the women's prison humming for days. The slightest deviation! What Tilly had done to Liza Spittle was no slight deviation . . . what would happen now to Tilly . . . what would the Prison Board do to her?

'Shall we go inside?'

The question cut across those thoughts spinning in Phoebe's mind, bringing her attention back to the man half smiling at her.

'There is no need.' She fished in her pocket then held out the folded square of white lawn. 'I can return this to you here. It is all I came for.'

'But that is not the only reason I wished you to come.' He regarded her from deep grey eyes. 'You have not yet been given a full explanation of the facts of what happened on that day, nor have you received my family's apology.'

'I have received my freedom,' Phoebe answered, her own gaze clear and steady, 'that is enough. Nothing more is necessary or wanted, therefore I wish you good day, Sir William.'

'Maybe it is enough for you,' his voice was suddenly hard, cutting through the quietness covering the beautiful valley, 'but what of my son? All he can do is apologise, Miss Pardoe. Would you deprive him of what little solace that can give him?'

Edward! How many times had he filled her thoughts during those long nights, how many times had she seen in her mind that handsome face, those vividly blue eyes? Yet strangely she had not once thought of him since meeting his father.

'Will you not at least let the boy speak for himself?'

Only a brief nod indicating her agreement, Phoebe followed him into the Priory. Dismissing all offers of attention, Sir William led her through the spacious rooms, each exquisite in its furnishings, until he came to a door concealed in an alcove in a corridor lined with portraits.

'My wife will be in here,' he said, pushing open the door and waiting until Phoebe passed inside.

Much smaller than the rooms through which she had already walked, this held a more intimate feel, the home of laughing children and shared secrets. Phoebe glanced quickly at the photographs in silver frames dotted on tables, the deep chairs carelessly scattered with bright cushions, the spectacles beside the newspapers that marked this a family room.

'Amelia, my dear, Miss Pardoe is here.'

Lady Amelia Dartmouth laid aside the book she had been reading. 'Miss Pardoe, do forgive my not welcoming you but I was not informed . . . William, why did no one tell me of Miss Pardoe's arrival?'

'Never mind that for now,' he replied as his wife drew Phoebe to a chair, 'ring for Edward and Sophie.'

'You will take tea, my dear?'

Phoebe looked at the elegant woman, remembering her from the evening market, only then her bonnet had hidden the traces of gold that still shone among the carefully dressed fading hair and her cloak had covered the stately, tightly corseted figure.

'Thank you,' she murmured as Amelia Dartmouth issued softly spoken orders to the man who responded almost immediately to the pull of a bell cord.

'Phoebe!' Edward was first into the room, rushing to where she sat in a deep brocade chair. 'Oh, Phoebe, I'm so sorry.'

'Edward!' his father cautioned as a maid entered with a silver tray. 'We will wait for your sister.'

He had grown. Phoebe glanced over to where Edward stood beside his father. He was taller than she remembered but still lacked three or four inches beside the older man. He had the same blue eyes and golden hair of his mother but the stance of his father, the assurance that a life of wealth and position bestows.

'Phoebe . . . Phoebe, I'm so happy to see you!' Sophie burst into the room like a boisterous puppy, grabbing both of Phoebe's hands and pulling her out of the chair. 'Was it positively awful in that prison?'

'Sophie!' Lady Amelia's voice was sharp.

'Sorry, Mama,' she said, giving Phoebe's hands a squeeze before releasing them.

'Miss Pardoe,' Sir William said as Phoebe accepted the delicate porcelain cup Sophie handed her, 'my son has something to say to you.'

'Yes, Phoebe.' Edward's blue eyes clouded. 'That day I met you coming here to return a necklace you told me you had found caught up inside a dress that Sophie had given you, I said I would return it in your stead.' He looked at his mother and Phoebe thought that despite his height he seemed just like a little boy, seeking encouragement in making a confession.

'Go on, Edward.' His mother smiled, a world of understanding in her eyes.

'Well, after I left you, The Prince caught his foot in a root or something and came down heavily.'

'The Prince?' Phoebe questioned.

'The bay I was riding,' Edward replied, 'he was a son of Satan, my father's black, and sometimes he showed it. He did that day anyway . . .'

'He was restless, I remember.' Phoebe put the delicate cup and saucer aside, her tea untouched.

'He always reacted to a sudden breeze that way.' Edward glanced at his father, still standing before the Adam fireplace. 'As if he wanted to race the wind. Anyway he got the bit between his teeth and set off like a bat out of hell. We were half across the valley when he came down, and when I couldn't get him to his feet I went for help. By the time it was all sorted out I had completely forgotten about the necklace in my pocket.'

'The Prince was a particular favourite of Edward's.' Amelia Dartmouth stretched a hand toward the tall young man who was her son. 'His father gave him the foal when it was born, you could say they grew up together were it not to sound so sentimental.'

'Edward was devastated when they had to shoot The Prince,' Sophie put in. 'It was days before he could bring himself to speak to anyone.'

'By that time,' Lady Dartmouth took up the explanation, 'the chill I had caught that evening at the street market had worsened, and it was decided we should leave for Europe earlier than originally intended. So you see, Miss Pardoe, both Sophie and Edward were out of the country when you . . .' The explanation trailed off, his mother holding on to Edward's hand.

'What my wife was about to say was that she and our son and daughter were abroad when you were arrested and imprisoned, and I did not acquaint them with that information in my letters to them. Therefore the fault is mine . . .'

'William,' Amelia Dartmouth's brow creased in a small frown as she turned to her husband, 'my dear, you were not to know the necklace would be found.'

'As you say, Amelia,' he nodded, 'but that does not excuse my behaviour. When James Siveter informed me that a young woman had been found guilty of stealing the necklace, I did nothing to ascertain the truth of what had happened.'

'But what could you have done?' his wife asked. 'You must accept the law.'

'As we all must,' his already dark eyes seemed to darken further, 'but we need not accept that the law has been presented with the true facts. I should have set in motion my own investigation.' He turned to Phoebe. 'As it was I did not, and therein lies my guilt. I was too ready to believe the friendship of my family had been abused and for that I offer my profound apology, Miss Pardoe, and ask in what manner I may make reparation?'

Phoebe rose, her plain brown garments a stark contrast to the elegant testimony to wealth that lay all about her.

'Sir William,' she said quietly, 'I told you yesterday that a mistake had been made. It was a mistake for which I attribute no blame and require no reparation. I know that as soon as you were told the truth you lost no time in securing my release. I know also that neither your son nor daughter would have wished for such a thing as my imprisonment, but now the truth is out and the necklace retrieved there is no need for the subject to be raised again.'

She turned to the woman who still clutched her son's hand, as if thinking he might be marched away to some prison. 'Thank you for receiving me, Lady Dartmouth. Now I must return home.'

'May I come to see you tomorrow, Phoebe?' Sophie was on her feet. 'I do so enjoy talking to you.'

'Sophie,' Lady Dartmouth smiled for the first time, 'Miss Pardoe may wish to rest for a few days before being concerned with callers.'

'I should be happy for Sophie to call at Wiggins Mill whenever you feel she may, Lady Dartmouth.' Phoebe dropped a polite curtsy.

'Does that invitation hold for me too?' Edward released his hand from that of his mother.

'Again, only when your mother permits it.'

'Don't bother ringing for Compson.' Sir William stepped forward as his wife made to pull the bell that would ring for a servant. 'If Miss Pardoe will allow, I will see her out myself.

'I really cannot permit you to refuse to take some form of compensation for what we have done to you.'

They had passed once again through rooms Phoebe would have loved to linger in and stood now at the foot of the curving stone steps that fronted the great house.

'You can't force me to accept either.'

'As it seems I could not force you into waiting for my carriage to collect you this morning.' William Dartmouth looked down into a face too pale and too thin but one that nevertheless whispered of beauty and character, and he smiled. 'Perhaps you will permit it to take you home?'

'Thank you, Sir William, but I prefer to walk.'

'What!' He laughed then, low in his throat. 'And get another stone in your shoe?'

'I may even take them off and walk barefoot.' Suddenly Phoebe too was smiling. 'That would give your servants even more cause for conversation. Good day, Sir William.'

Sir William Dartmouth watched the slight brown-clad figure walk away and found himself admiring the courage and honesty of the girl, the resilience that had brought her through months of imprisonment yet blaming no one at the end of it. He remembered the astuteness and honesty of the man he had known in the world of business.

'Yes, Miss Phoebe Pardoe,' he murmured, watching her disappear along the drive, 'you are truly Abel's daughter.'

Chapter Nine

Phoebe put the last of the breakfast dishes back on the kitchen dresser then settled the kettle over the coals. She would make a broth later against Lucy and Mathew's return from town. They were both trying so hard to make a living, Mathew trudging the streets in search of odd jobs and Lucy baking every night then selling scones and pies in the market place by day, while she . . . Phoebe looked around the small kitchen, its red flagstones boasting a pegged rug against the door, dresser arrayed with an assortment of plates and cups, the table whose twice-daily scrub had the wood almost white . . . apart from keeping the house clean, what was she doing?

She turned back to the fire, staring into its red heart. She couldn't go on like this, she couldn't continue to live off Lucy and her husband. In prison she had dreamed of being home, of earning her own living, of being beholden to none save herself yet . . . 'Why?' she whispered to the flames. 'Why can't I do it, why can't I at least try?'

The coals settled, sending a small glowing ember sliding between the bars of the grate. Phoebe watched the trail of sparks it made as it fell against the fender, sparks that glittered and then faded into nothing, as her life had once glittered only to fade.

If only her father's death had not come so soon, if she had been married to Montrose, her life would have been so different. Different! Reaching the tongs from the companion set that stood beside the range, she picked up the fallen ember, replacing it on the fire. Yes, her life would have been different but her world would still be empty for how long would happiness have lasted once she'd found out that Montrose's real reason for marrying her was her father's money? And now it seemed Sophie had been earmarked to become Mrs Montrose Wheeler.

Replacing the tongs, she walked restlessly into the small living room with its meagre pawnshop furnishings. Mrs Montrose Wheeler! Phoebe touched a finger to the blue glass top of the oil lamp sitting in the centre of the round chenille-covered table and knew which she would rather have.

The skirts of her brown dress swishing, she ran up the stairs and into the bedroom she had once used as a workroom, the lethargy that had lain over her since leaving prison falling away like a discarded shawl. She knew how she could make a living. Opening a chest that stood against the window wall she took out the small dresses she had made for Lady Dartmouth, dresses that had never been given as the presents they were intended for. They were pretty. She lifted them one at a time, holding them against the light from the window. There were women in Wednesbury who either hadn't the skill to make their children's clothes or else were too busy working to keep them to have the time to try. Lucy said there were customers for her baking, maybe some of those customers would buy clothing. Draping the dresses across a table she used for cutting out her patterns, she counted them. There were eight ready for sale now and she still had some of the dresses Sophie had given her.

Turning to a larger chest standing on the opposite wall she raised the domed lid and stood stock still. The pale green gown stared up at her.

'. . . *I find you guilty of wilful theft* . . .' Phoebe's hand tightened on the mahogany lid as the room swam away from her.

'. . . *I sentence you to be taken to a place of imprisonment and there you will serve a term of fifteen years' hard labour . . .'*

Hard labour . . . imprisonment . . . fifteen years . . . wilful theft . . . I sentence . . . fifteen years. . . . The words twisted and turned in her mind, louder and louder until they screamed in her head; life draining out of her, Phoebe's fingers loosed the heavy lid and it fell with a bang, the noise of it chasing away the ghosts of the past. She stood for several seconds, her breathing rapid and short. She was free of the walls but not yet free of the prison. But she would be free, determinedly she lifted the lid of the chest and took out the green gown, totally free.

Laying the gown across the one chair the room still held she hesitated at a sound from downstairs. Sophie? Edward? It couldn't be Lucy or Mathew, they would not return before evening. She crossed to the window and looked out to where the Dartmouth carriage would be standing . . . only there was no carriage.

It could have driven up unheard but it could not have left the same way. Maybe she had imagined the sound? She stood listening until the crash of breaking china told her she had not imagined it.

Maybe it was Lucy, maybe she was unwell. 'Lucy!' she called, running from the room and downstairs to the kitchen. 'Lucy, are you all right?'

'It ain't Lucy . . .' a voice behind her halted her progress toward the scullery '. . . it's me!'

Phoebe turned toward the voice. A man stood inside the kitchen, blocking the doorway to the living room. He was about five feet ten and aged around thirty, and eyed her brazenly.

'Who are you? What do you want?' Phoebe asked, suddenly knowing a new fear as his eyes wandered over her.

'Who I be don't matter.' He spoke through lips that seemed too thick for his narrow face. 'What I want, though, that be a different matter.'

'I have no work to give you.'

He smiled, spreading the thick lips, showing teeth that were strong but in need of a rub with baking soda. 'It ain't work I'm after.'

'I . . . I don't live alone here.'

'Oh, I know you don't.' His eyes glittered, he knew her fear and was feeding on it. 'I know about Lucy and 'er 'usband, same as I know about you and your visit to Sandwell Priory last week. 'Ow much did 'e give you?'

'I don't understand.' Phoebe tried to move into the scullery but the man was at her side before she had taken two steps.

'Don't play me for a fool, Miss Bloody Fancy Pardoe,' he grated. 'You understands all right an' comin' on all innocent won't pull the wool. My eyes am wide open. I knows the Dartmouths won't be lettin' things go wi'out payin' you somethin' . . . now wheer is it?'

'I did go to the Priory last week.' The fear in her was stronger now and she knew he sensed it as an animal senses fear. What would he do when he found nothing here of value? 'But I went there only to return a handkerchief Sir William had lent to me, nothing more. I . . . I took nothing from them.'

'So Phoebe Pardoe got nothing?' He moved closer. 'Look, I warned you, don't play clever wi' me. I know you done twelve months an' more on account of Mr Bloody 'igh falutin' Edward Dartmouth an' that last week you went to the Priory to collect. You talked to the 'ole bloody lot of 'em . . . compensation is what you talked and compensation is money. You got money an' it's that money I've come for . . . now wheer is it?'

One hand flashed upward, grabbing her hair, snatching her head backward. 'You might as well tell me,' he brought his face close, the thick lips only inches away, ''cos I'll find out one way or another and one of them ways you're gonna find very painful.'

'I . . . told . . . you,' Phoebe fought to speak against the constriction of her neck being pulled backward, 'I was given nothing . . . the Dartmouth family . . . they gave me . . . no . . . no money.'

'Lyin' bitch!' He released her hair, the same hand smacking viciously across her face, knocking her against the dresser, sending plates hurtling to the floor. Grabbing a poker, he thrust it deep into the glowing fire. 'If you ain't told me wheer you 'ave the money 'id by the time that's 'ot, you'll 'ave a face nobody will bear the lookin' at.'

He wouldn't believe her, he was convinced she had been given money by the Dartmouths and nothing she said would alter that. Phoebe swallowed hard, her thoughts unnaturally clear. If she could get out of the house she might be able to make a run for it.

'All right,' she said, wiping a hand across her smarting eyes, 'Sir William did give me money but it's not here . . .'

'Then wheer is it?'

He grabbed at her again, cinching her arm, pulling her forward. There was no smell of coal dust, Phoebe thought, and no tiny burn holes in his trousers so he was not a miner nor did he work in an iron foundry. That meant he wasn't local for there was little for men to do otherwise around Wednesbury. So how did he know about her being in prison or about her visit to the Priory?

'I said, wheer is it?' He reached his free hand to the poker, its steel tip indistinguishable from the crimson coals. 'But you can take yer time, it's gonna be a pleasure gettin' you to say.'

'It's outside.' Phoebe prayed her words would convince him. 'I thought it better not to bring it into the house. No one would expect so much money to be left out there.'

'Wheer outside?' He drew the poker out of the fire.

'In the old mill.'

'That's better.'

He dropped the poker, letting it rattle down the bars of the grate on to the stone hearth, dragging Phoebe with him out of the house and across the yard to where the windmill stood on a little rise.

'Wheer abouts did you put it?'

Phoebe winced as he jerked her arm. 'Up in the corn loft. There's a pile of empty sacks against the wall, I hid the money under them.'

'Yer best be tellin' the truth,' he threatened, almost frog marching her towards the door of the disused mill, 'yer'll regret it if you ain't.'

If only he would release her arm! Phoebe tried to form a plan: she could run back into the house and bolt the doors. But he did not release her. Kicking open the wooden door, he pushed her before him into the mill.

'The corn loft, you said?' He glanced upward then down to where a rickety ladder lay half buried in the dust of the floor. Holding her with one hand, he struggled to raise the ladder then rest it against the floor of the loft.

'You first.' He leered, his almost canine teeth taking on a yellower hue in the light streaming from the doorway.

Phoebe struggled up the ladder, her feet catching in her skirts, threatening to throw her off the narrow uneven struts.

'Stop there an' don't go movin' . . . if you know what's best for you.'

Pushing her as he followed from the topmost rung of the ladder, he kicked it aside, laughing as he made for the heap of sacks lying in a corner.

This would be her only chance. There would be no more tricking him when he found there was no money under those sacks. Moving slowly, holding her skirts so they wouldn't rustle, she got to her feet, inching towards the edge of the corn loft floor. He had kicked away the ladder but that wouldn't stop her.

'Go on . . . jump! Makes no odds.'

Despite her caution he had heard and was watching her, on his knees among the empty corn sacks.

'You'll break one leg at least, mebbe both, but you won't need legs for what I'm gonna do to you . . . after I've got yer money, that is. Go on, jump . . . you won't crawl far.'

He began to laugh again, a laugh that had her spine crawling. 'What I'm gonna do to you . . .' She had heard those words before; the image of Liza Spittle's birthmarked face floated before her eyes and the sour smell of her filled Phoebe's nostrils. Closing her eyes, she jumped.

Annie Pardoe slipped the key into her black bag and left her bedroom, going to her brother's studio.

'I am going into the town,' she signed, the movement of her hands setting her bag swinging from her arm. 'Doctor Dingley has prescribed a medicine for your headaches and I do not trust Isaac Jackson to send it before teatime. That man is not nearly the chemist his father was.'

Samuel put his brush on a table beside a palette smeared with paints and looked at his sister. He could hardly remember seeing her dressed in any colour other than black, as though she were in constant mourning; neither could he remember seeing her smile, he could only recall the bitterness that had eaten away at her over the years, a bitterness of her own making. Yes, Annie *was* in perpetual mourning, grieving for a life she thought duty had required her to forgo and nurturing bitterness against the brother she blamed for taking it.

'There is no need for you to go,' he signed, his long fingers moving in rapid succession, 'my headache is quite gone.'

'Yes, it is now,' Annie's fingers relayed words of care she had never truly felt, 'but what of the night-time, dear? You know how sometimes you cannot sleep for the pain in your head. I think it better I fetch your medicine myself.'

'If that is what you wish.' Samuel's fingers seemed to flow into each other, one sign blending into another with the practice of years. 'I will take a turn in the garden until you return.'

Going into the adjoining room that was her brother's bedroom, Annie took a lightweight coat from the panelled wardrobe. Returning to the studio, she held it out to Samuel.

'You must take care,' she signed as he took the coat and slipped it on, 'you know how quickly you take the influenza.'

Yes, he knew. Samuel followed her out of the studio, making his separate way into the garden. He also knew how much he wished the influenza would take him.

Annie drove her small trap along Walsall Road turning off when she reached Oakeswell End, directing the horse toward the chemist's shop that topped Dudley Street. She would collect the medicine Alfred Dingley had prescribed and then she would complete what she had intended all along.

Ignoring the sidelong glances of the women and the looks of dislike from men she had laid off from the pits on one pretext or another, and whom the iron foundries would not take on, she trotted the horse a roundabout route, avoiding where possible the more heavily frequented roads until she came to Bescot Fields. This part of Wednesbury was still mostly pasture with only a few farms holding out against the industrialisation that had engulfed the town like the black plague; here she had lived so many years before coming to Brunswick House, here at the end of a beaten track hidden by high hedges was the house Abel had given to her and Samuel. It had not been sold or let to tenants and neither would it be until her use for it was gone. Samuel took no interest in the property or businesses left to him by Abel and none in this house: his painting was his only interest, which suited her. She turned the horse off the track, driving round to the back of the house where the trap would be screened. Yes, it suited her very well.

Leaving the horse to crop at the overgrown flower border she took the key from her bag, letting herself into the house. She would not open the shutters. The years had taught her the geography of this house and she moved easily through its shadowed dimness. In her old bedroom she drew a box from the back of a narrow shelf obscured by a marble-topped washstand set in front of it.

A finger of daylight poked between the heavy velvet curtains. Annie carried the box over to it. She removed the lid and breathed deeply, a feeling of satisfaction coursing through her. It was still there. From the depths of the box she withdrew a small finely wrought glass bottle. By the finger of daylight she read the label: 'D'Amour'. Elias Webb had thought her his the day he gave her the bottle of French perfume. But the perfume and its giver had long gone from her life.

Discarding the box, she thrust the bottle into her bag and left the house, locking it securely before climbing into the trap and leaving her former prison to its silence.

Phoebe struck the packed earth with a jarring thud and lay still. Above her, his narrow face pulled into a grin, the man watched, then satisfied she was either unconscious or worse, turned back to searching the heap of sacks.

Hearing his movements above her, Phoebe knew he had not followed. Carefully, a prayer in every move, she pushed herself to her knees, then to her feet. By what miracle she had not broken her legs she didn't know and didn't stop to reason, her one thought was to make it back to the house and bolt herself in. Gathering her skirts in both hands she tiptoed toward the open door and was almost through it when she heard him shout.

Running the last few yards, she hurled herself out of the door, slamming it behind her, eyes skimming it in search of a bolt or securing bar. But there was no way of locking it; there had been no need for locks at Wiggins Mill.

'Hey! Come here, you bloody bitch . . .'

The shout was followed by a grunt. He was down from the corn loft, had jumped as she had.

'Think you could fool me, did you? You'll 'ave nuthin' to think with when I catch you!'

Phoebe heard the scuffle as he got to his feet. She was already halfway across the open ground separating the mill from the house when she heard the door slam open against the wall.

'You won't bloody get away . . .'

The shout followed her as she ran.

'You've got that money somewheers an' I'm gettin' it!'

The last came out in a gasp as he threw himself at Phoebe's back, his hands fastening in her skirts and dragging her to the ground.

'Would 'ave gone a lot better wi' you if you had just told me wheer the money is 'cos now I'm gonna knock the truth outa you . . .'

'I told you the truth.' Phoebe tried to move but his weight sprawled half across her was too much. Her face pressed against the earth, she went on, 'I was given no money at the Priory.' It would not be enough. Her brain began to work calmly; she had to be more convincing, tell him something his thieving mind would accept. 'They . . . they offered me a hundred pounds . . .'

She stopped as he rolled off her then snatched her over on to her back, a hand about her throat. ''Undred pounds!' His fingers tightened on her neck, lifting her head then banging it hard down on the ground. 'An' you told me you got nuthin', you bloody lyin' cow!'

'I . . . I didn't take it.' His fingers tightened about her throat and behind her eyes tiny fireworks began to explode. 'I . . . I told them . . . it . . . it wasn't enough.'

His fingers relaxed but stayed about her neck; above her his thick lips drew back. 'Not enough! You told 'im a 'undred pounds wasn't enough?'

'Y . . . Yes . . .' Phoebe coughed.

'You! You told the 'igh an' mighty Billy-me-Lord Dartmouth that a 'undred pounds wasn't enough?' He laughed. 'What a bloody cheek . . . I bet 'e 'ad near enough an' 'eart attack.'

'He . . . he wasn't pleased.'

'Pleased!' Her attacker laughed again, the sound rolling off the walls of the old windmill and away toward the canal. 'I bet 'e wasn't bloody pleased, 'is sort ain't used to bein' refused, not no way. So . . .' he stopped laughing '. . . if you didn't take 'is 'undred quid, what did you tek?'

Phoebe lifted her hands to the one still holding her by the neck and pushed. 'Nothing.'

The fingers tightened again, banging her head twice against the hard earth. 'You keep arsin' around wi' me an' you gets yer brains knocked out,' he hissed. 'I don't believe you didn't get summat, you was one of a sort once till that sister of yer father's took the lot from you . . . oh, I know all about that.' He grinned down at her, his yellow teeth parted. 'Same as I know you to be too smart to miss the chance of gettin' your 'ands on some of Billy's money, so don't tell me you got none.'

'I got a lot *more* than a hundred.'

The flicker of greed in his eyes told Phoebe this was what he wanted to hear, this would convince him, this he might just accept. Pushing against his wrist, she stared up at him.

Holding her stare for a full minute, he tried to gauge the truth of what she had just said then dropped his hand.

''Ow much more?'

'A lot.' She sat up, coughing as a stream of air gained free passage to her lungs. 'Only I don't get it until this afternoon.'

'Go on.' He watched her rub her throat, his eyes lowering to her breasts.

'They were all there, like you said,' Phoebe tried to ignore his look, 'Sir William and Lady Dartmouth and their son and daughter. They said they were sorry I had been inconvenienced . . .'

'Incon-bloody-venienced.' He laughed again, the noise of it rolling in waves from the mill to its outhouses before washing out over the low embankment that bordered the canal. 'That sounds just like 'im – somebody does twelve months in the shit an' '*e* calls it a inconvenience!'

Taking her chance, Phoebe got to her feet, brushing spears of dried grass from her skirts. 'I told him much the same. I also told him that this particular inconvenience was going to cost him ten thousand pounds or I would go to the newspapers. I said I was sure they would relish reporting how so prominent a member of the gentry had allowed an innocent girl to take the blame for a crime his son had committed.'

'But the necklace was found!' His eyes glittered up at her.

'Was it?' Phoebe flicked a dried straw from her sleeve, trying to guess how long she could stall him. Maybe Sophie or Edward would call and maybe not, reason told her, they had called only two days before. 'Or was it a replica? After all, who would know? And who would really care? The public's interest would not be in the recovery of the necklace but in the suffering of a young girl, and that suffering would only increase in the telling.'

'An' 'e went for it?'

He stood up, his tongue skimming his thick lips, and Phoebe stepped backwards, making a breathing space between them.

'Not at first. He argued that I would never be believed, but I argued that the damage to his family's reputation would be already done and that he might never be quite believed again in anything he tried to do. I said the aristocracy is a cautious breed. It cares to take no chances with the unreliable in case its own unreliability is brought to light.'

'Clever.' He smiled his approval. 'I said you was one of 'is own sort, y'ave brains as well as looks.'

Deep inside Phoebe shuddered at the glance he played over her but forced herself to stay calm. 'Clever enough,' she said, avoiding his eyes, 'to turn a hundred pounds into ten thousand.'

'Christ Almighty,' he breathed, 'ten thousand quid . . . it's a bloody king's ransom!'

'But it's a king's ransom I earned,' Phoebe said, 'over twelve months in hell I earned that money, and I told them either they pay what I ask or I tell the whole story plus more . . . much more.'

'So 'e agreed?' His eyes slid again to her breasts. 'Billy-me-Lord is payin' you ten thousand quid.'

'This afternoon.' Phoebe turned towards the house. 'He had to go to the bank. He said that he never kept that much money in the house, so if you come back around four o'clock you can have half.'

'Why go?' He grabbed at her, pulling her hard against him. 'It will be more pleasurable to wait 'ere . . .'

He pressed his face to the side of her neck, pulling at her flesh with his thick lips, and this time Phoebe could not hold her shudder inside. Grasping his hands, she tried to force them away, a sob of terror escaping her as he turned her in his arms. 'I . . . I'll give it all to you if you go.'

'I intend 'avin' it all,' he grinned, thick lips shining wetly, 'an' the money besides.'

Hooking one foot behind her ankle he brought her down, her spine hitting the ground hard, driving the wind out of her.

Already unbuckling the belt holding up his trousers, he looked down at her. 'Relax,' he grinned again, 'you'll enjoy what I've got fer you.'

Their hold released, his trousers fell around his ankles, revealing the naked flesh beneath, then he was on top of her, one hand clawing at her breast while the other slid her skirts above her hips.

'*You'll enjoy what Liza's got fer you.*'

Once more Phoebe was against that prison wall, the stink of Liza Spittle in her nostrils, the vileness of her touch rising like gall in her throat.

'Stop!' She struggled to push him away, to rid herself of the threat of his body. 'Please stop!'

'It ain't stop you'll be sayin' in a minute,' he said thickly, his hands fumbling at her underwear, 'you'll be sayin' more . . . please, more.'

'No . . .' Phoebe screamed as his fingers touched against her bare skin. 'Liza, no . . . o . . . o!'

Chapter Ten

Maudie Tranter slipped out of the back entrance of Brunswick House, her cloak covering a wicker basket.

Annie Pardoe would be gone most of the afternoon and there was little likelihood of Samuel's needing anything, poor man. Maudie shook her head. He seemed to become more drawn into himself every day, eating hardly enough to keep a sparrow alive, and those headaches! She reached the lane that backed the house, turning left towards Hall End. Yes, Samuel Pardoe's headaches just seemed to get worse despite the medicines Alfred Dingley regularly prescribed.

'Come in, Maudie.' Sarah Leach left off scraping the potatoes she had freshly pulled from the vegetable patch, wiping her hands on a square of white huckaback. 'It's good to see you, the seein' ain't often enough.'

'An' likely to be less.' Maudie followed her through to the kitchen, letting the basket on to the table with a groan. 'It gets to be a longer walk out 'ere each time a body comes, or at least that's the way it feels.'

'Give us yer cloak.' Sarah took the heavy woollen cloak, her eye on the basket.

'Eeh, ma wench!' Maudie dropped heavily on to a hoop-backed chair, its cane seat welcoming to her thin frame. 'Why do you still go on livin' out 'ere? You would be better off nearer the town an' Joseph wouldn't 'ave near so far to trot to the pit.'

'Try tellin' 'im that.' Sarah smiled, lifting the kettle from its bracket above the fire and scalding the tea in her brown earthenware pot. ''E says 'e is 'ere till they carries 'im up Church Hill an' settles 'im agen 'is mother and father.'

'P'raps 'e's got the right idea 'spite what I says.' Maudie watched the flow of dark brown liquid being poured into Sarah's china cups, kept for visitors. 'Wednesbury ain't the place it once was – all steel foundries wi' their smoke an' dirt messin' place up, an' now them newfangled toob works.'

'Toob works?' Sarah asked, adding milk to the tea before passing one of the cups to her visitor. 'What do toob works be?'

'They be factories as meks toobs – 'ollow stems of steel. All sizes they can mek – long an' fat, short an' thin, big or little.'

'What they be for then?' Sarah pointed to a small glass bowl filled with sugar. 'These toobs.'

'I'm buggered if I know!' Maudie spooned sugar into her tea. 'But I reckon 'er up at Brunswick 'Ouse does. Seems as 'er's dabblin' in a lot of things lately.'

'Is 'er buyin' these 'ere toobs then?' Sarah asked over her cup.

'Not buyin' 'em.' Maudie sipped her tea, savouring both it and the moment; she didn't see much of folk and when she did she enjoyed the glory of imparting news of the doings of Annie Pardoe. 'But I reckon 'er's puttin' money into the mekin' of 'em.'

'Well, 'er certainly ain't puttin' any into them pits o' their'n,' Sarah answered, placing home-cooked scones and a jar of her own damson jam on the table. 'Joseph says that Hobs Hill mine is near to cavin' in just about everywheer and that the Crown mine up at Moxley ain't much safer. What wi' all that an' their pay bein' docked, the men would pack in tomorrer if they could get set on anywheers else. Eeh, wench, what changes we've seen since Abel went!'

'There's been changes all right,' Maudie lifted a scone to the plate Sarah passed her, 'an' not all in them pits neither.' She sliced the scone, ladling it with thick dark jam. 'You knows 'ow long I've been wi' Annie Pardoe an' 'er brother, an' in all them years I ain't known 'er 'ave doin's wi' nobody other than tradesmen, but now . . . well, all I knows is summat is goin' on.'

''Ow do you mean?' Sarah helped herself to a scone.

'There's bin a caller to Brunswick 'Ouse several times over the last few weeks an' always when Samuel be sleepin' . . . 'e sleeps quite a bit, 'e does, these days.'

She paused but Sarah did not speak, not wanting to put her visitor off her stride. Maudie was easily diverted and any news of Annie Pardoe's doings was too good to miss.

Maudie drank the last of her tea and waited while the cup was refilled. Spooning sugar into it, she went on, 'It's always the same man: Clinton Harforth-Darby 'e says 'is name is, an' you should see Annie when 'e comes. All sweetness an' light 'er is, apologisin' for Samuel's absence sayin' as 'e regrets bein' unable to come down . . .' she stirred her tea vigorously as though the action would ease some of the contempt her words roused '. . . as if 'er would ever suffer the poor bugger to come downstairs. Keeps 'im up theer like a rooster in a pen, 'cept Samuel will never get to perform like no rooster.'

'Does 'e know what's going on?' Sarah chanced Maudie changing tack. 'I mean, the say-so in all business matters be wi' 'im surely? 'E must sign papers an' things, Annie can't do that.'

'That's what you think.' Maudie accepted a second scone. 'It's what a lot of folk think seein' as 'ow the lot was left to Samuel, but Maudie Tranter knows better . . .' Sinking her teeth into the light scone, her eyes fastened on Sarah's, relishing the interest she saw in them. 'I heard 'er tell this Harforth-Darby that 'er could sign in 'er brother's stead, that 'e 'ad given 'er power of a tur . . . I can't remember the exact word but it must be legal like 'cos Harforth-Darby passed her some papers an' I seen 'er sign meself.'

'You seen Annie Pardoe write 'er name on papers that man give 'er? Eeh, I wonder what they was for?'

Maudie touched a finger to each side of her lips checking for stray crumbs before sipping her tea. 'That I don't know,' she shook her head, 'but it was summat that set a smile on that man's face that stretched from ear to ear. An' there's another thing.' Maudie finished her tea, refusing a third cup with a shake of her head. 'Last time 'er went out, 'er bought a new frock . . .'

'Who, Annie Pardoe!' Sarah asked, disbelief plain in her voice.

Maudie nodded. 'Ar, an' not just a new frock but a new lavender-coloured frock.'

'God luv me, I don't believe it.' Sarah stared at the other woman. 'After all these years, Annie Pardoe in a frock that ain't black? I can't remember last time I seen 'er outa black.'

'Oh, 'er ain't wore it, it's hangin' in 'er wardrobe. 'Er don't know I've seen it – but then, there's one or two things as Annie Pardoe ain't knowin'.'

'P'raps they be goin' somewheer special?' Sarah swung the kettle on its bracket away from the fire as the hiss of steam became louder. ''Er an' Samuel, I mean.'

'Oh, ar,' Maudie smiled acidly, 'an' pigs might fly. That one never goes out nowheer, and garden is as far as 'e goes, an' I can't see as Annie 'as bought 'erself a new frock to saunter round the roses.'

'I never could understand that, Maudie,' Sarah said, sitting down again. 'From a babby 'e never went anywheer on 'is own, 'e was always wi' his mother, an' after 'er went 'e was only seen wi' Annie – an' that weren't often, poor sod. 'E was always kept close to their skirts an' yet from what I remembers of 'im 'e was a good-lookin' lad, same as Abel. Would 'ave been the mekin' of 'im to 'ave wed.'

'Ar, well,' Maudie sighed heavily, 'it be too late fer that now even if 'e 'ad the mind. That sister of his'n wouldn't 'arbour no other woman in the 'ouse an' I can't see Samuel goin' against 'er, not now.'

'Poor soul,' Sarah shook her head in unspoken sympathy,

'but whatever the reason 'e's been kept close all 'is life it couldn't a' been 'is brain or Abel would never 'ave left 'im everythin'.'

'It ain't 'is brain,' Maudie agreed, 'there be nuthin' wrong up top. 'E might not go out of that 'ouse but it ain't 'cos 'e's short of 'is marbles.' She tapped a finger to her forehead. ''E's just got no interest in nuthin' 'cept for 'is paintin'.'

'Seems to me 'e ain't never been allowed no interests. Eeh, that family am goin' to 'ave a lot to answer for, an' not only on account of Samuel neither. There's young Phoebe an' what they've done to 'er.'

'That were all Annie's doin', an' all,' Maudie replied. 'I tell you, Sarah, Abel Pardoe would turn in 'is grave if 'e knowed what 'ad 'appened to that girl of 'is'n.'

'There was no call to go turnin' the wench out of 'er own 'ome,' Sarah said, 'that were nuthin' short of vicious. Surely Samuel 'ad summat to say about that?'

''E might 'ave done,' Maudie rose reaching her cloak from the nail in the door, 'supposin' 'e knowed the truth of it but I 'ave me doubts about that. More likely 'is sister 'as filled 'im up wi' all sorts of lies.' She fastened the cloak about her throat. 'But like I said, Annie Pardoe don't know all. Might be as one day 'er will 'ave one or two surprises comin'.'

''Ow do you mean, Maudie?' Sarah waited for Annie's housekeeper to finish fastening her cloak.

'I ain't sayin'.' Maudie dropped a hand to the wicker basket still on a corner of the table; she wasn't one to give all her news in one sitting. If it were worth the telling it were worth the holding, for a while longer anyway. 'But mark my words, Annie Pardoe be in for a shock.'

'No . . . Liza, don't . . . no . . . o . . . o!'

Phoebe's screams ricocheted off the walls of the mill and its outhouses as she struggled to push the man away.

'You won't be sayin' no fer long,' he grunted, snatching at her drawers, the cotton of them tearing in his hand. 'You won't be sayin' anythin', you'll just be moanin' wi' pleasure when you gets this up you . . .'

'Somebody is goin' to get summat up 'em but I don't think it's goin' to be no woman!'

'What the bloody 'ell . . . ?'

'Is this yer 'usband, Missis?'

Her movements jerky, like a badly controlled puppet, Phoebe sat up, pushing her skirts down over her legs, grasping the torn bodice of her dress and holding it across her breasts, fear still bubbling in her throat. The man who had attacked her was jerked to his feet by the scruff of his neck.

'Am you married to 'im?'

'No!' Phoebe looked up at the figure dangling like a rag doll in the grip of a tall, broad-shouldered man.

'So you ain't 'er 'usband!' The tall man shook her attacker effortlessly. 'Then how come you be sprawled across 'er wi' your bare arse to the sun?'

'Let go, you interferin' bastard . . .'

Phoebe made to get to her feet as her attacker struggled to free himself, wanting only to get inside the mill house and lock herself away, but fell back as her legs refused to hold her.

'Oh, I'll let you go.' Placing two fingers in his mouth, the tall man gave a series of sharp whistles. 'When I've done wi' you.'

'You'll be sorry, you bloody canal rat.' The man who had come to rob Phoebe tried to kick backward but the trousers draped around his ankles prevented him. 'I've got mates . . .'

'An' do they all go around doin' what you intended doin' 'ere?' The tall man twisted the other around. 'You call attackin' a woman fun, I suppose? Well, I call punchin' the daylights out of scum like you fun – an' I'm goin' to 'ave me some fun right now!' One hand holding Phoebe's attacker by the throat, the other smacked into his yellow teeth with the force of a sledge hammer.

Her face turned away, Phoebe heard the cries as fists found their mark again and again.

'Bert . . . Bert, no more . . . you'm like to 'ave killed 'im!'

'I could bloody kill 'im lief as look at 'im.' Anger darkening his face, the tall man answered a woman in black skirts, a white cotton poke bonnet fastened over her brown hair, as she ran up to him. 'Makin' too free wi' what God give 'im.'

'Well, 'e won't make too free wi' it no more for a while.' The woman looked at the semi-conscious figure lying on his back, legs sprawled apart. 'Mind, the Lord weren't too lavish in first place wi' what he give this one.'

''E can still do more than enough harm wi' it all the same.' He dropped a hand to the handle of a knife tucked in his wide leather belt. 'I've a mind to cut the bugger off. That way 'e won't force it up no other woman as don't want it.'

'No, Bert!' The woman put a restraining hand over the one fondling the knife. 'I reckon 'e'll 'ave learned 'is lesson by the time 'e gets round to usin' that again. Best you do what you always do when you've knocked a man senseless an' I'll see to the wench.'

Turning away as the tall man caught the other by the collar, dragging him away, trousers about his ankles, the bare flesh of his buttocks scraping the rough ground, she moved to where Phoebe still sat, arms huddled across her chest.

'It's all right, ma wench,' she said softly, going down beside Phoebe and drawing her into her arms. 'It's all right, it's all over now.'

'Tilly . . .' Phoebe sobbed against the woman's shoulder. 'Oh, Tilly.'

'That's it,' the woman murmured soothingly, 'cry it up, wench, cry it up. You'll be better for gettin' it out.'

'We best get 'er inside.'

The man called Bert returned and stood looking at the two women huddled together on the ground.

'You be right.' The woman got to her feet, gently urging Phoebe to follow suit. 'A cup of sweet tea is what 'er's wantin'.' Then, seeing Phoebe flinch as the man made to help her up,

'It's all right, me luv, my Bert won't 'arm you, you'll be safe wi' us.'

''Er don't look as though 'er can make it on 'er own.' Bert stood still a moment then, reaching out, swept Phoebe up in his arms.

'Not in there, Bert,' the woman cautioned as he turned toward the house, its rear door still wide, 'we don't know what that bloke might 'ave taken out of there an' we don't want stickin' wi' the blame. We'll take 'er wi' us till 'er feels better. Might be somebody will be lookin' for 'er by then.'

'Try to drink some of that, ma wench, it'll do you good. You be in my 'ome.' Phoebe felt the cup held against her mouth.

'Tilly,' she cried, turning her face away, 'Tilly . . . it was Liza, oh God, it was Liza!'

'I ain't Tilly.' The woman placed the cup on top of a low cupboard built against a wall. 'An' it weren't no Liza as was 'avin' a go at you, it was a man.'

'Tilly . . . ?' Phoebe opened her eyes, looking for the first time at the woman who had helped her.

'No, ma wench, like I told you, I ain't Tilly an' it was no Liza sprawled across you, it were a man.' The woman smiled, her face kind beneath its bonnet. 'But you be all right, 'e's gone, an' after what my Bert give 'im I don't think 'e'll be back – not unless 'e be glutton for punishment.' Taking the heavy cup from the cupboard top she held it out to Phoebe. 'Try drinkin' this. It's only tea, but then our means don't stretch to alcohol.'

'Thank you.' Phoebe took the thick cup, swallowing the hot sweet liquid.

'Theer you go, Mam.'

Phoebe looked up as a lad of around nine years old squeezed into the narrow room, placing a prettily painted tin jug on the cupboard top.

'The water you wanted.'

'Eh!' The woman glanced at Phoebe. 'I 'ope as you don't

mind but I sent the lad for water from your yard. That was what brought Bert to your place earlier. 'E was supposed to be comin' to ask if we could 'ave a jug of water, this in canal be none too clean for drinkin'.'

Phoebe handed the cup back, her tea finished. 'What happened?'

'Me dad kicked the shit outa some bloke as was attackin' you,' the boy answered, eyes gleaming.

'An' you will get it belted out of you when I tells 'im what you've just said!' The woman aimed a swift blow to the side of the lad's head. 'What've I told you about that sort of language? You might live on a barge but you ain't no canal rat an' I ain't 'avin' you talk like one.'

'Sorry, Mam, sorry Miss.' The lad smiled, his face proud beneath a shock of brown hair. 'But me dad still kicked the s . . . stuffin' outa that bloke. Says 'e won't be maulin' no women for many a day.'

'Out!' The woman aimed a hand at the boy who ducked expertly. 'Get out and help yer father. Eeh!' She turned to Phoebe, 'Kids today. Their mouth be grown up afore their backsides be free of the napkin.'

'Was it your husband who . . . who pulled him off me?'

'Ar.' The woman nodded. ''E could tell from your screamin' that what that one was about 'ad none of your consentin' so 'e dragged 'im off you and give 'im a punchin' 'e won't forget in a 'urry.'

'Where is he now?'

'Who? The one as 'ad you pinned beneath 'is tackle?' The woman made a noise of contempt in her throat. 'Bert will 'ave chucked 'im where it'll go rusty if 'e don't get 'isself out, an' sharpish. 'E'll be in the cut, an' if 'e drowns I 'ope there's none to mourn 'im.' She poured more tea from a tall pot, pink roses and green leaves bright against its black enamelled body. 'I thought we should bring you 'ere to the barge, I didn't want nobody thinkin' we was in any place we shouldn't be, 'sides . . .' she placed the heavy platter cup on the cupboard top near to Phoebe '. . . if anythin' be missin' from your place, could be folk might think we took it.'

'He . . . he didn't take anything.' Phoebe picked up the cup, glad of something to do with her hands. 'He came for money, had the idea I had some hidden at the mill, and it was his intention to rob me of it.'

'An' did 'e?'

'No.' Phoebe shook her head. 'I didn't have any money at all, much less the amount he expected me to have.'

'You don't 'ave to say any more if you don't feel you want to,' the woman sipped her own tea, 'though usually it feels better to get it out like.'

'I was upstairs.' Phoebe stared into the tea. 'I heard him downstairs and thought it was Edward or Sophie. When I went to see he grabbed me and threatened to burn my face with a poker if I didn't give him the money.'

'But you 'adn't got any?'

'No.' Phoebe went on staring into her cup as if the events of the past few hours were being played out in its depths. 'But he wouldn't believe me. I thought if I could get him across to the mill I might be able to run away while he was searching it so I told him I had hidden the money in the old corn loft, but he forced me up there with him.'

'But you was outside when Bert come across you.'

'He kicked the ladder away,' Phoebe ignored the interruption, 'so I jumped. He didn't come straight down. I slipped out and made a run for the house.'

'An' that's when 'e catched you?'

'Yes.' It was little more than a whisper. 'I told him then that the money he thought I already had was to be brought to the mill that afternoon. I said if he would leave right away I would hand it all over to him when he returned.'

'An' 'e said 'e would 'ave the money an' a bit more besides,' the woman finished for her. 'The dirty swine! 'E deserves all my Bert give 'im an' more. The rope is too good for the likes of that one, but it ain't always the ones that am guilty as pays the price.'

'I find you guilty of wilful theft . . . you will serve a term of fifteen years . . .'

The Magistrate's words rang in Phoebe's ears. The woman was right: it was not always the guilty who paid the price.

Maudie Tranter let herself in at the rear entrance of Brunswick House and stood for a while in the kitchen, her ear registering the silence. The mistress wasn't back yet. Removing her cloak, she hung it in a cupboard in the scullery, sitting her bonnet on a shelf above.

She had timed her visit well as always, arriving back before Annie returned. Running her hands over her tight-drawn hair, she returned to the kitchen, a bitter smile touching the corners of her mouth as she replaced the wicker basket in its place beside the large pine dresser. Annie Pardoe had cut the wages of the miners to the bone; it was only fitting that some of the contents of her larder had gone to one of them.

Going out of the kitchen she crossed the hall, the slow tick of a longcase clock measuring her steps as she climbed the stairs. Halting outside Samuel's bedroom she listened for movement but, hearing nothing, moved along the corridor to the room used as a studio. Tapping the door out of respect for the man whose ears had been sealed in the womb, she went in. Samuel was not there. Maudie breathed more easily. He was still sleeping, so neither of them would know she had been out of the house.

She was halfway down the staircase when Annie let herself in at the front door. 'Mister Samuel must still be sleeping. I have just been to see if he wanted anything but he is not in his studio.'

'Has he woken at all while I have been out?'

'No, Ma'am,' Maudie answered. 'There 'asn't been a sound out of 'im the whole afternoon.'

'Bring his tray in about five minutes,' Annie turned towards the staircase, 'we will be in the sitting room.'

In her room she removed her cloak and bonnet, hanging them in a large wardrobe, letting her fingers caress the lavender silk of the gown the cloak would conceal. Soon she would wear no more black, soon she would wear the colours her lost youth had never known, soon now . . . very soon she would share a bed as Abel had shared his. Her body would know the touches his had known. Soon now . . . soon.

Opening her bag she took out the pretty glass bottle, holding it to where the light from the window caught the faintly golden contents, then crossing to a chest of drawers she placed the bottle in the bottom one, covering it with a layer of silk petticoats carefully wrapped in blue tissue paper.

Pushing to her feet, she gasped, clutching at a point below her left breast as a pain ripped through her. Her breathing rapid, she stumbled to the bed and sat for several minutes before taking the bottle of tablets from the drawer of the side table. Pouring a little water from the carafe that always stood beside her bed, she swallowed a couple of small white tablets. Two minutes later she made her way to her brother's bedroom, the medicine she had collected from the chemist in her hand.

In the kitchen Maudie laid a tray with tea and thinly cut sandwiches of salmon and cucumber. Samuel had taken salmon and cucumber for tea almost daily for the fifteen years she had served as housekeeper; in fact, everything remained the same in Annie Pardoe's household – or at least it had until Harforth-Darby had arrived on the scene. She scalded the tea, setting the white china pot on the tray. She didn't trust Harforth-Darby with his smarmy ways, he was buttering Annie Pardoe up sure as shooting, and just as sure she was in for a disappointment. Maudie set milk and sugar on the tray. If Annie thought she was going to get that one to the altar then she was shouting into an empty gulley, lavender frock or no lavender frock!

Carrying the tray to the sitting room, she set it beside Annie, her eyes taking in the tired sunken features and thin frame of the man who sat opposite.

'You be on your last legs, Samuel Pardoe,' she murmured, closing the door on brother and sister, 'an' it's my idea there be them as is ready to kick 'em out from under you.'

Waiting until the door closed, Annie poured tea, handing one of the cups to Samuel.

'It is just as well I went to collect your medicine,' she signed. 'I swear that Isaac Jackson took near enough an hour to prepare it. Seems tradesmen don't care how long they keep you waiting these days. I tell you, dear, things are no longer the same.'

Samuel smiled wearily. 'Things have not been the same since Abel died.'

Annie watched the rapid flickering of his fingers. 'What do you mean, not been the same?' Her own fingers formed the question.

'Let us not try to delude each other. You have always seen to my welfare, Annie, and I thank you for that though it has not been in the best of ways. It was our parents' thinking that turned my home into a prison. You have merely carried on where they left off. Oh, I know I could physically have forced my way out of this or our former home but what good would that have done? So in that way things have not changed.

'No, Annie, things changed when we heard Abel's will, when we came to Brunswick House. Feelings between you and me have never been what our brother thought them to be. You have always been bitter, blamed Abel for putting you in the position of nursemaid to me, blamed him for your never having married and saw his leaving me his fortune as a means of repayment for what he did. I can't blame you for those feelings, Annie, but since Abel died the bitterness in you has grown. I can never give you back the years you have spent with me but there are some things I can do . . .'

Annie sat stock still, her eyes on Samuel's dancing fingers, a feeling of alarm, fear almost, beginning to rise in her throat.

'. . . you see, I too feel that Abel acted wrongly, that your life was yours to do with as you wished and not as his money dictated. I know I should have told you this twenty years ago but I never found the way. That was my mistake and I'm sorry for it. I also think it was wrong of him to leave everything to us, literally denying his own daughter what was rightfully hers. That was Abel's mistake but it is one I can do something about . . .'

Samuel saw the apprehension on his sister's face deepen into something more at his mention of Abel's daughter and he felt a sudden deep pity. Annie had fed on her bitterness for years. What would she do when she heard all he had to say?

'It is my intention to return Brunswick House to Phoebe,' the movement of his fingers continued, 'together with the mines and partnerships in the Monway steel works and everything else her father willed to me, except a sum of money large enough to keep you comfortably for your lifetime and maybe recompense you somewhat for the years you have spent with me. You do, of course, have the house at Bescot. Whether or not you choose to live in it will be your decision.'

Annie stared at her brother, her brain numbed by what he had told her.

'As for myself,' he went on, 'I don't think Abel or Phoebe would object to my buying a small house somewhere. And not to worry,' the same weary smile touched his lips but the old sadness remained in his eyes, 'you and my parents can rest easily – I am not about to break my bonds. The shame I brought to the family will die a secret.'

The sharp sting of pain below her breast broke the numbness encircling her and Annie stood up, her glance sweeping the now empty room. Samuel was going to give everything back to their niece. She pressed a hand to the pain, will-power forcing the nausea out of her throat. But it was not only Samuel's to give, it was *hers*; she had spent half a lifetime earning that money, earning the power it brought, and Samuel would not take it from her.

''Ave you finished with the tray, Ma'am?' Maudie entered the room, one look at her employer telling her that the suspicion she had held for some time had proved correct, Annie Pardoe had been given a nasty shock. She smiled over the tray as Annie swept out.

'Ar, you've 'ad a shock, Annie Pardoe,' she whispered, carrying the tray to the kitchen, 'a big 'un. But there be more to come yet . . . much more.'

'Excuse me, Sir, but might you be Lucy's 'usband?'

'Who are you?' Edward Dartmouth looked at the tall well-built man coming toward him across the mill yard.

'My name is Bertram . . . Bertram Ingles.'

The reply was polite but there was none of the deference men usually adopted when addressing Edward.

'Might I ask what you are doing here?'

Edward looked at the man standing inches above himself, shirt sleeves rolled halfway between wrist and elbow, trousers held up by a broad leather belt blackened with wear, brass-studded clogs on his feet.

'I've come for water.' He lifted the black enamelled bucket painted around with a band of brightly coloured flowers. 'An' I asks you agen, Sir, be you Lucy's 'usband?'

'I am not Lucy's husband.' Edward's gaze circled the outbuildings. 'How do you know of her?' The gaze came back to the man now almost barring his way. 'And where is Miss Pardoe?'

'If Miss Pardoe be the young woman as lives 'ere then 'er is on my barge.'

'Your barge?' Edward said sharply. 'And how does she come to be there?'

'You've no need to come out fightin'.' Bert saw the flame kindle in the younger man's eyes. ''Er be wi' my Lizzie. I come for to ask permission to draw drinkin' water from the pump there earlier on today an' I found a young woman wi' a bloke sprawled across 'er, 'is trousers round 'is ankles . . .'

'Phoebe!' Edward interrupted. 'Did he . . . ?'

'Rape 'er?' Bert shook his head. 'Though it weren't for the want of tryin', an' 'e would 'ave an' all 'ad I not come across 'im when I did.'

'This man,' Edward brought his riding crop across the palm of his left hand, anger drawing his mouth in to a tight line, 'where is he now?'

'Coolin' what's left of 'is ardour in the cut,' Bert said, a nod of his head indicating the canal, 'though I doubt there was much of that left after I'd finished lettin' daylight into 'is guts.'

'You didn't give him enough!' Edward's eyes glistened with rage. 'You should have killed the swine, and even *that* would have been too good for him.'

'I think I near enough did do for 'im.' Bert smiled grimly. 'Leastways 'e won't be botherin' no woman for a long time yet.'

'More likely never again if I can find him, and I will!' Edward slapped his palm with the crop. 'I'll find the man and finish what you started . . . in the meantime, take this for your trouble.'

Bert Ingles looked at the sovereigns Edward drew from his waistcoat pocket and his face hardened.

'Any trouble I took on young wench's behalf was a trouble I would tek for any woman,' he said angrily, 'an' if it were a trouble then it be one I don't need payment for. You put your money back in your pocket, lad, an' put this bit of advice wi' it: next time you offer payment to a barge man for preventin' a wench bein' raped, mek sure you steps away pretty sharpish or you be likely to find yourself in the cut wi' the light shinin' on *your* innards.'

Edward stared. What was it with these people? First Phoebe and now this man. Both had refused money though it was obvious neither had any: both had almost nothing to support them but both burned with the same fierce pride.

'My apologies, Mr Ingles.' He slipped the coins back into his pocket. 'I had no wish to offend.'

'None teken, lad.' Bert smiled. 'Now if you'll wait till this bucket be filled, I'll tek you to . . . what did you say wench was called?'

'Miss Pardoe,' Edward answered, a liking for the tall rough-mannered man already formed. 'Miss Phoebe Pardoe.'

Edward followed, stepping gingerly from the narrow towpath on to the moored barge, picking his way through an assortment of buckets and ropes clustered into the small space between the prow and the cabin, almost three-quarters of the barge housing a cargo of coal on top of which sat a young boy and an even younger girl, both watching his progress through solemn eyes.

'You pair stop on top,' Bert said to them as he led the way down four steep steps that gave on to the family's living quarters.

'Phoebe,' said Edward blinking against the gloom, 'are you all right?'

''Er's all right.' Lizzie glanced at her husband standing on the steps, the confined space not enough to hold them all. 'Though 'er's 'ad a bad fright.'

Head and shoulders stooped against the low roof, Edward squeezed down the cabin that seemed barely a yard wide. 'Let me take you home, Phoebe.'

'I don't think much of you doin' that,' Lizzie said firmly. 'That wench 'as 'ad a shakin' up an' the last thing 'er needs is to be left on 'er own, so lessen there be somebody wi' 'er in that place of 'er'n then I says 'er's best left 'ere.'

'I think perhaps that would be best.' Edward looked at the bargee's wife, a white poke bonnet still covering her head even though she was in what was her sitting room. 'It would not be proper if I stay alone with her and neither can she be left on her own whilst I fetch Lucy from the town.' He touched a hand to Phoebe's, resting in her lap.

'Don't fetch Lucy, Edward.' She looked up at him. 'I have

suffered no harm and don't want her worried. If it is all right with Mr and Mrs Ingles I would prefer to stay with them until Lucy and Mathew return. They are always home about seven.'

'That ain't no bother to me nor Bert.' Lizzie caught the nod from her husband.

'Thank you.' Edward squeezed Phoebe's fingers gently before turning towards the hatchway. 'You may have refused my money, Mr Ingles,' he said when they both stood once more on the towpath, 'but surely you will not refuse my thanks for your solicitousness.'

'I won't refuse.' Bert took the hand the younger man extended, shaking it warmly. 'An' though it don't be necessary, it be appreciated.'

'Surprised me, that 'as,' he said, half to himself, watching Edward stride away towards the mill, its redundant windmill standing sentinel on the low rise that hid the house from the canalside.

'What 'as, Dad?'

'That one,' Bert answered his son, eyes following the figure moving rapidly away. ''E don't come from no miner nor no foundryman neither, that one 'as a different breedin', yet I thought all moneyed folk was above thankin' the likes of we. But 'e ain't.'

'Dad,' the boy asked as his father stepped aboard the barge, 'what's titty us ness?'

'Eh?' Bert glanced sharply across the expanse of coal.

'Titty us ness,' the boy's eyes gleamed roguishly, 'that's what that bloke thanked you for ain't it?'

'They ears been flappin' agen?' Bert picked up a nut of coal, 'they need a set o' doors fastened to 'em.' He threw the coal laughing as his son rolled clear, 'Cheeky young bugger,' he muttered fondly.

Chapter Eleven

Phoebe looked up from the small dress she was sewing, waves of fear flooding through her at the sound from outside the house. Putting her work aside she tiptoed to the window that looked out towards the track leading to the town, breathing her relief when she saw the trap she knew to be Sophie's.

Running swiftly downstairs she opened the door, her smile of welcome fading when she saw her caller.

'Good afternoon, Miss Pardoe.' Sir William Dartmouth inclined his head with a slight, barely perceptible movement. 'I hope I am not inconveniencing you by calling?'

'No . . . not at all.' Phoebe could not entirely hide her surprise.

'Edward told me of the unfortunate incident that took place yesterday,' he said when she did not ask him into the house. 'I trust you were not injured . . . in any way?'

'No.' The tiny pause so significant in its meaning was not lost on Phoebe; he had been told not only of the assault upon herself but also the nature of that assault. 'I was not injured . . . in any way.'

'I am relieved to hear it,' he said, watching the colour rise to her cheeks. 'My wife and I were concerned to hear of what happened to you, as was Sophie. Both of them were anxious to call upon you but my wife is ill with influenza and Sophie is not happy to leave her mother at the moment. But given your permission they will call once Amelia is well again.'

'I shall be happy to see them.' Phoebe stepped aside,

clearing the doorway. 'Forgive me, Sir William, won't you come in?'

Stepping inside, he allowed her to take his gloves, and when she set them on a small mahogany stand, followed her to the tiny parlour.

'Will you take some tea?' Phoebe asked when he was seated. 'I am afraid I have nothing in the way of wine.'

Tea. William Dartmouth smiled inwardly. It was every Englishwoman's placebo. 'No, thank you,' he said. 'I will not detain you. I came only to assure myself and my womenfolk that you had taken no harm.'

'None, I assure you.'

'That is as well, for the fellow who attacked you will pay hard enough when he is caught, and he will be, you have my word on that.'

'I think he has probably paid enough already,' Phoebe said, 'judging by what I hear Bert Ingles did to him.'

'Ah, yes, Edward told me of him. A bit of a rough diamond if I'm not mistaken.'

'You're not!' Phoebe's eyes flashed green fire. 'But then, diamonds are valuable rough or cut, are they not? And the Ingleses will always be highly valued friends to me.'

He glanced around the small room with its tired, well-worn furniture. This child of Abel Pardoe's might have little in the way of worldly goods but courage and integrity she had in plenty.

'You are not here alone, Miss Pardoe?'

'Of course I am, this is my home, where else would I be?'

'But I understood a woman and her husband were here with you.'

'Lucy and Mathew,' Phoebe nodded, 'but they go into Wednesbury every day.'

'Leaving you in this place by yourself?'

'Sir William, I am not a child.'

'That much is obvious,' he replied tersely, 'and therefore

the greater the danger. This Lucy . . . she must stay home, you must not be alone here again.'

'Sir William,' Phoebe said coolly, 'Lucy is the mainstay of this house at the moment. Her earnings provide most of their living and all of mine. Mathew works hard but odd jobs pay little in Wednesbury, so you see it is impossible for Lucy to stay here all day. My explanation is more for Lucy's sake than for yours. I would not have you think she left me on my own from choice.

'There is one more thing I have to say and it is this: do not ever use the word "must" to me. I have earned the right to be my own mistress and no man or woman will ever dictate to me again.'

William Dartmouth glanced at the down-at-heel furniture. 'Accept the money I still offer and neither of you would need to work again.'

'Don't seek to still your conscience with money.' Anger made Phoebe's voice sharp. 'I asked for none and I shall take none.'

'That is your prerogative.' He smiled. 'As will be your answer to my next question, always supposing you choose to give one for of course I should not dream of saying you must.'

'You can ask.' Phoebe caught the hint of amusement behind his grey eyes and her own mouth relaxed into a smile.

'This Ingles fellow – he told Edward that when he came upon that man attacking you, you were screaming about someone called Liza, and a little later you thought you were talking to a Tilly. Neither is a suitable name for a man. Tell me, was anyone else involved? Did the one who assaulted you have an accomplice?'

Phoebe's smile faded. 'No,' she said, looking to her lap where her fingers had automatically twined together at the memory of Handsworth Women's Prison. 'At least, there was no one with him when he . . . when he came here.'

'So who are the women whose names you called?'

She didn't have to tell him, Phoebe thought, he had no claim upon her, no right to ask questions. She could tell him that and then ask him to leave.

'Liza Spittle was a prisoner in Handsworth,' she said, surprised by the decision she could not recall making. 'She . . . she had certain tendencies . . . she . . . she tried . . .'

'You mean, she tried to force herself on you much the same as a man?'

'Yes,' Phoebe said, not knowing why she wanted him to know what Liza had done and grateful when he spared her the strain of the telling. 'And Tilly helped me . . . twice. She warned Liza not to touch me in . . . in that way again, and when she did try a second time Tilly tripped her up and Liza hit her head against the wall. I think she was hurt quite badly . . . she . . . she may even have died, and if so the Governors might say it was murder and Tilly would hang. But it wasn't! Tilly couldn't . . .'

'Is Tilly an inmate of the prison also?'

Phoebe nodded. 'She always will be. She is serving a lifetime sentence for manslaughter. They . . . they said she killed her husband but . . .' She looked up, her eyes defiant behind their cloud of unhappiness. 'I don't think she did. Tilly is no murderess no matter what any judge may have said.'

He rose, collecting his gloves from the small stand where Phoebe had placed them and opening the door himself.

'You are a very stubborn young woman,' he said, smiling. 'You refuse my offer of compensation, then you tell me never to use the word "must" to you again, and now you say you do not believe the verdict of a court.'

'It would not be the first time a court had been wrong, would it, Sir William?'

Pulling on his gloves, William Dartmouth looked at the girl whom he knew would openly defy him on any matter she felt to be right. 'Yes,' he inclined his head in a gesture of farewell, 'a very stubborn young woman, but one I admire. Good afternoon, Miss Phoebe Pardoe.'

* * *

'Me mam says to ask can I fill this from your pump?'

Phoebe smiled at the lad, his grin cheeky, his toffeedrop eyes bright beneath tumbling brown hair.

'Of course,' she answered. 'And when you're done come into the kitchen. I've got a big fat scone that is just asking to be eaten.'

''As it got sultanas in it?'

'Yes, big ones . . . this size.' She made a circle with thumb and forefinger.

'Oooh, bostin'.' His eyes gleamed with anticipation. 'I like sultanas. Our Ruth don't, 'er picks 'em out when we 'ave cake. Me mam says 'er shouldn't, it's bad manners to pick, but I don't mind 'cos our Ruth, 'er gives 'em to me.'

'I might be able to find one without sultanas for Ruth.' Phoebe recognised the barge man's word for something good or pleasant.

'Eh, don't do that, Miss!' He grinned, putting down the large flower-painted jug then wiping his palms against the sides of his trousers. ''Er enjoys picking 'em out as much as 'er does the eatin' of the rest.'

'In that case, we will find her one with extra sultanas.'

'We am leavin' tomorrer,' he said, perched on a stool in the kitchen, pulling sultanas from a scone and squashing them between his teeth, savouring each one before swallowing it. 'We as to tek them coals to London.'

'London?' Phoebe watched him work his way around the edge of the scone, the plate she had offered it on forgotten on the table. 'That's a good way off.'

'Ar, it is,' he nodded, recovering a crumb from his knee and stuffing it in his mouth beside a sultana. 'You ever been there, Miss?'

'No, I haven't.'

'I don't know as you'd like it.' He surveyed her over the scone. 'It's quite a big place, an' dirty the parts I've seen of it, an' folks pushin' an' shovin' as if they don't 'ave a minute to live.'

'It can't be much dirtier than Wednesbury.'

'It is, Miss, you can tek it from me. Wednesbury is a picture compared to London. Oh, the buildin's 'ere am black wi' smoke an' soot but the streets, well, they ain't filled wi' everybody's rubbish like, am they? I mean, they don't drop their paper on the roads or throw the peelin's out the windows here, do they?'

'They don't do that in London, do they?'

One foot tapping a half-laced boot against the leg of the stool, he considered a partly concealed sultana. 'I don't know about the places the nobs live in,' he twisted the scone, considering the sultana from all angles, 'but the ones we dock in, the basins like, well, you finds all sorts o' stuff throwed down there. Me mam, 'er don't like London an' I don't think you would either.'

'In that case I shan't go.' Phoebe placed several scones in a dark blue paper bag that had once held sugar. 'But I do quite fancy the seaside.'

'Me an' all.' He gave way to temptation, pulling the sultana free. 'An' our Ruth. Me dad says we might pick up a load that 'as to go to a port one day . . . a port is like the seaside, ain't it, Miss?'

'Mmmm.' Phoebe twisted the top of the bag to make a fastening. 'I imagine so. A port has ships and ships sail on the sea, so a port must be the seaside.'

''Ave you been to the seaside?'

Settling the bag of scones on the table, Phoebe went into the scullery, fetching a jug of milk from a bowl half filled with water to keep it cool.

'Not since I was a very small girl.' She filled a glass with the frothy white milk, setting the linen cover back over the jug before returning it to the scullery.

'Didn't your parents 'ave the money to tek you more than once?'

'It wasn't the money,' Phoebe placed the glass of milk before him, 'my mother died while I was still quite young and my father was too busy with his business to take me to the seaside.'

'Never mind, Miss.' He looked across at her, his eyes round and brown as a well-used penny, a seriousness in them that outstripped his years. 'Like me mam says, we all 'ave our cross to bear, but when we get that load for a port you can come with we. Mam an' Dad won't mind.'

'Speaking of your mother, Mark Ingles, she is not going to be at all pleased if you keep her waiting much longer for that jug of water.'

'Bugger me! I'd forgot all about the water.' He jumped from the stool, shoving the desecrated scone into his mouth.

Phoebe followed him into the yard, handing him the bag of scones as he finished filling the jug.

'An' you'll forget me language, won't you, Miss?' He grinned up at her, crumbs edging his lips. 'Go on, Miss, be a pal, say you ain't 'eard me say what I said?'

'All right,' Phoebe laughed, 'I didn't hear you say what you said.'

'Ta, Miss.' He sauntered off across the yard, raising the bag of scones above his head. 'Tara for now.'

'Miss Phoebe,' Lucy said thoughtfully, 'whoever it was come 'ere to rob you, 'e knowed about you bein' up at the Priory, 'e even knowed as you seen all of the family together, so it seems to me 'e is either a footman or else somebody who works in the 'ouse told 'im about you bein' there.'

'I . . . I hadn't thought about it.' It was true she had not thought of how the man had known of her visit, or of the fact she had been in prison, but she had lived through the nightmare of his attack again and again through the long night, jangles of fear setting her nerves dancing at every sound, only the knowledge that Lucy and Mathew were staying in the house preventing her from screaming.

'Well, I 'ave.' Lucy went on talking as she tipped flour into a bowl. 'An' if I 'ave then Sir William is sure to 'ave an' all. 'E ain't no fool that one, 'e can put two an' two together an' come up with 'alf a dozen.'

'Do you think that was the real reason for his coming here today?'

'Don't know.' Lucy spooned a small amount of salt into the flour. ''E didn't ask any questions about 'ow anybody might know, did 'e? But that don't mean anythin'. 'E might not 'ave said as much but you can take it from me 'e 'ad thought of it.'

He might have thought about it but Phoebe wanted only to put the whole episode behind her. She wouldn't forget, she would never forget, but right now she wanted only to leave it, to talk of anything except that.

Phoebe reached for the tongs settling fresh coals on the fire, then rinsed her hands and set about greasing pie tins with a dab of lard on a scrap of cloth.

'He asked whether I had suffered any harm from being attacked.'

'What the 'ell did 'e think? It certainly ain't done you no good. Bloody soft question to ask!' Lucy exploded.

'He said Sophie and Lady Amelia were concerned and that they would call later.'

'Huh!' Reaching a small shallow basin from the dresser, Lucy pressed it into the pastry, making a series of circles. 'Why didn't they come with him?'

'Lady Amelia has the influenza.'

Taking the circles she had cut from the pastry, Lucy pressed them into the tins. 'It was their son's fault you was gaoled but even so their sort don't usually call on the likes o' we.'

'The likes of us are as good as any Dartmouths, Lucy,' Phoebe answered, pounding a pot of boiled potatoes with a wooden spoon. 'The only difference is they have money and we do not.'

'*You* could have.' Lucy scooped the remnants of the circles together, rolling them with quick deft movements, making a further mat of soft pastry. 'You was offered it an' I think you should take it. It's nothin' you don't deserve.'

Phoebe lifted the large pot of mutton from the fireplace where it had stewed gently from early morning. Draining the stock into a bowl, she added the meat to the mashed potato. 'Accepting money will not alter what happened. I prefer to earn my living.'

'Well, I think you'm daft.' Tasting the mixture of meat and potato, Lucy nodded and Phoebe began filling the pastry-lined tins.

Finishing the filling of a dozen pie tins, she draped a cloth over the unused mixture, setting the pan in the hearth. 'Lucy,' she asked, passing a smaller basin the other girl had pointed to, 'do you think my dresses would sell in the town?'

Lucy pressed the basin into the pastry, cutting out smaller circles. 'The bits an' pieces I've managed to make 'ave gone well enough an' they ain't near so good as your'n. Mind, I couldn't make much, what wi' the baking.'

Phoebe watched smaller circles of pastry being placed over each pie tin, Lucy fluting the edges between finger and thumb. 'But what you did make sold each time?'

'Ar.' Lucy nodded. 'Could 'ave sold more but like I says, it's 'avin' the time to sew.'

Dipping two fingers into an egg she had beaten, Phoebe traced the lid of each pie. 'What about your pies and my dresses?'

'What you mean, Miss?' Lucy was already busy with the next batch of pastry.

'Put them together.'

'Eh?' Lucy paused.

'Well, not together as such.' Phoebe began to load the oven with pies. 'What I meant was, if you bake and I sew we could pool the money we make.'

'No, Miss Phoebe,' Lucy began, cutting out larger circles, 'your little frocks is worth much more than mutton pies.'

Closing the oven, Phoebe straightened. 'Your mutton pies have fed me since I came home, Lucy.'

'Oh, ar!' Looking up she ran her eyes over the girl she had once worked for. 'Well, they ain't made you much fatter. Anyway you give Mathew an' me a place to stay . . . well, you did in a manner o' speakin' 'cept you wasn't 'ere to speak to, an' then when you come out you didn't make we go. Way I sees things, a mutton pie an' the odd scone don't count for much against that.'

'It counts for a great deal with me,' Phoebe said, oiling more pie tins with a knob of lard, 'so we are equal, neither of us owes the other anything.' Lifting the pan from the hearth, she spooned the remainder of the filling into the pastry-lined tins then carried the empty pot into the scullery to be washed later.

'Do you really think my clothes would sell?' She asked again, uncertainty edging her question. 'Money is not all that plentiful in Wednesbury, is it?'

'Not in all quarters it ain't.' Lucy finished fluting the edge of the last pie. 'But then everybody don't work for Annie Pardoe. Some o' the men 'er finished at the pits as got taken on at Hampstead mine. Seem to be doin' all right an' all judgin' by the number of pies them women o' their'n buy.'

'But everyone has to have food,' Phoebe said, moistening pastry lids with beaten egg.

'Ar, an' they 'ave to wear clothes an' all or they gets a slow walk to Wednesbury police station wi' a bobby on each arm.' Lucy stretched her aching back. 'Tell you what . . . why don't I take them little frocks you made for Lady Dartmouth an' see if they sell?'

'I had thought of trying, I was getting them out of the trunk when . . .' Despite the heat of the kitchen Phoebe's face paled. The fear of what had happened was still vivid. It haunted her nights and filled her days but she knew if she admitted as much her friend would stay home and that would mean very little money coming in, and Mathew and Lucy had things hard enough. Going to the oven, she took out the cooked pies, hoping the action would cover her hesitation, masking what she could not say.

Lucy rattled the cooking utensils, gathering them for washing. If that bastard hasn't drowned in the cut then I hope he's dropped down a mine shaft! she thought. Either way may he rot in hell for attacking a woman. 'I will just get this lot shifted an' we'll 'ave us a cup of tea,' she said, rubbing her hands in the bowl of warm water on the hob. 'Put the kettle back over the fire, Miss.'

Phoebe swung the iron bracket, bringing the kettle to rest over the hot coals, then picking up the basin of water, followed to where Lucy had carried bowls and dishes to the scullery.

'I'll empty this in the yard,' she said, going to the scullery door. 'Will I give Mathew a shout?'

'If you will, Miss.' Lucy set the dishes against the large brownstone sink. ''E'll be just about gaspin' for a cup of tea.'

'Lucy . . .' The three of them were sitting in the kitchen of the mill house, cosy with the glow of the fire and the smell of fresh-baked pies and scones. 'What did you mean when you said not everyone in Wednesbury works for Annie Pardoe?'

'What do you mean, what do I mean?' Lucy asked in the tongue-twisting Black Country style.

'It seemed strange your using my aunt's name. She can't have anything to do with the business, that is solely Uncle Samuel's responsibility.'

'P'raps yer father thought it would be,' Mathew looked up from the fire, 'but Annie soon put the mockers on that. It's 'er as 'as all the say in what is or what isn't to be done, an' who is to be finished an' who ain't.'

'Aunt Annie might say things,' Phoebe nursed her cup between her hands, 'but she can't do more than that, she cannot sign her name to anything. Only Uncle Samuel can do that.'

'Seems like 'er can,' Mathew replied. 'I called in me mam's afore I come 'ome an' 'er said Maudie Tranter 'ad visited earlier. Maudie told 'er that Annie be gettin' a gentleman visitor . . . quite reglar it seems . . . an' Maudie 'eard 'er tellin' 'im Samuel 'ad given 'er some sort of power . . . power of a turn summat or other, me mam couldn't rightly say, but whatever it be it means Annie Pardoe can sign any business paper in place o' her brother.'

'Power of Attorney,' Phoebe said, suddenly understanding the sacking of men and the reduction in wages. 'My aunt has Uncle Samuel's Power of Attorney.'

'What does that mean, Miss?' Lucy asked.

Phoebe let her head sink tiredly against the back of her chair. 'It means my aunt has control of everything my father left to Samuel.'

'An' that means 'alf of Wednesbury,' Mathew said. ''E might just as well 'ave left it to the Devil.'

A loud knock on the scullery door jangled Phoebe's frayed nerves and the jerk of her hands set the tea dancing madly in her cup.

'You be all right, Miss,' Mathew said calmly. 'Just stop you theer, I'll see who that be.'

'I would like a word wi' Miss Pardoe, would you ask 'er if 'er will see me?'

Phoebe breathed out long and slow, feeling the tension loosen from her stomach as she recognised the voice of Bert Ingles.

'Come in, Mr Ingles,' she said, going to the scullery. 'I hope you don't mind the kitchen? It's a bit cramped but it's warmer than the sitting room.'

'I'm used wi' being cramped, there's not much living space on a barge.' Bert Ingles nodded to Lucy and Mathew as Phoebe introduced them.

'What can I do for you?' Phoebe smiled.

'I come to bring you these.' He fished in the pocket of a jacket that should have had a decent burial long ago, pulling out two brass locks. 'Me an' Lizzie got to talkin' after we brought you back 'ere yesterday evenin' . . . well, like we said, you can bolt these doors from the inside but we couldn't see 'ow you would fasten 'em on the outside, not so as nobody could get in like, an' Lizzie said there was bound to come times when you 'ad to leave the place, so we thought if you put these on the doors you would at least be certain nobody had got in while you was away. You would 'ave no more nasty surprises waitin' for you, if you follow what I mean.'

'That is very kind of you, Mr Ingles, I am most grateful to you and to your wife. It will be a great relief to me knowing the doors of the house are securely fastened.'

'They will be with these.' He looked proudly at the locks he held, one in each hand. 'Nobody will get them open wi'out the keys. These am no ordinary locks, I made these meself.'

'You made 'em?' Mathew took one of the locks, turning it over in his hands. ''Ow could you do that on a barge?'

'I didn't make them on the barge.'

'Oh,' Mathew looked up, 'then where?'

Shaking his head at Phoebe's offer of a chair, Bert Ingles went on, a strong hint of pride lacing his explanation: 'Them locks be my own design. You can't buy them in no ironmonger's. I made them just before me father died. You see, Miss. . .' he looked at Phoebe '. . . me father was a lockmaker out at Willenhall, an' 'e taught me the locksmithing.'

'But the barge,' Phoebe said, 'I thought you worked the barge?'

'So I do, Miss,' he answered, 'but I ain't always done that. I worked wi' me father up to three years ago. It wasn't until 'e died though that I found 'e had run at such a loss I couldn't pay the brass founders an' everybody else that claimed 'e owed them wi'out selling up.' He shrugged. 'So that is what I did. There were nothing for it after that but to get a job, any job that would feed the wife and kids. That's how I come to be working the canal.'

'What be so different about this?' Mathew turned the lock he was holding, sending darts of gold flickering from the polished brass.

'I'll show you.' Fishing a key from his jacket, Bert took the lock, inserted the key in it. 'See?' He turned the key, the action shooting out a metal bar.

'Ar, it's locked,' Mathew said, a quizzical frown pulling his brows together. 'I don't see nothin' different in that.'

'But it's not locked, not altogether.' Bert Ingles smiled. 'You see, this is a doubler.'

'A whater?' Lucy asked.

'A doubler, Missis.' Bert passed her the lock. 'Least that's what I call it. You see, it's a double barrel lock.' He took the lock back, turning the key a second time, and another bar shot out. 'Now,' he handed the lock to Mathew, 'try openin' it.'

Mathew tried turning the key but it wouldn't budge. He tried again then looked at the man watching him. 'It's stuck,' he said. 'The key must be jammed or summat.'

'It's not the key nor the lock that be jammed.' Bert retrieved the lock. 'That's what you are meant to think. You see, anybody not knowing how it works would think the same, and thinking they had got the key stuck would leave off trying to get in.'

'Well, if a burglar couldn't get in, all supposin' 'e managed to get 'old of the key, 'ow do you expect we to do it?'

'Like this.' Bert laid the lock on the table so they could each follow what he did. 'You turned the key anti-clockwise to operate the bolt,' he said, glancing at Mathew, 'that would be the normal way to operate a lock, but I reversed the mechanism. On this the key has to be turned clockwise to lock it.'

'Clever.' Mathew pursed his lips admiringly. 'But what about the doubler bit?'

'This is where the key does get stuck,' Bert answered, 'least you would think it had 'cos you won't pull it out at this stage. You 'ave to turn the key once more, that releases a second bolt an' also the key; it's a double safeguard. Even if a burglar cottoned on to the fact the key had to be turned back way round from usual, its getting stuck would cause him a bit of a headache.'

'An' pickin' the lock an' then findin' it still didn't open, 'e would likely pack in tryin' altogether?' Mathew grinned. 'That's what I calls useful.'

'It is a very good way of locking doors,' Phoebe said. 'They will save me a deal of concern whenever I have to go anywhere. How much do I owe you, Mr Ingles?'

'You don't owe me anything.' He laid three more keys beside the locks on the table. 'Me and Lizzie be just glad we could be of help.'

'But I couldn't . . .'

'Ar you could,' Bert Ingles looked suddenly embarrassed, 'just show me where you keep your screwdrivers and such and I'll have them locks on the doors in no time.'

'I'll give you a hand.' Mathew picked up the locks. 'Tools am in the barn.'

'Eh! What do you reckon to that?' Lucy asked as the two men left the kitchen.

'I reckon you are going to have to pay for those locks, Mrs Leach.'

'Me!' Lucy gasped. 'I ain't got but ninepence in me purse.'

'Bert Ingles won't take money,' Phoebe handed her a clean cloth from the airer strung across the fireplace, 'but I don't think he would refuse four of your mutton pies.'

Chapter Twelve

'I said to sell them . . . both of them.'

Annie Pardoe sat in James Siveter's office in his chambers in Lower High Street, her voluminous black skirts entirely hiding the small chair beneath her.

'You will have no trouble, I have been asked to sell them on several occasions.'

'Miss Pardoe,' the solicitor cleared his throat, 'does your brother know of this intended sale?'

Annie's eyes narrowed and her mouth tightened. 'If you want to continue to be our solicitor, James Siveter, I advise you to do as I instruct. My brother gave me his full Power of Attorney and that means I can act as I see fit, and I see fit to sell the Hobs Hill coal mine and the Crown. It also means I can replace you in your capacity as Samuel's solicitor. Your sort are two a penny.'

James Siveter rolled his long-handled pen between his fingers, experiencing a strong desire to tell the woman sitting opposite his heavy desk to take her business with her to the nearest canal and jump in with it! But it was a desire he curbed; she was right when she said she could replace him, and while not exactly two a penny solicitors were not hard to come by. He could not afford to lose business, however wrong he felt it to be.

'I will bring the necessary papers to Brunswick House first thing tomorrow.'

'No!' Annie's tight mouth showed no sign of slackening. 'You will not come to Brunswick House. I will sign an agreement of sale while I am here. You can get the purchaser's signature today – we have already agreed the price. I shall call here again tomorrow at three and I expect the business to be concluded.'

Why the rush? James Siveter thought, filling out the necessary documents. And why was Annie Pardoe here instead of sending for him to come to Brunswick House as he had always done? Power of Attorney or not, she obviously didn't intend Samuel knowing of today's doings.

'I will get this to the purchaser as soon as . . .'

'You will take it to him now!' Annie snapped. 'I want this finished and done. Three o'clock tomorrow.'

Holding the door for her to pass, the solicitor watched as she swept into the street. So she was selling both coal mines, and quickly . . . too quickly even for Annie Pardoe. Yes, it was a safe bet Samuel knew nothing of it, just as he likely knew nothing of what she had sold already: the shares in the Monway steel foundry, the Moxley iron works, together with a string of smaller businesses and houses. And what was she doing with the money she'd had for them? He had drawn up no new contracts. Whatever she had done, he, James Siveter, had not been consulted. Closing the door, he returned to his desk. 'I wonder?' he mused, taking up the papers Annie had signed and putting them into a small valise. 'I wonder, Samuel, do you have any idea just how close you are to having nothing?'

Leaving the solicitor's office Annie had turned her trap left along the bottom end of Lower High Street, guiding the horse left again into Finchpath Lane. This way she could avoid the wheels of the trap becoming caught in the tramlines. There was also less likelihood of her being seen by going back to the house via the heath. She flicked the reins, urging the horse into a trot. What the folk of Wednesbury didn't see they couldn't talk about, and she wanted no talk of what she had been about today.

Samuel had spoken of reverting his legacy to Phoebe, of

giving back what his sister's sacrifices had earned. How easily, she thought bitterly, how *easily* her brothers disposed of her life, ordering hers to the comfort of their own. Abel had enjoyed that comfort, enjoyed the pleasures of his pretty wife, and now Samuel wanted the comfort of a conscience cleared of taking Phoebe's inheritance and his sister was to have no part in that decision. But she would not let it happen again; she had been given a second chance at living, a chance to have all Abel had had in every sense of the word, and this time she would not let it go. Tomorrow she would have the money from the sale of the mines and the next day she would give it to Clinton.

She clicked her tongue, encouraging the horse, seeing the figure of Clinton Harforth-Darby in her mind. In his mid-forties, he was a handsome man, tall, always well dressed, his dark hair just hinting at grey, with clear intense eyes and a manner only real breeding bestowed. Calling to see Violet Wheeler at Oakeswell Hall she had first been introduced to Gaskell's cousin, and the next afternoon he had come to Brunswick House.

The reins forgotten in her hands, she let her mind play over the events of the past weeks, events that had led her to the threshold of a new life. With the death of his wife a year ago Clinton had sold his sugar plantation in the West Indies to return to England. Interested in the manufacture of the new metal tubes, he had come to Wednesbury to discuss with Gaskell the possibility of starting up a business. That was when he and Annie had met. From that moment she had, for the first time in twenty years, been treated like a woman and not a servile catspaw. Clinton was not like her father had been, nor Abel, treating women as though they didn't have the capacity to understand anything beyond the kitchen. He had talked to her about going into the manufacture of tubes, how he saw the business expanding over the years; he had told her how Gaskell had wanted to be a partner in the venture but Clinton had refused him. He had more than enough money to finance any business, he said. He did not want a partner, what he wanted was *her*.

Annie's heart gave the same crazy bounce it had when Clinton had said those words two weeks ago. He wanted to marry her, to make her his wife. She, Annie Pardoe, would become Mrs Clinton Harforth-Darby, *she* would marry into the Wheeler family not Phoebe, and she would take the Pardoe money with her. Clinton had brushed it aside when she had told him that Samuel owned everything. It was of no consequence, he had said, he wanted her for his wife not the paltry amount her brother might have bequeathed. However, if it interested her, she could go on being the legal representative for Samuel. It was then he had given her the ring, placing it on the third finger of her left hand, a square-cut amethyst the size of her thumbnail.

It was kept in a drawer in her bedroom. Annie thought now of the lovely ring hidden beneath layers of petticoats, the same petticoats that covered the perfume bottle that had been Elias Webb's gift to her. Clinton would announce their engagement at the Wheelers' house during the party they were giving before their son's regiment left for India. Until then she would not wear it, and by then everything that had once been Abel's would be hers.

They had often talked of the new premises he would build for the making of metal tubes during Clinton's visits, her interest seeming to fire his own as she suggested sites in or near the town, pointing out their nearness to the canal that would be needed to transport the tubes. That was when Clinton had said she would have made an ideal partner for his business except she was to be his wife, refusing to entertain the idea she could be both; it had taken her some time to get him to agree, Clinton eventually suggesting she become a steel tube manufacturer in her own right; the premises, the machinery, the raw steel, everything in her name. Only that way would he be happy.

And now the coal mines, the mainstay of all that had

once constituted Abel's wealth and then Samuel's were gone. Tomorrow she would have the money that would start her in her own business and the beginning of a new life.

'I was pleased to hear Sophie's news.' Phoebe glanced at Edward walking beside her. 'She was so excited when she called on Thursday.'

'Her coming engagement to Montrose Wheeler, you mean?' He stopped, picking up a stone and skimming it into the canal. 'I wish I could feel as happy for her.'

'But you don't?' Phoebe knew she was stating the obvious.

'No.' He sent a second stone winging after the first. 'The Wheelers are simply intent on making a good match, just as they were with . . .' He stopped awkwardly. 'I . . . I beg your pardon, Phoebe.'

'Just as they were with Abel Pardoe's daughter?' She smiled. 'You don't need to apologise for telling the truth, Edward.'

'You knew!' He turned to her, surprise lifting his fair eyebrows. 'You knew they wanted you for your father's money rather than for . . . for . . .'

'For myself?' She gazed at the circles spreading on the surface where the stones had struck the water. 'No, not at the time. I only realised that when his mother told me she had written to tell him of my Uncle Samuel's inheriting everything that was my father's, and he did nothing . . . he never even wrote to me to tell me he no longer wished to marry me.'

'He left that to his mother also?'

She nodded. 'It was a shock then but at least I have been saved from a marriage that could have brought me no real love, and I am grateful for that.'

'But what will save Sophie?' He kicked a boot savagely into the spongy earth. 'Her dowry will not be signed away to an uncle, she will be handed over like so much coal or wheat, she and all she has will become the property of Montrose Wheeler – and it will be God help her after that.'

'Does your mother know how you feel about Sophie's marrying Montrose?'

'My mother thinks that it is a good match. I truly believe she is of the opinion that love grows only after marriage.'

'And Sophie . . .' Phoebe watched the circles spread into nothing. 'Have you said anything of your feelings to her?'

'No, how could I when she is so happy? I can't tell her, Phoebe, I can't be the one to hurt her.'

Far better the bubble be burst now, Phoebe thought, than let it carry her to the moon only to break there.

'What of your father?' she asked. 'Have you confided in him?'

Edward plucked a blade of grass, twisting it between his fingers. 'I have said nothing to him but I think he knows I feel such a marriage would be wrong, and that like myself he would rather Sophie widened her social circle, met other young men before making her choice. But like myself Father could never bring himself to hurt her.'

'So Sophie will marry regardless of how you and Sir William feel?'

'Maybe not.' He rolled the blade of grass between his fingers then flicked it out over the water. 'My father has no wish to see Sophie hurt and that is why he has set the date for her betrothal to Wheeler to take place when we return from Europe, which puts it several months into next year. At least that way he is giving her a little time to find out if her emotion is love or not. And who knows? She may meet someone she would rather marry than Gaskell Wheeler's son . . . anyway that is what I hope, and I think it is my father's hope too.'

And mine, thought Phoebe, no trace of jealousy colouring it. No girl should marry a man only to discover his passion was for her money. She had been saved from that. Pray God Sophie would be too.

Returning the wave of a small girl on a passing barge, Phoebe turned from the peaceful lure of the water. Sophie's visits once a fortnight were not so disruptive to her work but Edward had begun to call at Wiggins Mill weekly and sometimes more than that. She had to find a way of telling him she could not spend a couple of afternoons a week out walking with him. 'I really must return, Edward,' she began. 'I ought not to be here, it's not fair on Lucy and Mathew.'

'How do you mean, not fair?'

'Surely you must see it is not right for me to be out walking when both of them are at work? I should be working too. I have a living to make as they do.'

'There's no need for any of this,' he waved a hand in the direction of the mill, 'you should not have to work for your living.'

'Then how would I manage?' Phoebe's laugh held more irony than humour. 'People need money to live, Edward, and it does not grow on trees.'

'You would not need money,' he caught her hand, his blue eyes intense, 'not if you became my wife. I love you, Phoebe. I have since that moment I helped you into the carriage the day you came to the Priory to collect those dresses. Marry me . . . say you will be my wife?'

What would that hold for both of them? Phoebe looked into his face, so like his mother's, and knew the answer. Sir William Dartmouth's son and heir married to a woman who had been in prison . . . what gossip that would provide! What houses would receive them merely to see his gaolbird wife, only to ignore them politely from then on. She knew Edward would argue his love was strong enough to withstand the attitudes of others, but would it be? Yes, he loved her now, she had seen it in his eyes each time they met, but was it real or just the misguided infatuation of a young man attempting to right a wrong he had caused, and would a year from now see him regretting such a marriage?

Gently she released her hands. She could not take that risk. She had too much respect for his parents, Edward carried too old a family line, too ancient a name, to have anything threaten it. And marriage to her, a woman accused and convicted of theft, however wrongly, would do him no good in the eyes of society.

'I won't marry you, Edward,' she said softly. 'I will not marry anyone yet.' She smiled up at him. 'Perhaps in a year or so, providing you feel as you do now, you will ask me again.' She turned away, the cloud of disappointment on his face hurting her too. Trying hard to sound matter-of-fact, hoping that way to lighten any embarrassment her refusal of his offer might have caused him, she went on, 'In the meantime, whether we like it or not, I have work to do.'

'Phoebe,' he said as she would have walked on, 'is there anyone else?'

'No, Edward,' she replied, the truth of it shining from her eyes, 'there is no one else.'

'Eeh, what a to do in the town today!' Lucy dropped into a chair as Phoebe dished up the evening meal she had prepared. 'You know Charles West, the jeweller in the High Street . . . well, 'e was robbed the night afore.'

'Robbed!' Phoebe stopped filling Mathew's bowl with the soup she had simmered all day. 'Who did it?'

'Nobody knows,' Mathew answered. 'It 'appened durin' the night by what I 'eard.'

'Heavens!' Phoebe finished filling his bowl then ladled soup into her own. 'Was anyone hurt?'

Mathew took a chunk of crusty bread, dipping it into his soup. 'No,' he said between bites, 'nobody 'eard anythin', not a sound. Charlie West never knowed it 'ad 'appened till he went for 'is cash this mornin'.'

'But the money from the shop,' Phoebe looked up from her meal, 'surely he doesn't leave the takings in the shop overnight?'

'No, 'e don't,' Mathew helped himself to more bread, 'an' 'e don't put it in no bank neither. Seems whoever broke into 'is 'ouse last night knowed that, 'cos money was all was took.'

'Were the police called?' Phoebe asked.

Lucy nodded but it was Mathew answered. 'Ar, they was called but them bobbies don't seem to know whether they be comin' or whether they've been. It seems Charlie West wasn't the only one to get 'is pocket lightened last night. Hollingsworth the pork butcher, 'e was 'ad, an' so was Samuel Platt the iron founder up on King's Hill.'

'All on the same night? No wonder the police were at their wit's end. I don't remember anything like this ever happening in Wednesbury before.'

'I don't either.' Lucy spooned her soup. 'Me mam says nothin' like it '*as* ever 'appened, least not as long as 'er's been alive.'

'Which is from the time of Adam, ain't it?'

'Watch it, Mathew Leach!' Lucy waved her spoon at her husband. 'You ain't so big 'er can't tan your arse.'

'Now *that* we would have to watch.' Phoebe joined in their laughter.

'Do you think it could be somebody local? The burglar, I means,' Lucy said finishing her soup.

'Won't know that till 'e be found.' Mathew cut a wedge of cheese from the block Phoebe placed on the table. 'An' Lord only knows if that'll ever 'appen. 'E could be miles away by now.'

Her sweet tooth preferring a sultana scone instead of cheese, Lucy spread it with the dark red damson jam Mathew's mother had sent from last summer's bottling. ''E could be,' she agreed, sinking her teeth into the scone, 'or 'e be down a disused mine shaft like that murderer we 'ad some years back. You know, 'e killed that woman Mary . . . Mary summat or other.'

'Mary Carter?' Mathew placed his cheese between two slices of bread, pressing the whole together with the heel of his hand. 'Bad business was that by what I've 'eard me mam an' dad say.'

'Any murder is a bad business.' Lucy popped the last of her scone into her mouth.

'Ar, that's right an' it ain't wrong, but that particular murder ended more'n one life, so it seemed, an' there was folks in Wednesbury was party to it 'appenin'. Me dad reckons there was no nicer bloke you would wish to meet than Joseph Bradly.'

'My father never spoke of a murder taking place in Wednesbury,' Phoebe said. 'At least, I never heard him speak of one. What happened?'

'Sit you down, Miss.' Lucy bustled up from the table. 'I'll get the teapot.'

Taking his cue, Mathew stayed silent but as the tea was poured Phoebe asked again.

'You don't want to be 'earin' about no murder, Miss Phoebe.' Lucy set the teapot firmly on the table. 'Anyway it all 'appened long ago.'

'Then my knowing can't hurt anyone,' Phoebe replied gently, realising Lucy wanted to protect her from anything she might find painful. 'Really, Mathew, I would like to know. There seems to be such a lot to this town I never knew of before.'

'If yer sure . . .' Mathew glanced at Lucy who lifted her shoulders resignedly. 'Joseph Bradly lived up along Church Hill, right against the old church. 'Is wife 'ad died while their daughter Anna was no more'n a babby an' Mary Carter used to go up to the 'ouse every day to do for 'em like. Well, 'er went missin' an' when 'er was found drownded in Millfields Pool folk said as 'ow Jos Bradly was one who done it; seems they kept on sayin' it till the poor bugger 'ad more'n 'e could stand.'

'What did he do?'

Mathew looked across the table at Phoebe then away to his mug of tea, his tongue stilled by sudden embarrassment.

'What did Joseph Bradly do, Mathew?'

''E . . . 'e got pie-eyed,' Mathew stared resolutely into the mug, 'too drunk to know what the 'ell 'e was about, then 'e . . . 'e went 'ome an' raped 'is own daughter.' The last came out in a rush. If he didn't say it quickly, he wouldn't say it at all.

'What a dreadful thing to happen!' Phoebe breathed.

'Ar,' Mathew nodded, ''er couldn't 'ave been more'n sixteen or seventeen accordin' to what was said. Left Wednesbury 'er did, left a babby . . . a lad, Aaron 'e was called . . . don't know what 'appened to 'er after that.'

'And her father, did he stay in Wednesbury?' Phoebe stirred milk into her own tea.

'Me mam said 'e couldn't do no other, not wi' a babby.'

''E could've put it into the workhouse,' Lucy joined the conversation.

'Me mam said that an' all.' Mathew leaned back, his meal finished. 'But me dad said 'e was too fine a bloke to leave a babby in the workhouse, no matter 'ow it was got.'

'Was anything ever proved?'

'Seems years after a bloke was brought up from a shaft 'e 'ad dropped into, and 'e said it was 'im killed Mary Carter.'

'So Joseph Bradly was cleared of suspicion of murder?'

'Cleared of suspicion by law but not by folk of Wednesbury,' Lucy said, collecting dishes into a pile. 'They 'ad got their claws into 'im an' wouldn't let go. Me mam said the same old tales kept flyin' around.'

'Did his daughter return?' Phoebe helped with clearing the table.

Lucy glanced at Mathew. 'Ar, 'er returned,' he said. 'At least Mam says 'er did, but only after 'er father 'ung 'isself.'

'Oh, how awful!' Phoebe looked from one to the other. 'What an awful thing to happen to a family.'

'Ar.' Mathew rose from the table, preparing to go to the workshop he had fashioned from one of the smaller outbuildings. 'First murder an' now these burglaries, there be some right crackpotical things goes on in Wednesbury.'

Burglaries! Phoebe helped carry the dishes to the scullery for washing. She had almost forgotten them. Thank God for the locks Bert Ingles had given her!

* * *

Samuel was sleeping. Annie had given him the draught Alfred Dingley had prescribed against wakeful nights, doubling the dose he had recommended. She wanted no interruptions. Everything had gone smoothly; her prices for both mines had been accepted, as she'd known they would be, and the cash for them paid without question. Siveter had wanted to ask questions, she knew, but had thought better of it; there wasn't much of Samuel's inheritance left for him to have the legal handling of, but words from her could still harm the lawyer's reputation and he would not risk that.

Reaching a box from beneath the fourposter bed Annie opened it, setting the contents in neat white piles on the counterpane. The last of everything of value apart from this house and the one at Bescot was gone, everything that had once been Abel's was sold and the money for it lay staring up at her. 'Everything!' Annie scooped the money together, the wads of notes thick in her hands. 'Everything you had, Abel.' She laughed low in her throat. 'Everything you ever owned is here in my hands, and tomorrow it will buy back my life.'

Leaving the money scattering the bed like a sudden snowstorm, she crossed the bedroom to the chest of drawers. Opening the bottom one, she took out the amethyst ring. Soon it would be on her finger for all to see, soon the whole town would know she was to be Clinton's wife. Carefully she replaced it, her fingers touching the perfume bottle, almost stroking it, before drawing one of the silk petticoats from its blue tissue paper.

Closing the drawer, she dropped the petticoat on the bed, watching several banknotes rise in the draught of air as it landed then settled back on the silk. That would be her life from now on, surrounded in money, covered in money . . . Abel's money.

Unbuttoning her black grosgrain town dress she stepped out of it. Throwing it across a chair, she slipped off her heavy cotton petticoat. She would not wear black for Clinton's coming . . . she would never wear black again.

Sliding the silk over her head, Annie let it down over her hips, her hands caressing the soft luxury of it. No, she wouldn't wear black again nor cotton either. Clinton would see her in nothing but silks and satins. Going to the wardrobe, she took out the lavender dress. She would wear it for his coming this afternoon.

The last of the tiny self-covered buttons fastened, she took a lavender fichu from her bag. She had bought it from Fosbrook's in Union Street before going to the solicitor's. Setting it on her head, she secured it with hairpins then stood looking at her reflection in the full-length cheval mirror. Stylish the dress might be but it did not give her back her youth, it could not remove the lines that bordered her mouth nor return the bloom to her skin.

Why was Clinton marrying her? She asked herself the question she knew others would ask. It wasn't for her looks. Annie touched a hand to her face. She had never been blessed with them; what there had been in the way of looks had been given to Abel and Samuel, not that they had done Samuel a lot of good. She turned away from the mirror. He had not fared much better with his life than she had with her own.

Annie gathered the banknotes, putting them neatly into the box and closing it. Looks and life, fate had denied her both, and Samuel had ideas of taking the latter away again, of returning everything to Phoebe. 'But you are too late,' she breathed, picking up the box. 'Just as it's too late for Abel's daughter.'

Phoebe put down her sewing, touching her aching back. [illegible]

Chapter Thirteen

Phoebe put down her sewing, stretching her aching back, listening to the quietness of the old mill house. Handsworth Prison had been quiet, every voice hushed to whispers save those of the wardresses, but it had been a harsh jarring quiet that left the brain reeling from its unsung staccato melody. Here it was gentle, its touch lenient to the mind, settling courteously over mill and heath. Here the quiet soothed and healed.

It wanted over an hour before Mathew and Lucy returned from their day's work, the meal was simmering in the oven, she had time for a walk. Running downstairs, cheating herself of time to change her mind, she slipped out of the back door, securing the lock Bert had fitted before slipping the brass key into the pocket of her brown dress.

Refusing to let her eyes linger on the brooding pile of the corn barn she turned in the direction of the canal. It would be pleasant there with the barges passing on the way to the ports Mark Ingles dreamed of.

Coming up out of the hollow that sheltered the mill house she looked toward the ribbon of water. There was no passing barge, only a finger of smoke spiralling toward the sky, the air too lazy to spread it. Shading her eyes from the remains of the sun, she stared. It had been an extra warm day but by no means hot enough to set the heath ablaze, so how come the smoke?

''Ow do, Miss?' The shout accompanied by a wave brought a smile to Phoebe's face and she walked on to where the

Ingleses sat grouped about a small fire above the towpath.

'I didn't know you were back.'

'Got back yesterday.' Bert took the shawl his wife handed to him, spreading it on the grass and gesturing Phoebe to sit down. 'Fetched a load of timber up from London way an' dropped it off at Moxley, shoring for the coalmine there.'

'But the barge,' Phoebe glanced to the empty waterway then back to Bert, 'where is it? You don't usually leave it while it's being reloaded.'

'Ain't no barge, Miss,' Lizzie said, staring at the fire trying its best to boil the kettle of water balanced over it, 'an' there ain't no load – least not for we there ain't.'

'No barge? I don't understand . . . what has happened to it?'

'Nothing 'as 'appened to the barge,' Bert poked the fire with a stick, 'barge is loaded an' off.'

'Mr Ingles,' Phoebe looked from one to the other, 'Lizzie, will you tell me what has happened, if not to the barge then to you . . . why are the four of you sitting here?'

'We come up yesterday . . . early on . . . wi' a load of timber for Moxley like Bert said,' Lizzie answered. 'We was expectin' to load coals for London like we usually does only the gaffer at the mine, 'e said there was no load for we an' that we was to get our things off the barge right away. There was already another bargee wantin' to take 'er off up to London.'

'But I thought the barge was yours . . . your home?'

'Our 'ome, yes,' Bert turned away, his face to the canal, 'but not our property. Now the owner 'as done a deal wi' new mine gaffer to put only 'is men on the barges.'

'New?' Phoebe looked at the man, his back still toward her. 'Do you mean Moxley mine has a new manager?'

'Not only a new manager.' Bert kicked out, sending a shower of grit from the path, spraying into the water. 'A new owner, an' that new owner 'as no place for Bert Ingles.'

The mine was sold! Phoebe sat back on her heels. Uncle Samuel had sold Moxley mine, and what of Hobs Hill? Was that also sold, was Joseph Leach too out of a job and a home?

'We would 'ave been further along but totin' our stuff as well as Bert's tools 'as slowed we more than we thought,' Lizzie said. ''Sides the walkin' is a bit tough on the little 'un. The lad 'e can manage it but the babby . . . 'er just ain't used to it.'

'Further on to where?' Phoebe asked, watching the boy go to stand beside his father. 'Where will you go? Where will you live?'

Lizzie glanced at her husband, his shoulders slumped forward. 'It ain't too bad, sleepin' out is quite pleasant, an' anyway Bert will find work soon.'

She smiled but behind the expression Phoebe read a different story. Sleeping out? They had slept out last night, and would again for how many nights? And what about food? No job meant no money and that in turn no food. She looked at the tiny girl huddled against her mother's skirts. How in God's name could people behave in such a way as to throw a man and his family out of their home? What sort of man was it who had bought her father's mine?

'Mr Ingles,' she got to her feet, 'why not stay here for a few days, give yourself a chance to try for work in Wednesbury? There must be something there.'

'An' if there ain't?'

'Then you have gained a few nights' rest and lost nothing.' She picked up the shawl, shaking it free of dried grass and handing it to Lizzie.

'I could go wi' you, Dad, mebbe we could both find work.'

Bert dropped a hand to his son's shoulder but remained gazing into the green depths of the canal.

'Best we stop alongside o' the cut, Miss,' he said. 'That way I can keep in touch, ask if barges 'ave 'eard of work to be 'ad in other parts. News travels fast along the cut.'

'A couple o' days wouldn't make no odds, Bert,' Lizzie

said gently. 'You need not traipse into the town, you could come down 'ere 'an wait o' the barges passin', but the little un . . . 'er could do wi' a few nights restin' in one place.'

'The barn is dry and there are plenty of corn sacks in the loft,' Phoebe said. 'It isn't much, I know, but you would be more comfortable than sleeping beside the canal.'

'Thank you, Miss.' Bert's gratitude was plain to see. 'We be grateful for your kindness. A few days an' then we'll be off . . . the Ingleses will be a nuisance to none.'

'I'm all for 'elpin' folk but four more mouths to feed . . . eeh, Miss Phoebe, 'ow we goin' to manage that?'

'It will be difficult, I know, but the clothes I have made sold well . . . I have the money from those.'

'True,' Lucy heaped flour into a bowl, 'but it won't last long spread over four of 'em.'

'I couldn't let them go any further, Lucy, that little girl of theirs looks far from well.'

'I noticed.' She rubbed fat into the flour. 'It can't be 'ealthy on them barges, all cooped up like rabbits in a hutch, an' the damp . . . it's a wonder they ain't all sprouted fins.'

'So can we manage?'

'Reckon so,' Lucy answered, 'but not for long.'

Phoebe began the ritual of greasing pie tins. 'We won't have to for long.'

Lucy looked up from rolling pastry. 'It won't be no easier, Miss Phoebe, watchin' 'em go, I mean, whether they be 'ere a short span or a longer.'

Phoebe took each circle of pastry as Lucy pressed it out, positioning it in its tin. 'Maybe they won't need to go.'

'Look,' Lucy stopped cutting circles, her eyes on Phoebe filling pastry cases with meat and potato, 'I wouldn't bank on Bert Ingles findin' work in Wednesbury. Joseph told Mathew that there might be quite a few men lookin' for jobs, wi' Moxley mine changin' 'ands.'

'Who has bought it?' Phoebe put the heavy pan of meat and potato in the hearth, covering it with a cloth.

Lucy reached for the smaller dish with which to cut pastry lids. 'Joseph couldn't say. Told Mathew nobody 'ad wind of the buyer, not yet. Let's just 'ope that whoever it is keeps 'em workin' . . . like Joseph says, there might be a few others lookin' for work in Wednesbury so don't go ratin' Bert Ingles's chances too 'igh.'

Waiting while Lucy placed the lids on the pies, Phoebe dipped her fingers in milk, spreading each with a thin film of moisture. 'Maybe he won't need to go to the town for work.'

Lucy refilled the bowl with flour, a fine white cloud mushrooming up to settle along her brows and lashes. 'What do you mean?' she asked. 'What you thinkin'?'

Phoebe turned from stocking the oven, her cheeks red from the fire. 'Locks,' she said simply, 'I'm thinking of locks.'

'I ain't with you, Miss.'

'I have been thinking a lot about those burglaries in the town.' Phoebe came to stand beside the table.

'Me an' all. They worry me they do. Who knows where 'e might strike next? Makes you scared to go to bed nights.'

'Well, if they worry us here . . .' Phoebe glanced around the kitchen with its worn chairs and mongrel assortment of second hand pots and dishes '. . . imagine how worried some folk in the town must be.'

Lucy began to make her second batch of pastry. 'Ar, there be plenty like we. An' if *they* be frightened, 'ow must all the nobs be feelin'?'

'Exactly! How must they be feeling . . . mine owners, iron and steel founders, brewers, grocers, tavern keepers? Think of it, Lucy, the list is endless and Wednesbury has plenty of them as well as plenty like us. All these people have something to lose, and all of them, rich or not so rich, would pay to make their home secure, don't you agree?'

''Course I do, but I still ain't wi' you.'

'People will pay for security.' Phoebe covered the batch of pies waiting their turn in the oven. 'We can give them that security.'

'We!' Lucy exclaimed. ''Ow?'

'Wait.' Phoebe wiped her hands on the white huckaback cloth kept 'specially for the baking then went out through the scullery, running across the yard to the barn where Mathew was helping the Ingleses settle in.

'Mr Ingles.'

Lizzie Ingles looked up from covering a heap of straw with her shawl, her face clouding with disappointment as she saw Phoebe standing in the doorway,cheeks red and arms crossed over her breasts.

'It's all right, Miss.' She picked up the shawl and began to fold it, the children watching from a corner. 'We understand, you can't let we stop 'ere after all. Just give we a minute to get we things an' we'll be gone.'

'I did not come to ask you to leave, Lizzie, I said you could stay here and you can. I . . . I only wish it were more like a home.'

'It could be.' Lizzie looked around the barn, at the rusting implements and unused flour sacks. 'If only . . .'

'If you ain't askin' we to go then what was you wantin' to ask, Miss?'

Phoebe smiled at the children, each sitting on a broken quern, then looked to where Bert stood watching her. 'Mr Ingles . . . Lizzie, would you come to the house, please? And you too, Mathew, I have something I wish to discuss with the three of you.'

'You two mind what you be about,' Lizzie pushed to her feet as she spoke to her children, 'no messin' wi' anything an' no larkin' around. You can finish makin' up this bed for the pair o' you.'

In the kitchen Lucy had finished her evening baking, the bowls and basins already stacked against the scullery sink and the brown earthenware teapot filled and waiting.

'What be all this about, Miss?' Bert asked as Phoebe reached cups from the dresser.

'It's about your locks, Mr Ingles.'

'Locks?'

'Locks, the ones you made for me.'

'They ain't broke, am they?'

'No, they are not broken,' Phoebe said, 'they work very well. I was wondering if you could make more?'

'I could,' he looked puzzled, 'but for what reason? Beggin' your pardon, you 'ave the doors to the 'ouse secured an' them barns don't 'old nought save a few old tools. An' if it's Mathew's place you was thinkin' of I already 'as a lock made for 'im, made it on me last trip to London. We intended leavin' it on your doorstep afore we moved on from the cut.'

'Thanks, Bert, that's good o' you,' Mathew said. 'I knows missis was worried about 'er bits an' pieces, we bein' out all day.'

'I wasn't wanting locks for myself . . . well, not for my own use.' Phoebe passed round the tea. 'The point is, do you think you could make . . . say a dozen . . . of the same sort as you fixed to my doors?'

'A dozen!' Bert set his mug on the table. 'That's a few locks, Miss.'

'Could you make them?' She asked, emphasising her words.

'Reckon I could,' he mused, 'I 'ave me patterns an' me files. I brought them wi' me.'

'What else would you need?' Phoebe caught the look of enquiry that flashed from Mathew to Lucy and the shrug of the shoulders she returned.

Bert pursed his lips. 'Brass or steel . . . place to work . . . a fire . . . a anvil . . . then you could manage.'

'How long would it take to make them?'

'Depends.' Bert thought for several moments. 'A week, p'raps, depends on 'ow much time you 'ave to give to the work.'

'If you had nothing else to do,' Phoebe asked, 'could you make a dozen locks in one week?'

'Ar,' he nodded, 'supposin' I 'ad a week.'

'Mathew,' Phoebe turned her attention to Lucy's husband, 'where could we get the metal Mr Ingles would need?'

'Bagnall's,' Mathew answered, his tone revealing the puzzlement this conversation was causing him. 'Bagnall's in Dudley Street will 'ave what 'e needs. I could tek 'im in wi' me an' Lucy tomorrow . . .'

'That be easy to say,' Bert interrupted, 'but money be needed to buy metals an' I've got precious little o' that.'

'Don't worry about money, Mr Ingles . . .'

'That's all right for you to say, Miss,' Lizzie put in, the same cloud of anxiety that Phoebe had seen in the barn settling over her eyes, 'but we 'ave the kids to feed an' no prospect of work to fetch more money in. I don't want to sound ungrateful, God forbid, but what bit o' money we got can't go bein' spent on makin' locks.'

'I think you have every prospect of work, Lizzie,' Phoebe smiled, 'or at least your husband has.'

Standing behind his wife's chair, Bert dropped a hand to her shoulder. 'What do you mean, Miss, I 'ave the prospect o' work?'

Phoebe looked at each of the people grouped in her small kitchen. 'I have a proposition to make, a proposition that will involve all of us. I will provide the necessary materials for the making of a dozen double barrel locks and a place for Mr Ingles to work. Food and keep for himself and his family will be his wage for the time it takes. For your part, Mathew, if you are willing, I would like you to show the lock to as many shopkeepers and tradesmen as you can. Given the recent robberies I don't think they will take much persuading to buy one, and the fitting of them could provide you with extra work.' She paused then. 'So both of you, what do you say, will you give it a try?'

'I'm game.' Mathew grinned.

'And what about you, Mr Ingles?' Phoebe smiled at the man who looked as though he had been kissed with a pole axe. 'Are you game?'

'A week off the road . . . food for the kids?' Bert grinned. 'Game? I'll say I'm bloody game . . . thanks, Miss, thanks for everythin'. I . . . I'll make you the best bloody locks ever to come out of Willenhall!'

Phoebe held out a hand. 'Then we are in business, Mr Ingles, and if things go as I hope, we will discuss a more usual wage for your labour.' She smiled at Lizzie. 'All, of course, provided your wife agrees to your settling here?'

'Oh, I agree, Miss.' Lizzie laid a hand over the one resting on her shoulder. 'An' my Bert will make you the best locks you ever seen.'

'You said your proposition included all o' we?' Lucy spoke for the first time since the Ingleses had entered the kitchen. 'So where be my part in all o' this?'

'You have the most important part.' Phoebe threw an arm around her one-time maid. 'Even the strongest of men can't work without food. We need your cooking to pay Mr Ingles's wages. What I have to ask you, Mrs Leach, is this . . . are you up to it?'

Picking up a pie warm from the oven, Lucy passed it to Bert. 'Here,' she laughed, 'you tell me, Bert . . . am I up to it?'

'Didn't you hear anything . . . anything at all?'

Maudie Tranter looked at the woman she had worked twelve years for, twelve years and not one good word in all of them. Annie Pardoe was a woman twisted with jealousy and spite, a woman who deserved all she got and more. And more she would get, Maudie could feel it in her bones.

'No, Miss Pardoe,' she said, her feelings well hidden. 'I slept all through the night, never 'eard nothing.'

Annie glanced around the dishevelled room, the mantelpiece relieved of its silver candlesticks and silver framed miniatures of her mother and father, and the desk littered with papers snatched from their drawers, strewn like white confetti over the carpet.

'You am a light sleeper, Miss, didn't you 'ear nothin' neither?'

Annie looked sharply at her thin angular housekeeper, standing with hands clasped together over a white apron that reached to the hem of her black skirts, unsure whether the woman's voice held a note of sarcasm.

'No, I did not!' she snapped. 'Mr Samuel has slept badly for several nights and I have stayed up with him. Last night I took a draught in order to get some sleep myself.'

''Course, Mr Samuel wouldn't 'ear anything, not the way 'e is.'

'Precisely.' Annie glanced once more at the room, just this one, the one with the desk and little else of interest or value apart from the few bits of silver. No other room had been disturbed, so what was the thief looking for? Whatever it was he'd expected to find it in the desk and had almost torn it apart in the search. 'Whoever it was must have come in through there.' She pointed to a door still open on to the garden. 'The Leathern Bottle gives right on to this property. He was probably drinking in there all night. I knew we should have had that dividing wall heightened.' She crossed the room, slamming the door shut. 'Go at once and bring the constables.'

Much good they'll do, Maudie thought, returning to the scullery and reaching her cloak from the cupboard. Whoever had been rummaging in that desk I doubt the bobbies will find him. That lot ain't sharp enough to catch a cold!

In the room Abel had used as a study Annie gathered up the strewn papers. Bills of sale for property that had once been Abel's but none that pointed to what had become of the proceeds of those sales. There had not been time yet for her to receive the title deeds for her tube works but, thank God, she had already given the money to Clinton.

'Sergeant down the station says as constables be out,'

Maudie said an hour later. She would have liked to take the time to call on Sarah but commonsense had warned against it. Annie Pardoe could time a walk to the police station and back almost to the minute; she would know for certain if there had been any gossiping on the way.

'Out!' Annie glared at the impudence of the man. 'What did he mean, the constables were out?'

''E meant they wasn't in,' Maudie enjoyed replying.

This time Annie was sure of the sarcasm. 'As you will be out of a position if you try your lip on me, Maudie Tranter,' she said, anger barely held in check. 'Now, if you don't want to go from this house a sight quicker than you came into it, you will tell me exactly what that fool at the station told you.'

I know what I'd like to tell you, you bad-tempered old cow, and one day, with God's help or the Devil's, I will! Maudie's thoughts gave her little consolation and she answered sullenly. ''E said as constables were out 'vestigatin' a break in up at Julia Hanson's place an' across at William Purchase, top end o' Chapel Street; said 'e would send 'em along 'ere when they reported back to the station, but 'e couldn't say 'ow long that was like to be.'

Julia Hanson and William Purchase, Annie mused as her housekeeper left the room, one a brewer, the other a grocer and general dealer, both likely to have money and like as not that money kept in the house. But what was the motive for breaking into Brunswick House? Unless . . . she touched a hand to the papers she had sorted ready to replace in relevant drawers of the desk. Unless someone knew of the cash she had got from James Siveter. She made her way to Samuel's room. And if they did, who but James Siveter could have told them?

'No, there has been no damage,' she signed in answer to her brother's question. 'Some papers scattered about the desk and the silver taken from the study. I have informed the constables. They will be here later.'

'Later?' Samuel's question flicked from his fingers.

'Two more houses were robbed last night,' Annie answered, 'Julia Hanson's and William Purchase's.'

'A brewer and a general dealer.' Samuel's fingers moved with the transient fluidity of a mayfly. 'Our burglar chooses his victims well, though why us?'

Annie shrugged. 'Who knows?' she replied her own fingers having none of the grace of movement her brother's held. 'Perhaps he thought to find money here. Thank heaven we keep little but petty cash, enough for small unforeseen events, no more.'

'This event was certainly unforeseen but nothing was taken that cannot be replaced – except, of course, for the miniatures of our parents and there is the possibility they will be returned.'

'We can always hope, but I do have my doubts.'

'No one was harmed, that is truly all that matters.'

All that mattered! Annie turned away, unable to disguise the contempt she knew must show in her face. How like Samuel to adopt that attitude . . . how typical of the weakness and ineffectuality he had shown all his life, the incapacity born of relying first upon their mother to attend to all then transferring that reliance to herself. And what of that reliance once she was married? And what of the condition that had kept Samuel confined to one house or the other for the greater part of his life? How would Clinton accept that? Would he accept it or would he . . . ?

'I must prepare for the constables' arrival,' she signed, quickly leaving the room before Samuel could answer. Clinton would not have to accept, Clinton would never know; no more would she be her brother's keeper.

Chapter Fourteen

'Ar, sold 'em both.' Sarah Leach looked at the young woman seated at her table. The years since her father's death had left their mark but it was the mark of confidence, of a sureness in herself; that prison had taught her a valuable lesson and not one any Magistrate would have expected: it had taught her that even in 1900 a woman had to fight and fight hard for any sort of life of her own. Many would have gone under given what this one had been dealt, but Abel Pardoe's daughter had learned how to fight.

'For what reason?' Phoebe's question caused the older woman to shake her head in a slow rhythm. 'Were the coal seams running out?'

'Joseph says they be gettin' thinner, but they 'ave a few years left in 'em yet.'

'Then why?'

'God knows, ma wench, an' 'e ain't tellin'.' Sarah stirred the tea she had poured. 'Who can tell what they at Brunswick 'Ouse might do next?'

'I can't understand Uncle Samuel's actions . . . to sell the coal mines!'

Sarah went on stirring, the spoon rattling against the cup. 'Who's to say it be yer uncle doin' the sellin'? Maudie Tranter said that aunt o' your'n 'ad the legal power to sign in 'er brother's stead, an' the Lord knows 'er would do it, tek 'er spite out on any 'er can. There's a few poor buggers lost their livin' 'cos of Annie Pardoe.'

Such as Bert Ingles, Phoebe thought, though he was one

of the lucky ones. The locks he made were selling as fast as he could produce them, there need be no more tramping the country in search of work for him and Lizzie had the comfort of a permanent place to make a home . . . but there were others not so fortunate.

'Sarah!' She pulled back from her thoughts, sudden agitation in her voice. 'Joseph . . . he hasn't . . .'

'Been given 'is tin?' Sarah intervened. 'No, ma wench, 'e still 'as 'is job at Hobs Hill. Seems to be just cut people as 'as been laid off . . . eh, what will them wimmin an' their babbies 'ave to live on? Meks my 'eart bleed to think on 'em.'

'Then you think my aunt is the one who has sold the mines?'

Twisting in her chair, Sarah swung the kettle from the fire, stilling its shrill hiss of steam. 'Think o' it,' she said, turning back to face Phoebe. 'Like you said you can't imagine yer uncle actin' in such a way as to put men an' their families on the streets, an' neither can I. It's true nobody 'as seen much o' him but 'e were a caring soul, never a bad word for nobody an' wouldn't 'arm a fly. But the other 'un, that Annie, 'er was a bad bugger from the start. No . . . if it was me 'ad to say who was the back of all this then it would be 'er as I'd name.'

Phoebe fingered her cup, looking at the tea she had not touched. 'Do you think Uncle Samuel knows what is happening?'

'If 'e don't then you ain't the one to tell 'im,' Sarah said sharply. 'That woman 'as 'armed you enough wi'out you givin' 'er the opportunity to do more. 'Er turned you out o' yer father's 'ouse, not carin' twopence where you went, an' naught but two frocks an' two pairs o' bloomers to go in.' She could have added that she had suspicions it was her aunt who had got her sent down for fifteen years, but bit this back. 'Mark my words an' keep well away from 'er, that woman is poison.'

What Sarah had said was true, her aunt had turned her out with virtually nothing, so perhaps it was true she was the one who'd sold off the mines. Phoebe stared at her tea, now cold in the cup. If only she could speak to Uncle Samuel, but she knew there was little chance of getting past his sister.

'So 'ow is it wi' you?' Sarah took the cup from Phoebe, going into the scullery and tipping the contents into the slop pail standing beneath the shallow ironstone sink.

'I am well, Sarah.' Phoebe watched a second cup of tea being poured.

'No after effects?'

Phoebe took the cup, adding sugar and milk. She knew what lay behind the question, knew it referred to the attack that had been made upon her, and knew also it was asked out of genuine feeling for her welfare and not morbid curiosity. 'No,' she answered, 'no after effects, though I am glad Mathew and Lucy are at Wiggins Mill with me.'

'And not only them, I 'ear.'

'You mean the Ingleses.' Phoebe sipped her tea, more from politeness than thirst. 'They were one of the families laid off. It seems the new owners had their own bargees. Mr Ingles and his wife and children were on the road when I came across them, I'm only thankful I could help them.'

'Turned out well for both of you so our Mathew tells me, but tek care, ma wench, don't get in so deep as you can't get out. 'Elpin' others is all well an' good so long as you don't get drownded in your own pity.'

'I'll try not to.' Phoebe smiled. 'And you and Joseph are always there to give me advice.'

'As long as you don't get too uppity to ask for it.'

'Joseph won't allow that.' Phoebe's smile widened. 'He never would allow Abel Pardoe's little girl to get above herself, and to him I am still a little girl.'

'Ar, Joseph always 'ad a soft spot for you.' Her tea finished, Sarah set her cup to one side. 'An' to 'im you always will be naught but a babby, but I knows an' you knows babbies 'ave a way o' growin', an' you be growin' to a beauty.'

'Has Joseph said yet who bought the mines?' Phoebe reached into the bag she had brought with her, her cheeks pink from the older woman's compliment.

'Nobody really knows, though Billy-me-Lord's agents 'ave been nosin' around for the last few days.'

'Sir William Dartmouth bought them!' Phoebe straightened up, her embarrassment forgotten.

'Like I says, nobody 'as spoke of 'im but I think as the facts says it theirselves. I reckon Billy-me-Lord be the new owner of the Crown and the Hobs Hill mines.'

Phoebe held the paper she had taken from her bag, her hand resting on the table, worry in her eyes as she looked at Sarah. 'I hope he doesn't make any more changes,' she said, 'people in the town need their jobs.'

'That be right an' don't be wrong,' Sarah agreed, taking two pots of damson jam from a cupboard. 'Pity that aunt o' your'n didn't 'ave the same feelin'.'

'What will happen . . . to men who might be finished, I mean?'

Sarah hesitated, a pot in each hand. 'Be my guess as young 'uns . . . they wi' no family to keep . . . will move on, the others'll like to stand the line.'

'Stand the line?'

'Ar,' Sarah nodded again, the movement slow and deliberate, 'men wantin' work gathers in the market place every mornin' an' stands in line 'opin' that any with work to be done will choose them. Some gets lucky and some goes wi'out . . .'

'The ones who are not chosen,' Phoebe's words dropped into the pause, 'what happens to them?'

Sarah sighed heavily. 'Work'ouse like as not, poor buggers.'

'Oh, no!' Phoebe's eyes widened. 'There must be something else.'

'Ain't nothin' else.' Sarah put the pots on the table. 'If you don't work you don't eat, not in this town. It's the work'ouse or starve, there be no such thing as charity in Wednesbury . . . things be too 'ard for them wi' next to nothin', an' them as 'ave plenty keep it to theirselves. That's the way of it, ma wench, an' you heed what I've told you an' don't go thinkin' you can tek on every man as gets 'is tin. That business o' your'n is doin' well enough but you ain't your father, you ain't Abel Pardoe.'

'No, I'm not Abel Pardoe,' Phoebe said quietly, 'but I am Abel's daughter.'

Phoebe walked toward Upper High Street, the pots of jam alongside the papers in her bag. She didn't get to visit Sarah as often as she would have liked and Joseph would be disappointed she had not waited to see him but as she had explained she was still not up to walking home alone, crossing the heath in darkness. This way she would finish her business and walk home with Mathew and Lucy.

She thought again of Sarah's pleased expression when she had shown her the poster now rolled up in her bag and told her how every shopkeeper she'd asked had agreed to display one in their premises. 'The Invincible', it proclaimed in two-inch type, 'Pardoe's Patent Locks'. They would be seen by all who used the shops, and for those who didn't she was on her way to the office of the *Express and Star*, an advertisement in the newspaper would reach every businessman in the town.

'Good day, Miss Pardoe.'

Phoebe turned at the sound of her name. She glanced first at the figure in tall hat and dark knee-length coat, then at the building he was vacating, and couldn't quite repress a shudder. The Magistrate had sentenced her to fifteen years from that building. 'Good afternoon, Sir William,' she returned.

'It was my intention to call upon you later in the day.' He replaced the hat held raised as he spoke.

'Perhaps I can save you the bother of the journey.' Phoebe wanted to move on, move away from that building and the memories it evoked.

'It is no bother, Miss Pardoe.' Grey eyes that could so easily be black regarded her evenly.

'Nevertheless it is some distance and an uncalled for journey if I can help you here.'

'I wished to tell you the man who attacked you has been gaoled. But we can't talk here . . .' He glanced at the women, their heads draped in shawls, who'd turned to look in their direction as Phoebe caught her breath sharply, a hand touching her throat. 'My carriage is to the rear.'

Gaol! Phoebe tried to breathe past the lump filling her throat. She would not wish a gaol sentence on any man, but for what he had tried to do to her . . .

'May I drive you home? I will give you the details on the way.'

'Home? No . . .' The spectres of that man's attack and of Handsworth Women's Prison fused together in her mind. 'I . . . I am not going home.'

'Then maybe we can talk inside.'

'No!' Phoebe's cry as he indicated the Green Dragon Hotel drew fresh inquisitive stares. 'I . . . I'm sorry, Sir William,' she said, 'I have no wish ever to enter that place again.'

He glanced first at the hotel and then at her, realisation dawning. The Magistrates' Court. Of course, she must have been sentenced from here. 'My apologies,' he said, 'I had not thought.'

'It is of no consequence.' Phoebe looked up, not all traces of fear gone from her face. 'If you have finished what you had to say . . .'

'I have not finished.' William Dartmouth interrupted what he knew to be a dismissal. 'If you will not allow us to speak somewhere else then it will be said here on the street. It seems one of my wife's maids overheard Sophie and her mother discussing our meeting that morning at the Priory. She presumed I had given you money and said as much to a man she was walking out with. He in turn thought to take it from you. That man is now in custody and will be spending a very substantial part of his life behind bars.'

'And the maid?' Phoebe asked. 'Is she to be dismissed her position as Lucy was?'

'Lucy?' He drew his brows together enquiringly.

'Mrs Leach, the girl you questioned at Wiggins Mill.'

'Why did she not come to me sooner with what she knew of what had happened to the necklace? Why say nothing until I questioned her?'

'Because she was warned not to.'

'Warned not to?' He frowned. 'Just what exactly does that mean?'

Phoebe looked straight at him. 'It means,' she said, her voice calm and clear, 'that Lucy was warned that to involve Ed— your son – in the affair would prove disastrous for her. She tried telling Lawyer Siveter what she knew but he said you would see to it she came to regret bringing the Dartmouth name under suspicion, then she was dismissed your wife's services.'

'She was in service at the Priory?' he asked, then before Phoebe answered, added, 'I was unaware of that, it had not occurred to me. Perhaps you will be good enough to tell Mrs Leach she will be reinstated immediately.'

No apology, Phoebe thought, no word of regret for what had happened to Lucy, just a calm proposal of her reinstatement.

'Does it not occur to you that she may have no wish to return to your employment?' she asked coldly.

Sir William Dartmouth looked at the young woman, her eyes cool and steady, and found the admiration he had first felt at their earlier meetings re-kindling in him. Not many men would speak to him as she did: his title and his money made no impression upon her and certainly did not intimidate her.

'That must be her prerogative – if you will forgive the use of the word "must".' The faintest hint of a smile appeared at the corners of his mouth. 'I wish you good day Miss Pardoe.'

'You said that?' Lucy asked later when Phoebe told her of her encounter. 'You said that to Billy-me-Lord?'

'I did,' Phoebe smiled broadly. 'Naughty of me, wasn't it?'

'Naughty or no, I bet it took the wind out o' 'is sails.'

'He did look somewhat surprised,' Phoebe said, still smiling.

'What did 'e 'ave to say to that?'

Waiting while Lucy served a customer to the last of her scones, giving her change from a sixpenny piece, Phoebe answered, 'He said that must be your prerogative.'

'My what?' Lucy shook her head as a woman, shawl drawn tight about her shoulders, enquired after a meat pie. 'What on earth does that mean?'

'It means that yours must be the choice. You can return to work at the Priory tomorrow if you wish, his wife will return you to the position you held there before.'

'Oh, ar.' Lucy sniffed scornfully. 'I'll be there bright an' early in me best cardi an' me boots blacked . . . like bloody 'ell I will! Go back to skivvyin' for the Dartmouths? I'd sooner go on the roads.'

'Were they unkind to you?' Phoebe watched the hurrying women pass from stall to stall, their purchases shoved into deep-bottomed baskets draped over one arm.

'The Dartmouths?' Lucy handed a broken scone she had placed to the side of her own stall to a small girl, her face pinched and thin, a ragged dress hanging from her bony shoulders, receiving a smile in payment. 'Not Miss Sophie or 'er mother, an' I never 'ardly seen Edward or the master. No, it was that lot below stairs. Talk about mean! They'd take the sugar out o' your tea an' then come back for the milk . . . no, I ain't goin' back there no more.'

''Ow much for this?'

A woman in skirts that had parted from their colour long ago and now hung like panels of rust from below her chequered shawl touched a finger to a child's white dress, its full skirts edged with a ribbon of cornflower blue, another of the same caught around the waist.

'Six an' eleven to you, luv.' Lucy smiled encouragingly. 'It's a lovely little frock an' all muslin.'

'It be pretty enough,' the woman ran a wistful eye over

the dress, 'an' my Ginny would look a picture in that come Sunday.' She looked at Lucy. ''Er's to be confirmed.'

Holding the dress closer to the woman, Lucy spread its skirts. 'Bein' confirmed, is 'er? Well, 'er couldn't 'ave a prettier frock for it than this.'

'That's right enough,' the woman fingered the dainty material, 'but 'er wouldn't get much wear out o' it after. It ain't the stuff to stand up to wear.'

'Muslin is stronger than it seems,' Lucy said, 'an' it's so easy to wash. You only needs to show this to the wash tub an' the dirt drops out o' it nor it needs no ironin' neither.'

'It *is* a special day.' The woman lingered. ''Er won't never get confirmed again, but near enough seven shillin' for a frock . . . that'd keep the kids for a week.'

'It might do,' Lucy withdrew the dress a fraction, 'but which would your little wench remember longest – a meal or the lovely frock 'er mother bought for 'er confirmation?'

'You'm right!' The woman drew a purse from the depths of her rusty skirts. 'I'll tek it, an' what me old man don't know 'e can't grieve over.'

Lucy wrapped the dress in a piece of brown paper, religiously saved from cloth Phoebe had bought from the draper and haberdasher in Upper High Street. ''Er'll do you proud in this,' she said, handing the woman a penny change.

'You know,' the woman wedged her package on top of those already in her basket, 'if I was the one made these frocks you wouldn't find me in Wednesbury for long.'

''Ow do you mean?' Lucy shot a sidelong glance at Phoebe.

'Well, they'm so pretty, ain't they? I tell you, if I 'ad the touch in me fingers to make such I would be in one o' they big fancy places like Brummagem or London. Folk there would pay twice as much for summat like this.' Returning the purse to her pocket, the woman turned away.

'You know, Miss Phoebe,' Lucy watched the customer, her old-fashioned black bonnet set on top of hair turned prematurely grey, disappear among the shoppers, 'I reckon there be some Wednesbury folk got more in their 'eads than coal dust.'

'But there is one at least with six shillings and elevenpence less in her purse,' Phoebe answered solemnly. 'Do you really think she should have spent so much on a dress? She said it would have kept the children for a week.'

'Don't you worry about that one,' Lucy said, after selling a woman a pink petticoat. 'If 'er couldn't 'ave afforded it 'er wouldn't 'ave bought it. 'Sides, 'er will sell it for four or five shillin' once 'er own kid be finished wi' it an' then when next one be too big for it, it will fetch a couple o' bob from somebody else, an' after they be done it'll still fetch a tanner or so from old Kilvert. There's always customers at the pawnshop either pledging bundles in or buying.'

'As I bought this.' Phoebe touched one hand to her jade green suit, the jacket trimmed with darker green frogging.

'You paid for it, didn't you?' Lucy said, a slightly indignant note in her voice. 'You didn't beg from nobody so you 'ave nothin' to feel 'shamed over. 'Sides it suits you, it really does. You look lovely, Miss.'

'Lovely enough to impress the printer?' Phoebe smiled.

'You'll knock 'is eyes out.' Lucy grinned. 'Just don't let 'im charge too much for that 'eaded notepaper an' order forms you be goin' to get 'im to print for you.'

'I won't.' Phoebe took the pots of jam from her bag. 'But could I leave these with you? I don't think Mr Simpson will be too impressed by my handing him two pots of damson jam with the designs for my bill headings.'

''E might take a bit off the price if you gives 'im a pot o' me mother-in-law's damson.' Lucy took the jam, setting it to the side of her stall. 'You never knows your luck.'

'I know I had better be off.' Phoebe closed her bag. 'I am putting off your customers.'

'Miss Phoebe,' Lucy said as she made to leave, 'mebbe you should wait for Mathew to come, let 'im go with you like? Might be best for a man to do the talkin'. After all, you ain't used to talkin' prices.'

'Then the sooner I get used to it, the better,' Phoebe said. 'I intend to be talking quite a lot of prices in the future and not all of them to a printer.'

Well, let's 'ope you stands up a bit stronger to that printer than you would to that woman just bought the frock, thought Lucy as Phoebe walked away. If I 'adn't been 'ere you would 'ave finished up givin' it to 'er. There's such a thing as bein' too soft . . .

'What did Simpson sting you for?' Mathew asked as the three of them walked home.

'A shilling a dozen.'

'A shilling a dozen!' Mathew was clearly disgusted. 'Why, that be pure bloody thievery. I'll go see 'im tomorrow an' tell 'im 'e can stick 'is bleedin' printin' wheer the monkey sticks its nuts. A shillin' a dozen! Who does 'e think 'e is coddin'?'

'He wasn't fooling me, Mathew.' Phoebe switched her bag from one arm to the other. Crammed now with butter and cheese, a pork hock wedged between the pots of jam, it weighed heavily.

'But a shillin' a dozen, Miss!' Lucy came in on Mathew's side. 'That does seem a bit steep.'

'I did not accept that price unconditionally.' Phoebe winced as her foot twisted against a stone. 'We came to an agreement.'

'An agreement?' Mathew sounded far from reassured. 'Like what?'

'Like fourpence a dozen when I order a gross or more.'

'Well, that's more like it.' Mathew hitched the hessian sack of potatoes higher on his shoulder. 'But will you ever be orderin' a gross?'

'I will be ordering many gross,' Phoebe answered, 'order forms, bill forms, receipts and notepaper, and the price will be the same for all of them.'

'Phew, steady on, Miss!' Mathew laughed. 'Lock business

be goin' well enough but I can't see it goin' on. After all, Wednesbury ain't all that big a town, it will only buy so many.'

'Mathew be right, Miss,' Lucy said. 'It don't pay to get carried away. Don't spend your money on fancy 'eaded paper you might never get to use.'

'Mathew *is* right,' Phoebe agreed, 'Wednesbury is not all that big a town. But then it is not the only town, and what we have sold in one town we can sell in another.'

'But 'ow?' Lucy made a detour, avoiding a puddle in the track. 'I mean, it takes folk to sell locks an' we . . . well, we all be busy doin' what we be doin'.'

'I have thought of that,' Phoebe said confidently. 'When the time comes I shall find somebody.'

'Always supposin' you find somebody to sell locks for you, Bert couldn't mek no more,' Mathew pressed home his point. ''E is workin' flat out now.'

'To say nothin' of 'avin' to buy in more metal,' Lucy supported her husband. 'An' that might be the 'orse you can't ride. Brass founders don't let stuff out on the strap, least not to likes of we they don't. You got to be big in business to get things first and pay later.'

What they were saying was perfectly reasonable. Phoebe trudged on in silence, but she had taken a gamble, made her play as her father would have said, and now she must follow it through.

Across the heath the windmill stood silent witness to one such as herself, Elias Webb, who had sold her Wiggins Mill, had made his play but for him the cards of fortune had not followed through. But hers would. Phoebe clenched her teeth, defying the laughter of the fates. One way or another she would win through, she had to if the Ingleses were not to be put back on the road.

''Ello, Miss, 'ello, Mrs Leach.' From the edge of the yard the Ingles children waved then raced to meet them, the boy leaving his sister in his wake.

'I will take that for you, Miss.' The boy took the bag from Phoebe, easing it on to his shoulder in imitation of Mathew before going to walk beside him, matching his step, in his own mind at least very much the man.

'I can carry summat as well as our Mark.' The girl looked up with serious eyes. 'I'm as strong as 'im.'

'No, you ain't.' Her brother sniffed scathingly. 'You be only a girl an' they ain't as strong as men, am they, Mr Leach?'

'They ain't that, lad.' Mathew grinned. 'But I reckon most of 'em be prettier an' our Ruthie be prettiest o' the lot.'

'But I am strong, me mother says my 'elp be in . . . in . . . invalible.'

'Well, I could certainly do wi' some 'elp,' Lucy said tactfully, 'this basket be fair breakin' my arm.' Lowering it to the ground, she took out a shank end of mutton wrapped in paper tied round with string, handing it to the child. 'If you could take that it would be a powerful 'elp.' She smiled at the small girl, the meat cradled like a doll in her arms. 'But you 'ave only to say if it gets to be too 'eavy. We 'ave two strong men 'ere can carry it.'

'I can carry it, Mrs Leach,' the child said proudly. 'I can do lots of things. I 'elped Mother make a 'ot pot today, peelin' 'tatoes an' carrots, an' 'er let me 'elp wi' jam roly poly.'

'That sounds like a real meal for a workin' man,' Mathew said. 'Jam roly poly, that's my favourite puddin', you'll 'ave to show Mrs Leach how it's done.'

'I will.' She looked up at Lucy, her little face wreathed in smiles. 'It's real easy.'

'I 'opes as you ain't fond o' too much jam in your roly poly,' the boy said, hitching the bag on his shoulder as Mathew hitched the potato sack.

'I like jam, the more the better,' Mathew answered.

'A pity that.'

'Why, don't you have any more jam?'

'Oh, ar, Miss,' the answer was jaunty, 'me mother 'as

another pot o' jam, but we don't get much on a roly poly. Least there won't be much on this'n.'

'Why not?' Phoebe asked as they crossed the yard to the house.

''Cos our Ruth keeps eatin' it!'

'So that's what meks 'er such a little sweet'eart.' Mathew lowered the sack of potatoes to the ground, sweeping the child into his arms and whirling round with her. 'Who wants jam when we 'ave our Ruthie?'

'It's time our Ruthie was in bed.' Lizzie Ingles came from the barn she had turned into a home, smiling at her daughter's delighted squeals. 'An' you too, my lad,' she said, looking at her son. 'I told the pair o' you more'n half an hour gone.' She turned to Phoebe. 'I never can get 'em to bed afore you all be back.'

'I wonder why?' Taking her bag from the boy, she drew out two fat round lollipops. 'It couldn't have something to do with these, could it?'

Shoving the joint of meat into Lucy's hands, the little girl jigged up and down, eyes shining at the promise of the sweet. 'I wants the red one.' She pulled at Phoebe's arm. 'It's my turn to 'ave the red one. Our Mark 'ad it last time.'

'Then if Mark had the red one last time it must be your turn to have it this time.' Phoebe handed her the sweet.

'I've got the red one!' The child jigged away, holding the lollipop in the air like some coveted trophy. 'I've got the red one!'

'You'll 'ave a red bottom, Ruth Ingles, if you don't say thank you,' Lizzie said sternly. 'You know better'n to take what somebody gives an' return no thanks. Whatever 'as 'appened to your manners, girl!'

The child stopped dancing. 'Beg pardon, Miss.' She came to Phoebe, her pretty mouth drooping. 'I'm mortal sorry.'

'That's all right, Ruth.' Phoebe caught the twitching of Lucy's mouth. 'I was always forgetting to say thank you when I was a little girl, and to tell you the truth I sometimes forget now.'

'Do you, Miss, do you honest?'

'Honest.' Licking a forefinger, Phoebe made the sign of the cross over her heart. 'Cross my heart and hope to die if what I have said is just a lie.'

'Ooh, you knows that an' all, you can't never say that if you 'ave told a lie.' The child's mouth lost its droop, turning upward in a smile. 'So you must be tellin' the truth, Miss, you do forget sometimes.'

We all do, Phoebe thought, bending to hug Lizzie's daughter, remembering playing the same scene so many times with her father. We all do.

'Now say goodnight.' Lizzie caught her daughter's hand as Phoebe released her.

'Goodnight.' The child lifted her face to each in turn, receiving a kiss on the cheek. 'Thank you, Mrs Leach, an' you, Mr Leach.'

'Why can't we make that Aunty Lucy and Uncle Mathew?' Lucy said, her face on a level with that of the child.

'I don't know if we could,' the answer came solemnly, 'it might not be 'lowed 'cos you ain't a real aunt, am you?'

'No,' Lucy said softly, 'but I love you as much as a real aunt, and Mr Leach loves you as much as a real uncle.'

'I'd like to,' the child said pensively, 'but I don't know if it's 'lowed.'

'Why don't we ask your mother?' Lucy looked up at the face of Lizzie Ingles.

'It's allowed.' The woman smiled, her eyes cloudy behind tears. 'It's allowed.'

Clasping her red lollipop in one hand, the other held by her mother, the girl walked away then stopped to look back at the three adults. 'I do love you all,' she said simply. 'I'm so glad we come to live 'ere.'

'I would like to call you Aunt and Uncle an' all if it's all right wi' you?'

Mathew looked at the face turned up towards his own, seeing the disappointments and knocks life had already dealt the young son of Bert Ingles, seeing apprehension of another. He held out his hand, shaking that of the boy offered to meet it. 'It's a sight more'n all right, Mark,' he answered huskily. 'That would mean more to me than a medal from the Queen.'

'*I'm so glad we come to live 'ere.*' The words echoed in her mind as later Phoebe prepared for bed. She was glad too. Having people about the place during the day gave her a feeling of security, and the knowledge they were close, combined with the locks on her doors, had given her confidence to sleep alone in the house, freeing Lucy and Mathew to go back to sleeping in their own home.

Yes, she was glad they had all come to live at Wiggins Mill. Picking up her nightgown from the bed, she held the soft cotton to her face, the memory of rough calico vivid in her mind. She was glad they were all here, Lucy and Mathew, the Ingleses with their children . . . if only she could have brought one more. If only she could have brought Tilly . . .

Chapter Fifteen

Annie Pardoe sat in the neat parlour of Brunswick House its graceful bay window overlooking well-kept lawns. She paid a man twice a week to see to the upkeep of the gardens and made sure he earned his money. Annie Pardoe paid no one to sit around. There had been little alteration since Abel's time though she had seen to it that no laburnum or yew grew there and had grubbed them out herself from the garden of the house at Bescot years before. She caught her breath, holding it till the twinge of pain below her left breast subsided. Yes, she had grubbed them out – but not until she had made good use of them.

'Papers, Miss.' Maudie Tranter entered the room, a newspaper neatly folded on a cloth-covered tray. Wait till you reads that, she thought as Annie took the newspaper, you'll have another shock. Making her way back to the kitchen Maudie thought of what she had seen in the *Express and Star* and how the woman in the parlour would react in the knowledge that her housekeeper always read the newspaper before taking it into her. Maudie enjoyed her thoughts.

In the parlour Annie spread the newspaper on the oval mahogany table, fixing on to her nose the reading glasses that hung on a silk string about her neck. She had made a lifetime's habit of taking the papers, reading thoroughly through them before allowing them to go to her brother.

'Hmmph!' she snorted, reading of certain elections to the town council. 'Not an ounce of brain between the lot of them.' Slowly she turned the pages, finding some reports of interest to her, others not, but reading them all until her eye caught the advertisement.

Annie's fingers dropped to the corner of the page she had been about to turn, her eyes devouring the large caption: 'The Invincible'. The heading topped a representation of a lock under the sub-heading 'Pardoe's Patent Locks'. She read the advert through once and then again. Phoebe! She pressed a hand to her side but it did not still the pain biting beneath her breast. It could only be Phoebe!

Her thoughts flew to the man who had promised to make her his wife. What if he saw the advertisement? The name was the same, Pardoe, how long would it take him to wonder if it carried with it any relationship to her? He was no fool, he would put two and two together sharp enough, then how long before he found Pardoe's Patent Locks was run by her niece?

The pain jabbed viciously, bringing her teeth together, nostrils flaring with the effort of controlling it as she read the advert through again. If he should find out . . . if he discovered her niece had not quit Brunswick House of her own choice but had been virtually thrown out . . . And what of Samuel? What would his reaction be to seeing that piece in the newspaper? He had already made clear his intention of returning everything to Abel's daughter, what would he do when he found there was almost nothing to return? But it didn't matter what Samuel thought. Annie's eyes stayed glued to the advertisement. She had taken care her brother would never carry out his threat. No, it did not matter what Samuel knew, but Clinton . . . Clinton must never know. She would kill this lock business stone dead before it got started.

Leaving the newspaper on the table she walked upstairs to her bedroom. Slipping a smart grey day coat over her matching dress, she pinned a feathered bonnet over her hair. Clutching her bag, she went downstairs without calling in on her brother.

'I am going out,' she said as Maudie appeared from the kitchen, 'I don't know what time I shall be back.'

Maudie watched her mistress wriggle her fingers into grey chamois gloves. I was right, she thought, closing the door after the departing Annie, you've had a shock right enough and it won't be the last. And you taking to dressing up in fine colours won't ward them off. There be others waiting on you, Annie Pardoe, ones you won't walk away from.

Annie walked briskly along Spring Head, following it into the market place cutting across toward Great Western Street. She had not taken the horse and trap, they would be too conspicuous left standing outside the Great Western Railway Station, for today she meant to take the train to Birmingham.

'You can sit in the ladies' waitin' room, Mum, it's the next door along the platform. There be a nice fire burnin' in there.'

The man in the tiny ticket office touched a finger to the peak of his dark green cap as he handed Annie a ticket.

Putting it carefully into her bag, she nodded. It might be best to sit in the room set aside for women, there would not be many of them using the train, not when the steam tram was a cheaper way to travel. But today the train suited Annie. The fewer folk to see where she headed, the better pleased she felt.

Choosing a seat that gave a clear view of the door and of any who might choose to enter, Annie sat in the empty room. It was a bind having to go to Birmingham but it was safest. She would not be known there and there would be few in Wednesbury who knew that town in any detail. The advertisement she had read only an hour before lodged in her mind, till she felt her mouth tightening like a trap. The hundred pounds she had paid the Magistrate had been a total waste of money. What had it bought . . . a fifteen-year sentence that had been set aside after little more than one! What had that fool been about? He should have made the sentence one that couldn't so easily be revoked. It was a pity they had ceased transportation, that way Phoebe would have been out of the country, but now her niece was free and broadcasting her presence by way of advertisements, one at least published in the *Express and Star* and God only knew how many in other publications and places. Annie pressed her hands together in her lap. If you want a thing doing right, do it yourself. This time she would do it herself, and this time it would be done right.

The conductor's call of 'Snow Hill' told of having reached Birmingham and Annie alighted. Who was stupid enough to give a name like Snow Hill to this place? she wondered, taking in the soot-grimed archways of the railway station. Black Hill would have been more appropriate. Leaving the station, she followed the line of shops beside it; tailor, draper, grocer, milliner, each jostled the other, elbowing for room in the narrow streets, but she passed them by without a second look at the overcrowded windows. Pie shop, beer hall. Annie walked on, her eye scanning signs painted over shop fronts proclaiming the name of the proprietor and the wares he sold until she read: James Greaves, Hardware and Ironmongery.

Annie caught the train back to Wednesbury, six pot menders and six mousetraps in her bag. The purchase of these would raise no eyebrows in Brunswick House: pot menders were often used in her kitchen to close small holes worn in iron pots and pans and mousetraps were always set in the cellar. Mousetrap! She gazed through the window at the dingy houses set regimentally close alongside the railway line. The trap she was setting would catch more than a mouse . . .

'Has Mr Samuel been downstairs?' she asked when she reached the house.

'No, Ma'am,' Maudie answered. ''E took 'is lunch in 'is room though 'e didn't touch it none, an' when I popped in the studio about three o'clock 'e was asleep in 'is chair. 'E seems to 'ave slept more than ever these past few days.'

'That will be his medicine.' Annie took the pot menders and mousetraps from her bag, handing them to her housekeeper.

'The doctor increased the strength a little . . . you have been careful only to give him the prescribed dose?'

'Two teaspoonfuls, measured 'em out meself, Ma'am, an' 'e swallowed 'em right off, then 'e sat in 'is chair an' 'as been there all day far as I know.'

'And he ate nothing?'

'Nothin' at all,' Maudie shook her head, 'not even a bite. I carried 'is tray down same as I carried it up . . . nothin' 'ad been touched at all.'

'Perhaps a cucumber sandwich will tempt him?' Annie turned to the stairs. 'I will go in to him when I have removed my coat. Prepare a tray now.'

'Perhaps a cucumber sandwich will tempt him,' Maudie mimicked under her breath as Annie went up the stairs. 'As if she cares whether he eats anything or not. It's all bloody top show wi' that one an' underneath it all 'er couldn't care twopence whether the poor bugger lives or dies!'

In the kitchen Maudie put the hardware on the dresser and stood looking at it. Pot menders and mousetraps, nothing unusual in that – 'cept Annie Pardoe never bought anything without it had been asked for a dozen times and she, Maudie, hadn't asked for either. And why walk into the town, why hadn't she taken the horse and trap as always? And why jaunt off down into Wednesbury to get them herself when she could have had them sent up with provisions? Taking out a tray she spread it with a freshly laundered cloth and set it with china. Annie Pardoe was up to summat as sure as God made little apples, Maudie told herself, and like as not Samuel wouldn't come out of it too well.

In her room Annie spread the newspaper she had brought up from the parlour. She had spent a couple of hours with her brother before leaving him for the night. She turned a page. He had not eaten a cucumber sandwich earlier and neither had he taken any dinner, but she had expected that. She turned a second page. She had told Maudie Tranter she would go herself tomorrow and ask the doctor to call. But that would do nothing for Samuel. Her eyes scanned the columns of print, coming to rest on the advertisement for Pardoe's Patent Locks. No, nothing would help Samuel.

Going to the marble-topped washstand she slid open the narrow drawer that ran almost the full width of it, taking a sheet of paper from beneath the pile of towels. Returning to the table, she placed it beside the newspaper then took from her bag the bottle of ink and the cheap pen she had bought before taking the train back to Wednesbury. Reading the advert through one last time, Annie dipped the pen into the ink and began to write.

Phoebe heard the crunch of carriage wheels along the track and put aside the dress she had almost finished making. Going to the window, she watched it drive to the front of the house, her feelings mixed. She liked Edward, liked him very much, and was happy for him to call . . . but if only he would call less often. She had tried to tell him of her need to work, to explain the strong necessity for it, but he only said to marry him and be done with tiresome necessities.

She watched him climb from the carriage, the light glinting on his fair hair. She knew he loved her and that he would do his best to make marriage to him happy . . . so why couldn't she say yes? Why wouldn't she marry Edward Dartmouth? Turning from the window, Phoebe left the room. She didn't know why.

'Phoebe, I am so glad you are home. I told Edward we ought to send a card before we visited.'

'Sophie, how nice.' Phoebe's smile was a mixture of pleasure and relief. She had turned from the window before seeing Sophie and now the pleasure of her visit brought the added relief of not having to walk with Edward.

'Don't bother with tea,' Sophie said when Phoebe offered refreshments, 'just sit down and listen. You are invited to a farewell ball.'

'A ball?' Phoebe was surprised. 'Where?'

'At the Priory.' Sophie's face glowed with delight. 'Where else did you think!'

'That's just it,' Phoebe said, 'you gave me no time to think.'

'What is there to think of?' Sophie rushed on. 'Father is giving a ball and you are invited. There is nothing to be thought about.'

Phoebe looked from Sophie to Edward. 'You said a farewell ball?'

'My mother is to leave for Europe sooner than had been intended.' He smiled, misreading the reason for the question in her eyes. 'The influenza she suffered recently has not cleared as we would have hoped and her physician has recommended a warmer climate.'

'I am sorry to hear your mother is not yet fully recovered,' Phoebe returned her gaze to Sophie, 'please give her my regards.'

'Oh, Mother is not too ill,' Sophie burst out with the thoughtless disloyalty of youth, 'she simply has an over-fondness for Italy, and of course we have to go too which means I will not see Montrose for several more months. The whole thing would be totally unbearable were it not for the shopping en route. You really can buy the most exquisite lace in Paris. I intend to buy my whole trousseau there. Montrose . . .'

'My mother and sister cannot travel alone,' Edward put in as his sister paused for breath, 'I am to travel with them to our villa in Tuscany then I shall return.'

'Will that not be doubling a journey?' Phoebe asked, knowing he had interrupted Sophie because he hated to think of her with Montrose Wheeler and wanting to spare him as much as possible. 'To have to return to Italy again to escort your mother home will be very tiring.'

He smiled, the thought of her concern for him deepening the vivid blue of his eyes. 'I will not be returning there a second time,' he explained. 'My father will be joining Sophie and Mother after Christmas. He will bring them home.'

'With us leaving in two weeks there will be no Advent Ball at the Priory this year,' Sophie burbled on, 'hence the idea of a farewell ball. Mother has sent invitations to absolutely everybody and here is yours.' She took a cream vellum envelope from her bag, handing it to Phoebe. 'It will be absolutely wonderful and I hope to persuade Father to let Montrose announce . . .'

'It is kind of your parents to invite me,' Phoebe cut in but this time it was not to spare Edward, 'though I cannot accept.' She could not attend a ball at the Priory, she hadn't a suitable gown for one thing, and to ask her to one which Montrose would be attending . . . hadn't anyone told Sophie the man she wanted to marry had already been engaged to the daughter of Abel Pardoe, and had broken that engagement when he found out she had no money?

'But why?' Sophie demanded. 'Is it because of Montrose? You have no cause for worry there, Phoebe. He told me what happened himself. Told me you asked to be freed from your engagement to him – that after the shock of your father's death you felt you could not marry for some time, and later you found you no longer loved him and begged him not to hold you to your promise so of course he did not. But now he loves me and we are to be married. And you,' she squeezed Phoebe's hand, 'are not to worry over my feelings. You are to accept Mother's invitation and that is that!'

So Montrose had told Sophie! Phoebe glanced at Edward, reading the distaste in his face. It was not her recollection of events she had just heard but what effect would it have on Sophie should she ever find out the true story? And what effect would it have should she discover Montrose was marrying her purely and simply for her money; that for him love played no part in marriage.

'I'm so excited,' Sophie trilled on, 'I am to have a new gown, pink, Montrose says I look ravishing in pink . . .'

I wore a pink gown on our last evening together. Phoebe's thoughts suppressed Sophie's voice, drowning it in waves of memory. Montrose said I too looked ravishing in the colour. He held me in his arms while he vowed his love for me, while he told me he could not wait for our marriage, while he told me the same lies.

'. . . he is to get leave from his regiment . . .'

Wrenching her thoughts back to the present, Phoebe glanced across to where Edward sat.

'Sophie dear,' he rose, 'we really must not take any more of Phoebe's time.'

The girl jumped to her feet, colour rising to her cheeks. 'I'm sorry, Phoebe, I do prattle on. Mother is always telling me about it.'

'And so am I,' Edward laughed, 'to say nothing of Father's efforts in that direction, all of which are wasted.

'You will come, Phoebe?' He hung back as Sophie reached the carriage.

'It's not possible, Edward.'

'Why not?' The intensity of his question was echoed in the pressure of the hands he placed on her arms. 'Is it because of my forgetting that damned necklace?'

Releasing herself from his grip, Phoebe glanced at his sister but her back was still turned to them.

'You know it isn't, Edward.'

He looked at her, frustration and the need to know lending his eyes a desperation she had not seen before. 'Then why, Phoebe?' he asked hoarsely. 'Why?'

'Edward,' she smiled patiently as though dealing with a demanding child, 'for a single girl to attend a ball she requires a female chaperone or a male escort. It might have escaped your notice that I have neither of these, on top of which I own no gown suitable for a ball.'

'The escort part might have eluded me,' Edward admitted, his eyes clearing, 'but it had not escaped my father. He has expressed the wish that you give your permission for me to be your escort for the evening, and I sincerely hope you will agree. As for a gown, I . . .'

'No.' Phoebe cut short the offer she knew would follow. She would take none of the Dartmouths' money, not even enough to buy a gown to attend their ball; she wanted no reparation and she certainly did not want their charity. 'Thank you, Edward, but I prefer to provide my own gown.'

'Then you will come!'

'I think you had better be going.' Phoebe avoided answering what was more statement than question. 'Your sister is waiting.'

'A ball, and with Edward Dartmouth your escort!' Lucy held the cream card with its gold edging as though it were a priceless object. 'Eeh, Miss Phoebe, how lovely. What will you wear?'

'Nothing.' Phoebe took the card, putting it behind a jug that held pride of place on the dresser.

'Well, that'll give the women the vapours and the men a rare treat, though I 'adn't thought it of you, to go 'ob nobbin' in naught but that you were born in, Miss Phoebe.' Mathew stood in the doorway of the scullery.

'Trust a man to be there with 'is ears flappin'.' Lucy turned a reproving look as her husband grinned. 'What you be in 'ere after anyway, Mathew Leach?'

Phoebe smiled, joining in with his infectious grin. 'Yes, what do you be in 'ere after?' she asked, using the same lazy dialect, 'listenin' to wenches gossipin'.'

'Well, you be wi' one can do that all right.'

'Don't push your luck, me lad.' Lucy stretched a hand ominously towards an iron pot set on the hob.

'All right, all right.' Mathew raised both hands in a gesture of surrender. 'Bert says to tell you, Miss, as brass for locks be runnin' pretty low.'

'He knows he can get more whenever he needs it.'

'Ar, 'e do know,' Mathew answered, 'but 'e still reckons to tell you beforehand like, says that's the way it should be.'

'Tell him to get what he thinks necessary,' Phoebe said.

'I will come see him myself as soon as I finish helping Lucy with tomorrow's baking.'

'What did you mean when you said you would wear nothing to the Priory ball?' Lucy whisked about the kitchen gathering utensils.

'What I said.' Phoebe lifted the pot from the hob, placing it on a cloth she had set on a corner of the well-scrubbed table, then set about pounding the boiled potatoes with a wooden spoon. 'I will be wearing nothing to the Dartmouths' ball for the simple reason that I will not be going.'

'Eeh, Miss Phoebe, whyever not?' Lucy was already wrist-deep in flour.

'I can't Lucy.' Phoebe attacked the potatoes with a new savagery. 'I . . . I wouldn't feel right. Everyone there will know what my aunt did.'

Lucy banged lard indignantly into the flour, sending it surging upward in a cloud. 'Ar, they will, an' they'll know what an old bitch 'er is an' all.'

Phoebe ladled cubes of mutton into the mashed potato, folding them in with the spoon. 'They will also know about the business of the necklace.'

'That an' all.' Lucy rolled the pastry. 'An' they'll see that the Dartmouths 'old nothin' against you . . . not that there be anythin' for 'em to 'old . . . but you see what I mean. Billy-me-Lord can't be apologisin' any more clear, an' that's what 'e be doin'. In front of the 'ole bloomin' county 'e's apologisin', an' your refusin' to go to that ball be like chuckin' 'is apology right back in 'is face. It do an' all, Miss Phoebe.'

She had not thought of it in those terms. Phoebe watched Lucy working dexterously at her pie-making. This could well be Sir William and Lady Dartmouth's way of proclaiming the fact she had been wrongly accused of stealing their daughter's necklace and that despite her lack of fortune she was accepted in their home. For her to refuse would be seen as churlish, and worse, in her own eyes, would rank as rudeness. But to attend . . .

'I realise how my refusal may be received, Lucy, but it can't be helped. I haven't a dress anywhere near grand enough for such an occasion.'

'Is that all? Lord, it would take a bloody sight more than that to keep me from goin' to a grand do like that. Surely you ain't gonna let a frock keep you from it?'

'Not a frock, more the lack of one.'

'That be nothin' as can't be remedied,' Lucy said, watching Phoebe carry pies to the oven and load them in. 'You can buy a frock easy as winkin'.'

'You can if you have money, which I have not . . . well, not to spend on ball gowns anyway. They cost a small fortune.'

'Spendin' some on yourself won't 'urt for once.'

'Spending that much would. I need that money to buy metal if we are to go on producing locks. I will not throw it away on a gown I will never wear again.'

'I seen a lovely bolt o' satin in Underwood's window,' Lucy sounded almost matter-of-fact, 'the loveliest shade of pale yellow you ever did see – just like butter cream. Make a bostin' frock it would.'

'Make!' Phoebe stopped filling pies to stare at Lucy. 'I couldn't make a ball gown.'

'O' course you could.' Lucy loaded her bowl with a fresh helping of flour, adding salt and lard. 'You already makes frocks, don't you?'

'Little ones, yes.'

Lucy looked up from rubbing fat into flour. 'Well, then! this will be the same 'cept bigger.'

Phoebe half smiled. Lucy made it all sound so easy, make herself a gown . . . as if nothing were simpler. Supposing she did manage to make a gown, that would only be a part of what she would need. There were other things.

'A dress is not the whole of it, Lucy,' she said. 'Given that I had one, I would also require gloves and shoes . . . a bag . . . a fan. And jewellery, what of jewellery? I have absolutely nothing in that line at all. The last of Grandmother's pieces went before . . . before . . .'

'Before you were sent to prison,' Lucy finished for her. 'Jewellery be a bit o' a sticky 'un. Wonder if Bert could make anything?'

Phoebe set the second batch of pies aside, spreading the white huckaback cloth over them until there was room in the oven. 'Mr Ingles is not a jeweller.'

'I know 'e ain't.' Lucy paused from mixing dough. 'But 'e makes things out o' brass, don't 'e?'

'Brass is not gold. If it were we would be quite wealthy for there is several pounds of it in the workshop.'

'Pity it isn't,' Lucy floured the wooden pin and board then scooped the dough from the bowl a few quick light movements rolling it into a creamy mat, 'I wouldn't mind bein' wealthy . . . not too much, mind you,' she grinned cheekily, 'just enough to make the 'ole of Wednesbury sit up and take notice.'

'Oh, I understand,' Phoebe laughed, 'nothing too blatant . . . just the odd million would do.'

'I just thought as seein' Bert was so 'andy with the brass like 'e might be able to make summat as would pass for jewellery,' Lucy said when they both stopped laughing.

'And how would I explain my neck turning a delicate shade of green halfway through the evening?'

'Oh, ar!' Lucy grimaced wryly but her eyes were laughing still. 'I 'adn't thought o' that. Mind, that would put you one up over the nobs . . . you'd 'ave summat they 'adn't got.'

'How very true. But I think I prefer to do without a green neck. It doesn't seem me somehow.'

'No! Well, p'raps you be right.' Taking the last remnants of dough Lucy shaped it into the figure of a man, giving it sultana eyes and four sultana buttons.

'Ruth doesn't like sultanas,' Phoebe said as Lucy blobbed jam where a nose would be.

'I know, but Mark does!' Lucy sprinkled the figure with

a coating of sugar before placing it in the tin alongside the scones, then looked across the table to where Phoebe was watching. 'Seriously though, Miss, apart from the jewellery there ain't nuthin' you couldn't get if you wanted to go to that ball.'

'I will not spend a great deal of money on . . .'

'You wouldn't 'ave to,' Lucy said quickly. 'Gloves you can get from Underwood's, ones that reach up over the elbow for no more than ninepence. An' they 'as feathers an' buttons. Eh, Miss, wi' your sewin' I reckon as you could make a lovely frock for little or nuthin'.'

'Hardly nothing.' Phoebe covered the scones then began to take cooked pies from the oven. 'How much is the material going to cost? Think how many yards it will take . . . Lucy, the whole thing is out of the question.'

'I don't know how many yards it'll take nor 'ow much the cost would be!' Lucy banged bowls and dishes together impatiently. 'An' neither do you 'cos you ain't asked so 'ow can you say it be out of the question? An' afore you says anythin' about shoes an' the costin' o' them you could always try John Kilvert's place.'

Phoebe straightened up, her cheeks reddened by the heat of the oven. 'A pawn shop!' she exclaimed. 'A pawn shop is not going to have dance slippers.'

'There you goes again!' Lucy rattled spoons and knives into the large mixing bowl. 'You'm a right one for reachin' a answer afore askin' the question, Miss Phoebe. Who's to say what old Kilvert 'as got stored away in that pawn shop . . . it ain't always the ones looks down an' out is down an' out, there be others 'ad to visit 'im, others popped pledges as they couldn't redeem.'

'But dance slippers?' Phoebe shook her head. 'Really, Lucy, I can't see there being such as that in a pawn shop.'

'You said that when that old brown cloak o' your'n got to be too bad off lookin' to go into town in any more, but you found that good green suit in one. What I says is if you don't try you won't know. Time to say a thing can't be done after you 'ave tried an' not t'other way round.'

She could always ask, she didn't have to buy anything. Ninepence for gloves . . . say threepence for second hand slippers . . . twopence for a dozen buttons . . . trimmings . . .

Gathering the rest of the used dishes from the table, she followed Lucy into the scullery.

Maybe it could be done, but jewellery, what of that? Phoebe smiled inwardly. Perhaps the Queen may have pawned the Crown Jewels.

'Lucy,' she asked, 'you did say the satin you saw in Underwood's shop window was a *pale* yellow?'

'Yes, Miss.' Lucy looked up from scouring pots. 'A lovely colour it be, like butter fresh from the dairy. Set your colourin' off to a tee it would.'

Pale yellow. Phoebe picked up the drying cloth and began to wipe the dishes Lucy had stacked on the board beside the sink. At least it wasn't pink.

Annie Pardoe wrote quickly, her well-formed copperplate hand rapidly covering the sheet of paper. She had bought the ink and the pen in Birmingham, that way she did not have to use that which was on the desk in the study, and the paper together with its envelope was the last of a birthday gift she had received from Abel many moons ago. She had kept one sheet of paper and one envelope, hiding them away for so many years, hiding them away but never forgetting them, knowing only that one day they would serve to hit back at him. Abel had died before she had found a way to strike, but that would not rob her of the revenge she had longed for all these years. Abel might be beyond her reach but his flesh and blood were not.

Folding the sheet of anonymously white notepaper she slipped it into the same self-effacing envelope, sealing it before writing an address across it in the same sure style. Abel was in his grave but his daughter was not. Slipping the envelope into her bag, she replaced the top on the bottle of ink, wiped the pen nib on a scrap torn from a corner of the newspaper, then slipped both into her bag alongside the letter.

Tearing the advert from the newspaper she slipped it into the drawer of the washstand, burying it beneath the towels. Abel was beyond her vengeance but she would destroy his daughter.

Thrusting a long hat pin through her hat, fastening it securely to her head, Annie checked her bedroom with a long seeking stare. The newspaper was folded neatly against her bag, the scrap of ink-stained paper was in the pocket of her coat, there was no sign of a letter having been written. Taking up her bag and the newspaper she left the room, passing that of her brother without looking in.

'Mr Samuel is still sleeping,' she said as she entered the kitchen, the lie sliding easily from her tongue. 'I thought it best not to disturb him. Take him a breakfast tray at eleven o'clock. I am going to ask the doctor to call, I am not at all sure Mr Samuel's health is improving despite the medicines.' Going into the scullery she deposited the newspaper with others kept in a wooden soap box alongside the stove to be used for lighting the house fires, then carried on, leaving the house by the rear door.

'Don't think Mr Samuel's health is improving?' Maudie watched from the scullery window. 'O' course it ain't improvin' an' you don't care for all you pretend to. You don't fool me, Annie Pardoe, you don't fool Maudie Tranter not for one minute you don't. You tell me you be going to fetch the doctor but it be my guess you be about more than that. You be up to summat, that much I be certain sure of, up to summat as sure as God med little apples.'

Standing to the side of the window so her watching presence would not easily be seen from outside Maudie waited until Annie had left, driving her small trap around to the front of the house. And still Maudie waited. She wouldn't put it past that sly bitch to come back into the house from the front. For several minutes she stood listening then, assured her mistress had gone, crossed the scullery to the soap box. Picking up the top newspaper she checked the date printed on the front page and smiled mirthlessly. 'You 'ave to get up early o' a mornin' to catch me, Annie, ma wench,' she murmured, then scanned the date on several papers until she found the one delivered to the house the day before. Turning to the page number she had made a mental note of, she smiled again. The advertisement for Pardoe's Patent Locks was missing.

Annie drove the trap at a steady walking pace, she was in no hurry and had no desire to draw attention to herself. She spoke to no one and none spoke to her, her long practice of ignoring people producing in them an almost total disregard for her. Passing to the left of Oakeswell Hall she skirted the black and white Tudor house, following the track across open ground the locals called the Mounts and coming around towards Hill Top. At the foot of the swell of ground Annie reined in the horse and sat looking at the black-grey water. Millfield Pool had formed when several gin pits had flooded, their vertical shafts filling with water which merged at the surface to form a large pond. The flooding of those shafts had taken many men, drowning them in their sludgy surging tide before they could scramble free, and it had taken others since.

Taking pen and ink from her bag she climbed from the trap and walked to the rim of ground overlooking the pool. 'You robbed me, Abel,' she whispered to the still menace lying at her feet, 'you robbed me of my life. Now watch while I rob your daughter of hers.'

Throwing the small bottle she saw it wing outward then thump into the water. She sent the pen after it, standing watching the spreading circles mark their watery grave. Taking the scrap of paper from her pocket, she stared at it for several moments. 'Vengeance is mine, Abel,' she whispered, rolling the paper between her fingers and letting it drop into her palm. Slowly raising her arm, stretching it out towards the water in macabre benediction, she tipped her hand, letting the balled scrap roll off the tips of her fingers. 'Vengeance is mine!'

Chapter Sixteen

'I wrote me name for it, Miss, I 'opes as that be all right? 'ad no way of knowin' 'ow long you would be like, an' he postman, well, 'e 'ad other letters 'e 'ad to be deliverin'.' izzie Ingles's features struggled between a worried frown nd an uncertain smile. 'I thought as if I wrote me name to ay as I 'ad taken it in place o' you it would be all right.'

'It is all right, Lizzie, thank you.' Phoebe smiled and the ther woman's face brightened. 'I wonder who it can be from?' he turned the white envelope but apart from the address vritten in neat flowing copperplate it bore no identifying nark.

'Only one way to find that out, Miss,' Lizzie said. 'That be o open it an' read it, an' that be best done over a nice cup ' tea.'

'I agree with you there, Lizzie.' Phoebe picked up the rown paper-wrapped parcel she had set down at her feet s Lizzie had met her. 'It's a fair walk from the Tipton Road. got a ride from the carter as far as there but even so I am eady for a sit down and a drink.'

'Would you like me to make it for you, Miss?'

'That's good of you, Lizzie, but you must have work enough vithout waiting on me.'

'Nothing as will take 'arm from waitin' a while.' Lizzie pened the door that led into the mill house through the cullery and waited for Phoebe to pass inside. 'Bert an' lark be in the workshop an' the babby be playin' around he back there.'

'Then you have time to join me. I will enjoy a cup of te the more for having your company.'

Phoebe placed the parcel on the table in the kitchen, th letter beside it, unbuttoning her coat and hanging it besid the old brown cloak she kept now for working about th yard. 'I will take it upstairs later,' she said, seeing Lizzie ey the coat she needed to keep looking its best.

'I'll run it up for you, Miss.' Lizzie released the coat fror its nail, her boots rattling on the stairs as she whisked up t Phoebe's bedroom.

'You really shouldn't,' Phoebe said as the woman skippe back in to the kitchen. 'You will have me too idle to scratc myself.'

'You, idle!' Lizzie poured boiling water on the fresh te leaves waiting in the pot. 'That'll be the day. I've yet t come across a wench as works 'arder'n you an' I've met few in me time. You sews most o' the day, then you 'elp with the filin' down o' the locks in the workshop, then c nights you 'elps Lucy wi' 'er cookin'. No, you ain't idle, Miss Whatever thoughts you might be 'oldin' about yourself tha 'un be wrong.'

'I bought the most beautiful material for a gown.' Phoeb began to untie the string securing the parcel, Lizzie' compliment painting her cheeks a ripe pink. 'It is ever bit as lovely as Lucy said and not nearly as expensive a I would have thought.'

'Eh, that's real pretty!' Lizzie made to touch the delicat lemony-cream fabric then pulled her hand away. 'An' it b just the colour for you with your hair.'

'There were others.' Phoebe added milk and sugar to th tea Lizzie poured for her. 'Green, blue, a really deep scarle and a soft sugary pink. They were all so nice I was spoile for choice.'

Sweetening her own tea, Lizzie sat opposite Phoebe i the warm kitchen. This girl must have had silks and finery, a the comfort and luxury her father's money could buy, and yet hadn't spoilt her. There was nothing bay-windowed about her, and nothing vicious either. Even the months spent in that rat hole of a gaol hadn't altered her nature. Lizzie drank her tea. That son of Dartmouth's came visiting too regular for it to be a way of apologising for what he had done. His sort might say it once if you were lucky but not a couple of times a week. There was more to his coming than that. He was looking to make this wench his wife and if he got to do it he could count himself fortunate. This one would be no high-faluting, sit-on-her-arse lady of the manor. This one would care for the folk who worked for her.

'I got these to go with it.' Phoebe delved into the basket she had carried, taking out an assortment of buttons and lace. 'I thought feathers might be a little too much, what do you think?'

'I think you made just the right choice.' Lizzie admired the lace and touched a finger to the pretty pearl buttons. 'You'll be pretty as a picture, Miss, an' no coddin'.'

'But a ball gown,' Phoebe said, holding the elbow-length gloves she had bought against the material, then looking worriedly at Lizzie. 'I hope I haven't taken on more than I can handle. A ball gown . . . it's so different from a child's dress.'

'A bit fancier, Miss, I'll give you that,' said Lizzie, gathering the teacups, 'an' a bit on the bigger side, but that be all an' that ain't different, not really.'

'You make it sound so easy,' Phoebe called after her into the scullery, 'I almost believe it myself.'

Lizzie returned from the scullery drying her hands on her rough apron. 'You believe it, Miss, 'cos it be the truth. Lizzie Ingles wouldn't lead you up the garden path, 'er tells you the way 'er sees things an' no lies. Now you best be gettin' that there cloth up to your workroom afore summat be findin' itself spilt on it.'

'Did the metal come?'

'Ar, Miss, brass founders delivered it about an hour after

the three of you left this mornin'.' Lizzie watched as Phoebe gathered her purchases into one parcel. 'Bert says as there be enough for a couple o' dozen doublers an' p'raps a bit left over as'll make a few close shackle padlocks, an' 'e says as it be good quality metal an' all.'

Thank heaven for that, Phoebe thought, remembering how she had declared to the brass founder that any dross delivered to her would be returned unpaid for and her business taken elsewhere. She had trembled inside, seeing the scorn in his eyes as he had listened to a woman trying to play at business, but the scorn had faded as she had declared the price she was prepared to pay for brass or steel, changing to veiled admiration as she stated she would pay not a penny more.

'Don't forget your letter, Miss.' Lizzie nodded to the envelope that had become hidden beneath layers of brown paper. 'I'll be off now.'

'Thank you, Lizzie,' Phoebe said as the other woman left through the scullery. 'I will just take these upstairs and then I will see what it is.'

'. . . *one gross of Invincible locks to be delivered by the close of business on the last day of the month* . . .'

Phoebe stared at the words written neatly across the sheet of notepaper, its heading boldly proclaiming James Greaves, Hardware and Ironmongery. An order for one gross of locks, the first in answer to her advertisement. She read the remainder of the letter: '. . . *should you find yourself unable to comply with my requirements please notify me by return post.*'

The end of the month. Phoebe made a swift mental calculation. That left twenty-one days all told, including Sundays. It could not be done. She sank heavily to a chair, the letter in her hand. Her very first order and it could not be met. The start she had prayed for and it was over before it had begun. Folding the letter, she returned it to its envelope.

'It is as I have told you before, your brother's constitution has been weak from childhood.' Alfred Dingley pulled on his chamois leather gloves. 'I can prescribe medicine to help him sleep or to relieve pain should he have any, but there is no real cure for what truly ails him. You know it, Miss Pardoe, and I know it, and sadly so does he.'

Picking up the black Gladstone bag that was his constant companion, the doctor pressed a hand to his patient's shoulder before leaving the bedroom. 'He is getting weaker,' he said as he reached the front door. 'You can try him with beef tea or with some chicken broth but nothing too heavy.'

'My brother eats so little,' Annie said with mock solicitude, 'I worry so for him.'

'Worrying heals no wounds.' The doctor raised his tall black hat the merest fraction. 'And seeing you fret will only add to his suffering. My advice is to treat him the way you have always done – give him no intimation of how things really stand with him, though it is my guess he needs none.'

'How do you mean?' Annie asked, her hands shaking just enough.

Placing his valise on the seat, the doctor climbed into the carriage. 'I mean your brother is probably already acquainted with the fact that he has just a few years left on this earth.' Taking up the reins, he raised his hat again. 'Good day, Miss Pardoe. I will call one week from today.'

A few years? Annie returned to the house. Alfred Dingley was wrong. Her brother Samuel did not have a few years left on this earth, he had less than a few days.

She had taken so much care. The seeds of yew and laburnum painstakingly collected from the garden of the Bescot house. Several seasons' worth gathered and stored before the shrubs had been rooted out and burned, leaving nothing that could be traced. Dried and ground to an ultra-fine powder and added to water, the seeds had produced a liquid that held death in its pale golden heart, death that had slept within a perfume bottle waiting the time to strike. That time had come on the day of the burglary.

Annie stood before her cheval mirror admiring the sheen

of her pearl grey dress. Samuel had said how nice it was to see her in a colour other than black. How much more becoming soft shades were to her, how particularly well the grey suited her. It had suited well that day. She touched her fingers to the pocket in her skirt, concealed by the folds of taffeta. She had taken the bottle from the drawer and put it in her pocket. Samuel had been so taken up with examining the other rooms in order to ascertain whether anything other than the few silver ornaments had been taken he did not see her add the liquid from the bottle to the glass of sherry she had poured for him. Clinton had arrived just at that moment. He had heard of the burgling of her home, he said, and had to call to satisfy himself no one had been harmed.

It had not mattered to her then. She had almost smiled as she had poured a second glass of the pale golden sherry for Clinton. It had not mattered that he had met Samuel, theirs would be only a short acquaintance. Placing the glasses on a small silver serving tray she had been interrupted by the arrival of the constables and had left the two men to their drinks while she showed the policemen to the study.

Clinton had been taking his leave when she returned and she had walked with him into the tree-shrouded drive. She would have the deeds to her industrial properties the next day, he had told her, then kissed her cheek before leaving.

Turning from the mirror she crossed the room to the chest of drawers. Sinking on to her knees she pulled open the bottom drawer, taking the box with its amethyst ring from beneath the tissue-wrapped petticoats. Slipping the ring on to the third finger of her left hand she twisted and turned her wrist, admiring the dancing spurts of purple flame shoot from the heart of the stone. Soon she would wear it beyond this room, soon it would shine where all could see.

She felt no regret for what she had done to Samuel, for bringing early the death that Alfred Dingley foretold. Any regret she might have felt was gone, eaten away by her wasted years; nor did she feel any guilt. That must be Abel's for the shackles forged by his money.

Returning the ring to its box, Annie slipped it back beneath the petticoats and stood up. She would be Clinton's wife and Samuel would be gone from her life. Soon she would be free from all she had despised for so long, free from all that had held her prisoner while her youth slipped away, a freedom that had no place in it for Samuel and none for Abel's daughter.

Abel's daughter! Annie turned away from the chest of drawers, catching her reflection in the mirror as she did so. She had once been as Abel's child, young, pretty enough, full of happiness, eager for life and the promise it held. But the promise had been broken, life had not been given to her, it had been snatched away, snatched by a brother intent on his own happiness to the detriment of her own; a brother who could not himself be made to pay for what he had done to her but whose daughter would pay.

Annie smoothed her grey dress but her eyes were on the reflection of her face, on the tired skin, on the lines about her mouth, on the creases across her brow, on the look of age. The gall of bitterness rose within her. 'The sins of the parents shall be visited upon the children,' she whispered. 'She will pay, Abel . . . to the very last penny.'

'It's just impossible.' Lucy read the letter then passed it to Mathew. 'Six or seven locks a day . . . it can't be done.'

'I know.' They were in the kitchen of Phoebe's house, the evening meal having been cleared, the table holding only the letter Mathew had placed at its centre. 'The first reply to my advertisement and I can't fulfil the order.'

''Ave you talked of this wi' Bert?'

'What is the use?' Phoebe glanced at the tall young man, shirt sleeves rolled above the elbow, a broad belt about his waist. His sleeked back hair was still wet from a wash at the outdoor pump.

'Maybe none,' Mathew answered, 'but you should talk to 'im all the same.'

'Like Miss Phoebe says,' Lucy turned to her husband, 'it ain't no use talkin'. Talkin' don't make no locks.'

'It don't cost nothin' neither.' Mathew's retort was sharp.

'You think I should have shown the Ingleses that letter?'

'I don't think as 'ow it would 'ave 'urt none even if it didn't do no good. Seems only right to me some'ow that Bert be told.'

'I don't see as tellin' Bert will make no difference no'ow,' Lucy said stubbornly. 'It might only make 'im feel bad 'cos 'e can't do what that order asks.'

'Lucy has a point, Mathew.' Phoebe picked up the letter, folding it into its envelope. 'Bert works so hard, I would not want him to feel that losing this order was due to him.'

'Nor you should.' Mathew's lower lip came forward as it always did when he felt his argument was the right one. 'But it seems the bloke 'as the right to know 'is locks not just be sellin' well but could be sellin' a damn' sight better.'

'An' that be supposed to make 'im feel good, is it?'

'It would bloody well mek *me* feel good!' Mathew frowned at his wife. 'A bloke slaves 'is guts out, it shouldn't be too much for 'im to know the job 'e be doin' is a good 'un.'

'You are right, of course, Mathew.' Phoebe stood up, the letter in her hand. 'Bert should see the order. I will take it to him now.'

'I realise it cannot be done but we thought you should see the order, it shows how well your work is being received.' Phoebe waited while Bert Ingles read through the letter.

'It can't given the way we be now,' he handed back the letter, 'but that don't mean to say as it couldn't be done at all.'

''Ow be that then?' Mathew asked, his broad shoulders almost blocking the doorway of the small workshop. 'I don't follow.'

'It be logical,' Bert answered. 'One bloke on 'is own can't be doin' everythin', but give 'im a little 'elp . . .'

''Elp?' Lucy squeezed in against Mathew. ''Ow can we 'elp? We be knowin' nothin' of lockmakin'.'

'Mathew do.' Bert smiled. ''E's picked it up real well, an' Lizzie does most of the filin' down, an' Miss Phoebe there 'elps out wi' that, an' the lad works the bellows an' fetches coals up from the cut.'

'Coals!' Phoebe asked, perplexed.

'Ah, Miss, coals.' Bert turned to her. 'You needs coal to fire the forge an' we gets it from the barges that pass along the cut.'

'You mean the bargees give you coal?'

'Not gives,' Bert grinned, 'they comes 'ere for fresh water an' leaves a few buckets o' coal the side o' the cut afore they goes. It's fair trade.'

'But . . . but don't they get into trouble? It . . . it's like stealing.'

'No, it ain't, Miss.' Lizzie smiled. 'The coal bosses, they knows as cut men can't carry everythin' they needs for trips to London or the coast an' they makes allowances like. They knows a bit o' coal 'as to be swapped for water an' such.'

And may the Lord shut His ears to your lies, Lizzie Ingles, she thought, glancing away. Any hint of a bargee exchanging coal for any reason would have the coal bosses slamming him into gaol, but then, what the eye don't see, the heart don't grieve over.

'So if we all be already doin' what we can to 'elp, 'ow come you says the fillin' o' that order could be done?' Mathew asked.

'I reckons as 'ow it could be given another bloke or two, a few more hours workin' a day, an' a bit o' proper machinery to work wi'.'

'But we don't 'ave another bloke!' Lucy stated the obvious.

'Then there be the metal, Miss,' Lizzie added. 'You 'ave to

'ave money for metal. Bert sometimes gets carried away. 'E don't always see obstacles till 'e cuts 'is nose on 'em.'

'I see this order could be the start.' Bert looked at Phoebe. 'This could lead to others. Get this done an' I reckon you will be lookin' at the beginnin' of a business that could grow into summat big.'

'Buying brass and steel is one thing,' Phoebe was touched by the note of hope in Bert's voice, knowing how his dreams had ended with his father's death, 'but buying machinery is another.'

'You wouldn't 'ave to.'

'Then how?'

'I think as Bert be thinkin' of 'is own,' Lizzie put in. 'The rest of 'is tools still be in a out'ouse back of 'is father's place. They were never sold . . . nobody 'ad use for 'em seemed.'

'Until now.' Phoebe's mouth set in a determined line. 'We are going to use them. What has happened once will happen again and next time we will not have to refuse an order.'

'What you thinkin' of?' Lucy asked, recognising the determined expression.

'I am thinking we should discuss this further but not here in the workshop. Come across to the house, all of you. And with your permission, Lizzie and Bert, I would like Mark to come too. He helps in the workshop, he should be part of any decision that is made.'

'So,' Phoebe looked at the circle of people grouped about her kitchen, 'we need metal, we need men, and we need equipment. Where do we find them and how much will it cost?'

'The equipment be no bother,' Bert said. 'There be several bench vices, an anvil, 'ammers, tongs, chisels, files, the lot in my old place. They only needs bringin' 'ere, and findin' space to work be no 'eadache.'

'Then we must find a way of bringing them here.'

'Reckon a couple of Lucy's best mutton pies would see to that.' Bert grinned as he had in the workshop, the excitement of regaining his own equipment showing in his eyes.

'I see,' Lucy laughed, 'it's bribery now, is it?'

'Summat like that.' Lizzie looked up from her chair by the fire, her daughter on her knee. 'Bert be good at that.'

'See, Miss,' he went on, 'the 'ole lot, bench an' all, could be brought 'ere by barge.'

'But you don't work the barges anymore, Bert, so how does that help us?'

'No, I don't work the barges any more,' he answered, 'but I knows many who does an' there be one alongside towpath who be goin' up to Wolverhampton tomorrow. That will take him through Willenhall and right past my old place, an' 'e will be back 'ere the same afternoon. 'E would cart the lot for nuthin' more'n a couple of pies.'

'Could the man do that? Alone, I mean. Some of the things you need must be quite heavy?'

''E would need another man. I thought as I might 'ave to go wi' 'im.'

'Would there be anythin' I wouldn't recognise?' Mathew caught the flavour of the discussion. 'If you give me a good description, could I find the things you want?'

Bert thought for a moment before nodding. 'Reckon you could, ain't nothin' special.'

'Then why don't I go?' Mathew looked at Phoebe, her hands resting on the table, still holding the letter with its order for one gross of locks. 'That way Bert could carry on with the locks 'e is workin' on.'

'But what of your own work?' Phoebe asked.

'Ain't much of it at the moment,' Mathew answered wryly. 'Don't seem to be anybody wantin' odd jobs done right now an' what locks I'd be sellin' round the town could be countin' towards the gross we be needin'.'

'We are still left with the matter of employing another man,' Phoebe said.

'I've 'ad me brain on that one an' all,' Bert said again, 'if it's all right to say?'

'You've 'ad nuthin' but good ideas so far Bert so let's be 'earing what else you 'ave to say.'

Bert smiled at Mathew's words but his eyes were on Phoebe.

'Mathew has said what we all feel.' She smiled encouragement. 'Without you there would be no lockmaking business. You have solved all the problems so far, I am sure you will be helpful again.'

'Well, Miss, way I look at it is this. Mathew there 'as a good 'and for the locks, 'e 'as picked the job up a treat, 'sides which 'e as the strength needed for usin' 'ammer an' anvil. Now 'e 'as said as 'ow odd jobs 'ave dropped off so why not give 'im the job of workin' along o' me?'

'I had never thought of that,' Phoebe said, 'but how would Mathew feel about it? And what of Lucy?'

'I wants Mathew to be 'appy in what 'e is doin',' Lucy said as her husband's eyes turned to her. 'Whatever 'e chooses I know 'e does it for the best.'

Reaching for her hand Mathew folded it in his own, his smile broad. 'I'd like to work wi' Bert, Miss. Tattin' for jobs be no way to mek a livin'. Seems this lock business is goin' to tek off an' bein' in on it would give a man a reglar job like.'

'So we have our new hand,' Phoebe tapped her fingers against the envelope, 'now what we must do is work out the finances.'

Almost an hour later Phoebe pushed across the table a sheet of paper covered with figures and leaned wearily against the back of her chair.

'If only I had not bought that material to make a gown we might just have managed. I'm so sorry, Bert.'

'Ain't your fault.' Lizzie handed her daughter across to Mark who placed a protective arm about his sister's thin shoulders. 'You wasn't to know about no order comin' in.' Taking the pot from the dresser, she set about making tea.

'Of course it ain't no fault of your'n.' Lucy turned to help Lizzie with the tea. 'It was your money, you 'ad a right to spend it any road you wanted.'

'What say we goes through it once more?' Bert intervened.

Her calculations were correct, Phoebe knew. To go over them a thousand times more would only bring the same result: she just did not have sufficient money to buy the metal and pay the extra wages and no amount of checking the figures would alter that. But she leaned over them again, not having the heart to say no as she saw the dream dying in Bert's eyes.

'Let's all have a cup of tea an' p'raps things will look better.' Lizzie handed out the steaming cups while Phoebe buttered a scone each for the children.

''Scuse me, Miss.' Mark pulled a sultana from the edge of his scone, eyeing it with the look of a connoisseur, 'but you said as since I was workin' along o' me father I should be paid a reglar wage.'

'So I did, Mark.' Phoebe saw the astonished face of the boy's mother and the tightening of Bert's hand on his broad leather belt.

'Well, Miss,' Mark kept his eyes on the sultana, avoiding the warning glare that was in his father's eyes, 'I don't want it.'

'You don't want it?' Phoebe glanced quickly at the angry face of his father then back to the boy. 'But, Mark, we all agreed that a shilling a week was a fair wage.'

'It's a bostin' wage, Miss, only you can keep it toward payin' for metals. But when you gets paid for them locks, I will tek a shillin' a week.' His toffeedrop eyes gleaming with the air of a satisfied businessman clinching a deal, he popped the sultana into his mouth.

His anger forgotten, Bert touched a proud hand to his son's shoulder. 'He be right, what you reckon to pay 'im do be a good wage. Reckon lad 'as shown the way we was lookin' for,' he said. 'You can 'old my wage over till job be done an' locks paid for an' all.'

'I could not do that.' Phoebe looked up, astonished at Bert's words. 'Thank you, both of you, but you cannot work for nothing.'

''T'wouldn't be for nuthin',' Bert answered solemnly. 'Look at it my way. As things be Lizzie an' me 'as a roof for the children an' food for their bellies. Anythin' over an' above that be a luxury, an' luxuries can be gone wi'out. I know Lizzie will agree to what I says an' it be this. We will do as we did the first week we come 'ere. We 'ave enough to live on for the next three weeks so Mark an' me will tek no wage. You can make it up once locks be paid for.'

'Lucy an' me be of the same mind,' Mathew came in quickly, preventing Phoebe's refusal. 'We can manage same as Bert an' Lizzie.'

'I don't know what to say.' Phoebe's eyes glistened.

'Ain't nuthin' to be said, 'cept get these cups outa the way an' let's go over them figures again.' Bert came to stand at her shoulder. 'This time we're goin' to make 'em work.'

'We are still short,' Phoebe announced later as Lizzie carried her sleeping daughter out of the kitchen, Mark at her heels. 'I don't see there is anything more we can do.'

'I do 'ave one more suggestion.' Bert ran a hand through his hair. 'You 'ave down there the wage for another workman along o' Mathew. That be countin' for 'alf a crown a week. Now Mark, 'e knows lockmakin' inside out. Long nights on a barge leave a lad wi' little to do. 'E 'as a good brain, an' what's better 'e listens to what 'e be told. 'E can do all I do 'cept for the anvil an' that be a bit too 'eavy for 'im as yet.'

'So what are you saying?'

'I'm sayin' this. You got to pay 'alf a crown a week for summat my lad can do, and on top o' that you will need a coupla weeks to show a new bloke the ropes an' a damn' sight more'n a coupla weeks afore 'e can be left to work on 'is own, where the lad can do that now.'

Phoebe pressed a hand to her back, more tired than she wished to show. 'I don't understand, Bert.'

'I think I do,' Mathew said. 'You will be payin' a man's wage for a job 'e won't be able to do for weeks, the same job as Mark can do now, so why not let 'im work on the locks an' get another bloke to work the bellows an' bring up the coal, right, Bert?'

'Almost.' He grinned. 'My way you will be gettin' job done quicker an' for less money.'

'But if Mark is doing what a man would do he must be paid the same wage.'

'That ain't the way of things, Miss.' Bert straightened from where he had been stooped over the figures. 'Lad won't be doin' quite all a man would 'ave to, like I say 'e ain't up to 'ammerin' on a anvil, not yet. An' anyway, young 'uns gets paid less on account of the trainin' they be given. I 'preciates your thinkin' but I would rather 'e learned the usual ways of the world.'

'Bert be right in what 'e says,' Mathew nodded. 'This be one o' the facts you 'as to learn if you be goin' to run a business.'

'I expect so.' Phoebe smiled. 'And I understand we have no time to train a man in the skills of lockmaker, but we will still have to employ one to do what Mark was doing so where is the saving in that?'

'I said Mathew was almost right.' Bert pointed to the column of figures. ''Alf a crown for a bloke against ninepence for a lad, so why set a bloke on doin' a lad's work? Pumpin' bellows be a lad's work so why not get a lad to do it? It will cut nearly two-thirds off what you will pay in wages.'

Phoebe ran a swift eye over the figures, her tiredness evaporating as the import of what Bert was saying struck home. Mentally deducting the wages of Mathew, Bert and Mark, together with the revised wage of a youth, she felt a tremor of exhilaration. She could do it!

'Supposing you can make that many locks in a day, then we can accept our first order.' Rising from her chair, she held out a hand to each of the two men. 'Thank you,' she said simply, 'thank you both very much.'

'An' I'll thank you both to leave,' Lucy bustled into the scullery in search of baking tins, 'otherwise there'll be no mutton pies for that there bargee an' that'll put the cobblebosh on the lot of it.'

Taking his flat cap from his trousers pocket, Bert held it in his hand. 'I'll go down to towpath now an' 'ave a word wi' 'im, but 'e will bring my stuff right enough, no need to lose sleep over that. Night, Miss. Night, Lucy.'

'Goodnight, Bert,' Phoebe answered as he moved toward the scullery door. 'And, Bert, you have a good son in Mark.'

'Aye, Miss,' Bert fitted the cap to his head, 'Lizzie an' me, we knows that.'

Chapter Seventeen

'I instructed my own barrister to look into the affair of your time in prison.' Sir William Dartmouth looked at the young woman standing before him, hands folded across the front of a print dress, hair that was neither gold nor brown caught back in a knot that tried in vain to add years to her face. 'The result, I regret to say, showed a lamentable lack of justice. I have here a warrant signed by a magistrate – not, I might say, the one who consigned you to prison in the first place. What I ask is, will you return to Handsworth Prison for Women with me or would you prefer the constables to escort you there?'

Instructed my own barrister, I have a warrant, will you return, would you prefer the constables . . .

The words whirled together, dancing a crazy fandango, whisking in and out of her understanding. Phoebe clenched her hands together, hoping the bite of nails into flesh would stop the screams rising to her throat. He had not forgotten though he had been told of her innocence of the theft of his daughter's necklace, he wanted vengeance, never mind if the victim be free from blame. He had pretended friendship, even to the length of asking that his son be her escort to a farewell ball, and all the time he had been searching for a way to send her back to hell.

'You . . . you say you have a warrant?'

'Here.' He tapped the folded sheet against a gloved hand. 'Do you wish to read it?'

'No . . .' Phoebe breathed long and deep, fighting the nausea that was laying claim to her stomach. 'There will be no need, Sir William.' She could read it, Phoebe thought, fetching her coat, but she could not alter it. This time the Magistrate would not be wrong. This man would have his revenge and would make certain there could be no way he would be cheated of it.

Thanking the coachman for the hand he held out to help her up, Phoebe climbed into the carriage, her gaze on her home until it fell away below the rise of the ground.

How long had he been planning this? Phoebe watched the passing landscape but saw only the devils of fear dancing in her brain. Was it in his mind when she met him outside of the Magistrate's rooms in Wednesbury . . . was he thinking of it when he sent Edward and Sophie to invite her to the ball? And Edward, was he party to his father's action? Had he known of it even when he had asked her to marry him?

She closed her eyes, leaning her head against the padded upholstery of the carriage. No one save Sir William Dartmouth would know where she had gone or what had happened. Lizzie had watched from where she had been hanging washing on a clothes line Bert had set up beside the old windmill to catch the best of the breezes, but it had been too far for her to see any distress which might have shown. How long would Lucy and Mathew wait before making enquiries as to her whereabouts? Tomorrow? The next day? No, not that long, they knew she would not stay away from Wiggins Mill that length of time unless she had told them beforehand. And what if they went to the Priory? Would he see them, or would he have them dismissed without a word?

'Miss Pardoe, Miss Pardoe, we have arrived.'

This was not happening, it was a bad dream that would vanish when she opened her eyes, but it didn't and as she stepped from the carriage to be faced by that blank wall with its solid oak door Phoebe came face to face with the nightmare she had thought was over.

The door opened in answer to a knock from Sir William's malacca cane and they were inside. Inside the jaws of Hell.

Phoebe followed the grim-faced wardress in her grey soulless uniform, their footsteps sounding sharp in the carbolic-laden air of the narrow bare brick corridors. *I sentence you to fifteen years* . . . The words seemed to echo from the brickwork. How many years would it be this time? How much of her life would be spent paying for a crime she did not commit?

'Begging your pardon . . .'

The wardress had led them to a small, sparsely furnished waiting room Phoebe had heard of but had not seen and now stood looking at her, a faint shadow of near-forgotten concern on her long, drawn features.

'. . . but are you feeling unwell, Miss?'

Sensing Sir William move toward her, Phoebe stepped away.

'We do 'ave a infirmary 'ere, Sir,' the wardress looked at Sir William, 'if the lady would like to rest? She do look pale.'

'Thank you, but I am quite all right.'

Phoebe forced the words past a throat tight with fear. Resting in the infirmary would delay her return to the dormitory and the laundry only for as long as it took the man who had brought her here to leave. It had to happen, she had to return to the torture of long days and nights locked in this Godforsaken place, so why delay the inevitable? Let her sentence begin.

'Then I will tell the Governess you are 'ere.' The wardress bobbed the tiniest of curtsies. ''scuse me.'

'Miss Pardoe,' catching her arm as the wardress left the waiting room Sir William pressed her to a chair, 'are you quite certain you are not feeling unwell? You were very quiet during our drive here and now . . . as the wardress said, you are looking very pale.'

Looking very pale? Phoebe wanted to laugh but stared at him instead, rage at his treatment of her suddenly destroying the fear that had been suffocating her.

Pushing his hand from her arm she stood up, her features calm and icy as if carved from some glacial peak. 'I am looking very pale, how unwarranted of me!' Every word clipped into the quiet room like ice cubes falling into a glass. 'Please forgive my thoughtlessness. How ungracious of me to look so when you were kind enough to escort me here personally . . . how ignorant to repay that kindness by looking pale! So tell me, Sir William, how do you expect a woman to look when she is being returned to the grave?'

'Returned to the . . . I don't understand?'

'Of course you don't understand!' Phoebe spat, anger and fear overcoming her reserve. 'How could you understand? You to whom a girl dare not come with the truth for fear of tainting the name of Dartmouth. You who have been protected from reality all your life, whom the people raise their hat to, the powerful Billy-me-Lord, how could *you* understand what it is to be imprisoned? The degradation, the total lack of privacy, the utter soul-destroying mindlessness of it, the complete waste of a life . . . how would you know the torment of being accused of something you did not do, of having your life ripped away, of being condemned to a living hell, to be released only to be returned? To have the torment begin all over again!'

'Miss Pardoe . . .' He made to touch her then his hand fell to his side. He stayed where he was, watching the shades of passion flit across her face. 'I am sorry my bringing you here has caused you distress . . .'

'Sorry!' Phoebe glared contemptuously. 'You are *sorry* to have caused me distress? What did you expect returning me to prison would cause?'

'I did not think . . .'

'You did not think!' Phoebe cut across him, her tone lacerating. 'Do not insult me with lies, Sir William. You could have thought of little else all the time you were planning your revenge.'

'Revenge? I . . .'

'Yes, revenge.' She refused to let him speak, anger still uppermost. 'You pretended friendship towards me, you and your family, when all you really wanted was to have me re-committed to this prison. Why, Sir William? Why when you know I am innocent, when you have the necklace back? Why . . . is it to show the great Sir William Dartmouth is not to be played with?'

'Miss Pardoe, listen . . .'

'To what? More lies?'

'Call what I have to say lies if you will, but you shall listen. I brought you here . . .'

'Good day, Sir William.'

He stopped in mid-sentence, turning to see Hannah Price standing in the doorway.

'Miss Pardoe, my dear, how are you?'

Habit bent Phoebe's knee to a slight curtsy as she faced the Governess of Handsworth Prison for Women, fear surging up through the anger.

'I am well, Ma'am,' she murmured.

'But you look so pale.' She glanced at the man standing tight-lipped beside the young woman who had spent over a year locked behind the walls of this prison, a young woman she had come to like, whose loyalty and courage she had grown to respect. 'Sir William, perhaps the infirmary . . .'

'No, Mrs Price, thank you but we will get our business over. I want no further delay.'

'As you wish.' The governess nodded to the wardress who had remained at the door and she stood aside, allowing a third figure to enter the room.

'You wanted to see me, Ma'am?'

Everything stilled in Phoebe: her mind, her heart, the very blood in her veins.

'Yes, come in. Would you wait outside, Mrs Marsh?'

'Yes, Ma'am.'

Phoebe refused to let the exchange register, waiting only for the voice that had stilled her world to speak again.

'I think you know one of our visitors?' Hannah Price said.

In the stillness of her soul, Phoebe waited.

'Phoebe?'

The voice was uncertain but Phoebe was not. She knew that voice, recognised it from the long months of her captivity. 'Tilly!' She whirled to face the gaunt-faced woman, her hair tied in the compulsory plaits, the regulation grey skirts hanging loose about her thin body. 'Tilly! Oh, Tilly!'

'Sir William.' Phoebe stood at the front entrance to Wiggins Mill, her cheeks pink with embarrassment of what she knew she had to say. He had remained silent during the drive back to the mill, watching her hold a sobbing Tilly in her arms, then had waited until she had been settled with tea in a china cup, the kindly Lizzie in attendance. 'Sir William . . .' Phoebe began again.

'You do not have to say anything.' He placed a hand on her elbow, leaving it there as he added, 'It was thoughtless of me to act as I did. There is no need for apology.'

'There is every need,' Phoebe said, her eyes still holding traces of the tears of relief and happiness she had shed. 'It was wrong of me to speak to you as I did.'

'I think harsh words a mild punishment given the circumstances.' His grey eyes grew warm. 'Were I in your shoes nothing short of a horsewhipping would satisfy my feelings, I do not consider you at fault in any way.'

'That is kind of you, Sir William.' The colour deepened in Phoebe's cheeks, 'but I was at fault. I should have asked your reasons for taking me back to that place before I railed at you.'

'What did you think my reasons were?'

'Revenge.' Embarrassed as she was, Phoebe forced herself to meet his gaze. 'I thought you planned to have me returned to gaol, to have me serve the sentence originally passed upon me or perhaps an even longer one.'

'You thought the warrant I had was an order returning you to prison?'

'Yes.'

'But you had not been brought before a Magistrate, there

had been no new charge laid against you, how could you have thought you were being returned to serve that sentence?'

'Fear makes you suspect many things you would not normally think. I was afraid – afraid of being locked into Hell.'

'Miss Pardoe,' his eyes darkened and the fingers holding her arm tightened, 'I would never have you afraid because of me. Believe me when I say I was thinking only of the pleasure my actions would afford you. Causing you fear or concern never entered my mind. You told me of the circumstances of your friend's trial, of how you suspected there had been a miscarriage of justice. I thought it would in some way make amends for the suffering my family caused you if I could get a review of Mrs Wood's trial. I put the whole of what I knew before my own barrister who set in motion a further investigation of the so-called murder of the husband. It appears that other occupants of the lodging house where they lived had witnessed the argument. They had seen the man strike his wife and her attempt to defend herself. They had seen him fall backward down the stairs, causing his death.'

'Why didn't they say so at Tilly's trial? Why didn't they tell the Magistrate that?'

'It appears the constables did not report there being witnesses to the fall.' He did not remove his hand nor did his eyes leave hers. 'Or at least that is what the prosecution claimed. My barrister pressed for a complete review of the trial on the grounds of suppression of evidence, with the result that Mrs Wood was given a Queen's Pardon. Had I thought to tell you of all this before we went to Handsworth Prison you would not have been subjected to so much worry. I am deeply sorry and apologise most profoundly.'

'You are sorry and I am sorry.' Phoebe broke into a smile. 'We are a sorry pair, you and I, Sir William.'

'Yes.' His fingers tightened fractionally and the grey of his eyes turned to smoke. 'A sorry pair,' he finished softly.

'Sir William,' she said as he withdrew his hand from her

arm and turned towards his waiting carriage, 'I will not forget what you have done, for Tilly and for me.'

I will not forget either, Miss Phoebe Pardoe, he thought, climbing into the carriage. I will not forget what you have done to me.

'Annie dear, tomorrow I would like to see James Siveter.' Samuel's fingers moved without hesitation. 'I told you I wish to return most of what Abel bequeathed me to Phoebe.'

Annie's mind moved like quicksilver. He could not know that Phoebe still lived here in Wednesbury. She scrutinised the newspapers closely before passing them to him, removing those advertisements that referred to Pardoe's Patent Locks, and there was no one who could communicate with him other than herself. She alone had learned to speak with her hands; even Abel had not troubled himself to do so, relying on her to relay what he wished to say to Samuel.

'I want the papers drawn up tomorrow.'

She caught the quick movements, her thoughts outstripping them. Let Samuel say all he wished it would achieve nothing. There would be no tomorrow. She had thought the poison she had concocted from the yew and laburnum seed would have acted more rapidly than this; she had tried it often in those early years, feeding it to mice then cats then a dog, and in every instance it had brought death in less than two days. But for Samuel it had not worked. He had shown no more than his usual signs of illness. Was that due to Alfred Dingley's potions? She doubted it. The medicines he prescribed were no more than coloured sugar water prescribed as a salve to his own conscience for the fees he charged.

'I will go to his office in the morning,' she signed. 'I will tell him what you want and ask him to bring the papers here to you when they are ready.' That way she could delay long enough, she thought. A day would be all she needed.

'No.' The shake of Samuel's head signalled his refusal while his fingers flashed the rest of his words. 'I do not wish Mr Siveter to call at the house. I intend to visit him in his office myself tomorrow.'

You may intend to visit him, Annie thought, but I intend you do not.

'Will you be kind enough to drive me there in the trap, Annie dear?'

'Of course.' She smiled, her hands moving nimbly. 'If you are feeling as well tomorrow as you are today then certainly we will visit Mr Siveter.'

If he was well. Annie resisted the temptation to laugh. He would not be!

Samuel looked about him, the colours of late summer glowing the borders to the lawns. He loved the garden in all its phases but perhaps this was his favourite time.

'Brunswick House is such a kind house,' he motioned, 'it is almost a shame to leave it.'

A shame for you, Annie's thoughts raced, but not for me. I shall not be sorry to see the last of this place, to see the last of Wednesbury. I shall have a home of my own at last, a home with Clinton.

'Like you say, Samuel,' her fingers answered, 'it will be a shame to leave, but if it will give you peace of mind then of course that is what we must do.'

'Thank you, dear,' he smiled his weary smile, 'you always were so understanding, I will ensure you are well provided for.'

'Nonsense,' she returned, 'whatever makes you happy is all I want. But tell me, dear, how do we go about finding Phoebe? We do not know where she went, she may not even live in Wednesbury any more.'

'I know,' Samuel answered, 'but I am sure Mr Siveter will have methods of enquiry. We may leave it to him to find her.'

'Then we will tell him to begin tomorrow.' Annie touched a hand to the pain below her breast. It troubled her more often as the days passed, forcing her to take the white tablets several times each day, waking her in the night with fresh demands.

'It's time for Mr Samuel's medicine, Ma'am.' Maudie Tranter set a tray on the wicker table set between the garden chairs. 'Will I measure it?'

'Yes,' Annie nodded, 'but carefully. Two dessert spoons, no more, we must not exceed the amount the doctor advised.'

Bloody hypocrite, Maudie thought, carefully filling the dessert spoon she had placed on the tray then pouring the liquid into a glass before repeating the process. 'Er wouldn't care if 'e swallowed the lot, bottle an' all. But the Lord missed nothing and he wouldn't be missin' Annie Pardoe's doings. There was evil in that one, an old evil that had festered from her mother's passing, an evil that wouldn't be quenched this side of the grave.

'Will I pour the tea, Ma'am?' she asked as Samuel took the glass, swallowing its contents.

'No.' Annie reached for the dainty flower-patterned milk jug. 'I will do it myself.'

Samuel would take his tea then would go to his room and rest, probably sleep for several hours. That would give her time. Annie took her own cup, sipping her tea as the seed of her plan germinated in her mind, temporarily banishing the pain from her side.

'I want you to go into town.'

'Yes Ma'am.' Maudie had answered the bell summoning her to the study.

'Mrs Gaskell Wheeler told me of a herbal tea she was sure would be of benefit to Mr Samuel,' Annie went on. 'I have written the name of it on this paper. Take it to the herbalist in Meeting Street and wait until it is made up, I want my brother to have it today.' She handed the paper to her housekeeper together with a florin. 'There will be change from that,' she said as Maudie turned to leave. 'That herbal tea will cost no more than sixpence.'

'I'll get 'im to mek a bill out,' Maudie said, and banged the door behind her.

Samuel had been sleeping half an hour, Annie looked at the fob watch she wore pinned to her dress, and Maudie had been gone five minutes. Opening the doors that led directly into the garden she walked its length, turning at the tall privet hedge that screened the brick boundary wall and making her way to the low bothy building housing garden tools.

It was not one of the days the gardener-handyman was employed at Brunswick House. What she was about to do would be observed by no one. Going into the building she searched quickly along the shelves. It was there, the cardboard carton the gardener had bought, a carton containing rat poison. He had shown it to her, labouring the importance of keeping it out of reach, stressing the potency of its contents.

Taking her handkerchief from her pocket, she tipped a little of the powder into it, wrapping it carefully in the folds of the small white square of cloth before pushing it deep inside her pocket. Then, after replacing the carton on the shelf, she left.

From his bedroom window Samuel watched his sister return along the garden and knew where she had been. The colour of the dress she wore had changed. She no longer wore black, but that was the only thing about his sister that was different. Inside the same bitterness that had plagued her youth plagued her still.

Entering the house through the scullery, Annie glanced at her fob watch, checking the time once more. Maudie Tranter would be another hour at least. She had time yet.

'What did you think when you knew there was to be a re-investigation?'

They sat together in the warm kitchen. The fire had settled low in the grate and one oil lamp spilled a pool of yellow light courted by shadows.

'I didn't know.' Tilly's eyes strayed for the hundredth time around the kitchen, not yet believing it would not disappear like some dream-built world at the chime of a clock.

'But you must have been given some hint? The Governess or the wardresses, surely they said something?'

'If they knowed they said nothin' to me.' Tilly returned her gaze to the glowing coals. 'You knows what it's like in that place. If anythin' good was goin' to 'appen then that lot would be as close-mouthed as a Jew in a presbytery. They'd keep it to theirselves on purpose, drag out the agony a bit longer.'

'I can believe that of the likes of Agnes Marsh but I had thought better of Hannah Price,' Phoebe answered. 'I always got the impression she acted fairly.'

'Ah, me wench, we all thought that, an' 'er was fair an' all. 'Er was a decent woman an' a good prison governess. You kept yer nose clean and you 'ad no worry from 'er.'

'Do you think she knew?'

'Can't say.' Tilly looked again to the rough wooden dresser, studying the motley assortment of cups and dishes. 'Maybe yes, then again maybe no. There was some comin' an' goin' about a week ago, 'er was off out somewhere two or three times, but we put it down to meetings wi' Prison Board.'

'Mary Pegleg heard nothing?'

'You can bet yer life 'er didn't.' Tilly stretched a hand to the lamp Phoebe had set in the middle of the kitchen table, running a finger over the gleaming brass body. 'Mary Pegleg gets to know summat an' 'er's like a cat wi' a maggot up its arse – 'er can't get it out quick enough.'

Phoebe bent over the spent fire, adding fresh coals, the move hiding her smile at her friend's rough language. Tilly had been in gaol a long time and the ways of others had touched her. It would take time for them to fade.

'If those meetings with the Prison Board concerned your release and Hannah Price said nothing of it to you, then she must have been told not to. I can't imagine there being any other reason for her to keep it from you,' Phoebe said, sitting down again.

'Like as not yer right,' Tilly nodded, 'an' come to think on it p'raps it were the sensible thing to do. I think if 'er 'ad told me there was a chance I'd be gettin' outta that place, then told me later that I weren't, I'd of got meself out another way.'

Phoebe looked perplexed. 'Another way? But surely there was no other way.'

'Oh, ar, there was, me wench.' Tilly looked up from the fire, her laughterless eyes haunted by the spectre of hopes long dead. 'A way I'd thought on many a time. A sharp knife across the throat gets you out of anywheer.'

'Oh, Tilly!' Leaning forward, Phoebe pressed the other woman's calloused hands. 'It's all over now.'

'For me it is.' Suddenly Tilly sounded far away. 'I'll never go back theer again, I'll put meself in me box first.'

Phoebe rose, kneeling before Tilly to put her arms about her. 'You won't ever go back, Tilly, I promise, I promise.'

Holding each other, the two women stared into the flickering flames of the rebuilt fire, each seeing their yesterdays in its heart.

'Phoebe,' Tilly asked after several minutes, ''ow come that man knowed about me an' what I'd done?'

'Sir William?' Releasing her, Phoebe stood up. 'I am afraid I told him after . . .' She broke off, the horror of the attack on her flooding back.

'After what?'

'Nothing.' Phoebe made a business of taking cups from the dresser and setting them on the table. 'Nothing.'

'Yer 'ands be shakin' an' yer face be the colour of a corpse. That don't be tellin' me it was nothin'.'

Locating a brown-coloured tin labelled 'Bournville', Phoebe spooned cocoa into the cups, spilling as much of the powder over the sides as went into them.

'A man came to the house,' she said, knowing Tilly would repeat her question until it was answered. 'I . . . I was upstairs. He thought I had been given money by Sir William and that I had it hidden somewhere.'

''Ad you?' Tilly watched the cocoa powder sprinkle like brown snow over the cups. It was her bet the girl had told nobody the full story of what had happened, and no matter what it had been it was better told and in the open; fastening it up inside herself would only see the fear grow.

'No.' Phoebe loosed the spoon into one of the cups, the clatter loud in the stillness of the kitchen.

'But 'e didn't believe you?' Tilly led her on, knowing each answer would relieve the pain.

'No, he didn't believe me. I thought if I could get him out of the house I might somehow escape him so I told him the money was in the old corn barn. He made me go there with him and while he was searching among the sacks I managed to run out into the yard, but he . . . he . . .'

Tilly rose from her chair. This was the part that was buried deepest, the core of the pain etched across that young face. Taking the tin from Phoebe's trembling hands, she stood it on the table then drew her into her arms. 'Get it up, ma wench,' she said softly, 'let it all come out, Tilly's got you.'

Slowly, between long shuddering sobs, the full story of the attack came out. Tilly listened without intervention. The dam was broken, let the water flow.

'I thought it was Liza,' Phoebe sobbed against her shoulder, 'I thought it was Liza!'

'Ssshh.' Tilly stroked her hair. 'Liza won't 'urt you no more, an' neither will anybody else so long as I be livin'.' She stood with Phoebe in her arms, holding her as she would a child until the sobbing had stopped.

'Now I think we're both ready for that cocoa,' she said, pushing Phoebe into a chair. 'An' I thinks I'll be meking it, you spills too much.'

'I never thought Sir William would do anything to help you,' Phoebe said, sipping the hot frothy liquid.

'An' why should 'e?' Tilly held her own cup cradled between both hands, savouring the heat on her fingers. ''E don't know me from Adam, so why put 'isself to all that bother?'

'He said he did it to try to make up for what his family had caused to happen to me.'

'Well, whatever 'is reason, I thank the Lord for it. 'E got me from Handsworth Prison when I never thought to see the outside of it never again.' She looked across at Phoebe, sudden concern in her eyes. 'Eh, wench, I've just thought! I never even said thank you. 'E's gonna think I'm a right 'un.'

'You didn't say anything as I remember,' Phoebe smiled at last, 'but I am sure Sir William will understand.'

'Do yer think as I might see 'im agen?' Tilly asked. 'Might 'e call 'ere agen sometime?'

Phoebe dropped her eyes to her cup, surprised at the answer rising silently within her. I hope so, Tilly, I hope so.

'P'raps it might be better to write 'im a note, just in case like,' Tilly went on. 'Would you 'elp me, Phoebe?'

'Of course.' She looked up. 'We will do it tomorrow and Lucy will post it for you in Wednesbury. The post office is just a stone's throw through the Shambles.'

'Is there work in Wednesbury?' Tilly asked. 'For a woman like me?'

'A woman like you!' Phoebe said sharply. 'What does that mean?'

'It means, will anybody employ a woman they know 'as been along the line.'

'If you are referring to a certain Tilly Wood,' Phoebe adopted her most cautionary tone, 'I advise you speak of her with respect. She happens to be one of my greatest friends and one who stands in no need of employment for she is to live, and work I might add, here with me at Wiggins Mill.'

'Oh, Phoebe, me wench!' Tilly choked. 'Phoebe!'

Carrying the cups to the scullery Phoebe washed them then returned them to the dresser, giving Tilly time to regain her composure, then she asked, 'Tilly, what happened to Liza?'

'Huh!' She snorted. 'A bad 'un that if ever I met one. It seemed for a long time as 'er wouldn't get over 'ittin' 'er face agen that wall, but 'er did. 'Appen there be no stoppin' the Devil's own, an' Liza Spittle was that all right. 'Er 'adn't been outta that infirmary no more than a fortnight when we 'ad a new inmate, pretty little thing wi' 'air the colour of corn fresh scythed an' eyes blue as a kingfisher's wing. Well, I don't need to tell it but Liza took a shine to 'er an' you won't believe this but so did Emily Pagett. You know, wardress as took Sally Moreton's place.'

'I remember.' Phoebe took a chair on the opposite side of the fire, resting her feet on the hearth.

'Well,' Tilly smiled sardonically, 'that pretty little thing looked like a angel but 'er weren't none. 'Er played them two women one agen another, lettin' both touch 'er up then tellin' each in turn the other 'ad forced 'erself on 'er. It would 'ave been summat for the rest o' we to laugh at if we 'ad any laughter left in we. Any road up, outcome was Liza 'ad the blue devils an' went for Emily Pagett wi' a knife.'

'Did she kill her?'

'No, me wench,' Tilly shook her head, 'though 'er nearly did. Knife just missed 'er lung so Mary Pegleg 'eard the doctor tell the Governess. Anyway, they took Pagett off to some 'ospital in Brummagem an' that be the last we seen of 'er.'

'And Liza?' Phoebe stared at the fire, seeing in its redness the birthmark that spread across the woman's face.

'Prison Board dished out thirty strokes of the cat.' Tilly's voice was devoid of emotion. 'No more than 'er deserved.'

'But is she all right?' Phoebe had to ask. 'She did get over it?'

Tilly was silent for a moment before answering the girl Liza Spittle had tried so many times to assault. 'Might 'ave been,' she said quietly, ''cept 'er 'ung 'erself wi' laces out of 'er own stays.'

Chapter Eighteen

Letting the fob watch drop back into place over her left breast, Annie listened. The house was silent, no movement from overhead. She breathed slowly. Samuel must still be sleeping.

Going into the pantry she brought out the one small chocolate-covered cake delivered to the house fresh each day. Samuel had never liked the taste of medicine, any medicine, complaining of the bitterness after every dose and the cake was a treat that took the taste away.

Annie placed it on a plate. Shaped like a cup, its thick chocolate sides daintily fluted, it was filled with a generous depth of fresh cream and topped with a thick chocolate lid embedded in which was a walnut. Working quickly, Annie removed the lid, scooping out the cream on to a saucer. Taking the powder from her pocket, she tipped it into the cream, mixing the two together. Would Samuel detect the taste? What if he left it uneaten after the first bite? Annie thought for a moment, then going back to the pantry brought out a box of finely powdered sugar. Adding a large spoonful to the cream, she folded it in then carefully returned it to its chocolate case, replacing the lid.

It was done! Putting cake and sugar back in the pantry, Annie cleared all traces of her activity from the kitchen then carried the plate to the scullery, washing both it and her hands and rinsing them in several bowls of water before drying them. Replacing the plate on the dresser in the kitchen, she returned to her chair in the garden, dropping her handkerchief in the stove as she passed through the scullery. Tomorrow she would not be talking to James Siveter, tomorrow she would be talking to Thomas Webb, Wednesbury's undertaker.

'The 'erbal tea, Ma'am.'

Annie opened her eyes, blinking rapidly, pretending to chase sleep from them. But she had not been sleeping though she had been dreaming – dreaming of her life with Clinton.

'The 'erbal tea.' Maudie held out a bottle in which a sludgy brown mixture reached almost to the cork. 'The 'erbalist said to give a small wineglass o' this twice a day.'

'Was that all he said?' Annie hitched herself straighter in the chair.

'No.' Maudie still held the bottle at arm's length.

'Then what else did he say?'

''E said we was fortunate to be 'avin' such fine weather though like as not we'd be payin' for it come winter.'

Snatching the bottle, Annie glared at her housekeeper. The woman deliberately tried to anger her. Was she hoping to be dismissed? Hope or not she would be in very few weeks from now. Rising from the chair, Annie stalked into the house, a smirking Maudie at her heels. 'I will leave this here.' She put the bottle of herbal mixture on the table Maudie kept well scrubbed.

'Will I be tekin' a draught up to Mr Samuel?'

'No.' Annie looked at the bottle then at Maudie, busy fastening the straps of her long white apron. 'No, you can bring a glass with the afternoon tray.'

'The bill for that be there on the dresser an' the change from the florin alongside o' it. You best count it.'

'Didn't you count it when the herbalist gave it to you?'

'Oh, I counted it,' Maudie looked bland, 'but then I ain't the one was worried over it.'

Sweeping to the dresser Annie snatched up the bill, reading the words 'One eight-ounce bottle of herbal mixture, sevenpence'. Scanning the change, one shilling, a threepenny bit and two pennies, she scooped them into her hand. 'Mrs

Gaskell Wheeler was confident this mixture would help Samuel.' She moved across the kitchen toward the door linking it to the rest of the house. 'And Mrs Gaskell Wheeler is most knowledgeable in the use of herbal remedies.'

Mrs Gaskell Wheeler this, Mrs Gaskell Wheeler that! Maudie grabbed the tea tray from beside the dresser, her thoughts acid. Annie Pardoe was possessed by that woman. Would kiss her arse if asked to.

'I think Mr Samuel would quite like his afternoon tea in the garden,' Annie went on. 'It is still so pleasant out there we should take advantage of the warm spell while we can. It is not often we get the chance with a climate such as ours. I will see if my brother is awake yet.'

She had thought of everything but as she moved up the stairs Annie went over it all again in her mind. The herbal tea had been Violet Wheeler's idea and Maudie Tranter had collected it. She, Annie, had left it unopened in the kitchen and would leave it to Maudie to administer it as she would leave it to her to give Samuel the cake. Should anyone question the cause of his death there would be no finger pointed at her and there would be no trace of poison having been added to either the herbal tea or the medicine Alfred Dingley prescribed.

And the cake? Who could prove poison had been added to that? Annie paused at the head of the stairs, pressing a hand to the pain that shot upward through her breast. The cake would be eaten. Samuel was too fond of sweet things to leave any of it uneaten. What if anyone asked the reason for there being just one cake? Annie pressed harder, clenching her teeth against the fire clawing at her side. Maudie Tranter would answer that. She could tell them Annie Pardoe never ate cake or sweet desserts. And the doctor? He would not look too closely, he had been expecting Samuel's death for too long. Pulling in a deep breath, she walked along the corridor to Samuel's bedroom. Yes, she had thought of everything, just as she had with that letter.

* * *

'They all be so pretty,' Tilly fingered the dainty dresses and lace-edged petticoats Phoebe had ready for market, 'an' they sells well, you say?'

'They have up to now.' Phoebe held a strip of ribbon against a length of delphinium-sprigged cotton cloth, matching the colours. 'Lucy says we could sell more.'

'Then sell more is what you must do!'

'It is not that easy.' Phoebe changed the ribbon for one of darker blue. 'I can't sew any more than I do already. I was hoping to buy one of Mr Singer's new sewing machines – I read about them in a newspaper Lucy had wrapped around some fish.'

'Bet that made a change from the smell o' brass filin's.'

Phoebe glanced across at Tilly, noticing the smile about her mouth, a smile that came more easily as each day passed.

'Then why ain't you?'

'Why haven't I what?' Phoebe went back to her first choice of ribbon.

'Why ain't you bought one o' Mr Singer's newfangled machines?'

'Money.' Phoebe spread the flower-strewn cloth on her workroom table and began laying paper pattern cut outs over it. 'I haven't got enough money. My clothing sells well but buying metal for locks swallows it as fast as I get it. I use every penny either on that or cloth or food.'

'An' what does this be for?' Tilly touched the delicate cream-yellow satin still lying in its paper wrapping.

'It was to have been for a ball gown.' Phoebe glanced at the gleaming satin then returned to her cutting.

'Was to 'ave been?' Tilly questioned. 'Why "was to 'ave been"? Why ain't it still goin' to be?'

'Because I will not have the time to make it,' Phoebe said, her lips pursed as she cut around a tricky piece of pattern.

Tilly waited until the manoeuvre was finished then asked,

'But won't the woman it be for be put out wi' your not mekin' 'er gown after gettin' that cloth an' all?'

'I don't think so.' Phoebe gathered the paper pattern pieces together, laying them aside. 'You see the woman was me.'

'You was mekin' yourself a ball gown?'

Phoebe gathered the pieces of cloth she had cut out. 'I had intended to do so but sometimes plans have to be set aside.'

'That means you ain't no longer goin' to mek it.' Tilly covered the cloth with its paper wrapping. 'Why?'

Sitting at her work table Phoebe began to pin the pieces of cloth together, matching sides to sides. 'Because it would be wrong of me to spend time sewing something that was not intended for sale, something that was bringing no money to Wiggins Mill when everyone else was working so hard.'

'But it must 'ave been special for you to 'ave spent money buying that cloth in the first place.'

'I have been invited to the Priory,' Phoebe explained. 'Sir William is giving a farewell ball in place of the more usual Advent Ball, the reason being Lady Amelia is leaving for the continent earlier than she would normally do. Her Ladyship took the influenza some weeks gone and is not yet over the effects.'

'An' you 'ad accepted the invite?'

'Not exactly.'

'Cockeyed way o' carryin' on, ain't it?'

'What is?' Phoebe asked, her mouth half full of pins.

'Buyin' stuff to mek yourself a fancy frock an' you not accepted the party invite exactly.' Tilly retrieved a pin from the floor, dropping it into the tobacco tin Phoebe kept them in. 'Strikes me you 'ad every intention of goin' to that ball. P'raps it could still be done if I 'elped you with the sewin' of it.'

'I did not know you sewed?' The words pushed past the pins still locked between Phoebe's teeth.

'There be a lot you don't know about Tilly Wood, me wench.'

Phoebe removed the pins from her mouth, putting them in

the tobacco tin that had once belonged to Mathew. 'This much I do know, you already work hard enough. You have taken on the running of the house and preparing the meals . . .'

'Lizzie does a fair share o' all that,' Tilly said quickly.

'And you do a fair share of the filing down of the locks.' Phoebe smiled gently. 'I wanted you to rest, Tilly, I didn't want you working just as hard as . . .'

'As hard as I had to inside.' She took up the words Phoebe couldn't say. 'Phoebe, wench, what I does 'ere at Wiggins Mill be paradise compared to Handsworth Gaol. I thank God every minute I breathes for what 'e done for me, an' 'elpin out wi' a bit o' sewin' ain't too great a burden. I'd like to see you go to that there ball.'

'Very well,' sorting a needle Phoebe broke off a length of blue thread, 'we will do a little each evening.' She looked up from threading the needle, her eyes smiling. 'Unless, of course, a fairy godmother should exist somewhere and decides to bring me a gown already made.'

'Oh, they exist all right.' Tilly picked up the tin of pins, staring into it. 'An' not all o' em be old neither. You be my fairy godmother, Phoebe. What you did for me be nuthin' short o' magic.'

'It was not I who got you released from prison, Tilly,' Phoebe reminded her softly. 'It was Sir William Dartmouth. He is the one who worked the magic.'

'Ar, wench, 'e is, an' grateful I be to 'im.' She replaced the tin on the table close by Phoebe's hand. 'Only some'ow I can't see 'im wi' wings an' wavin' of a wand.'

'Bert says the new lad Mathew got to work the bellows is doing very well,' Phoebe said when they had both stopped laughing.

''E is. Lad works like a little Trojan, nuthin' ain't too much trouble for 'im.'

'Do you think carrying coals might be too heavy?'

'No, wench, I don't. The lad be strong enough, Bert wouldn't set 'im no task 'e thought too much.'

'No, he would not.' Phoebe examined her line of stitching. 'Bert is a kind man.'

'They'm a nice family an' willin' workers the lot o' 'em.'

'Including Ruth. I have seen the way she gets under your feet, you can't do anything without her being there.'

'Ar, you be right.' Tilly smiled. 'But I don't mind that, 'er be a pleasant little thing, an' Lizzie 'as seen to it 'er knows 'er manners, never forgets a please or a thank you. An' talkin' of folk gettin' under other folks' feet, I better be off an' leave you to get on wi' what you be about.'

'How are the locks coming along?' Phoebe called after her.

'Nearly 'alf done,' the answer came back. 'Bert says you will 'ave 'em all on time.'

'How can you be certain?'

The evening meal finished, Lucy and Mathew sat for a few minutes before starting their evening's work.

'I can't, but it do seem strange me not seein' 'im once since 'e started.'

Mathew lit his pipe, sucking the stem much as his father did. 'P'raps 'e's found some other way.'

'Such as what?'

'Such as followin' the cut.'

'Could be as you're right but it wouldn't make a lot o' sense,' Lucy said. 'Cut would take 'im right out o' 'is way – 'e lives other end o' Wednesbury. Least that be what 'e told you, wasn't it?'

'Ar.' Mathew tapped his pipe against the heel of his hand.

'Then why would 'e be followin' the cut 'ome?'

'Who knows why kids do 'alf the things they does?'

'They does some daft 'uns, I'll give you that,' Lucy began to clear the table, 'but to go a mile or more outta your way 'ome after a day's work don't strike me as no kid's lark.'

'So what do you reckon?' Mathew blew down the stem of

his white clay pipe. 'You've got some bee in your bloomers, wench.'

'You watch the way you be talkin', Mathew Leach, I ain't no fish wife to be listenin' to your vulgarities.' Lucy flicked out with the cloth she had taken to the dishes but she was smiling.

'You ain't seen 'im, not once?' Mathew resumed, sucking his pipe.

'Not once,' Lucy affirmed. 'An' I thinks that be more'n strange. You know what I really thinks? I thinks 'e ain't goin' 'ome at all.'

Several puffs of blue-grey smoke curled into the room, suspended like a delicate veil above Mathew's head. 'Then where do 'e be goin'?'

Carrying the enamel bowl with its washing up water into the yard, Lucy emptied it into the drain running along its width then stared at the old windmill, secretive and brooding against the fading light. ''E be goin' there,' she whispered. 'It's my guess 'e be goin' there.'

Back in the outhouse they had made into a comfortable home Mathew finished his pipe, knocking the burned ash of the tobacco out against the bars of the fire. ''Ave you said anythin' to the others?'

Lucy fitted the cups and plates on to the rack Mathew had made and set on the wall, then folded the cloth she had dried them on and hung it across the length of string set across the grate. 'I thought as I would talk to you first.'

'You am sure?' Mathew put his pipe alongside the tin of shag tobacco on a cupboard that had come with a job lot of furniture from a tat man who had delivered it all for a shilling.

'Sure as I be talkin' to you.' Lucy reached for the white apron she wore only when baking, fastening the straps around her waist.

'Then we best tell the others.'

Phoebe listened, concern deepening on her face as Mathew spoke of Lucy's suspicions.

'He could not have crossed the heath without you seeing him?'

'I swear 'e couldn't, Miss Phoebe. A body can see for miles across there, it bein' mostly flat ground, an' I ain't seen 'im nowhere on it, not when I've been goin' in to Wednesbury on a mornin' nor when I've been comin' back at night. I be tellin' all o' you, that lad ain't passed me an' I says that shows 'e ain't goin' 'ome nights.'

'But his parents would have enquired before now surely?' Phoebe said. 'They must know where he is employed.'

'Maybe not,' Bert said. 'Maybe the lad 'as got no parents.'

'Was nobody wi' 'im that day I picked 'im out o' the line,' Mathew put in. 'Leastways nobody spoke to 'im when we set off.'

'If 'e don't 'ave no parents it could follow 'e don't 'ave no 'ome.' Lizzie looked at Phoebe. 'That would explain Lucy not seein' 'im on the way to an' from the town, wouldn't it?'

'It would.' Phoebe nodded. 'But if he is not going home at night, where is he going?'

Lucy's glance strayed to the rise of high ground, to the silent windmill painted black against the sky. 'I thinks 'e be goin' nowhere,' she said, 'not for the 'ole night anyway.'

'Then where is he spending his nights?' Phoebe asked, worry plain in her voice. 'I hope he is not sleeping on the heath.'

'I don't think 'e is,' Lucy glanced again at the windmill standing tall into the glow of the setting sun, 'I think 'e be sleepin' in there.'

'The windmill?' Bert followed the line of Lucy's eyes and her reasoning. 'Could well be. I could think of worse places a lad might get 'isself 'oled up in. You women wait indoors, Mathew an' me will go look.'

'You have been sleeping in the old windmill since the first day Mathew brought you here?' Phoebe said ten minutes later when the bellows boy stood in her kitchen, Mathew and Bert to either side of him.

'Yes, Miss,' the boy answered, chin on chest.

'But why? Is the walk from Wednesbury to here and back too much for you?'

'T'ain't too much!' The boy's chin came up defiantly. 'Ain't nuthin', that tiddly walk. I could walk six time further'n that wi'out feelin' tired.'

Bert placed a hand on the boy's shoulder, feeling the bones through his ragged coat. 'Tell 'er, lad.'

'Ain't nuthin' to tell.'

'If there ain't another reason you be sleepin' in that mill then Miss Phoebe be right in thinkin' the walk be too much for you, an' that bein' the case 'er might give you your coppers, lad, an' that means you'll be out o' a job.'

The boy looked quickly to Phoebe, the subtle warning Bert had given bringing fear to his eyes.

'You wouldn't, would you, Miss? You wouldn't go givin' me the sack?'

Phoebe looked at him. The sleeves of his threadbare coat were short of his wrists by several inches, his trousers halfway up his legs with more holes in them than sultanas in one of Lucy's scones, and her heart twisted with pity. What was it drove him to sneak back to sleep in the mill?

'I would have to if I thought it too far for you to walk, Josh.'

''T'ain't, Miss. Honest 't'ain't.' He looked down to where his toes peeped through boots that lacked the laces to fasten them. 'It's . . . it's . . . I ain't got no 'ome.' The reservoir of pride breached, the words tumbled from him. 'Me dad 'e buggered off years ago, left me mother to fend for 'erself an' me. We managed not too bad while she could tek in washin', then when 'er got sick we couldn't pay the landlord an' 'e chucked we out. It was the work'ouse or the road an' me mother wouldn't tek the work'ouse, least not till 'er could 'ardly walk no more. 'Er died the day after 'er went in. So you see, Miss, I ain't got other than the 'eath to sleep an' that windmill be a shelter from the wind.' He looked up at Phoebe. 'I didn't think as you would mind, Miss, I meant no 'arm, really I didn't.'

'And you did none.' Phoebe resisted the urge to take him in her arms, knowing that his fierce pride would resent any offer of childish comfort. 'But I wish you had told me.'

'You would 'ave chucked me out if I 'ad.'

'Miss Phoebe wouldn't 'ave chucked you out,' Mathew said.

'Mebbe 'er wouldn't,' the boy remained stubborn, 'but it was a chance I wasn't tekin'. Long as nobody seen me go in I 'ad a place to sleep.' He twisted free from Bert's hand. 'Who told you I was in there anyway?'

'Nobody told we,' Bert answered. 'Well, p'raps that's not strictly true. It were Mrs Leach not seein' 'ide nor 'air of you not comin' to work in the mornin's nor goin' back of an evenin'. Seemed strange to 'er that did, set 'er to wonderin' just 'ow you did get to Wiggins Mill.'

'I couldn't 'ave missed sight o' you, Josh,' Lucy said apologetically. 'The 'eath be mostly flat 'tween 'ere an' Wednesbury. You could spot a grass'opper a mile off.'

'I knows you didn't mean to drop me in it,' the boy tried to smile as he looked from her to Phoebe, 'an' I'm sorry to 'ave been the cause o' trouble, Miss. I won't go in the mill any more, you can be 'sured o' that. Just let me keep me job an' I'll bugger off every night cleaner than me father did.'

'You won't go nowhere every night, same as you won't be usin' that foul language no more.' Lizzie pushed further into the kitchen. ''E can't be sleepin' on that 'eath, Miss Phoebe, so unless you 'ave any objections 'e could bed down the side o' our Mark. There be room a-plenty in the corn loft, an' 'im an' Mark, they gets on well together.'

'Bert?' Phoebe looked at the man standing beside the young boy.

'That be all right by me, Miss Phoebe. Lad can stay wi'

Lizzie an' me long as 'e as a job at Wiggins Mill. An' if I knows Lizzie, 'er will look after 'im.'

'What do you say, Josh?' Phoebe asked.

A smile splitting his face, the boy looked at Lizzie. 'Bostin',' he breathed. 'I say that be bostin'.'

'I thought we would have afternoon tea in the garden, it is still quite warm enough,' Annie signed, finding her brother in his studio. 'And you do so enjoy the garden.' She stopped speaking, her mouth half open with surprise as she caught sight of the canvas on the easel. It was a finished portrait of Phoebe, only the paint that formed the signature still gleaming wetly. The face looked serenely back at her, a calmness beyond its years radiating from it. It was also the image of Abel's pretty wife, she realised.

'I . . . I did not know you had painted this.' Annie caught her brother's eyes on her and struggled to regain her composure. 'It is very good, especially considering you have seen so very little of Abel's daughter.'

Samuel's long narrow fingers moved rapidly. 'I worked from this more than from memory.' Going to a drawer set in a long bench-top table on the opposite side of the room, he drew out a photograph, handing it to Annie. 'It was in among some of Abel's papers. I found it when I went through them.'

Among Abel's papers? Annie stared at the photograph. She'd thought she had weeded everything out but obviously she had missed this and Samuel had said nothing of it, as he had said nothing of the portrait he'd now finished. What else had he said nothing of? What other secrets lay hidden from her? None that mattered, surely. She had held his Power of Attorney long enough to take everything from him save this house, and now it was too late for him to make good his intention of naming Phoebe his heir. She handed back the photograph. Their niece would get none of the wealth that had once been her father's.

'It is a very good likeness,' Samuel signed. 'We must hang it opposite the one of her father, they will look very well together. Perhaps James Siveter will find her and persuade her to come home. It would be nice to have her here with us, don't you agree, Annie?'

'Of course, dear,' Annie's fingers carried the lie. 'Nothing would give me more happiness than to have Phoebe return to us. We must pray that God will make it so.' She watched Samuel clean his brushes, immersing each in a jar of turpentine then wiping the bristles on a soft cloth. He could pray as much as he liked but he would find God as deaf as himself. She looked at the lovely painted face, her fingers curling into her palms. The portrait could hang with that of Abel but his daughter would never again live here.

She would sell this house, she thought as Samuel poured water from a tall flower-twined jug into a matching basin and washed his hands. She would sell it and give the money to Clinton to invest in more tube works. After all, there would be no need to keep this place on when she became his wife.

Clinton's wife. The thought stayed with Annie as they walked downstairs to the garden. How long would it be before they could marry? Not for several months that was certain, a suitable period of mourning for her brother must elapse before they could be wed, the proprieties must be observed. But Clinton would not mind the waiting, not when he saw her grief for Samuel's passing.

'Will you be wantin' tea now?' Maudie followed them into the garden.

'You have not mashed it yet, have you?' Annie asked sharply. 'I have no taste for stewed tea.'

You've no taste for anythin', if you asks me! Maudie sucked in her cheeks, looking at Annie's lavender dress with ill-concealed disdain.

'Tea ain't been mashed, not yet,' she replied. 'I knows 'ow you likes yer tea, an' so I should after all the years I've spent mekin' it.'

That won't go on for much longer, Annie thought. Once I am married you can count yourself dismissed. Aloud she said waspishly, 'Not long enough to do it graciously but I suppose we must make do. You may bring the tray now.'

Sour-faced old cow! Maudie returned to the kitchen. But then, that one had never had a good word for the doings of anybody other than herself – not that she had ever done good in her life.

'You have forgotten the herbal tea.' Annie looked at the tray her housekeeper set down on the wicker table.

'I ain't forgot nothin',' Maudie replied. 'I set it on a sep'rate tray. Seein' as 'ow Mr Samuel don't care for medicines I thought it might suit better for it to be on another tray altogether.'

'I see.' Annie began pouring milk into the cups. 'Then bring it out. It will do Mr Samuel no good left sitting in a bottle.'

'Yes, Ma'am.' Maudie turned away. If that mixture were only poison, she would gladly pour the lot down Annie Pardoe's throat!

'It is just a herbal tea, dear,' Annie's fingers signed rapidly to her brother. 'Mrs Gaskell Wheeler recommended it, she is convinced it will help you build up your strength, and I am sure Mrs Tranter has something that will relieve the taste should it prove unpalatable.' She looked at Maudie, carefully measuring the mixture into a cup, adding a little of the hot water from the tea tray. 'Have you something sweet?' she asked.

Maudie nodded a smile to Samuel, knowing he could not hear but wanting him to understand. 'Yes, Ma'am,' she said. 'I took a chocolate cake from the baker this mornin'. It be Mr Samuel's favourite sort.'

'Bring it for him then,' Annie said, 'he will take the herbal tea much easier with a chocolate cake to follow.'

Pouring the tea, she watched Maudie set the cake at Samuel's elbow then hand him the herbal mixture. Swallowing it in two long gulps, he handed the cup back to her.

'There now, that didn't be so bad, did it?' Maudie crooned to his silent ears. 'Now eat up your cake an' you'll soon forget the swallowin' o' that stuff.'

Annie picked up her own cup as Samuel took the cake, sinking his teeth into the chocolate-covered mound. Eat his cake and Samuel would soon be forgetting everything!

Chewing the last vestige of chocolate, Samuel touched his mouth with his napkin, eyes straying to the privet hedge that shielded the end of the garden. Annie had walked the length of it and when she had walked back she had held a hand close against her skirts.

It had gone as she'd known it would. Annie stood beside the four-poster bed that had been her brother's marriage bed. Samuel had eaten the cake. The ground yew and laburnum seeds had not worked, why she could not guess, but the poison she had mixed in the cream of that cake would. This time there would be no mistake. Come the morning Samuel would be dead and she would be free to enjoy her life as Mrs Clinton Harforth-Darby.

The pain that had gnawed at her all day spiralled up from her side and into her breast, the rawness of it stealing the breath from her lungs. Sinking on to the bed, she groped for the bottle of small white tablets, taking two into her mouth even as she poured a glass of water from the carafe on her night table. Waiting for the pain to pass, she checked the fob watch pinned to the shoulder of her dress. It wanted a quarter of an hour to nine o'clock. Samuel always retired at eight-thirty, he would already be in his bed.

Annie forced herself to stand. She must say goodnight to him as she always did. Tomorrow he would be beyond remembering whether she had or not but that sharp-nosed Maudie Tranter would remember the least thing that was different, and though you may not see Maudie Tranter, you could be certain the woman missed nothing.

Tapping on Samuel's bedroom door as her mother had

insisted everyone must though no sound passed his barrier of silence, Annie pushed open the door.

'Goodnight, dear,' she signed.

Samuel's hands rose like white wounded birds. 'Goodnight, Annie,' he signed, a slowness in his fingers. 'You always did what you thought best. Thank you, dear.'

What did he mean? Annie asked herself, leaning down to kiss his brow. Then in the soft glow of the oil lamp she caught the look in his eyes. He knew! Samuel knew what she had done. He was thanking her for giving him death!

Chapter Nineteen

Dead!

Phoebe walked across the heath toward Wednesbury, her mind still trying to reject the news Lucy had brought with her the night before. Her Uncle Samuel was dead.

She had not seen him since the reading of her father's will. In all that time he had not tried to contact her, not even when she was in prison. True she had never seen a great deal of Uncle Samuel, even as a child, but for him to ignore her very existence seemed somehow unnatural.

Reaching the town, she walked along Lower High Street, taking the turning that would lead her past Oakeswell Hall. She glanced at the black and white half-timbered building as she passed its curtain wall. Would Sophie live there when she married Montrose? The thought brought a twinge of pain, but it was pain for Sophie not for herself.

At the gate of Brunswick House she paused. This had once been her home, a place of happiness and love. Now it held neither. She had always been so glad to return here yet now she wanted only to turn and run. But she had to go in. Uncle Samuel was her father's brother and she must show her respects.

At the door she tugged the bell pull, her eyes avoiding the mourning wreath set at its centre. Her aunt hated her, that much had been made plain, but she was not here for the sake of her aunt.

'Eh, Miss Phoebe!' Maudie Tranter looked at the girl standing on the doorstep. 'What be you doin' 'ere?'

'Lucy told me my Uncle Samuel has passed away.'

'Ar, Miss, 'e 'as. In the night it was . . .'

'Who is it, Mrs Tranter?'

Inside Phoebe shivered at the sound of her aunt's voice but she stepped determinedly into the hall. 'It is me, Aunt.'

Annie Pardoe's hand flew to her side. She had not expected this, had had no intention of informing Abel's daughter of his brother's death. 'What are you doing here?' she rasped. 'You are not wanted in this house.'

'You made that clear enough more than two years ago,' Phoebe replied.

'That will be all, Tranter.' Annie glared at the listening Maudie, waiting until the door leading off to the kitchen had closed behind her. 'If I made it so clear,' she said, turning back to Phoebe, 'then how come you are here now?'

'I was given the news my Uncle Samuel was dead. I have come to Brunswick House to pay my respects, and that is the only thing I am here for.'

'Respects!' Annie let her gaze travel slowly over her niece. 'What respect does it show to come dressed in green? You have not even the respect to adopt mourning.'

'I apologise for the colour of my clothing,' Phoebe's chin came up, 'but this is all I have. You did not allow me an extensive wardrobe, did you, Aunt?'

'I want you to leave.' Annie placed a hand on the door handle.

'And I want to leave, Aunt, very much, I find you a most unpleasant person to be with, but I will not leave until I have done that for which I came.' Phoebe walked to the foot of the stairs. 'Is Uncle Samuel in his room?'

'No,' Annie looked towards the door of the parlour, 'he is in there.'

Phoebe stood for a moment, unmoving. Uncle Samuel had not wished her to visit him in life. Would he wish the same in death? Was her presence in this house an intrusion he would have resented? Somewhere deep in her heart she felt that to be untrue. He had been so kind to her on the few occasions they had met. Taking a long breath, she walked into the parlour.

Nothing had changed. The chiffonier held the same Staffordshire china figurines, the same high-backed sofa stood against the wall, only the mahogany table below the central ceiling gasolier was different. It stood where it always had but its heavy Brussels lace cloth was gone and in its place was draped the black velvet that had lain beneath her father's coffin and now lay beneath Samuel's.

Phoebe stared at the features that seemed to be cut from marble, her heart full of tears that would not reach her eyes. Though his eyes were closed and no smile lingered at his mouth the strange haunted look that had constantly drawn his face was no longer there. Her uncle seemed to have found a peace in death he had never known in life.

'Aunt,' she said softly, 'why do you hate me so much?'

Stood on the opposite side of the coffin Annie felt the breath catch in her throat but the rising gall of bitterness was too much for her to swallow.

'Your father stole my life!' she screamed. 'He took it, him and his fancy wife, and gave me this in return.' She struck the side of the walnut casket with her hand. 'I have had no life of my own now for nearly twenty years, I have known a living death all that time and it was your father's gift to me. He made me responsible for Samuel – Samuel who could not be cared for by any other than his own family, who could not be taken into your father's house for fear of causing distress to his pretty wife. Oh, yes, *she* must be shielded from his affliction.'

Phoebe looked from the face of her dead uncle to that of her aunt, twisted with bitterness. 'Affliction?'

'Yes, affliction!' Annie spat. 'That which kept him from leading a normal life, which kept him from taking a wife, which used up my life in keeping his secret.'

'But surely Uncle Samuel's deafness was not a good enough cause to turn him into a recluse.'

Annie's eyes burned as she answered, 'No, it was not a good enough cause. But it was not only deafness my brother suffered from – it was this!' Reaching into the casket she lifted the long white robe that covered her brother's body, snatching it open to the waist.

Phoebe gasped then turned away, her senses stunned.

'That was what made my brother a recluse!' Annie cried viciously. 'That was the shame that must be kept hidden from the world. That was what kept him from taking a wife for what woman would marry a man who was no man, who was neither male nor female, but had the genitals of both!'

'How strange we meet in the same place, Miss Pardoe. Miss Pardoe!' Sir William Dartmouth caught the arm of the young woman whose eyes set in a chalk-white face seemed to look straight through him. 'Are you feeling unwell?'

'Uncle Samuel,' Phoebe mumbled. 'Uncle Samuel, he . . . Lucy will . . . I must . . .'

Supporting her with his arm as she sagged against him, he helped her into the George Hotel. 'A doctor, quickly,' he ordered the attentive manager. 'Then a brandy. Move, man!'

'Nothing physically wrong,' Alfred Dingley said an hour later. 'She is suffering from some sort of shock, though . . . I have given her a sedative that will help but she needs rest and will get that better at home than she will here.' He nodded towards the door of the upstairs sitting room Phoebe had been taken to. 'I will have a carriage sent round to take her. Was there anyone with her, do you know?'

'She was alone when I met her in the street,' Sir William answered, 'so I presume no one was accompanying her, and as for a carriage there will be no need. I will see Miss Pardoe gets home. Send your account to the Priory.' He stood aside for the doctor to leave. 'Good day, Doctor.'

Tapping first at the door he went into the room where Phoebe sat, the wife of the hotel manager hovering at her elbow.

'Are you feeling better, Miss Pardoe?' he asked.

She looked up, the shock still showing in her eyes. 'Yes,' she said. 'Thank you, Sir William. I am sorry to have been so much trouble.'

'You were no trouble.'

'That is kind of you to say.' Phoebe stood up, her legs still not quite her own. 'But I have delayed you. I thank you again for helping me. I can manage on my own now.'

'Were you alone?'

'Yes.' Phoebe smiled at the woman handing her her bag.

'You said something about an Uncle Samuel and Lucy, were they not with you?'

Phoebe breathed deeply, her fingers curling tightly about the bag. 'My uncle is dead, Sir William. I have just come from paying my respects and I was going to speak to Lucy.'

'Lucy?' He frowned slightly. 'Is that the Lucy you told me was once in the employ of my wife?'

Phoebe nodded.

'Mrs Leach, so where is she now?' he asked.

'She will be in the market place.'

Sir William looked at the woman still hovering close to Phoebe. 'Send to the market place. See if Mrs Leach is there.'

'I know 'er, Sir,' the woman bobbed a curtsy, 'I'll fetch 'er.'

'There is no need,' Phoebe protested, 'I can go there myself.'

'Go to Mrs Leach,' Sir William spoke to the woman, ignoring Phoebe's protest, 'ask her to be good enough to come here, and tell your husband to have my carriage brought to the door.'

'Yes, Sir.' The woman bobbed again then disappeared through the door.

'I am sorry to hear of your uncle's death,' he continued to Phoebe, 'please accept my condolences. If I can be of assistance, do not hesitate to contact me.'

Phoebe walked from the room and down the stairs to the lobby. 'My aunt will be handling everything,' she said. 'She has cared for my uncle for many years.'

'Miss Phoebe, are you all right? What happened?' Lucy rushed in from the street.

'Lucy!' Phoebe caught her hands, holding them tightly. 'Lucy, I am so glad you are here.'

'Miss Pardoe has suffered something of a shock,' Sir William answered Lucy's enquiring glance. 'The doctor says she will be all right but she is in need of rest. Will you see her home?'

'O' course.' Lucy put an arm about Phoebe. 'You take a seat, Miss, while I finds the carter. 'E'll be 'avin' a drink in the Turks 'Ead round about this time. 'E'll give us both a ride as far as the Tipton Road.'

'Do not trouble yourself with the carter, Mrs Leach,' Sir William said as Lucy made to get a chair. 'My carriage is just outside. My driver will take you home and return for me here.'

'I'll collect your things from the market, Mrs Leach. They will keep 'ere till you collect them.' The manager's wife hovered nearby, eager to be seen offering assistance.

'Ta, Mrs Jinks.' Lucy led the way out of the lobby. 'I'll pick 'em up tomorrer.'

'Sir William, there is no need for me to take your carriage,' Phoebe hesitated at the door, 'a ride with the carter will do as well.'

He smiled suddenly, a light dancing behind his grey eyes. 'Miss Pardoe, you once told me that I should never use the word "must" to you again, but I will if I have to. Now spare me the retribution that would bring by accepting my carriage.'

Phoebe smiled. 'I would not have retribution fall upon you, Sir William, so I will accept. And thank you.'

Inside the carriage Phoebe leaned back, her eyes closed against the horror of what had taken place at Brunswick House, a house that had once held so much love and laughter and now held so much unhappiness.

Poor Uncle Samuel. She flinched as the picture of his thin disfigured body flashed before her closed eyelids. To have spent a lifetime with such a deformity would be terrible enough for any man to suffer, but knowing his sister's resentment, thinking that he was responsible, albeit indirectly, for her solitary life, as he must have done, could only have added to that suffering; and Aunt Annie, so consumed with her bitterness, so twisted with hate for her own family, had she ever made any attempt to hide her true feelings or had she shown them to Samuel as she had shown them to Phoebe?

Behind her closed lids a pale finely drawn face smiled back at her, a gentle kindly face, but one whose blue eyes held the shadow of pain.

'Are you all right, Miss Phoebe?' Lucy asked, feeling the shudder that passed through her.

Phoebe saw again the figure of her aunt standing over the casket which held that malformed body, her face distorted with the hate she held for her brother's child. All right? Phoebe turned her face, pressing it into Lucy's shoulder. Would she ever be all right again?

Five days to the end of the month. Phoebe looked at the calendar. She had crossed off each day as it ended, making a note of the number of finished locks. Now less than thirty were needed to make the gross. They had all worked so hard; even Ruth had helped put the finished locks in the wooden soap box Josh had got from the carter.

Brushing her hair, Phoebe remembered the grin on the boy's face as he had related his deal with the man. She had sent Josh with twopence to pay for the box. He had offered the carter one penny.

'A penny!' Zach Coates had laughed. 'It cost me more than that to cart it out 'ere.'

'It'll cost you twice as much if you 'as to cart it back,' Josh retorted. 'You might as well let me 'ave it.'

'Not fer a bloody penny I ain't. I might as well use it fer firewood, at least it'll keep me warm.'

'Why not swap it for this?' Josh had opened the sack he had carried with him across the heath, displaying the lumps of coal. 'It'll burn a lot longer than the few sticks that old box'll mek an' give off a lot more 'eat.'

'An' where 'ave you pinched that from?' Zach had demanded.

'Never you mind,' Josh told him. 'If I tell you you'll only get a 'eadache worryin' about it an' you'll 'ave to pay tuppence for a bottle of Aspro to cure it. So you see, you'll still be outta pocket.'

'You be a right bloody smart arse, don't you!' Zach grumbled, handing the soapbox down to Josh.

'Ar, an' you'll be a right 'ot 'un if you stands too near that coal,' Josh returned, handing over the sack. ''Eat that gives off is more than the fires o' Hell you've 'eard talk about.'

Tying a ribbon to the plait in her hair Phoebe could not resist a smile. Josh had bounced into the workshop, placing the box on the floor, his grin wide as the heath as he handed back the two pennies.

He was a nice boy. Phoebe climbed into bed, the smile still warm on her lips. Things were going so well, maybe he could stay on after the locks were finished.

Climbing into bed, she turned off the oil lamp that stood beside it on a table and lay back, staring at the moonlight filling her window. It was the same moonlight as filled the windows of Handsworth Prison only the spectres it held were different. In gaol the moonlight had brought memories of her life outside. Now it often brought memories of her life locked away behind those walls. How many women were lying behind them now, their freedom snatched away, and how many were staring at the moonlight?

She would never forget. Every moment spent in that place was etched deep in her soul, every word and every blow. No, she would not forget, nor would she forget Sir William. He had brought the release she thanked God for each night, but more than that he had shown her kindness at every opportunity. But why? For what reason? If he had been indebted to her because of her imprisonment he had more than made up for it. Or could it be her friendship with his son, did he know of Edward's feelings toward her? Phoebe looked away from the light of the window but the tall figure of Sir William Dartmouth remained lit in her mind. No, that was not the reason behind his kindness to her. A man with an ancestry graced by the best families in the county for so many generations would not allow his son to break with tradition. Whatever reason lay behind his friendship she was sure her possible marriage to Edward played no part in it.

Edward . . . Phoebe closed her eyes. Was he blind to his illustrious name? Could he honestly not see his parents could never accept her as his wife, a woman who had been in prison, or was he just too stubborn to accept it? He had asked her to marry him again when he and Sophie had called, bringing their mother's regrets that Phoebe would not be attending the ball and also her condolences for Uncle Samuel's death.

Phoebe turned restlessly, her eyes returning to the moonlit window. She had refused as gently as she could, trying not to hurt Edward, and now he was gone, left for Europe with his mother and sister. Painful as she knew it would be to him, she had felt bound to tell him she did not love him, her feelings were not those of a girl desiring to be his wife. He had smiled then, masking the hurt, and Phoebe had seen the strength of his father in him. Edward Dartmouth had been hurt but that hurt would never be allowed to affect his friendship toward her. Phoebe closed her eyes again but it was not Edward who stayed with her as she drifted into sleep. It was not his mouth that smiled or his eyes that watched her. The face that bent toward her was that of Sir William Dartmouth.

'That is the last of them, Tranter.'

Annie Pardoe folded the sheet of paper, slipping it into the envelope she had just finished addressing. There had been more messages of sympathy for the death of her brother than she would have expected and she had let a suitable time elapse before answering them. Let people believe her too grief-stricken to write replies before the two weeks that had gone by. Gathering the envelopes together, she handed them to Maudie.

'People will understand why it has taken so long before I answered their messages,' she said, wiping the pen nib clean of ink before moving from the desk. 'They will realise how much pain it causes me.'

Pain my arse! Maudie thought caustically. The only pain Samuel caused you was the pain of wanting him out of the way, and that pain worsened with the arrival of that Harforth-Darby!

'Take them to the post office now.' Annie took half a crown from a small black lacquered box, handing it to her housekeeper. 'That will be more than enough to pay for stamps.'

'Yes, Ma'am.' Maudie did not bob a curtsy. 'An' there'll be change an' all, I know that wi'out yer tellin'.'

Annie bit back the anger that rose in her as Maudie walked from the study. Maudie Tranter knew a lot of things and in a very few weeks she would know one more. She would know she was out of a job.

Following her from the study, Annie walked up the stairs. Maudie had seen her leave the study, she would think the last of the letters written as she had been told, but there was one more yet to do. Watching from the window of her room she saw Maudie leave the house by the rear door, crossing the yard and taking the path that led through the grounds to a door set in the garden wall. Looking at her fob watch, Annie remained at the window. She would give Maudie five minutes before writing that last letter.

The minutes gone she took the sheet of writing paper from where she had slipped it into the packet of her skirts. It was not exactly the same as the one that had lain so long in the drawer of her washstand but it was white and that was near enough. Going to the wardrobe she took her bag from the shelf, taking out a fresh bottle of ink and a new pen. She had thrown the others into Millfield Pool not thinking of the letter she must write now but her visits to Alfred Dingley's consulting room had afforded the opportunity to purchase more. Stress, the doctor had called the pain in her side, stress due to the passing of her brother but it would cease with time. She'd known it had to come, he had told her, slipping tablets into a small brown glass bottle. They had all known, even her brother himself. Annie levered the cork from the bottle of ink. Yes, Samuel had known. The look in his eyes as she kissed him goodnight had told her so.

Reaching once more into her bag, she took out the bill she had been given when she went back to that shop near Birmingham railroad station. It had been clever of her to pretend to have forgotten to buy pot menders when she bought those mousetraps. It had given her two receipts.

Fetching the small nail scissors she kept in a drawer of her dresser, she carefully cut the heading from the receipt. Quickly pouring a small amount of water from the carafe on her night table she placed it beside the ink then, drawing her handkerchief from her pocket, tipped into the water the spoonful of plain flour she had taken from the pantry while Maudie Tranter had been on her half day off. Using the long handle of the pen she mixed the flour and water to a paste then, with the tip of one finger, smoothed a little of it on to the back of the heading she had cut from James Greaves's receipt, attaching that to the top of the sheet of white paper. That done, she carefully washed pen and glass in the bowl on the washstand, wiping them on the towel folded beside it. Opening the window, she emptied the water she had used on to the flower border below. Maudie Tranter would find no trace when she came to clean.

Annie sat at the table and began to write. Tomorrow she would post this letter herself and the ink and pen would follow the others to the bottom of Millfield Pool.

The letter finished and sealed, all trace of its having been written hidden away, Annie returned her bag to the wardrobe, caressing the silk of the pearl grey gown and the rustling lavender taffeta. She must wear black for appearance's sake but once the period of mourning was over she would never wear it again. She would wear only gowns of coloured silk, the colours Clinton liked. Soon she would be with him. But how soon would that be? Annie tried to push away the thoughts that held sway in the shadows of her mind but they would not be denied.

Three weeks and more, it had been all of that since she had given him the money which the sale of the last of Abel's bequest had brought. Three weeks and she had heard nothing from him. He had told her she would have deeds of ownership to land on which to build her tube works in a couple of days, but those days had grown into weeks and she had seen nothing of him or the papers. But he would come, he would! She closed the door of the wardrobe, gritting her teeth as a spasm of pain bit upward to her breast. Clinton would come.

'Change from the post office.' Maudie entered the sitting room where Annie now sat, a newspaper spread across the table.

'Leave it there.' A nod of her head indicated the opposite side of the table but Annie did not look up.

'Do there be any mention of the Wheelers' trouble in the paper, Ma'am?' Maudie asked.

'Trouble!' Annie looked up sharply. 'What trouble? What are you talking about?'

'I 'eard it when I was comin' from the post office.' Maudie stood with hands folded in front of her. 'Two women was sayin' as 'ow Oakeswell 'All be in mournin', said as they 'ad it from one o' the maids.'

'In mourning?'

'That be what them women said, I 'eard for meself.'

'But for whom?' Annie asked, not quite believing what her housekeeper had said. 'Is it Gaskell?'

'Don't know, Ma'am,' Maudie replied. 'They said as nobody knowed.'

'How ridiculous! There couldn't be a death in the house without its being known who had died.'

'No, Ma'am, but there could be one as 'adn't took place in the 'ouse. That way could be the maid wouldn't know who it was 'ad died.'

'Well, it is no member of the family,' Annie glanced at the newspaper, 'otherwise there would have been an entry in the Obituaries column and there is none. Most probably it is a remote aunt of Mrs Wheeler's. She did sometimes talk of one living in southern France.'

'Likely that be who it is then.' Maudie turned to leave then paused as Annie spoke again.

'Nevertheless it is only polite to call and offer my sympathy, I shall go to Oakeswell Hall now.'

Fastening her cloak, Annie thought rapidly. She would go to the post office first and post the letter she had written. Then she would make her way to Oakeswell Hall, passing Millfield Pool where she would dispose of pen and bottle of ink.

From childhood she had been used to harnessing pony to trap and needed no help with either. Twenty minutes from hearing the news Maudie had brought, Annie was driving across the open ground that skirted Millfield Pool.

'I heard it being talked of in the town,' she said when she was shown into Violet Wheeler's sitting room, 'and felt

I must call and offer my condolence were it true for I saw no announcement in the newspaper.'

Violet Wheeler sat down, her black skirts flowing over the edges of her chair. 'Gaskell made none.'

'Then your husband is still with us, thank the Lord.'

Ordering tea from the housemaid who answered her ring, Violet looked at her visitor. 'Gaskell? But of course he is still with us.'

Uncomfortable beneath the other woman's gaze, Annie apologised. 'Forgive me, but with there being no announcement . . .'

'Of course,' Violet cut in, 'but as you say, Gaskell is still with us, thank the Lord.' Waiting as the maid reappeared with the tea tray, then with a bobbed curtsy left again, she went on, 'My husband is recently returned from London.'

'It is not Montrose, I hope?' Annie said. 'Not your son?'

Violet poured the tea with the grace of long practice. 'If you mean you are hoping it is not my son's death we are mourning, Miss Pardoe, then your hopes are fulfilled. My husband was in London on a business trip, not concerning our son.'

So it was Violet Wheeler's aunt who had died. Annie took the cup held out to her. 'It relieves me to hear your son is well.'

'Yes, Montrose is quite well though he is disappointed that given the circumstances we will not now be holding a farewell reception for him before his regiment leaves for India.'

Replacing her cup on the tray, Annie stood up. 'I will not intrude upon you any longer, Mrs Wheeler. I came only to offer my sympathy in your loss.'

'Before you go there is something here we believe was intended for your brother.' Crossing to an elegant mahogany sideboard she took a large envelope from a drawer, handing it to Annie. 'Gaskell saw his name on this but it bore no address so he brought it back with him from London.'

'Oh!' Annie turned the envelope in her hand but it bore no mark other than the name 'Pardoe' scrawled shakily across it.

'It was among Clinton's effects.'

Effects! Annie's hand tightened convulsively on the envelope. Why was Gaskell Wheeler dealing with Clinton's effects? Why was Clinton in London when he had told her he would be in Wednesbury? The answer was staring her in the face. Clinton had gone and her money had gone with him!

'Thank your husband for me.' Annie's lips struggled with the words.

'Gaskell's cousin was so ill before he left Oakeswell Hall . . .' Violet Wheeler's words followed Annie to the door.

'Ill?'

'Yes, it all came upon him so suddenly,' Violet answered the query in Annie's voice, 'stomach cramps and symptoms so akin to fever he thought it a return of the malady that struck him when he lived in the Caribbean. He went to London to consult his doctor there and we heard no more until a mutual friend wrote to tell Gaskell that his cousin was dead. Who would have thought it?' She fluttered a handkerchief to her eyes. 'A man as vital as Clinton, dead in a couple of days.'

Clinton was dead! Annie stood in her own bedroom with no memory of the drive back to Brunswick House. He had died after so short and so unexpected an illness. Clinton was dead! Taking the scissors she had used earlier that afternoon, she opened the wardrobe door. Clinton was dead and with him her dreams. Stabbing the scissors into the cloth, she slashed the grey and the lavender gowns. Clinton was dead, she would have no need of colours. The gowns in shreds about the floor, Annie slumped to the bed. *Such a short illness, so sudden, dead in a couple of days* . . . Violet Wheeler's words reverberated in her brain, circling round and round. What was it that had caused the death of a man who had appeared the picture of health when he had last called on her?

When he had last called on her. . . . Annie stared at the remnants of the pearl grey gown. She had been wearing that when he had been shown into the sitting room, when she had handed sherry to him and to Samuel. She had given Samuel the glass she always used for him, the glass with a small air bubble in the stem, one that she could not confuse with her own. She had handed it to him as Maudie had announced the arrival of the constables. But she hadn't! Fear closed her throat as memory returned. She had not handed Samuel his sherry. The tray had been taken from her by Clinton.

So sudden. . . . The words seemed to scream in her mind Stomach cramp followed by fever, the same symptoms the powdered seeds of yew and laburnum produced She had not handed Samuel his sherry, Clinton had after she had left the room. That explained why her brother had not fallen ill as she had expected. He had not drunk the poison, Clinton had. She had killed Clinton!

Pain surged into her breast but Annie ignored it. She had killed Samuel for nothing, she had sold his inheritance for nothing, she would never be Mrs Clinton Harforth-Darby And the money she had handed over to him, what had happened to that? Was it in some account that would most likely pass to Gaskell Wheeler? And the envelope Violet Wheeler had handed her, what lay in there? Reaching for it where she had dropped it on the bed, she looked at the name sprawled across it. Was it some lies as to her money or did it contain the barefaced truth? He had played her for a fool and now thank you, Annie Pardoe. Thank you and goodbye.

Breaking open the seal she drew out a letter, the writing spidery. '*Annie, my dear,*' she read, '*I wanted to bring you these myself but I am afraid I feel too ill. I will post them to you from London. You will be in my thoughts until I return. Yours, Clinton.*'

Taking the rest of the contents from the envelope, Annie ooked at the stylised wording . . . *land and buildings ppertaining thereto the property of Annie Mary Pardoe . . .*

Slowly she began to laugh, a low empty laugh that echoed ound the room, laughing as her soul died.

'They be a fine job, Miss, you'll 'ave no trouble wi' them.'

'Thank you, Bert, you have worked so hard.' Phoebe

Chapter Twenty

'They be a fine job, Miss, you'll 'ave no trouble wi' them.'

'Thank you, Bert, you have worked so hard.' Phoebe looked at the wooden soap box filled almost to the top with shining brass locks.

'I couldn't 'ave done it by meself, everybody 'as worked 'ard and that includes yourself.'

'Four days, Bert,' she reminded him, 'four days to delivery. Do you think we will do it?'

'We be good as done now,' he smiled. 'Mathew an' me we be on the last batch. Tomorrow will see the lot finished.'

'I must admit I had doubts when we started. It seemed impossible for you to have made so many in the time we were given.'

'Would 'ave been if Mathew 'adn't stepped in, an' them two lads 'ave worked like Trojans. I tell you, without that pair there would 'ave been no order to deliver in four days' time.'

'I wish I were the Queen."

'The Queen?' Mathew glanced up from the lock he was freeing from a vice attached to the work bench. 'Whatever do you want to be 'er for?'

Phoebe's eyes danced. 'Because then I could give you all a medal. You certainly deserve one.'

Josh looked up from pumping the bellows, his face red from his efforts. 'Medals be no good, you just 'ave to keep on cleanin' 'em. 'Sides, like me mother used to say, you can't eat medals.'

'In that case, Josh, I will make yours a fish supper.'

'That be more like it.' He looked across to where Mark was working alongside Mathew. 'What you say, Mark?'

'I say mek that two suppers, an' mek me eat both.'

'Them pair, eatin' be all they think on,' Bert joked. 'I swear neither of 'em 'as a bottom to their belly.'

'Hard work makes men hungry, which reminds me – Tilly and Lizzie said to tell you the meal was ready and waiting on the table.'

'I would rather 'ear news like that than that the Queen was to visit.' Josh laid the brass-studded bellows aside, running his palms along the sides of his trousers.

'Well, I might not be Queen, Josh White, but rubbing your hands on your trousers will not do for me nor will it do for Lizzie. You know her rule: no hands washed, no dinner given.'

Josh looked at his hands then at Phoebe, his grin cheeky. 'I might 'ave known there'd be a price to pay! Mind you, I wouldn't mind 'avin' a bath for one o' Mrs Ingles's dinners, only don't tell 'er I said so.'

''Ave you thought on what you be goin' to do wi' them locks when they be finished?' Mathew asked as they ate their dinner.

'Do with them?' Phoebe asked, a certain amount of surprise in her voice. 'I am going to deliver them to Mr Greaves, of course.'

Mathew chewed on some cheese. 'I know that be your intention but 'ow?'

'I've been wonderin' the same, Miss.' Bert looked up from his plate of cheese and pickles. 'Carryin' two or three o' them locks be one thing. Carryin' a gross on 'em be summat else.'

'Carryin' 'em be summat you ain't never goin' to do. You needs transport.' Mathew cut a slice of onion, sliding it into his mouth from the blade of his knife.

Across the long trestle table that the men had set up at one end of the corn barn, and where Lizzie and Tilly had laid the midday meal, Phoebe looked at them both, her brows drawing together in a worried frown. She had been so busy, so preoccupied with her sewing and with helping in the workshop, she had totally forgotten the need to arrange transport of the locks to Birmingham.

Mathew continued to eat. 'So what be you goin' to do?'

'I don't know,' Phoebe admitted. 'That part of it never seemed to enter my head.'

'We could 'ire a 'andcart?' Mathew suggested.

Bert nodded. 'We could, but it be a long push to Brummagem. It be all o' ten mile.'

'What about Zach Coates?' Mathew took a pull from the mug of beer he had brewed himself. 'If we could carry 'em between we up to the Tipton Road, 'e could put 'em on 'is cart down into Wednesbury and then on a train from there.'

Phoebe's frown turned to a look of dismay. 'That would mean paying carriage charges and a return fare for one of us to go with them.' She spread her hands on the table, defeat in the gesture. 'I just do not have the money.'

'Would it tek more'n four shillin', Miss?' Josh asked through a mouthful of food.

'I would not have thought so, Josh,' Phoebe answered, 'but I do not have four shillings.'

'I 'ave,' he swallowed noisily. 'Least I 'as three an' another 'un this comin' Friday'll mek four, so if as you says four shillin' be enough to pay to get them locks to Brummagem, then they'm as good as there already.'

'Those three shillings,' Phoebe looked at the tousle-headed boy regarding her with eyes like molten bronze, 'are they the same three shillings you have been paid as wages since you came to Wiggins Mill?'

'Ar.' He took another bite.

'And the fourth shilling is the one you will be paid for the work you have done this week?'

He nodded, the food in his mouth leaving no room for his tongue to manoeuvre.

'Thank you, Josh,' Phoebe said, her eyes grateful though her mouth would not smile. 'But I cannot take it. You will need that money to keep you until you find other employment.'

The boy's grin faded at her mention of finding work elsewhere but his eyes lost none of their brightness. 'I managed afore I come 'ere,' he said, allowing the food in his mouth to slide past his throat, 'an' I can manage when I be gone so you tek them shillin's an' get them locks to Brummagem. Could be when the bloke as 'as ordered 'em sees what 'e be gettin', 'e will up an' order another gross on the spot.'

Phoebe shook her head. 'No, Josh.'

'Why!' the boy demanded. 'That money be mine. I've earned it so I can do what I likes wi' it, an' I wants you to 'ave it.'

Pushing herself up with her spread hands, Phoebe rose from the table. 'You are right, Josh, that money is yours. You earned it and you are going to keep it, I . . .'

''Ang on, 'ang on!' he cut in on her refusal. 'I've been 'ere near a month as meks no odds an' in that time I ain't paid no board nor lodgin', I've 'ad three good meals a day an' supper besides, an' on top o' it all I've 'ad a bed. Now then.' Putting aside his knife, he held up his left hand, fingers curled into his palm. 'Three meals a day would cost tuppence a go an' they wouldn't be 'alf the tucker I've 'ad from Mrs Ingles neither, so wi'out supper I would 'ave been set back a tanner a day.' Two at a time he raised the fingers of his left hand, counting slowly before raising one finger of his right. Satisfied with his numbers he went on: 'A penny to 'ang the line in Joe Baker's lodgin' 'ouse would mek it seven.' He raised another finger. 'Sevenpence a day that would be, an' nowhere near the comfort I've 'ad 'ere so I reckons I owes you that money, Miss, an' a damn' sight more aside it.'

'If you owe anyone, Josh, it is Mrs Ingles. She is the one who has given you food and found a bed for you to sleep in.'

''E don't owe me nothin'.' Lizzie smiled at the boy. ''E 'as earned more'n a meal or two, the 'elp 'e gives me around the place, an' as for a bed, 'tain't nothin' outta me way lettin' 'im lie in the loft along o' me own so 'is money be 'is own to do whatever 'e likes wi' it.'

'There you am!' Josh grinned triumphantly. 'Now will you tek it?'

Phoebe shook her head. 'No, Josh, I will not.'

'What about the cut?' Mark had remained silent until now. 'You could get them locks straight into Brummagem if you sent 'em along the cut.'

''Course,' Bert nodded, 'I never give a thought to the cut.'

'What! An' you workin' the narrow boats this three year?' Lizzie smiled across at her husband. 'Some bargee you be, Bert Ingles. Back at the locks for a few weeks an' you forget the cut exists.'

'I 'ad forgot it an' that be no lie,' Bert said sheepishly, 'but Mark be right. Get that box o' locks on a boat an' you could bring 'em right into Gas Street Basin. An 'andcart from there an' you as 'em delivered.'

'It sounds easy, Bert,' Phoebe said, the worry in her tone not diminished, 'but will there be a barge going to Birmingham in the next day or two?'

'Sure to be.' The words were Lizzie's. 'Barges be up an' down to Brummagem as often as a barman serves beer on a Friday night.'

'Might be one comin' now.' Josh jumped up. 'Shall I go an' see?'

'Ar, lad,' Bert nodded, 'an' if one passes as ain't due for Brummagem ask if 'e knows when one is. An', lad,' Bert pointed a finger at him, 'no dawdlin'. There be work still to do.'

'Can I come?' Ruth scrambled up from the table. 'Take me wi' you, Josh, I want to come.'

''Old on to 'er,' Lizzie said as Josh looked at her for permission. ''Er can be off like a ferret down a rabbit 'ole if you leave go of 'er.'

''Er'll be all right wi' me, Mrs Ingles.' Josh caught the girl's hand. 'We'll be back quicker'n a navvy sups a pint.'

'There be a boat along o' the towpath.' Josh was back at the bellows in under five minutes. 'Bloke says if it be on for 'im to fetch water from the pump, 'e'll cart your locks up to Brummagem.'

'Can you carry on if I goes for a word wi' 'im?' Bert asked from the yard.

'Ar,' Mathew nodded. 'Mark 'ere can put me right should be I needs it.

'Settled?' he asked when Bert returned to the workshop later.

Sitting in his place at the workbench Bert took up a lock, removing it from the pattern mould. ''E goes up to Brum' wi' an empty boat, 'as a load to pick up from Gas Street in the mornin'. 'E 'as agreed to lay up 'ere for the night to give we the time to finish the last o' the order.'

'That be a bit o' good news for Phoebe.' Mathew put the lock he had finished on the pile set aside for filing down. ''Er was worried, you could tell that.'

'Well, the worry be groundless now,' Bert answered, 'but somebody 'as to go wi' them locks an' I don't think as Phoebe be the one. There be no other woman on that barge an' while I ain't sayin' as it be the bloke would touch 'er, I am sayin' as 'ow it wouldn't look right.'

'So what you reckon?'

'What I reckon is one o' we men should go wi' 'em.'

'It be the sensible thing,' Mathew agreed, 'an' that one should rightly be you, Bert. You can talk locks better'n me and you knows what they be worth. A bloke won't find it so easy diddlin' you as 'e would me.'

'Mmm.' Bert reached for a screwdriver. 'I'll go tell 'er when I've finished this, but we'll 'ave to bide by 'er decision.'

'It would have been the answer to our problem,' Phoebe said when Bert told her the reason for his being in her kitchen, 'but it will no longer be necessary. The locks are not going to Birmingham.'

'Not goin' to Brummagem?' Bert looked surprised. 'Then where do they be goin', Miss?'

'They won't be going anywhere, Bert. Perhaps you had better read this.' She handed him a white envelope. 'It came just a few minutes ago.'

Drawing a folded paper from the envelope, Bert read the neat copperplate hand. 'But why?' he asked. 'There be no reason given an' the month's end be three days clear away.'

'I do not know why.' Phoebe took the letter from Bert, her eyes scanning the heading James Greaves, Hardware and Ironmongery. He had given no reason in his letter, merely stating the gross of locks ordered on the second day of the month would no longer be required.

'I don't believe it!' Bert pushed a hand through his hair. 'I just don't bloody well believe it! Three days from finishin' an' the bloke 'as the gall to say 'e no longer wants 'em, an' not even a reason.'

'I am afraid we have to believe it.' Phoebe folded the letter, returning it to its envelope. 'But we do not have to accept it without a reason.'

'What you be goin' to do?'

'I am going to Birmingham, Bert.' Phoebe's chin came up. 'I am going to see Mr James Greaves.'

Phoebe sat on the slatted wooden seat of the steam tram, her bag with the one lock in it held close in her lap. The journey would take longer by tram but the fare by train was more than she had. The tram moved along Holloway Bank, complaining at the rise in the ground.

'Nice day, ain't it?'

A large woman in an even larger flowered hat nodded at Phoebe.

'Very nice,' she replied, her thoughts not with her words.

'It'll get nicer an' all if it don't get no worse.' The

woman's head bobbed, setting the flowers on her oversized hat wobbling dangerously.

'My rheumatiz says it be a-goin' ter rain.' A second woman joined the conversation.

'Oh, ar!' The flowers wobbled again. 'My old man says as 'ow 'e's goin' to get up off 'is idle arse tomorrer an' find isself a job – only tomorrer never comes, an' when it does 'e ain't in, so don't you go believin' all you 'ears.'

'You 'ave one o' them sort an' all, does you, wench!' The second woman laughed wheezily. 'I thought as I was the only woman wi' a bloke too idle to blow the froth off 'is beer.'

The large woman's assortment of chins wobbled in rhythm with the flowers on her hat. 'You knows what thought thought.' She laughed. ''E thought 'e weren't dead till they buried 'im!'

'Boundary,' the conductor of the tram called loudly. 'Boundary, all change.'

'Change?' Phoebe had been to Birmingham several times but always in her father's carriage. Now the conductor's call confused her.

'You 'as to get off 'ere, luv.' The large woman eased herself out of her seat. 'It's the boundary, did you want to go further?'

'I want to go to Birmingham.' Phoebe got out of her seat as the conductor called again.

The woman began to move along the narrow aisle separating the wooden bench-like seats, her ample hips brushing both sides. 'Wednesbury tram only runs as far as West Bromwich,' she said as Phoebe followed. 'To go on to Brummagem you 'ave to change at the boundary.' Alighting heavily, the woman eased her basket more firmly on to her arm then pointed. 'Just go a bit further down the road an' you'll see the tram for Brummagem. It be navy blue an' cream where this one be red, you can't miss it.'

Murmuring her thanks, Phoebe followed the way that had

been pointed. It took several more enquiries before she found the shop front announcing James Greaves, Hardware and Ironmongery. Taking a deep breath, she pushed open the door.

'Mr Greaves,' Phoebe took the letter from her bag, placing it address uppermost on the smooth polished wood of the counter that ran the length of the small dark shop, 'can you please explain to me why you have cancelled your order for one gross of Invincible locks just days before that order was due to be delivered to you?'

'I beg your pardon!' The man's smile faded to be replaced by a bemused look.

'I have no doubt you do,' Phoebe replied tartly, 'but begging my pardon is not enough. I require an explanation.'

'Are you sure you have come to the right shop?' He sounded almost apologetic. 'I have ordered no locks.'

'Yes!' Phoebe glared, her mouth tight with anger. A reason with or without an apology she would accept, but not bare-faced denial. 'You are Mr James Greaves, are you not?'

'I am, Miss,' the shopkeeper answered politely.

'And this, if I am not mistaken, is a Hardware and Ironmongery store?'

'It is.' He nodded, following Phoebe's cursory glance at the various articles of hardware hanging from every available space.

'Then this must be yours. Please read it and tell me if I am wrong.'

Taking the letter from the envelope, he fitted a pair of wire-framed spectacles to his nose, looking first over them to Phoebe's angry face then through them to read the words written on the paper. 'I am afraid you are wrong,' he said, after reading it through, 'I did not send this letter and neither have I sent any order for locks.'

'But it has your name and business address.' Phoebe took the letter, tapping a finger against the heading.

'I do not deny that,' he answered levelly, 'but I deny having written that letter. If you would care to look at this ledger you will see the handwriting is not the same as is on that letter.'

He could have disguised his writing. Phoebe glanced at the ledger. But why should he go to so much trouble? What did he have to gain from ordering a gross of locks then cancelling that order days before delivery?

'Then who?' Phoebe's hand fell limply on to the counter.

'I don't know who,' the man answered gently, seeing misery slowly spread across Phoebe's face, 'but it must be somebody who holds a grudge against you.'

Drawing in a deep breath, Phoebe folded the letter returning it to her bag. 'I apologise for having accused you of such an action, Mr Greaves,' she said, 'I should not have spoken as I did.'

'I understand, Miss. You pay it no more mind. These locks you spoke of, what be they like?'

'I have one here.' She took the lock from her bag, laying it on the counter where its polished brass gleamed against the dark wood.

'That ain't no botched up job.' James Greaves took the lock in his hands, examining it closely. 'This be a good bit o' work. Man as made this knows his job.' He looked up at Phoebe. 'Bet they teks a bit o' time making and all. And you have a gross, you say?'

He examined the lock again as Phoebe nodded. 'A man can be proud of making something like this,' he said. 'He's a craftsman and no mistake. Look here, Miss . . .?'

'Pardoe,' she supplied.

'Miss Pardoe,' he handed back the lock, 'I will be willing to take some locks off your hands.'

Phoebe sat on the steam tram, finding the journey home no less a strain than the outward one had been. James Greaves would take some of the locks but to whom could she sell the remainder? She looked through the window towards a sky that was already darkening. But it is not as dark as my horizons, she thought miserably. How do I tell

Mathew and Bert and Mark, and Josh there is no money to pay what I owe them?

'So there you have it.' Phoebe looked at Bert and the others grouped in her kitchen, their faces solemn. 'It appears that James Greaves did not send us an order for one gross of locks and neither did he send the letter that cancelled that order.'

'Then who the 'ell did?' Mathew had listened silently to all Phoebe had said and now his temper broke. 'Some stupid bugger wi' a twisted mind, an' if I finds out who it be 'e'll 'ave a bloody twisted neck to go wi' it . . .'

'You said as this Greaves bloke showed you a ledger of 'is 'andwritin'?' Bert said, interrupting Mathew's explosion, his own voice still level and calm. ''Ow good a proof do you take that to be?'

Phoebe looked up with eyes shadowed with disappointment and worry. 'Well, the ledger did go back several years and all the entries were in the same hand, quite different to this.' She touched the envelope lying on the table in front of her. 'I can't believe a man would go to so much trouble as to disguise his own handwriting to play a practical joke on someone he does not know, on someone he never even met before today.'

'There be no tellin' what folk'll do if they 'ave a mind,' Mathew cut in, his anger still hot.

'True,' Bert agreed soothingly, 'but what would the bloke be gainin' by doin' such? There was nothin' in it for 'im.'

'P'raps 'e thought 'avin' been turned down once 'e could get them locks cheap,' Tilly ventured her opinion. 'Mebbe 'e thought you would be only too glad to get shut of 'em.'

'There is no telling,' Phoebe answered wearily. 'The fact is I am left with a gross of locks for which I have no sale, and whether the ordering of them was a practical joke or not will not pay wages.'

'The ironmonger did offer to buy some of 'em and at the

price you first said. 'E made no attempt to cut you down, you told me?'

'None.'

'Well, to me that seems to say 'e wasn't tryin' to buy more on the cheap,' Bert thumbed the buckle of his broad belt. 'But like Tilly says, you never know 'ow a man's thoughts be turnin'.'

'Mine be turnin' to murder,' Mathew growled. 'Whoever it be 'as done this, pray God I never comes across 'im 'cos I won't be responsible for what I does to 'im – but it'll be a long time afore 'e walks again.'

'It's done now an' what's done can't be undone.' Lizzie took her daughter's hand. 'Best for all of you to get some rest. The problem will still be wi' us in the mornin', it can be talked on again then. Might be as you will see a way out when you be feelin' calmer.'

'Lizzie be right, Miss.' Bert followed his wife through the scullery to the yard. 'P'raps summat will make itself plain come mornin'.'

'I hope so, Bert, goodnight.' Phoebe stood as the Ingleses and Josh followed by Lucy and Mathew crossed the mill yard to their respective dwellings. They had all worked so hard, and for what! She looked up at the night sky, its inky void strewn with stars heavy with light. It could not all be for nothing, there had to be a reason. Why would someone want her to throw her last penny into a venture, only to see it sink? It didn't make sense. But then sending her to prison for a crime she had not committed had not made sense. She drew in a deep breath of the night air, carrying the sweet smell of the heath to her nostrils. She had been imprisoned but not defeated, and the failure to sell her locks would not defeat her either. Bert and Mathew had put their trust in her and it was up to her to ensure that trust was not in vain.

'But what can you do, wench?' Tilly asked later as she handed Phoebe a cup of steaming cocoa. 'It's all right you sayin' it's up to you to mek things good, but what do you reckon to do? You 'ave no money to pay the men an' none to buy more metals wi'. Not that you needs 'em with so many locks unsold.'

'I don't know what I can do,' Phoebe's hands shook as she put the cup on the table, 'I only know I have to do something. Mathew and Bert need their money to support their families and somehow I have to find that money.'

'Somehow, somehow!' Tilly fussed about the grate, banking down the fire for the night, the kettle already filled with water for the morning sitting on the hob above the oven. 'You can go on sayin' somehow till the cows come 'ome but it still won't put money in yer purse.'

'There has to be a way.' Phoebe closed her eyes, a thin film of tears glistening along the edge of her dark lashes.

'You could let James Greaves 'ave the dozen locks 'e said 'e would tek. That would be little, I know, but a little be better'n none at all.'

'And if I can't sell the rest, what then?' Phoebe spoke more to herself than Tilly. 'The Ingleses can't stay where there is no job to support them. They will have to move on, and that means being on the road for God knows how long, on the road with Ruth and Mark. And then there is Josh, what will he do? Go back to the streets of Wednesbury, standing in line for a job that breaks his back for a penny, sleeping under a hedge because that penny is not enough to buy him food and a bed. I can't let that happen, Tilly, I can't.'

'Mebbe you won't 'ave to, wench.' She rested a hand on Phoebe's slumped shoulders. 'The good Lord only lets we tek as much as we can bear then 'e teks the rest. 'E as give you a burden an' it be 'eavy for you, but 'e won't let it break your back. 'E'll lift it, you'll see. P'raps 'e won't tek it away altogether but 'e'll lift it enough for you to mek your way.'

'I don't mind for myself, Tilly,' Phoebe looked up, 'you and I have known worse, but I feel I have let the others down.'

'You've let nobody down, my wench!' Tilly said fiercely. 'You found 'em food an' a place to live when nobody else would 'ave 'em, an' they won't go blamin' you for what's 'appened. If it be as the Ingleses 'ave to move on then that will be 'cos the Lord is wantin' it that way.'

'No, Tilly,' Phoebe pressed the hand resting on her shoulder 'the Lord has no desire to see children suffering on the streets or men dragging their families from town to town in search of work. While we have food in the house we will share it, and with God's help we will stay together.'

'Amen to that,' Tilly answered fervently. 'Amen to that!'

In the moonlit shadows of her bedroom Phoebe slipped her nightgown over her head. They would go back to selling Bert's work one or two a day as before, but the profit from that would not be enough to keep his family and pay Mathew for toting them around Wednesbury. That in turn would mean extra work for Lucy, trying to cover the shortfall with her baking, and the strain of the past month was already showing in her face. She could not go on like this much longer. And then there was Josh. The Ingleses could not go on feeding him when they had next to nothing to keep themselves with.

Going over to the window she stared out over the silent night: over the windmill, its folded sails thrust out like a cross stark against the dark sky, over the corn loft into which she had been forced by the man who had come to rob her, and to the spot in the yard where he had almost raped her. 'Why?' she whispered softly. 'Why is all this happening to me?' But out of the quiet shadows there came no answer.

'Can I see you for a minute, Miss Phoebe?' Bert stood cap in hand at the doorway to the scullery.

Leaving the breakfast dishes she was drying as Tilly washed them, Phoebe laid the huckaback cloth aside. 'Of course, Bert. Come in, please.'

Nodding a greeting to Tilly, he followed Phoebe to the kitchen but as she made to go through to the parlour he held back. 'It will do 'ere, Miss.'

Phoebe's heart skipped a beat. She had lain awake the

greater part of the night trying to find a solution to their difficulties but none had come. If her burden was to be lifted it seemed the time was not yet, and if Bert had come to tell her that he and Lizzie must move on she had nothing to offer that would hold them to Wiggins Mill.

'It's like this,' he twisted his cap between his fingers, 'Mathew an' me, we been talkin', an' we thinks as 'ow p'raps them locks would be better taken down to Liverpool.'

'Liverpool!' Phoebe exclaimed.

'Ar.' Bert looked at her, his eyes candid. 'Mathew an' me, we says we got nothin' now so if we get nothin' there then we lost nothin'. We thinks it should be given a try, but we 'ad to ask what you thought. 'Ow you felt about it.'

'Liverpool.' Phoebe sat down, her hands together on the table. The night had brought her no idea of what to do with the locks but the same could not be said of Bert.

'Ar, Liverpool, Miss.' He reinforced the theme, his voice enthusiastic. 'You see, Liverpool be the docks from where ships sail to America. Mathew an' me reckon if we can get them locks over there, they will sell.'

'How do you reckon that?'

Bert shuffled from one foot to another, his hand nervously throttling his cap. 'Well, Miss, from what I 'ear tell, you can sell spectacles to a blind man in that country.'

Trying but failing to hide the smile his words brought to her mouth, Phoebe asked from whom he had such information.

'Word gets round the docks,' he told her. 'Sailors comin' in from America an' the West Indies talks of 'ow the country be growin' that fast an' 'ow they be 'ungry for all sorts o' goods. They tells the cut men you can find a market over there for anythin', an' if they be buyin' goods fast as we can ship 'em over seems reasonable they 'ave to be stored for a time in warehouses. An' warehouses need locks – good locks as can't be broken.'

'And you and Mathew think our locks will sell over there?'

Bert smiled. 'Like Mathew says, they might not be the first locks to 'it America but they'll be the best.'

'But it will take weeks, Bert, maybe months, and you have already gone a month without wages. You can't go for several more. It is different for Mathew, he can go back to oddjobbing in the town and they have the money Lucy makes selling pies, but you and Lizzie will have nothing and I have not enough money to buy more metals for you to carry on while you are waiting – not unless we let Mr Greaves buy the one dozen locks he offered to take.'

'We've thought of that, me an' Lizzie, an' we both say the same. Leave the gross of locks intact an' send 'em off to America. We will find a way to manage till we gets word back.'

'But if they should not sell as you think, Bert,' Phoebe added a cautionary note, 'Lizzie and the children . . .'

'Lizzie an' Mark knows the score,' Bert said quickly. 'They also knows that should it fail to come off we will be back on the road, but if we never takes a chance then we'll never 'ave the answer, one way nor t'other, so the final word rests wi' you, Miss.'

'Has Mathew discussed this with Lucy?'

'They spoke of it this mornin' as he walked 'er to the crossroads.'

'And Lucy was in agreement?'

'Sees 'er was,' Bert nodded, 'but t'would be better all round to talk the matter over wi' all concerned brought together. That way everybody gets to 'ear all the fors and all the agens, and gets to say their piece fair like.'

'Agreed. But in the meantime have you thought of the cost involved in transporting the locks to America? It is going to be a great deal more than getting them to Birmingham and I did not have sufficient money to do that.'

'I 'ave thought of it.' Bert stopped mangling the cap he had taken to wearing to keep the dust of the workshop out of his hair. 'An' if you agrees then I think as we 'ave the answer. You see, while you was off to Brummagem to see James Greaves I went down to the cut side an' a mate of mine was takin' a load o' coal up to London. From there 'e 'as to pick up a load that'll take 'im to Liverpool. 'E will call 'ere day after tomorrow an' if I asks 'im 'e will take them locks wi' 'im. Won't cost no more'n a couple o' pies.'

'A couple of pies might get them to Liverpool, Bert, but it will take more than that to get them across the Atlantic. How do you propose we do that?'

'This way.' Bert stuffed the cap in his trousers pocket. 'The bargee as will be passin' 'ere in a day or two 'as a brother-in-law who is first mate on a cargo steamer that makes a regular run to America. 'E takes aboard various items to sell over there.'

'What sort of items?' Phoebe asked.

'Anythin' the bargee picks up along 'is route.' Bert grinned. 'Anythin' they think will sell, which seems to be most things. An' this brother-in-law sells them for a cut of the profit.'

'Is he allowed to take things aboard the ship to be sold for his own profit?'

'Put it this way,' Bert smiled, ''e is allowed to take aboard anythin' that nobody else knows about.'

Phoebe looked at him, uncertainty in her eyes. 'There is something that does not seem quite honest about it, Bert. He is taking things on board to sell for himself and not for whoever is paying for the ship to carry cargo, and that can't be right.'

'Crew be allowed to take their own box aboard,' Bert explained. 'Don't nobody ask if it be 'olding clothes or anythin' else. One box be all they be allowed, it be up to them what they 'ave in it, so if this first mate wants to fill it wi' things 'e wants to sell that be 'is concern so long as 'e don't overdo it. It be a recognised thing, Miss Phoebe, that be 'ow seamen makes up for the low wage they be paid, same as do cut men.'

'This brother-in-law of your friend,' Phoebe asked, 'is he

to be trusted? I do not wish to call his honesty into question but . . .'

''E won't do the dirty, Miss Phoebe.' Bert's grin faded. ''E knows the cut men, an' 'e knows to cross one o' them is to wake up one mornin' wi' a knife in your ribs. No, if 'e sells 'em you'll get your money, an' if 'e don't sell 'em you gets the locks back, 'e makes nothin' an' we makes nothin'. That way benefits nobody so you can rest your mind easy: if them locks will sell at all in America then 'e will sell 'em. You tell 'im 'ow much you wants for 'em, that way 'e won't bring you less, then you pays 'im for 'is part.'

Phoebe sat silent, thinking over what Bert had said. She had little to lose either way. 'Very well.' She met Bert's quizzical stare. 'We will discuss it together this evening and if everyone is agreed, we will send the whole lot to America.'

Chapter Twenty-One

It had been a month. Phoebe picked up the bucket of water she had filled from the pump in the yard. A month since the locks had gone off to Liverpool, a month in which the small workshop had been silent.

She carried the bucket into the scullery, emptying it into the copper to heat for washing the household linen, feeling the empty pull of her stomach. The food stocks had diminished quicker than she had expected due to her giving more than a share to the Ingleses and she would take from Lucy only the small amount her needlework paid for. How much longer could it go on? she thought, slicing thin slivers of Sunlight soap from a thick bar and dropping them into the copper. A few shillings a week to feed herself, Tilly, the Ingleses and Josh.

Josh! She stirred the soap slivers into the water with a wooden stick. She had not yet found the courage to send him back to the town yet she knew she was merely putting off the moment, that it had to come. 'But not yet,' she whispered staring into the soap clouded water, 'not yet.'

'What be not yet?' Tilly came into the scullery, her arms filled with sheets.

'I was thinking we cannot keep Josh much longer.' Phoebe felt almost relieved as she said the words she had admitted to no one but herself. 'Lizzie is finding it hard to feed her own even with our help.'

'I've known that for some time, my wench.' Tilly took the wooden stick, using it to push the soiled linen into the wooden tub that stood beside the copper, pressing the sheets beneath the soapy water. 'An' I knows you won't be able to 'elp much longer. There be almost nothin' left in the 'ouse.'

'Has Bert gone looking for work?'

'Ar 'e 'as.' Tilly took the wooden maid to the clothes in the tub, banging it up and down on the linen. ''Im an' the two lads, same as they does every day, but it be a waste o' time. There be no work, not even in the foundries seems like.'

Phoebe watched the other woman pound away at the washing, her thin body bent by the weight of the heavy wooden wash tool that pressed the dirt from the linen. 'Do you think he will wait much longer before taking to the road?'

'Who can say what a man like that'll do?' Tilly brushed a wet hand across her brow. 'All I know is you can see it's gettin' 'arder day by day for 'im, comin' 'ome wi' nothin'.'

'But Lizzie and the children, he wouldn't take them on the road again, would he?'

Using the wooden stick she had taken from Phoebe as a rod Tilly fished the pounded sheet from the wooden tub, lifting it across to the brownstone sink, sloshing clean water over it and rinsing away the soiled soapy suds before carrying the sheet across to the copper to be boiled. 'Could be Lizzie would refuse to stay behind,' she said, recovering from the effort of carrying the water-soaked fabric. 'A woman like Lizzie Ingles ain't easy separated from 'er man.'

Nor from her children, Phoebe thought, lifting another sheet into the wooden tub. Lizzie would not leave her children at Wiggins Mill while she and Bert went to look for work.

'When you goin' to tell 'em?' Tilly took the maid to the sheet in the tub, pounding it with a steady rhythm.

'Yer goin' to 'ave to,' she said as Phoebe turned away. 'You 'ave to tell 'em that sewin' night an' day you still ain't got the means to support 'em more'n another couple of weeks at the outside, an' you try to do more'n you be doin' already an' you'll work yerself into the ground an' that'll be a lot o' good to nobody.'

Tilly was right. Phoebe made her way slowly to her sewing room. She would tell them tonight. To tell Bert and Lizzie she could help them no longer would be painful but what would she say to Josh? How do you tell a young boy he must leave the home and people he loves? That would not be painful, that would be heart-breaking.

Pausing before the brown paper that held the creamy yellow satin, Phoebe ran a finger over the cloth. She was to have worn that to the Dartmouths' ball where she would have been Edward's partner. Edward who loved her and wanted to marry her. Her life would be so different had she said yes, had she loved him as he did her. But she did not love Edward, she did not love any man. Closing the brown paper back over the satin, she walked to her chair, taking up the petticoat she was making, but the stitches were blurred by the face in her mind. The face of Edward's father.

Her thoughts going again and again over the problem of keeping the Ingleses and Josh, Phoebe sewed until the light from the window was too dim to see the tiny stitches clearly. The whole day and only one petticoat to show for the hours of work. She smoothed the narrow pin tuck pleating that wound around the skirt above the flounces of cotton lace. If only she could afford one of Mr Singer's sewing machines! Laying the petticoat aside, she stood up, stretching the aching muscles of her back. If only she could buy just enough metal for Bert to make one or two locks it would help, but money would stretch just so far and buying brass or steel out of what little she earned was that much too far.

Maybe I don't need money. Phoebe stood stock still, the words singing in her brain. Maybe she did not need to pay for metal when it was ordered. Maybe she could pay at the end of the month like her father's customers always had. She could but ask. Tomorrow, she would ask tomorrow.

She had walked across the heath from Wiggins Mill and now stood in the ledger room of Thomas Bagnall's iron foundry, conscious of the dust on the skirt of her green coat.

'This way, Miss.'

Phoebe followed a small man, his shoulders permanently stooped from bending all day over ledgers.

'In 'ere, Miss.'

The man stood aside, holding a door open for Phoebe to pass into an inner office.

'Miss Pardoe.' Heavy-jowled, his hairline way back from the front of his head, Thomas Bagnall pushed himself to his feet as the door closed behind her. 'I 'aven't seen you in a long time. Sit down, my dear, sit down.'

'Thank you.' Phoebe perched nervously on the chair he indicated, aware of the glance that took her in from boots to hair.

'So, my dear, you're well, I 'ope?'

'Quite well, Mr Bagnall,' Phoebe said, unable to furnish the words with a smile. There was something in Thomas Bagnall she did not like and the sooner their business was finished and she could leave the greater would be her relief.

'Then what is it Thomas Bagnall can do for you?' He smiled, the heavy folds of flesh on his face shuttering his small eyes. 'Nothing 'olds more pleasure for me than serving a pretty woman.'

'I want to order some metal.' Phoebe tried not to wonder how his eyes would re-emerge from the enfolding flesh.

'That's easy done,' Thomas Bagnall's eyes stayed buried by his broadening smile, 'you only 'ave to say what it is you want.'

'Twenty-four pounds of brass and half that of steel.'

'That don't be much.' The folds of flesh gave a little ground, allowing his eyes to show.

'No, Mr Bagnall, it is a smaller order than my previous one but it will suffice for now.'

Dropping a thick-fingered hand on to a bell set on his desk he bawled the requirements to the same stoop-shouldered man who came in answer.

'We will 'ave that out to you tomorrow, Miss Pardoe,' he said when the clerk had left for the second time, 'if you will pay Simms on your way out?'

'I wish to speak to you about that.' Phoebe fingered her bag, her nerve threatening to run out on her. 'I – I wish to settle my accounts monthly in the future.'

'Monthly!' He smoothed the whiskers that ran the length of his flabby cheeks, at the same time coming from behind his desk to stand beside her chair. 'Now that be a different arrangement . . .'

Phoebe eased her knees away from the figure standing so close his legs touched hers. 'I am aware of that, Mr Bagnall, and though I have always paid in advance when purchasing metal from you, I believe it is not unusual to pay a month after delivery.'

'It's not unusual,' his small eyes glittered, 'not unusual at all between men. But you don't be a man.'

'I do not see that it makes any difference, I can pay as well as any man.'

'Except you ain't got any money.' Thomas Bagnall's smile registered triumph as he saw Phoebe wince. 'If you had the money you wouldn't be asking to pay at the end of a month, now would you, Miss Pardoe? And that being so we need to talk terms.'

'Terms?' She hitched herself further from him, sitting almost sideways in an effort to avoid the touch of his legs. 'Do you mean a charge for interest?'

'Some might see it that way.' The small eyes hovered about her breasts and his podgy hands pulled at his side whiskers as if tearing away her clothes. 'I see it as a way of saying thank you for a favour.'

'Do you charge a man interest for the privilege of settling his account after a month?' she demanded.

'How I conduct my business is my business.' He smiled, sending waves of flesh coursing toward his eyes. 'And if you want my metal without paying cash on the nail, you must meet my terms.'

'Which are?'

He touched a finger to her face, stroking it across her cheek and along the side of her throat. 'A little of your company, a private dinner somewhere secluded. Not much to pay for a month's credit.'

Not much to pay? Phoebe felt her stomach reach for her throat. A little of her company? Thomas Bagnall would want more than that.

'I find your terms too much!' Phoebe pushed to her feet, moving quickly to the door and snatching it open.

'P'raps you do but when you find nobody'll give credit to a woman then come back to Thomas Bagnall. You'll find his terms easier to fulfil when you've no money in your pocket and no food in your stomach.'

Phoebe walked back across the heath. She had not gone to visit Sarah or to see Lucy at her stall in the market place, knowing the contempt and disgust she was feeling would show in her face. But why had she avoided both of her friends? She sat on a half-buried stone, her feet aching from the long walk to the town and halfway back again. Why did she not want either of them to know what had gone on in Thomas Bagnall's office? Turning her face to the sky she closed her eyes. She had not gone to visit them for fear of their finding out what she only now admitted. She could not let the Ingleses take their children out on the road nor could she allow Josh to sink back into the poverty and misery of living in the streets. She had to go back to Thomas Bagnall, she had to agree to his terms.

* * *

'You have no need to take me.' Phoebe smiled at the stoop-backed clerk who looked up as she entered the ledger room. 'I know where Mr Bagnall's office is.' Knowing his eyes were following her, she went along the corridor that led to the comfortably furnished room she had been in less than an hour before. Pushing open the door without knocking, she stepped inside.

'Well, now!' Thomas Bagnall's self-satisfied smile obliterated his eyes. 'You've come to your senses, I see. I thought you would so I didn't cancel your order for steel and brass.'

He moved around the desk to stand close, his body brushing hers, bringing a fresh surge of revulsion to Phoebe's throat. If she were to help Josh and the others she had to do it now for she would never have the courage to do it later. Her voice little more than a whisper, her legs trembling with weariness from her long walk but mostly from fear of what she was about to agree to, she said, 'Dinner with you one evening, that was what you proposed as payment for extending me credit, was it not?'

He lifted a hand, stroking his knuckles across her breast. 'One evening for brass,' he said thickly, 'an' one for steel.'

'But you said one evening!' Phoebe pushed his hand away, her cheeks flaming.

'So I did,' he agreed, his tiny fat-shrouded eyes sweeping the length of her before settling on her face, 'and I'm still saying one. One evening for brass, one evening for steel. Those be my terms. You may take 'em or leave 'em.'

She had no choice. Trembling she turned to the doorway, stumbling through it in her eagerness to get away from a man who revolted her, yet a man to whom she must submit. 'Mr Bagnall,' she said, her voice low and shaky, 'I agree to your terms.'

'And what terms might those be?' Sir William Dartmouth caught Phoebe's arms as in her haste to be gone from the office she cannoned into him. Steadying her, he released her, asking again, 'What terms?'

'Miss Pardoe an' me had business together.' Thomas Bagnall's eyes receded behind their barrier of fat as he glanced warningly at Phoebe.

'How interesting!' William Dartmouth looked from one to the other, his glance pausing on Phoebe's flushed face. 'I am always interested in business and in the terms that conclude it. Perhaps, Miss Pardoe, you will tell me of yours?'

'It was nothing of consequence.' Thomas Bagnall stepped back from the doorway, leaving it clear for the other man to enter the office, but he did not move.

'What do you call "nothing of consequence" Thomas?' Sir William asked the question of the iron founder but his eyes were on Phoebe.

'Twenty-four pounds of brass and half that of steel, a piddlin' little order!' Bagnall snapped, annoyed at being questioned.

'Little indeed,' Sir William nodded, 'though it could have been more politely described in the presence of a lady, don't you think Thomas?'

What little could be seen of his eyes glittering venomously, the iron founder looked at Phoebe. 'I beg your pardon, Miss Pardoe,' he ground, 'a slip of the tongue.' Then to Sir William, 'Miss Pardoe was just leaving.'

'So I see.' William Dartmouth remained blocking Phoebe's way in the narrow brown-painted corridor that smelled strongly of the foundry. 'And hurriedly. Is that because you have other business, Miss Pardoe, or is it due to the terms you have just agreed with Thomas Bagnall?'

'I . . . I asked Mr Bagnall to allow me to settle my account at the end of the month from the date of purchase.' Phoebe straightened the quaver from her voice though her cheeks still flamed.

'That is the usual practice.'

'Not for me, Sir William.' Phoebe raised her head, a mixture of pride and despair in her green eyes. 'I have always paid the full amount at the time of placing an order but today it is not possible for me to do that therefore I asked for the month of credit I knew it was usual to extend to customers.'

'And the terms?' he asked, the temperature of his voice dangerously low.

'There were no terms. She asked for a month. I . . . I gave her a month, that's all we agreed.' Thomas Bagnall glared at Phoebe. 'There were no other terms.'

'And there will be none!' Sir William glanced past Phoebe to the other man, a world of meaning in his cold grey eyes. 'Miss Pardoe's order will be delivered in the morning and paid for one calendar month following that day and there will be no extra charge any sort whatsoever. The same terms will apply to any and all future orders she may wish to place.' He turned to Phoebe. 'Do you find those terms acceptable?'

'Most acceptable,' she nodded, 'thank you.'

Inclining his head so slightly his eyes did not leave her face, he answered quietly, 'Then your business here is settled. Good day, Miss Pardoe.'

The brass and steel would be delivered tomorrow! Bert would have the means of earning a living again! Phoebe walked home across the heath, her tiredness forgotten. She had a month in which to get the money to pay for the metals and thanks to Sir William she would not have to dine with Thomas Bagnall or suffer the attentions she knew would have followed. It was more than fortunate Sir William had arrived when he did, it was heavensent. She breathed a long deep breath of air flavoured with the scent of ling and wild flowers. It had been many months since her release from Handsworth prison but she still felt the same wonder and relief at being free to walk across the heath, just to stand and listen to the hymn of a skylark rising to the sky or the chorus of crickets in the grass. William Dartmouth had brought her that freedom just as he had brought another different kind of freedom today. 'Thank you,' she murmured using her inner eyes to look at the tall dark-haired man whose grey eyes seemed to smile back at her. 'Thank you.'

'When did he go?' Phoebe asked Tilly, her voice throbbing with concern.

'About a hour after yerself,' she answered. ''E come swannin' into the kitchen an' said 'e was off somewheres else to find work 'cos there was none to be 'ad in Wednesbury. It wasn't till later I found that in the parlour.'

Phoebe glanced at the coins lying on the table, a tiny pool of silver glistening in the last of the daylight.

'Did he say where he was going?'

'I've told you what 'e said, word for word,' Tilly answered patiently, ''ad 'e said more I would 'ave told you more.'

'I know, Tilly, and I am sorry to keep on questioning you, it's just that I am so concerned.'

'We all be that, my wench, but I don't see as worryin' yerself sick will do any good – you already be worn out wi' walkin' to that town an' back. Sit yerself down an' wait for Mathew gettin' in. Could be 'e was told more'n me.'

But Phoebe could not sit down. The meeting with Thomas Bagnall had unnerved her, and now this.

'Has Lizzie said anything?' She looked at Tilly peeling potatoes in an enamel bowl, black chip marks leaving a pattern of dots around its white edge.

'Nuthin' 'er can say.' Tilly hacked a hole in a potato, digging out the brown rottenness attacking its heart. ''E be gone an' that be all there be to it. Talkin' will mek no odds to that.'

Phoebe had talked yesterday of not being able to keep them all together at Wiggins Mill; now she had found a way, only she had found it too late. If only he had waited just one more day.

'That be Lucy and Mathew 'ome.' Tilly dropped a half-peeled potato into the bowl, rubbing her hands on her apron. 'Could be they seen 'im somewheres.' Following Phoebe into the yard she heard Lizzie already asking the question and Mathew's answer.

'I seen 'im this mornin' afore Lucy an' me went into Wednesbury an' I ain't seen 'im since.'

'Neither 'ave I.' Lucy shook her head.

'It ain't 'ardly dark yet.' Mathew glanced at the golden-red rim of the horizon. ''E'll be back soon, you be worryin' over nuthin'. It ain't as if 'e ain't never been out in the dark on 'is own afore.'

'Mathew's right,' Lucy agreed, ''e 'as most like gone into the town an' met up wi' somebody 'e knows. Give 'im an hour or so an' 'e'll be back.'

'I 'ope you be tellin' true, Lucy,' Lizzie said tearfully. 'I 'ope you all be tellin' true.'

'Tell you what,' Mathew scooped Ruth into his arms as she came squealing with delight into the yard, 'let me give my best girl a cuddle and then I'll go look for 'im.'

'Who you goin' to look for, Uncle Mathew?'

Kissing the little girl's cheek he set her down beside her mother. 'I'm goin' to look for the prince who will marry my little princess, but not till you be older.'

'Can I come? Can I, Uncle Mathew?'

Mathew smiled at the child, her tumbling red-gold hair caught with a strip of cornflower blue ribbon Lucy had bought for her. 'We can't 'ave a princess walkin' the 'eath an' gettin' 'er royal feet dusty.'

'You could carry me,' she answered, her eyes wide and serious.

'I might be able to, Ruthie,' Mathew hid his smile, 'but I be gettin' very old. Could be as I couldn't carry you back.'

Catching his hand the girl smiled up at him, craning her head back on her neck. 'Don't worry, Uncle Mathew, I will carry you back.'

'Come along, miss.' Lizzie caught her daughter by her free hand. 'You can carry yerself to the wash bowl and wash yer 'ands an' face ready for bed. Say goodnight to everybody.'

'You will let me know if you find 'im?' Lizzie asked when the goodnights had been said.

'Don't worry,' Lucy smiled sympathetically, 'I'll come right over.'

'I think I'll go wi' Lizzie,' Tilly said quietly. ''Er 'as took this 'arder than I would 'ave thought. I'll stop with 'er till Mark be 'ome then I'll be back to finish them 'taters.'

'I will finish them.' Phoebe looked towards Lizzie leading her daughter to the corn barn that had become their home. 'Stay with Lizzie as long as she needs you.'

'Who would 'ave guessed Lizzie would 'ave been 'it that 'ard?' Mathew lifted his cap, running a hand through his hair.

'When you grow to love somebody it be 'ard when they ups an' leaves wi' 'ardly a word,' Lucy answered. 'Beats me why 'e did it. 'E ain't goin' to find no better 'ome than 'e's got 'ere.'

'He did it because he thought we could not keep him at Wiggins Mill any longer,' Phoebe said. 'He was no fool, he knew how long it had been since any money other than the few shillings my sewing brings had come into the house. He knew I could not support them all for much longer so he left.'

'Poor soul!' Lucy sighed. 'An' now 'e is Lord knows where, but at least 'e as *some* money in 'is pocket an' 'e is well used to mekin' it stretch as far as it'll go so at least 'e will eat for a week or two.'

'But he does not have any money.' Phoebe turned towards the house. 'He left what he had in the parlour.'

'What, all of it?' Lucy asked as Mathew set off to search the heath.

'All of it,' Phoebe nodded. 'All four shillings.'

'Poor soul!' Lucy said again. 'Poor little Josh!'

'If only he had waited, we will have brass and steel tomorrow enough for Bert to start again.'

'Eh, Miss Phoebe! How did you manage that?'

'It's a long story, Lucy.'

Catching her arm, Lucy hustled her towards the house. 'Then let's 'ave a cup o'tea wi' the tellin'. I'm that parched I couldn't spit a tanner.'

'Eh, the dirty old bugger!' Lucy exclaimed when Phoebe finished relating the happenings of the afternoon. 'I wonder 'ow the 'oity toity Rachel Bagnall would take to knowin' 'er old man be no better than a lecher!'

'I hope she never has to know.' Phoebe poured tea for both of them, handing a cup to Lucy.

'Prob'ly wouldn't worry 'er none.' Lucy blew indelicately into her cup to cool the steaming liquid. 'From what folk tell 'er ain't no better than 'er should be.' She looked up suddenly, shock slackening her mouth. 'Eeh, Miss Phoebe, you wouldn't 'a gone, would you? Wi' old Bagnall I mean!'

'I think that at the time I was prepared to do anything, Lucy,' Phoebe admitted.

'You would 'ave been called on to do more than eat a dinner wi' that dirty sod!' Lucy's shock retreated before an onslaught of indignation. 'Thank God Billy-me-Lord turned up when 'e did. Which reminds me,' she put her cup on the table, 'there was talk in the market today about the Dartmouths.'

'Sir William?'

''Im an' all,' Lucy said quickly, 'but mostly 'is family, about them comin' 'ome to England.'

Edward was coming home. The thought was pleasant but it brought no rush of excitement. It had been the truth when she had told him she was not in love with him but he had said that would change while he was in Europe, that when he returned he would ask her again to become his wife. But her feelings for him had not changed. Edward Dartmouth was a kind attentive man who would make a wonderful husband but she could never marry him.

'When are they expected?' Phoebe asked.

Across the table Lucy's eyes were bright. 'They ain't!' she said bluntly.

Phoebe's brows drew together with a hint of puzzlement. 'But you said they were coming home?'

'They *was*,' Lucy emphasised the last word, 'but it seems there was a almighty storm at sea somewheres an' the ship they was on was sunk. 'Pears there was quite a few of the passengers didn't find a place in them lifeboats an' was drowned.'

'No!' Phoebe's face blanched. 'No, not Sophie, she was to be married . . . she . . . she can't be drowned!'

'That seems to be what 'er father said,' Lucy continued. ''Cordin' to what be told in the market the ship was sunk some time ago but 'e wouldn't 'ave it that 'is family was drowned. 'E kept on waitin' for word that would tell they was still alive.'

'But it did not come?'

'Seems not.' Lucy picked up her cup, sipping the tea. 'Seems he 'eard to the contrary. 'E must 'ave for word to be goin' around.'

'I never thought when I saw him in Thomas Bagnall's foundry today, it didn't seem to register.'

'What didn't?' Lucy looked up from her tea.

Phoebe frowned as though trying to recall some inner picture. 'He, Sir William, he wore dark grey. The collar of his coat was faced with black velvet and he had a narrow ribbon of grosgrain about the sleeve. He was in mourning and I never noticed.'

'Don't blame yerself, Miss,' Lucy said soothingly, 'after what you 'ad just been through wi' old Bagnall, 't'ain't surprisin' you never noticed.'

'But *he* noticed.' Phoebe condemned her own oversight. 'He noticed my discomfort even in his own sorrow and I . . . he must think I am so heartless!'

Rising from her chair Lucy went to stand beside the girl she had once served as a maid, the girl whom life had moulded into a woman. ''E won't think nothin' like that,' she said, bending to place her arms about Phoebe. ''E could see you was upset an' 'e won't tek no insult from you not offerin' 'im sympathy. Billy-me-Lord be too fine a man to 'old a grudge, 'specially from summat 'e knows full well to be not meant.'

'I hope you are right, Lucy.' Phoebe turned to her friend, hiding her tears against her waist. 'He was so kind to me, I never wanted to hurt him.'

'You ain't 'urt 'im, Miss Phoebe.' Lucy stroked a hand across sherry-coloured hair, her voice gentle. 'You ain't 'urt 'im, an' when you be feelin' more like yerself you can write to tell 'im of yer sympathy wi' 'is loss, but for now go an' wash yer face while I finishes peelin' these 'taters. You will feel better for it.'

'Ain't no sign o'the lad,' Mathew was saying when Phoebe returned to the kitchen. 'Bert an' Mark went over towards Tipton way an' I went towards the Lyng but it be blacker than the devil's tongue out there an' wi' no moon I couldn't see no more'n a spit in front o' me an' same wi' Bert an' Mark. Ain't no more we can do tonight.'

'But he might be sleeping out in the open,' Phoebe protested.

''E might an' I can't say as 'e ain't,' Mathew answered, 'but it be no use our lookin' any more. 'Sides if it be as 'e left the parish like 'e told Tilly 'e was goin' to do 'e could be anywhere by this time. We can't tell whether 'e 'eaded for Brummagem or took Walsall way, an' in any case, even if we does find 'im we can't force 'im to come back to Wiggins Mill, not if 'e don't want to.'

'But he was happy here and the work with Bert interested him.'

'Ar, the work interested 'im,' Mathew looked from Phoebe to Lucy, 'but who knows 'ow long a lad's interest be 'eld by anythin'? They changes their minds quicker'n a kingfisher flaps its wings. One minute they be fascinated by one thing an' the next minute they wants no more to be doin' wi' it.'

'I don't think Josh was like that,' Phoebe said quietly. 'I think he left because he saw it as the only way to help the situation. He thought one less mouth to feed was one less to worry over. Why else would he have left every penny he had earned in my parlour?'

'You be right, Miss Phoebe.' Lucy added salt to the potatoes she had placed in a pan set over the coal fire. 'But so is Mathew. If the lad 'as med up 'is mind to go then there be nothin' we can do about it. We just 'ave to accept it.'

'Lizzie has taken it so hard you would almost think it was Mark had left.'

'Lizzie be a good soul,' Mathew said, ''er treated that lad like 'er treated 'er own. 'Tain't surprisin' 'er be tekin' it 'ard.'

'And Bert?'

''E were the same, treated Josh as 'e treated Mark.'

'One as worries me be Ruth,' Lucy said. 'That little 'un thought the sun shone out of 'is eyes, 'er followed 'im every chance 'er got. 'Ow do you explain to a child as young as that the one 'er took to be God 'as up an' left?'

'Lord!' Mathew breathed. 'Nobody thought about Ruthie.'

Phoebe stared at the window. The night sky had lightened into dawn and still she had not slept, her mind living and re-living the times spent with Sophie and Edward. Edward had loved Phoebe, and he had died knowing her love for him was not returned. And Sophie . . . she was so full of marriage plans, so happy at the thought of becoming Montrose's wife, and now she was lying somewhere on the sea bed. Son, daughter and wife, all taken in one swoop. Phoebe closed her eyes against the picture her mind formed yet again, a picture of people helpless against waves that engulfed then swallowed them. His whole family lost together, what must Sir William Dartmouth be feeling?

'Ruth . . . Ruth, where am you?'

Phoebe's eyes snapped open as Bert's voice rang across the yard.

'Ruth . . . Ruth, my girl, ah'll tan yer arse for yer if you don't come 'ere this minute!'

This time it was Lizzie's voice that rang on the dawn stillness. Flinging aside the covers Phoebe jumped from the bed, crossing quickly to the window that overlooked the yard. Bert and Lizzie, still in their nightclothes, were looking around the outhouses. Raising the sash, Phoebe called to ask what was wrong.

'It be Ruth.' Lizzie looked up at the window, her face a mask of concern. ''Er be gone from 'er bed.'

'Have you searched the barn thoroughly?' Phoebe realised the futility of her question only after asking it.

'We looked just about everywhere,' Lizzie said, her voice near to breaking, 'me and Bert been lookin' an hour or more.'

'I'll be down in a moment!'

'What be the matter?' Tilly came into Phoebe's room as she withdrew her head, leaving the sash open.

'Ruth.' Phoebe reached for her dress and petticoats. 'She is not in her bed and Lizzie and Bert cannot find her in any of the out buildings.

'Lord, not summat else!' Tilly threw up her hands in despair. 'If it ain't one thing it's another. When is it all goin' to end? I'll get me dress an' then I'll be down. That poor woman . . .'

Phoebe threw off her nightgown, scrambled into her day clothes. Unmindful of her unwashed face or her uncombed hair she thrust her feet into her shoes and ran downstairs to the yard.

'How long has she been gone?' she asked, reaching Lizzie's side.

'I don't know for true,' Lizzie answered, her face crumpling. 'I put 'er into 'er bed last night like always an' when I woke this mornin' 'er were not in it no longer.'

'Try not to worry.' Phoebe held the crying woman, realising the unreasonableness of her request but hoping it at least sounded confident. 'We will have her home in no time. She has probably gone over to the windmill to pick you some flowers. I noticed some very pretty ones around there the other day.'

'Or 'er might 'ave gone across by the cut.' Lizzie's body shook. ''Er might 'ave 'eard we talkin' after 'er 'ad been put to 'er bed. We said about Josh 'avin' left, an' Bert was sayin' 'ow 'e might never come back.' She stepped out of Phoebe's arms. 'You know 'ow 'er 'ad taken to the lad,' she said, her eyes darkening with fear. 'Summat tells me 'er 'as gone lookin' for 'im an' 'er'll 'ave little fear o' the cut. 'Er'll 'ave no understandin' o' the danger of it.'

'But she may not have gone to the canal.' Phoebe tried to sound reassuring. 'Why should she have?'

'I know 'er 'as.' Lizzie spoke more to herself than to Phoebe. ''Er 'eard Bert say the lad could well 'op a barge somewhere an' barges means the cut an' that be where my babby 'as gone! My Ruth be somewhere in the . . .'

'Don't talk like that!' Tilly snapped, coming into the yard in time to hear Lizzie's fear. 'That babby o' your'n be up to 'er arse in flowers over by that windmill an' 'er father will 'ave 'er back 'ere afore you 'ave time to blink, so stop yer snivellin' an' go mek 'er some breakfast to come back to!'

'Tilly is right,' Phoebe said as Mathew and Lucy joined them. 'Ruth will be back before you know it. Leave it to the men. You come with Tilly and me, a cup of tea will help.'

'Will it?' Lizzie sagged against Tilly. 'Will it 'elp that?'

Phoebe turned, following the line of Lizzie's stare. 'Oh no!' she whispered. 'Please God, no.'

'Ruthie!' Bert's agonised shout rent the quiet sky as he caught sight of his daughter, her white nightgown clinging to her small body, her red-gold hair a bright splash against a dark jacket. 'Ruthie!' he shouted again, running towards the boy who carried her in his arms . . .

* * *

'I were a few yards, along the cut,' Josh explained as Lizzie held her daughter, dry and in a fresh nightgown, tight in her arms. 'I know I'd said as I was leavin' Wednesbury altogether but when it come to it I couldn't, I just wanted to be near all of you, especially Mrs Ingles.'

'But why go in the first place, Josh?' Phoebe looked to where he sat, his fingers curled about the girl's hand.

'I knowed you was short o' money, Miss, an' 'ad been for some time. It sort of makes sense, don't it? One less body in the 'ouse meks one less mouth to feed so I went, but I come back when it was dark. I found a place to sleep the other side o' the lock. I would 'ave liked to have slept in the old windmill but I wouldn't 'cos I 'ad promised Miss Phoebe I wouldn't never sleep in that place again an' there were nowheres else so I kipped along o' the cut.'

'Thank the good God 'e put you there, lad.' Bert took the child from his wife, carrying her into the loft to her bed.

'But if you was sleepin',' Mark asked, ''ow come you knowed our Ruth was in the cut?'

'I was sleepin',' a puzzled look crept over Josh's face, 'an' I was dreamin'. I was dreamin' o' me mother only it were not me mother. Well, the face were not me mother's, it were Mrs Ingles's, but 'er were wearin' a lovely white frock an' 'er face were all shinin' like a light were on it an' 'er called me name.' He paused as if living the dream again. ''Er called me name two or three times an' then 'er told me to get up an' bring Ruth 'ome. I said as Ruth already be 'ome but 'er just smiled an' said it again. "Josh, get up and bring Ruth 'ome."'

He looked at the group of people watching him. 'I 'eard 'er say it plain as day an' then I woke up. I looked all around but I couldn't see nobody an' I was just goin' to lie down again when the water up along the canal by the lock went all bright wi' the sun an' I seen summat white floatin' in it. Well, I run like buggery to see what it might be an' . . . an' it were Ruth. I went in 'ead first an' brought 'er out but I couldn't bring 'er to wakin' so I carried 'er back 'ere to 'er 'ome like I was bid.'

'You did well, lad.' Tilly pushed a dish of thick porridge to each of the two boys.

'You did that.' Lizzie caught her husband's hand as he came down from the loft. 'An' don't you ever go leavin' we again, Josh, or I'll 'ave Bert 'ere belt the 'ide off you. This place or any other the Ingleses might find theirselves in be your 'ome an' we be your family.'

Josh looked up, a spoonful of porridge hovering at his lips, his eyes filled with something near to longing. 'Mrs Ingles,' he asked, 'could . . . could I call you Mother?'

'It was a strange dream Josh had,' Phoebe said as she walked with Tilly across the yard toward the mill house, 'strange but very fortunate.'

'It were fortunate all right an' a dream it might 'ave been.'

'Might?' Phoebe stopped walking and looked at the woman beside her. 'Now just what does that mean, Tilly Wood?'

'Mek on it what you will,' she answered, 'but to me that were no dream young Josh 'ad.'

'What else could it have been?'

'I ain't sayin',' Tilly's mouth set in a straight line, 'but the lad said as the sun shone on the water just about where that little wench was floatin', didn't 'e?'

'Yes,' Phoebe answered, puzzled by Tilly's attitude.

'Well, it 'pears to 'ave escaped everybody's notice but there ain't no sun, leastways none as can be seen through clouds that be thicker than a grorty puddin'.' She glanced skyward. 'There's been no break in them from first light. I knows 'cos I ain't been to bed. I sat watching against that lad comin' 'ome.'

Chapter Twenty-Two

'But this is more than I expected.' Phoebe looked at the banknotes on her kitchen table then to the man shuffling from one foot to another, clearly uncomfortable at being inside the house. 'It is more than I asked.'

'Ar,' he nodded, 'I knows that but my brother-in-law says they Americans were willin' to pay more for such good locks so 'e sold 'em for more. That bill 'e sent along wi' 'em be from man as bought 'em an' tells the price 'e paid. You will see when you check that it all be there.'

'I am sure of it,' Phoebe smiled, 'but why has your brother-in-law not taken his percentage?'

'You trusted 'im, Miss. Now 'e be trustin' you. If it be as you be satisfied wi' the deal 'e struck then you will be sendin' 'im what 'e earned, that be the way 'e looks at it.'

'I am more than satisfied and I think Bert and Mathew are too.'

'It be a right good deal so far as I sees it.' Mathew grinned delightedly. 'Bert was right to suggest it.'

'There be a market for many more, so I was instructed to tell you, an' they can cross over same way as before.'

'Take some time,' Bert said thoughtfully. 'We couldn't go on workin' flat out like we did to make that gross, not all the time we couldn't.'

'Well,' the man shuffled again, his clogs loud on the red scrubbed flags of the kitchen floor, 'I be away up to London termorrer and back this way along o' a week. I will call, if you allows, for water an' you can be givin' me yer answer then. An' if you don't mind, Miss, would you keep me brother-in-law's cut till I be comin' back 'cos it don't be doin' to 'ave money wi' you on the barges?'

'It'll be 'ere when you wants to pick it up,' Bert said, following the man from the kitchen, 'an' there'll be some for you an' all for the 'elp you 'ave been.'

''Elp where you can,' the bargee refastened the muffler wrapped about his neck, 'that's what me mother learned all 'er kids, an' if you can't be a 'elp then don't be a 'indrance.'

''Er couldn't 'ave learned you better,' Bert said, shaking the other man's hand. 'Safe journey to London an' I'll see you a week from now.'

'That went better'n I'd guessed,' he said as he re-entered the kitchen. 'Seems you 'ave a solid market if you wants to follow it up, Miss Phoebe.'

'We *have* to follow it up, Bert.' Phoebe glanced at the bill signed 'Hiram B. Rosmeyer'. 'It would be foolish not to. The only thing we have to decide is how many locks we can make in a month. As you have said, you can't work at the pace you were before so how many would you expect to make?'

'That depends,' he mused. 'As we be now I would say between a dozen or dozen an' a 'alf a week.'

'Half a gross a month,' Phoebe calculated quickly, 'two months before we could ship another worthwhile batch.'

'The market could be gone in that time,' Mathew said, 'could be somebody else will get a notion to do the same thing an' if they be quicker at it than we . . .' He shrugged his shoulders.

'I don't see we can do anything about that, Mathew.' Phoebe looked rueful. 'You all do your best and no one can do better than that.'

'Might be a way o' speedin' up the makin' . . .' Bert touched a hand to his chin. 'Mathew an' me 'ave both spoke o' the way young Josh picks things up. 'E be a quick learner an' already knows near as much of locksmithin' as do Mark. Now if we could tek 'im off the bellows an' set 'im to work on the benches along o' we three then you could turn that dozen an' 'alf into two dozen or more a week.'

'But who would work the bellows? You need those to keep the forge burning, don't you?'

Bert nodded. 'We need the bellows, that be right enough, but they don't need to be sat over full time. What I was thinkin', if Mathew be agreeable, was for each o' the four on we to tek the bellows to the forge when we uses it an' the two lads to tek a turn when Mathew an' me be too busy. An' as for the coal, I was of a mind to suggest that Mathew an' me hauls a load up from the cut each night.'

'Easy done,' Mathew grinned, 'I could knock up a cart on a couple of wheels to mek it less of a task.'

'I think though, Miss, in all fairness Josh should 'ave the same wage as Mark, learn the way o' the world ain't paved wi' gold like fairy tales would 'ave 'em believe.'

'Whatever you say, Bert.' Phoebe smiled her thanks. 'Pardoe's Patent Locks are in the export business.'

She had smiled confidently at Bert and Mathew but counting the banknotes later that evening Phoebe felt that confidence seeping away. Deducting the wages owed to the men and to Mark, and the money she would pay Bagnall tomorrow, plus setting aside even a minimum for food and household expenses, left the sum much depleted. Then she would need to order a further supply of metal if the workshop was to be kept in full production and that she would pay for in advance – she would take no more chances with the odious Thomas Bagnall. Phoebe counted in her mind. She was playing near the edge but she had done that before. Folding one of the white five-pound notes she shoved it deep into her bag. Perhaps it might be enough for what she wanted.

Leaving the iron foundry Phoebe smiled to herself. Thomas Bagnall had been surprised to find her settling one account two days before it was due to be paid and paying for a further, larger supply in advance.

With the five pounds in her bag she walked along Dudley Street, turning left against St James's Church, following Holyhead Road toward the Lodge Holes coal mine.

Joseph had given her the idea when she had visited on Sunday. He had mentioned that the old pit ponies were to be brought out of the mine and sold. Phoebe shuddered to think of these animals, most probably condemned to the glue works after years toiling underground, but that was the way it had always been.

Joseph had somehow seemed more than usually lame, needing Mathew's arm to walk around Sarah's tiny vegetable plot, and Phoebe knew they were worried for his job. If the new mine owner sacked him then they would have to leave their home.

Holding her skirts free of the dusty ground Phoebe left the road, striking left across open ground that gave on to the mine.

But Joseph had not been sacked as yet, and if she could only keep a supply of locks going to America, then maybe in a couple of years she could help Joseph and Sarah to find a new home.

'Please let things work out this time,' she breathed to the morning. 'Please don't let this order be a hoax.'

It was going to be hard work turning out the number of locks Bert had specified every week and she really ought to be at the mill helping all she could or at least busy on her needlework, Phoebe thought, feeling guilty at being away from the house. But for a few hours things were going to have to take their chances.

Reaching the large wooden gates that closed off the pit yard from nothing but open land, Phoebe saw her father's name, not painted out as yet. Nothing moved fast in Wednesbury. Loosing the skirts of her green coat, she took a deep breath and stepped hesitantly across the yard trodden black with coal dust. Today she would not be dealing with Joseph Leach, as she would have a few years before, now she would be doing business with a new yard foreman. Joseph had been dismissed when the mine had changed hands.

'Can I 'elp you, Miss?'

Phoebe smiled at the man who answered her knock on the door of the office. Of medium height but powerful across the shoulders, his splendid moustache wiggled as he spoke.

Phoebe swallowed the smile the dancing moustache threatened to bring to her lips. 'I have reason to believe you are bringing several ponies out of the pit today?'

'Ar, Miss, so we am.'

'Then I would like to purchase one of those ponies.'

'Purchase!' The moustache jigged. 'What do you mean, Miss?'

'May I step inside?' She glanced about the yard, seeing the heads of several men turn in her direction. Maybe Joseph would be in the office.

'Well, it be all dusty in 'ere like, it ain't clean for a lady.' The man hesitated, clearly unused to his working domain being encroached on by a woman.

'We won't let that worry us.' Phoebe stepped inside, glancing about the shed she remembered so well: at the heavy ledgers on a bench to one side, the row of nails hammered into one wall, each with a numbered tag that indicated a man underground, and the table where the dead Norton boy had been laid by his father. Pushing the image away she looked at the man who stood as if trying to bar her entry into a holy sanctum.

'As I said, I wish to purchase one of the ponies that are to be brought up from the pit.'

'You can't, Miss,' he said. 'Them ponies ain't to be sold.'

'What do you mean, they are not for sale!' Phoebe demanded.

'What I says, Miss.' The moustache danced indignantly at her question. 'Them ponies ain't to be sold, not to you anyway.'

'Not to me, but they are to be sold?' Phoebe pressed.

'Mebbe,' the man conceded grudgingly.

'Then why not to me? Why can I not buy one of them?'

''Cos you can't, that's all I know.' He touched a hand to his top lip as if to prevent the moustache leaping from his face. 'The ponies ain't to be sold.'

'You mean perhaps they have been sold already?'

'Maybe they 'ave, then maybe they ain't.' He held on to the moustache that seemed to want to lead a life of its own. 'All I know is what I'm told, an' I was told them ponies was not to be sold.'

'But they have always been sold,' Phoebe defended her case.

'They might 'ave bin, but that were before. This be now an' things am different. Seems new bloke don't want them ponies sent to no glue works.'

A tiny frown formed over Phoebe's eyes. 'Then what does he intend doing with them?'

'Look, Miss,' the man began to sound exasperated, 'I already told you I only knows what I'm told an' I ain't bin told that.'

'Then if you do not know perhaps you will direct me to someone who does?'

'You best talk to the manager,' he said stiffly, 'if anybody be told diff'rent it'll be 'im.'

Phoebe was taken aback. The pit ponies had always been sold off at the end of their working life to any who saw fit to buy them. It had nearly always been the glue works but others had never been barred from buying. 'Then please show me to the manager. Perhaps, as you say, I had best speak to him.'

'Can't do that.' The man grinned, triumphant in his small victory. ''E ain't 'ere.'

'Then where is he?' Phoebe felt a strong desire to slap both moustache and its owner.

'Could be anywheres in the pit, might be one place might be t'other, ain't no tellin'.'

'It is clear you did not win a Sunday school prize for honesty nor one for helpfulness,' Phoebe snapped.

'Maybe not, Miss Pardoe, but *I* did so perhaps you would do better to talk to me?'

Phoebe turned at the sound of a voice that echoed almost nightly in her mind, a faint hint of pink staining her cheeks.

'Might I ask what you are doing here?'

'Sir William,' the blush on her cheeks deepened at the unexpected encounter. 'I – I was told some of the pit ponies would be finished today.'

He waited, eyes taking in the bloom of her face.

'Oh!' His well-defined eyebrows lifted quizzically. 'Were you also told the ponies were to be sold to the glue works?'

'No.' She looked away awkwardly. What was he doing at the mine? Why did she suddenly feel like an erring child?

'But you presumed they were?'

Phoebe lifted her head, re-engaging his eyes defiantly. Wanting to buy a pony to save it from the glue works was no crime. 'Is that not what always happens to ponies taken from the pits?'

'Not all pits, Miss Pardoe.' He glanced at the yard foreman watching them covertly and the man turned back to his ledgers. Sir William led her out. 'Certainly not those belonging to me.'

'You bought my father's mines?' Phoebe asked, surprised.

'I did,' he nodded, 'and that means no more ponies from here or the Crown at Moxley will go to the glue works. Once their working life is over they will be returned to pasture at Sandwell Priory.'

'Then if they are to be put to pasture, why can I not buy one?'

Almost at the gates that closed off the pit head from the open heathland, he halted. 'Why do you want a pit pony?' he asked bluntly. 'When these animals have served so long underground they are virtually worked out. They will not be useful for heavy work.'

'I do not want a pony for heavy work.'

'Then what do you want it for?'

She did not have to tell him, of course, chances were he would not sell her a pony if she *did* tell him, but then she had nothing to hide.

'I wanted it for Ruth.'

'Ruth?' His brows rose again.

'She is the Ingleses' daughter – they live at Wiggins Mill,' Phoebe explained. 'There was an accident and she fell into the canal and though she seemed to suffer no serious injury she has not been the same child since. She used to be so full of life, always playing about the mill, but now she seems so withdrawn. I thought a pony of her own, one she would have the caring of, would give her something of interest.'

'How old is Ruth?'

'She is just a child, no more than eight years old.'

'Would she be able to handle a pony?'

'I am sure of it,' Phoebe answered. 'Her family worked the barges along the canal so she is well used to horses – that was why I thought a pit pony used to being handled by young children would suit her.'

He smiled, his eyes taking on a new warmth. 'Then perhaps we should discuss the possibility of furnishing Ruth with a pony, but here is not the most suitable of places.' He looked at the film of black dust covering her shoes and edging the hem of her coat. 'Might I suggest we go to the Priory?'

'The Priory is at least an hour and a half's walk and I have little time to spare, as I'm sure is the case with yourself, Sir William.'

'You are sure of so many things,' he said. 'Sure my ponies are to be sold off to make glue and sure I do not have time to discuss the provision of one for Ruth.'

'I beg your pardon,' Phoebe coloured afresh at his mild rebuke, 'but I have so little time and a walk to the Priory will take a great deal of it.'

'Not so much if you will accept a ride in my carriage.' He

smiled again. 'It would also relieve me of walking there as I must if you refuse.'

'But could we not just agree a sale here?' she protested.

'I think the pit ponies deserve the peace of the pasture,' he answered, 'even though Ruth would cherish one of them.'

'Then there is no cause for me to accompany you to the Priory.'

'There is every need if you wish the child to have a pony. Please,' he said, seeing the query on her face, 'there is a pony there that will answer your needs perfectly if only you will take enough of your precious time to look at it.'

It would take more of her time than she had accounted for. Phoebe thought of the others working at the mill. She really ought not to be away so long but Ruth seemed so dejected, so apart from them. If two or three more hours would serve to restore the child's interest in life then it would not be too much to pay.

'She's beautiful,' said Phoebe later, stroking the sand-coloured pony nuzzling her hand. 'What's her name?'

'Pippin,' Sir William answered quietly. 'Sophie gave her that name when the mare foaled. She said the newcomer was the colour of the pippins in an apple she fed to the mother.'

'I was so very sorry to hear of what happened to your family.' Phoebe saw the sadness shadow his face. Then in an effort to chase away a little of the shadows, she asked, 'Was this Sophie's horse?'

'The mother was Sophie's so I suppose the foal was too.'

'Then I cannot possibly take her from you.'

'Why not?' He signalled a groom who came and led the horse back to its stable. 'Sophie would have wanted the child to have it, and I want her to have it. I also want her to have this.' Leading the way to a long stone building set with graceful arched windows, he swung open a pair of heavy doors showing a line of broughams and carriages at the end of which stood a small blue-painted governess cart. 'This was my daughter's when she was a child,' he said, going over to it. 'Now I wish it to be Ruth's.'

'But I can't!' Phoebe thought of the five-pound note at the bottom of her bag. It could not possibly be enough to purchase horse and cart.

'Would the child not like it?' he asked, turning to her.

'I'm sure she would.' Phoebe glanced again at the cart, its blue-painted side edged with a pattern of daisies. 'But . . .'

'Once more you are sure,' he said gently, 'so why the "but"?'

'Ruth would love the horse and the cart would be her delight,' Phoebe decided only the truth would conclude this discussion, 'but five pounds is all I have and I know that to be insufficient to pay for them.'

'I am not selling you the horse or the cart, they are a gift.'

'No!' Phoebe's mouth set in a straight line. 'What I cannot pay for I will not take, whatever the need. Thank you for your kindness but I must refuse.'

Touching a hand to the pretty cart he seemed to see into the past, to the child who had once ridden in it so happily. 'If you will not accept a gift from me, accept it from Sophie,' he said softly.

Seeing the droop of his shoulders and hearing the pain in his voice, Phoebe's heart twisted with pity. If only she could take him in her arms and hold him until the pain had gone but she could not. Offering a gift on Sophie's behalf then having it refused would add to the hurt he was feeling. But such a gift . . . Phoebe hesitated, torn between her wish to spare him any more hurt and her decision to accept no man's charity.

Almost as if he sensed her thoughts he turned suddenly, a half sad, half amused smile at the edges of his mouth. 'I will make a bargain with you, Miss Phoebe Pardoe. You are, I take it, familiar with the handling of a horse?'

'I both rode and drove my own governess cart until . . .' She paused. 'Until a few years ago.'

'Then you take this.' He touched the prettily painted cart. 'Tell the child's parents I wish to make a gift of it to their daughter. With your permission I will drive over to Wiggins Mill tomorrow and if they do not wish to accept it I will have it taken away and no more will be said on the subject. Agreed?'

'Agreed.' Phoebe smiled, a part of her already looking forward to tomorrow.

'I ought not to have said I would do it,' she said that same evening.

'Then why did you?'

Why had she? She pondered Lucy's question. Was it because she wished to repay a kindness? Part of her owned to that but the greater part denied it. She had agreed to William Dartmouth's request, not to humour him but out of a desire she could not acknowledge.

'Why did you agree to be 'is 'ostess at the staff Advent Ball?' Lucy asked, her hands deep in flour.

'I suppose it was because he might otherwise have cancelled it,' Phoebe answered, 'and that would have been disappointing to his workers. It is the one really big celebration in their working year.'

'Why 'ave to cancel?' Adding water to the bowl, Lucy began to knead her pastry.

'Sir William explained he has no female relatives, no one he could call upon to fill the role of hostess for the evening.'

'An' so you said as you would do it?' Tipping pastry on to a board, Lucy began to roll it out. 'Was it 'cause 'e gave that 'orse an' cart to the Ingleses?' She looked up, her eyes asking a question she did not speak.

'It seemed churlish to refuse when he had been so kind.'

Phoebe avoided Lucy's eyes, knowing her own would betray the secret she had only fully recognised in the long reach of a sleepless night, a truth that had hit her like a bolt from the blue. She did not feel only pity for William

Dartmouth – she felt love. She had felt it for a long time, she realised, hugging the truth, trying to drive it from her mind as the hours passed. She could not love Edward because she had always loved his father!

'I reckon the ball'll do you good,' Tilly joined in. 'A chance to meet folk and mix a while wi' others will bring you no 'arm.'

'Perhaps not.' Phoebe spooned filling into pastry cases. 'But have you two thought about my gown? Brown grosgrain is hardly suitable for an Advent Ball.'

'Seems like that there satin'll 'ave a use after all.' Tilly carried pies to the oven, packing them inside in neat rows. 'And before you starts on about tekin' time from yer other sewin', I will tek that on till yer frock be done.'

'I don't have much choice, do I?' She smiled at Tilly.

'Not lessen you wants an argy bargy,' her friend replied, 'an' Tilly Wood don't lose no argument – 'er be determined to win.'

'An' you can forget 'elpin' in the workshop.' Lucy lined a fresh batch of pie tins with pastry cases. 'Me an' Lizzie can see to the filin' down.'

'Did I ever tell the two of you?'

'Tell we what?' Lucy asked.

'Tell you how dear you both are to me,' Phoebe said softly.

Annie Pardoe pressed a hand to the pain eating away below her breast. It was constant now, sometimes vicious, sometimes bearable, but always with her. Taking the bottle with its white tablets from the drawer of her bedside table, she eased the cork from its neck then angrily banged the bottle down on the polished mahogany surface. The pills did no good, they did not ease the pain, nor did the laudanum that fool Dingley had prescribed.

Her steps slow and heavy, she crossed the room, drawing a large brown envelope from the chest of drawers and carrying it held to her chest as she returned to sit on the huge bed. Her breathing regulated by spasms of pain, she stared at the sprawled writing before her. Her name in Clinton's writing, his hand shaking as a result of the poison she had given him. But it was not meant for you, my love! Her heart screamed. It was not for you. But he had taken it and had died and with him had died all her hopes, all her reasons for living. But Clinton would not be forgotten. Pressing the button mounted on the panelling beside the bed, she waited until Maudie Tranter entered the room.

'I . . . I have some letters . . . to write,' she said, pain interlacing the words so they came out haltingly. 'Bring . . . bring me pen and ink from . . . from the study. I . . . I will write them here.'

'Yes, ma'am.' Maudie glanced at the pill bottle, its cork still removed. 'Will you be wantin' paper an' envelopes?'

'Yes.' Annie paused, a sudden jab of pain forcing her eyes shut. 'Yes, bring paper and envelopes.'

It's a doctor you be needin', Maudie thought as she went to get the things Annie had asked for. And if you don't be callin' on one soon it won't be a letter you'll be writin' – it'll be yer will.

Drawing the documents from the brown envelope, Annie stared at the titles to properties Samuel's legacy had paid for, properties she was to have built a new life upon, a life shared with Clinton. But now he was gone and without him her life no longer held meaning.

'Will you be wantin' a tray in the garden, ma'am?' Maudie set the writing materials on the table that had been moved near the grate in which a fire was laid but as yet unlit. 'Or will I fetch a pot o' tea up to you 'ere?'

Annie glanced at the fob watch pinned to the left shoulder of her black dress. 'I will have tea here in . . . in about . . . an hour,' she said, pain snatching at the words.

'Very good, ma'am.' Maudie left the room. There don't be many hours left to you, Annie Pardoe, she thought, making her way to the kitchen. With or without the potions of old Dingley, you be walking the last stretch and how far that be only God in Heaven be knowing, and he won't tell.

Alone once more, Annie glanced at each of the documents Clinton had intended to post to her. She had doubted him, had judged him guilty of theft. But you will have it all, my love, she thought. You will have it all, every penny, as you would have had when I became your wife. I would have given it to you then as I give it to you now.

Crossing to the table she sat down, her black skirts rustling in the quiet room. Dipping the pen into the ink, she began to write.

Slicing cucumber sandwiches, Maudie placed the wafer thin triangles on a china plate, arranging a few sprigs of watercress across them before covering them with a food net. It had been an hour since she had taken the writing materials to Annie's bedroom and though she knew her mistress would probably not touch the sandwiches or even drink the tea she would take it up to her nonetheless. Annie had eaten less and less every day since hearing of that man's death. Maudie filled the tiny flowered jug with fresh milk, setting a dainty bowl of sugar beside it on the tray.

I guessed you would not be getting him to no altar, Annie Pardoe, she thought, scalding tea from a kettle bubbling softly over the kitchen fire. But I never thought he would avoid it by turning up his toes.

Taking the tray upstairs, she tapped at Annie's door with the toe of her boot, waiting for the call that would give her permission to enter and tapping more loudly when it did not come. Balancing the tray awkwardly on one arm when her second tap went unacknowledged, she turned the door knob and pushed open the door.

Annie sat on the bed, her voluminous black skirts spread over the cover like a storm cloud.

'I brought your tray.' Maudie crossed to the table set before the fireplace but seeing that the letters Annie had written were still open upon it, she took the tray to the washstand, setting it down beside the jug and bowl.

'Will I clear the table or will you take yer tea on yer bed?' she asked, shoving bowl and jug a little further along the marble top of the washstand. 'Do you want to tek yer tea at the table?' She turned, repeating her question when Annie did not answer.

'I'll pour you out a cup.' Pouring a little milk into the fragile china cup, Maudie filled it with tea then carried it across to where Annie sat on the bed, a large sheet of paper in her hands.

'Drink this up while it be 'ot.' Maudie held the cup towards Annie. 'C'mon, tek it.' She offered the cup again. 'It be fresh brewed, the way you like it.'

Annie carried on staring at the paper in her hand and Maudie tutted with irritation. Maybe she didn't fancy the tea now she had it but it was only good manners to answer a body. But then, when had good manners ever bothered Annie Pardoe? Never, unless that Clinton be about, and then it was all please and thank you. Clinton Harforth-Darby! Maudie put the cup beside the open bottle of tablets on the bedside table. What kind of a name had that been to go to bed on?

'Don't leave yer tea standin' there,' she said, the irritation she was feeling colouring her tone. 'It'll get stewed an' you knows you don't like stewed tea.'

Pausing as she turned to leave, Maudie looked at the woman seated on the bed. She hadn't spoken but that in itself was no surprise. Annie Pardoe often ignored her. But she hadn't moved either, not even to shield the paper she was holding from the possibility of being seen by another. That boded no good. But her eyes be open, Maudie told herself, 'er be readin' that paper so 'er be all right!

'Yer tea be to the side o' you,' she said again. 'Leave what you be doin' an' drink it afore it gets cold.'

Returning the few steps to the bedside table, she took up the cup with one hand, the other touching Annie lightly on the shoulder – only to draw away again quickly. Annie Pardoe was holding a sheet of paper and her eyes were open but she was stone dead.

'Oh my Lord!' Maudie breathed. 'Oh my dear Lord!'

Her hands shaking, she set the cup back on the table beside the still full bottle of tablets. Whatever had killed Annie Pardoe, it was not an overdose of them. She looked to where the body had fallen backward at her touch, the head lying a little sideways on the pillow, the open eyes seeming to watch her.

'I thought you was on the last stretch,' she murmured into the stillness, 'but I little thought you was *that* near thy end. May the Lord rest you, Annie Pardoe.'

Bending to lift the dead woman's legs on to the bed, Maudie noticed the hand that still held the paper had dropped palm down across her breast, showing a large amethyst ring on the third finger.

'That be yer weddin' finger!' she said as if Annie could hear. 'That must be a engageyment ring but I never seen you wi' it afore.'

She bent to look closer at the ring. 'Did 'e give you that?' she asked the silence. 'Or did you buy it yerself to mek it look like 'e was goin' to marry you?' Ignoring the open eyes, she eased the paper from the already cold fingers, reading the letter Clinton had written. *In his thoughts till he returned* . . . Carefully she replaced the single sheet of paper. Then he was going to marry her, seemed like. But if he was, it was unlike Annie to have let the fact go untold.

Glancing around the room, her eyes lit on the letters Annie had written that afternoon. Picking them up she read the neat copperplate hand. *'The Last Will and Testament . . .'* Maudie continued to read to the last word.

'You bitter, twisted old bugger!' she gasped, her hands falling to her sides. 'May the Lord see fit to forgive you for I never could.' She lifted the letters, looking unbelievingly at the second one. She could understand the feeling behind the first, if a woman wanted to leave her all to a man then that was her prerogative, but to write a letter like this to a girl who had done her no harm! Still unsure of what her eyes had told her, Maudie read again the letter addressed to Phoebe.

I want you to know whose was the hand behind the one that signed you to prison. I paid the Magistrate £100 to have you put behind those bars. It was I told Lawyer Siveter to advise Lucy Baines not to take what she knew of that necklace to the Dartmouths, and it was I paid John Kilvert to testify that you had pawned jewellery once before in his shop– jewellery he knew to have been stolen from another town altogether. But you were released, released from your prison though there was no release for me from the prison that held me. Abel's child was free but Abel's sister remained in the prison he had paid for.

Then there was the order for one gross of Pardoe's Patent Locks. How did you feel when you received that? I cut the heading from James Greaves's bill and pasted it to my own letter, and I did the same to the one you received cancelling that order.

And why? I will tell you why. Your father took my life. To me fell the task of living with Samuel, of ensuring no one would ever discover the twist of fate that held him and me prisoner in the same house, that none would ever learn of the affliction the medical world held out no cure for. Your father took my life so he might live his to the full. I could not make him pay so I exacted that payment from you, and though you might still live after I do not you will not have a penny of that which was first your father's and then Samuel's, for everything of that is for my husband that was to have been.

Signed, Annie Pardoe.

''Ow could 'er do all that to 'er own flesh an' blood?' Maudie said when she had finished reading. ''Ow could 'er do such bad things to a young wench who 'ad never done 'er no 'arm?'

Glancing at the first letter that was Annie's will she scanned the words again: '. . . *all land, property and jewellery belonging to me shall be sold, the realisation such land, property and jewellery shall produce is to be used for the erection of a monument to be dedicated to Clinton Harforth-Darby and is to bear the inscription, "Dear to the heart and to the memory of his betrothed, Annie Mary Pardoe . . ."*'

Maudie dropped the letters back on to the table. How could there be a spite so strong as to strike at a wench from the grave, as Annie Pardoe was here striking at her own niece? She had turned her from her father's house and even now was denying her the last of what should rightly be hers.

Maudie looked again at the figure on the bed and the papers spread about her. Going to the bed, she picked them up, quickly scanning words she did not understand but guessed to be legal proof of ownership of the properties they named. And all this was to be sold to build a monument to a dead man and feed the pride of a dead woman!

'An' Phoebe be to get nothin',' she said aloud. 'P'raps that be what you 'oped, Annie Pardoe, an' for all I know you may be 'opin' for it still but you reckoned wi'out Maudie Tranter. An' if you wants to stop me now you 'ave got to get up from that bed to do it!'

Seating herself at the table, Maudie began to copy the wording of the will until she reached the words 'shall be sold'. Careful to spell each word correctly, she changed the text to read 'shall become the property of my niece, Phoebe Mary Pardoe', then she signed Annie's name.

Taking both of Annie's letters, she pushed them into her pocket. They would burn on the kitchen fire. 'If what I be doin' be wrong, Lord, then you must punish me for I'll not change it,' she murmured. Then, slowly and methodically, she searched the room for any other paper Annie might have written and that could be compared with the Will now on the table.

Satisfied the room held no other documents she went to the rooms Samuel had used and searched them, finding nothing. She would collect the tray then search each of the downstairs rooms. Only then would she go for the doctor. Once more in Annie's bedroom she looked again at the dead figure, feeling no pity for the woman who could plot so much wickedness against her own kin. Reaching for the cup, she changed her mind. It would look more natural for it to be there; she would tell them she had left the tray earlier and on going back for it had found Annie lying on the bed and the letter she had said she wished to write on the table.

'You 'ave 'urt that wench enough, Annie Pardoe,' she murmured, leaving the room to go downstairs. 'You'll not 'urt Abel's daughter no more.'

It had been a month since Phoebe had agreed to William Dartmouth's request for her to stand as hostess for the annual party he gave for the household staff. The creamy satin falling in soft folds about her feet, Phoebe wondered if she had done right to consent to attend this evening at Sandwell Priory. Sir William had called at Wiggins Mill several times since the day he had shown her the little cart and the horse, each time saying he wished to enquire after Ruth's well-being, and with each of those visits she'd had to try harder not to read more into his grey eyes than friendship. That she loved him she could not deny, but to imagine that love returned was foolish as well as hopeless. Sir William Dartmouth might take another wife but he would not look for one at Wiggins Mill.

'You look beautiful, Miss Phoebe,' Lucy said, adding the last tiny yellow silk rose-bud to Phoebe's hair.

'Do you think he will expect jewels?' She looked at her reflection in the cheval mirror. The gown held her body in a close sheath, the satin drawn to the back in heavy swathes and the front of the skirt relieved by a trail of yellow roses

Lucy had spent hours making. The décolleté neckline was ornamented with one yellow rose, showing the swell of her breasts.

'That man 'as more sense than to go lookin' for jools other than the ones that be shinin' in yer eyes,' Tilly said, taking the gloves Phoebe had bought so many months before from the drawer and handing them to her. ''E don't need no finery – 'e can see what a woman be wi'out artificial 'elp.'

'Tilly's right,' Lucy added, 'you don't be needin' no jewels. They couldn't mek you look any more beautiful than you do now.'

'I hope you are right.' Phoebe took up her gloves and after checking one last time in the mirror, followed the two women downstairs.

'Afore you go, Miss,' Lizzie came hesitantly to the door of Phoebe's front parlour, 'the lads an' Ruth 'ave somethin' for you. Would you mind if they come in?'

'Of course I would not mind.'

'Eh, Miss, you look bostin'!' Josh was first through the door, his eyes round with admiration as he looked at her. 'Don't 'er, Mark?'

'Good enough to eat,' he grinned. 'I might even be tempted to tek you out meself, Miss.'

'Cheeky young sod!' Lizzie cuffed her son but could not help smiling.

'I think you looks like a princess!' Shy at being in the front parlour, Ruth pressed against her mother's side.

'Go on, Ruthie,' Josh urged the child, his hand gently taking hers, 'give Miss Phoebe what we got for 'er.'

The little girl looked up at her mother and at her nod allowed Josh to pull her forward. 'We buyed this for you, Miss,' she said, shyly holding up a fan of the palest lemon lace, each of its struts tipped with a tiny yellow crystal. Then as Phoebe bent to take it she piped, 'It be a new one, it ain't from the pawn shop.'

'Oh, you sweetheart!' Phoebe felt a rush of tears as she took the child in her arms. 'That is exactly what I needed.'

'We thought you might like a fan,' Mark's cheeky lopsided grin stretched across his mouth like a wedge of melon. 'You can 'ide yer yawns be'ind it if you gets bored.'

'I don't think I will be bored, Mark,' Phoebe said, giving Ruth one last hug before turning to him. 'Though I might need it to hide my embarrassment at having no jewellery.'

'No need for you to feel embarrassed,' Josh said gallantly. 'There ain't not one thing you could do would better the way you look.'

'Josh be right, Miss.' Mark wasn't to be outdone in the field of compliments. 'Ain't nothin' would mek you look prettier'n you look now. Ya looks real beautiful an' that be no lie.'

'When experts such as them two agree you look beautiful then you can be sure it's beautiful you look,' Lucy said.

'You could marry a prince,' Ruth said solemnly, 'you be beautiful enough to be a princess.'

'If I do,' Phoebe smiled, 'it will all be because of my lovely fan.' She flicked it open, holding it below her eyes. 'Any prince would be glad to marry a princess with a golden fan.'

But she did not want to marry a prince, Phoebe thought as she rode in the carriage sent to collect her. The man she loved held a title, albeit not a royal one, but he did not want her for his wife.

'Good evening, Miss Pardoe,' William Dartmouth greeted the young woman alighting from his carriage. 'Ruth is well, I hope?' He escorted her into the great hall of his ancient house.

'As well as she was when you called three days ago.' Phoebe smiled up at him, glancing quickly away as she met the look in his eyes, a look she so wanted to be saying what she knew he never would.

'And the boys?'

'Cheeky as ever.' Phoebe held out the fan. 'They bought me this.'

'Rogues, the pair of 'em.' He smiled. 'But rogues with good taste.'

'Mark said he might be tempted to take me out himself.'

'Did he!' Sir William laughed, the sound drawing the glances of his staff lined up to be presented to Phoebe. 'The young hound! There'll be many a man takes a horsewhip to that one before he settles, though I say again I admire his taste.' He glanced at Phoebe, seeing the colour steal the paleness from her cheeks. 'You look very beautiful, Miss Pardoe.'

'I think we should look to your guests.' She turned towards the line of waiting men and women.

'Our guests,' he murmured at her elbow. 'For one night at least allow them to be that.'

Later William watched the young woman dancing a waltz with his estate manager. For something like four hours she had mixed easily with the people of the estate, men and women alike, a smile and a word for each, her simple manner making her readily acceptable to them. Watching her now, the light from the chandeliers glistening on the bronze silk of her hair piled high on her head, tiny buds of yellow satin nestling in its coils, her slim body outlined by the lines of her gown, he felt a pang of jealousy that the arms holding her and the eyes looking down on her smiling face were not his. Impatient with his own thoughts, he turned to his steward.

'It is all going very well,' he said. 'Give my thanks to everyone in the morning and tell them I was very pleased at the effort they have all made.'

'I will, sir.' The steward smiled, pleased at these words of thanks.

'And now I think we should announce supper.' William watched the man make his way to the end of the great hall, to where the musicians were seated in a large alcove, not sure whether announcing supper or wanting Phoebe out of the arms of his estate manager was the real reason behind his having the music stopped. Watching the man escort her back to him, William carefully lowered his gaze, hiding the answer that throbbed in his heart.

'A glass of wine, Miss Pardoe?' he asked as the estate manager took his leave of them.

'I would find a glass of lemonade more acceptable,' Phoebe answered, a little breathless from the constant round of dancing.

'Lemonade it shall be.' He led her to the supper table. 'May I help you to a plate of something?'

Phoebe shook her head. 'Like the princess in the story, I am too happy to eat.'

'Unlike the princess in the story,' he said softly, 'don't disappear when the clock strikes midnight.'

'How does Pippin be gettin' along, Miss?' The groom who had led the horse from its stable to show to her smiled as Phoebe came up to the supper table.

'Being spoiled terribly.' Phoebe's own smile broke out spontaneously. 'She is loved by all of us but especially so by Ruth.'

'The master told us of Pippin's new mistress and with his permission we would like to send her an Advent gift.' He looked at Sir William and when he nodded permission the groom handed Phoebe a package. 'It be from all the 'ouse, an' we 'oped you would take it for we an' give it to the little girl.'

'May I peep?'

'Ar, Miss.'

The groom nodded and Phoebe peeled away a layer of brown paper, exclaiming with delight at sight of blue leather reins. 'How lovely! Ruth will be enchanted. Thank you all so much, it is so kind of you.' She smiled at the assembled staff, all of whom had their eyes turned to her and all of whom shared her delight.

Arranging for the gift to be placed in the carriage against her return, William Dartmouth accepted the glass of lemonade handed him by one of the housemaids, dressed now in a pretty print frock. 'You are a victim of your own popularity,' he said as Phoebe was kept continually busy answering the polite addresses of his staff, 'you have made too favourable an impression and I fear you will have to pay the penalty.'

'Talking to people as friendly as these is no penalty.'

'But you would like a quiet interlude before the evening resumes?'

She nodded. 'It would be nice. I have not been called upon to be hostess to a party before and it is tiring.'

'Exhausting would be my word for it. Let's go to the drawing room, it will be quiet there.'

He led the way to a room furnished with sofas and chairs upholstered in a deep cream brocade, the curtains over high arched windows echoing the same colour and the huge square of carpet patterned in cream and soft peach.

'I admit I prefer a glass of something other than lemonade.' Crossing to a large figured cabinet he drew out decanter and glass, filling the latter. Raising it to his lips, he looked at the young woman sitting on the sofa, her hair turned to glistening amber by the soft light, her lovely face smiling at him – and turned quickly away, staring into the fireplace.

'Miss Pardoe,' he said, the thickness in his throat not quite under control, 'I believe my son asked you to become his wife?'

Phoebe's smile faded. 'Edward did me that honour.'

'But you refused?'

'Yes.'

'Not once but several times, is that not so?'

Phoebe stared into her glass, the happiness of the evening draining away. Was this why he had asked her to come to Sandwell Priory? Was this why they were now alone in this room, so he could bombard her with questions? Glancing at a side table, she looked at the silver-framed photographs of his family, at Edward's face staring solemnly back at her. 'It is so,' she answered quietly.

He remained staring into the empty fireplace. 'Might I ask the reason or would that be considered too rude?'

Putting the lemonade aside, Phoebe took a long trembling breath. He had brought her to his home in order to question her and she would answer his questions, all of them, and then she would return to Wiggins Mill. 'No, I do not consider there to be any rudeness in your question. The reason for my refusals was simple: I did not love Edward in the way a woman should love the man she agrees to marry, and I would marry no man I did not love.'

'I see.' He waited for several moments, the silence marked by the ticking of a graceful clock on the mantel, above his head. Then: 'Was there someone else?'

Phoebe watched him, her emotions crying out to comfort him, knowing the pain these questions must be causing him, understanding his wish to know as much as possible of the son he had lost. 'When your son asked me to marry him there was no one else,' she said gently.

'And now?' He swivelled to face her, his question hard and sharp.

Phoebe hesitated, taken aback by the knife edge of his tone. 'I . . . there . . . no, I am not being called upon by anyone.' In the hushed light of the room Phoebe saw the play of emotion on his face, saw his fingers about the glass whiten with tension.

'I ask your pardon,' he said. 'I had no right to ask such a question.'

'No, you did not.' Phoebe looked at his face, still handsome behind the pain. 'But had I not wished to answer then I would not have done so.'

'Miss Pardoe . . . Phoebe.' He wrestled with the words, wanting to say them yet stubbornly denying them freedom. 'I, I . . .'

Phoebe remained silent. Whatever it was William Dartmouth had to say to her, he must say it alone.

'Miss Pardoe, had my family lived I would never have said to you what I must say now. Had Edward survived I would not have spoken, whether you had married him or not. You have told me there is no gentleman calling upon you, that you have promised marriage to no one.'

His fingers closed tighter, threatening to crush the glass in his hand, and a film of perspiration glistened on his forehead.

'That being so, allow me the honour of asking you to become my wife?'

Phoebe felt the rush of blood leaving her face, the fan falling from fingers suddenly without strength. Why did he want to marry her? Did he still feel Edward was somehow obligated to her, an obligation he must make good by making her his wife? That alone could be the reason, she decided.

'Sir William.' She spoke evenly though her heart was breaking. This was the thing she had dreamed of for so long; she loved this man deeply but he saw marriage to her only as a means of reparation. 'Edward was under no obligation to me, you have no debt to repay.'

'For God's sake!' He flung the glass from his hand, shattering it against the stone of the hearth. 'I love you. God help me, I love you!' He turned back to the fireplace, one hand on the mantel, his head bent, the anger in his voice replaced by a mixture of longing and recrimination.

'I have loved you since I brought you from that prison, may Heaven forgive me. It was wrong of me but I had no power to prevent it. I loved you even as Edward loved you, the thought of you married to my son or to any man haunted my days. I know it is useless to speak of it, I am afraid I allowed my emotions to override my judgement. It is unforgivable of me to have spoken to you as I have. I realise you would not dream of marrying me . . .'

'But I have dreamed of it,' Phoebe interrupted, her own voice soft with an answering surge of love. 'I have dreamed of it for many months and I dream of it still.'

'Phoebe!' He turned from the fireplace, his face lit with hope. 'You said you would never marry a man you did not love.'

She smiled across at him, her eyes tender with love. 'Nor would I, but I love you. I think I always have.'

'Phoebe!' He crossed the room with one bound, snatching her roughly into his arms. 'My love – oh, my love.'

He loved her, *he loved her*, and he wanted her for his wife. Phoebe leaned against him as he kissed her. But how would a wife who had been in prison be accepted among his circle? Would marriage to her slowly destroy his life? And children, what if they had children? What would they think of having a mother once accused of theft?

Pulling away from his arms Phoebe put her fears into words, asking each of the questions her soul told her she must.

He smiled at her, his grey eyes a deeper shade with the love he no longer feared to show. 'I want you for my wife because I love you. I love you so much I cannot conceive of life without you. I love your honesty and integrity, your loyalty and tenderness of conscience, your dignity and your constancy. I want more for my children than the emptiness of a society that prizes none of those qualities.

'The world is changing, Phoebe, and we must change with it. It might take some time for people to forget the past but give them that time and they will see for themselves that trueness of spirit that would never allow you to commit any crime.'

He drew her into his arms again, looking down into her radiant face. 'You told me once that I should never use the word "must" to you again, but I am going to do so one more time. Your father is unable to answer my request so you *must* do that yourself. Phoebe Pardoe, I ask for your hand in marriage. Will you marry me?'

Turning her face up to him, her eyes soft with love, Phoebe smiled. 'My father cannot answer you, William,' she murmured, 'but the answer would be the same. That answer is yes, you may marry Abel's daughter.'

If you enjoyed ABEL'S DAUGHTER, here's a foretaste of Meg Hutchinson's new novel, FOR THE SAKE OF HER CHILD:

For the Sake of her Child

Anna Bradly sat on one of the two wooden chairs that, together with a scrubbed wooden table, almost filled the tiny kitchen. Her feet, bare below the cotton of her blue print dress, rested on the drab hearth.

How long had it been? Leaning her head sideways, she let it rest against the rough brick of the wall. Light from the oil lamp on the mantelpiece caught the movement of her rich auburn hair. How long since Mary Carter had been pulled drowned from Millfield Pool . . . how long since the accusations had started?

Mary Carter had come twice a week to this house since Anna's mother had died in childbirth ten years ago. Mondays were given over to washing. The fire already lit beneath the brick-lined copper before she arrived, she would hang her shawl on the nail behind the kitchen door and go straight into the poky wash-house. Anna had been allowed to watch as she ladled heavy buckets of steaming water into the round wooden washtub and sometimes Mary let her help cut thin slices of yellow scrubbing soap and drop them like dusty curls in among the wash.

Thursday Mary baked.

Anna breathed deeply, remembering the smell of freshly baked bread and sugar-topped cinnamon cake. This had been her favourite day. A half-burned coal settled further into its glowing bed, sending flakes of grey ash falling into the hearth.

Anna looked back across the years since her mother's

death. Standing on a chair beside a table white from years of scrubbing, she would pour the liquid yeast and sugar mixture into the huge earthenware bowl of fluffy white flour after Mary had said the devil had been raised.

'Does yeast and sugar really raise the devil?'

She remembered the smile on Mary's face as she answered, but even more clearly remembered the answer she had never understood.

'There's more than yeast and sugar can raise that one.'

Only now could she see just how true that was.

The coals settled again and Anna stared into the depths of the fire, hypnotised. Oh, the devil had been raised all right! Only not in a cup of yeast and sugar water.

It had been on a Friday morning. Two men crossing the fields to work had seen the floating mass of clothes caught in the reeds; they had pulled the body on to the narrow path skirting the water-filled mine shaft . . . the body of Mary Carter.

'Death from misadventure' had been the Coroner's report but people hereabouts had called it murder, a murder they accused Anna's father of committing. That had been three years ago and not one of them had set foot in this house since.

At thirteen Anna had taken on the running of it, watching the taunts and jibes turn her father from a quiet man to a morose, withdrawn shadow.

He had murdered Mary Carter, they said, because she'd refused his advances. She would have nothing to do with his filthy suggestions so he had forced himself on her, then, knocking her senseless, thrown her into Millfield Pool.

Anna closed her eyes. Her father was innocent, that much she knew. Mary Carter had always arrived at the house after he had left for work and had long gone home before he returned. How could he have murdered her?

The hollow echo of the old tin bucket rattling across the cobbled yard woke Anna. The low fire now gave little light, and for a moment she could not make out the shape looming in the doorway as the door was thrown back on its hinges.

'Where are you, you bloody bitch?'

The harsh shout rang in the silence. Her father was drunk again. This had become the pattern of his life: trying to sink his pain at the bottom of a pint tankard.

'Where are you . . . you lying, stinking bitch?'

Stumbling forward, he half-fell across the table, sending the cups she had set out for tomorrow's breakfast crashing to the floor. Anna stood up, reaching for the oil lamp, turning the wick a little higher. She would help him to bed as she had done so many times; once there he would sleep off the beer.

'There you are, Mary Carter!'

He had pushed himself upright. Eyes glazed with alcohol and hatred stared at Anna. Her hand fell away from the lamp; he had called her by that name before, always when the accusations had been flying thick and his drinking heavy.

'No . . . it's me, Father . . . Anna.' She didn't move, watching the swaying of his head as he continued to stare at her.

'Do you know what you've done to me, Mary Carter?' The question was thick and slurred. 'Do you know what I've gone through because of you? The lies and insults I've suffered. Do you, you cow, *do* you?'

'Father.' Anna spoke softly, carefully. She had never seen him this bad before. 'Father, it's me, Anna . . . Mary has gone home.'

'Do you know what they are saying down there, those bastards!' He banged a heavy fist on the table, setting the knives dancing a crazy jig. 'I'll tell you what they're saying: they are saying I screwed you, forced you when you said no, then knocked you senseless and threw you into the pool.'

Swaying, he moved around the table, dim light filtering through the open door, turning him into frightening solidity. His hands hung at his sides, his head lolled tipsily forward on his neck. 'But that's not true, Mary Carter, and you know it. Screwed you? – Pah! – Christ knows I never laid a finger on you.'

Across the short distance Anna could smell the beery fumes exhaled with each breath. Something must have happened, someone in The Collier must have baited him more than usual for him to have drunk himself into such a state. Nervously she stepped forward, bare feet soundless on the flagged floor.

'C'mon, Father, I'll help you upstairs.'

His eyes continued to stare. Locked on her face, they did not see her, but what they did see contorted his expression to a twisted mask of bitterness. He moved slowly, head thrust forward, feet shuffling on the stone floor and Anna wanted to cry out but was afraid. If she remained calm he would recognise her and that terrible look would be gone from his face.

'No, by God, I never laid a finger on you. Was that why you did it? Was that why you told your cronies that every time you came to this house I made you lie with me? Was that pretence to cover the fact that I never did?'

He came closer. The dull yellow pool of light cast by the oil lamp flickered over his face, touching the long smear of blood on his left cheek, paling before the glitter of his almost transparent blue eyes.

'And why didn't I, did you tell them that, Mary Carter? Did you tell them Jos Bradly takes no whore?'

Anna clutched her hands tightly, pressing them against her sides as her father took another swaying step towards her. She had thought to help him to bed but now instinct told her to get to her own room. He would shout and swear for a few hours, smash a few dishes, but she could clear up in the morning. Right now she was safer out of his sight, for in his drink-fuddled mind he was seeing not her but Mary Carter.

'For months I've taken the brickbats,' he began again, but this time he didn't shout. His words were little more than a whisper, almost as if he were talking to himself. 'For months they've pointed the finger at me, accusing me of that which

I never thought to do. Well, now I've changed my mind. I've taken the insults so I might just as well take the pleasure.'

For the first time in her life Anna was afraid of her father. He would never harm her in his normal state. But tonight he was not normal, he was in drink. And there was worse than that wrong with him; the long months of mental torment since Mary's death, months of being a social outcast, treated like a leper by those who had called themselves his friends, had at last broken him.

Heart thumping, she stepped sideways. The light from the lamp, what little there was of it, was shining into his eyes. If she moved slowly, chances were he would not notice.

But she was wrong. One hand shot out, grasping the hair tied at the back of her neck and at the same time wrenching her forward, her scream muffled by the rough material of his jacket.

'You can go, Mary.' Above her head the words came out in a quiet sing-song voice. 'You can go, but this time it will be the truth you'll tell those bastards.'

Pulling back her head, Anna's anguished cries did not register on his fevered mind. Wiping his free hand across his face, mixing blood and sweat together, Joseph Bradly swore with the soft vehemence of one who has waited long for vengeance. Then, grasping the neckline of the cotton dress, he ripped it violently downward, tearing the cheap thin material to the hem.

For a moment he stared at the creamy skin above Anna's bodice then that garment too was torn away, his hand leaving a smear of blood across her breast.

'This is what you've talked of so often to your dirty-minded women friends, you filthy, bloody bitch! That you were crucifying a man didn't matter to you, did it? Well, now you're going to pay.'

'Father . . . please, Father, it's me, Anna. Father, please . . .'

Anna's screams died as a blow to the side of her head sent her spinning to the floor and the blackness of nightmare began. A nightmare that would stay with her for the rest of her life.

His weight pinning her to the floor, he dragged away her underclothes, freeing his own body as he did so. Then, with one knee forcing her legs apart, he drove deeply into her. Each thrust was like a red hot knife but Anna was already beyond pain. Her mind closed to what was happening to her body, she did not cry out. Eyes closed too, she waited while her father vented his rage and passion.

At last it was over and with a low grunt he rolled away from her.

Anna lay still, his sweat drying cold on her bare skin. Above her the yellow flame flickered a warning of the lamp's need for oil but she did not move. How long she lay there she could never later remember but at last, limbs as numbed as her mind, she pushed herself to her feet.

Her dress lay half under the snoring man stretched on the floor and there she left it. Pulling the remnants of her underwear about her, she walked slowly upstairs.

Moonlight silvered the tiny room that had been hers from birth, but Anna saw none of its magic. In a trance-like state she filled the bowl on the wash stand from its matching jug, unaware of the icy sting as she plunged her hands into the water, lifting palmsful to her face. For long seconds she threw the water over a face almost as cold, then stripping off her torn garments, reached for the thick greyish bar of soap. Again and again she scrubbed herself, covering every inch of her body, ignoring the sting of carbolic where the violence of his entry had lacerated her. She scrubbed her breasts, washing away the smear of blood; scrubbed her stomach where the flesh felt sticky; and still she scrubbed, trying to wash away the smell of his breath from her nostrils, the touch of his sweat-soaked flesh, the memory of what he had done to her.

Silver light turned a cold grey before Anna finally slipped a clean white calico nightdress over her frozen body. Her hair, still wet from the merciless scrubbing, dripped spots of icy water on to the front. In the small mirror hanging from a nail on her bedroom wall she watched them spread and join, forming a smear, the way the blood from her father's hand had smeared her breast. It was only then, hands blue with cold covering her face, that she sank into a heap on the bare wooden boards and cried: the desperate, hopeless crying of a soul doomed to everlasting torment.

The same grey light paling to opalescent pearl fingered past the undrawn curtains of the tired kitchen. The last embers of the fire had long settled and the lamp gave no more light. Groaning from the stiffness of his cold limbs, Joseph Bradly stood up. Shaking the last clouds of alcohol from his brain and remembering. That whore Mary Carter had got what she deserved. From now on the insinuations of the townspeople would carry some truth at last. Satisfaction in the grim set of his mouth, he reached for the poker, stabbing ash from the grate with hard jerky movements. Now she would have something to talk about, the bloody bitch. It was this last thought that halted his assault on the cold cinders. Mary Carter was dead! He had seen her bloated corpse laid on the path by Millfield Pool. He couldn't have been with her last night, it could not have been her, but he had . . .

Turning from the grate, he saw in the faint blush of morning the heap of torn blue cotton where he had lain. He reached for it, the iron poker dropping loudly to the stone hearth. He knew this dress. He had seen delight spread across the face of the child he had bought it for. Lifting the cloth to his face, he could smell the faint scent, as if the pattern of cornflowers gave off a living perfume . . . and then he knew. Last night he had not wreaked vengeance on Mary Carter. Last night he had raped his own daughter.

The long climb up Church Hill seemed never ending. [illegible]

Chapter One

The long climb up Church Hill seemed neverending. Glancing at the black, smoke-grimed walls of the ancient Parish Church that crowned it, Anna thought it still seemed as far away as when she began the trudge up Ethelfleda Terrace.

Back aching with the effort of freeing every step from mud that threatened to suck her down, swollen mound of a stomach making her lean awkwardly back, she willed herself on.

Pulling her foot from the squelching earth, she gripped the basket she was carrying, forcing the bamboo handle painfully into the flesh of her palm. But the pain went unnoticed, hidden beneath the breath-snatching agony that suddenly lanced through her.

Clutching at the nearest gate, Anna leaned heavily against it, her breath coming in short frightened gasps.

It had started, she thought through the pain. The long hopeless months of waiting were about to end. The child that had been set inside her with so much pain and bitterness was about to enter the world, about to begin a life that would be led the same way; could only continue in the malice and hatred that had been her lot since the finding of Mary Carter's body.

One hand gripping the grey splintered wood of the garden gate, Anna gasped, waiting for the pain that flared through her to diminish. Drawing in a long ragged breath, she lifted her head, glancing along the path of beaten earth that led to the door of the house. But though the curtain at the window twitched, no one emerged to help her.

She was Jos Bradly's daughter, his whore. No decent woman in Wednesbury would be seen helping her.

Sweat bathing her face, Anna pushed herself upright. She had to climb the hill. She must get home or give birth like some animal in the hedge.

Stopping every few yards, panting against the recurring stabs of pain, she dragged on to the house that once had held so much happiness for her, the house where her mother had loved and cherished her for the first seven years of her life.

Pushing open the door that gave on to the kitchen, she stumbled inside, grabbing the edge of the table that almost filled the little room, fighting the red hot spasms that threatened to cut her in two.

'Mother . . .' she moaned softly into the emptiness. 'Mother, help me . . . help me.'

But her mother could not help her. Her mother had died ten years before, died in the agony Anna was suffering now, the boy she had carried dying with her.

Letting the basket fall to the table, Anna breathed hard. She must fight the pain. She was alone and would be until past her usual bedtime. Only then did her father return to the house that had become his prison and her penitentiary.

Trying to keep her breathing calm and even, she took an enamel basin from the shabby wooden dresser. She was placing the eggs she had bought into it when fresh searing pain ripped through her, jarring every nerve with searing, brutal agony. The eggs jerked in her hands, splashing the front of her with oozing stickiness.

Anna gazed at her dress, the terror she had known once before returning with stark clarity.

Her stomach had been covered in the same slimy mess when he had finally lifted himself off her.

'No! No, mother, no!'

The cry was dragged from her as she rubbed at her dress in a vain attempt to wipe it clean.

* * *

It was too early to go back.

Jos Bradly walked out of the yard of the steel foundry in silence; no friendly wave acknowledged his going, no voice called a goodnight.

Shoving his hands deep into his pockets, he walked quickly in the direction of Church Hill. This was the wrong way, he told himself, he had never gone home before ten since . . .

He closed his eyes, momentarily trying to shut out the scene that never left him.

He never went back to the house until he knew she would be in bed, until she would not have to look at the man who had raped her. And he would not see, at least in the flesh, the hurt and fear in his daughter's eyes.

But tonight, try as he might to tell himself he must not return, his steps carried him home.

He could see from the gate that the door to the kitchen was wide open. Suddenly sick with new fear, Jos ran up the narrow path.

She was there, a crumpled heap on the kitchen floor, her red-gold hair covering her face – a face he did not need to see to know it was crumpled with pain.

'Anna! Anna, my little wench!'

Blood draining from his face, he stepped towards her then turned back to the open door.

Clear of the house he began to run, streaking away down the hill as if Gabriel's Hounds were already snapping at his heels.

'Will yer come, Polly?'

He fell into the tiny house that was one of a ribbon of tumbledown dwellings edging Trouse Lane.

'Say yer'll come? There's none other I can ask. I don't want none o' they touchin' 'er.'

Polly Shipton twisted round on her stool, her withered left leg dragging on the bare flagstones. She had wondered where he would turn when the girl's time came. Well, now she knew.

She looked up at the face she had known since childhood, a face smeared by tears mixed with the dirt of the steel foundry. Was it true what they said of him? Had he murdered one woman and then raped a young girl, and that girl his own daughter?

Polly sighed. She didn't have the answers and was never likely to have them.

'Please, Polly . . . yer must come.' At his sides, Jos's hands balled into fists. 'Anna, my little wench, 'er was on the floor. I . . . I couldn't . . . I don't know how!'

Shoving herself from the stool with her sound right leg, Polly reached for the heavy woollen shawl hanging on a nail in the scullery door. She pulled it close as she followed Joseph Bradly past the mocking eyes of the quickly gathered women – women who took care to keep their opinions in their mouths until he had passed.

Hobbling painfully, Polly kept her own head high. From this day on she would be as much an outcast in the town as the man she was following. No matter. Whatever else he might be, he was now a man sharing his daughter's agony, and the fact that she would be ostracised and ignored for helping either of them was of no consequence compared to a young girl's pain.

'It be all right, Anna.'

Pushing past Jos into the kitchen, she bent over the girl huddled on the stone floor.

'It'll be all right, me wench. Polly Shipton 'as come to be with you, Polly will take care of you. Come on now, there's a good wench, let's 'ave you upstairs.'

Hair plastered to her cheeks with sweat, Anna lifted her head and Polly saw the look of terror in her eyes as Jos Bradly bent to take his daughter in his arms.

'No . . . o . . . o!'

The scream filled the tiny kitchen and Polly Shipton knew she need go no further to find the father of the child struggling to enter the world.

* * *

Standing beside the wooden crib, Anna stared at the son she had borne a month ago, hearing in her mind the taunts and sneers that met her whenever she ventured out of the house.

She tucked the blanket closer around the sleeping child.

It had grown into something of a sport; women gathering in twos and threes as she approached, calling after her from the safety of their married respectability.

'That father o' 'er's . . .'

Words emerged from the shadows of her mind like silent wraiths.

'. . . 'e be bloody jailbait. 'Ow come the bobbies ain't fetched 'im afore now?'

They passed their taunts from one to the other, each woman raising her voice, ensuring Anna could hear.

'Ar, why ain't they? 'E killed Mary Carter, we all knows that, an' 'e be the one who 'as fathered that babby. That by blow belongs to Jos Bradly as sure as there be a God in 'eaven.'

'You didn't hear them, did you, sweetheart?'

Anna stroked a finger across her son's downy head.

'You didn't hear what they said or realise what they think, and you never will my precious . . . you never will.'

But those women had been partly right. Anna sat on her bed, one hand resting on the crib that her father had made for her own birth.

The child now sleeping in it was Jos Bradly's, in that they had been correct, but the rest of their accusations bore no truth. There was no God in heaven. She looked at the sleeping child, her heart filling with pain at what she knew was in store for him as he grew.

No, there was no God in heaven. Had there been she would not have been raped.

Rising from the bed, she lifted the child from the crib, a wild surge of love and sorrow sweeping through her as the tiny body touched her own.

'They have judged him too,' she murmured, her mouth against the tiny head, 'my father and yours. They have all judged him and, right or wrong, he will pay their price. All the years of his life will not wash away the sin of which he is guilty, even though he would have suffered death before committing it had he been sober.'

In her arms the tiny face crumpled, one arm freeing itself from the swaddling blanket, and Anna rocked gently back and forth, her lips touching her son's face, soothing away his complaining cry.

'Shhh,' she whispered, folding one finger into his clutching palm. 'Shhh, no one will hurt you. No one in this town will ever call lies and filth after you.'

But as she lifted the tiny hand to her mouth, Anna knew they would.